*Her dreams were born
of reckless passion . . . .*
*HER LIFE WAS BUILT
ON RESTLESS DREAMS. . . .*

CASTLES IN THE AIR

An enthralling generation-long saga as monumental as
the glorious epoch it portrays, *Castles in the Air* cap-
tures the heart of an American dream—and the soul of
the woman who transcends it.

"Something for every woman: romance and sex,
history and feminism. It just can't miss!"
Publishers Weekly

"A spectacular that may sell and sell!"

D0950310

CASTLES IN THE AIR

PATRICIA GALLAGHER

AVON
PUBLISHERS OF BARD, CAMELOT, DISCUS, EQUINOX AND FLARE BOOKS

CASTLES IN THE AIR is an original publication of Avon
Books. It has never before appeared in book form.

AVON BOOKS
A division of
The Hearst Corporation
959 Eighth Avenue
New York, New York 10019

Copyright © 1976 by Patricia Gallagher.
Published by arrangement with the author.

ISBN: 0-380-00570-0

All rights reserved, which includes the right to
reproduce this book or portions thereof in any form
whatsoever. For information address Avon Books.

First Avon Printing, May, 1976
Eighth Printing

AVON TRADEMARK REG. U.S. PAT. OFF. AND
FOREIGN COUNTRIES, REGISTERED TRADEMARK—
MARCA REGISTRADA, HECHO EN CHICAGO, U.S.A.

Printed in the U.S.A.

To Jimmy, Mary Kay, and Kellie,
with love and affection.

"These crazy women, and their castles in the air."
P. T. Barnum (1810–1891)

CONTENTS

PART I

But I feel sometimes such an impatience of my life and its narrow lot as I can scarcely describe. I want to go and see something better than I have ever known. I want to go, to take wings and fly and leave these sordid occupations. I think it is cruel to cultivate tastes that are never to be gratified in this world. . . .

> Entry in the diary of Cornelia Phillips,
> a young Southern girl,
> made shortly after the Civil War.

Were these the same people—these haggard, wrinkled women, bowed with care and trouble, sorrow and unusual toil? These tame, pale, tearless girls, from whose soft flesh the witching dimples had long since departed, or were drawn down into furrows—were they the same school girls of 1861? These women who, with coarse, lean and brown hands . . . these women with scant, faded cotton gowns and coarse leather shoes—these women who silently and apathetically packed the boxes, looking into them with the intense and sorrowful gaze that one casts into the tomb?

> Francis W. Dawson

Chapter 1

"Of all the damn fool female notions I've ever heard, this takes the prize," Daniel said. "Wanting a career as a journalist is bad enough—but New York! God knows what would happen to you up there without a man to guide and protect you. I know that town, Devon. I spent some time there before and after my Grand Tour. It's worse than New Orleans or St. Louis, and certainly no fit place for a decent young woman alone. My God, surely you're not that bold and adventurous!"

It was useless for Devon to argue. Daniel was adamant on the subject of New York—and no more amenable to the idea of her working now than when he had returned from Rock Island over a year ago. And, dear God, how he had returned! A skeleton in scarecrow rags with a chronic cough, a slight limp in his left leg and a nervous tic in his right eye: a gaunt gray ghost looking ten years beyond his twenty-nine.

Devon had had a sudden poignant vision of Daniel as he had left for the war—a dashing cavalier on a spirited white charger, captain of the elite Tidewater Guard, the best-uniformed, best-mounted troop in the Virginia cavalry. And in a rash moment of sympathy and despair, she had agreed to resume their courtship and marry him after a period of engagement.

So many young men were dead, maimed, consumptive, ruined—she was not the only frantic eligible Southern maiden. But this was what shamed and disgusted Devon most in retrospect: her dishonest emotions and motives in accepting Daniel's proposal—the simple irrational fear of being an old maid. Of all the reasons for a woman to marry a man she did not love, surely this was the most illogical, outrageous, and unforgivable.

Fortunately, Daniel seemed totally unaware that belated

conscience could be influencing Devon's rejection of him now. And although he had seen the burnt shell of her father's newspaper building, and knew the rubble and ashes contained relics of a century of publishing, he could read only feminine caprice and audacity and folly in her desire to escape Richmond and carry on a family tradition. The sensible thing for her to do, in his superior estimation, was to marry him and raise children, while he tried to raise tobacco on an equally ruined plantation. Provided he could beg, borrow, or steal the money to pay the delinquent taxes and buy the necessary mules and equipment; provided he could persuade some free-issue Negroes to help him plant and harvest and cure the crops.

"Now, then," Daniel was saying, "you are going to forget this foolishness about New York, aren't you? We'll be married immediately and go to Harmony Hill. The house wasn't burned, fortunately. But it was sacked and vandalized. The barns and stables will have to be restored too. It'll take time and hard work and sacrifice, but we'll succeed, Devon. Together we'll make Harmony Hill as big and beautiful and productive as ever, the finest tobacco plantation in Virginia, and its bright leaf and burley the best in the world."

"I'm sorry, Daniel."

"Sorry?"

"I can't marry you."

His arms fell away from her. His aggravated temper made him cough; he stifled it angrily. "Why not? Am I not good enough for you, Miss Marshall? Do you know of a finer family in this state, or the entire South, for that matter? My ancestors came to this country with the London Company, on the King James Charter! They sat in the House of Burgesses at Williamsburg. They helped to free and mold and govern Virginia, and they—"

She interrupted impatiently, "What difference does that make, Dan? We're all in the same sunken boat now!"

The ring she slipped from her finger had belonged to Daniel's mother, who, along with his sister, had fallen victim to typhoid during the final phases of the war. His father and two brothers had been killed on the battlefields; he was the last of his family—as Devon was the last of hers. But while mutual loss and tragedy might draw people together in empathy and compassion, it should not necessarily bind them permanently; to experience a common catastrophe is not to pledge a bond for eternity.

Doomsday, her father had called it in his last editorial. The apocalypse of the Confederacy. Armageddon before Appomattox. And to those who had witnessed the fall of Richmond, it was all of those things, and more. A nightmare from which there was no waking.

The first startling explosions had come from the waterfront in the darkness of night, where the gunboats, arsenals, and warehouses were destroyed to prevent their surrender to the advancing enemy. Driven by a high wind off the James River, the flames had swept swiftly from the harbor into the street, and by dawn the business district of Richmond was an inferno. Boiling black smoke mushroomed in the April sky, blotting out the rising sun, and fumes of sulphur and lead, oil and tar, tobacco, grain, cotton, wool, hides, paint, turpentine and varnish choked the air. The spectacle was awesome, the sounds ominous: popping and crackling wood, crashing brick and stone, the hissing of melting glass, the writhing of molten iron.

Miraculously, the Marshalls' clapboard Colonial had escaped the fire, which like an insatiable monster had devoured most everything in its path. And now, months later, waiting for the Northern gentleman a real estate agent was sending—a prospective buyer—Devon stood on the porch of the house and shuddered at the still vivid memory of that horrible day; it was as indelible as a birthmark.

Her father had finished writing his editorial, and then shot himself.

She had stayed in the newspaper office, holding her father's bloody body, numb with shock and grief and bewilderment, wondering how and when and where she would bury him, until the fire roared into Main Street.

Terrified, she fled home and managed to pack some valises and bandboxes and drag a trunk out onto the porch.

She had stayed in the house until the fire's eerie glow was flickering in the windows, knowing she would not—could not—return to face the memories, and then Devon took her hand luggage and headed toward the isolated safety of Capitol Hill. There, for two days and nights, sharing food and blankets with friends and strangers, she

ate and slept and wept and watched the triumphant blue
army enter the ruined city.

It was three days before the fires were extinguished and
the military allowed the civilians in the ruins. Some
Yankee guards helped her get her father's body out of the
newspaper office and buried in the churchyard. The body
had been nearly cremated, and with no coffins available,
they used a gunnysack. There was no funeral and no bells
tolling; the church bells had been melted down for cannon
early in the war. And there was no marker, either, because
the monument makers were all dead or gone.

A livery buggy drove up, and a tall well-dressed man
stepped out and tipped his high silk hat. But he left his
portfolio on the seat and kept his driving gloves on, obviously not intending to conduct business with her.

"Miss Devon Marshall?"

"Yes?"

"I'm Keith Curtis, and I'm terribly sorry to have kept
you waiting so long, but I was unavoidably detained. I'd
have sent a messenger, except that I didn't expect to get so
involved."

What could she say? "That's all right, sir."

"I'll be direct, Miss Marshall. The realtor gave me the
details of your property, and I'm afraid it's too small to
consider. I'm interested in a much larger tract, perferably
on the railroad or waterfront, to hold as an investment. So
perhaps you'd best cast about for another prospect."

Her chin quivered; she steadied it. "Do you know of
anyone else who might possibly be interested, Mr. Curtis?"

He pondered politely. "Not offhand, but I'll keep it in
mind and mention it to some of my friends."

"I'd appreciate that, sir."

"May I drive you somewhere?" he asked.

"No, thank you. It's not far. I'll walk."

"Isn't it late for a lady to be out alone?"

"I was here at three o'clock," she replied succinctly.

The sunset glare on the ruins gave the man's face a sardonic cast, increased by his arched black brows and faintly
smiling saturnine mouth. His features took on sharpness,
the lean bone structure visible in the chiseled planes and
angles, and his smoky-gray eyes had the alert incisiveness
of a night hunter. His spectacular looks were intriguing,
but more so his personality, for there was about him an

air, not of decadence, but of refined and elegant debauchery. Devon guessed him to be in his late twenties—he was young to be so obviously successful. A suit of such cloth and cut could not be acquired anywhere in the South now, not even in Charleston or New Orleans, and she knew no one who could have worn such finery with more aplomb.

"My apologies again, Miss Marshall, and I feel I should compensate your inconvenience. Permit me, please, to make amends over supper at the Richmond House."

"You don't owe me anything, Mr. Curtis. I'm only sorry we couldn't do business together."

"So am I," he said, chagrined. "However, if you should change your mind about supper—" The card he presented was personal, not business, with only his full name—Keith Heathstone Curtis—engraved in black English script on white vellum. "Good evening, Miss Marshall." He bowed, raised his hat to reveal a head of thick dark hair, and left without further ado.

Devon watched the buggy slip out of sight, conscious of the darkening hills on the horizon, tempted to call him back. Somehow the ruins always seemed more ominous at dusk, and they were utterly terrifying at night. The lifeless trees, the gaunt columns and chimneys, the twisted iron and tangled wire created a grotesque landscape, in which the gutted frameworks loomed like weird fossils from another age. Soon the moon would gleam eerily on the ashen skeletons and the river wind would rattle the loose bones.

The Chester residence, where Devon had been staying, was red brick with a slate roof. She was fond of Mrs. Chester, whose only son had been killed early in the war, at Bull Run, and whose husband had died at Fredericksburg. The three family slaves had departed when the Federals entered Richmond, and Agnes Chester, suffering from a long siege of ague, had welcomed the orphaned girl into her home in exchange for companionship and household assistance. It was one of many such expedient alliances in the South these desperate years.

A light glowed in the parlor, where Mrs. Chester sat with her mending. She was a small woman, with a shrunken bosom and dowager's hump, forced by necessity into dowdiness. Attended by servants from birth, she had had to learn at sixty to shift for herself. This she had done valiantly, as many of her generation had, confident that the worst was past and the future could only improve. Endurance was a victory in itself, she often said, and patience had its own rewards. But it was a philosophy more acceptable to age than youth, and in the twilight of life rather than at dawn or high noon.

"Did you sell your property, dear?"

Devon paused to catch her breath. "No, Ma'am. It was too small for Mr. Curtis' purpose. He's buying on speculation."

"Carpetbagger!" Mrs. Chester scoffed with all the hatred and contempt the word conveyed.

"Not this one," Devon said. "He's someone of consequence. If you could've seen his clothes! As fine as any President Davis or General Lee ever wore."

"It takes more than fancy duds to make a gentleman, young lady. They don't all come South with their worldly goods in a carpetbag. But they're still vultures feeding on the carrion of misfortune, and one will eventually roost on your property."

"I hope so," Devon murmured, pride bowing to poverty, "before it's auctioned for taxes."

"I was worried about you, out alone so late after dark. And in the ruins yet, where that poor girl was attacked only last week! Our streets are no longer safe at night, with all the Yankee soldiers and other trash abroad. You must be more careful, Devon Elizabeth Marshall. I'm responsible for your reputation as well as your safety, you know. Go eat your supper now—it's still warm on the stove."

Boiled rice and greens again. The horses and mules of the occupation forces ate better than the conquered people. The prolific Piedmont farms, the lush Tidewater plantations, the fertile fields and orchards of the Shenandoah Valley had all been plundered by the Union legions, the land so thoroughly devastated that General Sheridan had boasted that a crow couldn't fly through the region without a haversack. The few commodities that reached the civilian markets were controlled by hucksters and unscrupulous military agents, who seemed in league to rob, starve, and further humiliate and degrade the defeated.

Choking down the tasteless mess, Devon chided herself for a stupid fool. She could have been dining in style, at a hotel whose food and service had to be good, because it catered to Federal officials and officers. Such an attractive man—and surely Mr. Curtis would have treated her well. The finer things of life were still available to those able to afford and demand them.

Devon's kitchen chores were disagreeable—she washed the dishes in harsh lye soap, scoured pots and pans with ashes and swept the floor with a bedraggled rush broom. Yes, she could understand why some Southern girls consorted with the Yankees, married them, and even bartered themselves on the street for a few luxuries. A bar of castile soap, a bottle of cologne, some handkerchiefs, a package of hairpins—how cheaply and yet how dearly they sold their favors!

Returning to the parlor, she found Mrs. Chester repairing her best black poplin gown. Richmond was populated with females in perpetual mourning, anonymous shadows on the streets, their faces indistinct behind somber veils. They became adept and resourceful with needle and thread and dye substitutes, redesigning and dipping formal clothes for day wear. Those too elaborate for conversion were traded to secondhand dealers for necessities, and some elegant antebellum costumes now reposed in brothels. Occasionally a lady recognized one of her garments on a harlot plying her trade, and it was a mortifying experience.

Devon had lost most of her wardrobe in the fire and would have lost her hoops and crinolines too had she not been wearing them at the time. Much of what she had saved, however, was pretty but impractical, including the ball gown she had worn to President and Mrs. Davis' first formal reception in the executive mansion, which the press had naturally covered.

Busy with the serious news, her father, Hodge Marshall, had turned over the social aspects and distaff activities of the war to his daughter. Devon learned how to write, edit, and condense her copy when newsprint became scarce and then all but nonexistent, because the paper mills were in the North. By that time, however, there were fewer entertainments and victory celebrations to report, and more charity bazaars, hospital benefits, sanitary committees, fund-soliciting for widows and orphans, funerals, and prayer meetings. No tea for tea parties, coffee for Kaffeeklatsches, cloth for sewing bees. Mrs. Davis and the cabinet wives offered recipes for sugarless, saltless, spiceless, butterless cooking; formulas for medicines from roots and leaves and berries; substitutes for everything from condiments to candles, buttons to stays. Looms and spinning wheels emerged from retirement, creating a renaissance of butternut homespun. Family cobblers fashioned shoes from carpets and cardboard, and even whittled wooden clogs. It became such an ersatz society that life itself sometimes seemed like a substitute—a mere experiment in living.

"Don't you have something to mend?" Mrs. Chester asked.

"Everything," Devon answered glumly, pondering the new ugly tear in her skirt sustained on a piece of wire on her way home. Her underwear was a tissue of patches, and her stockings resembled webs woven by inept spiders. "But I don't feel much like mending now, Mrs. Chester. You see, I—I was counting on the money from the sale of the house to get me to New York."

The parlor was stuffy and smoky from the guttering tallow candle, for paraffin and beeswax were prohibitive in price. The wallpaper was faded, the ecru lace curtains had hung so long they were dingy tatters, and strips of carpet had been cut from the borders for shoes. The war had invaded, ravaged, impoverished every home in Richmond.

"Oh, I know you're worried about your future, and beginning to despair. So many of our young folks are leaving the South now, going North and West, to California and even the Indian Territories. And that may be well enough for an adventurous young man, but for a lone young lady"—she frowned, shaking her gray head dubiously. "If only your father were here to advise you!"

But he wasn't. Her father was dead, and she had broken her engagement to Daniel—refusing to see him—and she was alone and virtually naked in the world. It was like being born again, and though she couldn't explain it to Mrs. Chester, she had hoped the stranger would somehow be the instrument of her delivery into a new and hopefully better life. Now she felt stifled again. Suffocated. Stillborn.

"I think Pa would want me to stand on my own two feet," she said determinedly, hoping the old lady would not deliver one of her familiar homilies.

"Yes, he believed in freedom and independence for everyone, didn't he? And I remember how self-sufficient your mother was too, how well she managed her house with no slaves and only one servant. You're very much like her, you know, in many respects. What a pity that yellow fever plague had to come along that year! You were twelve, I believe, and away at school. But they're together now, your parents, and happy as only the dead can be." Mrs. Chester's needle wove through the black cloth, repairing the mourning weeds for another season or two, lest she not join her mate before then. "And perhaps your poor father sacrificed himself in that terrible way to make you more independent and self-reliant, force you out into the world, like a fledgling from the nest."

"Perhaps," Devon agreed, "although I'm inclined to believe he was seriously ill and afraid of becoming a burden on me."

Mrs. Chester pondered that possibility, and then asked, "Is there any chance that speculator might reconsider your property?"

"No, his refusal seemed final. But he did invite me to dine with him this evening at the Richmond House."

"Well, he may not be a carpetbagger, but he certainly has the manners of one! Inviting a young lady he has only just met to a public place! Such effrontery!" She clucked her tongue. "I trust you were properly indignant?"

"Oh, yes, indeed! Didn't I just finish dining on my proper indignation? And isn't a proper Southern lady supposed to starve rather than accept a crumb from an improper Yankee?"

"You sound petulant and regretful, girl. Surely you would not want to fraternize with the enemy?"

"They're not the enemy any more, Mrs. Chester. And they can't all be knaves and opportunists, either. There must be a few gentlemen among them."

"Possibly, and with Diogenes' lantern you might even find one in Yankeeland."

"Or Aladdin's lamp," Devon mused, rising to light her bedside candle on the mantel. "Good night, Ma'am."

"Good night, child. And try not to worry too much about tomorrow. The future has a way of resolving itself. . . ."

Chapter 2

If one believed in omens, the clear golden dawn would seem promising. After a dreary breakfast of unseasoned grits—out of which she had first to pick the weevils—Devon hurried through her morning chores, and then asked permission to go to town, which Mrs. Chester graciously granted.

She put on her best summer dress, a blue Swiss voile usually reserved for church. It was feminine and graceful, with a provocatively molded bodice and flirtatiously flounced skirt, and had she been wearing it yesterday, instead of her worn gray challis, the day might have had a different ending. For she was convinced now that she had used the wrong approach in trying to sell her property. She had been proud and haughty, as if she were doing Keith Curtis a favor. Naive fool, she should have appealed to his masculinity and played on his sympathy and chivalry, weeping and fainting if necessary. With artful persuasion she might have succeeded in selling him something he did not want, in the hope of acquiring something he did. For she flattered herself that he had looked at her with more than a casual interest, and that apology alone had not prompted his supper invitation.

Devon browsed in the vicinity of the Richmond House, where some new stores had risen and old ones reopened, gazing wistfully into the windows, as if she could actually afford to make purchase. Should Mr. Curtis leave or enter the hotel, he would likely see her and speak. Entering the lobby alone was, of course, unthinkable, lest she be mistaken for a harlot on assignation. Some stringent rules of chaperonage still had not been relaxed in the South, although the war had removed most of the eligible escorts. Her only hope was a chance meeting, but after idling

12

away two hours in vain, she feared he had already left town.

At noon she went into a little tearoom, which an enterprising matron she knew slightly had recently opened in her front parlor. Devon chose a table near the window, where she could watch passersby. Catching her reflection in the new plate-glass pane, she thought her eyes had the anxious gleam of a hawk awaiting some unsuspecting prey. It was hardly a pretty expression, and she quickly changed it; but then she looked like innocent prey awaiting a wary hawk, which was even less attractive. In a world of helpless, bewildered birds, who cared about one more lost lonely destitute chick? The predators were ruthless, greedy creatures.

The cakes cost ten cents each—United States coin, for the merchants no longer accepted shinplasters—so Devon ordered only tea and sipped it slowly. Mr. Curtis was probably enjoying a hearty luncheon at the hotel, and suddenly she was furious with him, as if he had kept her waiting on another appointment.

"Anything else, Miss Marshall?" the waitress asked.

"No, thank you, Rosemary. I have to leave now."

Outside, Devon unfurled her white muslin parasol like a tattered flag of surrender. The sun was high and hot and relentless, and the cloudless sky had a brassy glare, the kind of summer day the Negroes called "salt-sweatin'." Toward evening, cooling Chesapeake Bay breezes would sweep up the James River, but now the trees stood motionless, flies buzzed, and bees swarmed around the honeysuckle and roses.

Men were working in the ruins, knocking down gutted buildings with cannon balls, shoveling bricks and debris into wagons; much of Main Street had already been cleared. Some lumbermills were back in operation, and carpenters were busy with tools. Richmond's only iron foundry was blasting its furnaces again. Most of the activity centered around the docks and depots, however, for these had priority in the reconstruction program, and it was easy to understand why investors were more interested in such property. Wharves and warehouses were being rebuilt, rails repaired, boats and barges constructed as rapidly as materials became available. The massive destruction seemed wanton and futile now—the work of fanatics and lunatics.

Devon knew she should go home and help Mrs. Chester weed the garden. Instead, she went to the Richmond, Fredericksburg & Potomac Station to check the schedules. A train had arrived that morning and already proceeded southward; another was due to depart for Washington at 9:30 that evening. On a siding she noticed a fine private coach such as some dignitaries traveled in and wondered if the President could possibly be in town conferring with the military government, perhaps to set a date for the long-delayed treason trial of Jefferson Davis, who was still confined at Fort Monroe. The White House had ceased publicizing the presidential itinerary after Lincoln's assassination, and President Johnson often traveled incognito and always with a cordon of security operatives.

It was a kingly coach, actually, painted royal blue and gold, like a picture Devon had once seen of some European monarch's. The open door and windows afforded glimpses of the luxurious interior. A white-coated porter was busy inside.

"Is the President in Richmond?" she asked the dispatcher.

He laughed contemptuously. "I doubt if Andrew Johnson could afford that coach, Miss. The owner is a New York fella name of Curtis. Wall Street capitalist, I hear, and he's pulling out tonight."

Devon's stomach tightened and turned, but it was not the sensation of hunger or faintness from skipping lunch. What she felt was surging excitement, a sense of compelling urgency. It was imperative that she get on that northbound train tonight, or be stuck here until eternity. Intuition, compulsion—she knew it as surely as she knew her name: her future was on that train; if she missed it, she would miss the rest of her life.

Decisively, she returned to the house, packed her belongings and carefully tucked Keith Curtis' card and her small cache of coins—all that was left from the sale of her mother's cameo brooch and her own gold locket—into her reticule.

For the old lady's peace of mind, Devon explained that she had managed to mortgage her property, and after promising to write as soon as she was settled in New

York, Devon hired a black boy for two pennies and walked alongside as he carried her luggage to the train depot.

She sat on a long wooden bench, her resolution to leave still intact but vacillating—she knew she could not afford a ticket, since she must eat on route and find lodgings on her arrival. But another day was ending, another sunset etching the ruins, and she had to escape.

Some vagrant zephyrs had arrived from the Chesapeake, cooling the twilight, but cicadas still sizzled in the treetops. Moths fluttered around the depot lights, destroying themselves in panic and frenzy. She walked outside. Children were chasing fireflies, as she had at their age, pretending they were captured stars and the luminous residue they left in her hands was stardust.

Finally, as the porter was lighting the lamps, Devon approached Keith Curtis' majestic coach. The attendant met her at the door. "Yes, Miss?"

"Has Mr. Curtis come aboard yet?"

"No, Miss. He won't be here till the last minute, most likely."

"Oh, dear! He told me that, but I was hoping he'd finish his business sooner." She presented the engraved card. "Mr. Curtis said to give you this. I'm Miss Devon Marshall, and I'm traveling to New York as his guest."

The attendant registered no surprise, as if accustomed to such impromptu arrangements, and he stepped aside for her entrance. "Welcome aboard, Miss Marshall."

"Thank you. Will you fetch my luggage, please? It's in the station: the straw valises and floral bandbox." He obliged, and when he returned with her pathetic cargo, she asked his name.

"Rufus Brady, Ma'am."

Slaves gave only one name, but he was not and probably never had been a slave. She wondered how much Mr. Curtis paid him, and if attending this car was his only duty. "Thank you, Rufus. Now I'd like to freshen up a bit, if you please."

She had to get rid of him, at least until Keith Curtis came aboard. Then she would simply lay her cards on the table, explain her emergency, and offer him the deeds to the house and business lots for whatever he would pay. In lieu of that, she would put them up as collateral for her

fare. When he realized her plight, surely he could not refuse to help her. A word from him to the conductor would
secure her passage, and she would eat as little as possible
on the way. There was no sense attempting to plan beyond
that point—no sense burdening herself with exigencies that
might never occur. She would make do.

Restless, Devon began to explore. The railroad car was
as luxurious as a grand hotel suite. There was a double
bed covered in gold damask to match the draperies, a
built-in dresser and wardrobe, an intimate dining area with
servette and well-stocked cellaret. The private lavatory
contained a pedestaled white marble basin and porcelain
commode, racks of towels and chests of soaps, salts, colognes, tonics. Curtis had gall parking this symbol of wealth
and victory in the midst of poverty and defeat!

Devon dampened a towel and patted her flushed face.
She had never been able to do much with her hair; it just
curled as it pleased, fine and golden as a baby's, forming
cherubic ringlets on her forehead and cheeks and nape
when it escaped the pins. Her eyes were almond-shaped,
green with tiny gold flecks that glinted in excitement or
anger, and her skin had the color and texture of ivory. She
opened one of the crystal bottles and touched attar of
roses to her ears, throat, wrists, the cleft between her
breasts. Then she sat on the tufted velvet sofa, feeling like
Miss Muffet on her tuffet awaiting the spider.

He arrived, as Rufus had predicted, at the last moment.
The train with which the vehicle would rendezvous was
late, however. Evidently his valet had apprised him of her
presence, for he smiled faintly. "Good evening, Miss Marshall."

"Good evening, Mr. Curtis."

He carried a monogrammed leather portfolio, and as he
stripped off his gloves, the sight of his gold wedding band
at once relieved and disappointed her. "Rufus tells me I'm
to have the pleasure of your company to New York."

She swallowed. "I—I didn't know what else to tell him."

"Is there some problem?"

"No. I mean, yes."

"How does it concern me?"

"Mr. Curtis, I have to get to New York, and I'm short
of funds. The ticket costs more than I can afford, and I'll
have other expenses when I arrive."

"In that case, why are you going?"

"I must support myself, sir."

"How? As a governess? My dear, New England is full of governesses, and more arrive from the South every day. The competition is fierce. Furthermore, few wives are willing to employ a beautiful young woman in that capacity. While homeliness is not a prerequisite for a governess, it seems to be a preference. And you do not qualify in that respect."

"I'm a journalist, Mr. Curtis. I used to work with my father on our newspaper, the Richmond *Sentinel*. We lost the building and all the equipment when the city was burned."

"And your father?"

"He killed himself."

"I'm sorry," he said gently. "I'm truly sorry, Miss Marshall. And you have no inheritance?"

"Only the house and some worthless Confederate bonds. The entire South is bankrupt and destitute. The Yankees have all the money now!"

"The fortunes of war," he said, removing a bottle from the cellaret. "What do you want of me, Miss Marshall?"

"I—I want you to buy my property, Mr. Curtis, at any price." He was silent, pouring a drink, and she rushed on, "I hear you're a capitalist, sir."

"Among other things."

"Like butcher, baker, candlestick maker?"

"Like banker, broker, money maker." He smiled, swirling cognac in a crystal snifter. "How old are you, Miss Marshall? Seventeen, eighteen?"

"Twenty," she admitted.

"You want some sound advice, young lady? Get out of this car before it couples with the northbound train, which should be here any minute now. Stay in Richmond. It's your home, and there must be someone who can help you. You must have some relatives and friends."

"My relatives and friends are in the same straits."

"But surely there's a suitor—some young man who wants to marry you?"

She stared at the blue carpet, as if it were a pool in which, all else failing, she might drown herself. "No, he died in the war." She did not consider that much of a lie, nor even a gross exaggeration. A man whose dream had been destroyed was dead, or might as well be.

"Well, you can't possibly survive in New York in your present circumstances," he said. "It's a concrete dragon that feeds on pretty young girls. Devours them."

"I'm not afraid."

"Brave words, my dear. Many girls have uttered them, and lived to regret it."

"Will you buy my deeds, sir?"

"No."

"Will you take them as collateral for a ticket?"

"No."

"But you're a financier!"

"I don't finance folly."

"All right, then. I'll use what money I have to go as far as I can, until the conductor puts me off." She emptied her pitiful treasure before him. "How far will this take me?"

"About fifty miles."

Her face clouded. "That's not far enough. Please, couldn't you get me a pass? Sign a slip or something?"

"That would make me responsible for you," he declined. "I don't want the responsibility." They heard the whistle of the tardy train. He stood. "Is this all of your baggage?"

Devon remained seated, chin thrust defiantly, green eyes challenging. "I won't go—you'll have to throw me off!"

"Miss Marshall"—his hands reached down to assist, to urge, to dislodge.

"Please, Mr. Curtis—don't make me leave. I'll do anything. Anything! I don't care what, just let me stay on the train to New York." Tears splashed down her cheeks, and she caught frantically at his arms. "Please, sir, *please!*"

"Stop that," he said brusquely, "and listen to me. I'm not an ogre. I'm trying to help you, do what I think is best for you. Can't I make you understand? No, I guess not." He sat down beside her and held his glass to her mouth. "Drink some of this. Go ahead, it's not hemlock. Another sip. And stop crying." He offered his handkerchief. "Dry your eyes now, like a good little girl."

The train was pulling into the station. Some passengers debarked, others boarded, freight was loaded, unloaded. Trainmen yelled and signaled with lanterns. There was some switching, clanking, grinding of metal as the private coach coupled, and then a knock at the door and the valet's voice.

"Mr. Curtis, sir? You aboard?"

Curtis opened the door. "Stay in your quarters, Rufe. I'll ring if I need you."

"Yessir."

"All aboard!" the conductor called. The train jolted and moved and chugged, jolted and jerked and rolled.

"Have you had supper, Miss Marshall?"

"No."

"Luncheon?"

"Some tea."

"My God," he muttered. "I'll have Rufus fix something."

"Please don't bother. I'm not hungry."

"Trying to wean your appetite in the hope of longer survival? Slow starvation will only make it seem longer, my dear."

"You don't paint very pretty pictures."

"I don't believe in fairy tales, either. Do you?"

"I did once, long ago." When I believed that the moon was a gold ball for the angels to play with, and God lived in heaven and loved all good children. . . .

Replenishing his glass, Keith summoned his servant. "Prepare a buffet for Miss Marshall."

"Yessir." Rufus disappeared into the pantry, reappearing like a black genie with a tray of hors d'oeuvres, which he set in front of the guest before vanishing again.

Devon began to nibble: Smithfield ham cured in Virginia but unavailable to the average citizen, pâté de foie gras, caviar, imported cheese, olives, biscuits, pastries, confections, nuts. And she had thought she would have to eat crow and humble pie!

"You're spoiling me, Mr. Curtis. Feast today, famine tomorrow. Oh, I know the regular passenger fare and discomforts! Dry sandwiches and stale doughnuts and rancid peanuts from the news-butchers, and passengers have to sleep sitting up. But I won't mind, really. I'm so glad to be aboard this train, I'd sweep the aisles and scrub the galley if necessary."

His eyes, gazing at her intently, were like liquid smoke. "Did I misunderstand you earlier, Miss Marshall?"

Devon was spooning caviar on a biscuit; she had eaten

this delicacy only once before, at a presidential reception, and still was not sure she liked it, since it was apparently an acquired taste. "What do you mean, sir?"

"What I said. Did I misunderstand you?"

"Oh," she murmured, comprehending. It wasn't going to be a free ride, after all; she would have to pay the piper, and he would call the tune. She put the canape down, suddenly losing her appetite. "You're going to exact your pound of flesh?"

"Aptly put," he said. "I can almost believe you really are a writer. The question is, are you a welcher?"

"If so, I'll be dumped at the next station, right?"

"Wrong. I'll get off with you and personally escort you back to Richmond."

"Why would you do that?"

"Because I own stock in this railroad and don't want it sued. People are always hunting reasons to sue the railroads. Lawyers are beginning to specialize in such litigations."

The prospect of being delivered home to Mrs. Chester like a runaway child was too appalling to contemplate. She had gambled and lost, and her honor was forfeit. "Is that what you had in mind last night, when you invited me to supper?" she asked.

"More or less," he nodded.

"I see." She winced, abashed at her naivete. His only interest was in her body, to use and discard as he would a tart. He'd have propositioned her at the hotel, gambling then as now on her desperation. "I'll have some brandy," she said. "Some wine and whiskey, too."

He laughed. "Come now, you don't need all that fortification. It won't be that bad."

"But you're married!"

"Is that what you counted on, my marital fidelity?"

"Don't you love your wife and children?"

"I have no children, and my wife has nothing whatever to do with this."

"It's a common occurrence, I suppose"—Devon gestured significantly—"with such a convenience. . . ."

In the ensuing silence, the clicking wheels sounded like mocking tongues. Devon turned toward a window. The ravaged countryside lay peacefully asleep, the gray ghosts at rest. It must be near midnight, time for the coach to turn into a pumpkin, and the prince a pirate. Wordlessly, she rose and carried her straw valise into the dressing room, hoping the lights would be out when she returned. Her muslin wrapper was so shabby, her dimity nightshift faded and thin as cheesecloth. And she had not the vaguest notion of what to do with a man in bed; she knew only what she was supposed to do, not how to do it. And what if she would find herself pregnant and abandoned in a strange city. . . .

Keith was perusing some papers from his portfolio, and ignored her when she emerged. With a covert glance at his profile, silhouetted by the wall-lamps, she slipped quickly and quietly into bed. The mattress was deep and soft, the fresh linens sheer luxury after the coarse sheeting and often bare ticking of her beds the past few years. He continued to study the documents, frowning as if puzzled. Devon lay on her side and gazed at the passing landscape. There was something soothing about the atmosphere, the sounds and rhythms of the night, the aroma of pine and pasture and fertile earth wafting through the open windows.

Finally, he closed and locked the case and stepped into the lavatory. He came out wearing a crimson silk robe over his gray broadcloth trousers and poured himself a nightcap. He appeared to drink a great deal without actually consuming much—an acquired art, she suspected, useful in business and social life.

"There's something I—I must tell you, Mr. Curtis."

"Don't you think, under the circumstances, we might be a little less formal?"

"What should I call you?"

"My name is Keith, and yours is Devon. Good, serviceable names, wouldn't you say?" He finished his drink. "What is it you have to tell me, Devon?"

"You're going to be disappointed."

"Why?"

"Because I—well, I don't know what to do!"

"I didn't expect you would, my dear. I think I've known enough women to recognize a virgin when I see one."

Tremulously she watched him approach, the sheet pulled up to her chin, although she still wore her night clothes. "And still you would take me?"

"Now look here, Devon!" His voice had the impatience of an elder trying to reason with a deliberately difficult

child. "I did my damndest to discourage you in this impetuous adventure, to persuade you to stay at home, where
you belonged. But you would hear no counsel. In your
frantic desperation, you'd have sold yourself at auction for
a ticket to Manhattan and had to repeat the performance
immediately on arrival, to get food and shelter. It happens
every day to naive country maids in the big city. They all
think they can conquer it, and a few do—but a damned
few only. Without a protector, without friends or funds or
even a job, the majority end up walking the streets and
picking pockets, in brothels and jail. Some finish in the
harbor and rivers. I may be able to spare you that fate, at
least."

Daniel Haverston had tried to convey the same message,
in milder language, and while Devon pondered it, Keith
shucked his robe and sat down on the bed beside her.
Coarse black hair bristled on his broad chest; his belly was
lean and flat, and his muscular arms looked powerful
enough to crush any resistance. She expected to be taken
like Grant took Richmond. Suddenly all the horrible tales
of Yankee brutes raping helpless maidens sprang to mind,
and she was terrified and panicky and rebellious, thwarting
his advances, averting her face and compressing her lips
under his.

"Open your mouth," he commanded. "I know you've
been kissed before. Respond to me, Devon!"

She obeyed like an automaton, remembering a little tin
doll she'd had that performed when the key in its back
was wound; remembering, too, the whispered advice of
matrons during the sieges, that reluctance only stimulated
the male animal, maddened and made him more determined and ruthless, and the ultimate consequences harder
to bear.

"That's better." Removing the pins from her hair, Keith
put his hands and face in the sweet silky softness. "Now
take off those rags, they repulse me."

"I told you I was poor."

"I have some business in Washington," he said. "We'll
get you some clothes there."

"Please," she implored. "The lights."

"Let me see you first. You've nothing to hide, have you?
No defects or deformities?" His tone teased, but as her

eyes misted, he quickly apologized. "Forgive me. I'm not accustomed to so much modesty."

He rose to extinguish the lamps. When he returned she was naked under the sheet, her breasts taut and quivering, her whole being tense with dread expectancy, still hoping somehow to dissuade, divert, or evade him. He stripped and got into bed, hesitating slightly before embracing her, as if reluctant to proceed against her will. "This needn't be difficult for you, Devon. And it has to happen sometime, you know, unless you want to remain a virgin all your life."

"I expected it to happen with my husband," she quavered.

"Pretend I am tonight."

Resigned to her fate, Devon tried to relax and comply, while Keith sought to overcome her aversion, leisurely kissing and caressing and whispering endearments she had imagined a man would say only to his wife. Her response was gradual and involuntary, an instinctive awakening of sensuality in which she was too absorbed to protest or repulse him. Her nipples rose to his touch and tongue, and his mouth seemed as natural at her breasts as his sensitive fingers probing the moist folds between her thighs, and his swollen organ seeking entry. She was not sure just how he accomplished the ultimate invasion of her body, but she realized that she had inadvertently assisted him, if only by acquiescence. Her passive, silent yielding apparently surprised him as much as her, for he lay quietly with her, accustoming Devon to complete consummation, while the swaying coach rocked them like lovers in a hammock.

It seemed to Devon that they traveled for miles in that intimate coupling, that secret genital contact which was stimultaneously tender and violent, painful and pleasurable, and she was drifting into a vague trance, a strange and mysterious enchantment, which he shattered in an abrupt and desperate separation, spilling and wasting himself, trembling and heaving in some intense spasm that made her want to comfort him. None of her mild experiences with Daniel Haverston's suppressed passions had prepared her for the intensity of this man's. She stroked his back soothingly and waited for him to speak.

"Thank you," he said humbly. "You're a sweet girl, Devon, and I hope it wasn't too unbearable for you."

"No," she murmured, touched by his humility, as if the conquest and victory were hers.

From somewhere he produced a towel, applied it to her and then himself. And what now? she wondered. Talk, sleep, more sex? Would she become pregnant?

"It's strange how the moon seems to follow us," she said. "It's been outside the windows all along, and the stars seem low enough to touch."

"They're infinities away, however. And starlight is fire, you know."

"Yes. Astronomy was my father's hobby. He had a good telescope and used to let me look at the sky, to rid my mind of some childish notions gleaned from fables: that clouds were fairy castles, and rain angels' tears, and snow sugar strewn by elves. I especially liked to think the stars were fireflies to catch and hold in my hands."

"Childhood fantasies," he mused. "We all have them. Until I was six I believed there actually was a man in the moon and he lived on green cheese. Teachers have to remove a lot of nonsense from youngsters' heads in order to insert knowledge and logic. But I suppose little dreams are as necessary as big ones, and tiny expectations as important as great ones. Besides, children must lose their innocence and face reality soon enough."

"Too soon," Devon lamented. "Are we out of Virginia yet?"

"No, it's over a hundred miles to Washington, and many stops on the run. We won't arrive until morning."

"Do you always travel this way?"

"If possible. But I haven't had this convenience long, only since the war. I had it custom-built. The passenger cars were such abominations then, hardly fit for cattle, and they're not much better now. But it's no great novelty in New York. A number of other men—Jim Fisk, Jay Gould, Daniel Drew, Cornelius Vanderbilt, August Belmont, William Marcy Tweed—also have private railcars."

"How long will you be in Washington?"

"Several days. We'll stay in a hotel."

And when finally they reached New York, what then? A few greenbacks and goodbye? She sighed forlornly.

"You must be tired," he said, kissing her gently. "Good night, darling. Try to sleep now."

Surprisingly enough, she could and did.

Chapter 3

After some delay and confusion at Alexandria, the train proceeded across the Potomac trestle to the Baltimore & Ohio's Washington terminal, which was at the base of Capitol Hill.

Devon walked beside Keith, trying to assemble the jumble of emotions in her mind. It seemed like a dream. She had awakened in the morning on a train, naked in a stranger's bed, having paid her fare to New York with the only price he had wanted, and now she was in the middle of pandemonium.

Porters were toting baggage and bundles in and out of the station to the public and private conveyances and freight drays standing at the entrance. Keith pointed out a senator, congressman, an ambassador, and two lobbyists among the arriving and departing passengers; the crowd also included the inevitable hustlers, harlots, and soldiers. It seemed impossible there could be enough room in Washington to accommodate them all.

Keith engaged a hack for them, leaving Rufus with the rail coach.

"Where will we stay?" Devon asked.

"I keep a suite at the Clairmont, Devon. The Curtis Bank holds the mortgage. And don't worry. I don't sign registers. The Clairmont is my home when I'm in Washington, and I come and go as I please."

Keith was watching her, and she looked at him now. She liked his smooth bronze skin and the scent of his tonic, which was something superior to bay rum. The razor shortage had forced Southern men, young and old, to grow beards and mustaches, and she was tired of hirsute faces.

"What do you think of Washington so far?" he asked.

"I think," she replied succinctly, "that Richmond

25

would've been a much better capital for the country."

He grinned. "Careful, darling. Your rebel temper is showing. You didn't leave it behind, did you?"

But he sounded amused, and she saw herself as the object of his amusement, a mere titillation, and retreated into piqued frustration.

Getting settled in the hotel was less mortifying than Devon had feared. The atmosphere was gracious, the staff extremely courteous. She enjoyed riding up to the top floor of the hotel in an Otis steam elevator, her first such experience, and as they entered Keith's elaborate suite she rushed to a window to gaze out at the city.

Many government buildings, including the Capitol, were unfinished, in various stages of construction. Great piles of brick and stone lay in the streets, mingled with marble blocks, columns and statues, like the ruins of Carthage. The main thoroughfare, although broad and busy, was paved with collapsed cobblestones, dusty in dry weather, a bog in rain, and the White House, also incomplete, was surpassed by some of the antebellum plantation manors which it resembled.

Beside her, his arm curving about her waist, Keith said, "It's awesome, the power concentrated in those two buildings."

"And the corruption? My father wrote in an editorial once that American politicians have no peers in their field, and the ethics of the Roman Senate surpassed those of Congress."

"He was right in some respects. Still, the system has produced some of the greatest statesmen and patriots in history, unsurpassed even in the Forum. Many, as you know, from your own state. There never has been, nor ever will be, a perfect government, simply because there are no perfect people." He consulted his watch, a magnificent gold timepiece with several jeweled seals on the chain. "I have to leave shortly, but I'll try to get back early—is there anything you need?"

"May I borrow some paper? I'd like to record my impressions of Washington. If I'm going to find a newspaper job in New York, I should have some current work to show."

Keith's brows arched.

"I was quite serious about that. I have every intention of making my living writing. Didn't I make that clear?"

"It's a ridiculous idea, Devon."

"Why? You must know some publishers."

"Many."

"Well, then—you can help me get started."

He only frowned.

She persisted, "A letter of introduction would be helpful."

"My dear, the work you did on your father's newspaper could not possibly have earned you much reputation in journalism. I happen to know that it was a small paper, hardly in the class of the Richmond *Enquirer* or *Examiner*. Besides, there are veteran battlefield correspondents looking for jobs now. You're young and inexperienced ... and female. Now, let's call the issue settled."

She disengaged his arm and moved away, shaking her head vehemently. "Oh, no! I don't know the technical term for the agreement I made with you to get to New York, but it ends there. I am a single woman and I want to work and you are a married man and I won't be just another addition to your harem!"

"I don't have a harem, Devon."

"Collection, then. Mistresses, concubines, paramours—whatever you call them, they're all the same."

"No, my dear, they are not the same. And if you intend to be a writer, you had better learn the difference."

"I don't care about the difference!" she cried.

"I have to leave now," he said, picking up his inevitable portfolio. "Have you a formal gown of some kind?"

"One," she nodded. "I've been saving it, I never quite knew for what." But she did know. When she had rescued it from the fire, sacrificing more useful garments, she had visualized it as her bridal gown: ivory brocade flounced in Chantilly lace, all she would have needed was a veil of illusion.

"Good," he said. "We'll have dinner out if you're still here when I return."

"Where else would I be, Mr. Curtis?"

"Oh, I don't know, Miss Marshall. You might be out peddling your property on Pennsylvania Avenue. If you offer any other man that deed on the same proposition, he'll buy it sight unseen. Just remember, New York is still three hundred miles away. Think about it, Devon—and try to be more cautious than you were in approaching me. I might've been an ax murderer, for all you knew."

She wanted to scream and strike him. Instead she ran into the bedroom and locked the door and threw herself across the bed, attacking the bolster when he had gone. Damn him! He did not intend to liberate her when they reached New York—he intended to confine her in a plush prison of his own voluptuous design. And he would use the restraints that men had always used with women: dependence, security, helplessness, fear.

The fury spent, Devon rose and paced the room, like a prisoner a cell. No bars, yet she was immured. No ball and chain, yet she was restrained. Because money was freedom, and she was broke. How pitiful and incongruous her straw bags looked next to his leather luggage. Hopefully the management regarded her as a poor relation, for surely his previous companions had not been so obviously destitute.

There was a rap on the parlor door, and a voice called, "Chambermaid!" A uniformed young woman entered with her arms full of fresh linens. "Morning, Ma'am. I'm Mrs. Taylor. Mr. Curtis thought you might need me. I'm assigned to this suite."

"Well, yes. I'd like something pressed, please," Devon said, getting out the crushed ballgown.

"Is there anything else you wish me to do, Ma'am?"

"You can help me dress later, and fix my hair."

"Yes, Ma'am." Mrs. Taylor bobbed a curtsy and, after putting fresh sheets on the bed and fluffy Turkish towels in the bathroom, left with the ivory brocade gown.

Devon looked in the wardrobe and saw some masculine clothes, including many formal ones, but nothing feminine. Didn't his wife ever travel with him? Maybe he wasn't married at all, but just wore the wedding ring as another convenience.

When Keith returned at dusk, Devon was bathed and dressed and sitting patiently in the parlor. The lamps were lit. There were flowers in the vases and bowls, and a tray of canapes from the hotel kitchen. He paused, as if in surprise, and his eyes gleamed with quick admiration.

"God, I'm glad to see you! I was afraid you'd be gone,

Stand up, and let me look at you." She obeyed, posing for him, and he feasted on her beauty. "I don't know when I've seen a lovelier sight. You're beautiful, Devon."

"Thank you," she said demurely. "How did business go?"

"Hectic, like dealing with Ali Baba and the forty thieves. I swear, I never met a politician without larceny in his heart. They're all sons of pirates. But they didn't outwit or plunder me. I've got a portfolio of notes signed in blood."

"And a mortgage on the White House?"

He smiled, tweaking a golden curl. "The Treasury, my sweet."

"Is that possible?"

"Just about, by cornering the gold market—but I wouldn't try to do anything that drastic. That's how panics are made, and no banker wants that. Those of thirty-seven and fifty-seven almost destroyed the country."

"I don't understand economics and high finance," Devon confessed. "They confound me."

"But you do realize that's how the Confederacy went bankrupt? Not enough gold to support the paper currency. The mint was operated like a printing press."

"I remember drives to collect gold, and ladies donating their jewelry."

"Drops in the bucket," he scoffed. "How many such trinkets do you think it takes to make one ingot? The poor ladies were robbed. They'd have been wiser to hold on to their little treasures to barter in the black market."

"They were patriots," Devon bristled.

"And where are the patriots now? In rags and starving! Which reminds me—do we dine out or in this evening?"

"Whatever you want, Keith."

"Ah, you've finally said it."

"Said what?"

"My name. That's the first time, you know. You didn't even say it last night, when I made love to you. You haven't asked my age yet, either. Aren't you curious?"

"A little," she admitted.

"I'm thirty-one."

"You're very young to be so successful."

"I inherited most of the money," he said. "My ancestors, bless 'em, were shrewd enough to buy real estate and make other wise investments on Manhattan Island. My paternal great-grandfather was clever, a thrifty Scotsman. He established one of the first permanent counting houses, now the Curtis Bank, in Wall Street. My mother's family—well, they had a great many interests in England. I'd like to take credit for being a financial genius and self-made man, ascending by my bootstraps, but that's simply not the case. I was born to it."

"I think you're just being modest."

"You're a romantic little soul, aren't you? You like rags-to-riches, triumph-over-adversity stories, and want to be your own heroine."

"I will, too," she predicted. "Wait and see."

He removed a Havana cigar from a gold monogrammed case, lit it, and smiled at her through the smoke. "You delight me, Miss Marshall. Ours was the best deal I made in Richmond. Except for you, this would've been a damned dull trip. Now why don't you fix me a drink, please, while I change. Two-thirds Scotch, one water. In the marble-topped credenza. Should be some Madeira or Claret too, for you, if the help hasn't been pilfering."

Suddenly Devon felt like a plaything, a toy for temporary diversion. Keith did not take her talent or ambition any more seriously than did Daniel Haverston, although for different reasons, and it annoyed her. Worse even, he had taken advantage of her desperation, and this was contemptible. She should despise him.

He came out in black broadcloth and white linen, splendidly handsome and virile. The challenges of the afternoon had stimulated him, giving his skin a high color and his gray eyes a combative glint like honed steel. Evidently he thrived on the piratical confrontations, used them as duels to sharpen his financial wit and acumen. And yes, Devon had to admit it. He aroused emotions in her that Daniel Haverston had never touched, that she had not even realized she possessed. She was mortally afraid of falling in love with him, and having him plunder her body and take her heart as forfeit. It seemed immoral to even contemplate such a profane love, and a worse immorality to compare him with the beaten and broken veteran she had forsaken. Her hand trembled as she handed him the glass. He gazed at her curiously but made no comment, as if he sensed her fears.

"Will we go to Willard's?" she asked. It was the most famous hotel in Washington, and the only one she had heard of.

"Well, I'd like to show you off there, naturally, and at the National and Metropolitan, too. But I think Dijon's is in order this evening. It's the favorite restaurant of the French embassy, and often caters to the White House."

"Sounds perfect," she said, her eyes thanking him.

"I think you'll like the privacy."

Night life had never flourished publicly in Richmond, even before the war, and the entertainments were generally private affairs requiring invitations. Washington was a wide-open city. Something was going on in every hotel and hall, despite pigs rooting in the streets and putrid sewage flowing in canals. Both theaters, Ford's and Grove's, had capacity audiences. Since no food or liquor shortage existed, the restaurants and saloons were packed. There were also numerous private clubs and casinos and establishments with glowing red globes before them. Devon had never seen so many prostitutes brazenly soliciting and thought most of the camp followers of both armies must have ended up in Washington, which was still full of men in uniform. Carriages and hacks rattled over the cobblestones, and cavalrymen rode their mounts to their favorite haunts. Less a metropolis than an overgrown frontier town—wild, lusty, bawdy, Washington was apparently lawless—and if she managed to write an accurate appraisal of it, what ladies' publication would print it?

Dijon's was a serene and polished little island of crystal and silver and mirrors, of soft music and quiet voices. Devon had never dined in such fashion before: lobster, crab, capon, some wonderful entree called Cailles à la Grand Monarque, pastries, mousses and glaces, vintage wines, and fresh plump strawberries plucked from a tiny silver filigree tree in a salver of powdered sugar. Their table was in a small intimate alcove partially concealed by a beaded curtain, private but not secluded, for she could see into the main salon and hear the romantic violins. She ate too much dessert and drank too much champagne and stared at Keith too intently; and he smiled too charmingly and paid her too many extravagant compliments.

"How fair you are," he said softly, his eyes caressing

her pale hair and creamy shoulders and breasts above the decolletage. "Pearls would be perfect with your coloring, I think. Do you know your skin appears translucent, as if a light were shining through it? The glow of youth, I suppose. And I wonder if you realize how precious that youth is, Devon, and how desirable."

By the time they returned to the Clairmont, she was almost giddy, and he was amused again. Oh God, if only she could do more than amuse him!

"This tonight was a conspiracy, wasn't it?" she accused. "To seduce me to your way of life. You're really quite wicked, Keith. Something of a devil."

He laughed. "And you, my pet, are tipsy." He kissed her mouth. "Your lips taste like strawberries and wine."

"You're evading the issue. How many women have you brought to this hotel and said that to? How many have you seduced with your special charm and magic?"

"Are you jealous?"

"What right have I to be jealous, pray?"

"More than you might think," he said seriously, and then asked, "Would you like a nightcap?"

"Mercy, no! I'm spinning now."

"Do you need help undressing?"

"No, I'll manage."

"Go along, then. I'll join you shortly."

And when he finally put aside his work and joined Devon, his urgency swept away all pretense of restraint, and he urged her to reciprocate. "You're holding back, denying yourself and me. Don't do that, Devon. Indulge. Lust is a marvelous thing when released, and you want this as much as I do."

"How can you say that? Last night I was a virgin!"

"A passionate little virgin who almost reached climax her first time, and will tonight."

"I don't know what you mean."

"You will, when you experience it."

"Oh, you *are* wicked, Keith! Even lighting the bedside candles, as if for a ritual."

"Love properly performed is a ritual, Devon, and far too beautiful to be hidden or distorted in darkness. I want to see you, all of you—your body, your face, your expressions. I want you to see me and my reactions, and never again be ashamed of this natural and wonderful divine act."

"But I'm afraid, Keith! I don't understand myself any more. I don't know what's happening to me."

"You're falling in love, that's all. Welcome it, Devon. Liberate that slave to convention within yourself, and let me show you what this can really mean. It can be ecstasy in every sense of the word."

"And then I'll love you and never be free! I'll just exchange one slave for another. Is that what you want?"

"Yes, and is it so frightening, Devon? Hasn't it occurred to you that the same thing could happen to me? That it may already have happened?"

"For the tenth, twentieth, hundredth time?"

"This could turn into a filibuster," he said, "and this is cloture." His mouth silenced hers, and she embraced him with sudden delirious abandon, in which he exulted and she experienced the promised rapture, and still in triumphant possession of her body, he demanded, "Will you tell me *that* was coercion?"

"No, but it doesn't change anything, Keith."

"It changes everything, Devon."

"How? You're still married, how can this change that? Tell me, Keith. *How?*"

"Oh, you do have the inquiring journalistic mind, don't you? You want facts. Very well. The simple inescapable fact is that I'm in love with you, and I think it's mutual. I want you for myself, and I will not help you in any way that could make you independent of me."

"Then I'll do it on my own!" she cried defiantly.

"We'll see, darling. We'll see."

Chapter 4

Among Keith's more exasperating qualities were his honesty and consistency, for he said what he meant and meant what he said, and there was no getting around him with feminine wiles or witchery. He obtained a bill for every item he purchased for her in Washington, and though this was her own suggestion, it irked Devon to have him implement it so methodically. She determined to incur as little indebtedness as possible, but her wardrobe was so depleted and the temptations so great, she had difficulty resisting and choosing wisely. Nor did his criticism of the career clothes make it any easier for her. He said the demure Scotch-plaid gingham made her look like a frontier schoolmarm, the prim white-collared gray linen would be fine for a Puritan maiden, and the sedate brown merino belonged on a Quaker missionary. He delighted in her personal battles in which whim triumphed over thrift, indulgence over conservatism, and with the conspiracy of the clever modistes, she ended up with a wardrobe more suitable to pleasure than profession, and a handsome Saratoga trunk to carry it to New York in the opulent coach now attached to the Baltimore & Ohio caravan headed in that direction.

"Let me see now," he said, totaling a sheaf of receipts at his desk. "Your bill comes to seven hundred sixty-nine dollars and thirty-two cents."

"Seven hundred and ... oh, it can't be that much, Keith! You must've made a mistake. Add it again."

"Perhaps." He refigured the long column. "You're right, my dear. I did err. It's actually more than eight hundred dollars, plus ten percent interest. The total is exactly nine hundred two dollars and twenty-eight cents."

Devon sat down swiftly, her heart palpitating like a rabbit's with a wolf in pursuit. "You're charging me interest?"

"It's a business loan, isn't it?"

"But I'll never be able to repay so much!"

"I'll accept the deeds as collateral."

She scrounged in the trunk, angrily pawing the finery which now seemed like a tangle of traps, and flung the faded documents at him. "Here! Shall I prick my finger and sign the note in blood, Mr. Curtis?"

"May I remind you, Miss Marshall, that this arrangement is your idea, not mine? You can change it and cancel your debt with one word."

"I will pay for it," she vowed, "if it takes the rest of my life working in a sweatshop."

"And well it might," he drawled. "Do you know what shopgirls earn in wages? Two or three dollars a week, often less. Factories pay no better, and the hours are longer. And writers, my dear, rarely manage to support themselves; they starve in cellars and attics and die in obscurity and despair. Not the famous ones, but there are only a few of these. As for editors, a top one may make thirty to sixty dollars a week. Reporters often earn considerably less, and there is not to my knowledge one twenty-year-old female journalist on any major or minor publication in New York."

"Just the same, there are women in the profession! Some of them quite famous. Jenny June, Fanny Fern, Kate Field—"

"They're not callow young girls, Devon. Jenny June has been with *Demorest's Magazine* for years and was formerly on the editorial staff of the New York *World*, where her husband, David Croly, is managing editor. Fanny Fern is a pseudonym for the very mature wife of historian James Parton. Kate Field, of the *Tribune*, has published several books and numerous articles in leading magazines, including *Harper's Weekly* and *Atlantic Monthly*. Apparently you've only heard of the few successful ladies in the field, not the many failures."

"You can't discourage me, Keith Curtis. Journalism's in my blood, and my father said I had a natural flair for it. I was born with printer's ink in my veins and a quill in my hand. My great-grandfather, Cyrus Marshall, was a town crier and started in publishing by printing and distributing broadbills. My grandfather, Virgil Marshall, was a reporter during the Revolution; he followed the Continental

Army and was at Valley Forge and Yorktown when the British surrendered. His copy appeared in Whig papers all over the Colonies, and even some Tory journals used it as propaganda."

"That's an impressive heritage, my dear, but it hardly qualifies *you* for a post on a metropolitan daily."

"But you know the publishers, Keith!"

"Have you forgotten already, or imagine I have? I told you that I would not help you in that way."

Her eyes blazed in fury and defiance. "And I'm telling you now, I will not submit to you again under these circumstances!"

"Submit? I thought it was cooperation, Devon. But if you want to dissolve the corporation, you may do so officially at Baltimore."

"Without any money?"

"Get some. You know how now."

For a moment she could only stare at him, mortified. Then with a sharp cry of rage that brought him swiftly to his feet, she rushed at him violently, striking out in blind frenzy, clawing and crying incoherently.

Catching her flailing arms, Keith crossed them securely over her heaving breast and pinned her back to the wall. She struggled desperately, a wild spirit determined to be free, conquered and subdued only by his superior strength. Sick with humiliation and weak with despair, she collapsed against him limp as a rag doll. When she finally calmed down, Keith carried her to the bed, sloshed brandy into a glass and forced her to drink some, holding it to her mouth when she tried to push his hand away, until she swallowed a few gulps.

"Are you all right?" he asked anxiously.

She glared at him sullenly. "Your solicitude is very touching," she mocked.

He smiled faintly, shaking his head. "With fighters like you around, how did the South lose the war!"

"Maybe because we were fighting monsters instead of men."

"Maybe," he nodded, "and I'll admit that was a monstrous thing to say. But I was angry, because you keep implying that my interest in you is only sexual and that I'm holding you in white slavery, and you know better. Why do you persist in provoking me, Devon?"

"Well, I won't any longer, Mr. Curtis."

"Don't be childish," he said. "You're not getting off at Baltimore. Rufus will be serving supper soon. Do you want him to see you sulking?"

"I don't care!"

"Yes, you do, Devon. Pull yourself together now. How do you expect to cope in this competitive world if you get hysterical whenever you encounter an obstacle or disappointment because of your sex or idealism? If you insist on fighting your own survival battles, you had better toughen up a little. New York is not Richmond, and no allowances will be made for your Southern delicacy or inexperience. It will be one fierce challenge after another, and don't delude yourself that youth and beauty and charm can win them all. Somehow those weapons work best in gardens, parlors . . . and boudoirs."

She got up and began to arrange her hair and clothes. The Saratoga trunk had become her Pandora's box, and its prodigal contents her probable doom, but she effected a tentative truce. "How does one find a room in New York? Are they listed in the papers?"

"There are many hotels."

"I mean a boarding house, Keith. Or small flat, where I could shift for myself."

"And how do you expect to pay the advance rent?"

"Why, I—I shall have to borrow it from you."

"At the rate your debts are mounting, I'll have to hire an extra bookkeeper for your ledgers."

"I'm sure that would work a great hardship on you," she said morosely. "You must have millions."

"Millions," he agreed amiably.

"Is there anyone in New York richer than you?"

"One man. Cornelius Vanderbilt. But there are many other millionaires in Wall Street. Your Southern editors refer to them contemptuously as robber barons. Your father probably used the term in the *Sentinel* too." She nodded. "And no doubt he'd have put me in that category."

"No, I think he'd have had a different name for you," she quipped, and he only laughed.

Supper was kabobs of braised tenderloin alternated on skewers with succulent mushrooms, pearl onions, and cherry tomatoes; crisp green salad with a deliciously piquant dressing, and chilled burgundy, and Devon ate heartily, forgetting that she had considered a hunger strike to embarrass him before his servant. Afterwards, while he was occupied with his portfolio, she sampled bonbons from the huge box he had bought her in Washington. She had not tasted French chocolates in five years and could not seem to satisfy her craving. There were books and periodicals aboard, but she was still too upset with Keith to concentrate on reading, nor could she compose anything cogent on paper when she tried. At midnight, she began to nod and yawn.

"How long do you intend to work?" she asked.

"Another hour or so. Go to bed, Devon, if you're sleepy. And don't worry, I won't bother you."

Somewhere in the dark night it was storming. Clouds obscured the moon and stars. Distant lightning flashed like cannonade in the sky, and the remote rumble of thunder recalled the sights and sounds of Richmond under siege. Devon remembered her fear and apprehension during the Seven Days Battles, wondering if General Lee could halt the enemy advance up the peninsula, if the gunboats in the James River and battleships on the Chesapeake Bay could hold off invasion, if anything save God almighty could stop the Yankees. The terror-filled memories rushed back to mind now, and residual tremors shook her tense body. When finally Keith joined her, she was still restlessly awake and reached out a timid conciliatory hand.

"Don't be cross with me, Keith. It frightens me when you're angry and aloof. You'll be the only person I know in New York, my only friend."

"How naive you are, Devon. A child. In Washington I told you that I love you. We've been lovers. Do you honestly imagine that we could be only friends now?"

"But this thing between us is wrong, Keith! Sinful. Adultery for you, and fornication for me."

"That's puritanism."

"And what is love for the sake of love?"

"Hedonism, to some moralists. Sin and vice to preachers. I'm not trying to justify or sanctify it, Devon. I'm only telling you how I feel, as you've told me how you feel."

Her hand lay passively in his. A few yellow lights gleamed and flickered mistily in the village they were passing. The train whistled mournfully, as if saluting a cemetery. It began to rain, slowly and softly at first, then violently as the storm approached and broke.

"Do you want me now, Keith?"

"I'll always want you, Devon."

And what, dear God, if she always wanted him, reaching out when he wasn't there, finding only emptiness and silence and want and need?

She took his hand and put it on her breast.

None of Devon's preconceived notions of New York City stood up to reality, for it was simply beyond the realm of imagination. Before the war Richmond had had a population of forty thousand, that figure fluctuating with refugees. Keith told her that a million people lived in Manhattan, most of them concentrated in the tight narrow cramped southern tip of the island. Devon tried to think what she would have done had she arrived alone and broke in this fantastic place, which seemed a curious mixture of Paradise and pandemonium.

Compared to Broadway, Richmond's Main Street and Washington's Pennsylvania Avenue were village lanes. There were hundreds of shops and offices, restaurants and saloons and oyster bars, immense department stores with numerous plateglass windows displaying fabulous dreams for sale, and absolutely palatial hotels. People packed the horsecars, omnibuses, and sidewalks, and there were commercial caravans of merchandise vans and freight drays, butchers' and bakers' and produce wagons, vendors' carts, and great red-and-yellow brewery wagons drawn by the biggest horses Devon had ever seen, shaggy behemoths with banjo-sized hoofs. Liveried coachmen piloted elegant carriages, and sportsmen drove their own rakish pleasure phaetons, tandems and drays. There were hurdy-gurdies and harlequins and street entertainers. Beggars, bums, soldiers, seamen. And mounted police weaving in and out of the seemingly endless procession of hopeless confusion.

It took her breath away, and when once their hackney stalled and the driver began to bellow and rage at the impediments, she clutched Keith's hand, as if to make sure he was still beside her. He smiled at her anxiety.

"Welcome to Manhattan, Miss Marshall."

"It's awesome, Keith."

He cocked a dark brow. "Can this be the defiant little

rebel who assured me she wasn't afraid of the big bad Yankee town and would conquer it?"

"Oh, but I didn't know then how much there was to conquer! It's a whole new world."

"Many worlds," he said. "Sodom and Gomorrah and Babylon. Neronian Rome. London in the Restoration, and Paris before the Revolution. I warned you. It is a heartless dragon with an insatiable appetite for female flesh, and no tender young morsel could long survive without her special St. George."

Devon missed his last words, distracted by an organ grinder and his cute monkey, then a clown peddling balloons and pinwheels, and a bird-man toting a brace of wicker cages containing a squawking parrot and a singing canary. When the hack lurched on again, she was smiling, eager and excited, swept up in the magic spell of this Baghdad on the Hudson, this Roman carnival and Grecian fair.

Approaching some burned buildings and rubble, where workmen and machinery were busy, she was soberly reminded of the destruction of Richmond. "What happened here?" she asked.

"The draft riots. They were bloody and costly both in lives and property, and some scars will always remain. Surely they were reported in the Richmond papers."

"In what space they could spare. But their accuracy was doubted due to Northern censorship of Southern correspondents. The riots were caused by the inequities of the Union conscription laws, weren't they, which allowed rich men to buy military substitutes? Naturally, you were exempt."

He ignored the sarcasm, explaining quietly, "I was a financial adviser to the President, and I also loaned a great deal of money to the Treasury. I think I did my part."

So his gold had helped to defeat the Confederacy, she thought ruefully, as it had bought her temporary alliance. Then a spectacular white marble building confronted them, obliterating the argument. "Oh, what is that *palace*, Keith?"

"The St. Nickolas Hotel."

"It must have a thousand rooms!"

"Eight hundred."

"Mercy, what a prodigal place this is! So much of everything—food, clothing, wealth, grandeur."

"And poverty, squalor, crime and misery," he added, lest she forget his previous warnings. "Would you like to stay at the St. Nickolas, until you can find permanent lodgings?"

"Lord, no! I shouldn't want to get accustomed to so much luxury, and then have to leave it." She paused, to muster the courage to pose her next question. "Where do you live, Keith?"

"Gramercy Park."

This meant nothing to her. "In great splendor, no doubt?"

"The important thing," he said with a slight scowl, "is to get you settled somewhere, Devon."

"I've seen some signs. Rooms to let. There was one, Mrs. O'Toole's Boarding House. It looked right homey, and I bet the landlady is a fine Irish cook."

"Probably an old harridan with a drunken husband or lecherous son to pester you," he said. "These places have to be investigated before moving in, Devon. They are not always what they appear or advertise to be. Some are brothels, and worse. I think you should go to a hotel for the present. How much money do you have? Tell me the truth now."

"I showed you in Richmond."

"That pittance! Is that really all you have?"

"Did you think I was lying to get sympathy?"

He frowned. "I don't know what I thought. I guess I just couldn't believe that anyone, not even a naive young girl, would be foolish enough to leave home on such a small reserve. But you're here now and will need another substantial loan." His tone precluded any further debate, and she sat quietly staring at a church spire while he decided on her address, calling out to the driver, "Astor House, please!"

Devon stood in the splendid lobby, looking chic and almost cosmopolitan in a royal blue Florentine travel suit and peacock feathered cloche, while Keith made the necessary arrangements at the desk. Her Saratoga trunk, hand-tooled leather, preceded them up the grand marble staircase to the room, where Keith tipped and dismissed the porters.

"This is an American plan hotel, Devon. Your meals are included in the rate."

"What is the rate?" she asked curiously, glancing about the room, elegantly furnished in the Continental decor favored by European travelers.

"Never mind that now. If you want or need anything extra, just sign a tab. I've established some credit for you. And this"—he removed some greenbacks from his wallet and put them on the bureau—"is some pin money. I think you'll be comfortable here, Devon. Notice the view from your windows? You can watch Broadway—and that's City Hall Park over there." As he moved toward the door, panic seized her.

"You're not leaving!"

"Isn't that what you want?"

"Oh, but you can stay a little while, can't you? It's almost noon, and I—I don't want to go to the dining room alone."

"Have your meals served here," he suggested. "If you go down to supper, do it early—unescorted females are not allowed in the better restaurants after six o'clock."

"Keith, don't go yet, please!" Then, appalled at her tenacity and supplication, she turned away. "I'm sorry. Naturally you want to get home to your wife."

"Darling, it's not that—believe me, it isn't." Crossing the carpet, he drew her swiftly to him. "If you need me, send a message to the Curtis Bank. I'll come as soon as possible."

"Thank you," she said coolly, and the lips his touched were equally cool, like coral snow.

But the moment he had gone she sat down forlornly on a gilt chair and bowed her head on the carved arm. Already she was reaching out for him ... and he wasn't there.

The dining salon was full of luncheon guests, well-dressed men and women, and Devon wondered how many of the couples were husband and wife, and how many man and mistress. Some spoke in foreign tongues—world travelers—and she heard the names of exotic faraway places, and the language of businessmen and merchants, discussing markets and prices. Politicians from adjacent City Hall caucused in dynamic groups—hearty, vociferous men drinking brandied coffee and smoking expensive cigars. And there was also a round table of publishers and editors and journalists from nearby Park Row and Printing House Square.

Devon was one of the few unescorted females in the room. There were some elderly ladies, in severe black gowns adorned with garnet or cameo brooches, apparently permanent residents of the Astor House, sharing their loneliness and quiet desperation over luncheon and afternoon tea. Devon had seen enough of such lost lonely souls in Richmond to know they were widows. But at least they were old widows and evidently provided for, whereas Richmond now had numerous young and poor ones, some still in their teens. Her food stuck in her throat, and she had to wash it down with tea.

In the lobby she bought a couple of papers for two cents each and took them upstairs. One was the *Tribune*, a violently-hated paper in the South during the war, because its publisher had coined the slogan "On to Richmond!" to encourage the capture of the Confederate capital. Considered as treacherous as a Union spy, there was a price on Horace Greeley's head in Virginia. His politics notwithstanding, her father had regarded him as one of the best editors in the business and read the *Tribune* avidly whenever he could get his hands on a contraband copy.

Hodge Marshall had not, however, had the same esteem for James Gordon Bennett's yellow journalism, although his *Herald* was the largest and most popular of the New York dailies. And the latter's personal columns, in which prostitutes, abortionists, and charlatans advertised their lurid services, and illicit lovers made assignations, were notorious even in the South.

Neither paper was advertising for journalists, and it occurred to Devon, after two hours of disappointed searching, that perhaps this was not the way big city editors hired reporters. Nor could she judge the various lodgings offered in the classified sections, being unfamiliar with the neighborhoods.

She counted the greenbacks Keith had left. An even twenty dollars. How much freedom and independence could that buy in this town? She felt like a slave on a money-chain. He had not said how much credit he had established for her, but presumably it was not limitless. Nor had he said when, or if, he would see her again. That, apparently, was up to her. If she needed him she could summon him from his bank in Wall Street, thereby admitting helplessness, defeat, and dependency.

Damned if she would! And damned if she would sit around all afternoon feeling sorry for herself, either! She would put on her bonnet and promenade Broadway, window-shopping, pausing at a tearoom or ice cream parlor, idle away the hours before it was time for supper alone and bed alone. Dear Lord, how could she possibly have gotten used to eating and sleeping with a man not her husband in only five days!

Chapter 5

Gramercy Park, once a dismal swamp, was now considered the Mayfair of Manhattan, surrounded by massive brick and brownstone monuments to wealth. Bronze gas lamps supported by recumbent granite lions flanked the entrance to the Curtis mansion, on the south side of the exclusive park. The architecture was severely symmetrical, the sheer walls uncluttered, the tall narrow windows reaching from floor to ceiling. There were four stories and a basement, where a huge felt-lined vault held treasures of silver and gold and art too priceless for regular display and reserved for special occasions.

"Welcome home, sir," the butler said, taking the master's bags. "I trust you had a pleasant trip."

"Satisfactory, thank you, Hadley."

Keith stepped into the tessellated marble foyer, where ancestral portraits hung in ornate goldleaf frames on oak-paneled walls. The twenty rooms were all impeccably decorated and furnished with the finest pieces of French and English cabinetmakers. Brussels, Aubusson, and Persian carpets covered the floors, and the rich tapestries and hangings of velvet and damask might have come from a king's caravan.

"Mrs. Curtis has been asking for you, sir."

"I sent a message, Hadley."

"Yes, sir. It was delivered. But I think Madam expected you for dinner."

"Where is she?"

"In her rooms, sir."

His wife's rooms occupied most of the third floor and overlooked the private park now in summer greenness and bloom. The wallpaper was flocked in gold fleurs-de-lys, the windows draped in white satin and tied with heavy gold cords. Beside the queenly canopied bed, where Esther

Curtis sat propped against lacy pillows reading a French novel, stood a satin chaise longue and leather-padded wheelchair. The latter had become a part of the suite's furnishings five years before, although the physicians could find no valid medical reason for Esther Curtis' inability to walk. Also within easy reach were a teacart and lap tray, decanters of water and other beverages, dishes of fruit and candy, a portable library, games, jigsaw puzzles, a letter box, stationery, ink, and quills.

"Good evening," Keith said in greeting. "I'm sorry I'm so late getting home, Esther, but there was much unfinished business at the bank."

Esther closed the book, set it aside. She was almost twenty-nine, and strikingly beautiful, with raven hair, violet eyes, and skin pale as moonlight. The sun rarely touched her face, for she seldom used the solarium installed expressly for her; and since her pallor actually enhanced her fragile beauty, she worked at it with a portable vanity box.

"How was Washington? The usual summer madness?"

"The usual. Did anything unusual happen here?"

"No," she complained bitterly, "I'm still bored and confined in this elegant prison!"

"A prison of your own design," he said quietly. "You've had the best doctors in this country, Esther—in the entire world—and they all say the same thing. Your paralysis is in your mind, not your body. But perhaps they are mistaken, and it's really in your soul."

"Does it comfort you to think that, Keith? To delude yourself that you did not do this to me?"

"It was an accident, Esther—you know that. Had you not gotten in the way, trying to protect him, he'd have gone down those stairs instead of you. But what's the use recanting it all again? We've done it so often it's become a ritual of recrimination. I've tried to forget it, to live with it, but you won't let me. Why in God's name won't you let me!"

"Why should I?" she demanded grimly. "In my place, would you let *me* forget?"

Keith's facial muscles tensed and twitched, as if against a still sensitive injury. "Is there anything I can do for you now, Esther? I'm rather tired and want to retire."

"At this hour?"

"I have an early board meeting tomorrow and would like to be at least partially awake."

"Didn't you get any sleep this trip, darling? Perhaps your dissipations are catching up with you. Oh, I know about your affairs, Keith. I've known all along."

"Congratulations on your perception," he mocked. "I must confess I didn't know about yours. Giles Mallard was a complete surprise to me."

"I doubt that. You must have suspected—"

"That I was an artist's cuckold? No, my dear, incredibly enough, I trusted you. I knew you spent a great deal of time in art galleries and theaters, but I thought you were just a dedicated dilettante. Finding you together in his studio was a hell of a shock to me, and I reacted impulsively."

"Impulsively? You were a madman! And look at the result of your insane jealousy and rage. So primitive and unnecessary too. I wasn't even in love with him, merely infatuated."

Keith scowled and gestured impatiently. "Why do you persist in lying about it even at this late date, Esther? We both know the truth. You knew that bastard in Boston, before you met and married me. He followed you to New York, probably at your request. How soon after our honeymoon did you resume your affair? I've often wondered about that. And whose child did you lose in that fall, mine or his? I've wondered about that too."

"Fall? I was flung down those stairs during your wild attack on Mallard! You'd have killed him if I hadn't intervened, and you know it."

"The coward was trying to escape, and you were running after him. If you had remained in his bed, you wouldn't be confined to yours now."

Esther shut her eyes tightly, compressing her lips and resting her head on the pillows. "You'd better go, Keith. I'm about to have one of my fits, as you call them. Leave me alone, please. You buried me in this mausoleum—the least you can do is let me rest in peace."

"If it's any consolation to you, Esther, these walls also confine me. For all practical purposes, I'm just as dead and entombed as you."

"Ah, but your lusty spirit is still active enough! How many adulteries did you commit this time?"

"Good night," he muttered and turned to go.

His perfunctory visits always ended that way, with Esther accusing and carping and berating, and him walking out. The hostility between them was so intense and volatile, it often erupted involuntarily. And if Keith exercised better control over his emotions, it was only because he had releases and compensations which Esther lacked and bitterly resented. She gazed after him, trembling with rage, tempted to throw her book, to explode in the kind of tantrum he despised and had at first indulged but now ignored.

Bastard, she thought furiously, sorting among her medications for a palliative. Laudanum had been prescribed for the spinal pain of which she complained, and there were also various herbal tonics and elixirs, patent nostrums, and pills in every color of the rainbow. Esther rarely took any except the sedatives, however, and had discovered experimentally that one in particular not only induced sound slumber but marvelous and realistic dreams. It was this little gem that she sought and swallowed now.

It was winter and all was white loveliness, and Esther was skating on Jamaica Pond, flirting with an artist who was sketching the scene. "Am I in the picture?" she asked, pausing to admire his work.

"You inspired it," he answered.

"Really? Then I must see it when it's finished. What's your name?"

"Giles Mallard."

"Where do you live, Mr. Mallard?"

"Mallard," he said, which was how he signed his paintings. "In an attic, naturally. Where else do struggling young artists live?" He brushed her scarlet scarf on a female skater, and her red bladed boots under a bright swirled skirt, and his work took on dimension and vitality, as if she did indeed provide inspiration. When he topped the dark head with her white fur bonnet, she asked, "Don't you want to know her name?"

"I already do," he replied. "It's Esther Stanfield, and she lives on Louisburg Square, in a red brick Bulfinch, with violet-paned windows to match her eyes."

"Dear me! I didn't know I had a secret admirer. This is all very exciting!"

He feathered in some frosted trees, and a few crystal snowflakes falling from the bleak sky. "I expect to finish this masterpiece tomorrow, Miss Stanfield. If you'd like to witness the unveiling, come to my studio."

Esther accepted the invitation, expecting and willing to be seduced. Eager, in fact, for she had fallen instantly in love with Mallard, even though he possessed none of the qualifications of a proper suitor for a Stanfield, and she knew that what happened on her first visit to his studio would have appalled her mother. He was poor, the son of a carpenter living off a small legacy from his grandparents and whatever he could earn from his paintings. He roamed the New England coast, painting mediocre landscapes and seascapes, and passable portraits of peasant types, mostly old fishermen with squinting eyes, the workworn faces and hands of farmers and their wives, and barefoot youngsters with sunburned cheeks and windtossed hair. But his true talent lay in capturing still lifes especially in watercolor.

"Jack of all mediums," Mallard said ruefully. "Master of none."

Much of his work remained unsold, and Esther wanted to buy it all, less in appreciation of his art, however, than his artful lovemaking. Her infatuation was intense, consuming, demanding. Nothing mattered except being with him, and inventing ruses to escape her mother's vigilance taxed her ingenuity. Part of his attraction lay in his ineligibility, since the forbidden is always more tempting and desirable. But he was also excitingly different, intriguing in all the ways her approved beaux were not. She preferred spending one hour with the pauper artist, eating bread and cheese and wine, than an evening with any of her admirers dining on lobster and champagne and dancing in a grand ballroom. And she found him handsomer in his paint-spattered clothes and slouch hats and scuffed boots than other men in swallow-tailed coats, white ties, and high silk hats.

Mallard knew her parents by sight, and neither inspired him professionally. Mrs. Stanfield was a tall, thin, flat-chested aristocrat, with piercing steel-blue eyes, a disdainfully arched nose and imperious mouth, who wore her dated clothes with an elegance that made them seem modish. Mr. Stanfield was short, pot-bellied, beagle-eyed, and bald. To the artist, the improbable issue of this union seemed both a miracle and a mystery. With any other woman the paternity of the progeny might have been questionable, but the idea of a wild or random seed entering and rooting in Hortense Stanfield's private garden was ludicrous. That the family fortune had been diminished in the recent financial panic was common knowledge, but they were still far from bankrupt, and lived much as they always had.

"Mother let a couple of servants go," Esther said, "and Father hasn't bought a new carriage recently. They entertain and travel a little less, and have grown more ambitious for me. No expense was spared on my debut, and I get most of the new clothes and trinkets now. Naturally, I'm expected to marry expediently."

"Any prospects?"

"Several, but Mother's requirements are not easily met since the depression. Some of the best families are broke, and some of the others have only money to recommend them. That's why we visit relatives and friends in Philadelphia, Hartford, and New York. It's sort of a treasure-trophy hunt."

"Well, if you don't approve, why do you comply? You're not a child, Esther, to be forced into obedience. You could refuse."

"Oh, darling, you don't understand."

"What's to understand? I love you, Esther, and don't want you marrying some other man. I worry every time you go off on one of these hunting expeditions, afraid that you won't come back to me. I suffer hell in this goddamn garret, while you're prospecting at balls and promenades!"

"Things aren't done so crudely, Mallard. Mothers don't parade their eligible daughters like prize horses in a show ring. It's a subtle, sedate game played with discretion and finesse."

"But still a game."

"I suppose. Isn't life itself a game played against great odds? And marriage a lottery—cast your lot at the altar, for better or worse, win or lose. My parents just don't want to trust my future to luck or chance, Mallard. After all they've invested in me, you can't blame them for that." She paused, soothing his jealousy and chagrin. "Anyway, I always come back to you, don't I? I'm here now, aren't I? And not because I didn't make an important conquest in

New York. I did, and he's coming to Boston next week-end."

"That serious?"

Suddenly her face sobered, and she glanced away, focusing her eyes on the Jamaica Pond painting, which he could easily have sold but kept out of sentiment, because they were both romantically attached to it. "I'm afraid so, darling."

Mallard said nothing, but pinched out the candle flames and stood looking at Esther in the moonlight filtering through the skyglass. It was a miserable place by day, situated in the slums near the waterfront, cold and damp in winter and heated by a single stove on which he also cooked. Cockroaches lurked in the cracks, and they could hear rats scurrying between the walls. He rarely made the bed or swept the floor, although he did pay a woman to clean and do his laundry twice a month. In the interim, the studio was a shambles. Dirty dishes piled in pans, empty wine bottles with candles stuck in the necks, palettes and canvases everywhere, brushes in cans and jars of turpentine. Dirt and disarray—but at night it was magically transformed, for Esther at least, into an enchanted rendezvous.

Over a year she had been coming there, so she knew it in all seasons and elements. They had lain together watching rain wash the skylight, storms threaten it, and snow cover it, and birds cast quick shadows over it. Always there was a bottle of red wine beside the bed, a bowl of fruit and nuts, and often a little bouquet of flowers he had bought for her—violets to match her eyes, or daisies, marigolds, or asters. He waited now for her to undress, which she did hurriedly, for it was winter again and a bitter nor'easter was blowing off the Atlantic, and Esther was anxious to get under the covers and into the warmth of Mallard's arms. She was supposed to be visiting a trusted girlfriend, who conspired in her parental deceptions. She slipped into bed with goose pimples and chattering teeth.

"Let's not delay, darling. I'm freezing."

"Tell me his name first," he said.

"What?"

"This man. Who is he?"

"Later, darling."

"Now," he insisted, still not touching her.

"Oh, my God. I'm cold, Mallard."

"Tell me!"

"Keith Curtis."

"There's a Curtis Bank on Wall Street."

"He owns it, and a lot more."

"How'd you meet him?"

"At a party some friends gave," she said. "Do we have to talk about it *now*?"

"Yes." He reached for the wine and drank, resting on an elbow. "What does he look like?"

"Not at all like a banker."

"What does that mean?"

"Well, he's young and rather handsome, if you like the dark type. But I prefer yours. He's a Harvard graduate and was on the rowing and fencing teams. His father died last year, his mother and sister some years ago, and in his early twenties he inherited a vast fortune and responsibility. Oh, he's considered quite a catch, and plenty of Manhattan pussycats would like to scratch my eyes out."

He drank again. "You love him?"

"I love you."

"Then marry me."

"And live like vagabonds?"

"Like artists," he said. "Travel about, Go abroad, eventually. We wouldn't starve—my legacy would keep the wolf at bay. Maybe I could earn enough reputation on the Continent to make my work sought after here." He waited. "Esther?"

She sighed. "I'm not a gypsy, Mallard, and I couldn't live like one. Besides, I have a family to consider, and a name. You're alone, without ties or obligations to anyone but yourself. But I owe some allegiance to the Stanfields, and responsibility."

"Enough to sell yourself! If you love me, Esther, how can you do that?"

"Oh, good grief, Mallard! This has nothing to do with love. It would be a marriage of convenience, and it's done all the time. Nothing need change between us. We've met in secret here over a year, and can do the same in New York."

"You'll have a husband, young and presumbably potent. He'll take your nights, Esther."

"I'll still have my days. Love knows no time, darling."

Mallard's Nordic eyes, pale blue under flaxen brows, glittered like ice in the stark moonlight, and his hard cold voice was frost on her sensibilities. "What a greedy selfish conniving bitch you are, Esther Diana Stanfield! And your middle name suits you perfectly, you bloody little huntress."

"Does it help to insult and hurt me, darling?"

"Hurt you? What about me? What about him? I almost feel sorry for the poor bastard. If he loves you—and he must, to want to marry you—you're going to make his life one long hell. Wreck his dreams and illusions and hopes, rip out his heart and guts and soul. You're a vixen, Esther, and you were born to disillusion and destroy men."

"Have I done so to you?"

"Not yet, but you're trying, and I don't doubt you'll succeed. The only thing that makes it bearable for me is that I know you'll castrate Curtis, too. You'd make a great heroine for a British drawing room satire: Lady Esther's Eunuchs."

"But still you love me?"

"Like a satyr loves a nymph," he said, falling on her with sudden ravenous desire. "The devil take him! I saw you first."

When at last she was warm and languid in his arms, and he was relaxed and resigned to her future, she said, "My marriage could mean a lot to you, Mallard."

"How the hell do you figure that?"

She was in what he called her Mona Lisa mood, smiling the secretive, enigmatic smile that had intrigued him from the start and now enslaved him. "Well, you know there was never a wealthy person who didn't have his portrait painted and—".

He interrupted, "But I'm hardly a portrait painter."

"No Gilbert Stuart or Thomas Sully, perhaps, but good enough to get by," she insisted. "New York is not Boston, you know. Some of the best people there would be considered trash here. Many of the most successful men have risen out of gutters and garbage dumps, and their wives were washwomen and ragpickers, or worse. Just flatter the bulls and bears of Wall Street and their mates enough on canvas, and you'll earn enough in commissions to live comfortably the rest of your life."

"I'll have to meet them first."

"Leave that to me. In due time you can have an exhibit, and somehow I'll create a demand for your work, if I have to buy it all myself. Oh, I'll help you, darling! Wait and see."

Six months later, in Boston's and New York's wedding of the year, Esther Diana Stanfield married Keith Heathstone Curtis. And while they were honeymooning abroad, Giles Mallard found an attic apartment in an old two-story house on St. Marks Place, near Tompkins Square, signed a long lease, installed a skylight, and took up residence in Manhattan.

He followed the maritime news in the papers and managed to be sketching on the Battery the day the Cunard luxury liner steamed through Upper Bay, passing between Bedloe and Ellis Islands on the portside, and Governors Island on the starboard, finally docking at a pier in the East River.

Crowds welcomed every ship to port, just as they waved them off to sea. And the wharves were busy and noisy, a bedlam of shouting seamen and stevedores, confused stewards and pursers, harassed customs officials, and happy travelers relieved to set foot on land again, particularly if it had been a rough voyage.

Mallard first glimpsed Esther on the gangplank, regal in a purple velvet cloak banded in Russian sable, a crown of the same royal fur on her dark head and gloved hands tucked into an enormous sable muff. Her violet eyes were scanning the uplifted faces and waving arms. He was toting a palette and paintbox, an easel and several canvases, and she smiled faintly, then her husband took her arm to guide her off the ship, and she disappeared into the clamoring horde.

As prearranged, Mallard went directly to the *Herald* and inserted a notice in the personal columns. *"Artist starving in attic. 7 St. Marks Pl. G.M."* Then he went home and waited.

Within a week she responded, incognito, every vestige of her thick black hair tucked under a cossack turban with attached wimple, her eyes dramatically concealed behind a pair of lavender lensed stage spectacles picked up at the Paris Flea Market. Their reunion was swift and ardent

and ecstatic—sweeter, perhaps, because of the long interlude and its now adulterous aspects.

"Forbidden fruit," he grinned, handing her an apple and
biting into one himself, washing it down with red wine.
"How was the honeymoon, Mrs. Curtis?"

"Marvelous. I enjoyed Paris most of all. But London
was wonderful too, and Rome and Vienna. We were entertained by some very important people. Did I tell you
Keith's mother was of noble birth, the daughter of the
Earl and Countess of Heathstone? We visited the family
manor in Sussex, but he's very modest about his heritage
and never flaunts or boasts about it. I was presented to
Queen Victoria. And Napoleon and Empress Eugenie!
And the things he bought me—the clothes, furs, jewels. I
felt like a duchess."

Mallard frowned, pondering her marital rings. "That's
not what I meant, and you know it."

"Well," she hesitated, polishing her apple on the soiled
linen, "I didn't think you'd want to hear about that part.
But I won't lie to you—he's a good lover. Plenty of practice, apparently. Unfortunately for him, I'm in love with
you. But I'm going to be the perfect wife and hostess. I'll
make him happy, and he'll never suspect. It can't hurt
him, if he doesn't know."

"The happy cuckold. Well, he won't be the only one on
the Street."

"We're giving our first party next week," she said. "Oh,
I wish you could come, Mallard!"

He only laughed and reached for the dusty bottle again.

Sometimes she did not see him for a week or more, but
he was always waiting and primed by abstinence. And
Keith trusted her, so implicitly elaborate disguises were
unnecessary. Veils, high-collared cloaks, tinted glasses suf-
ficed, and she traveled in cabs. Mallard's studio was a little
better than the one in Boston, but not much, and he kept
it in the same haphazard maner. Nor was he producing
better in New York, and the commissions she had
promised him had not yet materialized. But Esther wasn't
sure any more that she wanted him to succeed. New York
had a way of lionizing and monopolizing celebrities in the
arts, and more than one lovely liaison was spoiled when an
obscure actress catapulted to fame, a struggling author's or
artist's genius was finally recognized and his work sud-

denly in demand. There was no privacy in the limelight of success, and the successful soon became not only public figures but public property.

Only once before the marital earthquake did Esther feel some ominous tremors, and that was when Keith began to speak of children. "Oh, there's plenty of time for that," she said. "I'm only twenty-two, darling."

"I understand it's easier when a woman is young."

"And I understand it's never easy, regardless of age."

"Do you fear pregnancy and childbirth, Esther? Is that why you resort to these damnable devices you think I don't notice, and rush frantically out of my arms to the bathroom?"

"Do I not please you in bed, Keith?"

"I'm not talking about sex," he said. "Marriage has other purposes and rewards, you know."

"Now you sound like a feudal lord, anxious to preserve the dynasty. My kingdom for a son! What if I produce only daughters, sir? Will you divorce me?"

She was teasing, hoping to divert him with banter, wondering how she could possibly tell her lover that her husband wanted a family. And how could she hop in and out of hackneys with a bulging belly, even if Mallard continued to love and want a pregnant paramour?

They had just returned from an elaborate reception in Washington Square, where Esther, in her cloth-of-silver gown overlaid with silver tiffany and her coronet of diamonds, had eclipsed every other woman present, including the debutante making her formal bow to society. She had danced every set. It was late, and she was tired and in no mood for lovemaking. But she had put Keith off for several days, with one excuse or another, and his intentions now were unmistakable.

He lounged in his chair, wearing a gray silk robe with a white scarf tucked in the neck, watching her go through the nightly ritual of hairbrushing and facial creams and lotions, which he had come to recognize for what it was—strategic delay to circumvent his advances. He had a brandy nightcap, but had to forego a final cigar, because she disliked tobacco smoke in the bedroom, and he had no way of knowing that her lover did not have this particular vice.

"I don't want to criticize," she changed the subject, "but

I think poor Letty's debut was a dismal failure, don't you? She looked like an over-risen biscuit in that bouffant white gown. Such a clabbery little creature, I can't imagine how she's ever going to charm a worthwhile man into matrimony."

"Oh, she has other attractions—about a million, in fact, some pure gold."

"She'll need them," Esther predicted. "Her own father told me I was the prettiest woman at the ball. Was I, Keith?"

"Mirror, mirror," he murmured.

"Well, you know I really was the fairest of them all!"

"You were the star, all right," he agreed, "even though it was Letty's premiere. Just as a matter of curiosity, how much did your gown cost?"

"Two thousand. It's a Paris original."

"Aren't they all?"

"Oh no, darling, I'm not *that* extravagant! My modiste makes many of my clothes, some from my own designs. I had a fitting today. Our anniversary gown—can you believe it will be two whole years in June? I won't tell you anything about the gown, however, except that it's blue velvet and Venetian lace."

"And sapphires would go nicely with it?"

"That wasn't very subtle, was it?" She smeared some Egyptian emollient on her face and removed the excess with a linen cloth. "I'm not much of a sophisticate, I'm afraid."

"Is the masterpiece nearing completion?"

Esther started. "What masterpiece? Oh, you mean the gown. Yes, it's nearly finished, and I'm not sorry, either. Fittings just exhaust me, and I have another tomorrow." He said nothing but she saw his disappointment when their eyes met in the mirror. "I'm sorry, darling. I haven't been much of a wife lately, have I? Be patient with me, Keith."

"Have I ever been otherwise, Esther?"

"Never, dear, and I appreciate your understanding. I've heard wives complain about their husbands in that respect. Janet Sloan says Percy is a regular pig. By the way, she showed me some pictures she had bought, by a new artist. His work is on exhibit at the Fenton Galleries. I suppose we received an announcement, but I didn't pay any attention. Janet bought one of his autumn landscapes—'Birches

in the Berkshires,' or some such title. She rechristened it
'Symphony in Gold.' She also bought a watercolor and
charcoal sketch. He's rather good, Keith."

"What's his name?"

"Mallard, if I remember correctly."

"Perhaps we're missing something," he said. "Why don't
we have a look after lunch tomorrow?"

"Oh, I have that fitting, darling. But I will meet you for
lunch. Shall we say the Brevoort, at one?"

Esther was late but every male head in the lobby
turned admiringly when she entered in a pearl gray cloak
and chinchilla toque pierced with an amethyst arrow, a
cluster of fresh spring violets pinned to her chinchilla
muff. The pride and pleasure in Keith's eyes convinced her
that he would forgive all her little faults—her habitual
tardiness, extravagance, pretexts to avoid intimacy, even
her unwillingness to reproduce—anything but infidelity,
and she determined to be extra cautious in her visits to
Mallard, perhaps even to resort to disguises again. She
chatted vivaciously over the meal, arch and flirtatious, and
while they were awaiting dessert, she reminded him of yet
another engagement that evening.

"Oh, Lord," he muttered. "Can't we forget it, Esther?
The Carltons bore me."

"It's just a musicale, Keith. It won't last long." She
waited to catch his eye. "We'll be home early ... and
don't *you* be the tired one tonight."

It was misting when they came out of the hotel. Keith
put his wife in a cab and then went to the Fenton Galleries, hoping to find a painting to give her in addition to
the anniversary jewelry. He considered the Mallard collection interesting, showing a good sense of color and propor-
tion, but otherwise undistinguished. There was a sensitive
blending of blue and green reminiscent of Renoir in the
landscapes when sky limned mountain and lake, or met
meadow and sea. But one could see almost as much talent
in some of the excellent murals painted on omnibuses or
minstrel and medicine wagons. The Boston scenes were
familiar to him from his Harvard days: Faneuil Hall, Old
North Church, the Common and Public Gardens, the
Charles River and the harbor. The best of the lot—a winter scene of Jamaica Pond—was not for sale, but perhaps
he could bargain for it.

The receptionist gave him Mallard's address, and rain was falling when the hansom reached Tompkins Square. Keith saw a skylight in the roof of the house on St. Marks Place. Entering the hall, he climbed the stairway to the studio and knocked.

"Are you expecting anyone?" It was Esther's voice, and Keith felt as if he had been kicked, unexpectedly, by a horse.

"Only my creditors," a man answered.

"I thought you had paid them off, darling."

"Not yet. I need a few more Janet Sloans."

Keith clenched his teeth and knocked again. The door cracked. "Yeah, what do you want, Mister?"

Keith pushed him aside, and Esther screamed. "Oh, my God! It's him, Mallard! Run!"

Half-dressed, Mallard made a game try, but he was not swift enough. Keith caught him at the landing and swung, clipping his jaw. The artist cowered, refusing to defend himself lest he injure his hands. Esther rushed out in her chemise and got between them, just as Keith swung again. She reeled backwards and tumbled down the stairs. Mallard sprinted after her, glaring furiously up at Keith, who was poised above them like an angry glowering colossus.

"You goddamn crazy fool!" he shouted, kneeling beside Esther. "You might've killed her!"

Descending, Keith shoved him aside. "Get away from her, you lousy sonofabitch!"

Esther was conscious but too stunned and terrified to speak or move, and obviously in severe pain. Mallard had fetched her cloak and hovered gravely, while her husband wrapped her in it and carried her swiftly to the waiting cab, ordering the driver to Gramercy Park.

"How did she get these bruises?" the physician asked, while examining the patient.

"She had a bad fall."

"Well, I'm sorry to have to tell you, sir, that she has miscarried."

"Miscarried?" Keith stared at him. "I didn't even know she was pregnant, Doctor."

"I doubt if she knew it herself. It was too early for symptoms, about six weeks, I'd say."

"Will she be all right?"

"Well, she's complaining now of numbness in her legs.

Probably just shock or hysteria, but there may be some spinal injury. We'll know in a few days."

Weeks passed, and months, and years. Doctors came and went and consulted, treated and prescribed, and recommended specialists in London, Paris, Rome, Vienna, Zurich. They crossed the Atlantic twice, and she was examined in every famed hospital and clinic in Europe and Great Britain. No reason could be established for her paralysis, and the physicians differed among themselves in diagnosis and prognosis. On stretchers and in wheelchairs, with nurses and servants in attendance, she drank the waters and took the baths at the famous spas. Keith spent a fortune on cures and still she was not cured, still she did not walk, and he could not divorce her.

Now, at last, there was someone else. Someone he cared for more than he had thought possible. Someone he wanted in a way he had never expected to want again.

Keith stood at a window in his rooms, smoking and gazing down at the shadowy park. He could not remember when last he had used his golden key to enter that sacrosanct patch of greenery, whose English-square aspect had so appealed to his British mother, for whom the house was built in 1848. (The old Curtis homestead, in which her children were born, was still standing on Cherry Hill, an unkempt rooming house now, victim of progress.) But she had enjoyed it only a few years before she and her younger child had died in one of the periodic cholera epidemics of the island, which respected no mansion walls or private fences. They were buried in the graveyard of Grace Church. Eventually, there was another marble monument to erect in the family plot, for Keith's father, Scott Byron Curtis, age fifty-seven, beside Beloved Wife Anne Heathstone Curtis, age forty-nine, and Beloved Daughter Elaine, age sixteen. And at twenty-three Keith became master of the house where, except for the servants, he lived alone until he brought his bride there.

Esther Stanfield Curtis was beautiful, gracious, accomplished, of "Brahmin peerage," and, he had thought, a fitting mistress to succeed his noble mother. The changes Esther made in the house were in excellent taste, her management efficient, her entertainments notable. A perfectionist, she demanded absolute order in her household, and the domestic staff was somewhat in awe of her. She would not tolerate a fallen flower petal, a tilted picture or uneven shade, a speck of dust or lint anywhere. She seemed to know instinctively when a piece of bric-a-brac had been moved an inch from its customary position, a dish broken in the kitchen, a book misplaced in the library. And when guests were present she kept a detail of servants in constant vigilance to prevent damage from accidents with food, drink, ashes.

Yet, ironically, he had found this fastidious creature in a squalid studio wallowing in a rat's nest of soiled linen, strewn clothes, dirty dishes, and empty wine bottles, garbage and a used chamberpot in a corner. The paradox never ceased to amaze and bewilder him in retrospect, nor his complete beguilement of her true character to anger and disgust him.

He tossed his cigar out the window and watched it fall like a shooting star to earth, then opened a decanter of Scotch and prepared for another restless night of insomnia. Only this time the cause was not something he wanted to forget.

It was one hell of a mess.

PART II

At present, in the more improved countries, the disabilities of women are the only case, save one, in which laws and institutions take persons at their birth, and ordain that they shall never in all their lives be allowed to compete for certain things. The one exception is that of royalty.

John Stuart Mill (1806–1873)
The Subjection of Women

The law took no cognizance of woman as a money-spender. She was a ward, an appendage, a relict. Thus it happened, that if a woman did not choose to marry, or when left a widow, to remarry, she had no choice but to enter one of the few employments open to her or to become a burden on the charity of some relative.

Harriet M. Robinson (1825–1911)

There is a vulgar persuasion that the ignorance of women, by favoring their subordination, insures their utility. 'Tis the same argument employed by the ruling few against the subject many in aristocracies; by the rich against the poor in democracies; and by the learned professions against the people in all countries.

Frances Wright (1795–1852)

Chapter 6

Newspaper publishing in New York was entirely different from anything Devon had ever experienced. There were no personal community enterprises operated, as so often in the South, by a single family and its descendants for generations. Here instead the newspapers were huge impersonal factories run by hundreds of gnomes in green visors and black cuff protectors and perpetual activity. And the equipment was such as her father had only dreamed of: great steam-powered rotary presses capable of printing twenty thousand sheets per hour and costing thousands of dollars.

Devon was discouraged by her inability to get in to see the busy publishers and editors of the metropolitan dailies, although she knew that discrimination against her sex was not the only reason. The fact that journalism ranked somewhere between gambling and espionage as a hazardous profession did not facilitate the entry of anyone, male or female, into the inner sanctums of the press. Precautions had to be taken against the lunatics and mendicants who hung around Park Row and Printing House Square. Fanatics preaching new religions, philosophers promoting seditious ideologies, clairvoyants with dire predictions for humanity, charlatans hawking magic nostrums, inventors and swindlers, all were convinced that free publicity was the way to success and prosperity. In addition, there were charity supplicants, outraged citizens threatening libel, enraged politicians demanding retractions, and irate feminists protesting persecution in print—gauntlets which the news staffs ran every day in one form or another.

A demure gown and gentle manner meant nothing, for some of the most militant suffragettes were perfect ladies. No one could fault the decorum of Susan B. Anthony, Elizabeth Cady Stanton, Lucy Stone, or the pious Quakeress Lucretia Mott. Nevertheless, few publishers would have considered hiring them, and eccentric Horace Greeley was about the only one who supported the Movement. But the *Tribune* never employed inexperienced journalists, perferring to recruit them after they had earned a reputation and some laurels elsewhere.

Nor was there room on the sophisticated weeklies, such as *Harper's, Leslie's Illustrated*, the *Independent*, and the *Ledger*, for someone trained in regional reportage. And certainly she lacked the special qualifications required by the fashion books, the three most important of which—*Godey's, Peterson's*, and *Author's*—were published in Philadelphia. New York had Demorest's *Mirror of Fashions* to promote the Demorest paper patterns and dress emporium, but it was staffed by the owners and the eminently successful Jenny June.

Finally, on the third day of her canvass, the city editor of a mediocre journal agreed to interview her, and Devon was admitted to a cluttered office with overflowing wastebaskets and cuspidors, half-filled coffee cups and partially-eaten sandwiches. The man behind the Matterhorn of copy was perhaps sixty, bearded and bespectacled, nervous and impatient and harassed. Inviting her to occupy a hardwood chair, he immediately requested her credentials, snapping his fingers when she hesitated. "Come, come, Miss Marshall! You do have a reference and résumé?"

"Well, no, sir. You see—" She began to explain about the Richmond fire, with which he was surely familiar, and her inability to salvage any files or copies of the *Sentinel* that contained her work. In the next offices she could hear male voices and robust laughter, as if at some lusty joke, and wondered if she were the only female in the building.

"I'm aware of all that, Miss Marshall. But surely you brought a character recommendation from one of your hometown editors or worthy citizens?"

Naturally any serious, sensible person seeking gainful employment in another city would have secured such a letter in advance and scoured the town if necessary to locate specimens of her byline. Appalled by her lack of foresight, Devon made matters worse by trying to rationalize her negligence. "There wasn't time, sir. I left in such a hurry—"

"Why such a hurry?" he interrupted suspiciously, as if

suspecting that she had been run out of Richmond on a rail. And at her embarrassed silence and dismay, he frowned and cleared his celluoid-collared throat. "I'm sorry, Miss Marshall, but we're not hiring any new reporters at present, and in fact have no females on our staff in that capacity. However, we do buy freelance, at space rate, and should you come up with an exclusive story, something really spectacular, bring it to us first, and we may be interested." He rose and opened the door.

Devon returned to her room at the Astor House, depressed and all but defeated. She had been chasing rainbows and mirages that evolved in chimeras—and Keith had either left town again, or abandoned her to her independence. She kicked at the Saratoga trunk, stubbing her toe so painfully she had to remove her shoe and chafe her foot. There were blisters on her heels, and her legs ached all the way to her hips.

Damn him! He had known this would happen, had predicted her failure just as Dan had, and he was waiting for her to call for help. So cocksure, both of them, that she could not make it on her own. And the worst part of it was, they might be right. But she wasn't beaten yet, not by a long shot. She would just have to reorganize, lower her sights a trifle, accept something less in another field and wait for an opportunity to arise. There were many shops and stores in town, and she had seen advertisements for help via placards in their windows. Tomorrow she would investigate some of them. There were also numerous factories, but she hoped to avoid the sweatshops if at all possible.

Unable to get to the dining room before six o'clock, Devon ordered supper sent to her room and sat by the window again, alone and lonely, watching the gaslights and activity on Broadway. Everyone, it seemed, had something to do and some place to go, except her. The only thing she had to do was take a bath, the only place she had to go was to bed, and neither prospect appeared exciting or fulfilling.

La Boutique Chic, on East Twelfth Street, just off Broadway, was in the fashionable shopping district known as The Ladies' Mile. It was small and intimate, with a white stucco façade, clipped boxwoods in white pottery jardinieres flanking the entrance, and a touch of Paris in the fringed green-and-white awning. The shop window was artistically draped in pastel gauzes and featured a wax mannequin in an exquisite satin negligee, with genuine human hair and eyelashes, so lifelike it seemed she might smile or wink at passersby.

Devon had gotten up with the birds in City Hall Park, and dressed prettily rather than practically, had spent seven fruitless hours canvassing the area. But, as in Richmond, she found male clerks preferred to female in most stores, and employed exclusively in shoes, drugs, furniture and hardware, as if merchants everywhere were in conspiracy against womankind. Male clerks manned the ice cream parlors, the bakeries, the groceries. They even sold ladies' millinery and notions—buttons, beads, ribbons, laces—in the novelty shops. And they predominated in the large department stores—A. T. Stewart's, Macy's, Lord & Taylor, Arnold Constable—where, along with dozens of other hopeful girls, Devon left applications.

Madame Joie, the proprietress of La Boutique Chic, was a petite brunette of an indefinite age, with thinly plucked eyebrows and a frisette of false curls, and she was just placing a poster in the window as Devon stopped to window shop and check her appearance in the glass. It seemed an omen, and Devon entered the shop and applied for the position.

The salary, five dollars a week, was stupendous for a clerk, and although Devon had neither references nor experience, Madame Joie liked what she saw—a stunning beauty in yellow India muslin with a sprinkling of black velvet bows on the swirling skirt, and a pert black velvet butterfly perched in her curls, which had the color and sparkle of champagne bubbles—and hired her on the spot.

Devon's duties would include selling, and occasional modeling for customers who had difficulty selecting off the racks. La Boutique Chic specialized in what she called "robes-de-chambres" and had a fashionable clientele.

In the morning Devon had to run to catch an early horsecar and stand up all the way to the Twelfth Street intersection without breakfast, for she had not allowed herself sufficient time to eat at the hotel and still report for work at eight.

Madame Joie was already in her office and about to sit

down to tea and croissants. She invited her new assistant, whom she called "Da-Von" to join her. "It is too early for the important customers," she said, "and Madame Wicks can serve the others." Mrs. Wicks was the alterationist, a small thin gray woman with birdlike eyes, who reminded Devon of a displaced wren. "Now then, cherie, tell me about yourself."

"Well," said Devon, breaking a pastry, "there isn't much to tell, Madame."

"No? I should think there would be a great deal, with one so young and beautiful. That gown you were wearing yesterday, tres chic! Not the usual shopgirl variety. Your family is rich, n'est-ce pas?"

"I have no family, Madame."

"But where is your home?"

"Richmond."

"Richmond?" She pronounced it "Reechmon."

Devon adored her accent and the way she talked as much with her expressive brown eyes and animated hands as her rouged mouth, and mixed her French and English. "That's in Virginia. It was the capital of the Confederacy."

"Ah, oui, in your Civil War, like our Revolution," she nodded. "And so your home is ruined, your family gone, your young men poor or sick or crippled—and you have come to New York to find a rich husband?"

"Well, not exactly."

"Ah, cherie"—Madame Joie wagged a knowing finger—"that is what every woman seeks—un rich mari! And if she cannot find him, she must settle for the next best thing—a rich keeper."

The bell tinkled, signaling a customer, and Mrs. Wicks ran out of the sewing room with a yellow tapeline coiled like a pet snake around her neck. But the lady was only browsing, which to the proprietress meant she could not afford to buy. "Le petit monde," she said, distinguishing such an unfortunate from the haut monde. "I remember them in my boutique in Paris—the eyes that yearn and covet while the lips deny desire, for the mari holds the pursestrings too tight, and there is no generous paramour to pamper and indulge."

"What shall I do, Madame?"

"Do?"

"Well, I presume I wasn't hired to sip tea and make pleasant conversation."

The Frenchwoman smiled. "No, but it is pleasant, n'est-ce pas? Come," she beckoned, placing her damask napkin on the little gilt Empire table and rising. "Some new shipments from Paris have just arrived. You may help unpack and tag them."

It was the sort of merchandise Devon had forced herself to ignore in the Washington shops, selecting only a couple of discreet wrappers and opaque nightgowns to replace the tattered garments Keith had called repulsive rags. The collection included lingerie exquisite enough for a princess' trousseau and seductive enough for a sultan's harem. Chiffon peignoirs in misty pink and blue and sea-green, lavender and mauve, peach and apricot and lemon and lime, coral and primrose and chartreuse, with gossamer gowns to match. Chambre-robes of jeweltone velvets, brocades, taffetas, and moirés antiques, really elegant. Chemises that were mere wisps of satin and lace, silk camisoles lavishly decorated with lace and ribbons, embroidered linen corset-covers, frilly drawers which had replaced pantalettes, bandeaus to reduce overly buxom bosoms and net puffs to supplement inadequate ones. There were boxes of silk and lisle hoisery in many colors, some with the new embroidered clocks; piles of handkerchiefs, scarves, shawls, reticules, parasols, veils, and other accesories.

Madame Joie, marking little tickets with big figures, passed them to Devon to attach to the designated garments.

"Five hundred dollars?" she questioned, astonished. "That is the correct price for this white set, Madame?"

"Mais oui, it is a bridal ensemble, cherie. French satin and Chantilly lace, an exact copy of the Empress Eugenie's . . . or was it in the trousseau of the Empress Josephine?" She shrugged. "No matter. The original of that cloth-of-gold chambre-robe once adorned Marie Antoinette. The cerise velvet peignoir is copied from one of Madame Dubarry's and the turquoise satin negligee was a favorite of Madame du Pompadour, both mistresses of King Louis." She winked and kissed her manicured fingers. "Oh, la-la! If there is one thing a Frenchwoman knows, it is how to dress in the boudoir!"

Keith's cynical comment concerning feminine youth and

beauty during their argument on the train—"Somehow these weapons seem to work best in gardens, parlors, and boudoirs!"—echoed like succinct wisdom, and Devon determined to vacate the Astor House as soon as possible. Keith had made no attempt to contact her, and Devon had been sleeping poorly, furious with herself for thinking of him—missing and even longing for him, and finally falling into restless sleeps in which he inhabited her dreams.

Mrs. Wicks told her about a place called the Gothic Arms, where she could get reasonable but decent lodging, and Devon checked out of the Astor House early Sunday morning. She suffered a few uneasy moments wondering what she should do if presented a bill she could not pay, before remembering that Keith has assumed responsibility for her hotel debts, presumably as a guardian for a ward. She told the management that she was moving to a relative's and wanted to leave a message for Mr. Curtis. She wrote, "I owe Keith Curtis $1000.00," signed the note, sealed it in an envelope and wrote his name on it. And while church bells rang, a hackney delivered her and the Saratoga trunk to her new and inelegant address.

The Gothic Arms, near Union Square, was an old garnet brick mansion turned rooming- and boarding-house. The large, high-ceilinged chambers had been partitioned to make more rentals and contained only half of their original space, windows, and appointments. The furniture consisted of the bare essentials, including in addition to the single spoolbed, dresser, and wardrobe, a small table and chair, washstand with pitcher and bowl, and a commode behind a catercorner curtain. Chambermaid service cost extra, so Devon decided to clean the room and empty the slops herself. There was a communal bathtub, a vintage relic resembling a zinc boat, with a twenty-minute monopoly limit.

The atmosphere of the Gothic Arms, with its ivied walls and courtyard, its neat cells and exclusive female occupancy, suggested an abbey run by a Spartan mother superior. Miss Cornelia Gibbons, the aging landlady, was every bit as circumspect as Mrs. Chester, though not nearly as maternal and congenial and sympathetic. Nevertheless, the "cloister" was now home to Devon and, she was confident, the last place on earth a sophisticated man would think of looking for her.

Madame Joie admitted to forty. She was born in Burgundy, France, the daughter of peasant vineyard workers. At fifteen she married a grape-picker, with whom she lived only a few months before running away to Lyon, where she met a wealthy silk merchant and soon became his mistress. After six years with him, and two abortions, he suddenly died, and his best friend took her into keeping. Unfortunately, he was killed in a duel with his wife's lover. Then she went to Paris, sold the jewelry both men had given her, and opened a boutique on the Rue de la Paix. There she met a nobleman, who had come in with his fat and ugly comtesse, and soon he had proposed an arrangement.

For some years she lived the gay glamorous pampered life of the demimonde who set the fashions at court, for the nobility made no secret of their affairs, and even the emperor's mistresses were well known in Paris. When, alas, the count's ardor cooled, he settled beaucoup francs on her, and she packed up and sailed to America. She had heard that the streets of New York were paved with gold and she wanted to make her fortune. Naturellement, it was just another of the gross lies told about Amerique, and she had found cobblestones instead of gold brick pavement. She had also found a succession of lovers, none of whom had offered to keep her à la le Comte, and now she was neither young nor attractive enough to interest a wealthy benefactor in that respect and was done with all men.

"So," she gestured resignedly, "I must work and save my money for the rainy day. But I have no regrets, none. I have lived and loved—and that is what life is all about, n'est-ce pas, cherie?"

Devon wanted to confide in Madame Joie, for she sensed the older woman would be a sagacious and sympathetic confidante. But she feared Madame Joie would consider her either a sorry liar or a stupid fool if she told the truth. For who would believe that a girl who had arrived in New York in a private rail-coach with a chic wardrobe, and was installed in the Astor House on credit, would prefer shop work if she had a choice? She doubted the cosmopolite could comprehend such provincial scruples; she could scarcely understand them herself and wondered if she were some kind of prude or imbecile, or both.

"Oui," she said simply.

Chapter 7

Devon was happy and reasonably content. She had found a comfortable, pleasant paying job while her real ambition was in abeyance, and some of her initial awe and qualms about the great metropolis were vanishing. Her days were full at the shop, her evenings busy cleaning her room at the Gothic Arms and attending her wardrobe. And no longer were her Sundays dull and lonely and routine, for she spent them in the exhilarating company of her employer, having dinner at her Murray Hill duplex, and then driving in the Central Park carriage parade—a Manhattan ritual, which the Frenchwoman said American travelers had imported from the Bois de Boulogne of Paris.

By the end of September most of the important people had returned from the popular domestic resorts—Saratoga Springs, Long Branch, Newport, Cape May, the Catskills—and the Continental spas where they spent their summers. Madame Joie knew them all by sight or reputation and identitied notable and notorious alike for her companion. Society displayed its wealth and prestige in the park in elegant clothes and elaborate equipages. Stage celebrities enjoyed the theatrics of the parade and the applause they received on recognition. Politicians used it to keep in the public eye, although some of them needed neither identification nor publicity.

On this particular occasion Madame Joie pointed out Mayor and Mrs. Hoffman riding in the official carriage of state, a dignified black barouche, which had transported both the Prince of Wales and President Lincoln on their respective visits to New York in '61. Accompanying them were William Marcy Tweed, whom Devon recognized from the woodcuts in the newspapers, and a petite and pretty blonde who was not Mrs. Tweed. She had been in the boutique only the day before and had spent a small fortune on exquisite lingerie, some of which Devon had privately modeled for her.

"Madame, isn't that—?"

"Oui, the same. She is supposed to be his niece." A sly wink of her mascaraed lashes. "The Boss also has a lovely brunette niece, and he is *vrai* generous with their allowances. Why not, since it is not his money."

"Whose money is it?"

"The taxpayers'."

"Isn't that against the law?"

"Monsieur Tweed has the law in his pocket, and as you can see, it is a big pocket."

It was, indeed. The man was huge, with a massive head and bearded face, and a merry mischievous twinkle in his bright blue eyes. He was said to possess the humor of Falstaff, the generosity of Santa Claus, the morals of King Henry VIII, and the ethics of Captain Kidd. He preferred to think of himself as a latter-day Robin Hood, robbing the rich city treasury to help the poor politicians; he had actually been depicted wearing a cockaded hat in a forest labeled Manhattan, surrounded by his Tammany gang. A man of enormous appetites, his lust equaled or surpassed his greed and gluttony, requiring a wife, two mistresses, and nobody knew how many whores to satisfy.

The flashiest participant in the parade, however, was the flamboyant financier, Colonel James Fisk Junior, driving a magnificent golden coach-and-six, with red plumes decorating the heads of the prancing black and white horses. "He's called the Prince of Erie," Madame explained, "because he and Jay Gould own the Erie Railroad. That's his mistress, Josephine Mansfield, with him. The August Belmonts are behind them. Monsieur Belmont is the American representative of the House de Rothschild."

Devon wondered how Keith Curtis had missed out on that appointment, but of course *he* was allied with the Bank of England! Did the Curtises ride in the carriage parade? Madame Joie would know, but Devon couldn't bring herself to ask.

Madame was a veritable fountain of fascinating knowledge, abreast of the latest gossip and rumors and scandals, the secret sins and vices and peccadillos of the haute monde and the bourgeoisie. Her clientele included some wives and mistresses of the same affluent men, and

some elegant ladies engaged in illicit affairs of the heart.
She could identify the popular theater and opera personalities: Charlotte Cushman and Laura Keene riding together
in a blue landau; prima donna Clara Louise Kellogg in a
canary-colored chaise with a fringed top; ballerina Maria
Bonfanti in a white wicker calèche as dainty as a tutu. She
knew the prominent equestrians on their sleek mounts, the
rakish sports and gamblers who raced their drags and cur-
ricles and sulkies in Harlem Lane, and the owners and operators of the most notorious casinos, brothels, and other
fleshpots.

"That man in the silver phaeton is Harry Hill," she said.
"The Beau Brummel of the concert saloons."

"They give concerts in saloons?"

"They are dance halls, ma petite, and some of the girls
are cocottes. The lady in the rose demi-d'Aumont is Josie
Woods, who owns the most exclusive bordello in town and
orders negligees by the dozen. Her clientele comes from
the aristocracy and must present credentials."

Suddenly a majestic purple victoria with two liveried attendants on the box rounded a rocky mound in the park,
its lone occupant regally gowned and jeweled. A handsome middleaged woman with dark grave eyes and silver-
streaked black hair, she exchanged polite nods with
Madame Joie, and Devon exclaimed, "My, she looks like
royalty!"

The Frenchwoman smiled. "You do not recognize her?"
And at Devon's blank expression, "I forget you are a naive
maiden from Reechmon. That is Madame Restell. She is
une accouchée—what you would call midwife."

"Business must be good," Devon observed.

"She does more than deliver bebes, ma cherie. She also
cures enceinte ladies."

"Cures? I don't understand." And then suddenly she
did. "You mean abortion?"

"Oui. Avortement. The most expensive treatments in
town. She built a new home a few years ago, a marble
palace on Fifth Avenue, just across from St. Patrick's
Cathedral. She outbid the Church for the property, to spite
them for condemning her practice. Now they are her neighbors, and she finds some private humor in this irony."

"You know her, Madame?"

"Oui, some of her clients are also mine. I attended her

housewarming reception. A grand ball, no less. Such splendor, her mansion! Master paintings and sculpture and rare *objets d'art*. Some furniture is inlaid with gold and ivory and mother-of-pearl, and the crystal chandelier in the salon has over a hundred gaslights. Her stables are lined in mahogany, and there is genuine silver on the trappings of her horses. And such food and wine she served that evening! There were many prominent guests, not all parvenus and nouveaux riches."

"She would be stoned in Richmond," Devon said.

"The press and pulpits stone her, but she is too powerful to be hurt by words. She knows too many secrets and could ruin too many important people. But I do not think it is so bad to help ladies in distress, do you? Almost every mistress has occasional need of such service. I did myself, several times, the last in Paris to keep from embarrassing le comte. Mon Dieu, the whole court of Louis Napoleon had need of them!"

And except for the grace of God, Devon thought guiltily, her eyes falling on a young pregnant woman walking alongside the lane. . . .

The poor and the working class came to the park on foot, by horsecar, and omnibus, tugging youngsters and picnic baskets. It was far uptown, a wilderness only partially developed. Farmers to the north continued to use it as pasturage for cows, pigs, and goats, and the squalid tents and shanties of the tenacious squatters clung scabrously to the fringes. The central thoroughfare was macadamized, but miles of rutted dirt lanes and bridal paths traversed the area. Landscaping was in perpetual progress, museums and statues and a zoological garden under construction, but scrubby natural growths and dangerous stone outcroppings persisted among the transplanted trees, shrubs, and flowers. The carriage parade was the main attraction, and most of the social activity centered around the mall promenade, the lake where London swans glided amid rowboats and canoes, and the Terrace House confectionery. Madame Joie spoke of summer concerts in the pavilion, and winter ice carnivals they would attend. Meanwhile, an admirer who attempted to approach Devon met a diligent and formidable chaperone.

"Ah, cherie!" Madame Joie cried, her dark eyes glowing passionately, "how I would like to show you Paris—and show you to Paris! All eyes would follow you on the Rue de la Paix and Champs-Élysées. Gentlemen would throw flowers into your carriage in the Bois, and send champagne to your table at the Cafe Anglais and Maison-Doree, and fight duels over your favor. Noblemen would pursue you and offer you fortunes and—"

"Oh, Madame," Devon interrupted, blushing, "you mustn't flatter me so! You will turn my poor head."

"But I do not flatter, ma petite. It is true, what I say. Paris would love you—and, alas, I would lose you." Her gloved hand curled intimately around Devon's. "You must not leave me, cherie. You must never leave me. I am so alone. And you are alone too. We are good for each other, n'est-ce pas?"

Touched by her pathetic plea, Devon murmured, "Oui."

The next day her salary was raised to ten dollars a week, half as much as some of the best metropolitan reporters earned, and Devon began to plan how she would repay her debt to Keith Curtis. At five dollars per month, it would take ... almost twenty years? Mother of God, she would be an old woman by then!

Autumn was on the island of Manhattan, burnishing leaves, purpling vines, ripening berries, unfolding late blooms in gardens. Devon snuggled deeper into her covers these chilly nights, and shivered on the early morning trips to empty the slopjar in the basement latrine, which somehow connected with the intricate metropolitan sewage system. The tenants also did their laundry there, and it was damp and dank, lighted by a single gaslamp. Generations of cockroaches dwelled around the odorous drains, and sometimes she saw huge rats—slimy, rheumy-eyed creatures that seemed to crawl out of the subterranean pipes.

"Filthy things!" said Mally O'Neill, when once they met at their chores. "You should see 'em in that place I work—big as rabbits, almost. And don't ever go to the harbor, they swarm on the docks. The ships bring 'em in by the hordes and, I expect, take some out too. If they carry plague, as the doctors think, only the Lord's mercy must keep this town on the map."

Mally O'Neill was twenty-two, the only roomer at Gothic Arms near Devon's age. She worked twelve hours a day packing boxes in a clothing factory. On Sundays she went to the Catholic church and then to visit friends in the Irish sector of the Fourth Ward, where many sweatshop employees lived. As most working girls who had not found ways to supplement their meager wages, Mally wore the cheapest of clothes and shoes, often secondhand, and Devon felt genuinely sorry for her, caught in the merciless and seemingly inextricable trap of poverty. She liked Mally, who was a sweet gentle person, and could have been a pretty pixie in becoming frocks and bonnets. Conversely, Mally admired Devon's stylish wardrobe and obvious breeding and imagined, along with other inmates of the Gothic Arms, that Miss Marshall was a well-to-do young lady, perhaps an heiress, who had run away from home or school to seek her own freedom and independence and had quite possibly assumed an alias.

The other residents were considerably older and far less friendly, suspicious of all strangers. One was a tight-lipped nurse named Ella Funston, who did night duty at Bellevue Hospital and slept all day. Devon rarely saw her, or the Widow Bixby, who sewed for a nearby seamstress and brought bundles of garments home to baste and hem at night, so exhausted when finally she retired that her snoring reverberated and echoed in the corridors. Two elderly spinsters, twin sisters, Ruth and Rena Judd, shared an attic room, which they seldom left except to attend spiritual meetings and seances, because the superstitious landlady would not allow them to "trance" in the house. Just below them lived a plump jolly Italian woman in her fifties, who claimed to have been in opera in her youth and sang arias while she bathed and emptied her slops, but who never said more than "ciao" to anybody.

What a pleasure and relief it was to spend her days at the boutique, selling and occasionally demonstrating exquisite merchandise for discriminating and appreciative customers, chatting and gossiping between sales with her charming employer, sharing her Continental breakfast, lunching with her at smart restaurants and tearooms where Madame always paid the tab, and dining and driving and promenading with her in Central Park on Sundays. If it was not the career she craved, it was almost as satisfying, especially when Madame began to speak of making her a partner in the business.

One cold November morning, when frost coated the city

like confectioner's sugar, Devon arrived at the shop to find
Madame Joie selecting an enormous wardrobe for packing. Devon was wearing the chic cloak purchased in Washington, the rich topaz wool and lustrous satin lining perfect with her cream-and honey complexion.

"Ah," Madame Joie said, "it is fortunate that you wear
your magnifique cloak today, for we go to show some deshabille to a very stylish lady. You shall model for her, in
her home."

"Why doesn't she come here, Madame?"

"She is an invalid, cherie. She cannot walk. She lives in
her boudoir and travels in a wheelchair. Twice a year, for
five years now, I give her private showings. She is one of
my best customers. We go at three o'clock. I have engaged
a hack. We will take many garments, without tags. The
lady does not concern herself with such trifles. The bills
are sent directly to her husband."

"And he never questions them?"

"Never."

"He must be a millionaire!"

"Many times over, cherie, many times over."

The cab arrived at two-thirty, and the driver carried out
ten of La Boutique Chic's distinctive glossy black boxes
lettered in gold. As he assisted the passengers, Madame
Joie said, "Gramercy Park, s'il vous plait. Number eleven
south."

Devon settled against the seat with a little jolt. "Did you
say Gramercy Park, Madame?"

"Oui. It is not far from here, we will not be late."

Devon crossed her fingers under her cloak and said a
prayer for good measure. Please God, don't let it be near
his house. Don't let him see us. Please, please. . . .

Madame Joie was preening herself to make the best possible impression in the haute monde neighborhood, although confident that her most effective advertisement was
sitting beside her. Never had she had a mannequin to
equal Mademoiselle Marshall, who not only possessed all
the physical prerequisites but an innate penchant for modeling. In her ten years in New York she had moved her
shop location twice and employed a number of assistants.
Most had been attractive and ambitious and soon went
into keeping by the husbands of her clientele. One had
married well, two had been forced into premature retire-

ment by pregnancies they either could not or would not terminate, and she never saw any of them again. One flamboyant little creature had become a successful actress and was now touring the Continent, another had opened a lucrative bordello on Mercer Street, a third had sunk to soliciting on the waterfront. They had showed no gratitude or loyalty to her and invariably disillusioned and disappointed her. Some had stolen what they could, slipping stockings, gloves, kerchiefs, perfumes into their reticules and under their capes. They were trollops and ingrates, and she was well rid of them. But this one—oh, she could not bear to think of losing this one! This lovely little doll she would keep, if she had to promise her the moon and stars—and give her the boutique!

The hackney halted before a ponderous brownstone mansion that appeared to brood in the wintry gloom, for the weather had turned suddenly cloudy and much colder, as if it might rain or snow. Devon gazed at the the granite lions guarding the entrance, the pedestalled gaslamps between their front paws already lighted against the overcast sky. The cabbie was assembling the boxes under Madame's direction. Finally they approached the great carved oak door, and Madame hammered the bronze knocker, a lion's head with a ring through its nose, possibly symbolic of the master of the house.

"Madame Joie and assistant!" she announced to the liveried butler. "We are expected."

"Yes, Madame. Mrs. Curtis is in her chambers."

Mrs. Curtis!

For a horrifying moment Devon thought her heart had actually failed, for she was weak and giddy and had to gasp for breath. Madame Joie glanced at her curiously, assuming that she was merely reacting to the splendor of the surroundings, and then the major domo was leading them up a wide curved stairway with an ornate banister, the cabbie behind him toting the pyramid of boxes, Madame in his wake, and there was nothing to do but follow the procession to its ultimate destination, though it be the gallows or guillotine. The merchandise was deposited in a private parlor that was all feminine elegance. Madame Joie ordered the driver to return in an hour, and the butler ushered him out.

Together they entered the boudoir of the mistress of the

house, and Madame greeted, "Bon après-midi, Madame," preferring her native tongue with clientele who might understand it, for she believed it enhanced her profession, and Mrs. Curtis responded in flawless French.

"May I present my new assistant, Mademoiselle Marshall? She will model for you. And I have an *exquis* collection, just arrived from Paris. Such dreams, Madame! Such bonbons!"

She rambled on about the marvels she had brought, while Devon stared hypnotically at the woman in the canopied bed. She was a Gainsborough portrait in blue: blue silk bedjacket and blue band in her long loose black hair. The sheets, pillows and comforter were blue satin, the canopy lined in blue cloth. She appeared delicate and exquisite as a porcelain figurine, the purple eyes in the white face like violets in snow.

Trying to ignore the wheelchair and other accouterments of invalidism, Devon said, "I'm happy to know you, Mrs. Curtis." She could not tell if her voice sounded as calm as she hoped, for she was trembling inside with rage and hatred against the woman's husband. With this beautiful wife, with this tragic helpless invalid, he had done what he had! Oh, God, she would never forgive him, or herself. She longed to run out of that room, out of that house, all the way back to Richmond.

"Thank you, Miss Marshall. It's nice to meet you. How long have you been with Madame?"

"Not long, Ma'am. About two months."

Madame Joie, whisking lids off boxes and displaying the treasures, inquired which she wished demonstrated.

"All of them, Madame. You know I never make impromptu decisions. Miss Marshall may use the dressing room to change, of course."

"Monsieur Curtis is well, I trust?" Madame asked politely, and Devon hoped to hear that he was out of town, or dead.

"Monsieur Curtis is quite well," came the somewhat taut reply, emphasizing the last two words. "The presentation, if you please, Madame."

Behind the dressing room screen Devon stripped down to her chemise and donned the first costume, consisting of nightgown, sacque, and negligee of mauve chiffon and rosepoint lace tied with satin ribbons. Madame Joie, sitting on a velvet slipperchair near the bed, narrated the virtues of the ensemble while Devon modeled. Mrs. Curtis did not gush; she merely said it was charming and she would take it.

The procedure was repeated with sets of eggshell satin and Valenciennes lace, lime mousseline de soie cascading in ruffles, Renoir-blue watered silk with portrait collar, and misty rose crepe de Chine embroidered in pale blue forget-me-nots. Mrs. Curtis nodded approval, Madame lauded her choices, and marked the prices in her ledger.

From the winter robe collection Esther Curtis chose a green moire antique with mink collar and cuffs; a free-flowing purple velvet with bishop's sleeves lined in amethyst satin; a pearl gray Lyon silk shot with silver thread; a sapphire taffeta with a standing collar embroidered in seed pearls and crystal bugle-beads; and for festive occasions, a silver brocade trimmed in ermine, and a cloth-of-gold with a deep yoke worked in semiprecious stones.

The most dramatic of the collection had been reserved for the finale, and Devon was preparing to present it when she heard the door open in the outer chamber and a familiar masculine voice saying, "Good afternoon, ladies."

"Ah, Monsieur Curtis! It is good to see you again. Madame has found much to her liking today, but I have one more jewel to show—and you have arrived at the propitious moment! It is à la mode in Paris, since the Empress Eugenie introduced it at a levee. Oh, la-la! It will lift the spirit and make the heart sing and—" She clapped her hands briskly for Devon to come out. "Mademoiselle! We are ready."

Esther said, "Madame Joie has a new mannequin, Keith, and she's absolutely adorable. I suspect some conspiracy on Madame's part, in that she knew I wouldn't be able to resist many things this lovely creature modeled."

Devon was cowering behind the screen, wishing she could somehow disappear. She couldn't, she simply couldn't go out there dressed like this! She would faint, or die on the spot.

"Mademoiselle!" Madame called again, a little impatiently. "Tout de suite!"

Devon emerged. The low-cut topaz satin nightdress was overlaid in amber tiffany fluttering with apricot marabu, the three shades blending in a kind of golden symphony.

She did not know how Keith reacted to the sight of her, for she simply refused to meet his eyes. She moved about the room as taught, slowly, gracefully, holding the sheer drapery lightly in her fingertips to flare like gossamer wings, turning languidly, pausing with one gold muled toe pointed before her, as if to curtsy. And whatever expression the Frenchwoman caught on the monsieur's face, it was enough to cause her to concentrate her sales efforts on him.

"La pièce de résistance, Monsieur!"

"Enchanting," he agreed.

"Yes, indeed," Esther murmured. "And what luscious, appetizing colors, rather like apricot mousse or frappe. It looks good enough to eat, doesn't it, darling? May I see the undergarment, please?"

Devon glanced at Madame, her eyes pleading to be spared this exposure, but she ignored her mannequin's modesty, considering this boudoir decolletage no more revealing than many formal gowns.

Devon stood perfectly still, controlling her breath as much as possible to curtail the voluptuous swell of her breasts, as embarrassed as if she were stark naked, and removed the peignoir.

Esther's tone taunted her spouse. "Do you like it, dear?"

"Yes," he said huskily.

"Are you sure, darling? It may not look the same on me. I've lost weight these long terrible years, you know, and am not so generously endowed in some respects as before. Come a bit closer, Miss Marshall. The light is somewhat dim under this canopy." Devon obliged, and Esther persisted, "Do you still like it, Keith?"

"Yes," he repeated in an even deeper timbre.

"But of course he does!" the Frenchwoman intervened, sensing a husband-baiting. "Mon Dieu, what man would not like it?"

"Very well," Esther decided. "I'll take it, Madame."

Madame Joie scratched in her collectaire and dismissed her mannequin. Without donning the overlay, Devon slipped into the dressing room and grasped the screen for support, hard enough to imprint the lacquered wood. Then she dressed as quickly as possible, folded the few garments Mrs. Curtis had rejected, and boxed them. The hackney was waiting, and Keith offered to carry the rejects out for them. But Madame Joie remained behind, to make sure she had listed every sale, as well as to discuss possible alterations.

In the hall outside Esther's room, Keith said, "I expected to hear from you."

"I'm sure you did. A one-word message: Help! Or perhaps, Surrender! Well, I don't need your kind of help any more, Monsieur Curtis, and I won't be beholden to you forever, either. Soon I can start repaying my debt."

He scowled angrily. "I don't want the goddamn money! It was never the money, and you know it. I've lost ten times that much and more on the turn of a card or roll of dice, and I was gambling on you too. Devon, look at me, please. Maybe you couldn't in there, but you can now. Have you any idea of the hell I went through, seeing you like that?"

"It wasn't exactly heaven for me, either."

"I know, darling, and I'm sorry. Some explanations are in order. I've been half crazy wondering what happened to you. Where are you living now? Tell me, quickly. I'll come to you this evening."

She was silent.

"I'll ask Madame Joie," he threatened.

"She won't tell you anything, if I ask her not to," Devon said. "She wouldn't want to lose your wife's business. Oh, how could you, Keith? With her in that condition!"

"You've jumped to some conclusions, Devon. They are not necessarily correct."

"I know what I see! A beautiful, helpless woman married to a—a monster!"

"Darling—"

"Don't call me that, and in her home yet! Oh, I feel so ashamed, Keith. So cheap and dirty."

Down the stairway they went, into the foyer where ancestral faces in wigs and ruffs and plumes peered at them from the dark paneled walls—some smiling, some frowning, some pensive, some serene and complacent, all aristocratic with noble brows and patrician noses—out the portal and into the gray November mist.

Keith put the boxes in the hackney and taking her arm to boost her in, said sotto voce, "I'll find you, Devon. You can't hide from me forever—this town isn't big enough for that."

"I'll just move again, Keith."

Madame Joie was coming now, stepping buoyantly; it had been a profitable day. "Merci, Monsieur, merci beaucoup," she smiled. "And until spring, au revoir."

"Au revoir," Keith responded, looking at Devon, who was staring straight ahead with the glazed eyes of the blind, seeing nothing. Had he touched her, she thought in disgust and self-loating, she would have melted into his arms—even in the presence of his poor wife.

Chapter 8

La Boutique Chic was decorated for Christmas. Holly wreaths tied with red ribbons, silver bells, tinsel festoons, evergreen boughs, and in the window a nostalgic Paris snow scene proclaiming, "Noel, Noel! Joyeux Noel!"

Business was brisk, for every item in the shop was an appropriate feminine gift. Perfumes and colognes and sachets, ornamental pillboxes and smelling salts vinaigrettes, ivory- and jade-handled parasols, tortoiseshell combs and fourchettes, opera lorgnettes, reticules, gloves, fans, muffs, silk scarves, paisley and cashmere and lace shawls, exquisite convent-made handkerchiefs—everything a whimsical heart could desire, or an acquisitive one covet. Many gentlemen purchased gifts for wives and mistresses in one convenient stop.

Devon sent Mrs. Chester a nice dark wool shawl along with the season's greetings. Remembering recent Southern holidays, the want and need and privation, she did not imagine things had improved much in the few months of her abscence. She had read in the papers that Richmond had been designated the Number One Military District, which meant the Federal government was even more firmly entrenched, and the carpetbaggers and scalawags more in favor.

Snow had been falling intermittently for a week, promising a white Christmas. Sleighs and cutters appeared on the streets, and the wheels of the horsecars and omnibuses were replaced with runners. Madame Joie had invited Devon to spend the holidays with her, and Devon looked forward to putting up a tree, which she had not done in several years. "How wonderful to feel such enthusiasm!" said Madame, whose own had long since vanished with her youth and naivete. "You have revived the spirit in me, ma petite, and I bless you for it."

She watched her young assistant a great deal, covertly for the most part, but sometimes with open intense yearning in her dark eyes, which Devon could not fathom and imagined was reminiscence or nostalgia for her own lost girlhood. And she was almost maternally solicitous of Devon's health, scolding her when she walked in the rain without an umbrella and the snow without boots. Her admonitions amused Devon.

"Madame, we had rain and snow in Richmond. Oh my, yes! Some fierce blizzards blow out of the mountains, and sometimes the rivers and lakes freeze. I enjoyed ice-skating and sledding on the hills. Richmond, like Rome, has seven hills. And I am not such a delicate flower as you may think."

"To me you are a white camellia, pure and sweet and perfect, and I would keep you in a conservatory if I could."

Devon smiled shyly. She could not adjust to such extravagant compliments from one of the same sex; they seemed unseemly and made her self-conscious, especially when Madame also caught and squeezed her hands and kissed her cheeks. Of course the innately affectionate French kissed and embraced impetuously, on the slightest pretext, and Devon didn't quite know how to avoid or cope with these increasingly frequent impulses.

While decorating the tree Christmas Eve, Madame suddenly decided that her mannequin should cease addressing her formally. "Je m'appelle Janette, cherie, and I wish you to call me so."

"Janette Joie," Devon mused. "What a charming name!"

"All my lovers thought so."

She had given her servant leave to be with her family in the French Quarter, where the emigrants celebrated the Gallic religious feasts and national holidays, including Bastille Day, in the traditions of the old country. And so they were alone in the gray stone duplex, which was furnished similar to the one the count had maintained for Janette in Paris.

The tree ornaments were exquisite: sequin stars, golden moons, crystal snowflakes, miniature angels of blown and spun glass, porcelain and china figurines, and gaily painted baubles. Janette had bought them and the elaborate Nativity *crèche* years before at the Santon Fair in Marseilles and brought them with her to America. Beneath the tree were brightly wrapped packages, which Devon knew had come from the shop and were undoubtedly for her. The rooms were pungently fragrant with juniper and bayberry and spice, and there was an elaborate buffet including a traditional Yule Log cake, a cornucopia of fruit and nuts and sweets, and decanters of vintage wine. The bache de Noel burned on the hearth, beside which sat an old wooden shoe from Janette's childhood. "The sabot," she explained when Devon inquired about it. "It is for gifts from le pere Noel and le petit Jesus. I had kept it so long, I could not bear to part with it when innocence was gone." And Devon realized that the sophisticated Frenchwoman was as sentimental about her homeland and as nostalgic for it now as the Virginian was for hers.

Murray Hill was a rapidly developing suburb of fine residences, north of Madison Square. To the east, in Kip's Bay and Turtle Bay, were wealthy country homes and estates. That Madame Joie could afford this prestigious address proved her business acumen and success, and Devon hoped she was serious about a possible partnership, although she had not mentioned it recently, perhaps saving it as a Christmas surprise. Janette had talked of expansion, of engaging an experienced milliner and talented modiste to design originals to bear her label, and eventually adding a custom bootery. Fortunes could be made in haute couture, she said, citing Monsieur Worth in Paris as an example. The risks were great, naturellement, but so were the rewards. And Devon was excited about the prospect; her future appeared bright, the New Year full of promise.

Now and then she glanced through the orieled window at the white roof and smoking chimneys of the house across the street. She could see the family decorating the tree and hanging stockings on the mantel. Some carolers passed, singing and ringing bells, their lanterns glowing on the snow. Tears of joy and gratitude filled her eyes.

"Merry Christmas, Janette."

"Joyeux Noel, Da-von." She filled two goblets with champagne. "A toast, ma petite. May we never part company! And now you open your presents. In France, they are given to adults on New Year, but I follow your custom here."

Her generosity overwhelmed Devon. Almost everything she had ever admired at the Boutique was there: Tuscany and Kasan gloves, an alligator purse, a blue fox muff, French perfume, an expensive cashmere shawl, and a pearly-white chiffon peignoir ensemble as frothy as whipped marshmallow. "Oh, Madame, I can't take all of this! It is too much. I will accept the gloves and the scent but—"

"Nonsense!" Janette quaffed her wine and replenished her glass. "I shall be angry if you refuse one single thing."

"But I've given you so little, a few handkerchiefs that are lost in this avalanche!"

"You deserve it all, and more," Janette insisted, her raised hand forbidding further protest. "And now I want to talk with you about changing your address, Devon. You do not like living in that place, do you?"

"The Gothic Arms? Well, it's not the Astor House but—"

"It is a convent," Janette said. "A cloister, and you do not belong there. There is much room in my home, and you could be comfortable here, no?"

"Of course. It's a lovely house, but I could not afford to pay what it would be worth."

"Pay? Did I mention pay?"

"But I couldn't be a permanent guest!"

"Think on it, anyway," Janette said, smiling. "It would make me *vrai* happy to have you here."

While they nibbled delicacies and sipped wine before the blazing hearth, Janette regaled Devon with fascinating stories of the Court of Napoleon III, which she had been privileged to frequent during her gilded life as the mistress of the Comte de Lyon. She was a vivid raconteuse, detailing the pomp and splendor, the magnificent clothes and jewels, risque amusements and vices, follies and affairs. She recalled the command performances of celebrated entertainers, the presentations of important people to the emperor and empress, and chuckled over the flamboyant bal masques in which wives and mistresses vied to outdo each other's costumes.

"Oh, it was a grand life," she said, "until the comte became enamored of another. But that too is the nature of the beast. Man, you know, is the most faithless of all God's creatures. I have developed an aversion to men for the unfair advantage they take of women, and retaliate by padding the bills I send for the purchases they make for their wives and mistresses. It is fair. Most are bêtes," she said contemptuously. "You cannot trust them, you can never trust them. They will betray you, always . . . and in the end, they will destroy you."

A strange sentiment, Devon thought, for the season of good will toward men. But she was inclined to agree with Janette. Hadn't Keith taken unfair advantage of her desperation? Hadn't he betrayed his wife as flagrantly as any husband could? How had she become an invalid? Presumably he had not married her in that condition.

"Did you send Monsieur Curtis a whopping bill?"

"Triple what the items were worth," Janette grinned. "I could be arrested for extortion."

"Mrs. Curtis is very beautiful, isn't she?"

"Oui, but beauty does not matter to l'animal when he tires of his mate and one can plainly see that Monsieur Curtis has lost interest in Madame."

"But still she buys seductive lingerie."

"All the boutiques de boudoir in Paris could not lure a disenchanted man."

"You don't think he makes love to her any more?"

"I would not think so, cherie. He does not look at her with desire, as he looked at you. I sense no love in that house at all, in the eyes or the heart or the bed."

"Because she's crippled?"

"I do not know how crippled she is," Janette said with a shrug. "I have never seen her out of her wheelchair."

"Do you know what happened to her?" Devon asked casually, selecting a frosted almond from the compote.

"Some kind of accident, I understand. She never explained to me and naturellement I did not ask. In my business one must have ethics. One must learn to listen without obvious curiosity and to keep secrets. If one does not learn these things, one will soon be bankrupt."

The wine and warmth of the fire made Devon drowsy. She lounged on the Empire sofa, her legs stretched on the cushion, crossed at the delicate ankles, her graceful turquoise taffeta skirt spread fanlike on the rose velvet carpet. The picture was one of pretty and appealing languor, and

Janette grew silent and pensive, thinking that only in youth could ennui be so attractive. The ormulu clock on the mantel was striking midnight when she suggested retirement.

The guest chamber was exquisitely feminine—bone-white furniture, delicately carved and touched with gilt. Roses and cupids entwined the headboard of the bed, which curved like embracing arms, and the dressing table wore the frilly white net skirt of a ballerina. A vase of fresh white flowers stood on a marble pedestal, and the steam heat intensified the fragrance of the spray of lily-of-the-valley in its center—rather like a bridal bouquet, Devon thought suddenly. Janette had brought up the white chiffon ensemble and urged her to put it on while she fetched "a little surprise." The partnership agreement? Devon wondered hopefully.

She was sitting before the mirror in the misty white garments, lovely as a virgin bride, when Janette returned with a demi-tasse of hot spiced Tokay and angelica on a Tole tray and yet another small wrapped gift. She paused and caught her breath in quick admiration. Then, as Devon sipped the relaxing drink, Janette picked up the brush and began stroking her hair, murmuring, "The curls of a bebe. Soft, sweet, golden."

Once, while making love to her, Keith had said much the same thing in the same caressing voice, fondling her hair and calling her a curly-headed baby. The intensity of his eyes in desire and the urgency of his touch, she saw and sensed in Janette too. With Keith she had responded passionately, but now she felt only revulsion and dismay. She put the demi-tasse aside and opened the package. It was a thin volume bound in white morocco stamped in gold: an English translation of some lyrics of Sappho of Lesbos, the flyleaf inscribed, *"Pour ma petite cherie, avec amour, Janette."*

Devon knew nothing of Sappho, except that she was a Greek poetess before Christ. But she could translate enough of the legend, and she knew what she saw in Janette's eyes, heard in her voice, felt in her touch. And it seemed incredible. What was wrong with her? Was she so lonely, so desperate, so starved for affection and companionship? Was she sick in some strange way? "Please," she said, taking the brush from her hand. "I'm rather tired, Janette. May I retire now ?"

"Cherie, the book. Comprendre?"

"No, Madame, I don't understand!"

"Janette," she corrected. "Ah, ma petite fleur. You are nervous, n'est-ce pas? Drink some more Tokay."

"I don't want any more."

Janette bent and kissed the crown of her head, whispering, "Adoree Devon ... la tindre fille de ma choix ... ma vierge ... ma belle mariée. ..."

Virgin? Bride? Girl of her choice?

"Madame, what are you saying?"

"Cherie, I think you do understand ... and it is not so terrible, is it? I will make you a partner in the boutique and the beneficiary of my will. I will take care of you, always, and never hurt you. And it is not like amour with a man, which can bring so much misery and unhappiness, and trouble and travail. You would never become endeinte. ..."

Her hands parted the peignoir and began to explore Devon's body, groping her breasts, fondling the nipples. Jesus, Jesus! What was she doing, what did she want, what did she think they could do together? And how could she escape? It was late and snowing again. The streetcars were not running, there was probably not a cab within a mile, she couldn't leave until morning, and the day after Christmas she would have to look for another job ... oh, God!

"Madame," she said desperately, "what you want of me is impossible! You see, I—I'm in love with a man—"

"What man?" she demanded with fierce jealousy.

"His name does not matter. But believe me, I love him."

"You have been together, in bed?"

"Yes."

"You are not virginal? The beast has deflowered you?"

"We've been intimate," Devon said. "Lovers."

"Where, in Reechmon?"

Devon nodded.

"But why did you leave him, if you love him?"

"I don't know, Madame. It was some wild impulse, some crazy fancy I had to come to New York. But I know now it was a mistake, and I must go home again. Soon. And then I shall marry him. ..."

Janette turned away with a deep sigh, as if she were suddenly weary, and she looked quite old and wretched.

"Go to bed, ma petite. It is not the end of the world. Not for you, anyway. Bonne nuit."

"Good night," Devon murmured.

Janette hesitated, sighed again, and left.

Devon lay awake most of the night, astonished at her innocence. Only a child could have been so beguiled by the gestures, endearments, presents. She was too naive to be out alone! Ignorant of sexual deviation, she could not understand how the woman had intended to consummate the relationship, and was almost as curious as she was repelled. What did she know of life? Certainly not enough to be a writer!

She left before dawn, creeping out of the dark house, and leaving the gifts behind. She suspected that Janette had remained in her room purposely, to spare them both any further embarrassment, and for that she was grateful to her. But she was beginning to wonder if she was born under an evil sign and doomed to disappointment, disillusion, and disaster.

She walked toward the city, lonely and bewildered and cold as a lost kitten in the snow. Church bells were pealing, carillons chiming. It was Christmas, the birthday of Jesus Christ, and she should go somewhere and adore Him. She met some early Christians on their way to worship. "Merry Christmas," they greeted, and Devon burst into tears.

Chapter 9

The streets were a gray slush of pulverized ice, the gutters awash with melting snow. Wearing a dark wool skirt and white tailored blouse under her cloak, Devon went to investigate a *Tribune* advertisement for an experienced clerk-bookkeeper, at Joseph's Books, on Broadway.

She found a small store sandwiched between a barber shop and an oyster bar. The proprietor, Ephraim Joseph, was an elderly man with a long thin high-bridged nose, weak eyes squinting behind square-lensed spectacles, and white hair brushing the collar of his black alpaca sackcoat. He mistook Devon for a customer. Apprised of her purpose, he peered at her narrowly, at once surprised and disgruntled, muttering, "I expected a man."

"The advertisement doesn't specify sex, sir."

"I naturally assumed, young lady, that an experienced bookkeeper would be male, since few females have any head for business and can scarcely count a dozen eggs correctly, or keep a household budget straight. I also assumed the applicant would be able to lift boxes of books, climb on ladders, make deliveries, and shovel snow off the sidewalk. As you can see, I'm not young or strong and need a sturdy assistant. Better find yourself a candy store or hat or dress shop."

"I worked in a boutique, sir, but it was only temporary, for the holiday rush. I received my discharge Christmas Eve." Hopefully, this explanation would eliminate the usual request for references.

"Well, I'm afraid there wasn't much seasonal rush here," he lamented. "People give books only when they can't think of anything else. Booksellers fare much better in Boston and Philadelphia, and actually flourish in London. But on the whole, this is a pitifully illiterate place. If it weren't for the perennials and standards of the trade—

the Bible, Charles Dickens, Shakespeare, and a few others—most of us would go out of business. If only Mrs. Stowe would write another *Uncle Tom's Cabin*! We did all right with that one."

Devon winced inwardly, as every Southerner did at the mere mention of that book; and the author's name was anathema in the South. "I should think Emerson, Longfellow and Whittier would move, sir. And I thought the works of Hawthorne, Washington Irving, and James Fenimore Cooper were highly popular in New England. And when you add Sir Walter Scott and the English classics—"

"Well, well," he mused, regarding her with new interest and some wonder, "what have we here—a pretty little bookworm?"

"I like to read, sir."

"Fiction, poetry?"

"Books," she said. "All kinds."

"Don't tell me you're a bluestocking!"

She despised this soubriquet, which had its origin in the blue hoisery affected by Elizabeth Montagu and the members of her literary society in England over a century before, and was still contemptuously applied to any female with an ounce of active gray matter and an iota of interest in learning.

"I have some education," she replied, "and my father was an intellectual."

"Are you a suffragist?"

Devon knew the expedient answer to this question: "I'm too busy for that, sir." Adding with dimpled smile, "Besides, I'm too young to vote."

"Don't misunderstand, Miss Marshall. I have no objection to a mind in a woman. At my age, I find it singularly attractive and stimulating, since I can still respond to mental attractions and stimulations. I take it you can add and subtract figures, and distinguish between credit and debit in a ledger?"

Devon responded affirmatively, as she would have to any other qualification required or desired. "I kept books for my father, and he said I was a competent accountant."

"Good. Inventory will be due at the end of this month, and I'll expect you to help with it. In addition, you must keep the shop clean, sweep and dust and so forth; keep the fire going in winter and the flies out in summer, if you last that long. You must also lend a hand with the snow shovel. I suffer from gout and lumbago, and sometimes find it difficult to negotiate the stairs to my quarters above. Do you think you can satisfactorily discharge all of these duties, young lady?"

"When shall I start, sir?"

"Immediately. The salary is three dollars a week, the hours from eight to seven, unless there are late customers, in which case you must remain. I can't afford to miss a prospect."

Devon had already removed her cloak and was hanging it on a wood peg in the stationery closet.

"I must say you don't look or dress like a bluestocking, Miss Marshall. That capote is indeed a handsome garment."

"I bought it at discount from the boutique," Devon lied. Was it possible for a girl to survive in New York without dissembling and mendacity and guile?

"Come, I'll show you the office."

It was a cramped, cluttered cubicle at the rear of the old building. No windows, only a transom over the door to admit light and air from the store. The gaslamp burned all day, and cleaning the globe would be another of her chores. There were several wood file cabinets, a rolltop desk with stuffed pigeonholes, and a Windsor chair with a tattered cushion. The only decoration was a current calendar on the drab walls and a dusty whatnot in a corner.

The stockroom was even more dim and dreary, with stacks of books and heavy wood crates of them on the floor. Seeing a crowbar to pry off the nailed lids, Devon suddenly understood why he had wanted a strong-backed employee; a pugilist's arms would have been desirable too.

"Still think you can handle the job, Miss Marshall?"

She hesitated, a shade less confident. "I'll try, sir."

"I admire your spirit, my dear. With your other assets, you should succeed in this world. But don't count on it. I'm afraid there's little reward for effort and perseverance. You will discover that yourself in time, and when you're my age, you'll be a skeptical cynic with few ideals and ambitions and goals left, and even fewer surprises."

Devon wanted to say that she had already discovered some of the injustices of life, and did not think there were many surprises left even at her age. Walking back into the store with him, she picked up the feather duster and began diligently cleaning the shelves and display counters and rearranging the merchandise, turned topsy-turvy by the previous day's browsers.

Being serious commodities by nature, there was little excitement or expectation in purveying books. The customers were seldom young (college students bought their texts at school and used the libraries) and generally ranged between middle age and dotage, primarily professors, ministers, tutors, governesses, lonely dowagers, and spinsters, as soberly garbed as the book jackets. Mr. Joseph told her that the wealthy with private libraries ordered directly from the publishers to be assured of first and usually autographed editions, and attended auctions in search of rare properties.

Compared to the stylish chattering clientele of La Boutique Chic, Joseph's was a morgue. Munching a sandwich and doughnut for lunch, with a fruit dessert off a peddler's cart, Devon yearned for the exotic cuisine of the sophisticated restaurants Madame Joie had patronized. Janette's unfortunate affliction, whatever it was, now seemed to Devon a great personal tragedy depriving her of a pleasant, comfortable, and interesting existence.

And then one fine day in the third week of the New Year, a scarlet-and-gilt carriage halted before Joseph's, breaking the monotony. The golden horses, with long silver manes and tails, were the most beautiful Devon had ever seen, although she came from a land of beautiful horses. A coachman and footman, in scarlet-and-gold livery, occupied the perch, the latter with a long jagged scar across his picaresque face, which might have been slashed with a Saracen blade or stevedore's hook. He jumped down to attend his master, a florid-faced giant in a fur-trimmed greatcoat and tall beaver hat. While Devon stared in fascination he entered the shop as if he owned it, or had the change in his pocket to buy it, and his Irish brogue was as thick as clam chowder. "Top o'the morn to ye, Miss!"

Devon could not recall seeing that spectacular equipage in the Central Park carriage parade, for Madame Joie would surely have identified it, and she had no idea who he could be. But her first impression was not favorable.

The man was perhaps forty, as sleek and well-fed as his horses, with deep-set blue eyes, russet hair, and a rusty handlebar mustache. His clothes were obviously expensive and just as obviously lacking in taste and refinement, from the too-wide beaver lapels of the coat and too-large diamond stickpin in his crimson cravat, to the fancy patent boots on his huge feet, and he reeked of bay rum and Macassar oil. If he was not the great showman, P. T. Barnum, he was certainly some lively competition for him.

"Good morning, sir. May I help you?"

"Indeed ye may, me pretty lass. The name is Trent Patrick Donahue, and I'm after buying a yard of books."

"A yard of books, sir?"

"Aye. Me shelves measure thirty-six inches across, and there be ten of 'em. I'll fill 'em a yard at a time, and when they be full, I'll install more shelves. So you see," his full-lipped mouth grinned, "I'll be a good customer for a long time. And I hear this store has the best stock in town."

"We like to think so, sir. What kind of books did you have in mind? History, philosophy, essays, biography, reference, poetry, fiction?"

" 'Tis no matter, Miss. I ain't aiming to read 'em."

"Oh, but you should, sir, and choose discriminately! Books are not mere ornaments for decoration; they're meant to be read and enjoyed and cherished, as friends."

"Only by folks that ain't got nothing better to do and enjoy and cherish," he replied. "I'll be leaving the titles up to you, Miss. 'Tis Miss?"

"Yes, sir. Miss Marshall."

"Miss Who Marshall?"

"Devon Elizabeth."

"I like the name. It's got class."

"About the books, Mr. Donahue. Mr. Joseph says that Shakespeare should be the foundation of every library."

"Me mither would argue that with him," Donahue said. "To her, the Bible is the rock on which to build."

"I assume you already possess the Good Book, sir. How about the philosophers? We have them all, from Aristotle to Voltaire, and Aurelius to Zeno, and—"

He raised a hand almost the size of a Virginia ham. "Those names mean naught to me, Miss Marshall. But I have heard of the Bard of Avon, so let us begin with him. One yard of Shakespeare, please."

"A wise choice, sir. And only yesterday we received a fine shipment from London. Beautiful red morocco bindings stamped in genuine twenty-four carat gold."

"Red covers? Good. That's me favorite color."

"These volumes are real treasures, Mr. Donahue, the kind to pass on to your heirs. But they're rather expensive, six dollars each. A yard would come to—let me see now—they're approximately an inch wide and shouldn't be crowded on the shelf. About twenty-four volumes to the yard, I would guess." She figured the cost on a scratch pad. "Oh, dear! That's one hundred and forty-four dollars! Now in plain buckram—"

"No, thankee, Miss Marshall. Nothing plain for Trent Patrick Donahue. I was raised on plain buckram, so to speak, in Ireland. Never knew nothing but mutton, potatoes, calico, and canvas. Now I can afford fancy stuff, and that's what I want. Take me new carriage, for instance. Custom-built, it is, and fit for royalty."

"Oh, it's very elegant," Devon assured him, although conspicuous would have been more accurate.

"Ain't it, though? I bet you never seen horses like that before, either? Palominos, they call 'em. 'Tis a color, not a breed. Very rare and expensive—came all the way from a Mexican rancho in Texas, up the Mississippi by riverboat. I got some fast trotters too that can take any in Harlem Lane. You ever go to the Harlem races, Miss Marshall?"

Devon had put a large cardboard box on the counter and was carefully packing the books. "No, but I've heard of them."

He said, "I'm racing Commodore Vanderbilt, August Belmont, and Robert Bonner this afternoon. If you'd like to watch, I'll send me carriage for you."

"I'm a working girl, Mr. Donahue."

"Where's your boss? I'll fix it with him."

"Oh no, please! Mr. Joseph wouldn't allow it. He's very strict. And he's in bad humor today, not feeling well. He just stepped out to pick up a prescription from his druggist." She scribbled an invoice. "Here you are, sir! One hundred and forty-four dollars, please."

He paid in greenbacks, peeling them off an immense roll. Opening the door, he beckoned the footman to carry out the purchase, growling at him when he bumped the box. "Careful, ye clumsy oaf! Them's valuable books."

"Books? I din't know youse could read, Boss!"

Donahue cuffed him and would have whacked him with his gold-headed cane, but the lackey dodged, grinning insolently at his scowling master, apparently accustomed to such treatment and even amused, as if brutality were a game they played. And Devon wondered again who this violent man was, and how he made his living. She was putting the money in the strongbox when Mr. Joseph returned with his medicine, limping slightly in pain.

"Guess what!" she said proudly. "I sold twenty-four volumes of that new shipment of Shakespeare!"

"Twenty-four volumes! Who was the customer?"

"He said his name was Trent Patrick Donahue."

"Donahue? That Bowery gambler!"

"Is that what he is, a gambler?"

"Only one of the most notorious in town! Where've you been, girl, that you've not heard of the Pot O'Gold and The Gilded Cage?" He scowled in disgust. "Bah! What an affront to Shakespeare. I doubt if that Irish boor can even read."

"But he buys books by the yard, Mr. Joseph. He wants the finest bindings, and he pays in cash."

The old man grunted. "Bring me some water, please. These blasted boluses get harder to swallow with every refill."

He liked her to wait on him, brew his tea and serve him, adjust his shawl, and prop his feet on the office ottoman. He seemed to think he had hired a nurse as well as a clerk and janitress, and Devon only hoped he would not dismiss his weekly charwoman and add his living quarters to her other cleaning burdens.

As every Sunday at Gothic Arms, Devon woke to the sweet sound of church bells. On the surface New York was a holy city, with a spire or belfry or campanile rising from almost every block. The houses of worship were the tallest buildings on the island, and a forest of steeples limned the horizon. Either Manhattan was a highly religious community, or one much in need of salvation.

Devon lay in her prim single bed, snuggled deep in the eiderdown, dreading to dress and go down to breakfast in the gloomy old dining room with the boring boarders. The conversation was invariably dull and repetitious, punctuated by physical and emotional complaints, scraping of plates and rattling of pots and pans in the kitchen. And though substantial, the meals were uninspired, the sort of hearty, heavy nourishment that encouraged fat, indigestion, and nightmares.

A convent, Janette had called the Gothic Arms, an impression heightened now by the extraneous chapel bells and the Italian soprano singing "Ave Maria" at the top of her powerful lungs. Devon gazed wistfully at the snow in the cloistered courtyard, despite which faithful Mally O'Neill had already gone to early Mass. She had probably fasted for communion—no great sacrifice considering the unappetizing fare.

After a bowl of tasteless gruel that stuck like mucilage to the roof of her mouth, and a slice of dry cinnamon toast forced down with weak tea, Devon did her weekly laundry in the freezing basement. She had just finished and was hanging her wash on the racks when Mally, back from St. Andrew's, came down and invited her to go skating in Central Park.

"The flags are flying on the streetcars," she said, "and that means the ball's up in the Park."

"What ball?"

"Why, the big red balloon that says the lake and ponds are frozen solid!" cried Mally, as if any resident should be aware of this important announcement. "It was zero last night!"

"Is that all? It seemed fifty below in my room, and this cellar is an ice-vault! Miss Gibbons claims the furnace went out during the night."

"Hah! That's the same old excuse every landlord gives the tenants. I nearly froze going to Mass this morning, and never would've made it if the man-of-war sleighs weren't running. They're ice-boating and cutting ice on the rivers too. Come on, Devon! We can rent some skates at the Park."

She seemed so eager, and Devon knew Mally's life was as dull as her own recently. "All right, just let me get into something more practical."

Soon they were off on a flag-flying runnered omnibus, with a score of others as anxious as Mally O'Neill to enjoy the sport. The Irish girl was bundled in a corduroy coat, her titian locks tucked under a fuzzy wool cap, a shamrock-green muffler hugging her throat. Devon wore a peplumed jacket of gold merino over a rust-and-brown plaid skirt flared to facilitate movement, warm flannel drawers and woolen stockings, and a becoming little gold tulip-shaped Dutch bonnet on her flaxen curls. Mally thought she resembled a picture she had once seen in the Astor Library, of a Holland girl standing on a dike of the Zuider Zee.

Alongside the public conveyances bound for the park, private sleighs and cutters transported merry parties wrapped in furs and afghans and fur laprobes. Prominent young ladies did not go to the ice carnivals unescorted, any more than they rode horses or went on picnics unchaperoned, but shopgirls often had no alternative except to forego these pleasures.

On both the main lake north of the mall and the pond at Fifty-ninth Street, skaters of all ages glided, whirled, spun to the music of calliopes, and couples cut fancy capers. Mally could hardly wait to strap on her rented blades and join them, for there were always some stags in search of a partner. She soon found one, a homely little fellow in a shabby mackinaw and tasseled cap, named Davey Thorne. His red misshapen ears looked as if they had been frequently cuffed in childhood, and his head appeared too big for his scrawny body, but his feet were as fleet on ice as the trotters' on the Harlem Lane turf.

Devon had not skated in several years and was unsteady at first, as a sailor readjusting his sea legs to land again. But soon she was navigating on her own power and drawn into a jolly group, which joined hands and then weaved over the lake like a mammoth caterpillar on crystal. It was fun, she laughed and sang, and was glad she had come.

Davey Thorne treated them to hot chocolate in the Terrace House, and Mally wanted to remain for the evening frolics, which were even more exciting, with the calcium lights sparkling on the ice and the finest folks in town coming to watch the spectacle. But Devon protested that they would be too late getting home, and besides she still had a blouse to press for work tomorrow, and some other tasks. Mally agreed, reluctantly, for she still had to wash, iron, and clean her room.

While waiting for return transportation, Devon noticed a man in a dark caped greatcoat and slouch hat, some feet away, who seemed familiar. Nudging Mally, who was munching chestnuts from the packet Davey had bought her, she whispered, "Wasn't that fellow on the bus that brought us up here?"

"You mean the one leaning against the lamppost reading the paper?"

"Yes. In fact, I think he got on the same block we did."

Mally shrugged. "So what? Half the city probably went to the park today. Maybe he lives in our neighborhood."

"Did you see him skating?"

"No, I wasn't aware of anyone but Davey. And there were as many spectators as skaters, anyway. What're you so edgy about?"

The omnibus arrived. They boarded. The man took a rear seat and spread the *Herald* before his face, as if its contents absorbed him. He got off at the same stop, followed them for a block, and then walked in another direction.

Relieved, Devon said, "I guess he's a neighbor."

Mally rolled her eyes and chomped another chestnut. "Did you think he was after us?"

"Well, it happens, Mally! You know what they say about girls being snatched off the streets and forced into—into white slavery!"

"They ain't all forced," Mally said. "Some go willingly. But I reckon I'd worry more if I looked like you. 'Tis a wonder you don't have a whole regiment of fellas chasing you, and no doubt would, if they knew where to find you." Approaching the Gothic Arms, she asked, "What do you think of Mr. Thorne?"

Devon hesitated, reluctant to disillusion Mally, who was plainly smitten with him. "He seems nice enough."

"Oh, I know he's no Prince Charming! But he's not exactly ugly, either, and he's got a good job as groom at a livery stable. I think he likes me too, and I ain't getting no younger. I came to New York to find a husband, because there wasn't hardly no young men left in my village after the war. Davey Thorne wants to see me again. I told him where I work, and I bet he gets in touch with me."

"Well, Mally, if that's what you want—"

"What do *you* want?"

Devon shrugged. "I don't know, Mally. A dream, perhaps, that's as hard to catch as a rainbow or will-o' the-wisp. Maybe I'm only chasing chimeras."

"You use pretty words, Devon. I don't understand all of them. But you can't marry a dream, and have baby rainbows. And what else is there for a girl? Marriage and children. That's all there is for us."

They had reached the house, icy and isolated behind its iron pickets and formidable walls, its shuttered windows blind to the world. "It seems that way, sometimes. But why, Mally? *Why* must it be all there is for us?"

"Because we're female," Mally replied resignedly. "That's what my poor sainted mother told me when once I asked her that same question. She's dead now, bless her heart and soul, and better off if you ask me, out of her misery. My pa was a brute that spent his money on whisky, whist, and whores. He never gave mama nothing but kids and the back of his hand."

"And are you willing to settle for that too, Mally?"

"I'm hoping I'll be luckier with my man," Mally said. "I'm praying too, and burning candles in church."

Devon sighed as they turned into the gate. "Light one for me sometime, Mally, will you, please?"

"Sure, honey. But with a face and figure like yours, there ain't much more Heaven can do for you. You should be able to make it on your own."

Chapter 10

So many things went wrong that day, Devon almost wished she had never opened her eyes on it.

To begin with, she had forgotten to set her alarm and could not get ready in time to leave with Mally, who had to be at the factory at seven-thirty, so she had to walk alone to the horsecar in the cold and fog. She hurried as much as possible in the weather, but it was like groping through a maze of wet cobwebs, and she was terrified of nameless terrors, for she sensed that she had uninvited company. Her hurrying footsteps echoed in the empty street, and her heart hammered in her breast. Hearing the streetcar, she lifted her skirts and ran, eyes straining to see her way, cape billowing, so that she was herself a phantomlike figure in the swirling mists. She reached the corner in time and was taken aboard breathless and about to collapse with relief. Paying her fare and taking a seat she peered into the dense opacity, seeing nothing and hearing nothing except the wheels grinding in the iron tracks and the staccato clopping of hoofs. The driver had to poke along, however, and she was late to work.

Mr. Joseph was already down from his quarters, stamping around impatiently. He had lighted the lamps and was trying to coax a glow into the banked coals in the Franklin furnace.

"I'm sorry I'm late, sir, but the fog—"

"Never mind that now. Just get this damned fire going! I seem to have lost my knack even with a stove."

Taking the bellows, she pumped up a flame, heaped on a scuttle of coal, and pumped some more. "Have you had your morning tea yet, sir?"

"Not yet. Make some, please. And then see if you can remember what you did with the statement from Reed and Company."

"Isn't it in the files?"

"No, nor the desk. I hope you haven't lost or accidently discarded it. I've already incinerated the refuse."

"I'll find it, sir."

She rummaged through the office, while Mr. Joseph stood helplessly about on his cane, favoring his gouty foot, his expression simultaneously impatient and indulgent. A search of the cabinets produced the elusive paper, mistakenly filed under S for Steed. Then she got out the ledgers and checkbook, so Mr. Joseph could write the creditors' drafts. When tea was ready, he invited her to join him, saying congenially, "You've been her two months now, Miss Marshall. Are you happy in your work?"

"Oh, yes, sir! Is it satisfactory?"

"Eminently," he nodded. "I've come to depend on you, in fact, perhaps more than I should. But I find it enjoyable, having a pretty young lady about during the day, and last night—well, do you believe in dreams, Miss Marshall?"

"Not really, Mr. Joseph. But I hope yours was pleasant."

"It had its pleasant aspects ... and its frustrations." He regarded her intently, drumming his bony fingers on the desk. "Ah God, how terrible it is to be an old man with the dreams of a young one!"

Devon sipped her tea in silence, afraid to pursue that.

He leaned forward, reaching out a clawish hand as if to touch her, then retracted it sheepishly, urging, "Tell me about your dreams, Miss Marshall. They're romantic, I suppose, about handsome young men? Princes and knights in shining armor?"

Staring into her teacup, at the dark dregs on the bottom, Devon sighed and shuddered. "Sometimes they're nightmares, of the war, and the Seven Days' siege, and Richmond in flames. My father's death, the newspaper and our home and everything we owned destroyed, and myself running wildly toward Capitol Hill. Sometimes I wake up crying, and even screaming."

"Nostalgia can be a sickness of body and soul, just as melancholia," he said. "Do you ever think of returning to Virginia?"

"Frequently," she admitted. "But I can't go back, and it

would be useless to try. There's nothing for me there now."

"No beau even?"

"There was a fiancé," she admitted, "and perhaps I made a mistake in not marrying him. But I left and must make the best of it now, without regrets. I only know I can't go home again."

His shawl had slipped off his shoulders. Devon rose to replace it. He thanked her and asked, "Have you abandoned your hope of finding a writing position in New York?"

"Temporarily."

"That's sensible, my dear. You should wait until you are older and wiser and know more about life. You are still too young and naive and inexperienced to produce much of substance or merit, although genius is not necessarily indigenous to nor dependent upon age. I'm reminded of a precocious young lady of a fine old Charleston family, who came to New York twelve years ago. Her name was Jane McElheney, but she changed it to Ada Clare. She used to buy poetry from me. Then she began writing poems and prose of her own, which appeared in the *Atlas*, a literary weekly of the day. Although only nineteen, she was brilliant, exceptionally talented, and truly lovely. Her hair was the color of yours and also curly, but she kept it close-cropped. Her skin had the same pale ivory texture, only her eyes were vivid blue and full of mischief. And she had the lithe form and grace of a ballerina."

"What happened to her?"

"She got in with the Bohemians—the crowd that met in Charlie Plaff's cellar restaurant before the war. Soon she was the uncrowned queen of Bohemia. All the men were wild about her, including Walt Whitman. Her verse shocked society, because it dwelt on subjects which seemed incongruous with her gentle breeding: love, passion, sensuality. She had an affair with the famous concert pianist, Louis Moreau Gottschalk, and bore his child in Paris. But the fickle fellow denied paternity, and abandoned her for someone else. She returned to New York and brazenly announced herself as 'Miss Ada Clare and Son.' She opened a literary salon in her home and held her special court attended by admiring writers, artists, and actors. Ada thumbed her pert nose at convention, scandalized elite social hypocrites who could not forgive her audacity, and was dutifully ostracized as a moral leper." He smiled at Devon's quizzical frown. "The point, my dear, is that she had lived."

"Indeed she had," Devon agreed.

"She was a feminist, believing that women should have the same rights and privileges as men, the same moral codes and ethics. She smoked and drank and loved freely. Whitman idolized her in one of his poems. Have you read *Leaves of Grass?*"

"Not yet. Pa considered it too mature for me. He never actually forbade me to read anything in the library, or locked up any books, but he did advise me on literature, and I respected his judgment."

"Well, I don't think *Leaves of Grass* is as scandalous and corruptive as it's supposed to be, and some of the criticism is puritanical and absurd. You should be mature enough to appreciate it now, along with other censored books. Some people tend to forget that the Bible and Shakespeare have also been intermittently banned. I have some rare editions I'd like to show you sometimes, and explain anything you don't understand. I collect rare books and manuscripts."

"That's nice," Devon said. "We had an excellent and extensive library too, but it was destroyed when the newspaper burned."

"How unfortunate. But you're welcome to read anything in the shop, my dear, and take it home if you wish. And tomorrow you may deliver a couple of books to the Cary sisters. I have an order from them."

"Alice and Phoebe Cary?"

"The same. Do you know their poetry and stories?"

"I do, and I'd love to meet them!"

"You shall have the opportunity, and a co-authored volume for them to autograph."

"Thank you, sir!"

She might have hugged him appreciatively, as she would a kindly old grandfather, but the bell signaled a customer, and he made a gesture of dismissal. Before leaving the office, she glanced over her shoulder in silent gratitude. He was smiling. His teeth were bad and stained, and though she knew it was ridiculous at his age, the smile struck her as lascivious. It gave her a queer sensation, a sense of impending unpleasantness, which she had difficulty shrugging off.

Devon was not surprised to see the Bowery gambler again; his appearance seemed in keeping with the other events of the day. Outside, a small crowd had gathered around his flamboyant equipage, as curious as if it were a circus or fire wagon, or General Tom Thumb's miniature gilded coach drawn by white ponies and piloted by liveried children.

"Good morning, Mr. Donahue. Have you come for another yard of books?"

Turning from the window, plainly pleased with the attention his turnout attracted, he swept off his black bowler. "That I have, Miss Marshall. Sure it was a wise choice you made for me before! Shakespeare makes a fine showing on me shelves. What would you be suggesting this time?"

"Well, an encyclopedia always adds substance to a library," she said, hoping to dispatch him swiftly, "and we have a handsome set of the Britannica still crated. Grolier bindings in hand-tooled leather. Now if you'll just summon your footman——." She started for the stockroom.

Donahue laughed, rapping his walking stick on the counter. "Hold on there, honey! I'm in no such hurry as that. I'd like to be browsing a bit, if ye don't mind."

"Of course not, sir. Take your time."

"What's them books stacked on the tables over there, the big ones?"

"Texts, sir. Histories and geographies."

"And on the shelves behind you?"

"More school editions. Grammar, arithmetic, spelling."

"How about the top racks?"

"French novels, sir. We have them in the original and translations."

"Let me see the translations."

"Yes, sir."

Devon mounted the ladder cautiously, one hand protecting the modesty of her skirts, made unwieldy by crinolines and petticoats. Her slipper caught in a ruffle, she lost her balance, and would have tumbled to the floor had not Donahue caught her. Her head thumped his barrel chest, momentarily stunning her. She blinked her eyes in surprise and embarrassed confusion. "I tripped! Thank heaven you caught me."

" 'Twas a lucky catch!" He grinned at her. "A prize, no less. Not since I left Ireland have I seen such a pretty sight. Your eyes are as green as the hills of Killarney, and you have the curls of a lamb in new fleece."

"You may put me down now, sir."

"Without a reward for saving your life?" he asked, and proceeded to reward himself. So spontaneous and aggressive was his ardor, her lips parted in amazement, which he mistook for response, until she gasped and pushed at him in protest.

"Mr. Donahue, please! This is a business house."

He sat her on the counter, reluctantly but gently now, as if she were a fragile doll. "I'll not say I'm sorry, me dear. 'Twas a taste of honey, and I'm craving more."

She ignored that, sliding to her feet and smoothing her hair and clothes. "Do you want the Britannica, sir, or not?"

"Aye, and anything else ye recommend."

"A book of etiquette might be in order. And a lexicon."

"I don't know those fancy words."

"Etiquette is decorum, Mr. Donahue: manners and social behavior. And a lexicon is a dictionary to define the apparently unfamiliar terms."

"So you think I'm ignorant and uncouth, Miss Marshall? Well, you're right, but 'tis not me fault. I never had much schooling and social advantages. Would you consider tutoring me? Teaching me to be a gentleman. I'd pay well."

"No, thank you, sir. I'm happy here."

"In this moldy hole, working for peanuts?"

She prepared his bill. "Here's your receipt, sir. Thank you very much. Good day."

"I'll be back," he said but she did not answer.

When he had gone, heckling his bizarre footman again, Mr. Joseph came out of the office to congratulate her on the sale. "You're a wonder, Miss Marshall, the best clerk I ever had! I believe you could sell ice to the Eskimos. Effective immediately you'll receive two percent commission on all your sales, which means you just earned an extra six dollars."

Six dollars, double her weekly salary! Devon didn't

know what to say, how to thank him. Then she remembered Madame Joie's generosity, her kindness and gifts. And Christmas Eve.

Some late customers and browsers delayed her departure, but she didn't mind, because she made a few extra pennies in commission, which was some incentive, at least, to work harder and longer. Many other shops and stores were still open when she left Joseph's at nine o'clock, and some factories operated night shifts.

Mally was not at their usual corner, and Devon supposed she was with Davey Thorne. They had begun a regular courtship, which Mally expected to culminate in marriage. How such a pretty girl could consider such a freakish fellow was beyond Devon, but that was none of her affair. She only wished she didn't have to go home alone so often these long dark winter evenings.

She waited under a gaslamp for the streetcar. A pale frosty moon glimmered over the harbor, and she could hear steamboat horns and whistles on the rivers. The fog had disappeared but would likely return before morning. That was more than evening haze in the cold crisp air, she thought, shivering under her cloak. She had just missed a ride and would have a long wait for another, and she considered spending some of her commission for a cab.

While pondering, she became conscious of a furtive figure in the shadows some distance away, surreptitiously observing her, but it was impossible to distinguish his features. He may or may not be the same person at Central Park, or the presence she had imagined in the morning mists, and may or may not be interested in her now. Nevertheless, on impulse, she approached the policeman on the beat and told him she feared she was being followed.

"By whom, Miss?" he inquired in a brogue thicker than Donahue's, and Devon wondered if half of Ireland had migrated to New York.

"A man, I don't know his name."

"Where is the suspect?"

"Over there, before that saloon." But when he looked, there was no one there, not even a shadow. "He must've gone inside."

"Well, if he comes out and bothers you, let me know."

"Does he have to bother me, Officer?"

"Well now, I can't be arresting every fella that looks at

a pretty colleen, can I? The Tombs wouldn't hold 'em all! 'Tis likely only your imagination, anyway. Everyone sees his own goblins at night. Why don't you just board your car and ride home, Miss? Sure everything will look brighter in the morning. Glory be, here come those drunken sailors again, higher than their ship's masts!"

The horsecar clanged to a stop. Devon climbed on. The stranger was nowhere in sight. She breathed easier. Talking to the law had been a good idea; it had vanquished him, if indeed he had been more than an illusion.

Chapter 11

The Cary sisters lived in a large handsome brick house on East Twenty-third Street, with a beautiful Colonial door and fanlight. A maid ushered the clerk from Joseph's into the vivid Victorian parlor with red roses on the wallpaper, red velvet sofas and chairs, and marble-topped tables. Soon one of the poet sisters came in, smiling as warmly as the fire.

"Miss Marshall? I'm Alice Cary."

She was in her middle years, a slightly-built woman with gray hair coiffed in a neat chignon, and deep pensive hazel eyes. Delicately feminine in rose silk scented with mignonette, she reminded Devon of a daguerrotype of her own mother.

"I'm honored to meet you, Miss Cary." She offered the package. "Mr. Joseph sent the books."

"How good of you to bring them in this wretched weather! Phoebe is working in her study but will be down shortly. You must have tea with us, Miss Marshall."

"I'd like that very much, Miss Cary. And I have a favor to ask of you both."

"A favor?"

"If it pleases you, would you inscribe your *Collected Poems* for me? Mr. Joseph gave me a copy."

"We'd be delighted, dear. You know our work?"

"Oh, yes! I've read many of your *Clovernook Stories* and Miss Phoebe's poems in the *Southern Literary Messenger* which, as you know, was published in Richmond, and unfortunately disbanded during the war."

"One of many such casualties," she nodded. "Were you there at the time?"

"Yes, Ma'am. My father published the Richmond *Sentinel*, also defunct now. I worked on the paper with him until his death, a few days before Appomattox."

114

"I'm sorry to hear that, Miss Marshall. And you were certainly a young journalist. But then Phoebe was published before she was twenty-five. Ah, here she is now."

Phoebe was younger by a few years, but still youthful and vivacious, with thick black hair and sparkling blue eyes, radiant in a burnt-orange teagown, which no fortyish spinster would have dared wear in Richmond. There was nothing about either woman to suggest maidenhood or the rural background that Alice extolled in her Clovernook idylls of country life. Phoebe's poems were influenced by the earthy realism of Walt Whitman, and the dark mysticism of Edgar Allen Poe. She wrote scathing criticisms of some of her literary contemporaries, including Longfellow, Lowell, and Whittier. The *Sentinel* had printed some of her essays and critiques, and Devon knew her father had considered the Cary sisters "advanced" women.

They were pleasant and friendly, and Devon spent an enchanting hour chatting over tea and cakes. Then they inscribed her volume, and invited her to attend their next Sunday evening reception, an established tradition in the artistic circles of Manhattan. She rushed back to the shop with the happy news.

"You'll meet some important people," Mr. Joseph told her. "Some peculiar ones too. They all congregate at the Carys."

He was right, and Devon was both awed and fascinated by the guests who wandered in and seemed to know one another well. Her father would have recognized some of them: William Cullen Bryant, whose eloquent editorials in the New York *Evening Post* he had admired; Herman Melville, a striking personality with long black hair threaded with silver and eyes as deep and restless as the seas in his great novels; and George Bancroft whose monumental *History of the United States* had been in the Marshall library, alongside Sir John Randolph's *History of Virginia*, and the works of Washington, Jefferson, Madison, and Monroe. Alice Cary introduced the historian as Ambassador Bancroft, explaining that he had recently been appointed minister to Prussia and was sailing in a few days to his new post. Congratulating him, Devon remarked that she had cut her wisdom teeth on his histories, and he smiled and nodded diplomatically.

But it was the women who impressed her most.

There was Madame Ellen Demorest, whose paper patterns had not only revolutionized the garment industry, but with the sewing machine enabled women everywhere in the country, even on the remote frontiers, to dress stylishly and economically, depending on individual talents and skills. Devon was flattered by the modiste's interest in her own Paris ensemble (acquired in Washington and still not paid for) of emerald Saxony with matching cape lined in chartreuse satin, and feathered Empress Eugenie tricorn now the rage on Parisian heads, as if she were mentally sketching it with an eye on the market.

Beside her stood her associate editor, Jenny June, who gave advice on fashion, beauty, etiquette, travel, and other subjects of feminine interest in the pages of *Demorest's Magazine*: she was an ardent advocate of women's rights. She espoused formal education for females, employment outside the home, and rejected the idea that a woman's identity depended on her husband's stature in the community, and that she had no social or economic status outside of marriage. Jenny June was thirty-five, her figure unspoiled by childbirth, elegant in iridescent silk as changeable as her blue-green eyes, her thick brown hair braided into a lustrous coronet. She was pleased when Devon told her how Southern women had cherished the few fashion magazines that slipped in during the war, living vicariously in the pages, and lending them to friends. "How nice to know we had such loyal fans," she beamed.

Devon met Susan B. Anthony and Elizabeth Cady Stanton—perhaps the most active of the suffragettes. They were trying to organize a newspaper to promote the Movement. Miss Anthony was tall and angular, of a severe countenance and bearing, utterly dedicated to her cause. Mrs. Stanton was plump, bright-eyed, mirthful, a happy wife and mother. "Phoebe tells me you've had some newspaper experience," she said.

"Some, yes. But not enough to interest the editors here, I'm afraid."

"Unfortunately, my dear, there's more against you than your inexperience. Men simply don't want women in the profession, and certainly not as reporters. The few publishers, including Robert Bonner of the *Ledger* and Horace Greeley of the *Tribune*, who do employ women on their staffs prefer those who have achieved success and recognition on their own first, writing novels or articles or essays. Like Fanny Fern and Kate Field." She glanced about the room. "Isn't Horace here yet, Phoebe? He rarely misses a Cary conclave."

"He'll be along," Phoebe assured her. "You know Horace the Perfectionist! He's probably still polishing Monday's editorial. You'd think he expected his every word to be preserved for posterity, and perhaps it will be. As for Robert, I saw him at the Bottas last evening, and his new contract with Fanny Fern for exclusive rights to all her work, at five thousand per year, makes her the highest paid female in the business. She will be making more even than her husband earns, which I hope won't cause dissension in the Parton household. But Fanny's not here yet, either, nor Kate Field. Have you met either of these ladies, Miss Marshall?"

Devon felt as if she had been in exile for twenty years, or shipwrecked on a remote island somewhere, out of contact with civilization. "I'm sorry to say I haven't. We were isolated in Richmond the last few years."

"Well, we're opening a women's bureau," Susan Anthony said, "and new young blood is always welcome in the Movement. Unfortunately, we're short of funds, and all services must be voluntary. So if you must earn your living with your pen, don't wait on our publication."

Miss Anthony paused as a radiant young woman swept into the parlor, wearing an azure velvet suit trimmed in blue fox. Her hair was burnished red, her eyes as brilliant as her sapphire jewelry, and her slender, supple figure showed her regular exercise at the Light Gymnastic School on Broadway.

"Kate darling!" cried Alice Cary. "We were just wondering when you'd arrive. Come, I want you to meet someone. . . ."

At thirty Kate Field looked twenty, and already had an enviable list of publishing credits, including several biographies and work in literary magazines. She was now doing features for the *Tribune*. She also lectured for substantial fees on Oriental mysticism—of which she was a devotee—metaphysics, and psychic phenomena. Her experiments in automatic writing had enabled her to write a treatise which was selling briskly, since spiritualism had become enormously popular, and the planchette was replacing the stereoscope as a parlor diversion.

"Well, my dear," she smiled, grasping Devon's hands in hers, as gracious as she was beautiful, "I'm delighted to know you! What an adorable costume—it must have arrived on the last packet from Paris. Don't be surprised if Ellen Demorest copies the design in a pattern." She winked and waved at Mme. Demorest across the room, saying nothing she would not to the other woman's face, for they were fast friends and Kate also contributed to her magazine. She called a cheery greeting to Jenny June, and then said, "Oh, I have the most exciting news, Phoebe! I'm going to hold another seance in the hope of contacting Margaret Fuller. Miss Marshall, are you aware of this great lady?"

"I've read her *Woman in the Nineteenth Century*," Devon said. Mr. Joseph, who had known Margaret Fuller when she was on the *Tribune*, had recommended the thesis.

"Well, I should hope so! No woman can presume to support the Movement intelligently without being conversant with that manifesto. I read it religiously. She was years ahead of her time, as Mary Wollstonecraft of hers, and we're all indebited to them for the little freedom we have now. I've been trying periodically to contact Margaret's spirit, hoping she might furnish some guidance from beyond. Horace still mourns the manuscript of the Roman revolution which perished with her in that shipwreck—it's history's loss. Of course it was all so long ago, back in fifty, but time is not of the essence there. . . ." Her eyes scanned the room, as if she had just realized something was missing. "Where are the men? Congregated in the library again? Cowards, they always retreat before forceful women!"

But she laughed liltingly, and Devon wondered how many marriage proposals she had refused in her determination to remain free and independent. "I can't stay long, because I have to be up bright and early tomorrow to interview the Sheik of Araby. His ship put into port today, with part of his harem, and I hope to persuade him to let me speak with one of his wives."

Phoebe teased, "Careful, darling, lest he invite you to join his seraglio."

"Not after he hears what I have to say about men who enslave women that way!"

At that moment a big burly man appeared on the threshold and boomed in a ringmaster's voice, "Ladies and—err—have you eaten the gentlemen alive?"

Kate lifted a gloved hand. "Hello, P. T. I thought you were off promoting another freak or something."

Phineas T. Barnum advanced, his great bulk shaking the parlor ornaments like the proverbial bull in the china shop, cobalt eyes flashing under craggy black brows, a massive head of dark boyish curls, and huge red bulbous nose resembling a putty clown's. "Now, Katie honey, you ain't gonna start on me again about exploitin' womankind, are you?"

"What else would you call your fat and bearded ladies, your snake charmers and belly dancers, you old huckster?"

"Don't I exploit the male of the species too? How about the fire-eaters, sword-swallowers, weight-lifters? Why, even little Tom Thumb—" He grinned ingratiatingly. "Say, I hear you're a clairvoyant. I could use another mystic, and you'd make a gorgeous one, with an East Indian robe and mysterious veil—"

"Oh, get out of here, you crafty rogue, before I organize a boycott and picket your unfair exhibits! You'll find your brother beasts cowering in the den." As Barnum departed, laughing uproariously, she hailed another arrival and fellow journalist. "There's George Ripley! I must tell him about the seance. He knew Margaret Fuller at Brook Farm, where both were disciples of transcendentalism." And off she sailed in a rush of scented velvet and fur.

Devon gazed after her wistfully, envying her poise and self-assurance. Would she ever approach her sophistication and keen wit? Not likely. Such women were rare as gems in a sandbox, roses in a cornfield.

Then Alice Cary was leading an arrogantly handsome young man toward her, whose pale hair shone like a silver helmet in the gaslight. He was carelessly dressed in brown canvas breeches, a red Garibaldi shirt laced with a leather thong, and cavalier boots. "Miss Marshall, meet Mallard. He painted that Cape Cod landscape over the sofa, and says he would like to do your portrait." She left them together, and the artist sat down across from Devon, studying her with Nordic blue eyes that sent icy prickles up her spine. She realized that he was slightly intoxicated, a condition he had reached somewhere else, since the Carys' punchbowl was not spiked.

"Would you?" he asked.

"Would I what, Mr. Mallard?"

"Mallard," he said. "Pose for me?"

Devon smiled wryly. "You'd be wasting your time, sir. With all the famous faces here, you picked the only anonymous one. I'm not rich, and I couldn't afford to pay you."

"Those duds didn't come out of a rag-bag," he surmised. "However, I'm not looking for a commission. I'll be glad to pay *you*. Not much, of course, because I, without a doubt, am the poorest person here. Not only money-wise. There's no poorer man on earth than an artist without inspiration, Miss Marshall, and until I saw you a moment ago that's what I was."

Something about him attracted even as it repelled. Was it the intriguing smile, the Viking appraisal that simultaneously warmed and chilled, the provocative personality? He was young, no older than Keith, and his interest was flattering. But he made her more nervous than the Bowery gambler, and she wished he would just go away and leave her alone.

"I have no desire to be immortalized that way," she said.

"Nor am I capable of such immortalization, Miss Marshall. But you have a fresh unspoiled beauty that I haven't seen in years. The quality of little-girl innocence and illusion that Renoir depicted so well. I'd like to try to capture it on canvas. If I succeeded, your face would be famous enough in New York, eventually, and you could earn fees as an artist's model."

"No, thank you, Mallard. I already have a job."

"Don't you trust my motives? While I couldn't promise not to try to seduce you, I can almost guarantee that you wouldn't fall in love with me. Why? Because, my dear, you are already in that state of human misery. No, don't bother to protest and deny. I see it in your eyes. Artists have especially keen vision and insight, you know, and it's quite true that the eyes reflect the soul. You have a beautiful soul, Miss Marshall, but sad eyes. It's a hopeless love, right? I know the feeling, I've had it myself."

"Many times, I suspect."

"No, only once. One can have many loves, I've found, but one loves only once. That's the love gospel according to St. Giles. I think Van Gogh cut off his ear because he couldn't cut love out of his heart. It would've been wiser and surely less painful to slit his goddamn throat." Her eyes wandered toward the door, and he turned to see what attracted her. "Oh, Jesus! Greeley has arrived. I hate that old bastard. He's always telling young men to go West, which is the same as telling them to go to hell. There's nothing west of the Mississippi but mountains and mirages—and he damn well knows it, because he's been there. Still, he assures me I'd get a new perspective on life in the Territories, presumably painting Indians and cowboys and buffaloes and dunghills. They say he's eccentric. I think he's crazy."

Devon knew Horace Greeley by sight. She had seen him frequently, hurrying along Broadway in his peculiar shuffling gait, as if his feet were too heavy to lift off the sidewalk, his small near-sighted eyes peering through rimless spectacles perched crookedly on his sharp nose. He had a pink moon face and a comical fringe of white whiskers along his jawline. He wore baggy trousers, rumpled frockcoats, and wrinkled cravats, and funny round hats set back off his bulging forehead.

But his editorial reputation was formidable, and his memory was reputed to be phenomenal. He had called Jefferson Davis a fanatical traitor and General Lee a misguided patriot, and undoubtedly would remember what the Richmond editors, including Hodge Marshall, had written about Horace Greeley. Devon had no desire to meet him, but it was inevitable, and immediately following the formalities, he addressed the sullen, glowering artist.

"You still here, young man? I thought I told you last week and the week before to go West."

"An ascetic of your age may not realize it, sir, but a man of mine needs more inspiration than cactus and cow skulls."

"Women, eh? Well, there're plenty of Calico Janes and Sunbonnet Sues out there too. And let me tell you this from observation. Nowhere does Mother Nature display a more magnificent and spectacular bosom than in the white peaks of the Rockies, Tetons, and Sierras. Our eastern elevations are flat-chested by comparison. So get a move on, Artist, and don't take my quotation out of context. What I said was, 'Go West, young man, and grow up with the country!' "

"I'm going, sir," Mallared muttered, bowing mockingly. "Right now, pronto. Can't get away fast enough."

"Well, fill your canteens with water," the teetotaler advised. "They've got enough sots out there already." Then he smiled at Devon. "How are things in Richmond, Miss Marshall?"

"I'm sure you know that better than I, Mr. Greeley, since I've not been there in six months, and you have correspondents on the scene. But it was bad when I left, and I've no reason to believe it has improved much."

"If you read the papers, you know they are preparing to try Jefferson Davis there soon. But did you know that I've been asked to sign his bond, along with several other Northerners, including Cornelius Vanderbilt?"

Devon was astonished. "You? But why on earth would—?"

"Because I've recommended amnesty for all Confederates, whether or not they take the oath of allegiance. I don't feel they should be regarded as criminals any longer, for supporting a concept they cherished. Such treatment only creates more dissension and discontent. Yet I've been warned anonymously and by friends that, should I go to Richmond even on Mr. Davis' behalf, I shall probably be assassinated the moment I step off the train, if not before. What do you think, Miss Marshall? Is the climate really that dangerous for me?"

"I think, sir, in your place, I should be inclined to listen to my friends."

The white jaw fringe waggled in a billygoat grin. "You speak your mind, don't you? I admire such honesty. It's one of my mottos, in fact, framed on my office wall: 'I speak my thoughts.' Did your father always speak his thoughts in the *Sentinel*? Surprised, Miss Marshall? I've read some of his editorials. Copies of the Richmond papers, as well as most others in the country, cross my desk. Hodge Marshall had a trace of genius, but he took the fool's way out. Think of all the good he might have done in his state now."

"The *Sentinel* burned in the fire," Devon reminded.

"So what? Other organs have risen out of rubble and ashes, to become greater than before. I have no patience with defeatism. But I won't judge his motives rashly—evidently he took them with him, leaving his daughter to write his epitaph."

"He wrote it himself, in his final editorial."

"And was it printed?"

"No, but it had his mark on it. His blood too. It was cremated with his body and the building."

"I'm sorry to hear that," he said sincerely. "A dead editor is always a loss to humanity and history, and a good one is more so. Did I understand the Carys to say that you worked on the *Sentinel*?"

"For several years, sir. Nothing significant, however. Social items. A few local features. And obituaries. There were many obits."

"But you were only a child then," he mused. "You are not much more now." One of his hostesses brought him a glass of diluted milk, the only beverage he consumed at parties; nor did he smoke, regarding tobacco as the devil's weed, evil and addicting, additional cause for Virginians to dislike him. "You've met Kate Field this evening, I presume. She writes for me, and I've had no more brilliant female journalist since Margaret Fuller. I'm sure you have similar aspirations, but I'm too old to take on a novice. Nor has the *Tribune* ever been a training school for cub reporters." He stood, bestowing a pontifical smile on her. "Good luck, young lady. Maybe you too should consider going West."

Then he searched out Kate Field, who was still bedeviling Barnum about his unfair exploitations of female flesh, and Devon heard the showman ask the oracle, "Man, why do you encourage these crazy women, and their castles in the air?"

The guests were beginning to leave, the unescorted ladies in their own carriages or public conveyances, together or alone, with no qualms about convention and propriety. At the door they were reminded of the next gathering of *artistes*, the Vincenzo Bottas' reception honoring the great Italian tragedienne, Adelaide Ristori, who had recently arrived in New York for her second American tour.

Chapter 12

Except for the war and reconstruction, Devon knew Adelaide Ristori would have played Richmond, where many international stars of stage and opera had appeared, and her father would have written about her in the *Sentinel*. Virginians were ardent drama enthusiasts, devoted to the theater since the Cavaliers had introduced amateur plays, pantomine, and minstrels, and the Colonials had established the first permanent American theater in Williamsburg, in 1718. Well-bred children were exposed early in life to all forms of culture, and Devon had been no exception. She was reading fairy tales almost as soon as she could talk, viewing puppet shows and comedies from her mother's lap and private art collections from her father's arms.

The Great Ristori's impressive repertoire included Queen Elizabeth, Mary Stuart, Marie Antoinette, Lady Macbeth, *Mirra*, and Legouvre's *Medea*, in which she had made her American debut the previous year, at New York's Lyceum Theater. The daughter of wandering street players of Venetia her marriage to the Marchese Capranica del Grillo was a theatrical romance in itself, and New Yorkers were as much intrigued by her title as her talent. She accepted only a select few of the many invitations she received, however, for she spoke little English, and had neither need nor desire to cultivate American society. Nor did she actually enjoy the company of those outside the arts.

She sat in queenly fashion on a velvet sofa in the Bottas' Renaissance drawing room, regal in gold brocade and the del Grillo family jewels, her adoring Roman consort at her side. Devon approached hesitantly, surprised to see neither a young nor beautiful woman but a rather homely and aging one, with coarse, almost masculine, features and

124

sallow olive skin. Her fascinating eyes made her face—dark, solemn, intense, brooding under a prominent brow, so full of smoldering emotion her audience understood her passionate portrayals through her articulate expressions and gestures, although her tongue spoke Italian dialogue. And it was easy to understand how her statuesque figure could command attention on any stage.

Devon made the curtsy due nobility. Professor Botta translated her compliments to the marquesa, who smiled and nodded noblesse oblige. And then Mrs. Botta promptly led her away, saying only, "You're the little friend of the Careys', aren't you, from Georgia or somewhere? How nice! Mingle now, dear, and make yourself at home."

The house began to fill with luminaries, all of whom seemed to have fame and success in common, and they made Devon feel conspicuous in her anonymity. What was she doing here, a nonentity among celebrities, a provincial among cosmopolites, a mere mortal on Olympus! She felt like a small girl at a grown-up party, pretty enough in her fancy dress, but too immature and unaccomplished to be interesting or even amusing; and like an ignored and disappointed child, she wanted to run away and hide. No one would miss her if she just quietly vanished.

Those not clustered around the honor guests were congregated in impervious groups of common interest. Ralph Waldo Emerson and John Greenleaf Whittier were in conversation with the newly-acclaimed poet, Edmund Clarence Stedman, whom Keith must surely know, since he was also a prominent Wall Street broker. Alice and Phoebe Cary encircled Elizabeth Stoddard, discussing her shocking new novel, *The Morgesons*, which criticized New England mores and hypocrisy so severely it was banned in polite society and not stocked by puritanical bookdealers. Mr. Joseph, however, was pushing it, and Devon kept an open copy under the counter to read in slack periods. In this way she was also reading the even more explicit and condemned *Miss Ravenel's Conversion*, which praised sin and vice and ridiculed virtue, and whose bold young author, John De Forest, was also present.

"Be nice to Miss Marshall," Phoebe warned the novelists. "She sells books at Joseph's." And immediately they pressed her for sales figures and recommendations of their works, and Devon made the stock responses to such supplications.

"Oh, they're selling very well! And Mr. Joseph recommends them to every customer he thinks would enjoy them."

Across the room two darlings of the Academy of Music, prima donna Clara Louise Kellogg and matinee idol pianist, Louis Moreau Gottschalk, were chatting animatedly, and Devon remembered what Mr. Joseph had said about the virtuoso's affair with poetess Ada Clare and his cruel desertion of her during her pregnancy. Pauline Markham and Maria Bonfanti, stars of *The Black Crook* ballet, were leaving to make an early curtain at Niblo's Garden, and Gottschalk kissed them goodbye. Soon he was kissing Laura Keene and Charlotte Cushman hello, possibly to console the aging Miss Cushman, who considered herself the finest tragedienne in the history of the theater, and who could barely conceal her professional jealousy and resentment of the European rival to whom she had ostensibly come to pay homage. Watching them, Devon recalled a comment Janette Joie had once made about frou-frou people composed of papier-mache and crepe paper. Keith would have said they were made of straw and sawdust. Oh, God, why should she think of *him* now! He could hardly restore her lost innocence and dreams and illusions, for he was the one who had destroyed them.

She was seeking a convenient exit when two people arrived whom no Southerner could ever admire or respect, and Devon cringed at the introduction. "Virginia?" said Mrs. Stowe, sedate in mauve taffeta flounced in black lace. "I understand it's in sorry straits now. You were wise to leave, but isn't that rather like abandoning a sinking ship, Miss Marshall?"

Phoebe looked embarrassed for her. "Oh that's all in the past, Harriet. Water under the Reconstruction bridge."

"You think so? Then I'm afraid you don't understand the South very well, darling. Even General Grant says Appomattox was only an official surrender. Unofficially, the South is still at war with us, and their hostility will probably endure for generations to come. Pardon me, I must go speak a few words with Mr. Emerson and Mr. Whittier— and of course congratulations are in order to the brilliant new poet among us."

Devon stared sullenly at the Reverend Henry Ward Beecher, a squat puffy man who, in spite of his religious preeminence, had impious eyes and a sensuous mouth. She longed to ask how he entertained his congregation, now that he could no longer "auction" slaves from the pulpit, and about the fate of the beautiful young mulatto girl he had smuggled from Virginia via the underground railroad. He had dressed her in white and urged the men to "purchase this lovely virgin's freedom, lest she be sold into concubinage by the white master who sired her!" That incident, recounted in all the Richmond papers, had aroused even her father's ire and contempt. Honest abolition sentiments were one thing, Hodge had said; sham and deception and cheap theatrics were quite another, and he had called Beecher an evangelical huckster, a revivalist showman, and the P. T. Barnum of religion.

"Have you visited Plymouth Church yet, Miss Marshall?" he inquired. His suit was sober black, conservatively cut and vested and he affected the narrow black ribbon tie of the circuit-riding frontier preachers, who breathed fire and brimstone. But she thought his pale blue protuberant eyes appraised her with more than clerical interest, and his full mouth was indulgently slack. "Most Southerners want to see what they call 'Beecher's Temple' and hear me preach. Out of curiosity, if nothing else."

"I have no such compulsion, Reverend."

"Tell me, how are the tobacco plantations managing to produce that vile weed without slave labor?"

"I wouldn't know, sir. My father was a publisher, not a planter. He was also an Abolitionist, although he did not express his ideology as theatrically as some."

"Perhaps his conservatism was dictated by his geography, and the expedience of the moment. In any event, I hope you will come to Brooklyn and attend one of my services soon. If you'll sit near the pulpit, where I may be aware of your pretty presence, I'll put extra effort into my sermon."

"Don't hold your breath, preacher," Devon muttered, and he smiled nonchalantly and moved off toward the literati.

"Oh, dear," Phoebe said in some distress. "I'm afraid you affronted them both."

"I'm sorry, but some of their remarks were provocative and offensive to me."

"Well, Henry is just naturally pompous and pontifical, but Harriet is generally more gracious. She is upset, I think, because her still unpublished biography of Lord Byron is causing shock waves across the Atlantic. You see, she is including the scandalous secrets about his incestuous relationship with his half sister by whom he fathered a child, which Lady Byron confided to Mrs. Stowe years ago. And though the British are well aware of all this and never esteemed Byron much, anyway, they bitterly resent an American exposing his clay feet—which, incidently, were also slightly clubbed and lame. So Harriet is being called a muckraker, scandalmonger, and troublemaker."

"The South would agree with England, unequivocally," Devon said vehemently. "They consider her brother a demigod too, and a hypocrite, and they say it's common knowledge that he preaches to at least a dozen of his paramours every Sunday."

The conversation obviously dismayed Phoebe, who was a staunch friend of the famous authoress. "Mrs. Parton has just come in," she observed with relief. "Fanny Fern is a nom de plume, of course, but everyone calls her that. Do you know her work in the *Ledger*?"

"Very well. I follow her serials faithfully."

In prewar Richmond, Mrs. Parton would have been relegated to the elderly matrons' and widows' parlor at social gatherings, to chat about her clubs, grandchildren, and servants. She was approaching sixty, but her ungrayed blonde hair, lucid blue eyes, and winsome smile subtracted years from her calendar. Modishly dressed in a misty gray moire and wide crinolines, she obviously did not regard age as a tragedy or obstacle. Aware of the fate of the *Sentinel* and its publisher, she expressed sympathy and regret. "Couldn't you find a spot on one of the surviving papers, Miss Marshall?"

"I'm afraid there's little need for society reporters anywhere in the South now, Mrs. Parton. Rags are the fashion, and entertainments are few and far between."

"Tragic, of course. And unfortunately there were many casualties in the Southern press, including some exceptionally erudite and liberal journals. But then publishing has always been a precarious venture, and today's competitor is tomorrow's applicant for employment. Our files, for instance, have applications from the staffs of the recently defunct *Gleason's Pictorial*, *Knickerbocker Magazine*, and *Graham's*, as well as your own *Southern Literary Messenger*, which was an excellent periodical and sorely missed by the arts."

They held a brief postmortem for the *Messenger*, once edited by Edgar Allan Poe, and then Fanny Fern said, "If you've written anything of consequence, Miss Marshall, I should be pleased to read it and pass it on to my publisher for consideration. I'm proud to say that Mr. Bonner has much respect for my literary judgment, and I've made some discoveries for him."

Devon shook her head regretfully. "I've nothing worthwhile to show anyone, Mrs. Parton."

"Well, don't despair, child. You're still young, your future is before you. And surely you don't lack for material! Why, you've lived through a great war, in the capital of the Confederacy! If you could put that experience to work . . . you did keep a diary?"

"Yes, but both my father's personal journals and mine were lost in the fire."

"How unfortunate! But you still have your memory, and I urge you to consign your memories to paper while they are still fresh and vivid. Then you will always have them for future reference. It won't be easy, of course. It's never easy for a writer, and particularly one of our sex. But at least we don't have to disguise our identities under mannish pseudonyms any more, like George Sand and George Eliot. It took me twenty years to succeed. Do you happen to know Louisa May Alcott?"

"No, I've never had the pleasure."

"Well, she has been struggling since girlhood, even with a brilliant father to guide her. She has enormous talent, and is currently writing a novel about her sisters and herself during the war, although she experienced it only indirectly, from a safe distance in Massachusetts. But it promises to be the success she has so long striven for, and we hope to serialize it in the *Ledger*." She smiled and patted Devon's hand reassuringly. "Just don't give up, dear. And write when you can."

And when was *that*? Devon wondered. Clerking twelve hours a day, six days a week. Washing, ironing, cleaning, mending on Sunday. Sometimes she was too tired at night to think, even to dream. She felt like a mouse on a tread-mill to oblivion.

She wandered into the dining room, where some guests were sampling the Continental buffet. But she wasn't hungry and moved instead to the French doors leading to the terrace, wondering if she could slip out unnoticed, hail a cab, and return to the Gothic Arms. She had a now familiar compulsion to cry for her naive mistakes, lament her foolish failures, and abandon her childish chasing of will-o' the-wisps.

Some male camaraderie penetrated her despair. "Hey there, Wait! When did you blow into town? We thought you were a confirmed Washingtonian now."

"I am, dear fellow, I am! Just here for a respite, visiting publishers and old friends. Ran into Vincenzo at the university and got invited here this evening."

The man who had spoken was filling his plate, and the one called Walt approached the girl standing alone at the glass doors contemplating the dark garden. "I'm Walt Whitman," he said, and Devon turned to see a big ruddy-faced man with bushy hair and beard, wearing a shabby tweed suit with a wilted flower in the lapel. He looked like a redneck farmer, a muleskinner, a stevedore, anything but a sensitive poet.

Devon had heard much about him from Mr. Joseph, who had known Whitman long before he had published anything and was one of the few booksellers in New England to stock the first edition of *Leaves of Grass*. Considered obscene, the work was neither a critical nor financial success. People refused to embrace the sensual Whitman as they had the mysterious and tempestuous Poe, who had died in poverty and despair. And twelve years later Walt Whitman was also still poor and despairing of acclaim, in debt, and ignored except in a few artistic salons.

"I'm pleased to know you, Mr. Whitman." Ephraim Joseph had described him as somewhat raffish in his youth, but at forty-eight the poet was gray and stout, with somber eyes under languid lids, and faltering movements suggesting physical debility and pain. He had publicly embraced mysticism, pantheism, and asceticism, and there were dark rumors about his private embraces of young men.

"Anything interesting out there?" he asked.

"Only the night, which is supposed to fascinate and intrigue all poets, isn't it?"

"Ah, yes, what would we do without the moon and stars for inspiration! Although Shelley claimed to beget his from quite different sources—wine and flesh of women, I believe. Your name, pretty one?"

"Devon Marshall."

"Lyrical," he said. "Perfect for an ode or sonnet."

"Some of my ancestors came from Devonshire, England."

"And what are you doing here now, Miss Marshall? Are you in the theater? Have you written or painted something of which I am ignorant?"

"Nothing so illustrious, sir. I sell books at Joseph's."

"Than which there is no more noble or necessary occupation," he said. "And so old Ephraim is still in business? His health hasn't forced retirement yet? I used to buy from him when he supplied the gang at Charlie Plaff's cellar, and did not dun us mercilessly." He grinned out of his mossy brush. "You want to watch that old rascal, though," he warned. "Eph always had an eye for youth and beauty. He admired Ada Clare and Lola Montez, and it broke his heart when Adah Menken sailed off to Paris and fell in love with Alexandre Dumas. If he offers to show you his rare books—well, just watch him."

Studying him from the shadows of her long lacy lashes, Devon replied, "I've discovered, sir, that most men bear watching."

He laughed. "And some women too, perhaps?"

Her cheeks flamed and she turned again to the terrace, wondering if he could possibly know Janette Joie.

"What a lovely profile," he complimented. "Just enough tilt to the nose and petulance to the mouth and haughtiness to the chin. I should like a silhouette. And of course you are aware of your enchanting voice. Virginian, aren't you?"

"You really are a mystic."

"I've been living in Washington since sixty-two," he said. "I've met many natives of that state, and they have a slightly different accent from other Southerners. I also recall Poe's telling me once that Virginia had the most beautiful belles in the country, and he was right. Have you read *Leaves of Grass*, Miss Marshall?"

"Not yet, Mr. Whitman. I'm sorry."

"No need to apologize, Miss Marshall. Millions of people haven't read it. Would you like a copy?"

"Mr. Joseph stocks it."

"Selling poorly, no doubt," he said ruefully. "Nevertheless, permit me to send you an inscribed volume. I have a surfeit of them, and it might prove valuable to your descendants some day. I shall also send you and Ephraim autographed first editions of my new collection due this year, including my memorials to Abraham Lincoln."

"That's very kind of you, sir. Thank you, and I hope it's a tremendous success."

"So do I, considering the deplorable state of my finances. Never write poetry, Miss Marshall. It's slow starvation. For some peculiar reason posterity demands the extreme penalty of its poets—all its artists, in fact—and like martyrs they must often die to gain recognition and appreciation. I'm working now as a clerk in the attorney general's office, and lucky to get that position, after the secretary of the interior dismissed me upon learning that I was the Whitman who had written that 'notorious' book. Granted that it might shock some delicate maidens, I doubt it could corrupt many. Art does not corrupt—ignorance and bigotry do. And truth does not demoralize—that is the province of subterfuge and hypocrisy." He paused and regarded her with his strange opaque, half-hooded eyes. "Perhaps you've heard unsavory rumors about me."

Devon shook her head negatively, although she had heard a few whispers at the Cary reception, and several sly insinuations this evening, none of which she fully understood.

"No? Well, I doubt not you will before this night is done, and increasingly if you move in these circles. They are rife in Washington, which is a grist mill for scandal. They say I have much affection for some of my fellow men." He shrugged heavy shoulders in the worn tweeds. "Well, perhaps I have. Indeed I am a lover of all mankind, all humanity!"

Mrs. Botta—a very lovely and liberated lady who had once served as private secretary to Henry Clay, and now wrote and lectured at the Brooklyn Academy for Women —interrupted with an announcement that Mr. Gottschalk and Miss Kellogg were about to entertain in the music room, and the poet smiled and whispered, "I believe this is a command performance, Miss Marshall, and we are obliged to attend. . . ."

Chapter 13

It was time to get up. Devon could hear Mally stirring in the next room. But the windows were still dark with the last remnants of winter night, and she was reluctant to relinquish her warm bed and pleasant reverie. She had been dreaming of spring in Virginia. Blue hills and pink laurel and rosy azaleas; meadows bright with golden daffodils and valleys fragrant with frothy fruit blossoms. Sweet lindens blooming in Richmond, and honeysuckle and roses in the garden, where she was a child again chasing butterflies and glowworms. She was wearing a frilly white pinafore and blue ribbons in her hair, and her parents were smiling fondly at her antics. The apocalyptic horsemen had not yet ridden over the South, delivering their terrible prophecies and scourges. She was happy and carefree and content in her childhood innocence, and she longed passionately to retreat into that safe serene comfortable cocoon and forget all that had happened since her hapless emergence.

Yesterday the weather had been beguilingly warm and balmy for early March. She had noticed new green tipping the lilacs in the courtyard, and tiny yellow buds opening on the bare forsythia branches, and sparrows nesting under the eaves. But Mally had assured her that winter was not over in New York, and Devon was convinced when she went to empty the slops in the predawn chill, shivering all the way.

"My pot runneth over," Mally giggled. "I swear I must've peed all night! Hardly slept a wink, either. I was in such a dither. I got the most wonderful news, Devon! Davey proposed last night, and I accepted. We're going to be married in summer and go to Coney Island on our honeymoon for three whole days!" Mally was as thrilled and excited as if they were going to Europe for three whole months. "Isn't that divine?"

"Divine," Devon agreed, hugging her. "And you know I wish you both every happiness, Mally, although I'll miss you here."

"Especially these latrine sociables," she grinned impishly. "Lord, I pray we can afford a flat with a toilet, so I'll never have to empty another chamberpot in my life! But such luxuries cost money, and with my luck I'll just be emptying slops for two and eventually more. We'd better hurry now, Devon. And wear your waterproof and galoshes, it looks like rain."

On the streetcar, which crept through the dismal mist with its single lantern glowing smokily and the filthy winter straw not yet swept out of the aisle, Devon asked, "Will you go on working after the wedding, Mally?"

"Until the babies start coming," she nodded, pulling the bellcord for her stop.

Devon continued to hers. Mr. Joseph had the fire going, the teakettle on, and he had been watching for her. Lately he complained less of his ailments and acted spry and vigorous, patronizing the oyster bars regularly and dosing himself with patent elixirs and mysterious nostrums. Now he flung the door wide and bowed her in as gallantly as if she were a princess royal.

"Good morning, Milady! At last you're here, safe and sound. I worry about you on the streets before dawn and after dark, and think I shall shorten your work hours. I must protect you somehow, for I could not get along without you."

"Nonsense, Mr. Joseph. You managed before I came."

"But not nearly so well, my dear. You've brought me luck, and something far more important. What the French call *raison d'être*: reason for being, for living. Each morning now I tell myself, 'Wake up, Ephraim, and get dressed! Wake up, old man, and live!' But nothing really happens until you arrive. Then immediately I feel younger and stronger and happier, and glad to be alive. Your youth and beauty are my most potent stimulants."

The kettle was steaming, and Devon prepared the tea. "It's messy out today, and rather blustery."

"Just March coming in like a lion," he smiled, affecting a pathetic roar. "If it doesn't rain, perhaps we might go to the park this afternoon. I could close shop early and hire a hansom—"

"And miss the overflow from the spring sales? Stewart's is running their first big one of the season, and naturally Macy's and Lord & Taylor and Arnold Constable are competing. Some shoppers are bound to pass this way. I thought I'd fix up a remainder table and put some new novels in the window."

He wagged a bony finger. "Poetry, my dear, poetry! That's what people buy in spring. It's the time of inspiration and renewal, you know. The spirit soars, the heart sings, the blood quickens. . . ."

Devon ignored his soaring spirit and quickening blood and served his habitual tea. But when she tried to adjust his shawl he shrugged it off, insisting that he had no need of extra warmth, nor would he elevate his reedy legs on the ottoman to improve their circulation. "I'm fit as a new fiddle," he declared. "I feel forty again . . . nay, twenty!"

"That's fine," Devon murmured, and left him to arrange the bargain table and window display.

"Don't forget *Leaves of Grass*," he called after her. "It's the perfect spring title."

True to his word, Walt Whitman had sent an inscribed copy to Devon at the shop, which she had now read and enjoyed and kept locked in her trunk, along with the signed volume of the Cary sisters. She had attended another of their receptions and been invited again to the Bottas but had not gone, primarily because she was ill-at-ease in such illustrious company. But also because she realized that merely mingling in a brilliant galaxy would not give her luminosity. She must shine on her own merits and accomplishments, polish her own star, weave her own laurel wreath; obviously, no one else could or would do it for her.

Preoccupied, she was unaware of any extraneous observation, until she glanced up and met a pair of familiar gray eyes through the glass. Her hands trembled, upsetting a carefully stacked pyramid of poetry, and she was trying vainly to rebuild it when Keith entered the shop. Mr. Joseph, thank God, was shut up in the office balancing ledgers.

"Surprised, Devon? I told you I'd find you, didn't I?"

She tried to flee past him to the stockroom, but he blocked her path. He looked every inch the Wall Street banker and member of the board of brokers privileged to deal in the gold room of the Stock Exchange. He was dressed in a tobacco-brown frockcoat cut to emphasize the magnificent breadth of his shoulders, fawn trousers, a wing-collared white shirt, a carefully knotted cravat of rich Damascus silk pierced with a pearl stickpin. He wore a high hat of brushed brown silk, and Cordovan leather boots.

"What do you want, Keith?"

"As if you didn't know! I have to talk to you, Devon."

"We've nothing to say to each other." She grabbed a novel off the counter. "Would you like to buy this for your wife? I'm sure she reads a great deal."

"She does indeed, and has standing orders with publishers in London, Boston, and Philadelphia. They ship her autographed first editions as rapidly as possible. Devon, when are you going to stop playing this game with me?"

"It's no game," she said.

"Hide-and-seek, cat-and-mouse—it is a game, Devon! I'm tired of it, and I should think you would be too. Let me take you to lunch. At Delmonico's?"

"I'm hardly dressed for Delmonico's," she snapped, indicating her gored black skirt over a modified hoop, and tucked white lawn blouse bowed in black grosgrain.

"The Brevoort, then. Or the St. Nickolas."

"They're just as fancy," she said, for she had dined at all of them with Madame Joie but never in the shopgirl "habit." "The working class eats at Goslings."

"All right, wherever you say. Nothing can happen to you in a public dining room, Devon."

"Nothing's going to happen to me with you anywhere, Keith, ever again."

"Darling, for God's sake! I can explain everything, if you'll just give me a chance."

She set her chin stubbornly. "What I saw in your home was self-explanatory, Mr. Curtis."

He ground his teeth. "You are without a doubt the most obstinate, exasperating female I've ever encountered."

"They all bend to your iron will, malleable as wax dolls, mesmerized by your golden charm?" She spun about angrily. "I must go to the stockroom for more books. If you're still here when I return, I shall ask Mr. Joseph to wait on you."

"That won't be necessary," he said. "Just promise me

one thing, Devon. If you get in a financial bind, you'll come to me before Trent Donahue. I assure you, I'll give you better terms."

"Donahue?" She stared at him. "How do you know—?"

"Never mind," he muttered and left, slamming the door.

Mr. Joseph came out of the office. "Who was that?"

"The Wolf of Wall Street," Devon murmured, using her handkerchief, "looking for Little Red Riding Hood. I told him we were out."

"Are we? I thought our fairy tale stock was fairly complete."

"I'll check again, sir."

"Is something wrong, Miss Marshall?"

"No, I—I just got some dust in my eyes. I'm all right now, sir. But the weather's getting much worse, isn't it? I hope a storm isn't coming. You'd better muffle up good before you go to the oyster bar."

"Why don't you bundle up and come with me, to that new tearoom down the block. The Blue Grotto. They have good food and gypsy fiddles."

"Thank you, Mr. Joseph, but I'd better finish those displays. And I wouldn't want to miss a commission."

By noon the temperature had dropped twenty degrees, and sleet was mixed with the rain. Devon had no appetite for her usual luncheon fare, and only drank some hot tea. All her resolutions to forget Keith had collapsed and dissolved at the sight of him. She had wanted desperately to touch him, and to have him touch her. She huddled by the stove now, longing for the warmth of his arms, the fire of his kiss, the feel of his body against hers. How had he known where to find her, and why had he mentioned that Irish gambler? Had he perhaps been watching through the window when she had tumbled off the ladder into Donahue's arms? What sort of game was *he* playing!

Mr. Joseph returned with a red runny nose and stiff joints, which he refused to pamper. "There was a coast-guardsman at the oyster bar said the Weather Bureau in Washington telegraphed the station that it's sleeting there and in Baltimore too. And Boston and Philadelphia report flying snow. Seems a late winter storm is brewing on the eastern seaboard. Put some more coal on the fire, and make a pot of sassafras tea with honey. I think I took a chill out there."

The wind, blowing simultaneously from north and south, drove sleet and snow up under the awning, hissing and crackling against the windowpane. Across the street a heavy wooden Indian toppled before a tobacco shop, and the proprietor struggled to upright it; almost immediately the painted brave bit the sidewalk again, and he dragged it into the store. Traffic stalled and snarled; horses and vehicles skidded on the icy pavement. Shoppers in town for the spring sales lost their hats and bonnets, had their umbrellas turned inside out and snatched from their hands by sudden violent gusts. Hoopskirts, always a hazard in wind, whirled women about like full-rigged ships out of control. Shrieking, sliding, pummeled, they sailed past Joseph's without a glance at the spring literature, and no thought except to get home to safe harbor.

The thermometer outside the door was steadily plunging. Devon hoped Mr. Joseph would close early and let her leave before it was too late. She had seen enough snowstorms in Richmond to fear and respect them. Several times she and her father had been stranded in the *Sentinel* office for a day or more, and the blizzards of '63, with the Army of Virginia crudely sheltered in tents and stockades along the Rapidan and Rappahannock, had cost General Lee almost as many troops as the enemy.

The sky began to darken in mid-afternoon. Flying snow obliterated the telegraph poles and church spires and blurred the buildings across the street. It was difficult to see their lights through the frosted windows. Shopkeepers and employees were out shoveling their sidewalks and spreading salt and sawdust to no avail. The horsecars and omnibuses, caught with their runners off, moved at snail's pace if at all. Devon was getting panicky. If she didn't leave soon, she would be marooned in the shop. Already the snow was banked to the windowsill and packing against the door. But the proprietor, sipping herb tea and perusing publishers' catalogs, seemed heedless of the March lion running wild in the streets.

"It's a blizzard, Mr. Joseph. A real blizzard!"

"We've had them before, Miss Marshall, though rarely so late in the season. It may peter out."

"I don't think so, Mr. Joseph, and I'd better get home before the streetcars stop running."

"They'll keep the main lines open," he said.

"But there aren't any shoppers, sir. No one has been in for hours. We might just as well close for the day."

He frowned, checking off titles he intended to order. "With your permission, Miss Marshall, I'll decide when to close. Come have some tea—sassafras soothes the nerves."

Devon spent the afternoon watching the blizzard turn the street into a frozen bedlam, knowing she was trapped, and unable to do anything about it. She busied herself dusting and straightening shelves and tables and pushing the cedar-oiled mop over the board floor, and Mr. Joseph's bespectacled eyes seemed to follow her every movement even while he studied and marked the brochures.

By evening the island was shivering and isolated in a savage storm. The raging wind had piled the snow into huge drifts and dunes, and Broadway resembled a boxed canyon crammed with abandoned covered wagons, half-frozen animals, and a few desperate wayfarers seeking shelter in the commercial caverns. Men patronized the saloons and taverns and brothels. Ladies huddled in tearooms, department stores, inns, and hotels. The policeman on the beat had stabled his horse because of the ice and patrolled on foot. He took temporary shelter under Joseph's corrugated awning, one of the few on the street still intact. Tapping on the hoarfrosted pane, Devon motioned him inside. But snow and ice jammed the door, and he could force it only a crack.

"Yes, Miss?"

"Is there any chance of getting out of here, Officer?"

He gazed at her as if he thought she was crazy. "Jesus Christ, lady! And where d'ye think ye could be going in this goddamn weather that ain't good but for one frigging thing, and how? 'Tis only a few cutters running, and the drivers are pouring whisky and gin into the horses to keep 'em from freezing to death. Every hostelry is full of stranded people. Stay where ye are, Miss. Even if the wind didn't pick ye up and dash your brains out against a building or post, ye couldn't be walking ten feet without snowshoes or skis. Sure there'll be frozen carcasses all over town tomorrow!" His breath steamed through the crack; he stamped his feet and rubbed his gloved hands together and swore lustily. "Ye see that bar across the street? I be going there now to get meself drunk, and if ye got any liquor in there, I'd be after advising ye and Grandpa to do the same!" And with a stiff salute to his frosted helmet, he fled to the haven.

The snow, piling higher against the window, blocked her view in a solid white wall. She tried the door; it wouldn't budge. She was sealed in a musty cave with a seedy old bear, who seemed to welcome and anticipate mutual hibernation.

"Shall we go upstairs and have some supper?"

Devon winced. She had never set foot in Mr. Joseph's overhead quarters, and had no wish to do so, even in this emergency. "I'm not hungry, Sir," she said.

"Still, you must eat, my dear. Come along now, and don't be shy."

The charwoman had been in the day before, so the place was neat and clean. The furniture, heavy old pieces of mahogany and black walnut and Jacobean oak, he said were family antiques. But the parlor settee was too small for sleeping, and Devon saw no couch or trundle to suffice. There was a bathroom with plumbing, and a closed door to another chamber which she did not care to investigate.

Her host was removing food from the pantry and placing it on the gate-legged table: ham, sausage, cheese, bread, and a dusty bottle of port. He filled two glasses, lit a candle, and pulled out a chair for her. Devon was almost too nervous to eat, but managed some bread and cheese and a few swallows of wine. For dessert he brought out a compote of chocolates, dried fruit, and glazed nuts, which Devon nibbled while he brewed and sipped a pungent concoction. The acrid odor was familiar; she had smelled it downstairs before, and frequently of late. Curious, she inquired what it was.

"Gingseng root and powdered ram's horn," he said.

Devon grimaced. "Medicine?"

"It has many properties, Miss Marshall. I buy it from a Cantonese merchant in Mott Street. This happens to be Genghis Khan's personal recipe, a long-guarded secret in the Mongol dynasty and discovered in the effects of Kublai Khan. But many mandarins use variations of it, for it promotes potency, health, and longevity. Would you like to try some?"

"Mercy, no! If it tastes as bad as it smells, I don't see how anyone could drink it."

"It's an acquired taste, but it's drunk more for effect than enjoyment."

Somewhere in the apartment a clock was chiming ten bells. Devon stood. "I think I'll go down and read awhile, Mr. Joseph. Why don't you retire. I'll keep the fire going and make a pallet beside it."

He put his cup down. "Don't be silly, girl. You couldn't rest that way, and you might catch cold. Let us be realistic about this situation, Miss Marshall."

"Realistic?"

"Practical," he clarified. "Surely you've heard of the fine old New England custom of bundling, practiced even by the Puritans during long severe winters? It's perfectly respectable, you know, because the clothes are not removed, and the couple merely share the same bed. It's better than freezing, isn't it? And what harm could an old man do you?"

"I'm from Virginia, Mr. Joseph, and we didn't go in much for that old custom there."

"There's nothing wrong with it," he insisted. "Don't be such a little prude, Miss Marshall. I'd sleep on the floor myself, but I strained my back lifting that box of books that was too heavy for you and have some pain now. Would you be kind enough to rub me with liniment?"

"I'm not a nurse, Mr. Joseph."

"And I'm not a patient, Miss Marshall. Just an old man with an aching sacroiliac, which might be yours except for my foolish gallantry. Ah well, it's my own fault. I should have hired a strong young man to begin with, and if you're not grateful enough to oblige me. . . ."

He made her feel responsible for his injury and her job dependent upon its treatment. "Very well, sir. If you'll tell me what to do, I'll try to alleviate your suffering."

"Thank you, my dear. I'd appreciate it very much."

Leading her into the bedroom, he handed her a bottle of oil of wintergreen. Then he stripped down to his red flannel underwear, lowered it to his waist, and lay face-down on the bed, issuing instructions as to location and procedure. His flesh was white and flabby, and it was like kneading fallen dough. Devon remembered another back, broad and bronzed and hard with muscle, and sensuous under her stroking hands. Oh, God! Why had she denied her heart and let her pride send Keith away? If only she had gone with him to lunch or anywhere else he wanted to take her, she'd probably be making love with him now, rather than humoring this repulsive old creature!

"Good, good," he murmured. "A little lower, please. Yes, there, that's fine. Massage harder, deeper."

As she obliged, he made moaning, groaning sounds of pleasure not pain, and Devon knew she was gratifying a senile lust. Then he turned over, presenting a sunken chest with sparse grizzled hairs that sent shivers of revulsion through her, inducing nausea. He bade her continue, saying there was magic in her deft touch, that she had the talented hands of a Japanese or Turkish masseuse. But when he tried to maneuver her hand below his navel, she quickly withdrew it and corked the bottle. "There now! I think that's enough, don't you?"

She handed him his robe and started for the door, but his voice stopped her. "Not yet, my dear. I want to show you my art and rare books."

"Some other time, Mr. Joseph."

"Now, Miss Marshall," he insisted. "It's a small collection, but select, and I'm quite proud of it." Clad in the smelly brown-plaid blanket robe and felt carpetslippers, he shuffled across the room to a closed door and beckoned her.

It was a miniature museum of erotica assembled by a dedicated or fanatical devotee, or both. Nude paintings and statuary, fetishes and aphrodisiacs, breast and phallic symbols, figures from Greek and Roman mythology in various attitudes of copulation and perversion, including sodomy and bestiality, naked Nubian maids and masters engaged in fellatio-cunnilingus, all exquisitely detailed.

"Now, now," he chided, as Devon blushed and turned away. "Don't betray your ignorance of art in embarrassment. The paintings and sculptures are reproductions of some of the world's great masterpieces. You don't recognize or appreciate Titian, Correggio, Rubens? Canova, Clodion, Michelangelo? These *objets d'art* are priceless." He touched a couple straining in ecstasy. "This is Apollo and Aphrodite, bronze. Here's satyr and nymphs, jade. The unicorn is pure silver, the centaur is Algerian marble, the cerebus is onyx. The other pieces are ivory, porcelain, mother-of-pearl, Venetian crystal. The rutting stag is solid gold! You disappoint me, Miss Marshall. I had hoped you

would realize the intrinsic value of this collection. There
are many men in this world who would gladly pay me a
fortune for it. I'm afraid your mind is much too narrow
and provincial to succeed in the profession you desire,
young lady. But perhaps the rare books will be of more interest to you. I have many, but several are outstanding."

From a locked cabinet he produced illustrated versions
of Ovid's *Amatoria* and the Marquis de Sade's *Justine* and
Histoire de Juliette in their original languages and em-
bossed leather bindings; also illuminated parchment
manuscripts of the Festival of Bacchus, and an unorthodox version of the seduction in Eden, depicting Eve's
breasts as apples and Adam's penis as the serpent. All
were so full of obscenity and perversion that Devon left
the room speechless after viewing only a few pages.

He continued, smiling lasciviously, vicariously enjoying
her embarrassment. "My poor child! It's art, all fine art,
and evil only if one considers art evil. Why, you could find
similar books and manuscripts in the Vatican library! And
never travel abroad if nudity offends you, for you will encounter it everywhere: in the museums, the public monuments, the parks and fountains, even some churches and
cathedrals. I fear your education has been sadly neglected
in this important area, and someone of age and wisdom
should enlighten you. How much wiser are the so-called
savages and barbarians in this respect than the civilized
world, for it is the duty of the elder mentors of the tribes
to instruct the maidens before marriage. And a similar
custom prevailed in feudal Europe, when the manor lords
had first-night privileges—jus primae noctis and droit du
seigneur—with the virgin brides of their vassals, to prepare
them for their ignorant and clumsy young grooms. Come,
child, sit down and don't be afraid. I won't hurt you. I
only want to talk to you, like a father."

Devon was not that naive; she perceived his intentions
well enough to realize they were not paternalistic. However rare and valuable, she knew her father would have
considered that art collection pornography, and the collec-
tor a decadent old lecher with a senile itch. He would
have warned her against Ephraim Joseph, as he had
against the friendly old fellows in Richmond who liked to
hug and kiss little girls and dandle them on their knees.

The blizzard still raged, lashing snow and ice against the

building, the wind howling like some crazed animal in a sexual frenzy. The glazed windows were undoubtedly frozen tight, but even if she could manage to pry one open and jump into a snowbank in the alley, she would surely freeze to death before morning. Her stomach was queasy, and she thought she was going to be sick. Worse, she had to go to the toilet. Was there a lock on the bathroom door? Suppose he followed her? She had to risk it, or wet her drawers. She rushed in, threw the bolt, and relieved herself.

When she emerged, he was sitting naked on the bed, grinning at her. She stared in revulsion at the hideous thing between his rangy legs, brown and withered as a piece of dried-up sausage, his lopsided testicles hanging out of a nest of mossy hair. Vaguely, through her shock and horror and disgust, she realized that this had been his intention all along: to outrage her innocence and modesty by exposing himself. Oh God, he was sicker than Janette Joie, and in a much worse way! Perhaps he was even dangerous, and she had to get out of there. . . .

"Come here," he coaxed, fondling himself. "Come play with me, and I'll play with you. It'll be fun, Devon. I've got a fine finger for females. No? Maybe you'd prefer a nice ivory or glass phallus, or that big black ebony dildo? You'll like it, honey, you'll like it. Come on now, don't be shy, take your clothes off. Come here, goddamn you, and do as I say! I'm sure you've been diddled before—"

Suddenly galvanized into action, Devon grabbed some covers and fled the room to the shop. If he followed, she would lock herself in the office. She waited, her heart thumping in her throat and ears, but there was only some groaning and thrashing overhead, suggesting self-abuse.

Devon stirred the coals in the pot-bellied stove, added more fuel, and fixed a pallet beside it. Then she planted some books and boxes at the base of the stairs, to trip him and wake her should he venture down in the dark, and she kept the poker handy for good measure.

The scraping of shovels and snowplows woke her before dawn. The island was buried in some twenty inches of snow, which seemed like twenty feet in the drifts. She listened apprehensively for signs of life upstairs, dreading to face him again. When finally he appeared, however, he was his old self again, dressed in his familiar dark sackcoat, smiling benignly on the landing and inviting her to breakfast.

"I've already made tea down here, sir."

"Very well, I'll bring you a tray."

He brought buttered toast and jam, stewed apricots and figs, and set it on a counter. But remembering his busy hands pawing himself, Devon lost her appetite.

"Help yourself," he urged, "and eat hearty. You will have to help shovel snow when the doors are unsealed. Meanwhile, you can unpack those new shipments from England."

"Yes, sir. I'll attend to it promptly."

"You slept well, I trust?"

"Well enough," she lied.

"Good. I was afraid the storm might give you nightmares. Stir up the fire, it's chilly in here. And where did you put my shawl?"

"In the office, sir. I'll fetch it."

"Never mind, I'll do it myself. Eat your breakfast."

Devon stared after him, astonished, wondering if she could possibly have dreamed or imagined the entire fantasy. No, it had happened, all right. It was as real as his little museum, and the books Walt Whitman had warned her about at the Bottas. The sly old devil had just decided to ignore the whole episode in the hope that she would do likewise.

PART III

■—■—■—■—■—■—■—■—■—■—■—■—■—■—■—■—■—■

Women are told from infancy, and taught by the example of their mothers, that a little knowledge of human weakness, justly termed cunning, softness of temper, *outward* obedience, and a scrupulous attention to a puerile kind of propriety, will obtain for them the protection of man; and should they be beautiful, everything else is needless, for, at least, twenty years of their life.

Mary Wollstonecraft (1759–1797)
A Vindication of the Rights of Women

He has adorned the creature whom God gave him as a companion, with baubles and gewgaws, turned her attention to personal attraction, offered incense to her vanity, and made her the instrument of his selfish gratification, a plaything to please his eyes and amuse his hours of leisure.

Ah! how many of my sex feel in the dominion, thus uprighteously exercised over them, under the gentle appellation of *protection*, that what they have leaned upon has proved a broken reed at best, and oft a spear.

Sarah M. Grimke (1792–1837)

I am convinced that men in general, the vast majority, believe most seriously that women were made to gratify their animal appetites.

Angelina Grimke (1805–1879)

Chapter 14

Bright lights, brass bands, hucksters, and clowns gave the Bowery a carnival air at night that was absent in daylight. The street was lined with saloons, billiard parlors, pawnships, shooting galleries, rat-and-cock pits, brothels, cheap shops and department stores, tenements and homes—all huddled together as if blown there by a freakish wind. The stores displayed their tawdry merchandise on the sidewalks and badgered pedestrians to buy. The largest of them, the Red House, hired harlequins to lure patrons.

Devon heard German, Italian, Greek and Yiddish tongues, but Irish brogue predominated, as it seemed to almost everywhere in New York. Mally O'Neill—who had confessed to sleeping with Davey Thorne the night of the blizzard—had told her that the Fourth Ward, a Tammany stronghold, was the second toughest neighborhood in town. The first, said Mally, was the Gas House District of Five Points, where even policemen would not venture except in pairs. Devon pitied the legions of dirty hollow-eyed barefoot children spilling out of the surrounding slums, whose only future seemed to be in the sweatshops, prostitution, or thievery—provided disease, malnutrition, and abuse allowed them to grow up.

Near the theater district of Chatham Square both the entertainments and buildings were of a better caliber. The Pot O'Gold and the Gilded Cage stood side by side, twins with golden façades and fancy signs: a kettledrum overflowing with riches on the casino, a captive bird in a gilded cage on the cabaret.

Devon tried to guess in which establishment the owner would be at this hour, and if he were actually interested in hiring a tutor, or had only been teasing her. A few days after the storm, she had told Mr. Joseph that she had decided to return to Richmond. This was the same excuse she had used for leaving La Boutique Chic, and she wondered how often she would have to resort to it. His expression had been as skeptical as Madame Joie's had been, but neither had tried to dissuade her nor referred to the true reasons for her sudden resignation. It was as if Christmas Eve had never happened with Janette Joie, or the night of the blizzard with Ephraim Joseph.

Hearing music in the Gilded Cage, Devon decided to try it first. The interior was gaudily splendid with the glitter of gilt, the sparkle of crystal, the opulence of red plush. Against one wall stood a long white marble bar with a baroque gilt mirror behind it. Tables and chairs circled a polished parquet dance floor. Recessed at one end was a stage curtained in scarlet velvet and gold tassels. There were a number of large gilded cages equipped with red velvet perches, gilt swings, and golden feedcups; some hung from the ceiling on golden chains which could be lowered and raised by pulleys. Devon supposed they were symbolic ornaments.

It was much too early for supper customers, but the entertainment was already in rehearsal—dancers in red velvet tights, with buoyant bosoms and plump legs, glittering headdresses, and elbow-length red velvet gloves. Directing them, her back to the visitor, was a flamboyant young woman with the brightest blonde hair Devon had ever seen, even on the Richmond harlots.

"One, two, kick!" she ordered. "Three, four, kick! Five, six, turn! Turn, Bessie, and put a little zest into it! You're a stick this morning."

"Sorry, Miss Lilly. I was out late last night with Tim, got in at dawn, and didn't get hardly no sleep."

"That's your problem, sister. Mr. Donahue pays you to dance, not yawn. If Timothy Murphy is more important to you than your career, marry the bum and raise his brats. But don't come to rehearsal with your tail dragging again, or you'll be hunting another job. All right now, back to work, all of you! Firm up your butts, tighten your bellies, and thrust out your bosoms. This isn't a wake, you know. One, two kick! Three, four—"

One of the chorus noticed the spectator in the shadows near the entrance. "Miss Lilly, there's a lady over there—"

"Lady!" shouted the piano player with a roar of ribald laughter. "What would a lady be doing here?"

Lilly Day gave him a withering glare. She disliked everything about this impudent musician, from his bald head to his moon-toed shoes. "Maybe you don't like your job either, Mr. Clancey?"

"Sur-r-r-r-e, Miss Lilly," he stammered. "I'm cra-cra-crazy about me job. I-I-I was just making a little joke, ha-ha."

"Hereafter leave the jokes to the minstrels, Jake. You ain't funny. You ain't even a good piano player."

Turning her attention to the stranger, Miss Lilly moved slowly toward Devon. Her gown, as everything else in the place, was spectacular, scarlet satin sprinkled with gold spangles. The tight, deeply-cut basque emphasized a small waist and voluptuous breasts. As she walked, her smooth round hips undulated beneath the shimmering material, and red satin shoes peeped from under the split skirt.

Devon stared in fascination, wondering how she had gotten her hair that color, for surely it was not naturally so, any more than her vivid lips and cheeks were natural, or the jet lashes framing her large dark flashing eyes. If she was not a raving beauty, she had something more important in her business: flamboyance.

"Yes, Miss?" Her voice, a throaty contralto, was most effective rendering sultry and sentimental ballads to the accompaniment of her gilded guitar. "I'm Lilly Day. May I help you?"

"Is Mr. Donahue here?"

"No, he isn't. But if you've come about employment, I do all of the hiring here. What's your name?"

"Devon Marshall."

It rang no bells with Miss Day, who was probably unaware of Joseph's Book Store. "You looking for work?"

Devon nodded.

"What have you done?"

"Well, I've done some writing and clerking," Devon said, adding before the other woman could laugh, "and modeling."

"For artists?"

Devon swallowed, unable to say she had demonstrated lingerie. "Yes, for artists. Portraits. I—I sing a little too."

"Do you indeed? Well, that's fine, Miss Marshall. But I'm the songbird here, so if you're seeking that limelight,

I'd advise you to take your talents elsewhere. Do you dance?"

"Not on stage."

"Too bad. I could use you in the chorus. The only other thing open here would be a cage."

"Beg pardon?"

"This place is called the Gilded Cage, you know. We put pretty girls dressed as various birds on display. No particular talent is required—they don't sing or talk or even twitter, and need only be decorative and beautiful and graceful when they pose or sit on the swing or perch. Having modeled for artists, you should know about posing and, in fact, artists occasionally come in to sketch the girls. I could use a new bird. I had to send one flying last night for soliciting from the cage. Flirtation is permissible, but we can't allow actual solicitation on the premises. It's bad for the image, you understand, since some men bring their wives or sweethearts." She paused, shrugging. "Naturally, what a girl does on her own time is her business, and we don't care, as long as she observes the house rules on duty. We furnish costumes, of course, and some girls prefer to conceal their identity with masks. We have some timid souls, you see, who must supplement their meager shop or factory wages and don't wish to be recognized. The cages pay five dollars a night, one night off a week if desired, without pay, and the birds are let out for brief respites twice during the evening. Well, Miss Marshall, what'll it be—the cage or nothing?"

"The cage," Devon decided, "and I'll need a mask."

Her smile mocked such modesty. "I thought so. My, how shy and virtuous some birds are, and yet how eager for the scratch. They do quite well too, with the extra feed put in their cups and tossed into the cages, and we don't demand a kickback of gratuities, as some places do. Mr. Donahue is very generous in that respect. Can you start this evening?"

"Yes, I can, Miss Day. What time?"

"The birds go into the cages at eight sharp. Nothing much happens before then. We close at one o'clock."

Devon frowned. "The streetcars stop running at midnight. Getting home will present a problem."

"Not for a clever bird," the other winked. "Very few have to fly or hop home. There's always some cock eager to escort them. In lieu of that, many hackneys and hansoms run all night, and you'll clear enough in tips to afford cabs both ways. I suggest that you be here by six-thirty, to select a costume and get some instructions. Having modeled, I assume you know enough to keep your legs and armpits shaved. No offense, but it's amazing the number of fuzzy-wuzzies I get. By the way, that's a Southern accent, isn't it?"

"Virginia," Devon nodded.

"What town?"

She hesitated. "Richmond."

"A capital bird, eh?" Lilly smiled her cool mockery again. "Well, you should feel at home here, dearie. We've had former belles of Charleston, Atlanta, Montgomery, Vicksburg, and New Orleans. A regular migration of Southern birds to the North since the war. One of them did a specialty act, a spectacular primitive dance whose wild rhythms she claimed to have picked up observing the slave festivals on her father's plantation. She created quite a sensation in her painted feathers. Unfortunately, we couldn't keep her long—a Tammany politician promptly acquired her for his personal pet. All but two have flown the coop now, taken into keeping by other Yankee fanciers of Rebel birds, including some of the aristocracy. You'll meet Natchez and Savannah this evening. And, Richmond—there's a stage entrance in the alley. Please use it hereafter."

"Yes, Ma'am."

"Don't call me ma'am. This isn't the South."

"I'm sorry, Miss Day."

"Lilly will do," she said. "I'm not old, you see. I doubt if I'm five years past your age."

More like ten, Devon thought, but she said, "I doubt it too." This woman could be friend or foe, and she certainly had no need of the latter.

Afraid she might be late or that Lilly would change her mind if she delayed, Devon arrived before six o'clock and knocked on the alley door.

Mike Brophy, the bartender, admitted her, polishing a glass. "Christ, you're early, chickadee! You the new bird?"

"Yes."

He whistled softly. "Lilly sure knows how to pick 'em! She says to wait in the dressing room."

"Thank you."

As she would have brushed past him, Brophy caught her arm. "Got a fella?"

"Yes. A strong-arm wrestler."

He grinned. "I get it, sweetheart. Hands off, eh? Well, you can't blame a man for trying." He popped the towel at her bottom and pointed to a corridor. "Down that way, honey. And good luck on your premiere."

Devon smiled in spite of herself, indignation vanishing. Why did she always suspect the worst in men's attentions? He was only trying to be friendly. She had to learn to distinguish between compliment and insult.

Soon Miss Day appeared in another theatrical creation, this one of vermilion velvet fluttering with crimson marabou, and her ruby jewelry looked genuine. Her mood was friendlier than before, and Devon decided she had just been aggravated by the bungling of the chorus.

"Let's go to the wardrobe," she said. "I've been trying to decide what sort of costume would suit you best, Richmond. Naturally, all the birds are gorgeous. We don't go in much for the domestic species, unless colorful, such as the redbird, bluebird, orange oriole, goldfinch, and painted bunting. We prefer the exotic tropical types: flamingos, egrets, the parrot family, and birds of paradise."

Lilly opened the door on racks of feathered costumes with elaborate headgear, in brilliant colors and designs, yet authentic enough for bird buffs to recognize.

"No canaries?" Devon asked.

"I'm the only canary here," Lilly reminded. "The girls may wear a different costume every evening if they wish and change during intermissions, to break the monotony. And it can get monotonous in those cages. I know, because I started in one myself. Some girls prefer to be known as one particular bird; they're usually the ambitious ones hoping some impresario will fancy them enough to make a stage offer. Naturally, they don't wear disguises. Neither do those who want to become the pets of wealthy bird keepers." As she talked Lilly removed costumes from the racks and held them before Devon. "What do you think of this cockatoo?"

The plumage was white tinged with rose, deepening to

salmon under the graceful wings, the headdress a high scarlet crest. "Lovely," Devon said.

"Here's an exquisite scarlet flamingo. And consider this gorgeous green-and-yellow macaw. What do you think of this adorable turquoise parakeet, or this bright little love-bird?"

Devon was puzzled. "They're all so beautiful, it's hard to choose. Perhaps I belong in something simple and domestic. I don't feel very exotic."

"I can't imagine why," Lilly said. "You could be a glamorous creature if you learned how to make up your face. You have such damned delicate features, but with rouge on your mouth and cheeks, Egyptian fard on your eyebrows and lashes, and gold dust in your hair—well, I'll show you about cosmetics later. And I think I have the perfect costume for you too. A bird of paradise. We have many, and most girls would wear them exclusively if allowed. But then the customers would tire of them, so we reserve them for special occasions, such as holidays, and to introduce a new bird in the aviary."

These costumes occupied special racks, and Devon caught her breath when Lilly whisked off the dust-covers. "Oh, how fabulous! They're works of art!"

"Almost as expensive too. This is my favorite, and the one I think you should wear tonight. It's called the great bird of paradise, and no wonder."

The colors were exquisitely hued and blended, pale cinnamon and fawn and beige and cream, with resplendent golden-whitish plumes cascading over the back from the sides of the breast. Not to detract from the magnificent plumage, the headdress was simple: a small sleek gold-feathered cap. And since the bird had a natural deep-green throat, Lilly suggested an emerald velvet eyemask, which she called a vizard.

"It's simply gorgeous, Lilly."

She grinned conspiratorially. "If you don't garner the most tips this evening, and make every male wonder who the new bird is, I'll eat my feathers! Just remember, the birds are for observation only, and do not speak to the viewers, even if they know them. You'll be admired, coveted, teased, propositioned. You may want to peck and claw the familiar hand that feeds you, but you only smile and pose and ignore the familiarites. And I'll grant you, it's easier to do masked."

At seven o'clock the company began to report. Lilly introduced Devon Marshall. The others appraised her with professional curiosity and jealousy, recognizing real competition when they saw it, for while they were all attractive and shapely, few were genuinely beautiful. Still, they were friendly enough, particularly the Southerners, who welcomed "Richmond" as a comrade and ally in enemy territory.

Maybelle Compton, the Mississippian, was called Natchez; she had blue-black hair, turquoise eyes, and gardenia skin. Devon could easily visualize her dancing at balls, flirting at barbecues, riding to hounds. Darlene Dumaine, tagged Savannah, spoke with the soft liquid drawl of the Georgia coast. Her eyes were as changeable as the sea she had grown up with, her hair the color of the sandy shores and rippling in waves.

"Come along, honey," Natchez said, taking Devon's hand, "we'll help you dress. What's your costume?"

"A bird of paradise."

"The great one, I bet," Savannah said. "It suits your tawny coloring perfectly, and it's the finest of the lot."

The dressing room, lined on three sides with mirrored tables lighted by gaslamps, was noisy with chatter, gossip, the usual fretting and grumbling over lost or pilfered rouge-pots, fard sticks, beauty patches, hairpins, powder-puffs. Lilly, the arbiter and body-inspector, was checking for hygiene, a routine to which they were all subjected.

"You didn't bathe today, Nan," she accused.

"Couldn't, Lilly. Indisposed."

"That's no excuse. You could've washed your underarms and dusted with talcum or alum. Go into the lavatory and do so now, at once. And you'd better be wearing enough protection—you know the penalty for ruining a costume. In case you've forgotten, the fine is a week's salary."

"Jesus," Nan muttered, "how I wish some wealthy cock would take me out of that goddamn cage."

"It'd have to be a sea hawk," Lilly told her, "to put up with your foul mouth. Commodore Vanderbilt speaks your language, but I doubt he'd want an albatross around his neck. He takes 'em on the wing."

"That old coot?" Nan scoffed. "I'd think it more likely he had to trap 'em with gold nuggets for bait."

"Don't fool yourself," said Opal Haskell, a cute little pixie type from Hartford. "They say no maid is safe in his house—he gets 'em all in the featherbed. Anyway, it's not so great having a keeper. They put you in a cage too. A mistress, I've found, has even less freedom than a wife. The first thing they do is clip your wings, band your legs, and try to put a hood over your head. Mine got livid if I so much as looked at another cock. After nine months of such confinement, I couldn't stand it any longer. I told him I wanted out, and I thought he would wring my neck in his jealous rage. Oh, they can't bear to be jilted! And would you believe, the old rooster had a hen and several chicks in a fancy coop on Long Island! Men are bastards, every last one of 'em."

"Naturally," Nan agreed. "They're all sons of bitches, aren't they?"

"Nan's family are Quakers, and Opal has a sister in the convent," Savannah said behind the screen. "But they talk and swear like a sailor's parrot."

"And so will we, probably," Natchez grimly predicted, "when we've been caged long enough. Wasn't there anything else you could possibly do, Richmond? No other way to make a living? I mean—well, you don't look as if you belong here any more than Savannah and I do."

"Oh, I don't expect this to be permanent," Devon assured her. "I have other plans for myself, but it'll take awhile for them to materialize."

Savannah sighed sadly. "Sure, we all have other plans, Richmond. So did General Lee . . . but even he had to surrender, eventually. And I'm beginning to think Manhattan is my Appomattox."

"Why did you come?" Devon asked.

"I thought I could teach school or govern children. I'm a graduate of Savannah Female Academy. But there are schoolmarms all over New England without classrooms, and governesses without charges. Someone suggested that I go West, where the competition for positions and men is not so keen."

Natchez nodded sympathetically. "I came hoping to find a solvent husband, now that all the Confederate gold ended up in Yankee pockets. Lots of Southern girls had the same idea, apparently. I've had some proposals, all right, but not of marriage. You may fare better with your plans, Richmond, whatever they are. I hope so."

They were helping her into the costume, which fastened at the side with hooks and eyes. It fitted her perfectly, and the shades blended with her cream-and-honey coloring as if they had been dyed expressly for her. Devon tucked her curls under the gold-feather cap and put on the green velvet mask, which made the visible irises of her eyes glow greener, like emeralds flecked with gold. Her arms were tucked into the delicate wings, and sheer beige silk stockings with gold-tipped claws covered her legs and feet. The transformation was amazing. Surely no one could recognize her; she hardly recognized herself in the mirror. Nevertheless, she was tense and nervous, dreading confinement in the cage and hoping it would not induce claustrophobia. Except for the fastidious secrets gleaned from Madame Joie, including the astringency of alum powder, perspiration would have been gushing from her armpits and between her thighs.

Most of the girls complimented her, but a few only stared sullenly, anticipating fewer tidbits in their feedcups. Even Lilly Day was somewhat surprised. "Good Lord, we may have to post a guard at your cage! The hawks and eagles and falcons always hover over a new chick, and I don't know when we've had a more delectable one. Now why don't you practice a few poses? You're not a mocking bird, remember, so don't try to imitate anyone else. Be individual, original—you'll attract attention enough if you merely sit in your swing, or on the perch. Use your own judgment, Richmond. Pretend you're having your portrait painted. You'll be a sensation."

Lilly left the room then and Nan, now dusted with talcum but still sulking, said to Opal, "Her Highness must be damn sure of her favor with the Bowery King to dangle that rare bird before him, especially when she knows he admires breeding."

"That's because he ain't got none," replied Opal, "and neither has Lilly. But Donahue couldn't run this place without her. She's managed the Cage so long, he depends on her completely. Besides, she seems to keep him satisfied and happy enough. Look at the baubles he gives her!

Those are real rubies she's flaunting tonight. And he hardly ever looks at the birds."

"He'll look at *that* one."

"If he comes tonight. He don't always, you know. He stays mostly at the Pot O'Gold, where the big money rolls in. This is just chicken feed to him. But it makes Lilly feel important and independent. Some mistresses get hat or dress shops. Lilly got a supperhouse."

"Hush," someone warned. "She'll be back any minute now."

And she was, clapping her hands briskly. "Cage time! Come on, you lazy birds! Get your tails out of here!"

The flock trooped out: a redbird with sequined wings and tail; a bluebird in sapphire velvet and silver-dusted feathers; a flamingo in vermilion plumage; a snowy egret with flowing white plumes; a brilliant green-and-red parrot; a magnificently crested cockatoo; and a tawny bird of paradise.

The cages were made of wicker, rattan, and ornamental metal, all lavishly gilded. The occupant could sit on the foldaway gilt perch, in the bright velvet swing, or stand and pose, as long as she made a pretty spectacle to edify and entertain.

Devon entered the cage Lilly assigned her, struck a graceful pose and froze her features into an artificial smile. The mask had several advantages—it protected her identity and modesty while enabling her to observe the patrons surreptitiously. They appeared to have one common factor: money. Most of it was obviously new gold, glittering, ostentatious, conspicuous in its display—what Madame Joie would call vulgar parvenus and nouveaux riches. But some was undoubtedly old wealth: family affluence, inherited, assured, elegant, the haute monde.

It was easy to tell the men of either class who were regular customers, for whether boldly or covertly, they glanced expectantly at the cages, as if hoping to glimpse some new and exciting creature inside. Their eyes ran the gamut quickly, and then returned to linger and speculate on the bird of paradise. Devon assumed various artistic attitudes as affected as her costume and expression, feeling like a freak in a carnival sideshow. Oh, God, they were all crass flesh-worshippers, who saw nothing beyond a pair of pretty lips, breasts, and legs. Hedonists at the shrine of youth and beauty and sensuality. And though she was not indecently exposed, their covetous lust made her feel stark naked. She wanted to scratch their leering eyes out.

She longed for the ten o'clock intermission, when they were freed from the cages to rest or change costumes and recoup their emotions, while Lilly Day presented her revue and sang a couple of popular ballads strumming her golden guitar.

It was midnight before Donahue strolled in from the Pot O'Gold. Lilly had not mentioned the new attraction to him, and he was there a good half-hour, moving from table to table, greeting guests, ordering champagne on the house for some, before he noticed her, apparently because somone had inquired about the bird of paradise. Devon saw him shake his head as he glanced in her direction, and then he moved toward her. He was wearing a crimson brocade evening jacket and ruffled silk shirt and he flashed with diamond studs, stickpin, cufflinks. Her mouth quivered and she wet her lips again, but it was difficult to maintain the moist parted-lip smile that Lilly demanded. He stood before her cage curiously, staring as if he could penetrate the mask, and finally asked, "Who are you?"

"Bird of paradise."

"I know that, birdie. What's your name?"

"Richmond."

"Change it," he said. "It don't suit you. How long have you been here?"

"I started this evening."

"To replace that little titmouse that disgraced her cage last night? Well, I must say ye're a fine replacement. The men like you, and no wonder. You got class—sure it sticks out all over you, no offense. Got a way home, sweetheart?"

Devon hesitated slightly. Her feedcup was full of coins, and there were some greenbacks and more silver on the floor of her cage, along with several notes begging introductions and favors. "Yes, sir."

"Husband?"

"No, sir. A friend."

Donahue fondled his mustaches, twisting the waxed ends into stiff little horns. "Ye know, your voice sounds familiar, unless me ears deceive me. Have we met before?"

She shook her head, surprised, for she had tried to disguise her voice. "No, sir."

"Well, welcome to the Gilded Cage, me fair beauty. I hope ye'll be a permanent fixture."

"I rather imagine that will depend on Miss Day." Lilly's eyes were at that moment trained on them from across the room, literally glinting with suspicion and jealousy.

He grinned noncommittally and returned to his role of genial host, greeting, nodding, pumping hands.

Including her tips and wages, Devon had earned over fifteen dollars for less than five hours' work. More than three dollars an hour! How much better the body paid than the mind. It was incredible, fantastic. At this rate, she'd be rich before long, able to begin repaying Keith, and be her own mistress.

She removed the costume with assistance from Natchez and Savannah, assisting them in turn, and the trio went out through the alley and around to Chatham Square. The Southerners shared an apartment in a nearby tenement, which Savannah described as a rookery, and asked, "Where do you roost, Richmond?"

"The Gothic Arms."

Natchez said, "I know someone who lived there once. It's a sanctuary for indigent birds compared to Gotham Court. You should see those coops and what they call Paradise Alley! A cholera plague would wipe out the whole block."

Devon rode home in a hansom, with a pocketful of money. In the morning she would order a ream of foolscap and a gross of pencils from a stationer and get busy preparing for the career she really wanted.

The late hour and largely deserted streets made her vaguely conscious of another cab, always a half-block or so behind. She tapped at the glass window. "Driver!"

He slid the glass open. "Yes, Mum?"

"Is that cab following us?"

"I'm not sure, Mum, but I think we picked it up on the Bowery."

It turned off shy of Gothic Arms, however, and Devon relaxed. No need for fear or apprehension now; she would not be walking alone on dark streets or riding horsecars and omnibuses any more.

Chapter 15

Lilly Day was constantly disciplining disobedient or errant or tardy or flighty birds and threatening to discharge them. But keeping the cages occupied with choice specimens was not easy, for they were constantly raided by impresarios seeking potential talent and gentlemen seeking potential pets, and concert saloon operators and brothel madames also tried to recruit the birds for their establishments. Their scouts hung around the stage door, approaching any and every prospect with alluring offers. Unable to distinguish between legitimate producers and the pimps, Devon cautiously ignored them all. As Natchez and Savannah assured her, nothing disastrous could happen inside the cage; it was on the outside that ambition beckoned and danger lurked. Convinced that her immurement was only temporary, anyway, Devon could resist the temptations that tricked and trapped some desperate birds into far worse and more hopeless captivity.

On her fifth evening, however, she arrived to find Miss Day in foul humor, and Savannah said it was because she and Mr. Donahue had been quarreling earlier.

"I heard 'em too," Nan said, "and I eavesdropped enough to know what it was about."

"What?" asked Natchez, getting into a goldfinch costume, feeling domestic this evening and hoping some decent fellow hunting a mate for a vine-covered nest would discover her.

"Richmond, what else!" Nan cried gleefully, eager for a contest to develop between the two women.

Startled, Devon asked, "Me? What have I done?"

"It ain't what you done," said Opal, donning blue-green cockateel feathers. "It's what the Duchess of Chatham Square is afraid the King of the Bowery might do."

"I don't understand?"

162

"Christ," muttered Nan, smirking. "Ain't you the naive one, though? As sweet and pure as the Virgin Mary, I doubt not, with your maidenhead still intact. Donahue wants to move you out of the cage into the limelight, give you some kind of solo act. He said maybe you could do more than look pretty, that maybe you had a voice and could warble a note or two. When Lilly laughed, he told her she needn't cackle so superiorly, because she wasn't exactly the Swedish Nightingale, Jenny Lind. Well, she flew at him like a wet hen then, clawing and pecking, threatening to quit and let him manage the Cage himself, until he soothed her ruffled feathers and promised not to interfere again. She accused him of personal interest in you, but he swore he'd never even seen you outside the cage or unmasked, and you might have crossed eyes and a hooked beak for all he knew. Then they billed and cooed a bit, and he promised to buy her another trinket and take her to the Harlem Lane races tomorrow and driving in the Central Park carriage parade Sunday."

"How could you hear all that without their knowledge?" demanded Natchez skeptically.

"I was behind the stage curtain and couldn't leave without betraying myself, for which that vampire bat would have my blood. Oh, they were fighting, all right, but Lilly won, as usual, because she knows this business better than him. And at least he can trust her not to cheat him, like the manager before her that he shot."

Devon caught her breath. *"Shot?"*

"Oh, not to kill, just to wound the thieving vulture. His right wing is crippled now, and there's a talon missing from the claw that was dipping in the till. Donahue ain't killed nobody since his last duel on the riverboat run from Cincinnati to New Orleans. That's how he made most of his money, you know. He got off the Mississippi just before the war wrecked his trade, and teamed up with Johnny Morrissey in Saratoga Springs for a couple of seasons. Then he went into business for himself."

Savannah eyed her suspiciously. "How do you know so much about him?"

"How d'you think?" quipped Nan. "I knew him before Lilly, only she doesn't know how *well* I knew him. She'd singe my tail and boot me out if she did. I hate that bleached bitch and would love to pluck her feathers!"

Nan swallowed her tongue as Lilly entered the dressing room and went directly to Devon. They had previously decided that she would be a different bird of paradise every night for the first week. In addition to the introductory number, she had already portrayed the superb bird of paradise in a dark velvet body, breast shield of iridescent green feathers and cape of delicate black fronds spread about the green-capped head, and black vizard; the magnificent bird with orange back, erect yellow ruff just behind the head, glistening green satin breast, and pair of long curled plumes from the tail; the Emperor Rudolph's beautiful blue bird of paradise spreading a fan of delicate blue plumes from the sides of the breast. This evening she was to be the King of Saxony's famous pet, a fabulous creature with a splendid dark bib, bright gold body, and twelve long recurved wiry plumes from the tail.

"Good evening, Richmond. All ready for exhibition?"

"Just about. It's not time yet, is it?"

"Not yet. Come over here, please. I want to chat with you." She motioned Devon to a corner. "Has Mr. Donahue said anything to you about leaving the cage?"

"Why no, he hasn't."

"Has he asked about your talents and ambitions?"

"No."

"I just wondered," Lilly mused. "He thought perhaps you might have some voice, but I assured him you couldn't do more than cheep and chirp. I believe I made it clear when I hired you that I am the chanteuse here, and I don't think we need two songsters, do you?"

"No, I don't," Devon promptly agreed. "And the only singing I ever did was in the church choir at home."

"Well, there's no choir here, my dear. But I have a feeling that Mr. Donahue might invite you to watch him race his trotters tomorrow, and accompany us in the Sunday carriage parade. You won't be able to accept, will you?"

Her dark eyes challenged and defied. "No, I have to wash my hair and do my laundry."

"Smart girl," Lilly said, unsmiling. "I think he's getting curious about your face too, so you'll keep your identity secret, won't you? A mask always adds to a woman's mystery. And you do want to remain anonymous, don't you?"

Devon nodded assent, her throat tight and cotton-dry.

"We understand each other, then, Richmond?"

Another silent affirmation.

"Good. Now why don't you change costumes during the first intermission. Put on the scarlet king bird of paradise, or the great bird again, which you wore your first night. Because tomorrow you go into the regular costumes. Some of the girls are complaining about favoritism, you see, and I must keep peace in the coop. Besides, it's not fair to them, since you naturally reap more rewards in this regalia. Wear a dark mask with that, and put more carmine pomade on your mouth. Gaslight tends to fade out colors, you know."

"Whatever you say, Lilly."

"Dumb dodo," Nan hissed after her nemesis had departed. "Why'd you let her bluff and intimidate you? You should've slit her goddamn craw."

That Saturday evening brought a number of well-known personalities. Mayor Hoffman and a small party. August Belmont with a lovely young companion definitely not Mrs. Belmont. Big blond mustached financier Jim Fisk and his striking brunette mistress, Josephine Mansfield. Madame Restell, elegant in black velvet and pearls, escorted by the handsome young chemist, half her age, who concocted her guaranteed "infallible" abortifacients.

Boss Tweed arrived with the same petite blonde for whom Devon had once modeled Paris lingerie, now sparkling with gems from her dainty head to her tiny toes. Tweed himself sported a huge diamond stickpin and ring, and a unique ruby-eyed gold tiger emblem in his broad satin lapel. His reputation for lavish largesse occasioned anticipation in the cages, for he was fond of real birds and kept canaries and parakeets in his home and office. He liked other pets too: dogs, cats, the cunning monkeys of the organ grinders, and thoroughbred horses. He never passed up a beggar on the street, or a disabled veteran peddling pencils and shoestrings, and Tammany charity to the poor made him a heroic humanitarian in the destitute wards. Such a generous and kind-hearted man couldn't be all bad, these folks said, no matter what others might think.

During the ten o'clock respite Devon changed into the tawny costume of her initial appearance, which was her favorite and decidedly more comfortable than the one she had just removed, whose tall wired tail made it difficult to sit or swing, since she must be careful not to crush the delicate quills, and so she had stood for most of the two hours.

A waiter brought in coffee and tidbits for their refreshment, and they had forty minutes of leisure and relaxation while Lilly and the chorus entertained.

"The house is packed with swells tonight," Opal remarked, sugaring her coffee. "Some gentry too."

"Slim pickings, though," Nan complained sourly. "They all brought mates, legal or otherwise."

"Well, the night's still young. Wait till the gamblers leave the Pot. They're always alone, because the only birds allowed in there are the decoys."

"It's damned unfair to our sex," declared Nan, who envied the open opportunities of the shills to make personal contact with wealthy prospects. "Why don't the suffragettes do something about our right to patronize casinos and saloons if we want? What good would the franchise do women, anyway? They'd still have to vote the way their goddamn menfolk told 'em! The injustice is at the altar, not the polls."

Savannah, leaning against a support to protect her costume, drawled languidly, "In that case it's easy enough to avoid—simply refuse all honest proposals."

"Oh, listen to the Savannah Sage! If you're so smart, honey-chile, how come you ain't teaching school like you want? And if Natchez was such a Mississippi Belle, why didn't she wed some big King Cotton? And with all Richmond's assets, she should've been First Lady of the Confederacy! You Dixie-keets ain't no better off than us poor ignorant Yankeets that didn't have your fancy advantages."

"You make a perfect parrot, Nan, always squawking."

Natchez sighed wearily. "More like a screech owl, if you ask me."

"Peck, peck," Nan mocked, "and naturally the birds of a Southern feather flock together. No doubt your families owned their share of blackbirds and hunted their runaway field crows with bloodhounds! Well, how do you like being your own slaves now?"

"You're giving tongue like a bitch at bay," Natchez said. "Down home, we'd shut you up with a hush puppy."

A loud knock on the door interrupted the tirade, and

Nan muttered, "Oh, shit! There's the five-minute call, and I still have to go to the toilet."

"Better hurry," Opal advised, "or put some newspaper down in your cage," and the flock twittered with giggles.

The revue was in its finale, the house lights turned up again. Lilly was taking a final bow and throwing kisses to her appreciative audience. Devon seated herself daintily on her perch. At a single table in a secluded corner, an artist was sketching between sips of red wine; she recognized him as the one she had met at the Carys.

Tweed and his "niece" left shortly after the entertainment, first sending his compliments to the cages in crisp greenbacks, and other guests were almost as generous. It was Devon's most lucrative night so far, and she was mentally calculating her bounty when a familiar figure walked in, giving her instant heart flutter. Formal black suit, top hat and white gloves, with a long white satin lined black cape flipped casually over one shoulder, Keith might have just come from a ball or the opera. Ordering a drink at the bar, he stood half-turned with an elbow leaning on the white marble counter, surveying the salon, as if he knew precisely what he was hunting but hadn't yet found it. Panic seized Devon, and an urge to escape her cage, but it was latched from the outside and only an emergency would open it during exhibition.

The casino patrons were wandering in now, to celebrate or commiserate their luck, and their tips would acknowledge their individual fortunes. Keith seemed to know some of them, and Devon wondered if he too had been gambling. And then, according to male custom, with drink and cigar in hand, he began to inspect the cages, as if prospecting for a pet, lingering before those that interested or amused him, rewarding each as he passed. Recognizing quality when they saw it, Natchez and Savannah smiled as charmingly as their vizards permitted, while Nan and Opal preened and flirted flagrantly, but Devon couldn't gauge his reaction.

She watched him approach apprehensively, wishing she could disappear in a puff of his cigar smoke. He appraised her impassively, without apparent interest or recognition, while she contrived equal indifference behind her green velvet mask, though her heart was beating like wild wings against her ribcage. His eyes traveled leisurely over her costumed body, pondering the full feathered breast and silk-netted legs, and she thought she detected a faint flicker of his facial nerves and jaw muscles. Feeling giddy, she clutched a swing-rope for support, afraid her involuntary tremors would betray her. He left without depositing a gratuity, a deliberate humiliation, since she was the only one he slighted . . . and she almost collapsed with relief.

But he did not leave as she had hoped and prayed. Instead, he returned to the bar for another drink. Once he spoke to Lilly, who smiled and shrugged her bare shoulders. Apparently he was waiting for someone, and Devon knew whom when Trent Donahue came in from the Pot O'Gold. They shook hands and began to talk, immediately and seriously. The gambler frowned some, the banker scowled some, and ultimately Donahue nodded and came to her cage.

"The gentleman at the bar wants to escort you home this evening, Richmond."

"Tell him I'm not interested, Mr. Donahue."

"Sorry, sweetheart. I don't want to release you, but Curtis insists. He has his fangs bared, and they don't call him the Wolf of Wall Street for nothing."

"I don't care! I won't go with him, and he can't make me. Who does he think he is, anyway?"

"He knows who he is," Donahue said. "He knows what he wants too, and usually gets it."

"Not this time! Send him away, Mr. Donahue. Please?"

"Can't, sugar, much as I'd like to bounce him. His bank holds some of my notes, payable on demand. If he called 'em in, I'd be in a bind."

"Let me out of here, then," Devon pleaded. "I'll return the costume tomorrow. Hurry, sir! He's coming!"

Shaking his leonine head regretfully, Donahue waited for Curtis before releasing the latch. "You can take her out through the office," he said. "That door behind you opens on the street. Lilly'll take care of your money for you, Richmond."

"Never mind that," Keith told him, and to Devon, who was glaring mutinously, "Don't make a scene, Miss, just come quietly."

In the office he swirled off his cape and draped it over her, opened the door and hailed a hackney on Chatham Square.

"This is abduction, Keith!"

"Charge me."

"I'll scream," she threatened.

"Go ahead. There's an officer on the corner. I'll say you tried to pick my pocket. We'll see which of us he believes. Would you rather go to jail?"

"Oh, you're contemptible!" she fumed, as he handed her into the hack and got in beside her.

"Rhinelander Gardens, Driver!"

Devon still wore her mask, as if coming from a masquerade. "How did you recognize me, Keith?"

"Your lips, of course. You think I could forget them, even under all that paint?"

"But how did you know I was there?" At his silence, she accused, "You had a spy on me, didn't you?"

"For your own protection," he admitted. "I was afraid your mania for self-reliance would get you into trouble. But you were safe enough, even in dark streets and alleys, because an armed guard was always near. Why did you leave Madame Joie?"

"That's personal."

"No doubt. Oh, I saw the way she looked at you that day in Gramercy Park! She wanted you as much as I did. And I bet the little old bookseller turned out to be a great big lecher, so you left him and went to the notorious Bowery gambler, after I'd explicitly asked you to come to me first. You just don't give up, do you, my stubborn rebel?"

"I only wanted to be free," she murmured.

"By putting yourself in a cage? It's a worse indignity than your Southern slave block was, and most men think those girls are for sale to the highest bidder! How could you do it, Devon?"

"I did it for five nights!" she cried defiantly. "Where were you then, my gallant Yankee knight?"

"Washington. I just got back today. The operative had an interesting dossier on you. He knew you were one of the birds, but wasn't sure which, because of the mask. He didn't have the mouth experience I did."

The cab halted before a row of beautiful houses in Greenwich Village. They were brick, three stories high and recessed from the street by front gardens. The connecting galleries, trimmed with ornamental ironwork, recalled sketches Devon had seen of the Vieux Carré in New Orleans.

"Another of your conveniences, Mr. Curtis?" she asked sarcastically. "Your homes away from home!"

He got down wordlessly and paid the cabbie. When Devon refused his proffered hand, he inquired if she would prefer to be carried. She acquiesced, suffering his assistance up the walk to the door, where his key admitted them to a wainscoted hall lighted by gas wall-sconces. On one side was a pleasant parlor with a smoldering fire on the hearth, which he immediately rekindled, explaining, "I was here earlier this evening. Take off that mask, Devon, and sit down. I want to talk to you."

"I won't listen, Keith."

"You will listen, Devon! You've condemned me on circumstantial evidence, without benefit of trial or jury. Now I'm going to present my case, and I won't countenance any interruptions. I'll give you an exclusive story that James Gordon Bennett would gladly buy for his scandal-sheet. You can do as you wish with it, but you're going to hear it!"

She removed her cloak and her mask and sat down on the gold damask sofa. He gazed into her face a long moment, and then began his defense as earnestly and eloquently as if he were pleading in court, pacing before the bench, pausing occasionally to reflect or reiterate, grasping the mantel once to release tension on the wood. Devon remained obediently silent and attentive, compassion gradually overwhelming all other emotion, until at last he concluded, "That's all, everything . . . the whole rotten truth, so help me God."

"I—I don't know what to say, Keith."

"Just say you believe me, Devon."

"I do, Keith. I believe you."

"What're we going to do about it, then?"

She shook her head in bewilderment.

"I rented this place the day after we arrived from Washington," he said. "I waited a week, hoping you'd send a message to the bank. Then I went to the Astor House and found you'd gone, leaving only that cynical promissory note. I hired the Pinkerton Agency to find you. But I didn't have a photograph, so a portrait had to be drawn from description. It didn't do you justice, however, and the operative was working under a handicap. You were located shortly before you came to the house with Madame Joie, and have been under surveillance ever since."

"I never suspected until the Sunday Mally O'Neill and I went ice skating in Central Park, and then I thought it was just some culprit following us. Naturally you know about that."

"Yes, it's in the report. So are the receptions you attended at the Carys and the Bottas; you were followed home from both of them, and to and from the Gilded Cage. I also know you were marooned at the bookstore during the blizzard—the agent spent the night in the bar across the street. And since you left old Ephraim Joseph promptly thereafter, I assume you had good reason. Did he molest you?"

"He tried," she admitted. "I kept hoping you'd come back and rescue me."

"I was stranded at the bank, with a lobby full of employees and customers. Besides, you didn't give me much incentive to return when I was there earlier."

"I know, Keith, and I regretted it."

"Have you had enough of freedom and independence, Devon, and fending for yourself? Do you see now not only how foolish and futile it was, but hazardous? You've been flirting with danger. And will you continue running and making me chase you? Because I will, you know, from here to eternity." He waited, while she picked nervously at the tawny-gold feathers. "Answer me, Devon."

"You win, Keith. I can't fight you any longer. I don't even want to any more."

"At last," he sighed, pulling her to her feet. "Oh God, at last!"

"I feel silly in this costume," she said, half laughing, half crying.

"There's something more comfortable in the wardrobe."

"Oh?"

"Don't say 'oh' that way, as if you expect to find shopworn merchandise."

"Well, after all—"

"After all, nothing. Come on, I'll show you."

But in the bedroom she blew out the match he struck to light a lamp and slipped her arms around him. "You haven't even kissed me yet."

"I was afraid of ravishing you," he said. "It's been so damned long. How do you get out of this thing?"

"Hooks, on the left side. Careful, don't tear it."

"Help me!"

"Yes . . . oh, wait! I'll do it. Do yourself."

Somehow they were naked and in bed and embracing, and she was murmuring, "This isn't a dream, is it? I've had so many dreams! I love you, Keith, I love you . . . and sometimes I think this is all that matters . . . the only really important thing in life . . . to love and be loved. . . ." Then, "Now, darling, now!" And finally, "I've been chattering like a magpie, and you haven't said a word."

"I was busy."

Soft secret laughter, radiant afterglow, languid euphoria. How good it was to lie together in the warm sweet tender intimacy, touching, teasing, playing—a man and a woman in love, reciprocating and rejoicing in each other.

"So you were, lover. Did you miss me?"

"I've been a man with a problem for seven months."

"Don't lie to me about that, Keith."

"I've never lied to you about anything, Devon. It's true. I couldn't be unfaithful to you even when I tried. And I did try, most recently in Washington. I got the willing lady as far as my suite in the Clairmont, and couldn't go any further. I sent her away with embarrassed apologies—I'm sure she thought me either impotent or queer—and got morbidly drunk. I nursed a fiendish headache all the way back to New York, remembering that first night out of Richmond with my little virgin Rebel. That's how much you've spoiled me for anyone else."

"I think I loved you even then, Keith."

"How could you? I took ruthless advantage of your predicament, and perhaps I'm still taking advantage. But I wanted you from the moment I saw you and hoped to effect an alliance via the supper invitation, or bind you financially, if all else failed. Faulty reasoning, of course, and my biggest mistake. Love is the only true binder any person ever has on another, and then only if it's mutual. Is this place all right, Devon?"

"It's fine, Keith."

His hand lay on her breast, gently cupping. "It's only temporary, you know. Eventually we'll have a home together."

"Let's not talk about that now, darling."

"All right." He waited in the darkness. "Would you like to cruise the Hudson when the weather settles?"

"On a riverboat?"

"Yacht."

"Yours?"

"Yes."

"Is there anything you don't have, Mr. Curtis?"

"You, Miss Marshall."

"You have me too."

"Not the way I want you," he said.

Within an hour he reached for her again, and toward dawn she reached for him, whispering, "Could too much of this be harmful? How'll we know when to stop?"

He laughed. "Nature will stop us. Me, anyway."

"How?"

"Never mind, you'll find out."

"Tell me."

"Later, darling. Make love now, while it lasts."

Not until morning did Devon realize what a truly perfect rendezvous the house was, tastefully furnished and decorated, with all the conveniences and many luxuries. It was a place meant to be shared with a man. Obviously he had been using it as a personal retreat, for there were leisure clothes in the armoire, a desk and an easy chair and ottoman, ample supplies of food, liquor, and tobacco; there were books and journals and his inevitable portfolio.

"There are some mews for these apartments," he said, as they sat enjoying coffee before the fire. "Do you want to help pick out a carriage and horses, or leave it to me?"

The equipages of the kept women Janette Joie had pointed out in the carriage parade sprang instantly to mind. "I won't be going out that much, Keith, and I can use cabs. I'd need a driver and groom and—it's too much trouble and expense."

He smiled, unbeguiled. "I can afford it, Devon."

"I don't want a carriage, Keith, and that's the end of it! Nor do I want a maid or other servants."

"Very well, it's up to you, darling. I'll establish a checking account for you at the bank and credit at the shops and department stores of your choice. You can hire a laundress and charwoman as you need them."

She did not like discussing the financial arrangements, which seemed to her mercenary and even sordid. "I'm sure you know what to do," she murmured. "No doubt you've done it before."

"Not to this extent," he said. "Oh, I won't deny I've had some fleeting affairs, Devon. Nothing serious, though, and certainly none I wanted to stabilize or perpetuate. I had to go to Richmond to want that kind of commitment."

"And I had to come to New York."

"No regrets, I hope?"

"At first, but not any more."

"Then there was someone at home? I thought he was killed in the war?"

"No, he survived, if you could call his condition survival. And he wanted to marry me and live on his ruined plantation on the James River. I—I just didn't love him enough."

"I suppose he'd want to kill me, challenge me to duel?"

"Probably."

"And your father?"

She shrugged, eyes downcast. "I'm not sure. He didn't hold much with that kind of chivalry."

"Not even to defend his daughter's honor?"

"Perhaps, I don't know. He was idealistic but nonviolent. I wish you had known him, Keith."

"So do I, Devon." He watched her arrange the soft white satin folds of the negligee and the rosepoint ruffles at her throat and wrists. "Do you like that ensemble?"

"It's lovely, the sort of lingerie I used to model and sell at the boutique. Did you buy it there?"

"No, in Washington. It's been here for months. I was afraid I'd never see you in it. When I learned you'd gone to Donahue, I was furious. I'm not sure what I'd have done, Devon, if you hadn't come with me."

"I didn't go there to become a bird in a gilded cage, Keith. Mr. Donahue had previously asked me to tutor him, and he was assembling a libriary he wished me to index."

"Tutor him? That's ridiculous! And what does that moron want with a library? I doubt he got beyond the primer in school. He'll never make it as a gentleman, if that's his aim, any more than his mistress will make it as a lady. But if he had noble intentions toward you, how did you end up in a cage?"

Devon couldn't feel too superior to the other woman, whose position with the Bowery gambler was equal to hers with the Wall Street banker; if there was a difference, it was in the foundation of the relationship, not the structure. "Miss Day unwittingly hired me. She was ignorant of his offer, and I was afraid to enlighten her. I didn't have much choice, Keith. I couldn't stay on at the bookstore, and I needed a job. But Donahue never realized who I was, unless you told him."

"No, but I wondered why he called you Richmond."

"That's what Lilly and the girls called me. And Donahue never saw me out of costume and mask, although he did say my voice sounded familiar. I think he liked me."

"I know damn well he did! I had to apply pressure to make him release you from that cage."

"I have to return the costume, Keith. It's very expensive; they all are."

"You can return it by messenger, Devon, and then pick up your things at the Gothic Arms. You still have the Saratoga trunk?"

"Yes, and all the clothes. Do you still have the deeds you took as collateral?"

He grinned sheepishly. "Jesus, what a villain! I did everything but tie you to the railroad tracks. I was saving that for the last resort."

"A detective, even! All that worrying I did, thinking some fiend was after me."

"You had no business going out alone at night . . . and to those Bohemian affairs, yet."

"They were artistic and intellectual," she corrected indignantly. "I met many people in the arts. But they were all so much older and wiser, I felt like the proverbial babe in the woods. Some were characters too. Horace Greeley is peculiar, and P. T. Barnum is a clown. And Walt Whitman—" She hesitated, picking up her cup from the low rosewood table between them and sipping her coffee pensively.

"What about Whitman?"

"Well, he's brilliant but somewhat strange."

"Strange?"

"Odd. They say—"

"That he's homosexual? That rumor got started when he

was nursing soldiers in the Washington hospitals during the war. Seems he was fond of kissing them on the mouth. They gossip as much in the capital, if not more, than in New York, and there're muckraking journalists who deal in sensationalism. I read insinuations about Whitman's association with naturalist John Burroughs, and a certain handsome young horsecar conductor, a former Confederate corporal, on the Pennsylvania Avenue line."

"I pity him, then," Devon mused, "although I don't actually understand such things."

"You didn't suspect Janette Joie's interest in you?"

"No, she was so nice and kind to me, and spoke of a partnership in business. Then, Christmas, she gave me a great many expensive gifts and a book of Sappho's poems, as if she thought that would explain everything. But it didn't, really. The lyrics are beautiful and sensitive and tragic, and the preface says that she committed suicide by leaping off a rock into the Aegean Sea but not why she killed herself."

"My sweet innocent, she was a lesbian. That's how the word originated. Sappho of Lesbos. And when I saw Janette coveting you, I knew she was a Sappho too. I wondered where you'd go when you found it necessary to leave her employ."

"But she was married at fifteen, Keith, and she had many lovers, including a French count. They must all have disappointed and disillusioned her terribly to turn her so completely against men. Oh, I don't want to talk about it any more!" She stood. "Shall I cook breakfast?"

"Not just yet." Catching her hand, he drew her down on his lap. "There is something we have to discuss, Devon."

"Money? We've already discussed that, Keith!"

"Not money, my dear."

"What, then?"

"Contraception. Birth control. There are some other methods besides the one I've been using."

"Is that why you—?" She couldn't finish.

"Yes, of course. What did you think?"

"I couldn't imagine. I'm so ignorant, Keith."

"Naive, darling. Be quiet now and listen."

She nodded agreeably, for above all she feared pregnancy.

Chapter 16

By May the trees were in leaf, flowers and shrubs in bloom, and clusters of purple wisteria hung grapelike over Village walls and balustrades and courtyards.

Devon did everything she could to make the apartment cheery and inviting. Pots of greenery in the hall, hyacinths in the parlor, bright red geraniums in the kitchen. She bought some Currier & Ives prints, a beautiful hooked rug, charming bric-a-brac for the étagère. Quite the little homemaker, aren't you? her conscience chided. For someone else's husband!

When thus self-reproached she fled to the improvised study and scribbled busily on her manuscript, until her fingers ached and were numb with writer's cramp. If work did not silence the nagging voice, she went shopping for things she didn't need, telling herself how wonderful it was to be able to buy on impulse and fancy rather than necessity, to have almost anything she desired simply by chanting three magic words: "Charge it, please!" If the guilt still persisted, she strolled to pleasant Washington Square, once a grim potter's field and public hanging ground, with thousands of skeletons buried in its landscaped grounds. Wasn't it nice to have so much idle leisure, to sit alone on a bench and read, to watch old folks taking their constitutionals, and youngsters at play? Some came with nursemaids and governesses, from the row of stately red brick mansions with white marble doorways and iron-railed stoops on the north side of the square. From the Gothic-towered university on the east came students—bold young blades who pitched horseshoes, tossed balls, scuffled and teased one another, and ogled and flirted with the girls, their youthful blood full of spring sap.

She bought bouquets from the Italian flower women and a canary in a bamboo cage from a Chinese bird man. But it wouldn't sing while confined, so she let it fly free. One day it flew out a window and was caught by a sly tomcat. She wept at its fate, but would not accept a replacement from Keith, nor the dog he offered, either. She remembered too well the kept women who had brought their pets to La Boutique Chic—perfumed poodles and Pekingese and Pomeranians that looked as silken and pampered as their mistresses, and often as forlorn and lonely, too.

Farther west, on the bank of the Hudson, sprawled the great teeming Washington Market, which Keith likened to London's Covent Garden. She seldom shopped there, however, for vendors plied the Village streets from dawn to dusk, and she could make most of her food purchases at Rhinelander Gardens. Dairy wagons brought fresh milk, butter, cheese, eggs. Butchers in soiled ulsters hawked beef, fish, poultry. Vegetable and fruit peddlers trundled laden carts. Having no budget restrictions, Devon could afford out-of-season fruit and ice to make ades and frozen desserts. Quite the life of ease and luxury!

Sometimes she cooked supper for Keith and fixed breakfast when he spent the night. But he did not visit her every day, considering it unwise to establish routine habits; also, he had business and social obligations he could not expediently ignore or escape. And though he owned many carriages and horses, he generally used cabs with Devon lest one of his equipages be recognized. The consummate skill with which he managed the affair made her skeptical that she was his first mistress in the true sense of the relationship, but she wanted with all her heart to believe it and curbed her curiosity to question and probe.

Sometimes he took her to dinner and the theater, or some other amusement. She finally saw *The Black Crook,* which was still running at Niblo's Garden, and enjoyed the spectacular scenery and dancing of the prima ballerina, Maria Bonfanti. *Mazeppa,* staring the notorious Adah Isaacs Menken, was another current rage breaking attendance records. A superb equestrienne and acrobat, as well as an accomplished actress, her performance while strapped in flesh-colored tights simulating nudity to the back of a raring white horse in the dramatic version of Lord Byron's famous poem, eclipsed all previous theatrics. And since she was already known in Paris as one of

Alexandre Dumas' mistresses, and in London for her amorous escapades with some of the nobility, La Menken became the femme fatale of two continents.

"I wonder where she learned to ride like that," Devon marveled, sitting tensely on the edge of her seat.

"Not in Virginia," Keith responded.

Because she liked melodrama, he took her to see Charlotte Cushman as Nancy Sykes in *Oliver Twist*. Miss Cushman was considered the American counterpart of Adelaide Ristori, although critics familiar with the Italian tragedienne's repertoire proclaimed the comparison absurd and presumptuous.

As for *East Lynne*, at which Devon sighed and wept, Keith whispered, "Darling, it's only a play ... and hardly worthy of such emotion. Lucille Western is a trivial Lady Isabel, at best, and the whole thing is trash, actually."

"Why is it trash?" she challenged him over supper at Delmonico's afterwards. "Because it's about adultery?"

"Because it's sentimental garbage that purports to point a moral, just as the insipid novel that inspired it. But it makes women sob and mourn—and for some strange reason they love to languish in suds. Therefore, I predict that *East Lynne* will enjoy perennial popularity."

"That's cynical," she accused. "Perhaps you subconsciously resent the parallel in your own life—your faithless 'Lady Esther' and her paramour?" She had spoken impetuously, prompted by her own seething jealousy and resentment of his wife, and immediately regretted her pettiness. "I'm sorry, Keith."

"You need a better appreciation of the theater," he said. "Tomorrow we'll go to the Winter Garden for Edwin Booth's *Hamlet*."

Affronted, she retorted, "I appreciate good drama, and I've seen all the Booths perform. They appeared in Richmond during the war, for Preisdent Davis and his cabinet. I know that Mr. Booth went into temporary retirement after his brother assassinated President Lincoln, and I've read that the family tragedy has given him new insight and emotional intensity, so that he's an even greater Shakespearean actor now than before, on a par with Edwin Forrest and William Macready. Virginians are quite civilized, really. We never were backwoods barbarians.

Besides, the South didn't originate sentimental trivia and trash in books or plays—the North did, with *Uncle Tom's Cabin!*"

"All right, let's forget it. I don't want to fight that war again."

"You never fought it at all, did you?"

"I've already explained that to you, Devon. I helped to finance the goddamn thing, and I'm not going to apologize for giving my money instead of my life. Where are all your bloody heroes now? In hell, most of 'em!"

"Oh, Keith." She gazed across the candle flame, her eyes moist and tender, but his face was closed, dark and moody and faintly angry. "We're quarreling, and it's all my fault. I shouldn't have mentioned her name."

"It's not that, Devon." He was sipping some pale green liqueur that looked like liquid jade. "I suppose we have to talk about it sometime. I just wish you wouldn't be so tragic about us, you and me. You're Juliet and Isolde and Hester Prynne and every other hapless heroine in the books, and I think you anticipate an unhappy ending to this romance."

"Oh, now really!" She blushed deeply. "I'm not that dramatic, am I? Or maudlin? What's in that pretty stuff you're drinking? Maybe I should have some."

"It's chartreuse, and what you should have is more faith in love and your lover," he told her. "Shall I confess some of my fears? That one day you will leave me for someone or something else. I know you still have ambitions for a career, Devon."

"Well," she shrugged, "I have to do something with my time, Keith. The days can be awfully long."

"And the nights never long enough." Suddenly he reached for her hand. "Let's go home, darling."

Home, she thought wistfully. Once it had meant a fine old white Colonial house in Richmond, with ivy-hung chimneys and boxwoods at the door, roses on the garden gate and clematis on the fence, a scuppernong arbor and Albemarle pippin reaching to her dormer windows; her father and the *Sentinel* and a thousand other nostalgic memories. Now it meant a fancy new apartment in New York, on which a Yankee paid the rent and shared her bed at his convenience and contrivance.

A few days later they were watching the trotter races in Harlem and when Devon asked why he didn't participate in this popular sport, which seemed to engage so many wealthy and prominent men, he replied, "Oh, I used to, as eagerly and competitively as any of them. I had a curricle built in London and a pair of trotters even Commodore Vanderbilt's couldn't beat. Then the thing with Esther happened, and we spent so much time in travel, consulting doctors here and abroad, and I was so involved with business otherwise, practically commuting to Washington, racing seemed a frivolous and expendable hobby. But I know the Virginian passion for horses, and if you'd like to ride in the park, it's easy enough to rent a mount."

"Will you ride with me?"

"Of course."

"When, Keith?"

"Soon."

"Tomorrow?"

"If I can get away from the bank."

Devon knew the Carys and the Bottas still held their literary teas and receptions; she read about them in the *Ledger* and felt she would be welcome, but they were evening affairs and she could not attend. This did not bother her, except when she read about some social event Keith had attended, or hosted in his home, for although Mrs. Curtis seldom left Gramercy Park in her wheelchair, she did occasionally entertain and have out-of-town guests, and Keith was expected to play his part. Devon's sympathy for the woman had vanished in her knowledge of the circumstances of her invalidism, and the unfair and even vicious advantage she took of her husband, the tenacious octopus-hold she kept on him—particularly since none of the specialists could determine either the cause of her paralysis or a cure for it. Still, it was inconceivable that a sane and healthy person would engage in such a long and morbid pretense out of revenge, and it all seemed terribly perplexing and immoral and hopeless.

When several days passed without a visit from Keith, Devon was sick herself with worry, senseless suspicions, and even fear. She walked the floor, unable to write or read or rest at night. She did not dare leave the place, lest he come in her absence, nor try to contact him lest the message go astray.

The clock had just struck two in the morning, and she was still awake, tossing and fretting, when she heard his key in the lock. She pretended to be asleep, but when he bent to kiss her, with champagne on his breath and Paris perfume on his clothes, her tensions suddenly snapped, and she demanded furiously, "Where have you been?"

Her outburst startled him enough to straighten and peer at her. "Did you forget? I told you the Belmonts were honoring an officer from the London branch of Rothschild. Every banker from Boston to Washington was there. Naturally, I had to represent my interests."

"It was a ball?"

"Yes."

He removed his swallowtail coat, hung it on the valet and began untying his white tie. She watched him in the ray of light from the hall sconce, tormented with love and longing, jealousy and frustration. "Well, I hope you had fun drinking and dancing!"

"I thought of you the whole time."

"Oh, sure." She was fighting tears with fury, loneliness with accusations. "You smell as if you'd been in a French boudoir or bordello!"

"Expensive scent clings," he said. "Don't you feel well, Devon? Would you rather I left?"

"After I've waited four nights!"

"Three, and I've waited too, you know."

"Have you, Keith?"

"Now, Devon, you know damn well—"

"I'm sorry, I'm sorry." She extended apologetic arms to him. "Come to bed, darling. Oh, please, come to bed!"

She was frantic in her embrace, her desire transcending his, driving him wildly, and while he exulted in her passion, he exhausted himself. When at last she was sated, he was spent in his own lust and violence. Still she clung to him, as if he were trying to escape, reveling as much in his climax as her own. She liked to think no other woman could possibly give him such intense, vital pleasure, nor any other man so excite and satisfy her. As always she stroked his back until his orgasmic tremors subsided, dreading the inevitable separation. Finally, he raised his head from her breast.

"My God, darling, what got into you besides me?"

"Was I wanton?"

"No, of course not. It was wonderful, like that night in Washington when I first knew you loved me. But I was worried for awhile, afraid I might be too old for you. I'm almost thirty-two, you know."

"Oh, and that's ancient, isn't it? How do you get around without a cane?"

He laughed, ruffling her curls. "I think I drank a mite too much tonight. As Macbeth said of alcohol, 'It provokes the desire but takes away the performance.' No doubt Shakespeare experienced a few such anxieties himself."

"It was a marvelous performance, lover. One of your best. Oh, Keith, I love you so much, and miss you so terribly when you're away! Did you really think of me at the ball?"

"Constantly, and I kept wishing you were with me. There wasn't a lady there to hold a candle to you for beauty, grace, or charm. Some were ugly and boring, in fact, and clumsy as cows."

"But still you danced with them?"

"It was a ball, Devon."

"Did they flirt with you?"

"Well, there were a few coquettes."

"There always are! And a few cocottes too?"

He kissed her petulant mouth. "Don't worry, I didn't make any assignations. Good night, my love."

"Keith . . . when are we going on the cruise?"

"Next week, perhaps, if the weather holds. Now go to sleep, darling. I'm wasted."

Chapter 17

Devon was in a flurry of preparation, consulting *Godey's Lady's Book* and *Demorest's Mirror of Fashions* for the current vogues. The experts recommended travel suits of gray and blue poplin, strolling dresses of English hound's tooth, buff nankeen, and tissue wools; tea gowns of watered silk and shantung; evening costumes of satin, peau de soie, chiffon. A cashmere shawl, a natural linen polonaise, a romantic lace mantilla for moonlight nights on shipboard. Colored leather walking boots, white sailcloth shoes, silver and gold kid dance slippers, exquisite lingerie, and accessories—she bought so much she needed another Saratoga trunk to accommodate it all. Her shopping expeditions were agonies of indecision, but she had to be correct, for Keith was very discriminating about her wardrobe; he associated with fasionable women and knew the difference between style and fad, chic and gauche. Consequently, she bought nothing she did not instinctively feel he would approve, and he would know how knowledgeable she was in the world of fashion when he got the bills.

She had seen his yacht, the *Sprite*, from shore—a sleek green-and-white vessel berthed in the North River—and could hardly wait to go aboard. Keith introduced her to the captain, Dolph Bowers, a tall bearded man with a prow-sharp nose, shark-keen eyes and barnacled skin that added ten years to his forty. A retired naval officer, Bowers had seen action on a Union gunboat. The crew were also former sailors, as easy to obtain in the harbor as army veterans on the streets, most of whom were idle and indigent since the war. Rufus Brady had come aboard earlier, as familiar with the Curtis yacht as the railcar, and as efficient on water as on land.

For Devon it was a maiden voyage. Although she had

lived on a navigable river and port, she had never been on a craft larger than a plantation barge or finer than a rowboat. Her father had traveled by steamer to Hampton Roads, Charleston, and Savannah, but the war had spoiled the Chesapeake cruise he had so long promised her. The *Sprite*'s smokestacks told her she was steam-powered, but there were no visible paddlewheels or sailing canvas on the masts, only the United States flag fluttering in the June breeze, and Keith's own colorful standard.

"How does it move?" she asked curiously.

"Screw propeller. That's the modern method. Most transatlantic steamers are being built that way now. Paddlewheels will eventually pass from the scene. We'll be casting off in a few minutes. Let me show you around."

The comfort and luxury exceeded her expectations, from the finely appointed dining and lounge salons, to the ten well-fitted cabins, and sumptuous master stateroom. The walls were paneled in Honduras mahogany with striking touches of white holly and silver hardware. The richly carved oak furniture included a fine old Spanish cabinet from a conquistador ship, a heavy brass-studded sea chest once used to store a buccaneer's booty, and a unique teakwood and ebony desk acquired at a salvage auction of sunken treasure. A tapestry lambrequin decorated the large double berth in Keith's quarters, and the chairs were covered in leather or tapestry. Bronze brackets supported converted whaler lamps, and the deep soft green carpet invited bare feet.

"Oh, Keith, it's beautiful! A royal yacht couldn't be finer. I hope we sail forever."

He smiled. "Be careful of your wishes, my dear. That's supposedly what happened to the *Flying Dutchman*, you know."

"That's just a legend, isn't it?"

"Not to superstitious sailors. Ask any who's sailed the Cape of Good Hope, and he'll swear he saw the phantom ship and her mad captain at the helm."

Devon put her arms around him. "I wouldn't care, as long as we were together."

"Well, I hope eternity isn't the only way for us, Devon. Oh, God, if only she'd get well! Get out of that wheelchair and walk again!"

The *Sprite* was moving upstream, into the Hudson channel. They parted and now Devon stood at a porthole, gazing out. "Why do you torture yourself, Keith? You know it's hopeless, and she wouldn't divorce you even if she were well, would she?"

"Probably not," he grimly agreed. "Surely not without a hellish court battle, and you'd be dragged into it. Sometimes I think her mind is affected. She got a slight concussion in the fall . . . perhaps it damaged her brain. The physicians say not, but they don't know everything, either. Only Esther knows the truth, and she's not revealing it. Like icebergs that wreck ships, ninety percent of her danger is submerged."

He was treading the stateroom with scowling face and clenched fists, in one of the dark restless desperate moods she had come to dread, always afraid that some inadvertent provocation would trigger the violence that seemed to lie just beneath the surface, suppressed but not dormant. The prospect of its ultimate release both terrified and intrigued her. And there were times, she knew, when he used tobacco, liquor, and lovemaking in restraint as much as indulgence.

She went to him. "Relax, Keith. This is supposed to be a pleasure cruise, remember, with problems and worries left behind. I'm anxious to see the scenery—the mountains and the great river estates you said were like castles on the Rhine."

"They're a long way upstream. The Palisades are the first interesting sight you'll see." He smiled wryly, taking her arm. "We may as well go topside. I had other ideas when I brought you in here, but the witch spoiled them. She was born in Boston, but I think she had ancestors in Salem."

Rufus had set up canvas chairs and tables under a striped deck awning and brought drinks, trays of delicacies, and binoculars for Devon to better enjoy the picturesque stone cliffs along the New Jersey shore. She was wearing a smart blue faille suit, with a red silk scarf knotted under the white pique sailor collar. Keith lounged beside her in white duck trousers, nautical brass-button jacket, and billed seacap, smoking and sipping Scotch on crushed ice, while she drank lemonade and sampled the canapes which he ignored.

The Hudson bristled with commercial and pleasure craft, and Devon remarked on it.

"New York is the largest port in the country," Keith said.

"Really?"

"Yes, really. Did you think Charleston was the biggest, or Norfolk, or New Orleans?"

"Well, I remember that Grant said whoever controlled the Mississippi would win the war, and he fought like a demon to take Vicksburg."

"Had the situation been reversed, he'd have fought just as fiendishly to take the Hudson, because it connects via the Erie Canal with the Great Lakes."

"It is a tremendous river," she acknowledged.

"On behalf of the Chamber of Commerce, I thank you."

"Is it always so busy?"

"Busier in spring and summer, perhaps, but never idle at any season, even when frozen over. Ice is the winter crop of the Hudson Valley, and its harvesting and storage is a major industry. Farmers and villagers work with the city crews, cutting and transporting the slabs to the barns along the riverbanks, where it's preserved in straw until warm weather. Valley ice is cooling your lemonade and my whisky now, and there's ice cream in the galley packed in it."

"And so the owners of the cutters and warehouses make fortunes every year off a commodity provided by nature and therefore in the public domain," Devon said. "That's smart business, I suppose?"

"Hell, yes! The same thing is done with timber, ore, coal, salt, sulphur, marble, granite—hundreds of natural products belonging to the universe, but also quite useless to humanity in their raw states. They have to be processed to be exploited, and this is expensive. The enterprisers not only deserve a fair profit on their investments but could not exist without it. For instance, I have petroleum interests in Pennsylvania, which are worthless in the ground. It costs money to drill wells to extract it, but the real gold is in processing the crude into commercial products—oil, kerosene, paraffin, drugs, chemicals, which is why I also invested in a refinery." He paused and grinned at her. "Trees do not grow naturally into houses, my dear. I never heard of a sheep spinning wool, a cotton bush weaving cloth, a wheat field bearing flour, a cane patch blooming sugar and molasses, and not even in Virginia do tobacco plants produce readymade cigars."

"I know all that," she protested, feeling like a naive child receiving her first lesson in economics. "Why do men always assume women have no business sense?"

"Because most of them haven't," he said. "You are the rare exception . . . and you spend money so wisely, too. How many trunks did you bring along for one week, half of which you'll spend in bed?"

"Hush," she whispered. "Rufus will hear you."

"You don't think he suspects?" Keith laughed. "My precious pet, joy and light of my life—what would I do without you! Pray God I never have to find out."

Devon determined to endure his jesting and teasing gracefully, as long as it relaxed him and jettisoned some of the cares he had brought aboard. If her naivete amused him, she would oblige; and if it pleased him to consider her a pretty pet, she would play that role too though it rubbed her mentality the wrong way. He needed a buffer, a sounding board, a receptacle, and she would accommodate him. Be anything, do anything, to bring him pleasure and happiness these seven days, ease his tensions and indulge his desires, soothe and solace and succor him . . . and make him as dependent on her for these human essentials as she was on him for the exigencies of life. According to the feminists, true feminine wisdom and freedom lay in manipulating the almighty male without his knowledge or realization of the fact. But there was more than selfish expediency in her manipulation now; she was also acutely aware that this brief interlude on the green-and-white floating island might be as close to Paradise as she would ever come with Keith. Only a stupid fool would mar or jeopardize it.

They left the country estates of Yonkers, the Revolutionary ramparts of Fort Tryon, the rocky ledges of Inwood behind. Soon Manhattan Island itself receded and, hopefully, the dilemma in Gramercy Park. Now they were approaching Tarrytown, and Keith sketched a brief history as they passed the lighthouse. Like a good reporter, Devon had briefed herself with available information on the subject beforehand, only to discover as usual that imagery fell short of reality. For then the river widened into the vast Tappan Zee, the shores shrinking away, the horizon a distant blur. More and more vessels appeared on the wide blue water, and suddenly she focused her binoculars on the aft deck of a drab gray steamer, where several men in black-and-white striped uniforms leaned against the bulwark, staring hopelessly into the river. They were chained together, hands and legs bound in irons, two armed guards keeping watch.

"Convicts," Keith said, "bound for Sing Sing Prison. Look toward the east bank, you'll see it."

Glimpsing the formidable walls, the granite for which the prisoners themselves had quarried, Devon sighed. "Poor souls! All this magnificent scenery, and they can't enjoy it. I hope they're not going to be executed?"

"Possibly. That's the state penitentiary."

"I think it's barbarian and medieval, hanging or shooting people, no matter the crime."

"Capital punishment? Oh, I don't know. I think I'd prefer death to life imprisonment. It's hard to imagine worse torture than permanent confinement in a cell."

Even if the cell is a bedroom, Devon thought, all silk-and-satin luxury and comfort, master paintings on the walls and a view of an exclusive park, but still seclusion and confinement—a prison without bars or locks. Don't, she told herself. You can't think of her now, it'll spoil the trip. But why did she keep intruding, haunting them that way, as if she really was a witch!

She tried to sublimate her mind in the elevations on the western horizon. A breeze whipped the flags on the mast, making their shadows dance macabrely on deck . . . and suddenly Esther was between them again, a specter of which both were conscious but neither would acknowledge.

Her spirit hovered through Haverstraw Bay and around Peekskill Bend, past Iona Island and Fort Montgomery and Highland Falls. Devon was tense and wary of any reference that might materialize her, give her vitality and power to diminish their pleasure and destroy their happiness. The brooding cynicism she had seen in the master stateroom darkened Keith's face again, and his smoky eyes pondered a massive complex of fortified buildings and stone walls off the port bow.

"That's West Point, Devon, established before the Revolution, and the site of the United States Military Academy since just after the turn of the century. Of course you know General Lee and some of your other Southern officers were trained there."

Immediately nostalgia flooded and threatened to inundate her. General Lee had been a familiar figure in Richmond during the war, riding in from the peninsula by train or on his famous gray horse, Traveller, to confer with President Davis and the cabinet, or attend some public function where his presence was necessary to boost civilian morale. Every schoolchild could recognize his finely caparisoned mount, and young boys would run alongside their hero in the street, begging to enlist and return to the front with him. His arrival always incited rumor and speculation. If he appeared confident, hope soared; if he seemed troubled, there was despair. He was idolized and lionized by the people, and hounded by the press. For everyone, especially Jefferson Davis, knew that the fate of the Confederacy hung on Robert E. Lee. If the Army of Virginia perished, the South would perish with it.

"Oh, yes," she answered dolefully. "The North never let us forget that. Your papers did their best to make our West Point men seem like traitors."

"And so they were, my dear, technically and morally."

Devon refused that gauntlet, turning her attention instead to the grandeur of the Hudson highlands. Rising hundreds of feet above the river the granite cliffs, so sheer even the eagles had difficulty building nests, blocked the sun and cast dense shade on the water. And crowning the crests were mansions of majestic design and dimension: a Tudor palace of terra cotta sandstone; a gray stucco Gothic manor, turreted and towered; a white marble-pillared Italian villa rambling among dark green trees, its landscaped walls hanging like the gardens of Babylon; a French chateau of spired bluestone.

"Oh, you were right, Keith! There are castles on the Hudson! Do people actually live in them?"

"Yes, indeed. Some of the river estates were Dutch baronies. The bank holds the mortgage on one, in fact . . . and if the heirs don't recoup the loan, I'll own a decaying castle on the Hudson myself. It's vacant now and most of the land has been sold to the tenant farmers who worked it under the patroon system."

"Does it have a name?"

"Tulipwyck, which means 'place of the tulips' in Dutch. The patroon had brought thousands of the bulbs from Holland, and the garden was one of the botanical wonders and delights of the region, but it's in ruin now. Like some of your once grand plantations—that's what happens, you know, when a culture fails. War doomed slavery, and law abolished patroon manorialism, which was almost the same thing."

"Could I see Tulipwyck, Keith?"

"Of course, if you don't mind dust and cobwebs. But it's farther upriver, near Kingston. I'll show it to you tomorrow."

Evening was drifting down from the mountains and settling over the river like a pale blue mist when they went in to supper, an excellent meal prepared under Rufus' supervision, and Devon learned that the black man had received his culinary training under the chef of the Astor House. Captain Bowers, dining with them, began recounting one of his wartime gunboat experiences when Keith interrupted, "Miss Marshall is a Virginian, Dolph."

"Oh? You don't say. Great state, Virginia . . . and none had braver men. Nowhere was the blockade harder to enforce than on the Chesapeake and James."

"Bowers has salt water in his veins," Keith told Devon later. "He was born on Nantucket Island, the grandson of a whaler. His father saw service against the Barbary pirates and was with Commander Perry in the Battle of Lake Erie. He's a damn fine pilot, and his retirement is the navy's loss and my gain. I never worry with him at the wheel."

Devon only wondered how many Confederate ships the man had destroyed, how much contraband he had seized in peninsula waters, and how much desperately needed cargo he had prevented from reaching Richmond. "I'm sure he's very competent," she said, brushing her hair at the dressing table. "And he was obviously embarrassed and disappointed when you mentioned my background. No doubt he had some exciting stories to tell. Did he perhaps witness the battle between the Monitor and the Merrimac, at Hampton Roads?" She remembered the *Sen-*

tinel's account of that singular event, the first clash of ironclads in the history of naval warfare.

"As a matter of fact, he did, but it was all in the line of duty, Devon."

"I know, Keith, and I'm sorry I can't appreciate his accomplishments and provide a proper audience for him. I wonder what he really thinks of me?"

Keith was having a nightcap. "That you're lovely and charming . . . what should he think? As for the crew, even that one-eyed sailor can see how we feel about each other. They all admire you and envy me."

Suddenly she asked, "Is the *Sprite* seaworthy, Keith? I mean, could she cross the ocean?"

"Easily, in fair weather, but no ship is guaranteed safe in a storm. We'll go downcoast this summer—to Charleston, if you like, and Savannah."

"And upcoast to Newport and Boston?"

"Not Boston," he said gravely, as if even Esther's birthplace aggrieved and embittered him. "I go there on business sometimes, but never pleasure."

Did it still hurt to remember? If so, perhaps he was still subconsciously in love with her. If not, why was he pouring another drink?

Devon's eyes focused on a vivid landscape, one of several in the stateroom, and hoping to divert him from the bottle, she said, "That's a beautiful scene. Who is the artist?"

"Thomas Cole, of the Hudson River School. He also did the mural in the dining salon. Some of his other regional paintings decorate the cabins, and there are some Durands, too."

"I met an artist at the Cary sisters' reception," Devon reflected. "I think his name was Mallard."

"What?"

"I met an—"

"No, the name!"

"Mallard, I believe."

"Giles Mallard? Tow-headed fellow, Nordic type?"

"Why yes, he has light hair and blue eyes."

"He's the one," Keith said grimly.

"The one?"

"Her lover! I told you he was an artist, didn't I?"

"Yes, but not his name."

"Well, it was Giles Mallard."

"My God," Devon murmured, rising from the table. "He was sketching in the Gilded Cage the night you came in, Keith. You didn't see him?"

"No, I wasn't looking for anyone but you. I had no idea he was still in New York. I imagined and rather hoped the bastard had starved in an attic somewhere—he's not much of a painter." Pausing to replenish his glass, "How well do *you* know him, my dear?"

"Oh, really Keith! We talked only a few minutes, and he was somewhat in his cups—not from the Cary punch but, I suspect, his hip-flask. He was morose and philosophic, muttering something about having many loves but loving only once. I don't remember, exactly, but he's probably still in love with her."

"The sonofabitch," he muttered. "I should've killed him, killed them both and pleaded the unwritten law."

"Don't talk that way, Keith."

"Why not? At least I'd be free."

"Would you, with murder on your conscience?"

"I had the right—"

"No," she shook her head vehemently. "Nobody has that right, Keith, no matter the reasons."

"What about war killing?" he asked sardonically. "Didn't the Rebs worship their military heroes and kiss the Yankee blood off their hands! 'I could not love thee, dear, so much loved I not honor more?' Is that how they rationalized their treason and other crimes?"

"There's no comparison," she replied, gazing pensively at the river. The *Sprite* lay at anchor for the night, in the shadows of the awesome cliffs, the water shimmering mercurially in the moonlight, so that they seemed to be moored in a chasm of quicksilver. "Don't drink any more tonight, Keith. Please."

"I'm sorry I'm such a macabre boor," he drawled.

"I didn't say that, and you're not. But I worry when you brood like this. I'm afraid you'll do something desperate."

"Banish the fear, my love. I should have acted when I found them together. It's too late now. It would be homicide, and I could hang for it." Draining the glass he flung it furiously through an open porthole. Devon saw it splash and sink in the water. "What the hell! Let's hit the bunk—"

He used her brutally at first, suggesting some indomitable anger and frustration within himself, but then he grew tender and humble, nuzzling his face in her breast and chanting a litany of love and contrition and dark despair, and she cradled and rocked him in her arms like a baby.

"Raptures of the deep," he murmured. "You know what happens to a diver who descends too deep in the sea? He goes into narcosis, the bends, and loses consciousness. Love is a form of narcosis too, I think, and a man can lose himself in the raptures of a woman's body."

"And she in his," Devon said. "That's what happens to me with you, Keith. It's some kind of enchantment and exquisite torture and ... Oh, darling, don't ever frighten me that way again! I don't think I could live without you. I think I'd just waste away without these periodic infusions of love and life—"

"Life? I wish I could do that, Devon . . . plant a new life in you. I wish we didn't have to take all these goddamn precautions! I die a little every time I pull out. . . ."

When at last he slept, she was still awake, listening to the river sounds and watching the lighted silhouettes pass the portholes: night passenger steamers to and from Albany, cattle to the Yonkers slaughterhouses, fruit and vegetables from Cornwall-on-Hudson for the Manhattan and Brooklyn markets, Great Lakes and St. Lawrence River and Canadian freight to the Battery. Paddlewheels churned and engines puffed and horns and whistles blew all night. And at dawn, when the sky was faintly pink above the gray cliffs, the banked boilers were restoked, and the *Sprite* steamed northward again.

Most of the large river estates had private landings, and Captain Bowers knew Tulipwyck's from previous trips.

Keith and Devon went ashore, climbing the long stone steps hewn into the precipitous west bank, pausing on the various ledges to rest and view the river, which diminished with ascent, until the yacht looked like a white toy boat on a green brook, while the mansion grew more massive and imposing. Reaching the pinnacle, Devon could only gasp and stare.

Tons of gray granite slabs formed Gothic wings and gables under mansard roofs, the walls rising three and four stories in the towers and cupolas, out of a forest of chimneys. The gardens, where once thousands of brilliant tulips had bloomed in spring, were rank with weeds; saplings sprouted under the arches and colonnades, the fountains and ponds were choked with leaves and debris, and the marble statuary and urns were covered with lichen and vines. A summer pavilion, its decaying columns entwined in ivy and crimson ramblers, crowned a promontory commanding a spectacular view of the countryside, including the misty-blue mountains in the west. And though a decade of vacancy and neglect had ravaged the grounds, it had scarcely affected the century-old manor which, built like a citadel to withstand the onslaught of time, had only accumulated an enhancing greenish-black patina of mildew and moss.

Awed, Devon whispered, "Do you think we could go inside?"

"You needn't whisper, darling. No one but the ghosts can hear us. And we're not trespassers—I'll likely be master of this monstrosity someday. Yes, I brought a key along. I thought you might be interested."

There were thirty enormous rooms, some the size of banquet halls, with columns and vaulted ceilings. The covered furniture, gray with dust, sat spectrally in the shadows. Spiders had spun floss about the chandeliers and sconces, across the corners and stairways and hearths. Dust motes floated in the sunlight filtering through the mullioned windows and stained glass panels. But the musty dampness had a sepulchral chill, and the silence was overwhelming and spellbinding.

"Does it intrigue your literary instincts, darling?"

"It scares the chemise off me! I wouldn't want to explore it alone. What a great ego the builder must've had! And the patroons deserved their fate. They were mortals living like gods."

"That's what some people thought about your planters."

"Well, they've been deposed."

"Some of the Hudson River deities still reign, however. To them, these elevations are Olympus. And if you ever witnessed a storm in the Catskills, you'd think you were somewhere between heaven and hell." He paused and looked at her seriously. "Would you like to live here, Devon? If you find it inspirational, I'll line a tower with ivory."

"Oh, I don't think so, Keith! All this solitude and loneliness . . . I might go mad."

"One of the mistresses of Tulipwyck did, according to legend, and took her own life . . . that wing is supposedly haunted. Romantic lore, of course, like Washington Irving's headless horseman and other fantasies of the Catskills. It has always been fashionable for a great house to have a ghost in residence, you know. Travelers will cross oceans to guest in one reputed to possess a spirit . . . and Southern plantation manors reportedly abound in them."

Their voices echoing in the halls and stairwells, and their footsteps resounding on the marble and tiled floors gave Devon an eerie feeling, as if they were not alone, and she began to whisper again. "It's spooky in here, Keith."

"Wait until you hear the squirrels in the attic and birds in the chimneys," he grinned. "I spent a night when I came up to appraise the loan value of the property. An owl outside the windows of the room I used kept hooting and there was a loon cackling atop the tower. After listening to them for hours, damned if it didn't sound like a hysterical woman laughing or crying, or both. Then a storm blew up and—well, I didn't get too much sleep."

"And you wonder if I'd like to live in this mausoleum?"

"I didn't mean alone."

Devon was immeasurably relieved when they walked out into the warm bright sunlight again. "I'm glad we came, though," she said. "I'm enjoying everything, Keith."

"Are you, darling?" He took her hand as they started down the precarious stairs. "For God's sake, be careful," he warned, and she saw somber anxiety cross his brow— the shadow of memory, the recurring horror of the fall that haunted him.

Chapter 18

Captain and crew were at liberty in Albany, while Keith and Devon entrained to Saratoga. Devon's only previous experience at a spa was during her ninth summer, when she had traveled with her parents to Hot Springs, Virginia. It hadn't been much fun, however, for a regiment of mammies had ridden herd on the youngsters while their elders had taken the waters, which smelled and tasted unpleasantly like their spring tonics of sulphur and molasses. The trip was memorable in later years only because it was the first time she had seen Robert E. Lee, who had brought the rheumatic Mrs. Lee there with her wheelchair and crutches strapped atop their coach.

Ironically, Keith Curtis had once brought his ailing wife to Saratoga Springs under similar conditions, trailing a retinue of attendants, including two maids, a footman, a nurse, and an eminent Boston physician. The entourage had occupied ten rooms at the United States Hotel, while the patient was daily bathed in a private stall at the Congress Spring bathhouse, and consumed gallons of the famous mineral waters purported to cure or alleviate many rare maladies and infirmities, but to no avail. The saline content had affected her adversely, as both emetic and cathartic, producing simultaneous retching and purging, and she had merely grown weaker, paler, thinner. She had been a wan wraith, still immobile, when finally the doctor had decided to halt the aquatherapy.

Unaware of all this, Devon was blissfully happy just sharing an uninterrupted rendezvous with Keith. He engaged a luxurious suite at the Grand Union Hotel, a massive array of towers, verandas and pavilions, grander by far than Hot Springs' Homestead and its humble cabins and cottages. This resort, quite obviously, was as much concerned with pleasure as health.

The horseracing season did not begin until August, but the casinos were open, and gamblers crowded around the roulette wheels and faro boxes, the poker and whist and dice tables. Keith, attentive as a bridegroom, did not indulge himself, for ladies were barred from the gaming rooms. When Devon assured him he could play if he wished, and she would entertain herself a few hours, he said, "I didn't bring you here to amuse yourself, darling. Besides, I do enough gambling at my clubs."

They went sightseeing in a brightly-painted hotel omnibus with a fringed top, and to High Rock Spring to drink the efficacious waters that bubbled out of a huge cone-shaped stone. They cantered on the bridal paths in the foothills of the Adirondacks, now fringed with wild flowers, Devon looking fashionably British in a black-and-white habit and veiled postilion, gracefully sidesaddled. Complimenting her equestrian ability, Keith asked how she had learned, and if she had ridden to hounds.

"Riding was required curriculum in every girls' school in Virginia," she said. "Presumably they would all fox-hunt, eventually. And I did a couple of seasons at Harmony Hill, when it was the finest plantation in the Tidewater."

"And except for the war and me, you'd be mistress of it now, wouldn't you?"

"Probably," she nodded.

"Well, I'm mighty glad I happened along when I did."

In a hired pony trap he drove her through the pungent pines, which reminded Devon of the forests of the Blue Ridge and the Shenandoah, to Saratoga Lake, where he rowed her romantically in a Seneca Indian canoe. The picnic basket prepared by the hotel kitchen contained cold turkey and Westphalian ham, Dutch cheese wedges, French pastries, the crisp fried potato curls called Saratoga chips, and a bottle of vintage wine.

In the evenings they dined and danced in the magnificent ballroom, slept late, and enjoyed breakfast in bed. The allotted time passed all too swiftly, and Devon was sad at the thought of leaving. Lounging in the pavilion one afternoon, watching other guests stroll in the gardens, she overheard a young couple talking about Niagara Falls, where they had spent their honeymoon. Devon asked

Keith if he had ever been there. He nodded, knocking the ash from his cheroot.

"Is it as marvelous as they say?"

"It's something to see, all right. But it's several hundred miles west of here, on the Canadian border, and a mean trip by rail and stage. When we make it, I'd prefer to go in the comfort of my coach."

Sunlight sparkled on the crystal fountains, and masses of white lilies, pink peonies, and blue delphinium banked the walls. "It's so beautiful here, Keith. I wish we could stay forever."

His mouth contrived a smile, while his eyes brooded over her, as they frequently did. "A few days ago you wanted to sail forever."

What she wanted was more than this brief interlude, this pretense at marriage, these few days of happiness and joy drawing inexorably to an end. What she wanted was to be together, always, no matter where or how. Didn't he understand that? Didn't he realize how completely, desperately, eternally she loved him? And didn't he feel the same way?

"You sound amused, Keith. Am I being naive again?"

"Romantic and idealistic. Nothing lasts forever, Devon."

"Not even love?"

"It's a human emotion, therefore mortal."

"That's cynical," she accused.

"Realitsic. I've experienced its mortality, remember."

"And you can't forget it, can you?"

"Not when you keep reminding me."

"I'm sorry," she murmured. "But why can't we stay here longer, Keith?"

"Captain Bowers is expecting us back in Albany tomorrow," he said. "Besides, there's a place in the Catskills I want to show you. It's called the Mountain House, and I tihnk you'll like it as much as this, darling."

"I believe I've read some of Washington Irving's and Harriet Martineau's writings about it," she said. "Oh yes, I'm sure I'll like it, Keith!"

The *Sprite* docked at Catskill-on-Hudson, and they boarded the Mountain House stage, along with some steamboat passengers from New York.

It was a long rough ride in the heavy Concord coach,

trailed by the baggage wagon, but the scenery was so spectacular, so wondrous and breathtaking, the occupants
hardly noticed the physical discomforts, and even those
who had seen it before were silent except for exclamations
of admiration or awe. They rumbled over rustic bridges,
through columns of timber giants' embracing limbs, across
sunny meadows where sleek cattle lazily grazed. Waterfalls
frothed out of hills into foaming streams. Misty-blue
ridges limned the sky; cresting one was a barely visible
white structure, which someone said was their destination.
They came to a peaceful plateau and a half-way tavern,
whose sign told Devon she was in the fabled Rip Van
Winkle country.

The stage climbed precariously on the spiral road, lurch-
ing and bouncing and swaying in the ruts of the narrow
path hewn into the mountainside. Devon glimpsed an
abysmal gorge below and knew a misstep of the horses, a
skidding wheel, or sliding rock could plunge them into
eternity. Apprehensively, under her reticule, her hand
sought Keith's, and he pressed it reassuringly. They rounded another bend, and suddenly the Greek-pillared building appeared, as startling as a temple in the clouds, and
she knew why he had saved it for the finale of their holiday.

They alighted at the rear of the hotel, where crews of
uniformed porters and maids waited, along with the genial
host, to welcome them. And soon Keith was ushering her
through the long central corridor to the Corinthian-
columned piazza for the view of the Hudson River Valley
that had made the Catskill resort famous abroad and
enticed as many travelers to America as had the great falls
on the Niagara. Devon gasped, speechless, and clung even
harder to his hand than she had in the stage.

"Well?" he prompted, "was it worth it?" She could only
nod mutely, and stare. "That weaving trace down there is
the road we just traveled. That toy village in the distance
is Catskill, where we landed, and that strip of shimmering
quicksilver is the Hudson. It's eight miles away, now."

Directly below the hotel, which rested on a twenty-five
hundred-foot rock ledge, were twin lakes, placidly blue,
and deep green forests and white cascades. The farms and
fields, orchards and vales and hedgerows created a patch-
work design that seemed to have originated in Genesis.

And hazily etched on the horizon, as if conceived in the mist and smoke of infinity, lay the Berkshire Hills of Massachusetts and Connecticut.

"It's like being in heaven," Devon whispered, "looking down on earth. And to think, God sees this sight every day."

Keith smiled. "He created it, darling."

"I want to see it at sunrise, Keith, and sunset."

"They're rituals here, Devon. Everybody watches in the evening, and rises early no matter how late in retiring. Tomorrow we'll explore some of the trails—there're miles of them. But now I think our rooms are ready. We'll dress for dinner, of course."

Her gown was shell-pink satin festooned in silver lace, and her silver slippers had the new pointed toes and two-inch French heels. Despite her protests against gifts of expensive jewelry, Keith had given her Tiffany pearls and emeralds, and installed a wall-safe in the apartment to protect them. He had also brought along some pieces from his late mother's priceless collection, kept in the bank vault, including some antique bracelets of Florentine gold, a sapphire pendant and brooch, a set of marital rings, and the magnificent diamond parure which she now wore with as much regal dignity and grace as the noble lady for whom it was designed.

"No Lady Heathstone ever did those jewels more justice," he said. "Not even the countess herself."

"Nor your mother?"

"I didn't know her at your age, of course, but she was a different type. Dark hair—darker even than mine. Crystal-gray eyes. There's a portrait of her at Gramercy Park, and some of her ancestors. My father's too. I'll introduce them some day."

Dusk was settling on the valley, soft and purple and faintly luminescent. Lights winked in the farmhouses, smoke wisps trailed from the chimneys. Now and then a barking dog could be heard, and the plaintive lowing of cattle. Soon the lakes below the dining room windows were dark mirrors reflecting the moon. But far off in the mountains there were glimmers of lightning and the muted echoes of thunder.

The cuisine was excellent: trout amandine, veal aspic, asparagus in Hollandaise, and strawberry meringue. But

Keith was restless, eating little, concentrating on the champagne. His eyes guarded Devon so possessively, no other man present dared venture more than an admiring glance in her direction. He was eager to go to the second-floor ballroom, where the orchestra was already playing.

While they danced, the wind began to blow and the clouds to scud across the moon. During an intermission they watched from the ballroom gallery, which faced the western mountains, and Keith said pleasedly, "It's going to storm."

"You arranged it, did you?"

"Just for you," he nodded. "It's a spectacle no visitor to the Catskills should miss. Ah, there's the music again! Strauss' 'Roses from the South' . . . I ordered that too, my love."

The storm broke shortly after midnight, as they were preparing for bed, and Keith quickly snuffed the candles and drew Devon to a window to watch. "Fascinating, isn't it? Like a vixen in a heat rage. There'll be some busy beds tonight; love has no friend like nature on a rampage." His arm tightened about her waist, and she felt an elemental response surging in his blood, swelling in his groin. He clutched at her peignoir. "Take this off, before I tear it. Everything! I will too. Let's stand here together, naked and unashamed, as God made us. . . ."

They stripped and stood in embrace, tracing each other's bodies intimately, his hands on her taut breasts and hers on his erect penis. "This is what it means to be male and female, Devon. This is the greatest thing a man and woman can experience together. It's the true belonging and merging, the only way they can actually become one in flesh and spirit. And it may be all we'll ever know or have together, for the rest of our lives. You realize that, don't you?"

"Yes," she murmured.

"And you're not ashamed of loving and wanting me? You don't think it's wrong any more? Wicked or sinful?"

"No, darling, no."

Together they sank to the floor and fused in a violent reckless passion heedless of consequences. In a flash of lightning she saw his dark face above hers, eyes glittering with lust, nostrils distended, teeth brilliant in a ravishing smile.

"Oh, my Lord," she cried, "what're we doing, Keith?"

"Making love, the way it was meant to be made."

"Not in bed?"

"There were no beds then, Devon. Only man and woman, and this—" And plunging, thrusting, rotating deep in her body, he finally exploded inside her.

When at last they returned to New York and Keith left her at Rhinelander Gardens, Devon felt like an abandoned bride. He was once more immersed in business, making up for lost time, and she began to hate the Curtis Bank, the Stock Exchange, Wall Street, and everything else that kept him from her. They were rivals worse than other women, demanding more of his time and attention, necessary evils which she did not know how to combat. She was left alone to seek her own diversions, and she resented her limitations and limited resources.

She reread her manuscript and was dissatisfied with what she had accomplished so far; it seemed to her juvenile, like pages from a schoolgirl's diary, not nearly as interesting or comprehensive as some Southerners' memoirs already published. Fanny Fern had advised her to incorporate her wartime experiences into an autobiographical novel, but that was easy advice for a mature and accomplished novelist to give a novice. Even if she could succeed, how could she compete with the far more brilliant female writers who had difficulty getting published? Besides, her real talent, if any, lay in journalism.

One morning in July she sat idly at her desk watching the rain splash the windows and the wind twisting the elms in the garden. A sudden summer storm had seized Greenwich Village, reminding her of the frenzy in the Catskills, and she longed for Keith with the same intensity she had that night. Was it storming on Wall Street and was he remembering too? She thought of the *Sprite*, snug in her Hudson berth, and craved another cruise. But Long Island and Cape Cod and other places he had promised would have to wait until he was less involved, which might mean the rest of the season.

Out of loneliness she wrote a long letter to Mrs. Chester begging news of Richmond. And another to Mally O'Neill asking if she had set her wedding date yet. The letter, addressed to the Gothic Arms, was returned marked "Deceased." Certain there was some ghastly mistake, Devon went to investigate.

But there was no mistake. Mally O'Neill had taken her own life by breathing gas fumes from the lamp-jet in her room, a convenient means of suicide.

"But why?" Devon asked, stunned and dismayed. "Why would she do such a terrible thing!"

"Why?" the landlady compressed her thin virtuous lips. "She was in trouble, what else? And the man responsible jilted her. Girls never seem to learn from the lessons of others."

"She told you she was in trouble?"

"She didn't need to tell any of us. We all knew it when she began puking in the morning and couldn't empty her slops or go to work. Finally she admitted it to Moira Thompson, the lady who rented your room. We tried to help Mally, but she just lost the will to live. Miss Thompson talked to the police when they came to investigate, and we agreed beforehand to call it an accident, for poor Mally's sake and the reputation of the house. We said the gas had somehow gone out, while she was asleep, and accidently asphyxiated her. But I know she did it purposely, and a wonder she didn't blow us all to kingdom come!" Miss Gibbons peered at her former tenant suspiciously, appraising her stylish clothes. "Mally wondered what had happened to you, where you had gone so suddenly, as if you had vanished into thin air. We all wondered, my dear. Obviously we needn't have worried. You seem prosperous enough," she added succinctly.

"I came into a small inheritance," Devon dissembled.

"Did you indeed? How lucky for you! Too bad Miss O'Neill never had similar good fortune. At least she might've had a decent coffin, instead of that pauper's box. Poor soul, died penniless and in debt, owing me a month's rent. The city had to bury her in Potter's Field."

"Oh, no," Devon whispered, her hand on her throat.

"Oh, yes. Miss Thompson and I went, and a couple of the other ladies out of respect and decency and pity. But we couldn't locate any relatives."

"She had no family, Miss Gibbons, except a worthless father whose whereabouts were unknown to her."

"Men!" the spinster hissed contemptuously. "A woman

can't even trust her own father not to abandon or betray her. As for her husband or lover—"

Devon interrupted, "When did it happen, Miss Gibbons?"

"Two weeks ago."

Two weeks ago, while she was cavorting up and down and around the Hudson, in silks and satins and jewels, poor pregnant Mally O'Neill was desperately inhaling death from a lethal jet. Devon shook her head inrcedulously. "I can't believe it, Miss Gibbons. I just can't believe it!"

"You better believe it," the landlady said grimly. "Mally O'Neill is dead and in her grave, and sure as there's a God above and a judgment to come, she put herself there."

Devon dug some money out of her reticule. "Take this, for what Mally owed you. I borrowed from her once and forgot to repay," she lied.

Miss Gibbons hesitated slightly, but accepted the greenbacks and sighed her thanks. "You don't seem to need it, Miss Marshall, and I do. It is still Miss, isn't it?"

Devon nodded.

"Well, say a prayer for the poor creature. It's all any of us can do for her now."

PART IV

The history of mankind is a history of repeated injuries and usurpations on the part of man toward woman, having in direct object the establishment of an absolute tyranny over her.

> Elizabeth Cady Stanton (1815–1902)

That your sex are naturally tyrannical is a truth so thoroughly established as to admit of no dispute; but such of you as wish to be happy willingly give up the harsh title of master for the more tender and endearing one of friend. Why, then, not put it out of the power of the vicious and lawless to use us with cruelty and indignity with impunity? Men of sense in all ages abhor those customs which treat us only as the vassals of your sex.

> Abigail Adams (1744–1818)
> *The Letters of John and Abigail Adams*

When the men who make laws for us in Washington can stand forth and declare themselves pure and unspotted from all the sins mentioned in the Decalogue, then we will demand that every woman who makes a Constitutional argument on our platform shall be as chaste as Diana. . . .

We have had enough women sacrificed to this sentimental, hypocritical prating about purity. Let us end this ignoble record. If Victoria Woodhull must be crucified, let men drive the spikes and plait the crown of thorns.

> Elizabeth Cady Stanton (1815–1902)

Bravo, my dear Woodhull! Go ahead, bright, glorious, young and strong spirit, and believe in the best love and hope and faith of S. B. Anthony.

Susan B. Anthony (1820–1906)

There is a great stir about colored men getting their rights, but not a word about the colored women; and if colored men get their rights, and not colored women theirs, you see the colored men will be master over the women, and it will be just as bad as it was before. So I am for keeping the thing going while things are stirring. . . .

Sojourner Truth (1797–1883)
Freed slave and dedicated feminist

Chapter 19

The Women's Bureau was a large brownstone house on East Twenty-third Street, just off Fifth Avenue, donated by a wealthy benefactress of the Movement. Over the entrance was posted the credo of the gestating journal: THE TRUE REPUBLIC—MEN, THEIR RIGHTS AND NOTHING MORE; WOMEN, THEIR RIGHTS AND NOTHING LESS. It did not seem an unreasonable goal or request, nor its aspirants worthy of scorn, ridicule, and persecution even by some of their oppressed sisters. As in any crusade, there were some firebrands and fanatics, radicals and rascals. But the majority were sane serious intelligent women seeking primarily their own betterment, and the essential human rights, freedoms, and qualities supposedly guaranteed to all American citizens in the Constitution.

Devon was not sure exactly what had brought her here this morning: interest, curiosity, sympathy, frustration, despair, escape. Perhaps all of these, and more—plus a haunting guilt and grief about Mally O'Neill, for the knowledge that she had been the girl's only friend and had deserted her was an incubus on her heart and conscience. She loathed Davey Thorne, seeing him as the bête noir that Janette Joie depicted all men. Apparently he had wanted Mally until her seduction, after which she became a pregnant burden to brutally abandon. Perhaps chastity was the only virtue the beast really esteemed and appreciated in a prospective mate. Prematurely surrendered, it lost its intrinsic value. The personal columns of the *Herald* listed midwives and charlatans willing to aid such unfortunate victims of male treachery—for a price, and invariably it was a high one. But Mally had been poor. Devon visualized her pleading with Davey to marry her when she discovered her predicament, callously rejected, and turning to suicide as the only solution. She determined to take all possible precautions with Keith.

"Well, Miss Marshall!" Mrs. Stanton greeted her at the door. "Welcome to the bureau! Phoebe Cary and I were thinking of you only last week, wondering what had become of you, if you had returned to Richmond."

"No, I've just been busy earning a living. But I'm happy to see you again, Mrs. Stanton. I hope things have been going well with the Movement."

"Oh, it's a long hard pull, my dear, and uphill all the way! Miss Anthony has been on an arduous lecture tour in New England, concentrating on her home state, since Massachusetts women are among the most enslaved in the country. Susan was telling me about the tragic case of an old friend of hers, the wife of a prominent Boston physician, who had discovered his many adulteries. But when confronted with her proof, he merely accused her of delusions and had her committed to an insane asylum! She lost her children, because Massachusetts' domestic laws—and indeed those of most states—give the husband, no matter how faithless or drunken or brutal, complete control of his wife's person, property, possessions, and children. Could there be any more unjust and cruel and barbarous law in this so-called civilized age and democracy?"

"It's a man's world," Devon affirmed ruefully, "and always has been, from the cave."

"The Garden, my dear. Even the Creator discriminated against womankind, else why did He blame Eve entirely for the temptation and seduction? Adam was equally guilty . . . if indeed the whole account wasn't twisted by some chauvanistic Before-Christ scribe. Why did God curse woman and decree her to bear children in pain and sorrow? What was Adam's punishment beyond expulsion from Paradise? Women have been suffering and sorrowing at the hands of men who consider themselves gods ever since!"

Amen, thought Devon, and she almost burst out with the sad saga of Mally O'Neill. "What can I do to help, Mrs. Stanton?"

"Many things, Miss Marshall. Write letters, knock on doors, distribute handbills, collect funds, parade in the streets, ride on bandwagons. Susan is making some speeches today, in fact. Come with me now. I'll introduce you to the other ladies."

They entered what was once a large formal drawing room, with French wallpaper above the satinwood wainscoting, crystal chandeliers and sconces, and luxurious carpeting. Now it held sofas, tables and chairs and benches, where dedicated volunteers of many ages and backgrounds worked harmoniously at various tasks: sorting pamphlets, reviewing news clippings, pondering written accounts of victimized and abused women, counting coins collected on recent canvasses. In the library across the hall, a conference unit discussed legal aspects and issues and perused copies of various state and federal constitutions, most of which granted more protection and consideration to a man's material possessions and even his animals than to his wife and children.

Acknowledging the introductions, Devon promptly sat down and gathered up a sheaf of leaflets, stuffing them into envelopes which several others were addressing. Those with legible penmanship were assigned to copy formula letters appealing for donations to take the fight to Congress. Brave souls, Devon thought, defying husbands, fathers, brothers, lovers. What would Keith think of her joining them?

Brunch of sandwiches, cakes, tea, and lemonade was served from picnic baskets brought by the refreshment committee as if to a church social, and afterwards Miss Anthony appeared, as soberly clad as a missionary. One had to read her burning tracts and hear her impassioned lectures to understand the fire that imbued her. On the platform she became a radiant personality, her plain face illuminated and transformed with ardent purpose, her slender body an intense liberty torch. She made a brief rallying speech, and her enthusiasm was contagious. Every woman in the building caught it. They clapped and shouted her praise, stood on chairs and benches vowing eternal loyalty and support, marched through the rooms waving flags and singing battle hymns, and Devon Marshall was among them.

"Freedom!" she cried, venting pent-up emotions of Mally O'Neill and her own dilemmas and frustrations. "Give us our freedom! The slaves have been emancipated, now liberate women! We demand the franchise! We demand the right to control our own minds and bodies and ambitions! No ballots, no babies! We'll be at the polls a hundred thousand strong in November!"

Impressed with her fervor and enthusiasm, the captain of the street campaign pinned a red banner across Devon's breast and marched her out of the barracks onto the battlefield, where a caravan of wagons and buckboards waited at the curb. Women piled into them, settling on the board seats in tangles of skirts and petticoats and crinolines. Miss Anthony boarded the lead vehicle and the driver, a grim-visaged old pioneer matron in a prairie sunbonnet, took up the reins as if embarking for the frontier. A standard-bearer and skirted band preceded them, and a contingent of pots and pans and placards followed.

"Where're we going?" Devon asked her seat-companion.

"To the lions' dens! Broadway, the Bowery, Tammany Hall, Wall Street! We'll show the merchants and moneychangers and politicians that we mean business!"

"Wall Street?" Devon repeated, some of her exuberance vanishing.

"Certainly! It's the citadel of masculine power and dominance. Money is the master that makes slaves of us, isn't it? They buy our bodies and souls with it, don't they? We live at their mercy, sustained by their almighty gold. I don't have a cent to my name—my husband controls all our money in his tight fist, including what I inherited from my family! He keeps it in the Curtis Bank, and I shall protest plenty when we pass it!"

"Oh, damn," Devon murmured.

"What?"

"Oh, dear. I'm getting a headache. The heat, I suppose. I wish I'd worn a larger hat, and a veil to protect my face. I burn so easily."

"Yes, you do have awfully fair skin, and it's getting pink already. You should have brought a parasol."

"I didn't know I was going to parade."

"Well, if you feel faint, use your smelling salts. But try not to exhibit such feminine weakness publicly. Some of us are indisposed and pregnant, but we dare not let these handicaps betray or defeat us. Remember Joan of Arc!"

Remembering that lady's fate, Devon was tempted to jump out of the vanguard. But she couldn't do anything so cowardly or traitorous and, besides, she might break her neck. She sat still, curious as to what special significance was attached to the scarlet pennant, feeling as if she had been decorated for valor on her way to the firing squad.

The campaign was thwarted at Union Square by the police, and harassed and threatened by "centaurs"—as Miss Anthony dubbed the mounted officers—all along Broadway for stalling traffic and parading without permission. Spectators laughed and jeered; some brave women cheered. The brass band blared. The command signaled, and the troops obeyed. The target now was Bowling Green, where Miss Anthony determined to make a stand, come hell or high water.

Her impromptu stump speeches were powerful but expediently brief. She would speak for tireless hours on her lecture tours, to generally attentive audiences, who had paid for the privilege. But speaking unbidden to a predominately hostile audience was somewhat inhibiting, and every terse word counted. So when she rose in the wagon at Bowling Green, once popular with orators of the Revolution, it was to denounce the oppression of the female by the male, her subjugation and degradation in her servility, and to demand her liberty as fervently as the Washingtons, Jeffersons, and Monroes had demanded the Colonists'.

"Is woman free in a house where man is lord and master, and eminent ruler of his domain? Is a wife bound to a husband by bonds of holy matrimony, or unholy bondage? Is she his helpmeet, or his helpless mate? His companion, or his chattel? His partner, or his indentured servant? Does he acquire a bride at the altar to love, honor, and cherish ... or a slave to possess, command, and abuse at will? The average woman knows all too well the unhappy answers to these pertinent questions! She knows she may be governed, disciplined and punished by her man, denied her property and even food and clothing, forced to bear children against her will, often at the risk of her health and even her life. She must endure his drinking and gambling and adultery, but he can divorce and even murder her for infidelity, and go scot free!" She concluded by assuring her female listeners that all these injustices, abominations and atrocities could and would be changed through suffrage, for then women could elect representatives willing to champion their causes and lead them like Moses out of their bondage. "And why not, pray? If we

are good enough to share their beds, to be their mothers
and wives and bear their children, why then are we not
good enough to cast our votes at their sides?"

A grizzly old man, ruminating a tobacco quid, stepped
up to the wagon. "You scrawny ugly old maid! What do
you know about marriage and kids? Go back to your cats
and knitting!" And clearing his stringy throat, he spat onto
her gown.

Miss Anthony ignored his remarks as if inaudible, and
the spittle as if invisible. Through insult, contempt, threat,
she maintained remarkable composure and dignity. Her
driver, however, was not so poised. She raised her whip
menacingly, eager to lash the old tormentor, but Miss Anthony forbade any violence and ordered the parade to continue.

Passing the Stock Exchange on Broad Street, Devon hid
behind her poster, uncertain what bold or hilarious challenge it carried, and hoped that Keith was occupied in the
gold room. Wall Street was next—a narrow cobbled canyon lined with imposing buildings, not the least of which
was the Curtis Bank. As they came abreast of the monumental marble structure, with fluted pilasters flanking the
great bronze portals, the martyr beside Devon went suddenly berserk, screaming that her inheritance was on de-
posit there in her husband's name and untouchable by her.
Unable to calm her, Devon glanced up at Trinity Church
steeple and prayed that Midas was not in his countinghouse.

En route to Tammany Hall, at Frankfort and Chatham
Streets, the procession suffered a pelting with garbage and
manure, and derisive catcalls. Miss Anthony seemed as impervious as she had to the old graybeard's demonstration
at Bowling Green. A rotten tomato burst on her breast,
crimson as blood, followed by a fresh moist horse biscuit
to the head. "Faith, ladies!" she encouraged. "Jesus Christ
was crucified on the way to Calvary. He died to redeem
mankind. If necessary, we must die to redeem womankind."

The band struck up "The Battle Hymn of the
Republic," and Devon sang as fervently as if it were
"Dixie." But as they approached the Bowery district, she
grew tense and apprehensive, remembering the breed of
rabble who congregated there. They occupied the benches

and ground under the trees in Chatham Square, lounged on sidewalks and in doorways, perched on stoops and stairs. Hostile, belligerent, clannish, they roamed in tribes and thrived on trouble, challenging all foes and strangers. They were as fierce as the gamecocks and ferocious terriers and rats on which they bet in the bloody pits, when not otherwise amusing themselves in the gambling dens, concert saloons, gin-mills, and whorehouses. They carried knives and daggers, brass knuckles, iron pipes and other cudgels, and guns. They robbed, raped, molested, murdered, and disappeared into the convenient underground catacombs, the subterranean bowels of the Bowery, where even the most fearless lawmen feared to pursue.

Devon thought it extremely unwise to enter this danger zone, although she knew the Movement was aiming at the fleshpots that demeaned and enslaved females, who must depend on them for existence, including the Gilded Cage, which exploited them like captive birds in fancy cages. The chorus, trooping out of rehearsal to watch, formed a small phalanx on the sidewalk. Recognizing a former comrade, they waved and cheered, and Devon longed for the anonymity of a mask. "Hey, Richmond! Hooray, Rebel! Give 'em hell! Strike a blow for us! Remember the cages!"

That was all the incentive the hoodlums, spoiling for action, needed to attack. A barrage of refuse and manure, corncobs and oyster shells, water and beer bombs exploded over the wagons. The occupants were struck; some were injured. Devon ducked her head in her lap, and felt rough hands tugging at her arms and legs, boldly exploring under her skirts, trying to pull her off the wagon. The driver lashed her whip across the man's back and stabbed the handle in his mouth, and he fled like a yelping dog. Others used parasols and purses and shoes, hatpins and nail files and hairbrushes to ward off the brutes, cracking skulls, gouging eyes, raking faces.

Several policemen watched the fray for awhile, wary of the gang that had started it, but finally came to the ladies' assistance, yelling and blowing whistles and brandishing billies. Their interference only incensed the thugs, who hated cops more than anyone else, and turned their wrath and vengeance upon them. But soon precinct reinforcements arrived via several paddywagons with clanging bells. The rioters scattered into their rookeries and secret sanctuaries. The women were arrested for disturbing the peace, and those in the leading wagons were hauled off to jail.

There was no panic or hysteria among the crusaders familiar with such treatment. But it was Devon's first offense and ride in a Black Maria, and she was petrified with fear and horror, shame and indignation. Her straw hat was askew, flowers and ribbons ripped off. Her white collar had a beet-juice stain, and a flounce hung loose on her skirt. Her companions had missing bows and sashes, trailing ruffles and laces, ruined bonnets, lost slippers, tattered parasols. A thief had stolen Devon's reticule, and she had no money to pay a fine, if that was to be the extent of her punishment.

They were not taken to the convenient Ludlow Street Station, as Miss Anthony expected, but to the awesome Tombs. Devon had seen this ponderous pile of granite before, occupying an entire block in its Centre Street hollow and resembling a massive Egyptian mausoleum, and having read of the kind of justice administered in its grim confines, she was utterly terrified.

But if Miss Anthony's raiment was in disarray, her emotions were not. She maintained stoic equanimity throughout the ordeal of booking and incarceration. She tried to explain that they had not started the trouble but were deliberately and viciously attacked, while peacefully demonstrating, and had resisted and retaliated only in self-defense, when some of their young members were molested and threatened with violation. Unfortunatly, most of her explanation eluded the menial mentality of the desk sergeant, an illiterate man with mutton-chop whiskers.

"Yeah—well, youse fanatics is got to learn youse can't run wild in the streets, drummin' up recruits for yore ridiculous rebellion! I know youse and yore crazy idears about votin' and temperance and gamblin' and wantin' to wear men's pants. But you shouldna invaded the Bowery, cause there ain't no place in town wants reform less, and youse can jest blame yorselfs for the fix youse is in now. I got to charge youse with incitin' to riot."

"Inciting to riot? I deny that charge, Sergeant! We are innocent victims."

"You're crazy females with illusions of grandeur."

"Are we charged with sedition too? And treason?"

"That ain't for me to decide," he drawled. "But youse is

rebels, sure as shootin', and bent on startin' yore own dang revolution."

"How long will we be here?" a young mother inquired.

"How the hell should I know? I ain't no judge. All I know is we got to lock youse up."

"But I have to get home," she protested. "I have small children to look after."

"Youse shoulda thought of that before, Ma. Who's mindin' 'em now, yore hen-pecked husband? Bah!" He spat into an overflowing cuspidor. "Youse make me sick, all of youse!"

"Naturally," Miss Anthony reasoned, "we will be separately immured, to prevent any further intrigue or conspiracy against the mighty male dominion."

He stared at her blankly. "I'd advise youse to keep a civil tongue in yore head, lady."

Devon found herself in a cell with two other women, who introduced themselves as Marge and Lou, alias a dozen surnames. Marge was a hook-nosed, pock-marked creature with rheumy black eyes and stringy black hair hanging on her hunched shoulders; she reminded Devon of Hallowe'en. Lou had orange hair, inexpertly dyed, and jaundiced eyes. She wore a tawdry purple satin gown stained with food, liquor, and sweat. Scabby sores covered her face and arms, at which she intermittently scratched. Both smelled like spoiled fish.

"What'd you do, sister?" asked Marge.

"Nothing," Devon answered. "Nothing at all."

"Yeah? That's what they all say. We had a fancy dame in here last week, Miss Hoighty-Toity herself. Butter wouldn't melt in her mouth. Turned out she was the bait to lure rich dudes to their doom—a thug's accomplice, and one of their victims didn't survive his clout on the bean. She's in solitary now, waitin' trial. She'll be convicted and hung, or sent to rot on Blackwell Island. If she's smart, she'll jump off the ferry into the East River on her way over. Jesus mercy, what a chamber of horrors!"

"Well, this ain't exactly no resort," said Lou. "You heard of Newgate and the Bastille? Welcome to the Tombs, Milady! Here you get buried alive."

Devon believed it. The cell was five feet by eight, hardly larger than a grave. Mold and mildew covered the damp walls, and the air was as putrid as death. The daylight slanting through the narrow slit in the wall only increased the gloom and confinement. "I didn't do anything criminal," she said. "I was just parading with Miss Anthony."

"Who?" asked Marge.

"Susan Brownell Anthony, the lady who's trying to get the vote and other rights for women."

"Oh, yeah, I heard of her. Nerve and guts, and plain as homemade soap. But personally I think she's wastin' her time and breath, fartin' in the wind, so to speak." Marge scratched her lice, pursuing them into the bodice of her dress, between her pendulous breasts. "You heard about the Anthony, ain't you, Lou? Saint Susan, patron of oppressed females."

Lou was lounging on her cot, chewing snuff which oozed from her slack mouth. She hawked and spat some brown, bloody phlegm on the floor, spattering Devon in the process. "I reckon, and I wish she'd do something about the right to solicit in peace. I was mindin' my own business, scoutin' the Battery for a sucker, when they nabbed me. It's my body, ain't it? Why can't I use it how I please in a free country? Why do I always have to be harassed and threatened and locked up?"

"Because you ain't got no pimp to protect you and garnish the law," Marge told her. "And I wouldn't be here, either, if I hadn't tried to steal on my own. The cops don't hound the packs, they concentrate on the loners. This is our punishment for trying to be independent of men!"

"I had a pimp, once," Lou reflected grimly. "The dirty dog left me when I got pregnant and peppered. I got a poor blind imbecile kid in Bellevue. Why do you think I work the waterfront at night? So they won't see my cankers! I bet I gave every sailor from here to Tripoli the clap and French pox, and I hope to hell they all die of it. It'll be my revenge on the fuckin' bastards. You can't trust 'em. They'll betray you every time, and desert you when you need 'em most."

Devon sat forlornly on her bunk, staring at the filthy floor. In a corner was a pitcher of drinking water with foreign matter floating on the surface, and a nearly full chamberpot. Devon thought she would rather die of thirst than drink the water, or soil herself rather than use the slopjar. Her stays bound her excruciatingly, her head throbbed, and she feared she would vomit from the formidable stench. She felt weak, sick, giddy, and rather hoped she would faint, for then she might be taken to the infirmary.

Despite the summer heat outside, the cell seemed chilly. She shivered and wished for a wrap. Reaching for the blanket she noticed crawling vermin and pushed it aside, horrified. A sense of doom pervaded her, and she was filled with hopeless despair and bewilderment. Suddenly a huge rat darted across the cell in pursuit of a cockroach. Devon lifted her feet and clutched her skirts, and Lou burst into laughter, choking and sputtering on her cud.

"Better get used to it, honey. Them's our pets. Better get used to the stink too, and the screams at night, and a few whacks from matron now and then."

"Ah, stop scarin' her," Marge relented. "She ain't no common tramp or felon—anyone can see that. And somebody'll come to get her outta here, maybe the commissioner himself. She's too pretty to languish long in this dungeon."

"Well, if she ain't fetched before mornin'," Lou predicted glumly, "them lovely curls will be so thick with lice her head'll have to be shorn bald. Boy, wouldn't that bitchy old bawd love to work on her, though! And wait till she eats that swill they call food and tries to sleep on that straw mattress with them bloodsuckin' bedbugs. Oh, it ain't no home sweet home, I can tell you! It's Newgate and the Bastille combined."

Devon sighed and waited forlornly for the next development, for some miracle to save her. Intent on her miseries, she scarcely heard the key grate in the lock and the iron door creak open, and the harsh female voice startled her.

"Hey you, Marshall!"

Devon glanced up at the buxom matron, with her keys, cudgel, and leather strap dangling from her wide waist. "Me, Ma'am?"

"Ain't your name Marshall?"

"Yes, it is."

"Well, come on, then! There's a gent here says it's all a mistake, your arrest."

The prostitute sniffed. "Ain't she the lucky one!"

"Didn't I tell you?" the thief gloated, as triumphantly as if it were her own release. "Some sonofabitch with a guilty conscience has come to pay her fine with blood-money—

some gent will always save her from disaster, long as she has that pretty face. Don't forget to tell Miss Anthony about our rights, honey!"

"I will," Devon promised, following the matron.

It had to be Keith, of course—and of all that had happened to her that day, this was the supreme mortification, the ultimate horror and shame and agony: facing him in this place and condition, looking like a bedraggled hoyden or worse, fearing his temper, which she expected to explode the instant they were alone. Which it did.

"I'm sure you have some explanation for this, Devon, but I'm not sure I want to hear it. Just tell me what the devil you're trying to do!"

"First tell me how you found out." She wondered if he had a network of spies around town to report on her, or sleuths still shadowing her.

"How do you think? I was watching from my office windows when that petticoat platoon passed, and heard some wild creature shouting the name of the bank and something about her impounded funds. I thought I was having hallucinations, but holy smoke! sure enough, there *you* were in the front caisson, with the general, a red banner across your breast and a sign saying, NO BALLOTS, NO BABIES!"

"Is that what it said? I wasn't sure."

"When word got back to the Street about the Bowery riot and Miss Anthony's clique in the clink, I knew you were entombed too."

"Oh, Keith, don't fuss at me, please. Just get me home quickly. I want to bathe and wash my hair. That jail is a dreadful place! If it's any criterion of the prison system, it needs reform desperately. Keith, do you think you could get Miss Anthony and the others out too?"

"Devon, I'm a banker, not a bondsman! Let their own embarrassed menfolk bail them out. Miss Anthony would probably prefer to stay there awhile, as a symbol of persecution. Think of all the disciples she'll convert out of sympathy. I've got an industrialist waiting to discuss a loan."

"What did you tell the jailer?"

"That you were an employee inadvertently caught in that ridiculous charade. I ought to spank you, Devon. And if ever you get your pretty little posterior into the pokey again, I'm going to let you languish there awhile. You hear me?"

"Yes, sir."

"Don't be cute. Can I trust you to behave now?"

"Yes, only take me home, and hurry! I'm beginning to itch, and my hair will have to be cut off if I don't get it washed. But thanks for coming, Keith. That's the second time you've rescued me from a cage."

His scowl dissolved in a grin. "Men are good for something, after all, aren't they?"

Chapter 20

Keith was en route to a banking conclave in Chicago. Devon had wanted to accompany him, anxious to see the city on Lake Michigan, which some travelers considered as exciting as New Orleans, San Francisco, and even New York. But he insisted that women never attended business or professional conventions, and any man who brought one along, wife or otherwise, would be a laughingstock. To mollify her, however, he promised to take her on future trips to Philadelphia, Hartford, and Washington, and encouraged her to amuse herself shopping during his absence. Lonely, disappointed, frustrated, unable to make headway on her manuscript, she had already run up sizable bills at Lord & Taylor and Stewart's, when she met Kate Field at Demorest's.

The irrepressible journalist was assembling a new wardrobe for her second trip abroad that year. She had spent the entire month of April in Paris, reporting along with other Stateside correspondents on the opening of the World Exposition. Her vivid newsletters in the *Tribune* describing the glamour, fashions, fads, novelties, entertainments, and important Americans received at the court of the Second Empire, had thrilled her female readers who, like Devon, could only long and hope for such wondrous experiences.

Kate Field invited her to lunch, and now they were sitting in the sky-parlor tearoom of the St. Nicklaus Hotel, six marble stories above Broadway, and Kate was saying, "The Demorest exhibit created quite a sensation in Paris, particularly the paper patterns, corsets, and new demi-hoops. Crinolines are shrinking to a more manageable girth, finally, and we won't be so vulnerable in the wind any more, thanks to Ellen Louise. Her designs and clever inventions are a tribute to the ingenuity of American womanhood, and she is now internationally famous."

"And you're going back for another glamorous and exciting adventure of your own," Devon said. "I envy you, Kate. I envy all of you. Madame Demorest and Jenny June and Fanny Fern—"

"Oh, darling, don't be silly! You'll hit your stride one of these days, and find your niche. You're still young—who knows what lies in your future? You may surpass all of us! But I'm not sailing for several weeks yet, and right now I'm more excited about something else," Kate bubbled over her terrapin soup. "Margaret Fuller's death anniversary is only two days away, and there's going to be a seance aboard Commodore Vanderbilt's yacht in another attempt to contact her spirit. Did you know she died at sea in a hurricane?"

Devon nodded. "I've read more about her since we met at the Carys. What happened at your other sitting, Kate?"

"Nothing, unfortunately. I just couldn't get through to her. Nor can I imagine why, since I'm a dedicated believer. Perhaps my netherworld control is lax or somehow inhibited. However, Victoria Woodhull is conducting this seance—and she has Demosthenes, no less, guiding her! Have you met Mrs. Woodhull or her sister, Tennessee Claflin? All New York is buzzing about them now."

"No, I haven't, but I read the papers, Kate. And it's fantastic what they've accomplished in such a short time!"

"Oh, they're terrific, both of them, but they also have Demosthenes directing Victoria. It's a fascinating story, and proof positive of a hereafter. As Vicky tells it, her powerful Greek friend advised her to come to New York, and apparently everything was predestined and prearranged, just as he promised, from the lovely home in Great Jones Street to the brokerage house on Broadway. Not mere coincidences, you understand, but spiritual guidance and arrangements."

Kate seemed fairly convinced of this, and listening to her Devon was partially persuaded too. There seemed no other logical explanation for the phenomenal success of the spectacular sisters who had recently descended like blazing comets upon Manhattan from "somewhere in the Midwest" and dominated the local news almost as completely as a common catastrophe. Their origins were hazy, nebulous to the point of obscurity. But diligent newsmen, probing the available fragments left along their erratic trail, discovered a few pertinent and provocative facts: they had traveled across country as clairvoyants and spiritual leaders, preaching and practicing free love; Victoria's intimate companion was one Colonel Blood, a handsome ex-Confederate officer, while both had spouses elsewhere; and Tennessee Claflin's appointments for magnetic treatments were more in the nature of assignations. They supported a disreputable family consisting of a crafty one-eyed father, an illiterate religious fanatic mother, and assorted indigent, indolent inlaws, morons, and idiots. Nevertheless, their flagrant feminism and immorality might have been slyly winked at by sophisticated Manhattan men, and even encouraged, if they had not had the audacity and effrontery to trespass on Wall Street; and if Cornelius Vanderbilt, long a devotee of spiritualism and dupe of empiricism, had not seen fit to sponsor them, staking their financial enterprise and supporting their efforts, either to amuse himself or antagonize his enemies, or because he actually believed in their supernatural powers and efficacies.

As every female yearning for individual recognition and independence, Devon had an avid curiosity about those who achieved these goals and ambitions. She knew that Keith, along with hundreds of other businessmen, had made a courtesy call at the Broad Street office of the Bewitching Brokers, as the press labeled them. But despite her pestering she could learn little beyond what she read in the papers and heard at the Women's Bureau, where she continued to go without Keith's knowledge. Did they really wear the shirts of their mannishly-tailored walking suits only ankle length, sometimes even higher, exposing their boot tops? Did they tuck fresh flowers into their shirt bosoms and gold pens behind their dainty ears? Was Tennessee's hair boyishly bobbed? Keith's answer to all these foolishly feminine questions was a disgruntled frown and an abrupt, "I never noticed."

Devon doubted this, since he had a quick keen eye for a pretty face and shapely figure, and persisted, "They must be terribly smart, though, to run a brokerage firm."

He gave a contemptuous snort. "They don't know a damned thing about the business! Mrs. Woodhull's husband or lover, or whatever Blood is to her, manages the firm on advice from Vanderbilt. The women are just figureheads and decoys, because he's convinced of Victoria's clairvoyance and enamored of Tennessee. The consensus on the Street is that Old Corneel is in his dotage. Senile, or worse."

"I'd like to meet the ladies," Devon said tentatively.

"Ladies? They're a pair of clever and cunning whores who've hoodwinked that old fool. The Commodore was always greedy and prurient, and as unscrupulous in his private life as he is publicly. He has little either of business ethics or personal integrity . . . ask any man who's ever had commerce with him. He's a scoundrel, and age hasn't mellowed him."

"Is he ill? Why does he need a magnetic healer?"

"Darling, there's no such thing! The bitches are frauds and charlatans. They're catering to the old lecher's lusts and superstitions. Tennie Claflin is twenty-four, and he's past seventy. Figure it out for yourself."

"And what is our connection, Keith?"

He stared at her, the nerves in his jaw flickering as always in anger or impatience. "Well, surely you don't put it in *that* category?"

"No, but it's a form of free love, isn't it? Illicit and illegal. Adultery."

"Oh, for Christ's sake, Devon! Are you suffering another attack of conscience and religion? I thought after our exchange at the Mountain House that we were done with puritan recriminations."

"I'm not recriminating or recanting, Keith. It's just that I wish things could be different for us."

"Don't you think I do?" he asked miserably, and once again they were commiserating, consoling, reassuring each other in bed. Hadn't they agreed that this was the most important aspect of their relationship? Didn't they realize and accept that it might be all they would ever share together? They renewed their vows of eternal love and devotion, Devon clinging to Keith, grasping and straining in ecstasy which, no matter how hard she tried to sustain and prolong, inevitably vanished with climax and physical separation, leaving her alone, lonely, and longing for the next sensual union.

*

"Do you know Mrs. Woodhull and Miss Claflin, Kate?"

"Oh, yes! The press, along with the money moguls and thousands of ordinary curious citizens, attended their opening reception. They've advised me on some railroad and marine stocks, which have already advanced. If you can afford to invest in the market, get their counsel. I understand they've already coined a tidy fortune for themselves."

"Is it true that Vanderbilt is advising them?"

At Kate's signal the pastry-cart was wheeled to the table. She selected a meringue filled with caramel custard and toasted almonds; Devon chose a Napoleon. "Not only advising, my dear, but manipulating his own securities to their advantage."

"Is that ethical?"

"Well, its business. And the Commodore isn't the only capitalist who engages in such machinations and chicanery. Witness Gould, Fisk, Drew, Belmont, and a host of others. Wall Street is a brotherhood of greedy gold grubbers, whose fraternal rites and practices often astound and bewilder the uninitiated. The Street literally abounds in rogues, rascals, and renegades, and there are as many wolves as bulls and bears. Nor is Old Corneel the only petticoat fancier; they all deal in that commodity, more or less. Most men do, you know."

"At the bureau, they say male hostility toward the Claflin sisters is due primarily to challenged ego and wounded pride."

"Undoubtedly. They have penetrated, thereby usurping the phallic prerogative, the masculine domain at its fiscal foundations, its tenacious taproot of superiority—the almighty dollar with which the money-masters buy and control womankind, as if she were any other essential commodity on the market. Furthermore, they have made themselves financially independent, a feat neither of their drunken, faithless husbands accomplished before being dumped in divorce, perhaps the most 'scandalous' and 'unforgivable' of all their actions. Their names are anathema in the pulpits. Religion is as important in New York as gold, and its purveyors almost as powerful. Trinity Church is considered the godfather of Wall Street, blessing their fortunes. And while sin, vice, and corruption flourish in high places, open honest profligacy is vigorously and consistently condemned by the pious hypocrites. We live in a censorious society."

"I suppose," Devon agreed. "But wouldn't it be the end, the supreme triumph if Woodhull and Claflin could somehow acquire a seat on the Stock Exchange?"

"It would be the feminine coup of the century—indeed, the millennium! Hardly likely, though, since women aren't even allowed to observe the proceedings in that bloody bastion. I tried to crash the gold room—the sanctus sanctorum—once disguised as a man and using counterfeit credentials, but was caught at the door and treated like a foreign spy on sabotage, as if I were trying to bomb or set fire to it." She paused in a pensive frown. "Female journalists are taboo even in the Press Club. Jenny June, Fanny Fern, and I have been besieging that male rampart for years without avail. Perhaps there's something to the 'Woodhull witchery and Claflin magic,' after all. At any rate, they've breached some barriers for us, and we should all be grateful and inspired. By the way, I heard that you were among the suffragettes arrested with Susan Anthony."

Devon nodded, sipping her tea.

"I was out of town on assignment at the time, or I'd have been at the dungeon to cry up my support." Kate forked some pastry into her delicately curved pink mouth. "It had already been reported when I returned, although the majority of papers either ignored or ridiculed it as 'another Anthony antic to gain publicity and public sympathy and support.' They always impugn the Movement's motives, no matter how noble and sincere. Imagine arresting the ladies rather than the rabble that incited the riot! Persecution, no less, and a wonder they didn't have to stand trial. Was it a dreadful experience?"

"Horrible," Devon reflected, shuddering. "They locked me in a cell with a thief and a prostitute. And the filth and degradation . . . oh, Kate, it's appalling!"

"Well, the Tombs has never been noted for hospitality. And Jefferson Market Prison is known as the 'black hole of Calcutta.' Margaret Fuller tried to initiate prison reforms here twenty-five years ago, while reporting on the *Tribune,* but her efforts fell by the political wayside. Unfortunately, the public has always been apathetic, if not downright lethargic, about social reform, and antagonistic toward reformers. They seem to regard change and progress as radical and revolutionary. The bigots invented status quo and invariably protest and contest any infringement on their patent. One wonders how the Revolution ever developed and succeeded, and the answer is that the entire populace was oppressed then, not only selected minorities. It was collective bravery, defiance, and perseverance. Well, thank God, there are still some courageous women to rally around our cause."

"Not enough, however, nor well enough organized."

"Unfortunately not. I met Dorothea Dix in Hartford last week, and she is still crusading for the helplessly insane. She tells me that the majority of states continue to confine paupers and lunatics in their penal institutions, as if they were no different from the criminals. And the medieval and barbaric treatment would be inhumane even for animals. It made me ill to hear some of the gruesome details. In some respects, Miss Dix is an even more remarkable woman than Miss Fuller was. A kind of saint, actually, who will probably never be beatified." Kate sighed wistfully, reverting to her ideal again. "Would you like to attend that seance, Devon?"

"Oh, I'd love to, Kate!"

"Are you interested in spiritualism?"

"Avidly," Devon lied, "and I've often tried to contact my father's spirit. Could you possibly get me an invitation?"

"I'll try," Kate promised, winking conspiratorially over her teacup. "The Commodore, you know, has a penchant for pretty young girls. Where can I reach you?"

Devon gave her address. Kate was visibly impressed.

"Rhinelander Gardens? Good heaven, Vanderbilt is practically your neighbor! He lives at Number Ten Washington Place, just off the Square. You must have had a turn of fortune yourself."

A demure tongue-in-cheek smile. "I have some property in Richmond, which I mortgaged to the Curtis Bank."

"Really? Then you should meet the man who holds your mortgage." Kate rolled her lucid blue eyes. "Oh, Lord, what a dream! One of the few males in this town who could persuade me to abandon my freedom and independence. Married, alas, and permanently, it would appear, his wife being invalid."

"Do you know them, Kate?"

"Well, I used to cover some of their social affairs in Gramercy Park, before her accident. They don't entertain much any more, rarely, in fact. Nor as lavishly as before. Teas, soirees, musicals—the sort of receptions she can manage in a wheelchair. And she used to dance so beautifully at their brilliant balls! I saw them abroad too, at the spas—Liege, Vichy, Ems, Baden—and the mineral resorts here. He must've spent a fortune trying to cure her, but apparently it's hopeless. I feel sorry for them both. He seems such a vigorous, virile man ... and she's so pathetically handicapped. But c'est la vie!" Kate picked up the tab, her gloves, and reticule.

"Thanks for the treat, Kate."

"Thank Greeley, darling. I'm putting it on my expense sheet. Now I must dash back to the office. You'll hear from me, dear."

The next morning, true to her word, a message arrived. It was arranged. Devon was to meet Kate at the Vanderbilt pier, at two that afternoon, and be prepared to spend the night at sea.

Morocco portmanteau in hand, Devon boarded the Vanderbilt steamer for the ghostly rendezvous off Fire Island with as much excitement and enthusiasm, though of a different nature, as she had on the *Sprite* for the romantic excursion up the Hudson.

She had seen the Commodore before, many times. He was a familiar figure in town, driving his drag and high-stepping, white-footed trotters up and down Broadway, often at breakneck speed, and out to Harlem Road, where he bested many a sport half his age in the races. An impressive, indomitable man, tall and spare of frame, with shrewd hazel eyes under craggy brows, and formidable features that looked as if they had been blasted out of stone. His hair was white and flaring, and he wore a raffish ruff of white whiskers. He was dressed in his customary habit: black suit and high white stock long out of fashion, but as much his trademark as the gold-hilted walking stick.

"Every vile adjective in the lexicon has been applied to his character," Kate confided, "and most of them accurately so. I'm afraid he *is* vulgar, profane, lusty, avaricious, ruthless, vindictive, rapacious . . . and utterly fascinating."

The new women in his life, both young and beautiful, flanked the titan. Victoria Woodhull had long, thick, dark hair, exquisitely fair skin, brilliant blue eyes, and perfect white teeth that gave her a dazzling smile. She was wearing a flowing purple silk drapery simulating a Grecian chiton, with a fresh white tearose at her throat. Her younger sister, Tennessee, was even lovelier with her soft brown curls shorn pixishly, her mischievously sparkling gray-blue eyes, her dewy petal-pink complexion. And no doubt her magnetic ministrations agreed with the Commodore, for he was in fine fettle and frisky humor, joking, teasing, flirting, cursing, bellowing, and roaring with laughter.

When Kate introduced Devon Marshall, Vanderbilt welcomed her aboard heartily, clasping her hand and buffing her cheek. Sedate Victoria responded as cordially as a duchess, but vivacious Tennessee hugged her impetuously and chuckled and warned the Commodore about ogling her. "Careful, old boy," she grinned, flicking his stock. "I'm mighty jealous, you know."

Vanderbilt laughed and squeezed the dainty hand tucked through his arm, assuring her that he was quite content with his current alliance. He never bothered with pretense or formality, one reason why he was scorned in formal society, and addressed his new acquaintance, a delightful goldenhaired doll in yellow India muslin and floppy leghorn hat bowed beneath the chin, informally. "Kate tells me that you're interested in the occult, Devon."

"Isn't everyone?" she asked archly. The fad was, in fact, sweeping the country.

"Yes, indeed," Victoria agreed. "It's never been more popular. So many people are trying now to contact loved ones lost in the war."

"And I can vouch for Vicky's mystic powers," Vanderbilt said. "Only last week she contacted my mother's spirit for me, and God knows Phoebe Hand was difficult to communicate with even in life."

Kate, still disappointed at her own failures in this area, smiled at Mrs. Woodhull. "Let's hope you succeed with Margaret. I'm sure she must have many significant messages for us."

"Undoubtedly," Victoria concurred. "But even without her assistance, we must never falter in our goals, nor fail to pursue them whatever the cost to ourselves."

"Where the hell is Greeley?" Vanderbilt suddenly exploded. "I thought he'd be the first one aboard. After all, he knew the lady better than any of us, except George Ripley. I only met her a couple of times myself—too damn busy those days making money to bother with much else."

"Horace'll be along," Kate assured him. "Poor dear, he's getting a little slow. And his eyesight is so impaired, he probably went to the wrong pier."

"Rubbish!" Vanderbilt scoffed. "He's still shy of sixty, should be in his prime. I've got a dozen and more years on him, and behold me! What Greeley needs is the kind of magnetism and energy Tennie dispenses. She's a marvelous healer, this little girl. Absolutely miraculous."

Kate winked at him, and he grinned and pinched her pretty cheek. He liked her sophistication, which masked no demure prudery or coy deception; she knew the Commodore for what he was and did not sit in judgment on him, and this he found almost as exhilarating as Tennie's stimulating touch.

Greeley and Ripley were ascending the gangplank now, the publisher in a baggy white linen suit and round Panama hat, his literary critic in striped seersucker and string tie. "Get the lead out!" the Commodore yelled. "You expect to be piped aboard maybe, Greeley, like some goddamn dignitary!" And when the pair made deck, he signaled the captain. "Ahoy, skipper! Launch this blasted tub on the waves!"

Luxurious as was the Curtis yacht, this floating palace overshadowed it if only by sheer bulk. In size and concept the salons were as majestic as Queen Victoria's *Britannica*. Polished marble walls, frescoed ceilings, Venetian chandeliers, Oriental carpets. Among the paintings, medallions, and marble statuary were framed engravings of historic Vanderbilt vessels, including the family's first ferry, first Hudson River steamboat, first yacht, and first transatlantic liner. And the deep-throated whistle was a far cry from the conch horn that had signaled the maiden voyage of his father's two-masted periauger from Staten Island to Manhattan.

Teetotaling vegetarian Greeley eschewed the gourmet buffet, munching celery and carrots and drinking diluted milk, while the others feasted on roast beef, pheasant, capon, caviar, and Dutch cheeses among other delicacies, and drank the finest of imported wines.

"God almighty, Horace," their genial host muttered, "is that rabbit food all you gonna eat? I'm insulted! Can't you suspend your crazy diet for one day, at least? It sure as hell ain't making you healthy, from what I can see. You get more puny and feeble every goddamn day."

Greeley shrugged. "I was never robust, Corneel, and that stuff you're stowing and swilling would kill me."

"Well, I ain't aiming to die of thirst or starvation, man. I expect to depart this earth with a full belly."

"And full arms?"

"Yeah, full of something warm and soft and sweet and pretty. You know a better way to go?"

The commodore enjoyed baiting the editor, whose prudery and views on monogamy were well known. Greeley's criticism of Brigham Young's "harem of wives" was harsh and severe, and his agitation for legislation to outlaw Mormon polygamy was intense and relentless. He couldn't abide evil or wickedness in any form.

"Stop teasing Horace," Kate scolded Vanderbilt, although she too was often amused by some of Greeley's puritanism and idiosyncrasies. "Anyway, he does break his diet commandments occasionally." She repeated the story currently circulating newsrooms about Greeley's having eaten a thick juicy steak at the Astor House, in the supposed mistaken belief that it was a slice of graham bread, and everyone laughed, including Greeley.

They sat about on velvet and damask sofas and chairs, trying to relax in an atmosphere at once convivial and apprehensive, conscious of the ultimate experiment. Although not aloof, Victoria was detached and quietly meditative. Tennessee occupied a sultan-like couch with Vanderbilt, who seemed utterly infatuated with his vibrant young mistress. If he was senile, as Keith had implied, it was not the kind of senility Devon had encountered in Ephraim Joseph; for however avid the Commodore's lust, it did not appear abnormal.

Devon was the only member of the party who had never participated in a seance, and she could barely

suppress her excitement at the prospect. She sat with Kate
Field, Horace Greeley, and George Ripley, a non-practic-
ing Unitarian minister whom some still addressed as Reverend. From a biography of Margaret Fuller, Devon knew
Ripley had met her during his Brook Farm experiment
days, a commune founded on transcendentalism, of which
many intellectuals including Greeley and Emerson and
Bronson Alcott, were either members or frequent visitors.
The biographer had also hinted that Greeley was in love
with his lady editor, a chaste and honorable love, whose
temptations he had avoided by sending her to Europe as a
foreign correspondent; he had received the news of her
marriage to the Marquis Giovanni Angelino Ossoli sorrow-
fully, and her death at sea had sent him into a severe mental depression and physical decline, from which he had
never fully recovered. His estate at Turtle Bay, where
Margaret had resided during her tenure in New York, was
called Castle Doleful, because of Greeley's brooding marital miseries, with a more than strange wife who lived
mostly in a "spirit world," caring nothing for her husband
and not even grieving at the loss of her children. Much
concerned with spiritualism himself, Greeley often discussed it with his religious friends and theologians, particularly George Ripley.

He said now, "Margaret was the most brilliant woman I
ever knew," and Kate did not take exception or offense,
aware that the lady had been a scholar with few equals in
either sex. "Emerson, Hawthorne, Lowell, Whittier, Bryant
all acknowledged her brilliance. Unfortunately, there are
only a few such prodigies in any one generation. I often
wonder what great things she might have accomplished,
for surely she had not reached her zenith at death."

"I've tried so many times to raise her," Kate confessed
ruefully. "One night I thought sure she was going to give
me a message via the planchette, and another time I almost felt her hand trying to take over my automatic writing. I've summoned and implored her in every conceivable
method and mood, but still she eludes or ignores me. Do
you suppose that's because I never knew her personally?
After all, she must know I'm trying to reach her. She was
a transcendentalist too, and she had tremendous psychic
perception, didn't she, George?"

Ripley nodded. "But don't feel slighted, Katie dear.

We've all tried to communicate with Margaret on many occasions. I myself wonder why she is so elusive. Perhaps it's the circumstances of her passing. Souls who cross over in water may be more difficult to contact. There may be some kind of karmic barrier of which we are unaware."

The conversation made Devon's flesh prickle and tingle. They spoke of these things as if they were fact rather than fancy or supposition, and she had nothing intelligent to contribute, for she was woefully ignorant on the subject. Ashamed of her ignorance, she wisely kept her ears open and her mouth shut.

Kate asked, "Do you think Victoria will have better luck, George?"

"Possibly, with Demosthenes as her guide."

"If he is," Greeley muttered skeptically. He was not as convinced as the Commodore of Mrs. Woodhull's supernatural gifts and talents, nor that the great Greek orator, dead some four thousand years after biting off the tip of a poison pen in the temple of Poseidon, had been making periodic visitations to Victoria since childhood and directing her life. For a shrewd man, Vanderbilt was sometimes uncommonly simple and gullible, he thought. Still, undeniably, he was charged by Tennessee's electricity, and certain that Victoria had summoned his ancestral spirits for him, whether by second sight or subtle sorcery.

"Now, Horace," Kate reproached him, "You know very well a negative attitude is detrimental and impeding to any medium. We must all hold positive, receptive thoughts and make our psyches readily accessible. Isn't that right, Georgie?"

"Right as rain," Ripley agreed. "And we might just have some rain tonight too."

"Good," Kate said. "I hope it storms a little. That's the best possible atmosphere for a seance. And since Margaret perished in the violence of a hurricane. . . ."

The steamer had cleared the Narrows and Lower Bay and was in the Atlantic. They could see the lighthouse on Rockaway Point. The sea was somewhat choppy, agitated. Strong winds were blowing from the southeast. It had been an unusually disagreeable day, hot and muggy—the kind of weather that sent wealthy New Yorkers to the summer resorts, and only this event had kept Vanderbilt from his Saratoga cottage. Soon a fuzzy haze gathered on the evening horizon. But there was nothing to fear; the yacht was an ocean liner, actually, with an able crew and sturdy lifeboats, and they would always be within sight of land.

Nevertheless, Devon was tense and began to think poignantly of Keith somewhere on the rails to Chicago. These people were virtual strangers to her, strangers on a weird and fantastic voyage. She had nothing in common with them, really, not even their intense occult interests. What, then, was she doing in their company? Sometimes it seemed that she was not entirely her own mistress, in complete control of her faculties and emotions, but impelled and compelled by unknown forces.

Keith was right to be angry and aggravated over the situations in which she sometimes involved and even imperiled herself, and she knew he would be absolutely furious about this escapade. He had already vehemently expressed his opinion of Woodhull and Claflin. And there were three Wall Street men, whom he referred to variously as the Terrible Trio and the Tovarich Trinity, and for whom he had little use and even less respect: Jay Gould, Daniel Drew, and Cornelius Vanderbilt. And here she was on a ghoulish treasure hunt with the Commodore!

Chapter 21

Victoria was contemplating the individual countenances, gazing at each intently, her compelling blue eyes narrowed incisively, and Kate whispered to Devon, "She's studying our auras."

"Auras?"

"The subtle radiation that emanates from every being. Mediums are highly cognizant of this ethereal nimbus, and sensitive to it. Vicky's studying yours now."

The scrutiny made Devon nervous; she smoothed her hair and skirts, as if she were being photographed. "Did you tell the Commodore anything about me, Kate?"

"Only that you were a sympathetic friend I'd met at the Carys. Your interest in the Eternal Search was reference enough to secure your invitation. Why?" she teased. "Afraid Victoria might rattle some family skeletons?"

"Oh no, nothing like that! On the contrary, I hope she also contacts my father. He may be in Margaret Fuller's sphere or periphery, since they were in the same profession." She hesitated, her skin creeping whenever she thought of the hereafter. The concept of eternity baffled her young mind, too profound to comprehend, too fantastic to placidly accept or dismiss. "But it's all rather mysterious and eerie, don't you think?"

"Not at all, dear. Death is perfectly natural, and there's no logical or valid reason to assume that life ends at the grave. What a senseless and tragic waste if this short sojourn on earth were our only destination, and fertilizer our only purpose! The great minds of the ages have never subscribed to that pagan theory, nor doubted spiritual existence—" They were distracted by the scene across the salon, where the Commodore was teasing Tennie, tickling and fondling her, while she giggled and tugged his whiskers coquettishly. "No need to wonder how they'll spend the night," Kate murmured. "Does it seem to you that the boat is rocking more?"

"Decidedly," Devon agreed, shuddering. "I wish we'd hurry and get there."

"So do I," Kate said. "I feel that we're on our way to an important rendezvous." Fantasy inspired and intrigued her. "I wonder if Victoria could possibly be Margaret incarnate?"

Greeley, who had been relaxing with his head back and eyes closed, preparing himself psychically, smiled gingerly. "According to the ministry, she's the devil incarnate, or his wife."

"Or mistress? The pious hypocrites, how eagerly they focus on women's faults and trangressions while ignoring men's!"

"Don't brand all clergy with the same iron," Ripley said.

Kate smiled benignly. "You're an exception, Georgie, but you're also not a cleric any more. And you know very well there are demigods in the pulpits, and the green pastures abound with wolves in shepherd's clothing. As Vicky so succinctly says, many a voluminous sacred robe conveniently conceals an erect phallus! Oh, don't look so aghast, George, and close your mouth, Horace. Hasn't hypocrisy always existed in the cloth? What of Abelard, Kierkegaard, St. Augustine, and some of the profligate popes of Rome, including Alexander VI, whose lusts gave the world the Borgias. And considering our Brooklyn contemporary, every journalist has heard rumors about the pastor of Plymouth Church and his subtle seductions of his female parishioners."

Greeley raised a flaccid hand, warning, "Careful now, Kate. Remember the slander and libel laws."

"You're not saying or printing it, Horace. Furthermore, I doubt seriously that Reverend Beecher would ever make an issue of it, lest the truth emerge. After all, the Beecher-Bowen business is hardly a secret in the trade." (Henry Bowen, publisher of the eminent religious journal, the *Independent*, had confided to his editor, Theodore Tilton, that his wife had confessed on her deathbed to an affair with the pastor of Plymouth Church.) "Isn't that how Henry justified his remarriage so soon after his wife's death? Why remain faithful to the memory of a faithless woman? Imagine how he felt at her obsequies presided over by his cuckold! Theodore had to hold him back at the grave, not to keep him from falling on her casket but from leaping at her lover."

"That story is grossly exaggerated," Ripley temporized. "I attended Mrs. Bowen's funeral, and Henry was gravely stoic. Dry-eyed, too. I never saw him shed a tear."

"Would you, under the circumstances? And if you ask me, Theodore is a worried man himself. His Lib is so young and lovely, and he's away so much on his lecture tours . . . perhaps he suspects their pastor of comforting her more than spiritually."

"We'd better drop that subject," Greeley decided, and turned to Devon, who had been fascinated by it. "Our little Katie can be quite a firebrand in pursuit of women's rights. Do you subscribe to the Movement's gospel?"

"Yes, of course. The slaves were freed, why not women?"

"Well, I don't think any of you need worry about your light failing with torchbearers like the Anthonys, Stantons, Motts, Stones, Bloomers, Carys, Woodhulls, and Claflins. That's a mighty impressive and formidable vanguard."

Ripley said, "Victoria could not be Margaret's incarnate, however, since she was alive at the time of her death. Reincarnation takes pace at birth."

"Spirits also possess, release, and repossess," Kate reminded authoritatively. "There are temperamental souls there, as here."

"Undoubtedly," Greeley agreed, and addressed Devon again: "You're the little Richmond rebel, aren't you?"

"I'm a native Virginian," she retorted crisply.

"No offense, Miss, but I was in your territory recently, posting Mr. Davis' bond, and their sentiments haven't mellowed much. I wasn't shot, however, although I'm still not sure whether that was a favor or a flattery."

His droll humor mitigated his irony, often making him the intentional brunt of his trenchant wit, and Devon could not be angry with him for long. "Perhaps it was both," she said.

He laughed, nodded, closed his eyes and sank back into reverie again, capable of withdrawing even in a multitude.

The captain reported their position to the Commodore, who announced that they would be anchoring soon. "The steward has already assigned your staterooms, and if you want to retire and rest until the seance, please feel free to do so." And pulling Tennie to her feet and grinning, "Come along, my little sparrow, we'll meditate together."

Devon's cabin parallelled Kate's. Greeley and Ripley were separately quartered across the passageway. Victoria occupied Mrs. Vanderbilt's seldom used stateroom, and the commodore escorted Tennie to the master suite.

The wind was rising, flinging spray across the decks, the sea churning like the paddlewheels. Devon could see nothing outside her porthole except the raging waves and increasing fog. The accommodations were opulent, if not sybaritic. The walls were paneled in satinwood, with gold traceries and intaglio on the white plaster ceiling. Crystal hurricane globes protected the candles and oil lamps of the wall-sconces. The berth was generous and comfortable, but her stomach was queasy from the undulating vessel. How terrible if she should have to miss the seance due to seasickness. Perhaps Kate had a remedy. She knocked at her door. "I'm sorry to disturb you, dear, but I'm feeling somewhat nauseous."

"Oh, my! We can't have such a contretemps, can we? Don't you know the sovereign cure for mal de mer? Just suck a lemon, darling. Should be some in your cabin. Here, take one of mine."

"Thanks, Kate. I never thought of that."

It worked. She felt better, able to return to the salon when the steward sounded the gong.

The yacht was now anchored a safe distance from the sandbars of Fire Island, yet as near as possible, according to the captain's calculations from the maritime records, to the location where the merchant ship *Elizabeth*, carrying the Marquis Ossoli, his wife Margaret, and their baby boy Angelino, had broken up in a hurricane, July 21, 1850, within sight of the Long Island and New Jersey shores.

Darkness, conducive to seance, was settling on the sea. But the Commodore, displeased with the worsening gale and fog, roared at the captain, "Bannon, what the hell is this weather? Didn't you get a forecast before sailing?"

"I did, sir. And there was no mention of a local coastal disturbance. It's just a squall, Commodore, nothing to worry about. The ship is well lighted and the foghorns operating."

"I'm not worried about our safety, Captain. But we intend to conduct a seance, and it'll be damned distracting with the dishes and bottles rattling and jumping out of the racks. How can we hear the spirits rapping through all this goddamn racket?"

Bannon stared at him, nonplused, wondering if he was expected to somehow control the elements, banish the mists, calm the sea. "I should think it would be advantageous to the experiment, Commodore. But I'll order every loose item removed or secured. And the crew, except for the watch, requested permission to observe, sir."

Vanderbilt consulted Victoria. She agreed, aware of the superstitions of the sea inherent or acquired in every sailor; perhaps their presence would help to summon the denizens of the deep. Victoria was growing increasingly anxious herself, her pale skin flushing as it invariably did in emotional excitement, for she was genuinely convinced of her extraordinary powers. Hadn't she performed some amazing feats under the guidance of her Athenian mentor, accomplished some fantastic successes against tremendous odds, and brought some monumental mortals into her camp? And it was not as if she were a novice sybil; she had conducted productive readings over much of the country in a decade of travel with her nomad family and her free lover, before Demosthenes had directed her to go to "a place surrounded by ships," which she had immediately interpreted as the Isle of Manhattan, and he so promptly delivered such promised fame and success that even she was astounded.

The pragamatic press, however, was obviously dubious of her destiny. Thus, when the Commodore had informed her of Horace Greeley's interest in occultism and his sittings some years past with the famous Fox sisters of Rochester, along with James Fenimore Cooper, William Cullen Bryant, George Bancroft, and other prominent citizens, in his home in Turtle Bay, Victoria had suggested a seance at sea, on the death anniversary of Greeley's departed idol, whose shipwrecked body had never been recovered from Davy Jones' locker. If she could succeed in summoning Margaret Fuller's spirit, the *Tribune* might become her oracle in her future campaigns, for it was Victoria Woodhull's ambition to be President of the United States. Indeed, Demosthenes had told her that she would become "the leader of her people," a prophecy which Victoria *expected to fulfill in the White House*.

She welcomed the storm as an elemental asset and convinced the Commodore of its propitiousness, declaring, "The spirits willed it."

The large round dining table had been cleared and the chairs circled around it. All but one wall lamp was extinguished, this situated at Victoria's back and simulating a mystic halo about her lustrous head. She directed them to be seated and clasp hands to increase the mood and vibrations. Then she closed her eyes and slipped into a trance, seemingly oblivious of the banshee wails of the wind and the ghostly mists hovering at the portholes.

Tense and frightened, Devon longed for Keith's steadying influence. If only it were his hands she clung to, instead of Kate Field's and George Ripley's. Both of their pulsations were vibrant and expectant. Her eyelids fluttered open, and she had a glimpse of the medium.

Victoria appeared in deep hypnotic slumber, her magnificent breasts swelling rhythmically beneath the purple silk drapery, the white rose incensing her person. Gradually a serene smile touched her soft sensuous lips, revealing her beautiful teeth, as if she recognized an old friend whom she was about to greet. Then a voice spoke, similar but not identical to Victoria's, and her personality seemed to undergo metamorphosis as well. The hands around the table grasped one another tighter, as the medium murmured a name: "Demosthenes."

"He's come," the Commodore whispered gutturally. "By God, he's here!"

"Shh," Tennessee hissed, clutching his hand.

Ignoring the interruption, Victoria announced, "Demosthenes is among us," and for a few moments she carried on an intimate conversation with the invisible man, as if he were a lover come to a spiritual assignation, then surrendered her mortal body to him, that he might possess her immortal soul. "You know for what purpose we are assembled, my dear Demosthenes! Do not forsake or disappoint us. It is the spirit of Margaret Fuller we seek, she who perished in these very waters . . ."

There was a long tentative silence, during which everyone listened for her Greek discarnate's voice, and heard instead one perceived as Margaret Fuller's by those who had known her intimately. No one was more amazed than Greeley, since mimicry seemed impossible. Victoria, only thirteen at the time of the other woman's death, could hardly have met or remembered her.

"Horace," the spirit voice spoke, "I think of you a great deal here, and am so sorry that my manuscript, *The History of the Roman Republic,* perished with me. Ossoli regrets exceedingly that he was unable to meet my beloved friend and editor, whom I praised so highly and loved so devotedly. But we are happy and content now, and our little Angelo is with us. We are together in eternity."

Greeley, frowning in puzzlement, his high-pitched voice squeakier than usual, asked, "Why did you stay with the ship, Margaret? Why didn't you leave with the other passengers?"

"The lifeboats were swept away early. Of the passengers and crew who jumped overboard with life preservers, only a few survived and reached shore. We watched the unfortunates drown, and did not want to risk our baby's life. But why do you ask, Horace? Did you not receive my letters detailing my presentiment of the disaster long before I left Italy? Did not my dear friends, Robert and Elizabeth Browning, inform you of my premonitions, and that I had inscribed a Bible from my son to theirs, 'In memory of Angelo Eugene Ossoli.' Did not I also advise the Brownings of a savant's previous prophecy that the marquis would die by drowning? We were merely fulfilling our destinies, Horace. The *Elizabeth* was an ill-fated ship from the beginning of the voyage. Captain Hasty's death of smallpox was the first bad omen, and his burial in the deep waters off Gibraltar and our long quarantine in port, which delayed our departure for the States long enough to throw the *Elizabeth* into the jaws of the Caribbean hurricane. . . ."

Oh, Devon thought excitedly, I should be writing this down! And here I am holding hands instead of a pen. I'll never be able to remember it all, never!

"Tell us, please," Kate beseeched, "about the place you now inhabit."

"It is a state of mind," the voice informed. "It is a progression via levels, from lower to higher planes of wisdom and understanding, depending on the maturity of the soul.

It is a spiritual evolution through which every soul must evolve to attain sublimity."

"My God," the Commodore exclaimed, "we are witnessing a revelation! Victoria Woodhull is a miracle worker!" Vanderbilt firmly believed in miracles, for his own progression up the ladder of life, from abject poverty to supreme wealth, had always struck him as miraculous.

George Ripley inquired about his former profession. "How important is religion, Margaret?"

The wind whistled, the waves crashed against the ship. But it was so quiet and expectant in the salon, they could hear the heavy breathing of the entranced crew behind them, from the boiler stokers to the first mate.

The spirit voice replied, with a touch of whimsy or irony, "Not as important as the clergy would like to think, George. Far more important are love and compassion; love of God and of all humanity, compassion for the less fortunate. Intrinsic human worth and values. Truth, honesty, lack of hypocrisy. Unity, loving and helping one another; denying *no one* his inherent freedoms, rights, and privileges."

Kate took this as a cue for her next question. "Have you any advice for your earth sisters in their continuing struggle toward these liberties?"

"You refer to women's rights, and you have many dedicated souls in your campaign. But soon one will rise, preordained to lead you to ultimate victory, destined to deliver womankind to her proper throne. The answer lies in Constitutional amendments. Article Fourteen is a start, but still inadequate. There must be an amendment *guaranteeing* the vote to every citizen of the country, and this must be your relentless dedication. A series of pronunciamentos, in which the leader of my prophecy will excel and is even now pondering, will be necessary to incite action in Washington. Indeed, a memorial must be presented to Congress!"

"Oh, I knew it!" Kate cried excitedly. "And it shall be! Thank you, Margaret. If only you were here to help us!"

"I am with you in spirit," the voice assured.

Caught up in the spell, Devon was trying to muster the courage to ask about her father, when the spirit again assumed uncanny command. "I have a message for a girl among you. One of her names is the same as the ship on which I perished. The message is from her father, a member of my profession, and we have many enlightened discussions together. Will she please identify herself?"

"It's me ... I," Devon murmured, her voice barely audible, her breath almost suffocated in awe. "Devon Elizabeth Marshall. My father, Hodge Marshall, was publisher and editor of the Richmond *Sentinel*."

"Yes," droned the voice, as if this were superfluous information in the spirit world. "He wants you to know that he is happy here, but he is also sorry that through self-destruction he did not bide his allotted time on earth."

"Oh!" cried Devon, aghast, "how did you know *that?*"

"It is common knowledge *here*," came the somewhat impatient reply. "But he wants you to know that he loves you deeply and is always watching over you."

Tears moistened Devon's eyes, but she could not blot them with her occupied hands; they spilled down her cheeks onto her gown. "Thank you," she whispered humbly. "Tell him that I love him too, and understand and forgive what he did."

"Forgiveness is not in your realm," the voice rebuked.

"Well, tell him—"

But abruptly, apparently on signal from Demosthenes, the spirit announced that it was time to return to the higher elevations, poetically described as "The Mystic Mountain of Eternity overlooking the Enchanted Valley of Time, where the King of Peace and Serenity rules supreme and eternal."

A steward was rushing around lighting the lamps and candles again. The chain of hands was broken. Victoria was waking from her mesmeric trance with a dreamy-eyed graceful languor, as if she were on stage, as indeed she had been during a brief sojourn in San Francisco, where she had appeared in some of Anna Cogswell's presentations. She smiled at her awed audience and said, "I know Demosthenes came. Did he raise Margaret?"

"He did indeed!" Kate declared, jubilantly. "Not only raised but delivered her to us! Oh, Vicky, you are an absolute marvel! My mediumship is nothing by comparison— but then, unfortunately, I don't have a Greek sage in my service. My poor guide is only a witch burned at Salem."

The Commodore was pumping Victoria's hand and beaming at her. "I never saw you in greater form, honey.

By God, Demosthenes is not only your servant but your slave. I want another sitting first thing next week. And I think you should go to Washington and read for that nincompoop in the White House. He's leading the country up a blind alley to ruin. Somebody's got to warn, stop, guide him!" Grinning complacently, he slapped Greeley's shoulder. "Well, Horace! What do you think of my seeress now?"

"Did you say sorceress?"

"You know damn well what I said! Are you satisfied of her psychic ability? You knew Margaret Fuller well—was that her spirit, her voice?"

"If not, it was a reasonable facsimile," Greeley reluctantly conceded. He realized, of course, that the information given was all recorded and available to anyone for the effort of research, but he could not explain the similarity of voice, for Margaret's had possessed a unique cadence, full of high octaves, and he would not have believed himself easily beguiled or persuaded by even a clever imitation. Still, it had been many years, almost twenty. And more astute minds than his had been confused by the rappings and levitations of the Rochester sisters ten years ago.

"I had many questions to ask," he complained.

"And I," Kate lamented.

Ripley said, "We all did. But nobody reminded her of the date, that this is her special anniversary."

"Don't you suppose she knew it?" Vanderbilt chided. "God, what an experience! It calls for a celebration. Steward, break out the bar!"

The seamen were ordered back to duty without the demijohn of rum they had hoped to share, for the Commodore would tolerate no crew intoxication on any of his vessels, particularly his yacht, though passengers might inundate themselves.

While all except Greeley were toasting Victoria in champagne, the storm broke in full fury. But the Commodore, now stimulated by spirits and the elements, assured them that there was no danger. "It's only a summer squall, friends, not a tropical hurricane such as wrecked the *Elizabeth.* Let it deluge, we're in a safe ark. So relax. Eat, drink, and be merry, for tomorrow we *live!* Tonight we live," he added, gazing at Tennie.

Devon alone seemed frightened. She shunned the food and merely pretended to sip from the glass she held with both trembling hands, to prevent an accident. She hoped that Kate would suggest sharing one of their cabins. But later, as they walked together in the passage, the journalist only recalled a violent storm she had once witnessed in the North Atlantic, which made this one seem mild by comparison, and remarked that she was going to remain up awhile recording the events in her diary. She advised Devon to do the same, and they parted at her door.

Devon undressed and, leaving a light burning, crawled into her berth and pulled the covers over her head. But the phantoms and fantasies conjured in the seance had been too stimulating, and sleep eluded her. Had Mrs. Woodhull actually summoned Demosthenes, and he in turn Margaret Fuller? How had Victoria known about her father's suicide? Horace Greeley and Kate Field knew, of course, but Kate insisted she had not told Vanderbilt anything about Devon, so who could have briefed Victoria? And was the storm a coincidence, or a sign? What if the vessel broke up, as had that other, and the lifeboats were swept away, and they all drowned? Keith would have dispelled her specters and superstitions with a few calm, rational explanations, but Devon shuddered and burrowed deeper into the covers.

Terrified, she did not immediately hear the tapping on her door, and then her apprehension became ominous. She smiled at herself, when she recognized George Ripley's voice.

"Miss Marshall? Are you awake?"

Devon donned her negligee before answering. "Yes, Reverend."

"I thought you might be afraid and need comfort," he said. "Spiritual comfort. Would you like me to pray with you?"

She hesitated. How did one refuse such an offer? "Come in," she invited.

Ripley stepped inside and closed the door. He was sixty-five years old, a tall personable man with silver hair and a warm personality. His smile was tender, perceptive. "You are afraid, aren't you?"

"A little," she admitted. "Perhaps a lot."

"Don't be, child. No harm will come to you. This is a

very seaworthy craft. Mrs. Woodhull gave an impressive performance, didn't she?"

"Performance?"

He nodded. "Acting is one of her talents, you know."

"No, I didn't know."

"Yes, she had a brief career on the stage, out West."

"You think it was just an act?"

"I'm not sure, one way or the other. I knew Margaret well, and the voice was remarkably similar, as I recall it. Certainly I believe in life after death. And Horace is just as confused and bewildered about tonight's revelation, if such it was, as I. The thing that makes it suspicious, however, is that so little time was allotted to individual questioning, as if inquiries might arise for which there were no ready answers. But then spirits are believed to return to earth only briefly, if at all, and to be imminently on the verge of evanescence. They are not easily captured in bottles or otherwise."

His levity relaxed Devon. She felt more at ease, although she did not understand how she could, sitting in deshabille on a berth with a night-robed stranger beside her. "Do you suppose she researched and rehearsed all that, and recited it like an actress in a play?"

"Oh, undoubtedly she read a biography of Margaret Fuller. And your father's fate is known in journalism, and she did not elaborate on it, remember. She's extraordinarily clever and talented. Certainly the Commodore is convinced."

Devon's hands lay idly in her lap. Ripley picked them up and pressed the palms together in prayerful attitude, holding them thus in his own. Devon gazed at him expectantly, waiting for him to commence praying. His eyes began to glow. He said softly, "What a lovely little creature you are, enchanting as a sea nymph in that misty green thing. I hope it's true that your father is watching over you. Someone definitely should."

"Reverend—"

"I'm not a minister any more, Devon. It's been twenty years since I've preached in church. No, I wasn't defrocked; I resigned to pursue a dream. Do you know anything about Brook Farm?"

"Not much."

"Well, it was an experiment in socialism. Communal liv-

ing, and also transcendentalism. Mrs. Ripley and I founded, the commune at West Roxbury, Massachusetts, before
you were born. We had many famous members, advocates,
devotees. Nathaniel Hawthorne, Albert Brisbane, Charles
Dana, to name a few. We had some distinguished scholars
in the school, and many renowned visitors. Emerson,
Lowell, Whittier, Greeley, Margaret Fuller. Brook Farm
thrived for six years, until a fire destroyed our phalanstery.
We could not sustain or recoup the loss, and so had
to disband. Now it's only a memory, and sometimes seems
but an illusion that didn't quite manifest, a dream that
couldn't endure. Nevertheless, it was a noble experiment,
of great benefit to those able to share in its brief existence."

"I'm sure it was," Devon agreed.

"A high-minded, highly principled and motivated organization," he continued. "Greeley was a convert, and
then a disciple. He subscribed to the basic concepts and
precepts of Brook Farm, and under the auspices of
Charles Fourier established a community at Red Bank,
New Jersey. Horace is very idealistic, albeit a bit peculiar
at times. But then, visionaries, as geniuses, are often eccentric."

"I suppose," Devon said, wondering if this was what he
had come for at this hour, to enlighten her about Brook
Farm.

"Tell me," he urged, still imprisoning her hands in his,
"do you think what the Commodore and Tennie are doing
now is wrong?"

"I don't know what they're doing," she hedged.

"You have imagination, haven't you? You should, if
you intend to write."

"Well, then—yes, I do think it's wrong."

He nodded, releasing her hands. "You're right. It's damn-
ably wrong. And rest assured, I was only testing your
morals, which are equally as staunch as Kate's. You're a
golden-haired angel. But Victoria and Tennessee, I suspect,
are something less. They appear unburdened by virtue or
propriety. One is a merry little trollop, the other an ambitious adventuress, and I do not believe either will ultimately triumph, even with such a giant as Vanderbilt
championing them. As for myself, I had better return to
my quarters before that ascetic next door makes a bunk
check and draws erroneous conclusions. Sometimes I think

Horace is a nonsectarian monk." He stood, tall and straight and strangely imposing in his dark robe. "Good night, my dear. There's an old seafarer's prayer that begins, 'O Lord, Thy sea is so great and my bark so small.' Do you know it?"

"Yes," Devon murmured, although she did not.

"Say it," he said, opened the door and left.

When she awoke, the sky was a clear washed blue, the sun sparkling on the calm green water. Devon could see the tall white lighthouse on Fire Island, the desolate dunes bristling with reeds and salt-weed, and scattered with the bleaching bones of dead ships. The seance, the storm, the whole strange night might have been only a dream, a fantasy.

The bells announced breakfast. Devon was hungry. She dressed in a summer printed voile and carried her leghorn hat. In the dining salon their genial host, flanked by the radiant sisters, was obviously energized, full of vinegar and joviality.

Kate, chic in a deck costume of white pique with a red polkadot scarf, nudged Devon and whispered sotto voce, "I'm tempted to ask *him* how he slept, except that he's frank enough to tell me," and she chuckled vivaciously, in high spirits herself.

Ripley arrived. A steward had steamed the wrinkles from his seersucker suit, shined his shoes, and he wore a fresh white shirt and blue ascot. He smiled warmly at Devon. "Did the sea monsters plague your sleep?"

"No, I banished them with prayer, Reverend."

"I had to exorcise some demons of my own," he confessed ruefully. "Come with me to the grill, please. Help me select."

"If you wish. Maybe you can help me."

Finally, the rumpled Greeley appeared, mumbled his greetings, and peered near-sightedly at the prodigal table for the meager fare he fancied, disappointed to find no bran, stewed fruit, or curds. "Bacchanalia even at breakfast," he muttered. "Disgusting. Disgraceful. Steward, get me some oat gruel and prunes, if you must ransack the gallery!"

At the helm of the table, feasting on a ham omelette, potato pancakes, muffins, honeydew melon filled with fresh strawberries, coffee, and thick cream, the Commodore announced that they would circle Long Island before returning to Manhattan. Devon regretted this, aware that it was a cruise Keith planned in the *Sprite*, and for this reason she enjoyed it less.

When at last they docked in New York harbor again, at the Vanderbilt pier, and Devon was thanking him, he said brusquely, "Not a'tall, not a'tall! Pleasure to have had you aboard. But I'm curious to know, pretty minx, if you have any kind of specialty."

"Specialty?"

"Well, Tennie here is a magnetic healer. Vicky there is a clairvoyant. If you don't have a specialty, girlie, I'd advise you to develop one promptly. A female can't go very far in this man's world without a specialty." And lightly, with his cane, he tapped her buttocks and winked. "Know what I mean?"

"I think so, Commodore, and I'll try to invent one."

His laughter boomed across the Battery. "When you do, look me up, honey. I ain't hard to find. . . ."

Chapter 22

St. Andrew's Church stood on the corner of Duane and Cardinal Streets, near City Hall and Newspaper Row, convenient to Catholic politicians and printers. Mally O'Neill had worshiped there because many of her factory friends were members, and she had not felt so alone among them on Sundays. Devon had come now to burn some devotional candles for the Irish girl's soul, hoping also to allay her still haunting memory. She had not dared mention Mally's name after her father's had been introduced at the seance, since suicides, according to occult belief, were restless spirits roaming in ethereality, therefore easily contacted, and Devon still was not sure whether Victoria Woodhull had merely hookwinked them all, or not.

At first she thought she was alone in the great domed and pillared cathedral, with its dark oak pews, grilled confessionals, and ponderous choir loft, and was wary and apprehensive, half-expecting some Quasimodo creature to creep out of the Gothic gloom. Then she distinguished the silhouettes of several nuns, their black habits blending into the ephemeral shadows, and a scattering of widows in somber weeds, long black veils or mantillas draping their heads. Why were the mourners usually women? One rarely saw a man prostrate in grief. Most widowers removed their black armbands promptly after the funeral, and some she remembered in Richmond had remarried so rapidly one would suspect they had anticipated and prepared for the eventuality. Hodge Marshall had been a rare exception, assuaging his loss and loneliness and grief through his work and child.

Devon deposited some coins in the cache attached to the votive rack, lighted several candles, and watched them flicker in the cranberry glass receptacles. Then she sat in a rear pew and said some Protestant prayers for Mally

O'Neill and all female victims of male monsters. Painted images with outstretched hands and weeping eyes and mysterious expressions stood about on pedestals, in an exotic atmosphere of burnt beeswax and incense from the last benediction. The sun made mystic mosaics of the stained glass windows, and she could see the faint golden gleam of the crucifix and candelabra on the high marble altar. Peaceful, tranquil, and somehow enchanting. Did the virgin nuns attend the vestal lamp in the sanctuary?

She remembered Mally's great faith in the esoterica of her religion, her superstitions and amulets, how she had clung to her rosary when in distress. In violent weather she had burned sacred candles and sprinkled holy water about her room and tied blessed palm leaves to her bedposts, murmuring prayers and litanies and crossing herself. And she had kept a little shrine to her patron saint.

Where was she now? Languishing in limbo, expiating in purgatory, burning in hell for having taken her own life? Her mortal remains were excluded from the churchyard, the consecrated earth forbidden by canon law to suicides. But it was the devil who had tempted and seduced her who should be denied the Sacraments, excommunicated, damned for all eternity. And sacrilegiously, Devon cursed in this holy place. God damn you, Davey Thorne! May you burn forever and ever, Amen.

Preoccupied, she started walking, her parasol forgotten in the pew. The blazing sun almost sent her back into the cool dim haven. New York summers were violent compared to Virginia's. Unbidden, she remembered the prewar barbecues and picnics in the shady groves, picking berries and mushrooms in the fragrant pine woods, cantering leisurely across bluegrass meadows and along flowery lanes, boating on the river. And for the first time in months her nostalgia included Daniel Haverston. Was he managing to survive Reconstruction, succeeding at Harmony Hill? Had he forgotten her by now, replaced her as easily as she replaced her lost articles? Keith's generosity not only made her careless with her possessions and spoiled her thrift but marred some of the pleasure of acquisition, since things easily acquired were usually less appreciated.

The fetid Manhattan miasma of manure, ammonia, and garbage steamed from the teeming streets, compounded by beclouding factory and steamer smoke, boiling pitch from the docks, and the sulphur fumigation of a nearby pestilent tenement. Faint from the heat and odors, she began to weave and wander, bumping into several pedestrians, who mumbled and grumbled and cursed her. Then a brash young British sailor caught her arm familiarily. "Lookin' for company, sweetheart?"

She gazed at him blankly, and his eager grin faded in disappointment. "You sick, lady?"

"No, just dazed, I think. And lost. Where am I?"

"Search me! I'm new in this port myself and forgot my compass. But you seem headed on a collision course."

"I'm sorry. It's this wretched weather."

"Well, don't swoon, Ma'am, because they'll just let you lay in the gutter. This is some goddamn unfriendly place! The reactions I've had, you'd think my ship was flying the Jolly Roger and under plague quarantine." He gave her a jaunty salute and ambled off, eyes casting about for a more amenable prospect with which to pass his liberty, and Devon realized she had better get out of the neighborhood, fast.

But as usual when needed, there was no hackney available. Orienting herself by St. Andrew's steeple, she moved in that direction, and did not see the scarlet coach and prancing palominos until they were almost on top of her. The driver yelled and hauled on the reins, and the occupant leaped out just as Devon jumped back onto the curb. It was Trent Donahue.

"Miss Marshall, isn't it? Are ye hurt?" He bellowed at the bizarre pair on the perch, "Stupid fools! Watch where ye're going! You near ran down this lovely lady!"

"It was her not lookin' whar she was goin', Boss."

"Shut up!" Donahue growled. Taking Devon's arm, he boosted her into the carriage and she, still disoriented and shaken by her narrow escape, went without volition. "Drive on, Patch! Don't be blocking traffic!" The coach lurched forward, and Devon settled into a nest of red plush permeated with Lilly Day's narcissus scent. "This is the best luck I've had in a month of Sundays, finding you again, Miss Marshall. That scurvy old buzzard at the bookstore told me you'd left town."

"Just for a visit, Mr. Donahue."

"But what're you doing in the Fourth Ward? 'Tis no fit place for a lady, I can tell you."

"I was at St. Andrew's Church."

"St. Andrew's?" He arched a russet brow. "Be ye Catholic?"

"No, I went in memory of a friend."

Donahue smiled. "Had I known you was there, I'd have paid old St. Andy a visit meself. I'm on me way to a picnic now, and you're coming along."

"Oh no, I couldn't, sir! I'm not invited."

"Everybody's invited," he said. " 'Tis a political shindig, and all Tammany'll be there, including the Boss. 'Tis his rally, in fact. He's ticketed for state senator this year, and his campaign is on."

"I've noticed," Devon said.

Tweed's great yellow barrage balloons floating over Tammany Hall were visible for miles. His posters and handbills plastered every available wall and fence. His banners waved from horsecars, omnibuses, drays, minstrel and medicine wagons. Children flew kites bearing his name and wore feather-bonnets distributed by the Wigwam. Tweed's personal flag fluttered from the mast of his yacht, and he had also bought advertising on steamboats and trains making the Albany run.

"The bastard's not content to control the city," Keith had said on one of the rare occasions he discussed politics with her, for he considered it a brutalizing, defeminizing subject. "He wants to control the state and eventually the country."

"If he's so corrupt, why do the people elect him to public office?"

"Don't tell me a newsman's daughter never heard of political corruption? Some historians say voting tombstones and stuffing ballot boxes originated with your crafty Southern politicians, who killed their opponents in duels when they couldn't beat them at the polls."

"You're evading the issue."

"I'm saying the practice of stealing elections didn't originate with Tammany, but has existed since this country became a republic. Tweed merely organized it into an efficient, unbeatable machine, which doesn't function on honesty."

"You don't do business with them?"

"Business, yes. They all have accounts with the Curtis Bank, because they know their loot is safe. We withstood the universal financial panic of thirty-seven, and hardly felt the tremors of the fifty-seven quake that destroyed so many other firms. Besides, I make money lending theirs at interest, and that's what banking's all about, you know. But I wouldn't trust any of them with a penny of mine, because they plunder one another and ruin their friends as readily as their enemies. Fortunately, I don't have to cater to the pirates in any respect. I have treasure in far-flung places which they can't touch or threaten, and I owe no man anywhere allegiance or favor."

"How wonderful to be so independent," Devon mused, and he glanced at her sharply, as always when she spoke of independence, for she had once accused him of espousing freedom for everyone except her. "How did you get your soubriquets, then?"

"Machiavelli, Merlin?" He grinned. "By anticipating and outwitting the Wall Street rascals at their own bloody games. I know, for instance, that a monumental battle for control of the Erie Railroad is shaping up with Jay Gould and Jim Fisk allied against Commodore Vanderbilt, and regardless of who wins, the stockholders will lose. Consequently, I intend to pull out and offer my shares to the highest bidder. The competition will be lively between the rivals, and I stand to profit handsomely on my original investment. There's nothing unscrupulous or mesmeric about that—it's just sound business judgment and acumen."

"And the 'Wolf of Wall Street'?"

"Oh, that got started when a female journalist—Kate Field, to be exact, a clever and lovely little witch—covered a Curtis ball and wrote with tongue-in-cheek, I suspect, 'The host was so handsome and charming he could have persuaded Little Red Riding Hood to surrender her cookies,' or some such trivia, at which she excels. Allegory is a popular press game, and cartoonists thrive on it. But the wolf is a much maligned creature, actually, especially in his social habits. He's monogamous by nature and mates for life; he roams only when he's deprived or hungry." And he'd laughed and kissed her, nibbling at her ears and throat, declaring she was sweet and tender and tasty enough to eat.

*

"Miss Marshall?" Donahue snapped his fingers before her face. "Did I lose ye again?"

"No, I was just in a brown study, sir. Would you be kind enough to drop me off on Broadway? I have some shopping to do." Keith still had not heard about the seance with the Commodore and the Bewitching Brokers, and that was bad enough. But a picnic with Ali Baba and the Tammany Thieves—he'd probably kill her!

"Nonsense." Somehow he was holding her left hand and apparently testing for a ring under the white glove. "This won't take long. I just want to make an appearance, to show the boss I'm in his camp. I owe Tweed some favors. Besides, I got political ambitions meself. 'Tis a sorry Irishman that don't."

"How is your library coming?" Devon asked.

"Not so good, without you to advise me. But I've read some of those books and found 'em interesting, what I could understand, anyway. I still need a tutor, though, and the offer is still open," he said tentatively. "Would you be available now, Miss Marshall?"

"I'm afraid not, sir."

"You have another position?"

"Yes."

"And you're satisfied with it?"

"Yes."

"Must pay well," he observed. "Them's fine duds, and your slippers are Cordovan. I know good leather. All my boots are custom-made, and I have dozens of 'em. But once I owned only one cheap pair of brogans for church, and worked barefoot in the fields till I was almost a grown man."

As they approached the financial district, Devon shielded her face behind a scarlet velvet swag, although she knew it was that time of day when the board of brokers were ensconced in the gold room of the Exchange, and nothing short of fire or earthquake could rout them.

"Where is this picnic, Mr. Donahue?"

"Battery Park, and 'twill be cooler on the bay." Despite the open windows, the air in the carriage was stifling and the cloying scents of perfume, bay rum, and pomade sickening. Sweat glistened on Donahue's heavy florid face, and his mustaches drooped slightly under the melting wax. "There'll be refreshments—plenty to eat and drink. The

Boss puts on a hearty feedbag . . . and why not, 'tain't his oats."

"But why does he bother, if he's bound to win the election, anyway? Why waste the time and effort?"

"Good will, me dear, the politician's stock-in-trade. And Tweed is popular with the common folk. He's generous to charity and has naught but praise for religion, all creeds, though he follows none himself. He eats wurst and sauerkraut at the German fests, pasta at the Italian feasts, kosher at the Jewish ones, and on St. Patrick's Day the Scotsman dons a green coat and shamrock and marches in the Irish parade. He became the Nigras' friend when they got the vote, and he'll be the ladies' champion when and if they get it. The Boss spreads himself around, and there's plenty of him to spread."

Devon glanced longingly at Bowling Green fountain, wishing she could splash her face and dangle her bare feet in the cool water. She felt wilted, and as captive in the gambler's coach as she had been in his cage. How had it happened, when she had only wanted to burn some candles for a poor dead girl?

She could hear a loud brass band playing in Battery Park, and the steam calliopes of the carousel and happy squeals and laughter of the youngsters. There was a huge milling motley crowd. Poor people, mostly: men in shirtsleeves and cheap factory-made pants or bibbed overalls; women in gingham and calico; barefoot children in Onasburg shoddy. And a small brigade of Union veterans in ragged blue uniforms and frayed forage caps, many disabled, hobbling on crutches and peg-legs, empty sleeves dangling uselessly, black patches on sightless eyes. A potpourri of misery and despair, a polyglot of tongues and accents, with Irish brogue predominant. Anyone who offered them something more or better than they had was a hero to be hailed, a saint to be revered, and voted into office by whatever means necessary, fair or foul. They came for the hope and promise so vital to life, and the food and fun and games they could not otherwise afford.

There were hundreds of hams and sausages, enormous wheels of cheese, crocks of coleslaw, sauerkraut, potato salad, pickles; tubs of butter and gallons of jam, mountains of bread and cakes and cookies, tanks of lemonade with ice floes, and barrels of beer on canvas-covered ice wagons. A carload of army surplus tincups and plates and cutlery had been previously delivered, and there were no limits on doles. Already some men were leaning unsteadily against trees, or lying prone beneath them. Mothers stuffed themselves while infants nursed at their breasts, and gorged·kids were throwing up.

The provider of this prodigal feast had not yet appeared, however, and Donahue said, "The boss won't show till folks have had time to get their fill and fun. He knows ears listen better when mouths are full and hearts happy. Empty bellies and disgruntled minds make distracting noises."

"My father used to say that hunger was the primary cause of revolution, oppression only secondary."

"Your pa was a smart fella, then. Some kind of oracle, maybe. Because wise men have known that since Christ performed the miracle of the loaves and fishes, and changed water into wine. I think if Jesus was alive now, Tweed would try to make Him a Tammany Democrat. But let's get out of this stampede."

He ushered her to the shade of a pavilion near the seawall, and preempted a bench for her. Then he brought her a frosted cup of lemonade, and beer for himself. Refreshed by the cool drink and the breezes off the water, Devon felt better. Wisps of amber curls had blown about her face, and the chin-ribbons of her chic French hat, small and flat as a crepe suzette, fluttered flirtatiously. Donahue, leaning against a pillar beside her, smiled admiringly, and asked, "Who was this friend you was remembering at St. Andrew's?"

"Mally O'Neill."

"A fine Irish colleen, no doubt. What happened to her?"

"She . . . had an accident."

"And you went to have Masses said for her soul?"

"No, to burn some candles, which she believed in. Sometimes she deprived herself of lunch to buy votive lights. She was very religious."

"Like my family," he nodded. "I think it's nonsense, but then I'm not much of a Catholic any more. Sure I've been a thorn in me poor mother's side since I first ran away from home, at fourteen."

"So young?"

"Aye. They couldn't understand why I wasn't content to

work the land, or apprentice meself to some village trades-
man; why I wanted decent clothes and good shoes and
something better to eat than mutton stew and potatoes.
Well, I didn't have much schooling, only seven years at the
convent, but I found there was other ways of making
money than by the sweat of the brow. In the big towns
there were men living comfortably off taverns and gambling. So I went to Dublin and hung round the pubs till I
learnt the tricks of the trade and earned enough to buy
passage to America. I put me wits to work here, and I
managed. Sure it wasn't easy, at first. I worked in saloons
and slept on pool tables and lived on the free lunches. Then
I went on the riverboats and won me fortune at poker.
There's no man alive can beat me at that game."

Devon removed an ivory-spoked fan from her reticule
and plied it leisurely, and he watched her hand as if it
held a spread of cards. "And your family?"

"Pa had a seizure at the plow and died in the field,
broke and in debt. Mum now lives with me sister and her
husband on a farm in County Wexford. I send 'em money,
but they send it right back. 'Tis tainted, ye see, got by
unholy means, and they'll have no part of it. They'd rather
break their honest backs tending sheep and hoeing potatoes
and praying the crops won't fail and bring another famine,
and more persecution and terrorism from the English ogres
and Orangemen. I've begged them to come to America
but—" He shrugged and stared off at the horizon, as if
he could see Ireland there, and Devon sensed that he missed
his homeland as much as she missed hers.

The harbor was full of ships, foreign and domestic, and
more were coming in. She recognized the *Richmond
Rogue*, once a dashing blockade runner, now a disreputable tobacco tramp. She averted her eyes to the islands,
Ellis and the old fort on Governors, to Bedloe, and the
hills of Staten. Ferries plied between all points, and to
Brooklyn and New Jersey. The Vanderbilt yacht had traveled that course to Fire Island, and the *Sprite* was moored
farther up in the North River, out of sight but not mind.

"Fine view, ain't it?" Donahue said. "But I can tell you
from experience, it's terrifying to the poor devils arriving
in steerage and herded ashore like cattle to the Castle
Garden pens. Twenty years ago, I was one of 'em, and so
damned scared of failing in the Promised Land, I was sick

most of the voyage, if you could call it that—packed like spoiled fish in a slimy tub we were, stinking and sleeping on the floor with vermin and rats, eating moldy bread and thin gruel, watching some passengers die of disease and starvation and dumped like galley-garbage into the sea. Talk about haunted ships—every one carrying immigrants is full of the ghosts of them that didn't make it. For six weeks it was like living in a floating coffin, and sailing in netherland. No priest aboard, and didn't seem to be no God aboard, either. As for the luck of the Irish—" He laughed shortly. "Some folks knelt and kissed the earth when we landed. Trent Patrick Donahue fell on the ground and puked up his guts."

"But you did find luck, eventually," Devon said, her eyes indicating his white linen suit and broad-brimmed Panama hat, his diamond jewelry and gold watch with ruby charms.

"I made my luck, honey, with a deck of cards and pair of dice. And if I didn't give every sucker an even break, neither did I get many. But I've got everything I want now, or almost." There was a long pause during which he studied her speculatively. "Do you have everything you want, Miss Marshall?"

"Not quite, Mr. Donahue."

"Tell me, where d'ye come from? Ephraim Joseph wouldn't say. But I know 'tis the South, from your voice. What state? Shall I guess?" She shook her head negatively. "Ah well, maybe you'd rather forget."

Just then the band struck up the national anthem, and shouts and cheers hailed the arrival of the city's official barouche carrying the mayor and the Boss. Close behind, in a Tammany vehicle, rode the three most important members of the cabal: Chamberlain Peter Barr Sweeny, Comptroller Richard B. Connolly, and the elegant A. Oakey Hall, district attorney.

"They're here!" Donahue announced excitedly, urging Devon to her feet. "Come, you must meet them."

"Oh no, you go ahead, sir! I'll wait here."

She intended to leave during his absence. But he had her hand firmly and insistently, escorting her through the crowd, elbowing a path as if she were a dignitary, until they reached the men alighting from the carriages, some of whom Devon had seen from behind her mask at the Gilded Cage.

Despite the heat, all were finely dressed and groomed, for they knew the power of appearance—the awe and respect that wealth created in poverty. Whatever a man's private ethics and morals, he must project the proper public image to reach the top at Tammany, and Tweed surrounded himself with gentlemanly rogues and scholarly scoundrels.

Of the Ring, Pete Sweeny was the most picaresque in appearance, of average height and build, with coal black hair and fierce black eyes glittering in a swarthy face. He was born on Park Row, in the rear of the saloon still operated by his father. Now a competent lawyer and politician par excellence, Sweeny typified the kind of clever brain and cunning craft that Tweed admired, respected, and recruited.

Dick Connolly was a schoolmaster's son, a scholar, poet, and former bank clerk. He had been drafted into the organization two decades before, to coordinate the dissident Irish vote, which was then split into fighting factions of Connaughtmen, Meadmen, Galwaymen, Kerrymen, Corkmen. It was Connolly's job to harmonize them into Tammanymen. His laughing Irish eyes, his keen Irish wit and humor and folklore, his jolly good fellowship unified and solidified the discordant wards, and he was recognized as a master of the art of persuasion and coercion.

All were charter members of the exclusive Americus Club, founded by Tweed at beautiful Indian Harbor, Connecticut, on Long Island Sound, where they relaxed, yachted, gambled, and romped with the women they kept in elaborate beach cottages. The emblem of this secret brotherhood was a two thousand dollar gold tiger's head with genuine ruby eyes, and it was Trent Donahue's ambition to wear this symbol of power and distinction in his own lapel. Why not? Hadn't his former partner at Saratoga, gambler-pugilist Johnny Morrissey, been elected to Congress under Tammany's aegis, beating out Horace Greeley in the race? The Boss could work political miracles for any man who impressed and interested him enough in that capacity, and affected the right public image.

And he obviously approved of the lovely young lady the

Bowery Boy was presenting now, for he smiled with the instant delight he took in all feminine youth and beauty. Handsome Hoffman was gallantly suave. The elegant Oakey, of English and Southern ancestry, bowed and kissed her hand chivalrously. Sweeny's piratical eyes ravished her, and out of a long curling mustache as dark and thick as his cohort's, Connolly bestowed a poetic smile. Then Devon overheard Tweed whisper to Donahue, "Your taste in women is improving, man. There may be some hope for you, after all, and a place in the Indian Harbor sun."

A signal from Sweeny to the bandmaster brought a drumroll for silence. The speakers mounted the platform, which was draped with patriotic bunting and banners. Their speeches were similar to those Devon had heard at Richmond rallies, county fairs, and community festivals. They promised more jobs and higher wages, lower taxes, greater freedoms, less crime and vice and violence, more schools and parks and pleasures—everything the deprived heart craved and the starved and abused body coveted. All were skilled orators who knew the value of brevity, the boredom of harangue, and had the sense and wisdom to realize when they had accomplished the one and approached the other.

In elevation they looked like a tableau of giants and geniuses centered by a corpulent colossus. Once Tweed's shrewd eyes focused on Donahue, as if evaluating his possible worth to Tammany, and then calculated his companion. But his bearded face was inscrutable. "And now, good friends, we'll tire your ears and try your patience no longer," he concluded. "Return to your picnic, and show us your appreciation at the polls in November!"

The applause was thunderous. Hands reached out to shake his as he descended from the mount, or merely to touch his garments, as a savior's. Acknowledging Donahue's congratulations, he said, "I'm having a little party at my place this evening. You and the lady are invited." He smiled at Devon out of his salt-and-pepper whiskers. "I hope to see you later, Miss Marshall." He bowed and moved on, his entourage and body guards following.

Donahue was elated. An invitation from William Marcy Tweed was practically an initiation into the Americus Club. He could visualize the tiger's head in his lapel, a position at Tammany, and eventually a place on the ticket. "You'll come, of course," he asked anxiously.

"No, I'm sorry, but I have another engagement this evening," Devon told him.

The band was playing again, and some people were dancing on the grass and pavement—Irish jigs and American reels, polkas and and schottisches, Hebrew folk dances.

"Come over here." He escorted her back to the pavilion, deserted now. "Don't you realize who the Boss is, Miss Marshall? Nobody ignores or spurns his invitations, not if they want to get anywhere in this town. He can open doors for you, and close 'em, too. He admires you, and considers me in the right company, for once. Sure he could give us both a bright future, together or separately, and I would hope together. I've got a sort of jealous woman on my hands at present, but I can handle her. Please say you'll come."

"I'm terribly sorry, but I can't, Mr. Donahue."

"There's someone else?"

"Yes."

"Who is he, and why don't he marry you?"

Devon glanced at the harbor. An East Indian merchantman was arriving, laden with silks and tapestries, ivory and jade and pearls and porcelain, incense and spices. She watched the golden vessel wistfully, as if it were the Holy Grail, and said softly, "He will. Some day."

"When his ship comes in? When he makes his fortune? I've already made mine, Miss Marshall. My treasure's in the bank. Sure now you've heard of my establishments on Chatham Square, the Pot O'Gold and the Gilded Cage?"

Her smile was so vague and elusive even the gambler's sharp eyes missed its significance. "Yes, I've heard of your places, Mr. Donahue. They say you put pretty young women in gilded cages."

"Not without their consent." He bit off the tip of a long black cigar and chewed it to tail-feathers. "They're dressed as gorgeous birds, and they earn plenty of scratch in those fancy coops. They're the natural prey of hawks and eagles, sure, and some end up as the spoils of vultures. But I try to protect them from predators on the premises, and only one has ever been snatched in my presence. She was a bird of paradise, a rare species called Richmond—" Suddenly he paused and peered into her face, as if trying to penetrate a veil or vizard. "She had a soft sweet voice, like yours. And her mouth might have been as delicate and pink under the coarse red paint. Perhaps she also had gold dust in her emerald eyes and a pretty nose and honey-colored ringlets. I don't know. She always wore a mask and feathered cap."

"What happened to her?"

"A goddamn poacher got her! Just wandered into the preserve one night, decided he wanted her, and took her against her will. Stealing, I'd call it. I never saw her again."

"I have to leave now," Devon said.

"Let me take you home."

"No, thank you. I'll catch a cab."

"Your friend is jealous, eh? Well, I can't blame him. But I expect to see you again, Miss Marshall. Somehow, sometime, somewhere. I don't give up easy."

"The picnic is over, Mr. Donahue. Goodbye." She smiled and turned away, walking toward the bandstand, where some hacks and hansoms waited.

Donahue watched her receding shadow. Richmond and the Wolf of Wall Street? Was she laughing at how cleverly she had fooled him? Impossible! They were similar but not the same person. No mask could have disguised her that much. Or could it?

Chapter 23

The Village vendors were already making their rounds.

"Milk! Get your nice fresh milk, butter, cream, cheese!"

"Need eggs today? I got fine fresh farm eggs for sale!"

"Cabbages and turnips, carrots and peas; peaches and pears and plums you can squeeze!"

And the delightful young herb girl chanting, "Rosemary and thyme, parsely and dill, mint and rue; if you don't cook with herbs, shame on you!"

Devon needed some things, but lacked the will or energy to put on a wrapper and signal from the gallery. She lay motionless, concentrating on the rosy rectangles of dawn at the windows, hoping the nausea and dizziness would pass. Not that, she told herself. No, it was something else. Digestive upset, greensickness, vapors, perhaps even too much lovemaking last night. She reassured herself, as she had last month, when the date had come and gone on her calendar, that other causes were responsible for her delay and malaise: that shower she had gotten caught in without an umbrella, those too-cool baths she had taken in the summer heat, her perennial worry and anxiety and frustration over her future.

Then she remembered Kathleen Melton, her best friend in Richmond and roommate at Rosewood Female Academy in Charlottesville. They were of the generation that had flowered during the war, Rosewood's last graduating class after Fort Sumter. And they were innocent as all sheltered young ladies, curious but ignorant about their budding bodies and the mysteries of life and womanhood, exchanging girlish confidences while snuggled in cozy feather-beds, in a dainty dormitory with pink rosebuds on the wallpaper and billowy white organdy curtains like bouffant party dresses at the windows that looked toward the sweeping vista of the Blue Ridge Mountains. Carefree and happy

and safe in their own little world, before it was rudely
and violently split asunder in the apocalypse of the Confederacy.

A year later, at sixteen, Kathleen had married her childhood beau, Wade Truman, a merchant's son, the day before he left to join the Army of Northern Virginia. Two
months later she fainted at the medical complex, a con-
glomeration of makeshift buildings and tents housing
thousands of patients from all over Virginia and the
neighboring states. Their particular section occupied a
bluff above the James River and the busy wharves and
harbor defenses.

The hall had been full of busy chattering women, for
every adult female volunteered several hours each day to
nursing or making supplies, and some brought their slaves
to assist them. Cheesecloth and gauze, in short supply,
were rationed for surgical dressings, necessitating the do-
nation of household linens for bandages. But cotton was
plentiful, and bales of it absorbed rivers of blood in the
surgeries and wards, and the burned refuse stank abomina-
bly of infection, gangrenous flesh, and putrid body wastes.
The stench made strong stomachs queasy, and weak ones
ill.

Reluctant to surrender to her symptoms, Kathleen had
sat pale and glassy-eyed, bravely scraping lint, which
swirled and drifted and encompassed them in a miniature
cotton blizzard. The white fuzz settled on their hair and
clothes like snowflakes, reminding them of happier times.

"Remember the winters at school," Kathleen reflected,
"when Rosewood looked like a great frosted cake?"

"A spun sugar fairy castle," Devon recalled, "and the
hills sparkled like rock candy mountains."

"And the only men in our lives were made of snow."

"Or gingerbread," Devon laughed, for the campus had
been off-limits to the local male schools, and the head
mistress and her staff were assiduous chaperones.

"Now I'm married, and you probably will be soon. On
Dan's next furlough, perhaps?"

"Perhaps."

"And we'll have our first babies together."

Then Kathleen had pitched forward face down into the
pile of swabs before her. She recovered quickly enough,
but her face had the greenish pallor of some young girls

during menses, and Devon assumed she was just having her cycle, which was never a picnic for either of them. They suffered with headaches, cramps, aching backs, and sore breasts, for which they drank herb tisanes and took paregoric and patent medicines, and carried smelling salts. Kathleen was inhaling hers now.

"Bad time, Kay?"

"No time," she murmured.

"I mean, period."

"That's what I mean. No period."

Devon stared at her. "Kathleen, you don't think—? Oh no, it couldn't be that, could it? You were together only that one night—"

"Maybe that's all it takes!"

Kathleen's mother had told her nothing except that she must submit to her husband in bed, and the virgin bride was as astonished to find herself pregnant after one inept experience with her virginal groom as her naive young friend was to realize that pregnancy could result from a single sexual contact with a male. Seven months later, Devon was horrified when Kathleen died in childbirth and was buried in her white bridal gown with her dead infant like a swaddled doll in her arms. She had sat stunned at the wake, staring incredulously into the coffin, and was dazed for months after the funeral. To alleviate her grief, her father had increased her assignments on the *Sentinel*, and that was when Devon had begun to think less of marriage and motherhood and more a career.

Now she was in New York without either, and probably caught in the oldest female trap in the world.

Keith's pillow lay beside hers, the imprint of his head still visible, his masculine scent still fresh in her nostrils. Her breasts had been tender to his touch, her whole body tense and sensitive with what he had imagined—and she had hoped—was premenstrual tension. He had left shortly after midnight, having an early morning business appointment and not wishing to disturb her. She embraced his pillow now, burying her face, and wept. And then, in a sudden passionate rage, as if he had betrayed her, she beat it with her fists and flung it on the floor.

Tony the Ragman was trundling his clumsy wooden cart past Rhinelander Gardens, singing, "You got rags, bones, bottles, old clothes? Geeve 'em to Tony, he needa dem, God knows!"

But there was no one collecting unwanted babies; they must be taken to orphanages, or left on doorsteps.

She got up and fixed tea. The little yellow kitchen was bright with early sunlight, and there were fresh blooms in the windowbox. Her spirits revived slightly. Then she saw Keith's nightcap glass on the sink-drain, a few dregs of brandy at the bottom, and burst into tears. She was not sure, had he been there then, if she would have kissed or killed him. She sat down at the table, gazing morosely at the empty chair opposite, and sucking a sour lemon to settle her stomach.

She would have to go to a doctor, and she had noticed the shingles of several on her walks in the Village. But she was reluctant to exchange the small comfort of doubt for the discomfort of certainty. Once confronted with reality, she would have to cope with it, and her experience with unwed motherhood was limited to the few cases she had known or heard of in Richmond, where not even the war had excused unchastity in decent society. That was for whores and sluts, and the bastards of such wantons were treated with the same community scorn and contempt. Premarital pregnancy rarely occurred in respectable families, for the daughters were generally chaperoned; if it did, the couple married promptly and the birth of the child, not its conception, was considered premature.

Devon drank a cup of tea and ate a piece of dry toast. Then she dressed and put on the wedding ring she had used in the resort hotels. Undoubtedly one of their wild, reckless passions on the Hudson was responsible, possibly that stormy night in the Catskills, when they had copulated on the carpet, like frenzied rutting animals. Such a primitive union could only spawn a vixen or savage better left unborn.

The doctor's office was on Greenwich Street, between an apothecary and a chandlery. His name was Virgil Palmer, and he was old and gray and clumsy, for his hands shook with palsy. His manual examination hurt, and the tortuous instrument he introduced into her tense vagina made her cringe and cry out in pain. "My goodness," he frowned sympathetically, "most women hardly feel the speculum. You're sensitive as a virgin. I hope that won't mean a difficult labor."

Devon clutched the side of the table and pushed her feet hard against the iron stirrups. "Then I am pregnant?"

"Oh, yes. Definitely."

"You couldn't be mistaken, Doctor?"

"After fifty years in medical practice?" He smiled, helping her off the table. "You may dress, now, Mrs. Marshall."

When she emerged from the old wicker screen in the corner, he was consulting a worn chart. "You can expect confinement early in March, but come and see me again in a few months."

Why? she wondered. Expectant mothers did not frequent doctors. In wartime Richmond, they had been delivered by midwives, female relatives, and mammies. "Is something wrong, Doctor?"

"No, no. You seem quite healthy. Unusually small pelvic structure, however, and it's a first pregnancy. I like to watch such cases."

Devon caught her breath. Kathleen had had slender hips. Kathleen had labored for three days, until she was unconscious with exhaustion, and the suffocated fetus was forcibly extracted, and her womb ruptured, and she died.

"Dr. Palmer—"

He was preparing a card for his files. "Yes?"

She hesitated, wanting to confide the truth and throw herself on his mercy, but in hesitancy courage failed. "Nothing. I'm just a little nervous."

"All new brides are," he said gently. "Try nibbling soda crackers for the nausea. Ginger ale helps too. The vertigo and other peculiar sensations are normal symptoms, and will eventually subside. The delivery fee is twenty-five dollars, but let Papa worry about that. Good day, Mrs. Marshall."

By the time she got back to the apartment, Devon was sick enough to vomit. Afterwards she glimpsed herself in the bathroom mirror, eyes dull, face wraith-pale. Kathleen had looked and felt that way for several months, and being properly married had not prevented her discomfort or her death in delivery. But the dreadful escapes sought by disgraced girls were even more tragic and awesome to contemplate. One had reportedly drunk lye and died in agonized convulsions; another had swallowed carbolic acid and strangled on her burned, swollen tongue. A farm girl had jumped off a cow-shed and bled to death in the barnyard. A planter's daughter had galloped wildly on her horse, hoping to lose her burden in a foxhunt, only to bear an idiot. And poor Mally O'Neill had gone to sleep with an unlit gas jet open.

But there were other, less drastic alternatives. The personal columns of the *Herald* listed positive cures for such female distress, although Janette Joie had condemned these as mostly frauds that rarely solved the problem and often complicated it. The best and safest solution, according to the Frenchwoman, was an accommodating midwife, and Devon knew she would have recommended one who catered to the carriage trade. If only she could talk to Janette now! But she could almost hear her voice scolding and lamenting, "Ah, cherie, didn't I warn you that the beast would make you enceinte? See what I would have spared you? This terrible thing could never have happened with me. . . ."

Decision brought some relief but also anguish, for there was something abhorrent about this last resort of desperate females. Maternal instinct rebelled, and she knew she must be resolute, or remorse would defeat her. Nor could she procrastinate. The sooner the better, according to Janette, who had said the operation if performed early was no worse than a difficult menses. Madame Restell was expensive, of course. But Devon had money enough and could get more from Keith, if necessary, and he need never know anything about it.

When he came that evening, she was not dressed. She had, in fact, forgotten their plans to go to supper and the concert at Steinway Hall featuring the brilliant Negro pianist, Blind Tom. "You're not ready? We'll be late, Devon."

"Could we go another time, Keith?"

"Yes, certainly, but I have tickets for this evening, and I thought you were looking forward to it."

"I don't feel well," she murmured. "I'm sorry."

"That's all right, darling. I'll dismiss the cab." He went out and when he returned looked at her worriedly. "Is it worse than usual this month? Maybe you should see a doctor, Devon?"

She had spent the day in mental turmoil and anxiety, lounging on the bed and chaise and sofa, restless and resentful, bewildered and brooding. Her life seemed like one long dilemma and frustration. Suddenly her emotional dam burst, and the secret rushed out furiously. "I saw a doctor, Keith! Today. I'm pregnant!"

He started forward but stopped, held by the indignation and despair in her voice, the anger and accusation in her eyes. "How far?" he asked quietly.

"Two months."

"The Catskills," he nodded. "I was afraid of that."

"I won't have it, Keith!"

Swiftly he closed the space separating them and grasped her shoulders, bruising her flesh. "What are you saying, Devon? Have you done something? Tell me!"

"Not yet, but I'm going to! Tomorrow. There are things. Madame Joie told me—"

"Abortion? That's against the law."

"So is adultery and fornication! But that doesn't seem to bother you. And I don't see how abortion could be any more criminal than bringing another bastard into a world that seems amply populated with them already!"

"Jesus Christ, you sound more like the feminists every day! That's Woodhull and Claflin philosophy, which reminds me of an interesting little ghost story I heard in the Street today. About a seance on the high seas, and the fascinating passenger list aboard Commodore Vanderbilt's yacht!"

"Now, Keith, don't be angry. I can explain everything. You see, I met Kate Field while you were in Chicago. We had lunch and she—"

He interrupted, "Never mind that now, Devon. This takes precedence."

"I won't bear an illegitimate child, Keith."

"The alternative can be fatal, Devon. Women die that way."

"They die in childbirth too, and kill themselves in disgrace!" she cried hysterically.

"I won't let you do it," he said.

"You can't stop me!"

"I can, and I will . . . if I have to chain you to me."

She gave him a defiant glare. "You want a child so much, even a bastard?"

"I don't think of it that way."

"But that's how the law thinks of it, doesn't it, if you want to drag legalities into it?"

"You little fool! Don't you realize I love you and don't want to lose you on some butcher's block?"

"Butcher?" Some of her audacity and defiance vanished. "Janette Joie said there wasn't much to it. She'd been through it herself several times, in France. And one of her mannequins entertained her lover the day after her appointment with Madame Restell."

"Madame Restell? My God, she's the worst of them, Devon! Don't you read the papers and see the cartoons of her? They call her Madame Killer and depict her as a bloody bat with a dead infant in her maws. She'd be hanged at Sing Sing, if she didn't have influence at City Hall!"

"Isn't she a doctor of midwifery?"

"She's a charlatan with a self-conferred degree," Keith said. "More than one corpse has been carted out of her human abattoir on Chambers Street under cover of darkness and disposed of in the rivers, or God knows how. And abortion isn't her only business, nor murder her only crime. She also practices blackmail and extortion. Scores of prominent people are buying her silence. The women confide their secrets in her, and she threatens the men responsible with exposure. How do you think she can afford that palatial home on Fifth Avenue, and all the other refinements with which she is trying to purchase a place in respectable society?"

"Are you worried that I might betray you, Keith, and leave you open to blackmail? I won't, I promise you."

His face turned livid, and she thought he would strike her. "Goddamn it, Devon! Can't you get it through your thick little skull? I'm worried and afraid that she might kill you! It's a dangerous operation even in the hands of a skilled surgeon. If you insist on being aborted, I'll find a physician. There're enough whose ethics are for sale. And when you get that part of me out of your body, I'll get out of your life."

Her defenses collapsed. "Oh no, Keith! That's not fair. You know I love you."

"Do you, Devon? What's love? And what's fair in a situation like this? Is it love to want me and not my child? Is it fair to waste my seed?"

"You've been wasting it yourself."

"Not by choice, my dear."

"But the child can't bear your name, Keith!"

"It can, Devon—through adoption."

"And what would that make *me* in the eyes of the law?"

"I'll fix that," he promised grimly. "By God, Esther will free me, one way or another."

This frightened Devon more than anything else, and subdued her anxiety and desperation in his. "Don't talk that way, Keith. It's insane. I'll have the baby." She rushed to the cellaret to pour him a drink. "Here, darling. Sit down, please. We'll discuss it rationally." She put the glass in his hand and urged him toward his lounge chair. "Did you hear what I said, Keith? I'll have the child."

He sat down heavily, swallowed the whisky and set the glass aside. Her hand, still wearing his mother's gold band, touched his shoulder. Seeing it, he drew her onto his lap. "You told the doctor you were married?"

"Yes."

"Who is he?"

"Dr. Virgil Palmer, on Greenwich Street."

"Does he seem competent?"

"Well, he's rather old, perhaps seventy, and sort of shaky. And he said I—I might have a difficult time."

His arm muscles tensed. "Why?"

"Oh, something about a narrow pelvis and first pregnancy."

"We'll get someone else," he decided. "The best man in town. And I want you to hire a housekeeper, Devon, one who can live in. I don't want you alone any more."

"That's not necessary, Keith. Not yet, anyway. Dr. Palmer says I'm perfectly healthy and shouldn't have any trouble, if I take care of myself."

"And that's what you're going to do, isn't it? And I'll take care of you too."

"Just don't abandon me, Keith."

"Good Lord, did you think I would? Because Madame Joie told you all men are beasts, and Mally O'Neill's experience convinced you she was right? Is that what caused your hysteria and panic?" He shook his head at her. "I thought you knew me better than that, Devon."

"I was afraid, Keith. I'd suspected it for several weeks, and when I woke up sick this morning and you weren't here—"

"I knew something was wrong last night," he said. "You were nervous as a cat. But I thought ... why didn't you tell me, Devon? I'd have stayed."

"You had business at the bank."

"Nothing more important than you or this," he said, drawing her head onto his shoulder and stroking her hair. "Don't worry, Devon. Things will work out for us. You'll see."

Something in his voice made her draw back and regard his face, which was in partial shadow, dark and impassive. "Keith, you're not going to confront *her*, are you? Demand a divorce?"

"I told you not to worry, darling." Smiling, he kissed her mouth. "Have you eaten anything today?"

"Not much."

"I'll fix something. Oh yes, I can cook. I have many unusual accomplishments."

"And you do love me?"

"Both of you," he said.

Chapter 24

If Esther Curtis' domestic schedule was rigorous, her personal one was ritualistic.

Each morning at precisely eight o'clock her breakfast was served on a silver tray garnished with a fresh flower from the conservatory at the rear of the house. Her toilette began promptly at ten, and she was attended like Cleopatra by her handmaidens: bathed in scented water clouded with milk, dried with scented towels, rubbed with cologne, and dusted with talcum. Then her long black hair was brushed and arranged as she wished, her fingernails and toenails were filed and buffed, and she was clothed in whatever boudoir costume she had chosen for the day. Afterwards, she might rest on the chaise, or inspect the house in her wheelchair, escorted through the maze of halls and rooms by servants, transported to the various levels including the basement via a pulley-operated elevator. Occasionally she went into the solarium on the top floor and employed her binoculars on the view. In pleasant weather she might venture into Gramercy Park, always with an entourage of at least two maids and a footman. Most often she returned to bed to read, record her diary, correspond, play solitaire, fit jigsaw puzzles, receive visitors; to languish and brood in frustration and resentment. Except for these diversions, and a few others she had discovered or invented, Esther thought she would have died of languor and boredom. Her friends, however, marveled at her fortitude and forbearance, her tolerant endurance of a seemingly hopeless situation.

Once a week, on separate days, her hair was dressed and her body massaged. Monsieur Dubonnet came with a hoard of idle gossip relayed while his delicate hands worked wonders with brush and comb, falsettes and fourches, and absolute miracles with artifices and cosmetics.

275

His services were much in demand in Manhattan society, and the ladies bribed him outlandishly and engaged him far in advance of their needs. Esther knew that the eccentric little Frenchman—with his plucked eyebrows, puckered lips, and obviously curled hair—amused Keith, who was so flagrantly virile that any man the least bit foppish appeared effeminate by comparison; and he had once remarked that the monsieur was less masculine than the masseuse.

Hilde Swengard was a tall, large-boned, ruddy-faced blonde with the muscular physique of a wrestler, and Mrs. Curtis was her most satisfied client. Various nurses had performed this medically recommended therapy over the years, but Esther had never been pleased with any of them. The last, dismissed for incompetence, had complained to the patient's husband: "She claims I hurt her legs, Mr. Curtis. But how could I, if they're paralyzed? Paralytics have no sensation in wasted muscles, no reflexes, and certainly no nerves. You can stick pins in them with no reaction. Furthermore, unused limbs wither, eventually, and hers definitely have not. Frankly, sir, I don't believe there's anything whatever wrong with her health. If so, it's mental, not physical. I daresay she could walk, even run, if she wanted. Let the house catch fire, she'd probably be the first one out. And in your place, sir, I believe I'd be tempted to smoke her out."

Esther's diagnosis of the nurse, when Keith apprised her, was insolence, sadism, and insanity. And when once a new maid had excitedly reported to the master, "Oh, sir, Madame seems much improved today! I saw her standing before the mirror!" Esther accused her of malicious delusions and promptly discharged her sans reference.

This was massage day, and Hilde arrived with her satchel of exotic oils and balms and professional expertise. Mrs. Curtis was stripped and salved and covered with a soft white linen cloth, under which Hilde's knowing hands performed their trained skills and complementary pleasures. Intent on her art, she appeared oblivious of any extra benefits derived from her stimulations and manipulations of breasts and buttocks and more erogenous areas, heedless of intense sighs and moans, allowing the recipient to retain her pride and dignity while enjoying her ecstasy. Neglected wives were especially responsive to this surreptitious gratification, and appreciative enough to bestow large largesse. Hilde's discreet practice of voluptuary in the luxurious boudoirs of elegant ladies had enabled her, a penniless immigrant twelve years before, to own her own comfortable home and equipage in which to make her house calls.

She lingered over her treatments in the Curtis mansion, for the mistress was young and desperate enough to desire an encore, and Hilde concentrated on evoking a second sensual spasm, before removing her hands from under the cover and returning her accouterments to the satchel. With a terry towel she wiped away the residue of emollients and assisted the lady into her negligee. Her fee, plus gratuity, was in an envelope on the dresser. Hilde tucked it into her huge bosom.

"Next Thursday, same time, Mrs. Curtis?"

"Yes, thank you, Hilde."

"Thank *you*, Madame," the masseuse said and smiled and left ten dollars richer.

Esther plumped the pillows and relaxed against them. There were some compensations for a man's neglect, and she had found them. But they were only substitutes, and she still craved masculine embrace. Keith had been an entirely satisfactory sexual partner, when she was not too tired or sated by her potent lover to welcome her husband to her bed, and she would have welcomed him now, gladly, had he shown the slightest interest or inclination. But he only seemed amused by her subtle attempts at seduction, and repulsed by her obvious overtures. She knew he had been deeply and passionately in love with her, and the abruptness and apparent finality with which he had turned off his affection and desire puzzled and defeated her. Naturally, he had other accommodations, including, she suspected, some of her perfidious friends.

Lorna Hampton, the brazen bitch, flirted with him before his wife. And Judith Lipscomb, who lived in a red brick Greek Revival on Gramercy Park West, timed her afternoon visits to coincide with Keith's arrival from the bank so accurately that Esther assumed either she or one of her servants kept the Curtises under surveillance. Both were married and mothers, but also young and attractive, and Judith had exceptionally large breasts from suckling several children, refusing a wet nurse as any sensible, self-respecting woman would. Utterly without shame or modesty, she nursed her child in Keith's presence, and he lacked the decency to leave the room or even look away. Rather, he played with the infant in her lap, tickling his toes and talking to him, as if he were the proud and ridiculous father. A disgusting and embarrassing spectacle, and unforgivable on Judith's part, flaunting her fertility and bosom before a childless invalid whose dimensions had been greatly reduced by confinement.

"Where did John Lipscomb find Judith?" she had once asked Keith. "In a concert saloon or brothel? Her manners are absolutely atrocious."

"The baby was hungry. Should she have let him cry?"

"She should have excused herself and left, or you should have. It's time she weaned that brat, anyway. Only poor women nurse their own children in Boston."

"This isn't Boston, and I believe some queens and empresses have been known to nurse their young."

"You envy her husband, don't you? And Lorna's too. Because they have heirs to their kingdoms."

He had not answered, but Esther knew this was one of his great disappointments, just as she knew he was inherently monogamous and preferred a permanent attachment to promiscuity. He had no relatives in America, and only a few in England and Scotland. Thus, he longed for a family of his own, and eventually she would have obliged him with a child or two, although under no circumstances would she have become a brood mare. Whoever's seed she had lost in that fall—and the law of averages favored Mallard—Esther had felt only intense relief and gratitude. Not until Keith had requested a divorce had she realized the emotional and financial advantages of motherhood, and then it was too late. Nothing could lure him back to her bed.

She still thought of Mallard, missed him and wondered what had become of him. She read the art news avidly, but his name never appeared in the Studio Row exhibits. Perhaps he had gone abroad to wander with other vagabond painters, or had colonized somewhere in Paris or Rome or Madrid. They had never seen each other again after that hideous day, for Mallard could not come to her nor she go to him. There was simply too much confusion and bewilderment. Doctors and nurses hovering, her mother's hysterical arrival from Boston, her long convalescence . . . and then the tiresome traveling and treatments in search of a cure. And through it all, Keith's bitter remorse and despair.

The diversion provided by the masseuse was only temporary, and soon Esther was sunk in desolate dilemma and dejection again. The knock on the door revived her morale somewhat. She would welcome a visitor, anybody, even the audacious hypocrite or the buxom cow and her drooling calf. After a quick glance into her hand-mirror, she opened a book on her lap. To keep her French fluent, she read all the popular Gallic novelists in the original (Lorna and Judy had to wait for the tedious and usually tepid translations) and often spoke to the servants in French, although only the parlormaid, Minette, could understand her.

"Entrez, s'il vous plait!"

Keith entered, and she murmured. "Oh, it's you."

"Were you expecting Napoleon, Camille?"

She felt foolish; he had an irritating habit of making even her accomplishments seem affected and absurd. "Well, I certainly wasn't expecting Casanova! After all, how often does *he* visit me? My chances of a levee with Napoleon are better."

A bland smile. "Another invitation?"

"You're my husband, Keith."

"No, Madam, I'm your exchequer, and it is in that capacity that I'm calling now."

"Is my household account overdrawn?"

"It always has been."

"You want me to curtail my extravagances?" she parried, and abruptly he abandoned the persiflage.

"I want you to give me a divorce, and I expect to pay for it. Any price you demand. This isn't a marriage we have, Esther. It's a dog-in-the-manger arrangement on your part."

"You're the dog, Keith. The night prowler leaving your property unprotected, and you could sleep in the home manger if you wished. That part of me isn't paralyzed, far from it."

He scowled in embarrassment, as always, at her flagrance. "Shall we get down to business, Esther? You married the Curtis fortune, and I'm prepared to give you a tidy share of it in exchange for my freedom."

"You sound desperate, darling. Don't tell me you're in love and want to make an honest woman of her?" She laughed, a hollow sound, brittle as the shattering of glass. "Or is it more urgent than that?"

"Esther, could we please discuss this matter intelligently, and try to arrive at an amicable agreement?"

"For whose benefit, Keith? Yours, and the current object of your slippery affections? Does she know how liberally you've spread them around these past five years? Or has one of your many seductions finally entrapped you, Lothario? If so, you can spring the trap easily enough, you know. Just send her to Madame Restell!"

"Shut up," he said darkly. "Just shut your goddamn mouth, and listen to me. I want an end to this sham and farce, do you understand? I want out! Name your ransom, I'll meet it."

"My word, you *are* desperate! In a panic, I suspect, to legitimize one of your bastards. But I'm afraid all that tempting treasure has little value to me now. What could I do if I owned a mint or the Treasury? Where could I go in a solid gold wheelchair?"

"Home," he suggested.

"This is my home, Keith."

"I meant Boston, Esther. You could live there as well as here, and do as much."

"A cast-off cripple? Oh no, Keith! My family is not aware of our estrangement, and I'll never disgrace them with a divorce. Mother would have a stroke!"

"Too bad you didn't consider her health when you were fooling with that paint dauber."

"Dear Lord! Does that little indiscretion still rankle in your proud flesh?"

"Little indiscretion? Good God, Esther! You were in love with Mallard when you married me—the marriage of convenience of the year, though I was too beguiled to realize it."

"Oh, don't be so medieval! You weren't a virgin. Why do the bachelor whoremasters always expect chaste brides?"

"I knew better than that, my dear, despite your elaborate pretenses to the contrary. Planning the wedding night to coincide with the menses is an old trick of deflowered brides, and some bumpkins are fooled by the stuck-pig squeals and show of blood. It was all so unnecessary, Esther. I wouldn't have quibbled about your affair had it ended at the altar. But you wanted to have your wedding cake and eat it too, with your lover, and *that* I did mind, particularly since he got the lion's share."

Her purple eyes mocked him. "You should have been more aggressive in your marital rights, darling."

"I had some gallant idea that they were privileges to be granted, not demanded. What you resented was my refusal to play the convenient cuckold and wear my horns meekly."

Her hands picked at a satin rosette on her sacque, pulling the blue petals apart. "Not really, Keith. But I was surprised by your violence on discovery. I expected more savoir faire from a sophisticated gentleman. Urbanity. But I suppose every man reverts to savagery when he thinks he's defending his honor and hearth. Why not? Basically, he's still a jungle primitive protecting the sanctity of his hut with spears and poison darts, a Neanderthal guarding his cave with a stone club, and dragging his woman around by the hair."

"And a cannibal devouring his enemies," Keith nodded. "But I'm in no mood for a seminar on atavism and ancient history, Esther. Please be reasonable. We've lost seven years in a misalliance that should never have occurred. What happened to you was an accident, and I've never stopped regretting it. But whether you languish here or somewhere else is immaterial, as long as you are comfortable. And a million dollars should provide adequate comfort and care. You needn't live in New York or Boston. There are other cities, you know. And other countries."

"I loved England on our honeymoon," she reflected wistfully, "and I loved you in Europe."

"You loved being presented at court," Keith said. "Mingling with royalty and nobility, being entertained at palaces and castles and noble estates. I saw how you admired and coveted Heathstone Manor, and fawned on the old earl, even though he is my own grandfather. You flirted outrageously with Napoleon and every courtier at the Tuileries and every baron of the Bourse, especially Alphonse de Rothschild."

"Nevertheless, I fell in love with you in Paris. You were so suave and debonair and had learned so much on your grand tour. We made a handsome couple and were admired everywhere we went. I was happy, Keith. Oh, don't sneer—it's true and humanly possible. Can't a man love two women at once, his wife and his mistress? Well, a woman's emotions are just as vulnerable and flexible, with respect to her husband and her paramour."

He made a deprecating gesture. "Esther, I no longer care if you loved an entire army and had as many affairs as Lady Castlemaine! Will you accept this settlement?"

She shook her head negatively. "What pleasure could living abroad be for me now, even in a castle with a hundred servants? Even a queen or empress in my condition would be a mere curiosity and object of pity. No, thank you, Keith."

"That's your answer?"

"That's always been my answer," she said.

He began to pace. Her eyes followed every imprint of his boots in the deep velvet carpet; when he kicked furiously at a hassock in his path, Esther winced as if it were herself, so personal and precious were her possessions. "And if I refuse to countenance this travesty any longer? If I dismiss the servants, put the house on the market, and you in an institution?"

"Asylum, you mean? Perhaps the same one in Flushing, where the Commodore committed his wife twenty years ago, when she objected to his treatment of her and would likely still be, if his own mother hadn't rescued her!" She smiled tremulously, convinced that he was bluffing but nevertheless disturbed that his desperation was driving him to such extremes. "I come from a prominent family, remember, not like poor peasant Mrs. Vanderbilt. The Stanfields have powerful connections in law and politics. If you imagine my parents would stand for anything like that, you are the lunatic, Keith, not I. And I promise you—oh, I promise you!—your mistress would suffer far more than your wife in any public scandal in the courts. You would succeed only in branding her a whore before the world and your child a bastard. Because I'm certain now a child is involved, either born or unborn. What a shame! Fatherhood at last, and you can't acknowledge paternity."

"The hell I couldn't, if such were the case. Kings do and create titles for them. I could do better than that. I could adopt mine, make it my legal heir and disinherit you completely. Think about that, Mrs. Curtis."

Her mind dwelt on the neuter pronoun. "You said 'it,' meaning you don't know the sex yet, and 'it' is still in gestation. Who is the mother, Keith. Anyone I know?"

He gazed at her in sardonic silence.

"I can find out," she challenged.

"I wouldn't advise hiring a detective, Esther, unless you want to continue this vendetta to the death of one of us."

Her eyes defied him. "Is that a threat?"

"A warning," he muttered. "Don't give me any more trouble than you already have, Esther. My patience is long, but not endless." And with that serving of ominous malice, he left her to digest the spoils.

Esther felt a sudden chill. She knew he was capable of violence and had no doubt he was also capable of murder; indeed, he would have killed Mallard had not she interfered. She knew too, despite her bravado about her family's prestige, that this was New York, not Boston—his bailiwick, not hers, and she could not hope to match his power and influence should he choose to exert them. He could apply tourniquet-pressure to the jugulars of the Wall Street men dependent on the Curtis Bank for their vital blood supply, financially garroting them, since in New York, more than anywhere else on earth, money was the eau de vie. Should he decide to commit her, his physicians would agree that she was unbalanced and belonged in a madhouse. After all, specialists here and abroad had pronounced her paralysis nonorganic, some diagnosing it as hysteria, others as melancholia, all insisting it was imaginary. Oh yes, he could get her certified insane! He could dispose of her in some more drastic and permanent fashion too, if desperate and determined enough, and either avoid suspicion entirely, or escape with no more than some lurid publicity.

The suffragettes were right: a man could do anything he pleased with his wife, use her, abuse her, intimidate and incarcerate her, tyrannize and terrorize her, even murder her, and go unpunished. The law favored him, and a woman had to devise her own protection and reprisal. Well, damn his threats and his male immunity to punishment! She ought to invite the Bewitching Brokers to tea, spill the beans, and let them dump the Curtis manure in the Street! Ruin her, would he? Sell the house and lock her away in some dingy tower or dungeon? Oh, that whorehound and his pregnant slut! Don't give him any more trouble? What was she supposed to do, docilely divorce him or conveniently die, so he could have a legitimate pup?

She twisted the rings on her finger. His tobacco-tonic-leather scent still lingered in the room, mingling sensuously with the flowers and her own perfume. She had longed to claw his saturnine face, gouge his mocking eyes—but even more, she had wanted to be brutalized in bed. Mallard had once accused her of perversity, and the supposition had neither disturbed nor distressed her. Rather, it had intrigued and stimulated her.

Vendetta, was it? Very well.

She reached for stationery, dipped her raven's quill in India ink, and wrote: "I, Esther Stanfield, do hereby accuse my husband, Keith Heathstone Curtis, of intentions to harm me; and, in fact, of having made verbal threats on my life. I charge him with numerous adulteries, and the paternity of at least one illegitimate child. I further accuse him of demanding divorce under duress in order to marry the mother of this bastard. Therefore, should untimely or violent death befall me, I request and direct that this statement be delivered into the hands of lawful authorities."

Affixing the date and her signature, she sealed the statement in a personal envelope, which she inscribed, "Last Will and Testament of Esther Stanfield Curtis." Then she wrote to her mother and asked her to keep the document in a safe place, assuring her that she felt fine but wanted to prepare for any eventuality and didn't want to worry Keith with premature plans. Implying that her parents were her beneficiaries would insure their confidence and keep them at bay.

A yank of the bellcord brought a young maid on the run, straightening her white mobcap and apron before entering the sanctum. "You rang, Ma'am?"

"Of course I rang, Lurline! Who else? A ghost or phantom? What took you so long?"

"I came as fast as I could, Ma'am!"

"Never mind excuses. Look in the top drawer of the highboy. You will see a dark leather case bearing my initials. Bring it to me, please."

"Yes, Ma'am." The servant obeyed.

"Thank you," Esther said. "Now go out and post this letter, and mind you don't lose it."

"I'll guard it with my life, Ma'am."

"Just mail it, Lurline."

"Right away, Ma'am."

Esther opened the monogrammed case. The derringer lay like an ominous jewel on the crimson velvet lining. Ironically, Keith had given it to her shortly before the war—when moods were tense, tempers explosive, and no one knew what to expect—and taught her to handle it. The mother-of-pearl stock was constructed to her individual grip, inlaid with silver filigree, and her initials were engraved on the silver barrel: an exquisite little weapon, precise and compact enough to carry in a reticule, but nonetheless deadly. He had taken her to a private shooting gallery for instruction, and then to the country where he had put up targets for her, while he practiced with his dueling pistols.

Esther tucked the gun into the drawer of the bedside commode, beneath a stack of scented handkerchiefs. She hoped she would never have to use it, but she intended to be prepared. Perhaps she was only being morbid; still, eventually and inevitably, one way or another, this horror between them must be resolved.

PART V

Where there is marriage without love, there will be love without marriage.

Benjamin Franklin (1706–1790)

I have said that this problem of sexual love is the most important one that ever engaged the human mind.

Sexual intercourse that is in accordance with nature, and therefore proper, is that which is based upon mutual love and desire, and that ultimates in reciprocal benefit.

To what does modern marriage amount, if it not be to hold sexual slaves, who otherwise would be free?

I am a Free Lover!

Victoria Woodhull (1838–1927)

The very foundation of our existing social order is mutual deception and all-prevalent hypocrisy; and this will always be the case until we have freedom; until we recognize the rights of nature, until we provide in a normal and proper way for every passion of the human soul.

Tennessee Claflin (1846–1923)
Sister of Victoria Woodhull

Although for my part, I would rather pass the rest of my life in a dungeon than marry again, I know of love outside marriage which is so lasting, so imperious that nothing even in the ancient civil and religious law can make the bond more solid. . . .

George Sand (1804–1876)
The Letters of George Sand

In education, in marriage, in religion, in everything, disappointment is the lot of woman.

Lucy Stone (1818–1893)

Chapter 25

Devon watched a shadow on the parlor wall. The days were waning sooner, and the equinoctial sun struck her Village windows at a different angle. It had been pleasant sitting in the mauve twilight, but now she was eager to light the lamps.

Keith helped her and when he sat down again, began to prepare a pipe. She enjoyed the little ritual of stuffing, tamping, puffing, and the aroma which lingered like incense after he had gone. But it made her nostalgic too, for tobacco meant home: the green fields outside Richmond, the curing sheds, the wagons and boats hauling the hogsheads of bright leaf and burley to the warehouses on the rails and the river, to be shipped all over the world. Virginia had been founded on that one crop, had traded and prospered on it, as South Carolina on rice and indigo, Georgia and Alabama and Mississippi on cotton, and Louisiana on sugar cane. Plantations such as Harmony Hill had grown internationally famous on that commodity, which had brought buyers and speculators and agents, foreign and domestic, to Richmond well in advance of the annual auctions. But she had no business remembering any of that now, and especially not Daniel Haverston. Pregnancy made her retrospective, sentimental, and sometimes weepy.

"I've been looking for a country place," Keith said.

"An estate?"

"A home for you and the baby, and I've found one."

"Not that haunted castle on the Hudson!"

"No, this is a marvelous old Dutch farmhouse, once the manor of a sizable bouverie, farther up the island. It has been completely renovated, and there's a beautiful woods ... an ideal environment for a child. I've leased it with an option to buy."

"But I like it here, Keith."

"Darling, I think you'd be better off in the country, for the next year or so, anyway. And you won't be alone. There'll be servants and caretakers."

"Keith, what's wrong?" she asked suspiciously. "Why do you want to get me so far out of town? Does Esther know something? Please tell me the truth."

"She knows a little, and suspects a lot."

"You told her?" She was appalled, mortified.

"Of course not! But she sensed the truth, and threatened to hire a detective. I made counterthreats to thwart her, but she's unpredictable. We have to be careful, Devon. Esther's vicious and vindictive."

"But she's paralyzed, Keith!"

"The doctors are not convinced of that, and neither am I. I'm inclined to believe she has used invalidism as a conscience club over my head all these years—since I was ostensibly responsible for the accident—and that she could walk if she wanted to, or had enough motivation. This might be the incentive to get her out of that wheelchair with a vengeance."

"Well, if she's determined enough, the country won't hide me from her any more than the city did from you, Keith. A sleuth could trail you there, couldn't he?"

"Not as easily as here," he said. "I'd be aware of a hound that far and lead him on a wild goose chase. Why make it easy for her?"

"Even if we must make it harder for us?"

He smoked in silence awhile, and she heard his teeth grinding the pipestem. "This isn't such an isolated place, Devon. There's a village and farms and estates in the vicinity. Dr. Blake, the obstetrician I have engaged in place of Dr. Palmer, has a weekend place nearby and there's a local doctor in case of emergency, but naturally Blake and a nurse would come ahead of time for the delivery. He's a personal friend, you know, and understands the situation. Trust me, Devon. I think this is the best procedure, and most expedient."

Dissent flared and faded, unvoiced. Lately, it seemed, she lacked the ability, and even the volition, to make her own decisions. Where was the free spirit, the initiative and individuality, that had brought her to New York in the first place? Determination had dissolved into diffidence, courage into cowardice, independence into dependence. She had become the pathetic creature-thing she had sought to escape, the female vine clinging to the male pillar. She might as well have stayed in Virginia and spread her tendrils around the columns of Harmony Hill. At least her sprout would have had a surname and identity!

"Don't worry, Devon. You'll be safe and comfortable there. I'll come as often as I can and will be with you during confinement. Meanwhile, you can get a message to me promptly at the bank, through my private telegraph wire. Just send one of the servants to the Hudson River Railway station in the village."

"What if it's night, or you're out of town?"

"The company will deliver it to my home," he said, "and I don't plan to do any traveling for awhile. I can send a bank officer in my place. Now then," he said authoritatively, as if all obstacles and objections had been magically vanquished, "how soon can you move to your new home?"

"Whenever you say, Keith. I don't have much to pack." At that stage her cargo was primarily emotional. But in less than six months there would be a human burden that might become a helpless pawn in some bitter contest between him and his wife. She shuddered, pondering the glowing ember in his briar, the tenuous wisps of smoke, and the dark lengthening shadow on the wall.

"Just be careful, darling. Don't lift anything heavy. Let the draymen do it."

"Why don't you just lock me in the bank vault until I deliver?" she asked wryly.

"I would, if it could insure your safety. And the baby's."

"I suppose you want a boy?"

"It doesn't matter, as long as it's healthy."

"What if it isn't healthy?"

He regarded her intently. "Why do you say that? We're perfectly healthy, why shouldn't our child be?"

"Well," she frowned, oddly embarrassed, "the way it was conceived—"

"In sin, you mean? And we might be punished? That's an old wives' tale, invented by old wives in fear of young women and straying husbands."

"It was more than just sin that night in the mountains, Keith. We were animals."

"Oh, now, Devon! A little wild and uninhibited, maybe, if that's when it happened."

"Animals," she insisted.

"All right, animals. So what's the benighted backwoods theory? Animals beget animals? Savages spawn savages? Violence breeds violence? A damned good copulation is cursed? More silly superstitions, Devon, and you're much too intelligent to believe such nonsense." He paused to draw on his pipe. "As for the sinful aspect of your conception, aren't we all born of original sin, according to Scripture? It's supposedly our heritage from Adam and Eve. Furthermore, some of the most brilliant and famous people in history were conceived by adulterous parents. I couldn't begin to name them all."

"But it's also true, isn't it, that peculiar and afflicted people are born every day? Twisted in body, strange in mind and character, and nobody can explain why. Preachers rationalize it as God's will, or His curse. Physicians blame bad eggs or seeds. P. T. Barnum exploits them as freaks of nature and curiosities to the morbid public. How do you explain such deformities and monstrosities?"

"Misfortune, of course. People are either lucky or unlucky, blessed or deprived, victors or victims of life."

"That's fatalism."

"Then I'm a fatalist. Devon, I'm sure we've created a perfectly beautiful and normal child. But if it's a freak or monster, we'll just drown it in the river." And at her horrified gasp, "I was joking, darling! Lord, what a complicated creature is a pregnant woman."

An unwed pregnant woman, she brooded.

"Forgive me, Keith. I guess maudlin thoughts and anxieties go with the condition, like peculiar cravings. I ate three artichokes today, and I never cared for them before."

"Well, that's normal enough, isn't it? What would you like for supper this evening?"

"Oh, I don't know. Something exotic. French, I think. Surprise me."

"I'll let Delmonico's chef do that," he said. "Then we'll see the new comedy at Wallack's Theater. I hear it's a laugh a minute, and we could do with some laughter."

"Some loving too," she murmured, meeting his eyes.

"For an appetizer, or dessert?"

"Both." Winding her arms about his neck, she drew his mouth toward hers. "Don't you realize, my darling, that I crave *you* most of all?"

"Bon appetit!" he smiled and kissed her.

The house was built of fieldstone and oak timbers silvered with age. Over a hundred years old, it had an aura of peace and permanency, but of loneliness and isolation too. The rooms were all large and square and completely furnished, the paint and wallpaper and curtains so fresh Devon knew it had been in renovation long before Keith had mentioned it to her, and certainly before her pregnancy. Apparently he had been planning this move for some time and hoping to convince her of its necessity.

She loved the fireplaces framed with colorful Delft tiles, the corner cupboards with gingerbread trim, the paneled doors and polished wood staircases and beamed ceilings. The big bright airy kitchen had a terra cotta floor and open hearth with blackened iron cranes and gleaming copper pans and kettles, and two brick ovens. But a new Franklin range had also been added, along with a modern sink and convenient water supply, and a massive carved oak hutch full of china and pottery.

The windows of the master bedroom overlooked the Hudson. Devon could see the palisades across the water and watch the endless commercial flotilla. The adjacent nursery contained some of its original furniture, including a quaint hooded cradle and enclosed bed for the nursemaid. Tiny figures in Dutch costume—bonnets and pinafores, pantaloons and clogs—played on the sunny yellow wallpaper, and the cabinets and chest were gaily painted with tulips and windmills.

"Traditionally, Dutch wall-coverings and tiles tell folk stories," Keith explained. "Nursery rhymes and fairy tales for children; feasts and festivals and mythology in adult rooms. The architects and decorators tried to restore the authentic atmosphere, but feel free to change anything you wish, Devon."

She smiled with tears in her eyes. "I wouldn't think of doing that, Keith. It's all just perfect."

"I've hired some domestic help. A housekeeper and her

young daughter. Mrs. Sommes is a widow with excellent references from her last employer. The girl's name is Enid, and her mother says she's a well-trained maid. They're coming up on the train tomorrow. One of the handymen will meet them at the station."

"Do they know——?"

"Know what?"

"About us?"

"Of course not!"

"But won't they wonder?"

"They're servants, Devon. It's not their place to wonder, and this isn't the South, where mettlesome old mammies may be tolerated and even humored. Nor is this living arrangement uncommon. Many people have more than one residence, you know, and many men maintain more than one domicile under these circumstances. Some of my friends have been doing it for years. One has three children and their mother at an estate on Long Island. Another has a second family in a Connecticut cottage. And your Southern gentlemen had them too, some in slave cabins. It happens everywhere, Devon, and to all kinds of people—kings, priests, presidents."

"Presidents?"

"Yes, my dear, presidents. They don't teach all of the historic facts and human failings in schoolbooks. You never heard that Thomas Jefferson had a mulatto mistress at Monticello, and several quadroons by her?"

"I don't believe it!"

"He never denied it, when accused. And you didn't know that Andrew Jackson lived in bigamy with Rachel Robards for years, thinking her first husband had divorced her? They eloped to Mississippi without waiting to learn whether or not the divorce from her first husband was granted in Richmond, or even filed. Sort of irresponsible of Jackson, wouldn't you say, considering he was an astute lawyer? When the scandal leaked, he had to fight some duels over it and killed at least one man. The press was well aware of it, and no doubt your father was too."

"I know he was an ardent duelist," Devon said. "But I thought he just had a hot temper."

"He was still defending Rachel's honor in a sentimental speech at her grave, a few months after his election to the presidency," Keith said. "George Washington was also in love with another man's wife, and there were rumors about Monroe and some cocotte when he was in Paris. So far Lincoln's fidelity hasn't been questioned, but I was in Washington enough during the war to know that his cabinet members had as many mistresses and courtesans per capita as Napoleon's court."

Devon winced. "A courtesan is a prostitute, Keith. Am I in that category?"

"Certainly not! I'm only trying to prove that our case is not unique, Devon. My God, there were concubines in the Bible!" But he realized he was only making matters worse, and took her hand. "Let's go outside and survey the property. Most of the land was sold off, but there are still a few acres left. The garden has long since gone to pot, but can be restored. A good landscapist could turn it into a paradise."

"You sound like a country squire," she said, as they walked about the estate.

He laughed. "I feel like one. The stables have been repaired, and I bought some horses, and a carriage and pony trap. When you're able again, we can go riding."

"What about the neighbors, Keith?"

"There are no near neighbors, and they don't visit without invitation. The farmers and villagers are friendly but not officious. They know city folks seek privacy in the country, and don't intrude or trespass. Besides, people who act married are presumed to be married. No one will demand to see a wedding certificate. Don't concern yourself with trifles, Devon."

"Trifles?" she cried angrily, raising her voice as they passed the caretaker's cottage, now occupied by Lars and Karl Hummel, middleaged bachelor brothers from Inwood. "How can you use that word in this situation?"

"Keep it up, darling, and we won't have to try to convince them we're married. That's just the tone a scolding wife would use. Did I carry you over the threshold?"

"Oh!" She stamped her foot in frustration. "What am I going to do with you, Keith?"

"I think, my love, you've already done it."

That night, lying together in the big Flemish oak bed with its carved wood canopy, Devon felt the first quickening of life in her womb, faint but distinct, like the flutter of tiny wings. She wanted to share the experience with

Keith, but he was asleep, arms relaxed around her, heart throbbing peacefully against her breast. She waited expectantly but the sensation did not soon recur, as if the embryo had merely wanted to declare its presence, dispel any doubt of its existence. And so, she thought ruefully, despair mingled with joy, the child conceived on the Hudson would be born on the Hudson.

Mrs. Sommes and her daughter arrived with neat bundles of belongings, and promptly donned plain dark dresses, starched white aprons, and unfrilled mobcaps. Devon assured them that uniforms were not required, but they were accustomed to them and therefore were more comfortable. The mother was perhaps thirty-five, with straw-colored hair twisted into a heavy knot on her nape, pale-lashed hazel eyes, and an air of brisk efficiency. The girl had thick butter-yellow braids and mottled blue-gray eyes like agate marbles. Devon liked them both instantly, and felt a little sorry for Enid, with her plain round face and too-plump figure, and humble amenability, so eager to please, as if already resigned, at fifteen, to a life of servitude.

The way they attended Devon—they would not allow her to help with any of the chores or cooking—made her realize that Keith had given them orders to pamper her. Mrs. Sommes even did the marketing, driving herself in the pony trap, depriving Devon of the excuse to go to the village. Never good at fancywork or sewing, being always handier with pen and ink than needle and thread, she found leisure heavy on her hands. She could not even make clothes for the baby, for a New York seamstress had been engaged to assemble the layette and purchase necessary supplies for the lying-in.

Her unfinished manuscript lay in a desk drawer like an unfinished dream, and she thought that foolscap was certainly the right name for the paper. She read avidly: books, magazines, and the New York papers.

Kate Field was still in Paris, reporting the doings at the French court, the latest fashions from Monsieur Worth's salon, and the American travelers abroad. In London, Queen Victoria was reported to be finally emerging from her long bereavement, if not her weeds, and the Court of St. James was almost as gay as it had been before the death of Prince Albert. Jenny June had gone to Washington to cover the Ambassadors' Ball, which traditionally launched the autumn social season at the White House. The Cary sisters were publishing new books of poetry, and Fanny Fern's latest serial was beginning in the *Ledger*. Still prospering on Wall Street and now living in an elabrate mansion, Victoria Woodhull and Tennessee Claflin were also active in the suffrage movement, creating controversy and sensation with their candid lectures on the even more explosive issues of free love, divorce, birth control, and advocating legalized prostitution and abortion.

Everyone seemed busy and successful but herself. Here she was languishing in the country, idle as a bump on a log—and as helplessly trapped as the child growing in her body.

Did Keith really believe they could live a quiet peaceful life here, a Darby and Joan existence, sufficient unto themselves, members of the community and yet separate from it? And did he imagine that she would simply forget every hope, dream, ambition she had to be more than his mistress? Oh God, the loneliness and emptiness when he was not there!

There was nothing to do but walk in the woods, now turning color, and across the meadow bright with goldenrod. She could see cows grazing there, hear their bells tinkling and the attendant's dogs barking. Sometimes she sat on the escarpment, gazing forlornly at the river and the massive bulk of Indian Head on the opposite shore, wondering how she had ever gotten herself into such a mess. Certainly she had not been raised for this kind of life; it was contrary to all her principles and ideals and religious training. She had not been to church since she had left Richmond, and had almost forgotten how to pray.

But most of all she worried about the future of her child. Were the two of them to be immured here indefinitely, perhaps forever? And was she not doing the baby a terrible injustice in giving it birth? What was so wrong about abortion that made it condemned as a heinous crime punishable by imprisonment? Its furtive practice was what made it dangerous and horrible, Victoria said, not the act itself, insisting that it was a far greater crime to bring unwanted children into the world.

Dusk came early now, and cold winds sweeping down

from Canada kept Devon near the hearth in the evening, and the morning mists often obscured the river, so that the foghorns seemed to moan on ghost ships. The almanac predicted a severe winter, and the handymen had already chopped several cords of firewood in anticipation.

"You needn't hire a nursemaid," Mrs. Sommes told her one morning, while Devon was watching her bake a chocolate cake. "Enid and I can care for the baby."

"I'm sure you can, Mrs. Sommes."

"Anna," she said. "Please call me Anna. Will Mr. Curtis be coming up this weekend?"

"I think so, unless business takes him elsewhere. He travels a good deal, you know." This was how they excused his absences.

"So he said, Ma'am, when he hired us, and I assured him that he needn't worry about you while away."

I should tell her the truth, Devon thought. She has a right to know the kind of people she's serving and decide for herself whether she wants to expose her young daughter to such an immoral household. But perhaps she had already guessed and chose to remain, out of loyalty or necessity.

"If your hand is tired, Anna, I can beat the batter awhile."

"No, that's all right."

"Well, I can make the frosting then, if you have a recipe."

"You'd better just have some milk and take your nap, Ma'am."

"Oh, Anna, two naps a day? All I do is eat and sleep. I'll grow big and fat as a sow."

Anna smiled. "All ladies think that with the first one. After two or three, the figure doesn't seem so important. And after five or six—" She shrugged, whipping the batter vigorously.

"They really look like pigs," Devon finished, "and lose their husbands, who caused them to get that way in the first place! It doesn't seem fair, somehow."

"Well, that's woman's lot. And a sorry one it is, sometimes. But I don't think you need worry about that with Mr. Curtis, Ma'am. He's a fine gentleman and very much in love with you."

He loved his wife once too, Devon thought darkly, and

now he hates her and wants only to be free. And I hate her too and want his freedom more than my life. . . .

Madame Joie was showing her fall collection at Gramercy Park. With a casual glance at the mannequin, a tall willowy brunette, Keith begged pardon for intruding and told his wife he would return later. When the French-woman protested that he would miss the "magnifique presentation," he smiled and politely replied that he would know how successful it was by the size of the bill presented to him, and retreated to the library.

Two hours later Esther sent a maid for him. "Christ," he said, surveying the mountain of merchandise left behind, "there's enough lingerie here to supply a harem!"

"You should know, darling. No doubt you've outfitted a few. What did you think of Madame Joie's new model?"

"I never noticed."

"Well, she's certainly not as lovely as that little cream-and-honey blonde she had last year. I asked what happened to Mlle. Marshall, and Janette said she had gone home to Virginia, presumably to marry some ruined Rebel. I thought you rather liked her, Keith, and definitely admired her in that luscious apricot ensemble. Do you know I've never worn it?" She bestowed a warm smile, her eyes the color of the lapis-lazuli lamp by the bed. "Have your supper brought up with mine, Keith? I'm so tired of eating alone and would appreciate your company."

"Come to the dining room," he invited.

"Will you carry me?" she asked archly.

"You can walk, Esther. You know you can."

"Oh, if only I could!"

"Try. I'll help you."

But she only frowned, shaking her head. "No, I'd just fall again, as I have so many times before." Her hand gestured toward the slipper chair. "Sit down, dear, and smoke if you like."

"Concessions?" he mocked. "You never welcomed my cigars before, Esther, and my pipe was as forbidden in here as a Turkish hookah."

"I'm afraid I was a shrew in some respects, Keith, and a fool in others. I understand now why men smoke, and some women too. I also understand why some people drink. It's relaxing, and makes boredom bearable. I've read that certain kinds of weed, notably hemp, can tranquilize when smoked or burned as incense. They call it ganji in India and use it as an anesthetic in pain. Indian women are said to smoke it before they commit suttee. It's also known as marijuana."

"Have you been reading the pharmacopoeia again, Esther? You have a coffer of sedatives and anodynes now, but if you feel you need another crutch—" He gave a careless shrug. "Tell me, have you given any consideration whatever to my proposition?"

"Some."

"I'll up the ante, Esther, to two million, plus the deed to this house. You'd be richer than I."

"Don't try to hoodwink me, Machiavelli. The only man in this country with more money than you is Cornelius Vanderbilt, and he's not interested in paralyzed women." She grinned at him, as if they were playing a game and she had scored. "Incidentally, I saw Woodhull and Claflin's advertisement in the *Tribune*, and it now reads brokers and bankers. Some competition for you, dear. Is the Commodore behind that expansion too?"

"Probably."

"Is Tennie Claflin really his mistress?"

"How the devil should I know!"

"What do they say in the Street?"

"Who cares? And who's going to object? Certainly not his wife, who learned her lesson on that subject twenty years ago. Which reminds me, Mrs. Curtis. I intend to ask some more physicians to examine you."

Esther tensed. "I won't permit it, Keith."

"Would you rather be declared non compos mentis without a medical examination?"

"That old bedlam bogey doesn't scare me, Keith. My parents would promptly rescue me. You see, I wrote them about your previous ultimatum."

"You're lying, Esther. If so, they'd have been here on the first train from Boston."

"Try to railroad me into an asylum, and they will! In fact, you'd better take very good care of me, Keith, and see that no harm comes to me. Because they also have a signed statement in which I express fear for my safety."

Keith had been sitting with his legs leisurely crossed but

now he rose and advanced on the bed, scowling in anger.
"You accused me in writing of intentions to harm you?"

"Do you deny threatening me? And you're even more
desperate now, aren't you? Is the bitch about to whelp?"

His hands rose involuntarily, as if to throttle her, and at
the same moment hers emerged from under the pillow,
with the Derringer pointed straight at him. His expression
changed from surprise to disbelief to disgust. "My God,
Esther! You've lied to me, deceived me, cheated me—and
now you pull a gun on me!"

"It's loaded too," she warned ominously. "You gave it
to me, remember, and taught me to use it. You said I was
a fair shot for a woman. Well, I still am, Keith, if the target is close enough. So pray keep your distance."

"So this is what it has come to," he said, shaking his
head. "This hideous contest of suspicion and threat. Did
you forget what I said about changing my will, Esther?
Well, I didn't forget, and my attorneys have already taken
care of it."

"You've stricken me?"

"Suffice it to say I'm more valuable to you alive than
dead, Mrs. Curtis. Unfortunately, I can't say the same for
you to me. And if you had the sense of a goose, you'd
take my generous offer and run like hell."

"Or what?" she taunted. "You'll torture me with threats
and insinuations in some weird duel of nerves?"

"You're insane, Esther, and should be confined for your
own benefit."

Her eyes glittered malevolently. "Just try it, darling, if
you want to know some real trouble."

"You think you have me in a box, don't you? That no
matter when or how you expire, if it's twenty or thirty
years from now, I'd still be suspect."

"I felt I had to do it, Keith, for my own protection.
You were a monster that day, and I was frightened. After
all, I'm helpless."

"As a tigress," he said grimly, "and you've been
mauling me in your 'helpless' fashion for years."

"Nevertheless, I still want you for my mate."

"Even if you have to tear me to pieces in the process?"

"Oh, I'm not really that vicious, darling. But naturally
I'm concerned about self-preservation. You can't expect
me to oblige you in this cruel wish to put me away some-

where, in the hope that I'll die promptly. The statement is sealed, however, and my parents think it is my last will. I can recall it easily enough, with the proper incentive. It's up to you, Keith."

"Me? How, Esther?"

"Very simply," she purred. "Forget the past, and the enmity between us now, and start over. If I can forgive your many affairs, why can't you forgive my one indiscretion? I'm still young, Keith, and I think I could be well and strong again, with your help and encouragement. Faith can move mountains, you know. Perhaps I just need a reason. I could walk and dance again. Yes, and even bear children!"

"By immaculate conception? I could never make love to you again, Esther."

Her vanity rejected his rejection. "How do you know, unless you try?"

"Forced by gunpoint?" His eyes indicated the pistol, its silver barrel glinting lethally in the lamplight. "This debacle gets more sordid and incredible by the moment, and you've destroyed all hope of salvaging anything from it. There's nothing left anymore, Esther, except bitterness and distrust, and that's not much of a foundation to rebuild a marriage on. Furthermore, I think I should move out of this house. Neither of us can have any peace or rest under the same roof."

"Nor any happiness while the other lives?"

"I didn't say that Esther."

"But that's what you meant!"

"Have it your way."

"Yes, I will have it my way, Keith! No separate domiciles. That's the same as desertion, and I won't add that humiliation to all my others. I deplore our estrangement and wish with all my heart I could change it. I'm willing to compromise, even crawl, but not sacrifice myself for another woman." A vehement shake of her head. "No, not even on an altar of gold would I do that! I'm even willing to share you with someone else, but not give you up entirely. You see, it's you I want, Keith, far more than your money."

"You're beating a dead horse, Esther."

"Perhaps—but he's still my horse."

Chapter 26

It was in secret and confidential matters that Esther felt most hampered and hamstrung. An individual in a wheelchair was hardly inconspicuous. She could not come and go as she pleased without an entourage of attendants who were also, unfortunately, witnesses to her every act, including some highly personal and private ones. Still, she managed to make furtive inspections of Keith's rooms (her chair was self-propelled and she needed assistance only in getting in and out of it), searching for clues to the identity of his social companions, still convinced that he was betraying her with one of her own perfidious friends. She tried, unsuccessfully, to pick the locks of his armoire and desk with hairpins and nail files, and even tampered with the dial of his wall-safe. She knew when his bed had or had not been occupied and the hours at which he returned, if at all, to Gramercy Park. Everything but what she wanted to know.

Despite his warnings, she would have engaged a detective had it been feasible to do so. But never having made any effort to win the affection and loyalty of the servants, she could neither confide in them nor trust them not to betray her confidence. And she knew the butler—who had been in Curtis service when Keith was a child—was completely loyal to his master. Hadley would never admit a stranger to the house without identification; thus, she could neither secretly seek the services of an agent, nor summon one to the house. There was nothing curious about her visits to her husband's quarters, for she had every right to go there at any hour of the day or night. For the servants' benefit she pretended that he also visited her privately, planting a robe or pair of slippers by the bed, and sprinkling some of his facial tonic on the pillows and linens.

So far, however, her snooping had availed her nothing

but bewilderment and frustration. And then one morning while she was hunting some reading material in the library, a vast repository of several thousand books and manuscripts, she noticed some volumes out of alignment in the science section, suggesting either someone's recent research or a servant's negligence in cleaning. The perfectionist, unable to endure the slightest irregularity in her household, proceeded to straighten the offenders, pausing when she noticed the provocative titles. There was one on poisons, chemical and botanical. Another, *A Common Sense Manual on the Extermination of Household Pests*, dealt with arsenic, Paris green, and nux vomica. The third was called *Zymurology: The Science of Fermentation*.

Periodically they were troubled with roaches and rodents in the storeroom, and she knew Hadley had a diligent control program. She summoned him and inquired, "Are we having pest problems again, Hadley?"

"Mr. Curtis saw some rats in the wine cellar, Ma'am, and I set out some bait for them."

"Why don't you use traps?"

"I'm using both, Ma'am."

"I see. Very well. Thank you, Hadley."

A few days later the protruding spines of several other books caught her attention. *Aberrations of the Unsound Mind; Coping With Mental Disorders; Suicide in Insanity*.

Keith was an avid reader, and his evenings at home were spent in the library, reading or playing chess with Hadley. He read primarily for knowledge, but he also liked to relax with bizarre or exotic literature, and he had been there last night. His pipesmoke still beclouded the air. The aroma of his special tabacco mixture permeated the heavy damask draperies, the thick Oriental carpet, and even the soft leather furniture had absorbed the distinctive scent.

How clever of him, and how crude! He had known she would discover the misaligned volumes before anyone else was likely to, if at all. Did he want to play games? What would he do next? Offer her a cordial as if it contained hemlock or nightshade? Present her with a rare plant supposed to emit noxious vapors? Spread some *Police Gazette*s around with gory details of unsolved crimes? Tease and torment her with wonder and uncertainty until she would be glad, indeed eager, to leave of her own accord? Well, she could play games too!

The vendetta had lapsed into boredom, and she wlecomed the new developments; they were challenging and stimulating, testing her wit and alertness. His lack of subtlety amused her, in fact, and suddenly she laughed aloud, wild rollicking laughter that echoed through the corridors, and brought a trio of scurrying servants and the curious inquiring butler.

"Are you all right, Ma'am?"

"I'm fine, Hadley. However, I want to see Lurline alone. Come in here, please. The rest of you are excused," she said with a gesture of dismissal.

Lurline shut the door and waited apprehensively, expecting reprimand and wondering what she had done to deserve it. Hoping to divert her mistress, she said, "Lord, Ma'am, what a fright you gave us, shrieking like that!"

"Shrieking? How dare you say such a thing! I was merely amused, Lurline, and laughing aloud. Were you on duty in the library this morning?"

"I was, Ma'am."

"You dusted the books and shelves?"

"I did, Ma'am."

"Did you perhaps forget to straighten some of them?"

"Perhaps."

"Well, please be more careful hereafter."

"Yes, Ma'am." The maid bobbed a curtsy and waited for punishment, but Mrs. Curtis had a surprise for her.

"How would you like to be my personal maid, Lurline, with an increase in wages?"

"Oh, I'd like that just fine, Ma'am!"

"Very well. Henceforth you alone will attend me. You will prepare my meals directly from the range and in cook's presence, and deliver them to me personally. Is that clear?"

"Clear, Ma'am."

Esther hesitated, reluctant to share her nocturnal privacy with a servant. "Also, until further notice, you will sleep in my rooms, on the trundle, so I won't have to disturb the quarters should I feel unwell or need assistance during the night. And please bring up some lamps and candles. I find that gaslight irritates my eyes and gives me headaches. The jets in my chambers will have to be sealed off, at least temporarily, to prevent possible leakage. Tell Hadley to summon a workman immediately. You will also store some wine and liquors in my cabinet, for the master's convenience. That's all at present, Lurline. You may go."

Another servile curtsy. "Thank you, Ma'am."

Her sudden suspicions and precautions should give *him* something to ponder! She considered ordering a trained dog from a kennel, but she had no use for pets, and Keith had such a way with animals that he would soon make friends even with the most ferocious mastiff. She saw that a chess game was in progress on the library table and toyed with the ornate ivory and ebony figures, finally deposing all but one. Silly man, he should know the queen was the strongest piece on the board, and always figured in checkmating the vulnerable king!

She laughed again, hilariously, but this time it brought no alarmed response from the staff, only wonder and curiosity and whispering in the quarters. Had the mistress gone into a decline? Was she hysterical, daft? Demanding supervision of her meals and beverages, ordering lamps and candles instead of gaslight. . . .

"Listen to her, cackling like a hyena," the scullery maid remarked to the newly-promoted personal maid. "What do you suppose got into her all of a sudden?"

Lurline shrugged. "She's always been nervous, Bridget. And finicky." ·

"Well, ain't I got enough to do polishing silver and brass and crystal? Now I got to clean lamps and candlesticks yet! And she's got cat eyes, can see a smudge or fingerprint across the room, and a speck of dust or lint in the dark!"

"And uneven books on a shelf," Lurline nodded.

"But you'll get extra wages. All I get is extra work."

"Hurry up with those lamps, girl—and don't forget the drop of attar of roses in the oil. She wants to use 'em tonight."

"Loony if you ask me," Bridget muttered. "Crazy as a loon."

When the master came in that afternoon, the butler requested an immediate audience in the library. "Madam developed some peculiar notions today, sir."

Keith was tired, having just left the board of brokers,

where he generally spent the hours between one and three. There had been the usual tensions and hassles over stocks and bonds in the gold room, the shouting and confusion and barely controlled violence. The furious trading in Erie Railroad issues had caused one member to suffer a heart seizure and brought several others to the brink of apoplexy. The board president had banged his ivory mallet desperately, pleading for order, but the pandemonium had continued at a deafening pitch, and the roaring and bellowing of the bulls and bears still echoed in his ears. He needed a relaxing drink in the worst way, and here was his major domo presenting him with yet another domestic problem.

"Peculiar, Hadley?"

"Yes, sir."

As Hadley related the events of the day, including Madam's erratic actions and demands, Keith realized that butlering had its bad moments even as banking and broking did, and he would have commiserated were he less weary and frustrated himself.

"Women are noted for strange ideas, Hadley, and Madam has had some before this day. However, gas fumes do affect some people adversely, you know."

"But she wants her jets plugged, sir!"

Keith scratched a long sideburn, bemused. "That does seem a bit extreme. But since it's only her jets, I don't suppose it matters. I'm sure Lurline has no objection to attending her constantly, if that's her wish. And if she wants some private stock handy, I see no reason to deny her that pleasure, either. She has little enough diversion, don't you think?" He paused, smiling at the victorious queen centering the board. "As for disrupting our chess game, perhaps it was accidental."

"I'm more inclined to consider it deliberate, sir. An unsubtle protest. I think she resents the time you spend at the game instead of with her."

"Feminine caprice, Hadley. We just have to ignore it, and humor her."

"Yes, sir. Dinner will be served at the usual hour. I'll fix your drink now."

"Never mind, Hadley. I'll do it myself."

On his way upstairs, glass in hand, Keith encountered Lurline carrying a branched candelabra tipped with tall white tapers. "For the mistress," she explained, adding significantly, in case he had husbandly ideas, "I'm to sleep in her rooms for the present too, and prepare all her meals personally. Has Madam suffered a relapse, sir? Is she worse?"

"What do you mean, worse?"

"Well, she gave us all an awful scare today, sir. Didn't Hadley tell you? We thought she was screaming in the library. But she said she was only amused and laughing to herself. But it was odd laughter, sir."

"Odd in what way, Lurline? Hysterical, maniacal, what?"

"Peculiar," Lurline hedged, employing Hadley's description. "Sort of shrieky. Perhaps we should've called the doctor."

"Perhaps," he agreed. "How is she now?"

"Oh, she seems fine now, sir! Resting comfortably."

"Then I shan't disturb her," Keith said considerately and proceeded to his own chambers.

Since their daughter's accident, the Stanfields had been celebrating the autumn holidays in New York, and this year Mrs. Stanfield wrote that she planned to remain from Thanksgiving through the New Year. Accustomed to the arrangement, Keith had accepted it and gone about his business as usual, and was even a genial host while his in-laws were in residence. This year, however, he advised Esther that he had other plans, and if she wished to avoid the embarrassment of his absence and a possible unfortunate confrontation with her parents, she had better go to Boston for the season.

"You can travel in the private car, and take Lurline and a footman with you," he said. "You'll be quite comfortable, and I'm sure your family would be happy to have you."

"Without my husband?"

"Didn't you hear me? I have other plans."

"Well, that's just too bad, darling. I'm afraid you'll have to cancel them."

"Damned if I will! You're going to Boston if I have to ship you in a crate."

She gazed at him sullenly, her eyes slanting catlike at the corners. "Don't you think I can see through that ploy,

Keith? Once I left you'd probably close the house and put it on the market, and I'd be stranded in Boston! Well, I'm not such a benighted fool as that, my dear husband. I'm also wise to your other tricks and schemes to intimidate and torment me, and must say they're rather obvious and clumsy."

"What're you talking about?"

"As if you didn't know! Those books you've been reading and trying *not* to conceal. I should think a genius like you would be more clever."

"You're raving again, Madam."

"Not at all. I'm in complete control of my faculties."

"Indeed? Then how do you explain your strange behavior of late? Your spontaneous, hysterical laughter? Your food taster and night sentry? Your sealed gas jets? Your searching of my rooms and tinkering with my locks? What're you seeking, or expect to find? Christ, Esther! Even the servants consider you eccentric, if not actually insane, and they are all afraid of you, wondering what you'll do next."

Her hand rose involuntarily to her throat. My God, he was right! To anyone unaware of their personal animosities and conflicts, her behavior must appear odd, to say the least. Outwardly, he was the soul of tact and kindness and husbandly solicitude, and no servant or friend could ever attest otherwise. Whereas she, in her efforts to outwit him, had made herself appear dim-witted. Irrational, and even mad. Protecting herself from imaginary fears, laughing boisterously at private humors—shrieking, Lurline had termed it. No doubt there was plenty of idle backstairs gossip concerning the mistress' idiosyncrasies. What a stupid, gullible fool she'd been, swallowing his bait as blindly as the mice in the basement!

"Why, you insidious rogue," she accused through clenched teeth. "This is precisely what you had in mind, isn't it? You hoped I would react to your subtle persecution this way, and make the servants think me a lunatic!"

"More delusions" he deprecated. "Too much medication, I suspect. And I understand you've also added spirits to your chest. For medicinal purposes, I presume?"

"Dr. Hawley prescribed an occasional brandy nightcap or wine caudle to promote relaxation and sound slumber."

"Yes, indeed. Alcohol has always been a sovereign

remedy for nervous tension and insomnia, and it's even more effective when combined with morphine or other opiates. Why don't you try a little absinthe too?"

"That's a vile liquor, and you know it. Deadly to some people. What a heartless brute you are, Keith! A pitiless hawk tantalizing a lame pigeon." As he stood to leave, she asked, "Has the egg in your illicit nest been hatched yet, or is she still incubating it?" He was silent. "You once said you intended to adopt the chick, but you don't propose to bring it here to live, do you?"

Still no answer, only wary speculation.

"And yet, it would seem quite natural and logical to our friends, wouldn't it, were we to adopt a child? I've been thinking about it, Keith, and you may believe me or not, but I'd be agreeable to adoption. Certainly I wouldn't be the first wife to achieve motherhood through her husband's mistress, and since you deny me the privilege—"

"Deny? There was a time I begged you, Esther."

"Well, I'm sorry about that, Keith, and have often regretted it. But I'm amenable now and trying to make amends. It's an opportunity to legitimize your heir with the respect and approbation of society."

"Hang society," he muttered.

"Does she share those sentiments? And will the fatherless child, when it discovers the truth? Think about it, Keith. You owe your offspring the obligation of serious consideration. Bastard is an ugly word."

Keith waited until mid-November to tell Devon that he could not spend Thanksgiving with her, and disappointment made her petulant and remonstrative.

"But Mrs. Sommes has already panned the dinner, Keith! The turkey's in the barnyard, the pumpkins are in the pantry, and we'll have chestnut dressing and cranberries and—"

"Darling, I've already explained the situation. Esther refuses to go to Boston, which means her parents will come to New York again. I can't use business as an excuse, because nobody does business on those holidays, so I'm stuck at Gramercy Park. I can't be in two places at once, Devon."

"And so I must spend Christmas and New Year alone too?"

"They're just days, Devon. Does it matter if we celebrate them a little early or late? We're not bound by a calendar."

"I am," she said miserably. "I'm bound by the nine-month lunar chart! I'm secluded in the country, like a social exile in Coventry. I'm helpless and dependent on you, and sometimes I think this is precisely the way you wanted and planned it, Keith, that you made me pregnant deliberately!"

"That's not true, Devon."

Devon knew she was being unreasonable, but couldn't check herself. She could see nothing ahead of her but years of acquiescing to Esther's whims and vindictiveness; a lifetime of waiting in secret places while Keith humored a vixen in the hope of eventual freedom. And it seemed grossly unfair of him to expect such submissive cooperation of her.

"Just the same, I don't like living alone in the wilderness, and I won't do it forever, Keith! I'm coming back to the city after the baby is born. You haven't given up the lease at Rhinelander Gardens, have you?"

"No, and you may return whenever you wish, my dear. I thought this place would provide security and serenity for you, but if you're unhappy—well, it's not a prison or cloister, Devon. And certainly it would be more convenient for me to have you in town. I'll take you back tomorrow, or whenever you say."

His rationality dissolved her petulance, and even made her ashamed of her temper. "I'm just ranting, Keith, out of capricious disappointment. I was counting on our being together at least one of the holidays."

"I was counting on being together all of them," he said.

He had come for the weekend, arriving on the *Sprite* and sending captain and crew back to port, saying he would return by other means. He varied his modes of transportation, for he trusted Esther no more than she trusted him, and was even more wary of establishing routine habits and patterns now than before. He could take the train to the village station, a steamboat to Inwood Landing, or the Marble Hill stage. He might sail himself up the Hudson in a rented yawl or scull and anchor it off Fort Tryon. If the weather obliged he could drive one of his sport rigs and fast teams, as if going to compete in the Harlem Lane races.

Now, as they prepared to retire, ice crystals pelted the windows and obscured the river. Winter had come in earnest. Keith stirred the coals on the hearth and added another log from the woodbox. Etched in flame, his face had a sanguinary glow, his smoky eyes a dark moodiness she saw too often of late.

"It's all right, Keith. Knowing you want to be with me is almost as good as having you, and I realize we must both make sacrifices for awhile." She stood before the mirror, removing the combs from her hair, which fell in soft gleaming masses on her shoulders. All the disagreeable early symptoms had passed, and she was now enjoying robust health. Her eyes sparkled, her skin glowed. And though her misty blue chiffon peignoir, cut in the voluminous Empire lines with cascades of Brussels lace, effectively concealed her pregnancy, she still felt awkward, misshapen, unattractive. She sighed wistfully. "I'm afraid I'm not very pretty any more, or desirable."

"Good Lord, is that what you think?" The poker clattered to the tile as he rushed to reassure her in his arms. "You've never been more beautiful or desirable to me, Devon."

"How can you say that? Look at me!"

"I am, and you're absolutely radiant. Everything about you excites me now, and I can't wait to make love to you. I think about it all week and get stimulated at the damndest times: during board meetings, at the Exchange, my clubs, and once even while making a speech to the Chamber of Commerce. Fortunately, the rostrum concealed my embarrassment. I admire the changes in your body, they fascinate me, and I doubt I'd notice another woman if she were naked in the street with her hair on fire. I especially like holding you this way and lying together, with our little creation between us."

"But I'm getting so big and clumsy. I'm afraid it's twins or triplets—and it kicks like a colt."

He laughed, nuzzling his face in her fragrant curls, parting the peignoir to fondle her full ripe breasts and taut nipples, pressing his belly to hers. "I know, I feel it. I thought you were rejecting me."

"Oh, darling, no!" She moved with him to the bed. "Be patient with me, Keith."

"*You* be patient with me, Devon. And love me. I'll make it up to you someday, I promise. I swear it by all that's holy—and the baby is holy, you know. Every child is an angel and sacred in the sight of God, no matter how it was conceived. If life is a miracle, then who else but God could create it?" His eyes focused briefly on the fire. "It's just that some people, like my witch of a wife, have the devil for a godfather. . . ."

Chapter 27

Dinner was at three o'clock, and at half-past two Esther still was not sure they would have a host for the traditional feast, which her mother had always thought more appropriately celebrated in pilgrim Massachusetts or Colonial Virginia. Of all days to take a constitutional, Keith had perversely chosen this one! To spite her, naturally. To torment her with anxiety, and to punish her for forcing him to do something against his will. Esther was tense and nervous, and kept an anxious eye on the drawing room clock, afraid her parents would sense the violent undercurrents in her surface tranquillity, and the hideous developments in her marriage since their last visit to New York.

She was exquisitely groomed. Monsieur Dubonnet, assisted by her maid, had done her long lustrous hair in a becoming chignon that very morning and painted her face so artfully the boxed bloom was imperceptible. Her robe-de-chambre, an Empress Eugenie copy from Madame Joie's Paris collection, was royal blue velvet with a standing collar of white ermine and matching cuffs on flaring bracelet-length sleeves. With it she wore the sapphires Keith had given her on their first anniversary and not yet taken away, as he had the coveted family jewels. He was exerting every possible pressure and aggravation, every conceivable strategy and finesse, in his campaign to force her capitulation. His every action seemed suspicious to Esther now, and she detected sinister motives in this patently innocent stroll, with which he apparently hoped to provoke a scene before her family. For if he could arouse her wrath sufficiently, drive her to irrational fury or hysteria before them, he would have some proof of her mental instability and necessity of treatment including commitment. Well, if such was his foul intention, he was going to be foiled! She would be the sweetest, gentlest, most under-standing of wives, impervious to provocation.

Mrs. Stanfield's gown was several years old, a gray fleur-de-lys satin with a discreet bodice and long tight sleeves pointed over the wrists, demode but still elegant, for a genuine Worth, like vintage wine, seemed to improve with age, and the antique amethyst jewelry was the perfect complement. Although she had never been pretty even in youth, there was about her an air of aristocracy and im-perious hauteur which attracted and even commanded attention. It was Hortense Clayton Stanfield's personal opin-ion that the world was improved by her presence, and would be diminished by her absence. She regarded Boston as the center of the universe, and Beacon Hill its axis, viewing life serenely and sublimely through the violet-tinted windows of her Bulfinch mansion on Louisburg Square, as if nothing vile or unpleasant existed beyond its periphery. She had no more suspected her daughter's clandestine affair with an impoverished painter than she did her hus-band's marital infidelities, for in her mind decent, well-bred people simply did not behave otherwise. She further believed that in character, decorum and discretion, Esther was an extension of herself, and would have been aston-ished to discover that since puberty she had considered herself a separate entity, an individual entitled to a person-ality and life of her own. In some respects, Mallard had been a challenge to the mother-image, as well as a revolt against the de rigueur of the Hill.

"What do you suppose is keeping Keith, dear?" Hor-tense asked, as another quarter-hour chimed.

"Don't worry, Mother. He has a watch, and an uncanny sense of timing." Esther was remembering his cataclysmic arrival at the studio, and her vehemence might have be-trayed her to a more sophisticated or less complacent per-son.

"Oh? Is he so punctual in his habits?"

"Perfunctory," Esther replied.

"Which is essentially the same thing," said her father, to whom marriage had long since become a perfunctory habit.

As usual, Henry Stanfield was enjoying his visit. The food was superb, the liquors and tobacco excellent, the servants solicitous of his comfort. The Curtis household was as well managed as the Stanfield's . . . and why not, since the mistress had been trained by the same meticulous mentor-martinet. Since his daughter's accident, however, Henry had sensed dissatisfaction and unrest in his son-in-law and felt a natural male empathy for a virile young man saddled with a physically incapacitated wife, no matter how lovely and charming and competent. He would not have been either surprised or condemnatory to learn that Keith had a mistress. Henry had one himself at that age, and still enjoyed other women when inclination and opportunity coincided, and he expected to continue doing so until he joined his ancestors in Mount Auburn Cemetery.

"I noticed the park from our windows this morning," Hortense remarked. "Most of the trees are bare, and it must be freezing out there now. What attraction could it possibly have to anyone on this occasion?"

"Perhaps he has problems to ponder," her husband suggested. "Any man who spends most of his time in Wall Street is mentally burdened. The Boston market is mild compared to the Manhattan madhouse. If women could realize the killing pressures men are under, there might be fewer widows around."

"Gracious, Henry! I was merely commenting on the wintry aspects of Gramercy Park, which has always reminded me of our own Louisburg Square, and even more of London's Mayfair, which was its inspiration. But what a blessing for any neighborhood to have its own exclusive park! I can't imagine living without one. Commons are so so . . . *common*."

Esther was about to send a servant after Keith, when the front door opened on an arctic draft, and he walked briskly through the marble-squared foyer, just as the butler announced dinner. He looked robust and vigorous, his skin ruddy from the cold, his movements quick and controlled.

"Did you have a nice walk, dear?" Esther inquired smilingly, as he wheeled her to the dining room.

Thinking of Devon dining alone in the country, his hands gripped the chair-handles hard enough to dent the wood. "I needed some exercise." Either that or a cold bath.

As he lifted Esther and seated her at the table, her arms slid possessively about his neck, and she planted a triumphant kiss on his cheek, pleased at his helpless anger and chagrin. After grace, he proceeded to carve the bird with a vengeance, yet precisely and methodically, as if the cutlery tools were surgical instruments and he dared not miscalculate or blunder; and only Esther realized the suppressed violence under his surface calm.

Mrs. Stanfield admired the beauty and richness of her surroundings as if they were mutual possessions: the repousse sterling and gold-plate brought up from the basement vault to gleam on the massive mahogany sideboards; the exquisite Marie Therese chandelier with cascades of rosetted crystal pendalogues glittering overhead; the master paintings and splendid wall-size tapestry of an English hunt scene commissioned for Heathstone Manor in Sussex; the Damascus tablecloth and Spode china and silver goblets ornate as cathedral chalices. All this, she thought proudly, and a bank on Wall Street too!

Midway through the banquet, Esther said unexpectedly, "Shall we tell them our news, darling?"

Startled, Keith glanced up sharply, laying his fork on his plate with a faint click. "What news?"

"Well, it's not definite yet," Esther said, addressing her mother, "but we may adopt a child."

Hortense stopped chewing and swallowed her turkey in an embarrassing gulp. "Did you say *adopt*, dear?"

"If it can be arranged," Esther nodded, her eyes challenging Keith across the flickering candles and silver bowl of hothouse roses. "Isn't that right, dearest?"

"I'm afraid," said Keith to no one in particular, "she's entertaining false hopes."

His father-in-law glanced at him curiously wondering if he meant delusions. "Where is this child?"

"More important," said his wife, "*who* is this child?"

"It hasn't been born yet," Esther replied, enjoying her husband's apprehension. "But the doctor knows of this girl, this poor unfortunate creature who got into trouble with a married man and—"

"Oh, mercy!" Hortense interrupted, scandalized. "You mustn't even consider a child of such uncertain parentage. Heaven only knows how it might turn out!"

"Mother, will you please listen? The mother is young and healthy, and was probably decent enough before her seduction. And the father, I understand, is of excellent blood. His lineage is supposedly the best, isn't it, darling?"

"I doubt that," Hortense said. "Certainly his character and morals leave much to be desired. A gentleman of honor and integrity and *breeding* would never—"

"Oh. Mother, it happens all the time!"

"In New York?"

"Everywhere," Esther snapped, casting a critical eye at her father, who promptly reached for his wine.

"Couldn't we discuss this later, daughter, over coffee? I don't think your mother considers it an appropriate dinner table topic."

"Do forgive me, please, if I've spoiled anyone's appetite." Esther apologized, tinkling the service bell. "Hadley, we'll have dessert and demi-tasse in the library."

She extended her arms to her glowering husband to perform the chair ritual again. He obliged but dropped her, hard, onto the leather-padded seat. "Oh, I'm sorry, dear. How clumsy of me! Did I hurt you?"

"Not at all," she glared. "Better luck next time."

Servants brought coffee and an array of desserts, and after Esther dismissed them, Mrs. Stanfield said, "I don't wish to interfere in any plans you and Keith may already have made in this matter, dear, but I do think you should give it due consideration. After all, you're still young, and it's quite possible that you will recover and be able to bear children of your own. And speaking of recovery, our own Dr. Danvers has learned of a new physician in Vienna, a nerve specialist whose advanced knowledge and treatment supposedly works miracles in cases like yours. The European and British medical journals have praised him enthusiastically, and Dr. Danvers recommends that you consult him." Her eyes beseeched her son-in-law. "Don't you think it's worth another trip abroad?"

"Certainly," he agreed, "if there's any hope at all. Unfortunately, I can't get away in the near future. But if you would like to accompany her, at my expense—"

"Oh, I think she needs her husband more than her mother in this instance!"

"It will have to wait, then."

"How long?"

"Six months or so."

"But she could be well by that time!"

"There's no hurry, Mother. I've been this way five years. Six more months won't kill me. Will it, Keith?"

"But, darling, if meanwhile you adopt this little waif or urchin or whatever—"

"Bastard," Esther said.

"What?" cried Hortense, shocked.

"Isn't that the proper word for a nameless child, Mother?"

Henry laced his coffee liberally with brandy. "This conversation is hardly an aid to digestion, daughter, and I see no necessity to continue it at this time. Why don't you and Mother go along to the parlor, and let us enjoy our brandy and cigars without dyspepsia. Hortense, take a hand with her chair, can't you?"

When they had gone, an irrepressible belch escaped Henry. "That woman—my wife—would frazzle an iron man's guts to fiddlestrings! I'd be shredded to straw by now if I hadn't learned long ago how to relax, and I hear New York is a harassed husband's haven. My friends tell me about a concert saloon—Harry Hill's, I believe—where the girls are all in their teens and wear short skirts and red boots with bells on them."

Keith was pouring the brandies. "That's the Louvre, on Broadway. Harry Hill's is on Houston Street, and the emphasis there is on bosoms rather than legs. Other men prefer to relax in the parlor houses—the Seven Sisters on Seventh Avenue and Flora's on Green Street are the most popular. If you need to relieve serious tensions, however, Josephine Woods has the most select clientele in town. Her establishment is located on Clinton Place, and is so exclusive that credentials are required."

"References, for a brothel?"

Keith handed him a drink. "It's a discreet house of assignation, Henry, and not every Phil Philander and Louie Libertine has access. Gentlemen only, and no perversions or other quaint titillations."

Henry grinned. "I presume you know the lady?"

"I've met her and recommended her house to discriminating friends and customers. As you surely know, Henry, supplying entertainment for prospective clients is a part of business."

"Would your name suffice as open sesame?"

"Probably, although you can safely use your Stock Exchange ticket for admission. Unlike some others in the profession, Miss Woods doesn't engage in blackmail."

"That's comforting knowledge, and the best recommendation any madam could have." Henry raised his glass appreciatively, as one sophisticated gentleman saluting another. "To discretion and discreet women!"

"Amen," Keith said, touching snifters and smiling at his concupiscent father-in-law, who had just compromised himself in the oldest conspiracy in the world. Now the old boy was securely in his camp and must either support him or remain neutral in any open battle between the sexes, including one with his own daughter.

The parlor, a rosewood and brocade room with flocked wallpaper and floral carpet, was as feminine as the library was masculine, and perfect for the sort of intimate mother-daughter conversation Hortense deemed vital and imperative now. "I don't recall your mentioning adoption in any of your letters, dear. Is it a recent decision?"

"Comparatively, and it's for Keith's sake more than mine, Mother. He wants a child, which is natural enough, I suppose. Unfortunately, with my infirmities—well, I fear I'm barren. Apparently the miscarriage sterilized me."

"Temporarily, perhaps, but I doubt permanently." Hortense contemplated a Sevres urn on a Boulle cabinet. So many priceless treasures, including a Louis XIV étagère of porcelains and cloisonné. "Can't you placate him somehow?"

"I'm trying, Mother."

"But aren't you afraid that he—well, that he might transfer his affections to some other woman's child?"

"And his fortune?"

"I didn't mean that," Hortense protested indignantly.

But her daughter knew her too well to dissemble. "In truth, I am a little fearful of that, Mother."

"Then you must insist on seeing this doctor in Vienna, and on his accompanying you!"

Esther stroked the fur on her robe with the sensuous pleasure she took in all luxuries. "He will, Mother, if I say so . . . and if you don't volunteer to take his place."

They exchanged smiles and nods of mutual conspiracy, and Hortense detected a touch of tyranny in her daughter's complacency. The result of ruling too long from a wheelchair? But what more effective persuasion and defense could an infirm wife have than her infirmity? Only a stupid fool would not take advantage of it, and her girl was no fool.

Henry remained in New York several days, spending his time somewhere in town, and then left for Boston with the expectation of returning for the later holidays, which were infinitely more lively in Manhattan. He especially looked forward to the traditional New York celebrations, in which men alone were privileged to make the circuit of open houses, going from one to another until midnight, by which time only a deacon or monk would not be thoroughly drunk and depraved. He had already made his reservation with Miss Woods. Keith had neglected to tell him how expensive her girls were, but they were worth it, and more. His had been only seventeen, gorgeous, and tight as a virgin.

Hortense dispatched him with wifely admonitions concerning his health and other moderations, then promptly forgot him and concentrated on her daughter. And not since adolescence had Esther felt such camaraderie with her mother. They spent hours together dining from trays in her suite, chatting and charting the future, and Hortense believed she had convinced Esther not to rush into anything rashly or prematurely. She remained during her toilette and while the odd little Frenchman shampooed and dressed her hair. But when the strapping masseuse came, Esther politely suggested that Mother take a walk or nap. Hortense had no wish to observe the procedure, anyway, and would never have submitted to it herself, though her muscles petrified from disuse. Evidently the massage had some therapeutic benefits, though, for the client always appeared relaxed and even languid when they met for tea afterwards.

"Does Hilde have some special magic in her touch, dear?"

"She's a marvel, Mother. Her treatments have made my life tolerable, at least. I don't know how I would live without her."

One day in December, Indian summer returned for a brief warm spell, and Hortense suggested that they enjoy it in the solarium. At great expense, part of the roof had been cut away and several large skylights installed along with a windowed wall. This was on the advice of an eminent British physician and amateur horticulturist, who theorized that if the sun could encourage stunted plant growth, it might also discourage, prevent, or reverse the withering of paralytic human limbs. He had specifically recomemnded nude sunbathing, but Esther feared prolonged or excessive exposure would blemish her flawless white skin. Thus she used the solarium infrequently, rarely naked, and seldom even unveiled.

Now, because she was bored, restless, and somewhat weary of her mother's officious company, she protected her face with a chiffon scarf and yielded to maternal persuasion. There were comfortable lounges and chairs, adjustable blinds and screens, and pots of flowers and greenery, hanging and standing, from the conservatory.

It was Sunday, the factory funnels were largely idle, and the view spectacular. A clear smokeless sky, Wedgwood blue with a few streaks of white cloud like tempera, an artist's sky, and Esther thought wistfully of Mallard. She could see for miles in several directions: the East River and Long Island, the Hudson and New Jersey. From the rear of the solarium she could locate, as she had before, the gabled roof of the house near Tompkins Square, where their secret world had ended in violent discovery.

"Look," Hortense said suddenly. "There's Keith in the park now, playing ball with those youngsters."

"Oh, yes. Kids adore him. They show him their toys and pets. The boys want him to roughhouse and referee their games, and the girls expect him to admire their dolls and dresses. He's the Pied Piper of Gramercy Park."

Soon Lorna Hampton and Judith Lipscomb brought their broods to play, and Keith made a fuss over Judy's little girl, a pretty moppet with wide blue eyes and a riot of taffy curls, picking her up in his arms. One cherubic hand curved easily about his neck, while the other held a Raggedy Ann against his chest. Then the Lipscombs' English nanny took over, and Keith sat down to smoke, sharing the stone bench with the congenial ladies.

"Hussies," Esther muttered. "Worse than bitches in heat."

"Oh, my dear, such language!"

"But accurate, Mother! They sniff around him every chance they get. I wouldn't trust either one alone with him. What's more, I think Keith has a mistress." There, she'd said it, and she felt better, though her mother obviously did not.

"Mistress?"

"Surprised, Mother? You shouldn't be. Adultery's no novelty even in Boston. Didn't the Puritans invent the red letter?"

A grim nod and compressed lips. "But only to brand women. Men were never punished that way, because they made the laws. But if you only suspect Keith at this point, take my advice and don't try to convince yourself. You'll regret it if you do."

"Ignorance is bliss?"

"It's security and protection, if you don't force the issue. A man rarely divorces his mate to marry his mistress, unless her pride and stupidity demand that he choose between them. Usually she is just a convenience, as a harlot, whose need will diminish with age and ultimately vanish."

Esther grimaced. "And what is a wife supposed to do in the interim? Be a patient Griselda waiting for him to return home, like a tired old dog to lie by the hearth? Is that what you've done with Father all these years? Oh, Mother, how could you bear it? Wondering who she is and where he keeps her, and what kind of gifts he gives her!"

"Your father's too old for that now," Hortense said hopefully. "Besides, he can't afford to maintain two households any more, if he ever did."

"Don't be an ostrich, Mother."

"Well, if your husband keeps anyone, I doubt the place could compare to this one. Count your blessings, dear. You still have a great many, you know. Millions, I would guess. And his gifts to *you* are the only important ones." She paused, touching a frond of Boston fern in a nearby urn. "Incidentally, I haven't noticed you wearing any of his family jewels. Of course I know they're priceless, but surely you have replicas."

"No, and the Curtis-Heathstone collection is locked in the bank vault. I rarely see them any more, Mother, much less wear them. And I'm not at all sure I'll inherit them."

"Oh, darling, listen to me! You must—you simply must try to have a child with him!"

Esther sighed. "That's easier said than done, Mother."

She raised her glasses again. Judy was holding his

cheroot while Keith removed his tweed jacket, which Lorna promptly folded and placed on her lap. "Bitches," she murmured with savage jealousy. "Sluts, and he has their scent!"

"Stop looking at them," Hortense said, "and send a servant to fetch him. It's time for tea, anyway."

"Will tea solve all my problems, Mother?"

"It'll solve the immediate one, daughter, which is breaking up that little conclave down there!"

That evening, when Keith made the perfunctory call demanded by Esther while her mother was in residence, she said tentatively, "We were in the solarium this afternoon, and saw you in the park, with Judy and Lorna. You seemed quite taken with Judy's youngest child. Is she yours, Keith?"

He stared at her. "Don't be ridiculous! Her husband is quite capable of fathering his own children."

"That doesn't mean she couldn't also have a lover. She flirts with you outrageously, and is obviously pregnant again."

"Is she? I hadn't noticed."

"Didn't you? She breeds like a peasant. Is Judith Lipscomb your mistress, Keith?"

"No, goddammit! I've never touched her. Nor Lorna, either. You're grabbing at straws, Esther. Good night."

"Go to hell," she said.

"I imagine we both will, eventually."

Chapter 28

Devon was reading the new novel by Louisa May Alcott that warmed New England hearts that cold winter. The success of *Little Women*, which incorporated the author's wartime memories and family experiences, inspired Devon to consider her own manuscript again. But the fetal motions in her body distracted and soon diverted her mind, and enthusiasm was stillborn. Miss Alcott had not labored under such an impeding handicap, nor had to surmount such a cumbersome obstacle.

Devon lay on the chaise gazing forlornly at the Hudson flowing past the windows, swiftly and relentlessly as time into eternity, time forever lost to her and as irretrievable as the river from the sea.

The housekeeper had to knock several times to be heard. "You busy, Ma'am?"

"Just resting, Anna. Come in, please. What is it?"

"A gentleman to see you, Ma'am."

"Gentleman? Did he give his name?"

Anna hesitated. "Daniel Haverston, Ma'am, from Virginia. But he asked for Miss Marshall ... and he seems to think you work here."

"What did you say?"

"Nothing, Ma'am. You look pale. Is anything wrong?"

"No, I'm just surprised, Anna. Mr. Haverston is an old friend from the past, whom I never expected to see again. Tell him I'll be down shortly, and send Enid to help me dress."

"She's just across the hall, Ma'am. I'll fetch her."

There was no mystery about how Dan had found her. Either he had pried her whereabouts out of Mrs. Chester, or the poor soul had unwittingly volunteered the information, still the vigilant duenna. Perhaps she had not believed Devon's last letter, that she had taken a position as companion to a wealthy old widow in the country. What a stupid clumsy idiotic lie, and now she was trapped in it!

Enid helped her into hoops and petticoats and full-skirted gown of dark linsey-woolsey, demure with a white lace fichu. Thank God for crinolines, which concealed advanced pregnancy so effectively even a physician could be fooled by mere appearance, and a clever woman could and often did go to delivery without detection by family or friends. Monsieur Worth was trying to outmode crinolines in Paris, but they remained popular at the European courts, possibly for the same reason that Devon appreciated them now, although a man could not be expected to understand this convenient camouflage.

He was warming himself at the parlor hearth when she entered and spoke his name softly. "Daniel?"

Immediately he turned and came forward, smiling, hands extended—a different man from the one she remembered. While his clothes did not compare to those he had worn before the war, they were of good fabric and fit. The prison pallor was gone from his face, the dullness from his blue eyes, the nervous tic. Straighter shoulders, fuller chest. His slight limp was a permanent affliction, souvenir of the minie ball caught in his leg at Gettysburg, but the rasping Rock Island cough had disappeared. His sandy hair was neatly cut, the long sideburns golden as bright leaf tobacco against his sun-bronzed skin. He looked healthy and vigorous and even prosperous, almost his old self again—the dahsing cavalier, the aristocratic planter and lord and master of his domain, the image of the antebellum Virginian. Perhaps things had not changed so drastically in the South, after all.

"My dear," he said, embracing her, kissing her cheek when she averted her lips. "How long it's been! And since you wouldn't come to me, I had to come to you."

"You're looking well, Daniel." It was all she could think of to say. "You've gained weight."

"So have you, a little," he teased, admiring her fuller bosom. "But it's most becoming. You're even prettier than I remembered, if that's possible. But what are you doing in the country? Is it true you're working for some old dowager? I thought you wanted a journalism career in New York."

"Oh," she shrugged, breaking out of his arms, "that'll

come later. Sit down, Daniel, and tell me about Virginia. Things must be improving under Reconstruction."

"In some ways. Of course the military government is still in full control, and the carpetbaggers and scalawags still in favor, thick as locusts in the Shenandoah wheat fields. But apparently Mr. Davis is not going to be tried for treason, after all. If so, the charges and penalty will be modified. Did you know some important Northerners signed his bond?"

"Several from New York," Devon nodded. "But what about yourself, Dan?"

"I'm managing, Devon, and even prospering. Many slaves returned to the plantations when they did not receive as much of the victory spoils as they had expected, all the free land and mules promised them, and now they must work as hard or harder to survive. Yet they don't seem to mind, as long as they have something tangible to show for their labor. It's really not such a bad system and arrangement, and even compatible. Tenant farmers and sharecroppers have always existed in the South, and are simply more numerous now. The world markets for our crops are greater than ever since American supplies were cut off by the war. The demand is so great, in fact, that my tobacco is being bought in the fields, before harvest."

"And you're restoring Harmony Hill?"

"Not completely. Full restoration of the house and gardens will take years and a fortune. I'm investing most of my time and energy and funds in tobacco culture, and a British importer has contracted for all I can produce. There'll be money for other things eventually, including the stables and kennels. I've already bought a fine Maryland jumper and plan to scout the New Jersey and Connecticut horse markets and auctions for some hunters. Hounds are easy enough to come by in Virginia; the Yankees didn't seem to want them—presumably because they couldn't be ridden, hitched to a plow, or eaten. I expect to host a hunt and ball before many more seasons pass, however, and naturally I hope you'll be my hostess." She only smiled, and he pursued, "Have you had your fill of Yankeeland, Devon? Are you ready and willing to come home, where you belong?"

"Where do I belong, Dan? I don't have a home in Virginia any more."

He leaned forward in his chair, his expression eager and hopeful. "You know what I mean, Devon, and why I've come. I want you to return to Harmony Hill with me, as my wife."

"Oh, Dan." A sad mournful sigh escaped her. "We've been apart a long time. Things change."

"Not for me, Devon. And you can't mean that you *like* living here, humoring some old lady. Where is she, anyway? Upstairs, confined to her bed, perhaps. You might as well have stayed in Richmond with Mrs. Chester. At least you'd have been among friends and your own people. Is it so much better with strangers and former enemies?"

Devon glanced away, at the wintry landscape beyond the windows, gray and bleak, with remnants of the last snow still clinging in sheltered places, although it was March. She knew her time was fast approaching, and could be any day now, for Dr. Blake had said first babies were often unpredictable and might arrive early or late, rarely on exact schedule.

"Have you had breakfast, Dan?"

"Yes, in the village. I'm staying at the inn there. You haven't answered my question, Devon?"

"You shouldn't have come, Daniel. It's no use, no use at all. I can't marry you, now or ever. Please, just leave. Go away and forget me."

Abruptly he rose, and his determination with him. "Don't you think I've tried? But it's not that easy, Devon, to forget someone you love. And I didn't travel all this distance to be rejected again by whim and caprice! You've had long enough to get your foolish fancies out of your head. You should be ready to settle down to a woman's life now, a home and children." He waited expectantly. "Say something, Devon."

Why must he be so persistent, so obtuse! "I've been trying to tell you, Daniel! I can't go back with you—I can never go home again. A lot has happened to me since I left Richmond. I've had my failures and troubles, just as you predicted, and I've changed, Dan. I'm not the same girl any more. Besides, there's someone else now, and I belong to him."

"Belong?" He stared at her, feeling pain more intense than the Yankee bullet had inflicted. "Lord, what a dense fool I am! But I think I understand well enough now.

There is no old dowager, is there? He's married, and this is his hideaway—your rustic rendezvous! You're *his* illicit companion, and the reason you've gained weight—" He turned away, shaking his head in disbelief, grasping the mantel for support. "How could you get involved that way, Devon? I thought you were an intelligent girl, too smart to be lured into such a foolish trap! But perhaps my suit of country morals is out of date here, and it's the fashionable, sophisticated thing to do in New York!"

She was growing increasingly wretched, twisting her hands nervously, tears glistening in her eyes. "I love him, Dan, and he loves me. I'm all right, and I'm happy. Really, I am."

"Is that why you're crying, out of happiness? And are you delirious with joy at the prospect of bearing his bastard?" He clenched his teeth and hammered his fists on the carved oak shelf. "The sonofabitch! I ought to kill him!"

"Don't be ridiculous, Daniel!"

"Who is he, Devon? Will you tell me his name, or must I inquire in the village to learn who owns this place?"

She knew he was angry and jealous and desperate enough to do so, and possibly embarrass them before the community. "Keith Curtis," she said.

"The Wall Street capitalist?"

At her nod, his mouth twisted grimly. "Were you trying to borrow money from his bank—and borrowed trouble instead, with nine months' interest? Never mind. It'll be a pleasure fighting a Yankee who helped to finance the war and defeat us. Perhaps you've forgiven and forgotten all your grievances against the North, Devon, but I haven't, nor ever will. And he'll pay for what he did to you, and me, and the South. But don't worry, I'll not kill him in cold blood. He'll have a chance to defend himself."

"Daniel, you fool! You're not going to challenge him? Dueling's against the law in this state!"

"It's against the law in most states," he said. "But that doesn't stop it, and only a rank coward would refuse a challenge, regardless of the penalty."

"Are you sure it's not your pride you want to avenge, Dan, more than my honor? That the real reason you hate and want to fight him is because he's a Yankee?"

"Do you hold your virtue so lightly now?" he countered.

"Have you lost all respect for decency and convention? Is that what the Yankee dog has done to you! They had no compunction about seducing Southern women, I know, and forcing those who wouldn't submit. They left victims in every town they invaded, and scattered across the countryside."

"Didn't our soldiers also, Daniel?"

"Only the trash and deserters, and they were promptly shot if caught. I killed three rapists myself. And I'll meet your suave seducer at his convenience."

"How bloodthirsty you sound," she said sadly. "And that's precisely what he'll expect of you, Dan. He once said that to the Southern gentleman the *code duello* is a way of life."

"When do you expect him?"

She shrugged. "I don't know. He comes when he can."

"That's the rule in these cases, isn't it?"

"It's different with us, Dan, but I don't expect you to believe or understand that."

"Understand what, Devon? Shoddy romance? A secreted mistress? We have them in the South too, you know. That was the purpose of the Quadroon Balls of New Orleans. And many planters had their slaves and mulatto brats. But to think that you ... goddamn that bastard, I *will* kill him!"

He rushed out of the house to the horse he had hired in the village, and she could hear the hoofbeats echoing in the lane long after he was out of sight.

Early the next morning Keith arrived, driving his cabriolet at high speed, the blooded bays steaming at the nostrils in the frosty air. Lars Hummel ran out to take the reins and lathered team, and Devon met him at the door. "What is it, Keith? What's happened?"

He pulled an envelope out of his coat. "This was delivered to me at the bank yesterday afternoon. Read it, and see what an arrogant fool your ex-fiancé is!"

Devon unfolded the note. It was written in Daniel's hand, scrawled in haste and fury.

Sir:
    You have dishonored a Southern lady in a fashion which no true Virginian can condone or ignore, and I

hereby challenge you to defend yourself by whatever means you choose, and time and place you appoint.

I shall await your reply at the Tryon Tavern, in the village near your country estate, and trust it will be prompt and honorable.

Sincerely yours,
Daniel E. Haverston

Her hand trembled as she returned it, and there was a tight constriction in her breast. "I'm sorry, Keith. I hoped he'd simmer down and reconsider. What are you going to do?"

"I telegraphed a message to the inn, inviting him to come here this morning and discuss it. I'll try to talk some sense into him."

"Oh, Lord, what a mess!" Devon sat down on the sofa and began to cry. "I think I shall die of mortification!"

He dropped on one knee beside her. "What did he say to make you so ashamed, Devon? Do you feel dishonored because *he* thinks so? What the devil is he doing up here, anyway? And how did he know where to find you?"

She explained, haltingly, blotting her eyes with his handkerchief, about her letters to Mrs. Chester, the foolish fabrications and falsehoods. "So she wouldn't worry, Keith. She was like a mother to me for over a year, and a strict chaperone and—well, I could hardly tell her the truth!"

"Stop crying, Devon. He'll be here soon. Go upstairs and rest. I'll handle this."

"How?"

"Never mind. Just do as I say."

"No! Your temper is as hot as his, Keith. You'll provoke each other. I won't let you fight!"

Impatience crossed Keith's face, but before he could command obedience Dan had arrived and was pounding the door impatiently. Keith admitted him and neither man spoke at first, merely stood measuring each other: mortal enemies, rivals for the same woman. There was no appreciable difference in age or height, although Keith was slightly heavier in the shoulders, if that was an advantage. And if Dan had a disadvantage, it was in his reckless rage and hostility, which was not as effectively concealed or controlled as Keith's cold bitter anger.

"At your service, Mr. Curtis!"

Keith temporized, "I've asked you here, Mr. Haverston, in the hope of settling this like civilized men."

"With a handshake and drink—and perhaps a toast to your conquest of the lady?"

At Devon's appalled gasp, Keith demanded roughly, "Do you want to hear insults? For God's sake, get out of here!"

She remained seated with the same adamant defiance Dan had previously and frequently encountered in her, and he smirked now at his opponent's obvious frustration. "I sent you a cartel, Curtis. Do you accept?"

"This isn't Virginia, Haverston! It's New York, where dueling has been outlawed since Aaron Burr fought Alexander Hamilton across the Hudson. It's a penitentiary offense and even if we fought to the death, the winner would still lose to the gallows or the cell. I don't fancy either fate for myself."

The Southerner's mouth curled contemptuously. "Spoken like a true Yankee coward."

Keith responded through clenched teeth. "I have no fear of meeting you, Rebel. Can you use a sword?"

"I fenced in college and belonged to a sword club before the war. We had matches with the Charleston club."

"And jousted with the Carolinians too? You Southern cavaliers! Will you consider this settled when blood is drawn?"

"Blood?" cried Devon, rising awkwardly. "Are you mad, Keith?"

"I'll consider it settled when one of us is dead," Dan replied grimly.

"Dear God! You're both crazy! I forbid it, Keith!"

He ignored her. "I'm sorry I can't oblige you in that capacity at this time, Haverston. But we're not alone in this, you know. There's a lady involved, and I'm concerned about her future. After the child is born, I'll meet you on your land and give you whatever satisfaction you demand or think you deserve. Until then, we'll fight with our fists. Fair enough?"

"Keith, he boxed at William and Mary!"

"I boxed at Harvard," he muttered.

"He was wounded in the war."

"He seems to have recovered."

"Oh, you're both behaving like schoolboys!"

"You just stay in here," Keith ordered, opening the door, and Dan grinned again as she disobeyed and followed them outside.

Already they had tossed aside their coats, eager to clash. Dan swung first, catching Keith's chin and jolting his head back violently. Keith retaliated with a blow to the jaw that sounded as if bone had shattered in his hand or his antagonist's face. They had tested mettle and strength, satisfied that they were equally matched, glared truculently and plunged into ruthless, unrelenting battle.

Devon had witnessed pugilistic exhibitions at county fairs, but this was no mere fisticuffs of skill and endurance. They were beating and battering each other mercilessly, in fierce senseless rage, slamming against trees and bushes, grunting and huffing like rutting bucks over a doe in mating season. The Hummels ran out of the stable but Keith warned them to keep out of it.

Suddenly Dan's game leg unbalanced him and flung them to the frozen ground, where they thrashed in the dirt and leaves. They rose and attacked even more viciously, using their hands like weapons to club, slash, chop. Keith's face was cut, blood oozing from his mouth. Dan had a bruised and swollen eye, scrapes on his chin and forehead, and a bloody nose. Still they fought and wrestled, bent on annihilating each other, until Devon could bear no more and screamed at the caretakers to stop them.

They hesitated, enjoying the bout as if they had a wager on the outcome. "But Mr. Curtis said—"

"I don't care what he said! Can't you see they're killing each other? Stop them, I say! Pull them apart!" And apparently more in awe of the five-foot-three mistress than the six-foot-two master, the brothers obeyed and intervened, taking a few licks themselves before succeeding in separating the violent men, for which Devon thanked them.

On his feet again, still scowling belligerently, Keith demanded, "Are you satisfied, Haverston? Do we quit on a draw, or continue this until we beat our brains out?"

Dan was surlily knocking debris from his hair and clothes. Both their shirts were torn, buttons ripped off, blood-stained. "This is how trash settle disputes in the South, Curtis, and rabble in frontier saloons. Gentlemen fight with pistol or sword. But I should have known better than to expect a Yankee to fight like a gentleman."

"Rest assured, Reb, the next time we meet it will be in a 'gentlemanly' duel in your territory. But this is my property, and you're trespassing, so get the hell off and away! Go back to your goddamn plantation, raise your goddamn weed—and find some other woman to fight over, because this one is mine!"

"Is she? Don't be so sure, Yank. She's still a Virginian, remember!"

Replacing his discarded garments, Dan walked to the horse, trying not to limp. He mounted and sat with his battered hands on the saddle-bow, gazing down at Devon, his expression at once tender and pitying, as though loath to surrender her to the enemy. But he only nodded rue-fully as her lips formed a silent goodbye, and she watched him ride off with the same mixed emotions she had felt long ago day in the rubble and ruin of Richmond.

Keith stood contemplating the battleground, shoulders slumped and arms akimbo. "Maybe you wanted to go with him," he said cynically.

"You know better than that." She took his arm. "Come in and get cleaned up. You're a sight. That shirt is ruined."

"So is his, and he ripped his pants, too."

"Well, and are you proud of yourself, brawling like a Bowery Boy in a gutter?" He followed her upstairs to the bedroom, where she wet a towel in the basin and wiped the blood and dirt from his face. "What a ridiculous spectacle! And what did it prove?"

He rubbed his jaw gingerly. "That he has a terrific punch, for one thing. But I think he felt mine too. And now you feel very superior and maternal, don't you, nursing your naughty little boy's wounds? Should I have let him think I was too cowardly to fight him on any terms?"

"No, your manhood would never have permitted that! But it didn't solve anything, Keith. Violence never does. If men could only realize that, this world would be a lot better off. But I suppose you and Dan were bound to fight each other eventually, over geography or politics or some other stupid reason. I was just a convenient catalyst." She dabbed styptic on his abrasions.

"Jesus, that burns! You're punishing me."

"Don't you think you deserve some punishment?"

"He started it!"

She smiled forgivingly. "Yes, darling, he did, and it's over now. But you can't go back to town in this condition. You'll have to stay here until you're presentable again, so maybe it was a blessing in disguise."

She expected that to please him, but he was preoccupied, frowning morosely. "Much as I hate to admit it, Haverston's a lot of man, Devon, and would have made you a good husband—if I hadn't come along and fouled up your life. And he was right, you know, in wanting to kill me for it. Maybe, for your sake, I should've let him. It might've been good riddance."

"Hush that kind of talk, or I'll think he scrambled your brains."

"But it's true," he insisted.

"Keith, don't. Please. I can't bear any recanting or post-mortems now." She sat down on the bed, suddenly tense and silent, and the look on her face alarmed him.

"What is it, Devon? Are you ill?"

"No, I—I just had a little pain, but it's gone now."

"That was too much excitement for you. I told you to stay inside! Lie down, darling. I'll help you."

"Oh!" Devon clutched his hand. "I think it's the baby!"

"But it's not time yet!"

"Almost. The doctor said it could vary a couple of weeks, one way or the other."

"I'll go telegraph him."

"No, don't leave me, Keith. Send one of the men. And tell Mrs. Sommes . . . she'll know what to do."

"Yes, and I'll send for the village doctor too. Don't worry, darling. Everything will be all right." But he was thinking, God help Haverston if she loses this child!

The messages off, he returned to the room. Mrs. Sommes had already brought up fresh linens, and a tray with twine, scissors, oil. Enid followed with a kettle of water, which she hooked on the hearth-crane, and then poked up the fire. Motioning the older woman into the nursery, Keith asked, "Did you examine her? How is she?"

"Well, I don't think it's false labor, sir. She has the slow and beginning contractions."

"Oh, God! That New York doctor couldn't get here in

time if he had wings. But the local man should be here soon. . . ."

An hour later Karl Hummel stood in the hall, with his cap in one hand and a book in the other. "Dr. Travers can't come, sir. He's sick in bed with grippe, running a high fever. But he sent this instruction book and this medicine."

"Thank you," Keith said, taking the obstetrical manual and bottle of ergot. "Did Lars get the telegram off to New York?"

"Yes, sir. Is there anything else we can do?"

"Not unless you can deliver a baby."

"No, sir. Never done that. We're bachelors, you know."

"Well, just be available for errands."

"You bet, sir. And good luck."

Keith summoned Anna for another consultation. "We may have to deliver her, Anna. Have you had any practice in midwifery?"

"Some," she said. "My sister, and several nieces."

"Good. I've read some medical books. Nature is supposed to do most of the work. But I don't want to alarm her." Pausing, "How much do you know about this situation, Anna?"

"Beg pardon, sir?"

"Has she told you anything about us?"

"Nothing, sir."

"But you know, don't you, why that man and I fought?" She nodded slowly.

"Does it make any difference to you, Anna? In the way you feel about her?"

"She's a kind and gentle person," Anna said. "I'm very fond of her, and so is my daughter. We would do anything for her. And for you too, sir."

"Thank you," Keith said humbly. "Thank you both."

"I'll fix you some lunch, sir."

"I'm not hungry, Anna. But I would like some coffee, strong and black."

"Enid will bring it," she said.

Keith put on a sanguine smile before entering the bedroom and going to the bed. "Dr. Travers is on a case, darling, but he'll be here as soon as possible."

"What's all the whispering between you and Anna?"

"We didn't want to disturb you. Any more pains?"

"Yes, but not bad. Why don't you have a drink? It's traditional for fathers-in-waiting to get drunk, you know."

"I'll do my celebrating afterwards," he said.

They tried to joke and tease but a paroxysm of pain contorted Devon's features. She cringed and turned her face into the pillow to muffle her cry, and Keith said, "Don't be so brave, darling. Scream, if it'll help. That's traditional too, isn't it?"

"Anna says it's labor, but what if it's premature? A miscarriage, and I lose the baby! Oh, Keith, I'm scared!"

"No, Devon, no! That won't happen."

Another pain wrenched her, and she cried out hysterically, "Oh, God, it hurts! I'm going to die, like my friend in Richmond! Will you bury us together?"

"Anna!" Keith shouted. "Come in here! We need you. . . ."

Chapter 29

They worked with her for hours, and she tried to help them and herself. But most of the time she was either delirious or too weak with pain, incoherent, writhing, moaning, straining instinctively at the cords attached to the bedposts, as though she would tear her arms from their sockets.

"What's taking so long, Anna?"

"It's not so long, sir, for a firstborn. Some take all day, and more. Just be patient."

"Patient? She's the one suffering, and it's all my fault. If only I had left her in town, near the doctor! But no, I had to bring her out here, to this wilderness—"

"Children are born every day in the wilderness and on the frontiers," Anna consoled. "In covered wagons jouncing across prairies, in log cabins and adobe huts and hogans with wolves howling outside. They're born in fields and woods and jungles—"

"Yes, and they've been delivered by hack and horsecar drivers, train conductors and boat pilots and the women themselves . . . but this is *my* child!"

"And you're doing fine, sir. You have wonderful hands, so kind and gentle. You should have been a surgeon."

"This is one time I wish I were," said Keith, pouring sweat and seeming to share Devon's ordeal. "She's finally dilating, isn't she? If only we had something to ease the pain—God, I'd give a fortune for a little chloroform! Can you hear me, Devon? Bear down! Hard! Push! Harder, darling! Again! That's right! Again!" Her response was natural, her reflexes involuntary, and gradually the head appeared, then the shoulders, and soon they knew the sex.

"It's a boy, sir!"

"I can see that, Anna. How is she?"

"Well enough, I think, now it's over," Anna assured him,

already busy with the infant and summoning her daughter from the nursery to help.

But it was Keith who slapped the first breath of life into his son. "God," he murmured gratefully. "God."

"Enid and I can manage now, sir. Go have yourself a good long drink. You deserve it."

Reminding her to save the afterbirth for the doctor, as the manual instructed, Keith asked, "Are you sure she's all right, Anna? She's so still."

"Exhaustion, sir. She'll sleep now, for hours, and it's the best medicine for her. That was quite an ordeal."

"Quite," he agreed. "But he's a fine baby, isn't he?"

"I never saw a finer one."

"I was afraid he was premature. That stupid ruckus this morning—"

"No, he's full term, sir. Seven pounds, or more, and he wouldn't have waited more than a day or two for birth. Look at all his pretty dark hair, and just listen to him cry. Strong clear lungs! No weak mewing kitten, this one. Congratulations, sir."

"Thank you, Anna. For everything. But I think his mother deserves the credit." He smiled proudly at the squalling, squirming babe, vigorously protesting his arrival in an unfamiliar world, where he must endure the indignities of water, oil, clothing, handling, and the pangs of hunger. "I think I will have a drink."

Devon was still asleep when finally Dr. Blake arrived, at dusk. He looked in on the patient and infant, examined the placenta and fetal membranes, said he couldn't have done better himself, and proceeded to celebrate with the happy father. It had been a long hard drive from the city in threatening weather, and he was glad for the warm relaxing fire, and the excellent brandy and cigars.

Ramsey Blake was thirty-six, considered a young man in a profession of graybeards, and had decided to specialize in obstetrics and gynecology against the advice of his general practice colleagues. A handsome bachelor, with light wavy hair and intense blue eyes, many of his patients fell in love with him. He was also a personal friend and well acquainted with the Curtis domestic situation.

"I'm sorry I couldn't make it in time, Keith. But I was on a difficult case when your telegram reached the office.

Thought sure I'd have to perform a Caesarean and naturally couldn't leave the patient. Yours was a little ahead of schedule, I think. But physicians are not prophets and can only estimate, not predict, confinement dates."

"I understand, Ramsey."

"What happened to your face? Did she fight you? They sometimes do in the extremities of labor and revile the brute responsible for their misery. I've seen sweet gentle little creatures turn into veritable wildcats—scratching, biting, raving, threatening to mutilate their mates if ever they touched them again. So if she clawed you, just ignore and forget it."

"No, I ran into a door with knuckles," Keith wryly explained his facial injuries. "Devon was pretty docile, considering the agony she suffered, and a few times there I felt like gelding myself. I just hope our emergency midwifery didn't do any irreparable damage."

"I doubt it. Complications can develop in any case, but they're the exception not the rule. Less than twenty percent of births in this country are attended by physicians, actually. And don't believe that fallacy about the weaker sex; most of them are tougher than our beards or boots. They recuperate rapidly too, and soon forget their travail in the joys of motherhood. She'll want to get up in a few days, but keep her in bed two weeks." He paused, as Keith replenished their glasses. "This is fine stuff—those French monks really know how to make cognac, don't they? Like the Cubans know how to make cigars."

"About the child, Ramsey—the birth has to be registered in this county, I suppose."

"That's the law, more or less, but it's not strictly enforced, and there's no penalty for failure to comply. Nor is there any time limit in the statute. You can wait awhile. Plenty of births are never recorded at all. That's what made conscription so difficult during the war: lack of vital statistics to trace the men, or even prove their existence."

Keith sat with his elbows resting on his spread knees, hands cupping the snifter. "Unfortunately, my marriage is duly recorded in Boston, and there's little hope of dissolving it in divorce. You know Esther, and the hold she has on me. Now she wants to go abroad again, to consult that Vienna neurologist we discussed at the Harvard Club. I've postponed the trip waiting for the baby. Furthermore, she's aware of the child, although not the mother's name and, ironically enough, wants to adopt it."

"Well, that might be one solution."

"In her mental state?"

The physician shrugged. "Oh, I doubt her neurosis is any more real than her paralysis, Keith. I think she's just a helluva good actress, who has been playing a difficult but convincing role all these years. She would give Charlotte Cushman competition on the stage, and possibly even Adelaide Ristori. If you ask me, Esther missed her calling."

Keith nodded. "But I don't think Devon would agree to give her the child under any circumstances."

"Have you asked her?"

"No. I'm still hoping to coax Esther into domestic court. The only other alternative—and I swear I'm desperate enough to consider it—is to move to Utah and embrace Mormonism. If Brigham Young can have twenty wives, I should be allowed two, especially since I only want one."

"How do you suppose Solomon managed with a thousand?"

"Supernatural wisdom, I guess. I don't seem to have it."

"You've got the devil's own dilemma, and I don't envy you," Ramsey said. "But you're not the only man in New York with such problems. Most of your Street friends, as you know, have similar ones. Last week I delivered both the wife and mistress of one, only a day apart. We were both sweating in fear they'd have simultaneous confinements, and he'd have to choose which I should attend. I understand there were wagers at the Exchange on which lady would domino first. You market bulls and bears will gamble on anything, won't you?"

Keith smiled. "That was the wildest trading in the gold room since the Panic of fifty-seven! I won several thousand on the mistress. But poor Charlie was a nervous wreck, and now has another legitimate heir in his Madison Square mansion and another bastard in his Connecticut cottage. It's a case for polygamy, isn't it?"

Ramsey concurred, puffing his cigar. "I'll be at my country place for the weekend, Keith. If anything develops with Devon, send for me. Her milk will come in a day or two, and I don't anticipate any problems there—she's well equipped for nursing the baby. But if she prefers a wet nurse, I can recommend some healthy ones. I left a sedative and some instructions with Mrs. Sommes, and I'll stop by before returning to town. Of course you know you're taboo in the tent for awhile?"

"Oh, hell yes, Ramsey! What I'd like to know is, when are you medical experts going to devise some reliable contraceptives? You're still in the Dark Ages in that respect. The Egyptians and Romans knew about those mercury and sulphur salves before Christ. Cleopatra used that same cervical net with Caesar and Marc Antony, except that it was made of linen instead of lambskin. Our vulcanized rubber shields aren't much of an improvement over those damnable fishbladders Dr. Condom invented for King Charles and his courtiers, and coitus interruptus was Casanova's method and probably every other legendary lover's, including Don Juan. As for petroleum jelly and carbolic acid solutions—"

The physician laughed. "I see you've made an exhaustive study on the subject. But abstinence is the only positive protection." He stood, picked up his overcoat, hat, and leather satchel. "By the way, I'm only charging you a token fee."

Keith grinned, opening the door for him. "That's generous of you, Doc, considering you only rendered token service. You ought to pay me and my midwife housekeeper!" They laughed and shook hands, Keith stuck a cigar in the doctor's breastpocket, and waved him off in the cold dark windy night. His estate was less than a mile away.

It was midnight before Devon roused from her lethargic slumber, and then only because the breaking storm disturbed her. It had swept out of the mountains and down the Hudson like a precocious vixen in premature spring heat, howling and lashing the island in a frenzy of wind and rain and hail. Lightning struck near the house, splitting a huge oak tree, and Devon sat bolt upright and screamed in terror. Keith, dozing in the lounge chair, was immediately beside her and gesturing away Mrs. Sommes, who had opened the nursery door.

"It's nothing, Devon. Just a little storm. You're all right now. It's over, all over."

"The baby?"

"Born hours ago. A boy, and he's perfect."

Her eyes searched his anxiously in the lamplight. "Really? You wouldn't lie to me, Keith?"

"No, we have a fine little son, Devon."

In relief she collapsed on the pillow again. "Then I was only dreaming."

"Dreaming what?"

"Oh, a terrible dream! That I—I died and the baby too. I could see us in the coffin, at the wake, just like Kathleen and her child."

"Kathleen?"

"My best friend in Richmond, and my roommate at boarding school in Charlottesville. Her husband was at the front, and she died in childbirth and was buried with the baby in her arms. I went to the funeral and—"

"Darling, don't!" He held her and stroked her tumbled and matted curls. "You're not dead, you're alive and the baby too. You had a bad time, but Dr. Blake has been here and said you came through it fine and will be good as new in a few weeks. How do you feel?"

"Drained," she said. "Empty."

"I can imagine."

"Was I much trouble?"

"You were an angel."

"Hardly that," she said ruefully, turning toward the windows. "It's storming, like that night in the Catskills. Remember?"

"I'll never forget. Try to go back to sleep, dearest. The doctor left a sedative for you."

"I don't need it, Keith. But you must be tired, and you can't rest in that chair. Lie on the bed. Please," she insisted when he hesitated. "I want you here beside me, darling, where I can touch you and hold your hand. . . ."

The baby was a week old and nursing at her breast when Keith said, "You look like a Raphael Madonna and Child. Have you decided on a name yet?"

"Your father's," she replied. "Isn't that what we agreed for a boy? I wish we could have him baptized, Keith. Back home, a christening is a big thing, with a feast and presents, except when the child is—" His look stopped her, and she concentrated on her motherhood, guiding the hungry little mouth.

"I want to adopt him, Devon."

"Adopt?"

"Legitimize him through adoption, as I mentioned at the beginning of your pregnancy."

"I thought you intended just to—to acknowledge paternity on the birth certificate, Keith."

"He'd still be illegitimate, Devon."

"Well, what *do* you want? To take him away from me? To your home? To *her*?"

"It's just something to consider, Devon, should all else fail. I mean—well, his future is important, isn't it?"

"Yes! Too important to surrender him to a woman you said yourself is deranged!" Her bosom heaved, the baby lost the nipple and began to cry, screwing up his tiny face and flexing his fists, until he found it again.

"All right, darling, don't upset yourself. You'll curdle your milk and give him colic."

"Then you'll just have to walk the floor with him! What did you expect me to say, Keith? Yes, take him as soon as he's weaned, or maybe even before and put him to a wet nurse! Oh, I know I balked at first and considered abortion, because I was desperate and thought that was the answer. But he's here now, and I want him, and won't give him up to anyone, least of all your wife! Let her have her own baby."

"That's what she wants," he said tentatively.

"Well, oblige her! Go home and sleep with her. I won't be well enough for awhile, anyway."

"Do you realize what you're saying?"

"No, and you know I don't mean it." She reached for a napkin to blot her eyes. "I'd die if you did that, Keith ... but first I'd murder you!"

He smiled, shaking his head. "One thing I do know, life with you could never be dull or predictable, with threats like that and former lovers challenging me."

"Not plural," she corrected. "There was only one."

"He fought like the whole Rebel army! Too bad he can't see my little boy, though. He'd know the winner."

"Oh, you Yankee egotist! Don't you think he does? And I bet even God didn't look so smug when He said, 'This is my Son, in whom I am well pleased.'"

"Why not? I begot one in my image too!" He grinned and stood. "Now I think I'll go out and try to move a mountain."

"Mount Esther?"

"Yes, although I think Everest would be easier."

When Anna came in to take over the baby, Devon was holding him to her breast and weeping. "Something amiss, Ma'am?"

"No, I'm just blue, Anna."

"Postpartum blues," Anna diagnosed. "Natural enough. We all get them a few days later, and sometimes they seem worse than the labor pangs. I saw Mr. Curtis on the stairs just now. My, how proud he is of his son! And how wonderful he was all the time he was being born, doing most of the delivery himself. Never left you for a minute, or took one drink. So many men are sodden by the time their children arrive. Some go to taverns and play cards and others even to whorehouses."

"Anna, you needn't pretend any longer. Mr. Curtis told me about your little conversation that day, and I want you to know I appreciate what you said and did for me. I'm grateful to you and Enid. But if you want to leave now, I'll understand."

"Leave, Ma'am? And where would I go, pray, with my fatherless child?"

"Fatherless? But you said your husband was a fisherman, on the Grand Banks, and drowned at sea?"

"No, I was never married," Anna said, preparing the baby's bath. "Enid's father was the son of a family I served. He was young and handsome, and I was seventeen and madly in love with him. He teased and flirted with me, and I thought he cared for me too. One night, while his parents were out, he came to my room and often thereafter. When I got with child, he was sympathetic, but refused to marry me. He was a fine rich man, after all, and I was only a servant. He offered to arrange an abortion, but I couldn't do it. Then he gave me a sum of money and begged me to make no trouble for him, but go away and never try to see him again, and that's what I did."

"But you still love him?"

"I suppose so. There was never anyone else, anyway. And I still think of him, and dream of him."

"Oh, Anna! Life is strange, isn't it? And so cruel and contrary sometimes."

"For women," the other nodded. "But don't compare

your case to mine, Ma'am. There's a big difference. Mr. Curtis loves you and the baby. Jeffrey didn't love me or want our child. Your man can't marry you, and mine wouldn't marry me. So it's not the same, you see. Not the same a'tall."

"No," Devon sighed, handing the baby to her, "I guess is isn't, Anna. But that doesn't make it any simpler or easier to bear. It's all one great big puzzle."

Chapter 30

To Esther's immense relief, her mother had returned to Boston early in January. But they corresponded regularly, and Esther repeatedly promised to go to Vienna as soon as Keith could accompany her. She had not seen him in almost a week, however, and, aware that he was not away on business, assumed that he was with his mistress for the birth of the child. Where was the wench, anyway? The city, the country, on Long Island, in New Jersey or Connecticut? There were many places to hide her and ways to reach her by land or sea. Adulterous mates were often quite crafty and ingenious, she mused, recalling the disguises and subterfuge she had employed in her own affair. Indeed, his rendezvous, as hers and Mallard's, might be only a short distance from Gramercy Park. A provocative thought, this. Her pen faltered, spattering ink on the stationery. She crumpled the spoiled sheet, dropped it in the wastebasket beside the bed, and took a fresh one from the portfolio. A familiar knock interrupted her, and her husband entered. She smiled wryly.

"Welcome home, Mr. Curtis. Are congratulations in order? But of course they are, and no doubt it's a boy. Nothing else, I'm sure, could put that Cheshire-cat look of complacency on your face."

"Obviously, my absence hasn't dulled *your* claws any, Mrs. Curtis; they're as sharp and bloody as ever."

"Why not? I have four bedposts to sharpen them on!" The late winter day was cold and wet, and toward evening snow flurries swirled past her windows. But her rooms were warm and moist with steam heat, and a cozy fire crackled on the hearth. "How is the happy little mother?"

"Happy."

"Did you mention adoption to her?"

He hesitated before nodding.

"And?" she prompted.

"She refused."

"Can't you persuade her? Reason with her? Make her realize it's best for the child?"

"She doesn't happen to agree with you," he said.

"She'd rather condemn him to a life of illegitimacy? Then she's selfish and vindictive. Take the child from her, Keith. You'd have no trouble legally. She's an unfit mother."

His face tensed, darkened. "How dare you speak of fitness, Esther? She's a thousand times more decent than you ever were!"

"Your defense of her character is downright quixotic, Keith. You're an even more uxurious lover than you were a husband. But she wouldn't appear so prim and proper in court, before a judge and jury. And your fatuous gallantry can't alter the legal status of your son, either. He's still a bastard! But to show you I'm more interested in his future than his own mother, apparently, I'm going to give you your freedom."

He watched her warily, with cynical skepticism. "On what terms?"

"Very generous ones, I think. Go with me to Vienna, Keith, and regardless of the prognosis, I'll institute divorce proceedings on our return."

"If I thought you meant that, Esther—"

"I mean it, Keith. I'm as weary of this marital tug o' war as you, possibly more so, since I've had to fight it from the disadvantage of a cul-de-sac. But surely you don't imagine it's easy or pleasant for me, that I enjoy living under this armed truce? I'm miserable, wretched, and want desperately to escape. Once you suggested that I live abroad, and I've decided to take your advice. So the trip could serve a dual purpose, to consult the physician, and find another home for me. I give you my word, Keith. I'll swear on the Book, if you like."

His emotions, frozen for years, thawed slowly. "Your word and solemn oath haven't meant much in the past, Esther."

"Have I ever made this particular proposition to you before? On the contrary, I've been quite consistent in my attitude toward divorce."

That much, at least, was true. What seemed so incredible and suspicious now was that she should suddenly reverse that stand, retract six years of adamancy in amenability. But he wanted to believe her, believe that she had somehow softened, mellowed, relented; that the long bitter barriers of hatred and revenge had finally eroded. Above all, he wanted to renew his faith in human nature, its ability to change, to recycle waste into worthiness. And in his desperate need to be convinced, he was willing to go to any lengths and inconveniences, make any personal sacrifices to achieve her transformation.

"Perhaps I've misjudged you, Esther. If so, I'm sorry and beg forgiveness. You must know I'd be eternally grateful for this particular favor. And we'll find a place for you abroad, a castle if you wish and there's one for sale—even a palace, provided you don't covet Buckingham or the Tuileries." He smiled at his feeble levity, and she responded faintly. "When would you like to leave?"

"Not until winter is out of the Atlantic. You know my morbid fear of ice storms at sea."

"May should be safe enough and give you plenty of time to get ready. I'll make the necessary arrangements." He gazed at her intently, trying to penetrate her mind, fathom its strange depths and intricate recesses.

"You seem apprehensive," she observed.

"How do I know you're sincere, Esther, and this isn't just more of the beguilement you've so long practiced on me and the physicians?"

"Is that what you think?"

Shrugging, pondering, shaking his head, "I don't know what to think, Esther. I can't help wondering how Ramsey Blake would diagnose this development in your case."

"Ramsey? Do you see him often?"

"We belong to the same clubs, you know."

"Yes, how convenient for you. Did he deliver the child?"

"No, I did."

"Oh, of course," she scoffed. "You have many unusual skills and talents, haven't you?"

"Not as many as you," he countered.

"Touché, mon mari! But I'm serious now, Keith, and you can bank on my sincerity. This is the only answer for us, isn't it?"

"The only logical one," he agreed.

"We've made a deal, then. And it's customary, I believe, to seal it somehow."

He accepted her proffered hand with a brief light clasp, and asked, "What about that damaging letter your parents hold?"

"There's no such letter, Keith. I lied to you, out of fear and frustration. I'm sorry. Please forgive me and forget it."

Evening was coming on, and she bade him light the lamps and candles. Obliging, Keith recalled her reasons for sealing the gas jets. Esther watched him from the shadows of the canopy, but he could not assay her expression, nor deduce anything from her silky voice. "Will you bring your bride here to live?"

"What?"

"Will you live together in this house, or build another? After all, there are memories here. Your family, your youth. Us. Every house is haunted by the ghosts of time and memory, Keith. She can't possibly share your past experiences, and may not want to, even if she could."

"I hadn't thought about it," he said. "Until a few minutes ago, the possibility was so remote—" The last lamp and candle aglow, he returned to the bedside. "Frankly, I'll have to adjust to the whole idea, and so will she. We were practically resigned to our . . . present arrangement."

"Must we continue to discuss her anonymously, Keith? Surely she deserves the dignity of identification." She waited in vain. "Oh, very well. Keep her identity secret, as you've kept her secretly. Most men are not so squeamish about their mistresses, however. Jim Fisk parades his Josie Mansfield around town, and Vanderbilt doesn't try to hide his infatuation for Tennie Claflin, either. Why must you be the most discreet and conservative man on Wall Street?"

"Habit, I guess. I'm also cautious in my market affairs, and have never indulged in the wild speculations of some of my reckless colleagues. You were one of my few risky gambles. I lost, and it taught me a lesson."

"Nevertheless, your liaison will eventually leak out, Keith, and not many people will be fooled when you take a new wife with a ready-made family. And if you imagine the staid old Manhattan matrons will welcome her to their fat bosoms—"

"Not that it's important to either of us, but I can practically guarantee her acceptance, Esther. As you've so often told me, New York is not Boston. This is a mercenary society, and all that glitters here *is* gold."

Esther sighed. He was right, of course. She had almost forgotten how crass and mundane it actually was, and how superficial. She had been utterly astonished to discover on her arrival that the rector of Grace Church, a clergyman of humble origins, ruled Gotham society; that he was both the moral and social arbiter, in charge of all invitations to important events, and could transform washwomen into "ladies" and robber barons into "gentlemen" simply by including them on the preferred lists. Ancestry counted in Boston, Philadelphia and Baltimore. But in New York, a man's financial standing determined his eligibility to belong to the best clubs and circles, and fixed his wife's place in society. In this money-worshipping cult, members of the board of brokers were the elite. A seat in the gold room of the Stock Exchange was tantamount to a throne, and the occupant a king. And to possess noble blood in addition to wealth, as did Keith Heathstone Curtis, was to hold the scepter.

"How true," she conceded. "For a large enough contribution, no doubt the Reverend Brown would gladly solemnize the wedding, baptize the bastard, and arrange the reception and housewarming. He never fails, on his spiritual consolation visits, to mention his many charities. I've been tempted to propose that some of his prosperous male parishioners endow a home for unwed mothers, and let my husband lay the cornerstone."

"I thought we'd signed a peace pact, Esther."

"Sorry, dear, I just couldn't suppress my envy and petty petulance. But what if she resents this voyage, Keith? Refuses to consent to it? In her place, I'd be furiously jealous and suspicious. I'd forbid you to go."

"I'll try to convince her of its importance."

"Yet you couldn't persuade her to surrender the child. Not that I blame her. Why relinquish her strongest claim on you? She's not as naive and witless as I imagined. Oh, don't rush chivalrously to her defense again! Our bargain still holds. Shall we consummate it with more than a handshake?" Laughing, chiding his frown, "No, I'm not trying to seduce you, darling. I had in mind a friendly kiss. But if it's so repugnant to you, I'll settle for supper together. That shouldn't tax you too much. I'll have Lurline set up a table before the fire. We used to do that sometimes, remember? It was very pleasant, cozy and intimate, and afterwards we always made love and—"

He interrupted, "You'll take Lurline abroad, I presume."

"Yes, I couldn't manage without her. Why?"

"I need to know what accommodations to reserve."

"A suite, naturally. And, Keith, do try for that new Cunard liner. I understand it has some absolutely sumptuous staterooms. Oh, it'll be a wonderful voyage! And house-hunting in Europe will be delightful too. If I find the right place, I just may stay and file the suit in absentia. Tell her that if she frets, Keith. Reassure her."

His eyes regarded her seriously, with some of his former respect and admiration. "I will, Esther. And believe me, I won't renege on any of my promises to you."

"To be realistic, my dear, both of us have already betrayed our most sacred vows, haven't we? Otherwise, none of this would be necessary, would it?"

"No, I guess not." He glanced toward the windows, but the hoarfrost obscured his vision, and he saw only dark glazed blanks. "Esther, why don't you try to find Mallard again? He may still be single, and still in love with you. And Europe is a painter's paradise. You could be his patroness again, and his inspiration."

"Inspiration? In this condition!"

"What condition? You know you're still beautiful. Besides, every woman is more desirable and appealing in bed."

"Really?" She removed a scented handkerchief from her lacy bosom, touched her eyes. "Your sentiments are making me weep, Keith. Shall we skip the supper?"

"Not at all. I'll even play some cribbage with you afterwards, if you'll promise not to cheat."

Her eyes reflected poignant remorse. "I even cheated at the parlor games we played, didn't I? And you always knew, and let me win. So lenient and indulgent in my little vices, I was encouraged in the big one. But I've reformed, Keith. I've confessed and done my penance. You can trust me now." She overturned the pillow for his inspection, "See . . . no derringer! So relax your vigilance, please? Go put on a dressing gown or that handsome black velvet smoking jacket I gave you for your birthday, while I summon Lurline——" Reaching toward the bellcord, she added, "I think we should have champagne with supper, don't you?"

"No, no, no!" Devon cried, stamping her foot furiously. "Absolutely not! How could you even consider it, Keith, much less agree, if you love me?"

"Because I *do* love you, Devon, and it's our only hope. Can't you understand? This is our only possible chance to be together the rest of our lives!"

They had been discussing, and arguing for better than an hour, and Devon was neither convinced nor persuaded. "You believe her? After all she's done to you? All her lies and broken promises? When you yourself said she had been pretending paralysis all these years? Don't be a gullible fool, Keith! This is just a trick to get you to Europe with her. And if you go, don't expect me to be here when you return."

In three strides he was across the room, gripping her shoulders, shaking her slightly. "What do you mean?"

A defiant lift of her chin. "Exactly what I said! I'll take the baby and leave New York."

"And just where do you think you'll go?"

"I don't know or care. Anywhere, as long as it's away from here."

"Now, Devon, I'm trying to be patient, because I know this is hard for you to accept. But I won't be intimidated or coerced by threats or temper tantrums. There's too much at stake. You should realize that yourself. Do you want marriage, a name for our child, a home together? Do you want to be wife to me, or mistress?"

"You know what I want, Keith. But I don't trust Esther. I can't believe she's going to make it so easy for us."

"Easy? Has it been easy, Devon? We've had a little happiness, and a lot of hell. Wouldn't it be worth a few months of purgatory to get out of it? Listen to me, Devon. I intend to buy her a castle or a chateau—any goddamn thing she wants that will keep her three thousand miles away from us! If my freedom costs me five or ten million dollars, I'll consider it a bargain, and I'll still have forty or fifty million left."

She was flouncing about the parlor, her taffeta skirts swishing the furniture, her nervous hands touching the bric-a-brac, finally smashing a cupid-clustered porcelain vase against the stone hearth. "I don't care about that, Keith! Do you think I care only for your money? I love you and don't want you romping over Europe with her!"

"Romping, in a wheelchair?"

"That witch won't stay in a wheelchair! She has some scheme in mind, Keith, mark my words." She felt this, intuitively, a premonition she could not shake off as petty jealousy, and it filled her with suspicion and a sense of dread despair, which the broken bibelot could not negate or relieve.

"Well, if you think there'll be any intimacy between us, forget it. No amount of sorcery could revive my lost interest in her. This trip is strictly an expedient, Devon, a means to an end. I've even suggested that she try to locate her lover again. And if she can find the home she wants, she'll divorce me in absentia. Naturally, I'll have to assume full blame."

"Another of her demands and edicts?"

"Adultery is the only grounds in New York."

Devon whirled about in wide-eyed astonishment. "And am I to be named corespondent?"

"Certainly not! You think I'd allow that? It'll be an amicable, uncontested decree. No court battle, therefore no trial and jury and public washing of dirty linen." He approached her tentatively, coaxing her into his arms. "It should be over in six months, a year at the most. Then we'll be married and have our son's adoption recorded and—"

"Live happily ever after?"

"Don't you think so?"

"No, I don't, Keith. I think the witch will always be in the shadows, taunting us. Remember our first night together, on the train? We talked about fairy tales and childhood fantasies and said we didn't believe in them any more."

"I was disillusioned and cynical," he said, "and you had seen your hopes and dreams go up in the smoke of Richmond. Even so, I think we both knew then how it was with us, and would always be. Nothing can change that, Devon."

"Nothing," she murmured, pressing her body to his, offering her mouth, which he took and searched. "I wish I were well enough . . ."

"But you're not, darling."

"I know, but I wish I were. Oh, Keith, I'm going to miss you! I'm tempted to stow away on the ship—"

"I'll leave the *Sprite* at your disposal," he said. "If you want to go on a cruise, just notify Captain Bowers."

"What fun would it be without you?"

"Oh," he teased, "you might want to hold another seance off Fire Island." Grinning, he flipped one of her curls. "Just stay out of mischief, my little minx. Off the Commodore's yacht, away from the Bewitching Brokers, and out of the Tombs with the feminist firebrands. Remember, your hero won't be around to rescue you if you get tangled up in your petticoats."

"I'll be fine," she assured him. "Just be careful *you* don't fall under the witch's spell."

"Impossible, with a talisman like you." Their mouths met and clung again until, reluctantly, he wrenched them apart. "I'd better get out of here, go chop some wood or something—"

PART VI

PART VI

Why do they not discover, when in the noon of
beauty's power, that they are treated like queens only
to be deluded by hollow respect, till they are led to
resign, or not assume, their natural prerogatives? Confined then in cages like the feathered race, they have
nothing to do but to plume themselves, and stalk with
mock majesty from perch to perch. It is true they are
provided with food and raiment, for which they neither toil nor spin; but health, liberty, and virtue, are
given in exchange.

Liberty is the mother of virtue, and if women be,
by their very condition, slaves, and not allowed to
breathe the sharp invigorating air of freedom, they
must ever languish like exotics, and be reckoned beautiful flaws in nature. . . .

> Mary Wollstonecraft
> *A Vindication of the Rights of Women*

Many minds, deprived of the traditionary or instinctive means of passing a cheerful existence, must find
help in self-impulse, or perish.

It is therefore that I would have Woman lay aside
all thought, such as she habitually cherished, of being
taught and led by men. I would have her, like the
Indian girl, dedicate herself to the Sun, the Sun of
Truth, and go nowhere if his beams did not make
clear the path. I would have her free from compromise, from complaisance, from helplessness, because I would have her good enough and strong
enough to love one and all beings, from the fullness,
not the poverty of being.

> Margaret Fuller (1810–1850)
> *Woman in the Nineteenth Century*

Chapter 31

Keith's first letter from Europe, written largely at sea and mailed from Le Havre on landing, described an uneventful crossing on smooth waters and regaled her with pleasant shipboard anecdotes and incidents, while submerging the heart of the matter. And though Devon knew he could not betray either of them with love letters, and that she must read his sentiments between the lines, she was nevertheless curious about what was really happening and tormented by her jealousy and overactive imagination. He stated only that the situation was fairly stable, as if quoting the market, and the itinerary unchanged, meaning that the medical consultation in Vienna was still the first order of business.

From Austria came a postcard showing the snow-capped Alps and a pretty young blonde in Tyrolean costume, holding a bouquet of edelweiss, such as tourists sent home. The girl's obvious resemblance to Devon and the standard, emphasized message—"Beautiful scenery, wish you were here!"—were unmistakable, yet it infuriated her, for there was no mention of the outcome at the clinic. Subsequent communications were equally vague and brief and formal, as if composed with a censor over his shoulder.

From the beginning Devon had suspected Esther of trickery; now she suspected her of treachery and intrigue. She was too distraught and despondent to resume her writing, as she had planned. Nor could she devote every spare moment to motherhood and domesticity, although she knew this was what Keith wanted and expected her to do in his absence—and a nursing infant was certainly an anchor. As Victoria Woodhull charged in one of her candid lectures, the text of which Devon read in the paper, man had always confined, subjugated, and suppressed woman with either a full belly or full arms, simultaneously if possible.

As June passed into July with no encouraging news from abroad, Devon's discontent and depression deepened to despair, forcing her to seek alleviation in a shopping trip to the city. Clothes and baubles, the panacea for the morose mistress! But she was heartily sick of the maternity hubbards and nursing gowns that had composed her wardrobe for the past nine months. And she was also concerned about her figure, now that Keith was not there to admire and reassure her in bed, where he found her large breasts stimulating. In Richmond she had seen the damage done by prolonged suckling of children: the sagging, pendulous bosoms on young mothers as unattractive as the deflated bags of the menopausal matron, and dreaded similar deformity. Fortunately, as Anna said, she and the cow had come fresh at the same time, and her weaned babe thrived as vigorously on bovine milk as the bully calf.

Now, at last, she had some freedom and leisure during which no one could make demands on her time or person. She drove herself in the pony trap to the village, but there was nothing of interest there, only a market, general store, and blacksmith. She took long walks in the woods and across the meadows, pausing to chat with the old sheepherder tending his small flock. But she was lonely, restless, and bored.

She had not left the country since Keith had brought her there last October, not even for her postpartum examination, which Dr. Blake had performed at the farmhouse, pronouncing her in excellent health. "You may bid him a proper bon voyage," he'd said, aware that Keith was sailing shortly. "Just remember—contrary to that old wives' tale, lactation is not a contraceptive. Nursing mothers can, and frequently do, conceive."

They had an interlude of intense, almost desperate, lovemaking, as if each intimacy might be their last. And as the time to leave drew near, he held her achingly hard, as though his body could somehow absorb hers. "God, I hate to go! If only there was some way I could take you both with me!"

"That would be quite a coup, wouldn't it?" Nervous, apprehensive, struggling to control feminine tears and clinging, she adjusted his cravat and smoothed back a lock of dark hair from his forehead. "You'll miss your train if you delay much longer."

"I want to say goodbye again."

"Darling, we said that particular goodbye several times."

"Just once more, please?"

"Yes, of course. But I have to feed the baby soon."

"Feed me first," he said, locking the door.

"Like son, like father? You'd just better be weaned before you get on that ship tomorrow!"

"I've told you before, that's a barren breast as far as I'm concerned. Nothing! I'll starve until I return—"

"How long will you be gone?" Anna asked, as Devon packed the morocco portmanteau she had taken aboard Commodore Vanderbilt's yacht for a seance a year before.

"I'm not sure, Anna. I need some new clothes, and now my figure's back to normal I can splurge."

"You have loads of pretty clothes!"

"Last season's, and older, Anna. Styles change, you know. According to *Godey's* and *Demorest's,* a new fashion is blooming in Paris. It's called a bustle and will probably outmode hoops eventually and entirely. Of course, Monsieur Worth says crinolines have been moribund since the war, anyway."

Paris, she thought suddenly. Worth, the Empress Eugenie's couturier. Was Mrs. Curtis visiting his salon too, buying lovely things to make herself more alluring to her husband? *Why* didn't he let her know what was happening? Something more than those "friendly" notes, whose content could have been cabled or quoted verbatim in the daily press without arousing suspicion. He needn't be *that* cautious! There was no one intercepting his mail.

The housekeeper frowned. "Mr. Curtis wouldn't like your going off alone this way, Ma'am. He gave us all strict orders—"

"I'm sure he did," Devon interrupted. "He's good at giving orders, but that doesn't mean I have to obey all of them. Besides, he didn't tell me not to go to New York— he just assumed I couldn't if I was feeding the baby every few hours! Well, if he can gallivant over the Continent, surely I can shop in the city!"

"Oh now, Ma'am, that's not fair. You know he never wanted that trip. It's for your sake and the baby's he's over there now." Anna had become her friend and confidante, and sometimes her critic as well as her servant.

Devon sighed, ashamed of her caprice. "I know, Anna. But it doesn't make the waiting and worrying any easier." She continued packing. "I'll be in Greenwich Village, at the address I gave you. If you need me, send a telegram. Now go tell Lars I'll be ready to leave in twenty minutes. I just hope that steamboat is on time."

"Why don't you take the train? Those steamers are always racing and blowing up."

"Nonsense, Anna. I want to go by steamboat. I've been watching them pass for months, since they came out of winter dock, refurbished like ladies in their new spring finery. I wish I were going to Albany and back, just for the ride." She paused wistfully. "We took a cruise up that way last June, on the *Sprite*. Oh, it was so wonderful and romantic, Anna! Somewhere along the Hudson I got pregnant."

"That's what usually happens in romance," the other reflected. "Only for me it was a cold drafty garret, and the master's son sneaking up to me after the family had gone to sleep." Her haunted eyes wandered poignantly, focusing on something remote and gossamer as a cobweb. "It seemed beautiful, though, because I was so much in love."

"Do you ever plan to tell your daughter the truth about her birth, Anna?"

"I used to wonder about that," Anna admitted, "but not any more. No, her life will be hard enough without that burden."

"The stigma of illegitimacy?" Devon glanced guiltily toward the nursery. "Suppose he had wanted to adopt her, Anna? Would you have agreed?"

"I don't know, I honestly don't know. It would've been best for the child, naturally, but I never had to make that decision. He didn't suggest marriage or adoption, only abortion."

The *Water Witch*, which Devon boarded at Inwood Landing, was packed with passengers from Troy, Albany, and other upriver towns, bound for the metropolis. They occupied deck chairs, leaned against the bulwarks, or strolled the promenades, enjoying the sunshine and scenery: the Jersey palisades, ruby-colored in the striations, and the emerald woods and gray stone escarpments of Manhattan island; the cozy cottages with gardens and orchards running down to the shores, and the elaborate country estates like private resorts in landscaped parks. Some ladies lounged in the luxurious salons or dining rooms reached by grand staircases, while their men patronized the bars: still others remained in the seclusion of their staterooms and cabins.

Devon stood on deck, savoring it all. Not in months had she felt so happy at merely being alive, so young and free and vital and completely her own mistress. No qualms of guilt or compunction about leaving the baby assailed her, for she knew he was too young to miss her and would be well cared for by Anna and Enid, who, with Keith's encouragement, had already fairly spoiled him. Never had Devon seen a man so wild about a child. Often she had found him in the nursery standing by the cradle watching Scotty sleep, bending to kiss the small flushed face and touch the downy dark curls, as if to make sure he was real, flesh and blood, not merely an image he had dreamed or imagined.

A deep masculine voice penetrated her reverie, startling her. "Miss Marshall?"

Passengers often spoke without introduction, but this one knew her name, and she knew his face. There was no forgetting that dark picaresque countenance, those fierce black eyes, and that thick black mustache.

"Peter Barr Sweeny," he said. "Do you remember meeting me, Miss Marshall?"

"Why yes, I do, Mr. Sweeny. Last summer, wasn't it, at Mr. Tweed's picnic in Battery Park?"

"You were with Trent Donahue," he nodded. "We missed you at the party that night, and the victory celebrations in November. I've just come from Albany. Dick Connolly and Oakey Hall are also aboard, and some other fellows caucusing in the saloon. The smoke got so thick I came out for air. The legislative session has just closed, and Senator Tweed'll be back in New York tomorrow, for the dedication ceremonies of the new Tammany Hall and opening of the Democratic Presidential Convention, on the Fourth of July."

Devon had read of these upcoming political events, as she had of the Republican nomination of General Ulysses S. Grant at the May convention in Chicago. Her Virginia blood boiled at the thought of that man in the White House, and she fervently hoped the Democrats would win the election. "Congratulations to Tammany," she said. "And good luck to your candidate."

"Thanks." He smiled. "Jim Fisk and Miss Mansfield are having a pre-convention ball ... I suppose Donahue told you?"

"I haven't seen Mr. Donahue since that day in Battery Park," Devon said.

"Lovers' quarrel?"

"Oh, no! Nothing like that. We're barely acquainted."

"I got that impression at the rally, although I'm sure the Bowery Fox would prefer it otherwise. But where've you been all this time?"

"In a sort of ivory tower."

"Secluded in the country? I saw you come aboard at Inwood."

"A friend of mine has a retreat near there," she explained. "I borrowed it to work on a book."

"A book? Aren't you a little young for that?"

"Not really. And I'm just keeping in practice, mostly, and marking time. I'm a journalist, you see—or was, on a defunct Southern paper. I came North seeking opportunity, but there isn't much in that field for a woman."

"I should think that would depend on the woman," Sweeny said. "Her connections, experience, and ability."

"In that order?"

"More or less." He gazed downriver, at the piers they were approaching. Suddenly Devon sighted the graceful *Sprite* moored in her berth, gently lolling in the waves created by the *Water Witch*. Her heart lurched, as if they'd struck a reef, and her hands gripped the bulwark harder. "Anything wrong?" he asked.

"Nothing," Devon murmured. "But you forgot to mention talent, Mr. Sweeny."

"A minor factor, Miss Marshall, and only relative. The world is full of hidden talent and lights under bushels, where most of it remains except for rare occasions of fate and coincidence. Smart people make their own destiny, turn their own wheels-of-fortune. They hunt opportunity, not wait patiently for it to knock on their doors. They don't woo Lady Luck; they chase her down, seduce or rape her if necessary. Do you imagine Mr. Tweed would be where he is, if he had depended on chance and fortune to find and bless him?"

"Well, I'm hardly in that category."

"No, but you're obviously not content in your present status, either, and it's up to you to change it, my dear. You get what you want by going after it." He allowed her time to assimilate that rationale, and then said, "I take it you've heard of the Claflin sisters and their success on Wall Street? But there are other ambitious ladies in this town who know how to take the bulls and bears by the horns and tails, and manipulate them to their advantage. Do you happen to know Josephine Mansfield?"

"Not personally," she said.

"The press is well aware of her," he said. "But you're presently inactive, aren't you?"

"I've applied at dozens of papers and periodicals," she said. "There were no positions available."

"In most offices, Miss Marshall, including mine at City Hall, the applications of unknowns are filed in the wastebasket. Personal recommendations are required. I know some publishers. I could introduce you."

She stared at him. "But why should you?"

Sweeny shrugged tailored shoulders, as impeccably dressed as the day she had met him, but still a rather terrifying man in appearance and personality. Forceful of mind, ruthless of purpose, she could not imagine him deviating from any personal goal, shrinking from any compromise, deterred by any obstacle, showing mercy or forgiveness to any foe. The ruby eyes of the gold Tammany tiger in his lapel winked in the sun. "Perhaps I have ulterior motives, Miss Marshall. Then again, I may just want to give you a lift up the ladder. All of us at Tammany can be helpful, you know, when we take the trouble. Unfortunately, some folks don't see us as Good Samaritans, and we don't always shine in the press. Nevertheless, we do have friends in journalism, staunch supporters, and even admirers. Why don't we discuss it at the ball tomorrow evening? It's fancy dress, and I can fix it for you with Miss Mansfield."

"I'd need a costume."

"Well, a mask, anyway. The actress in Josie and the clown in Jim like masquerades, and there'll be some guests from Pike's Opera House company, which Fisk is negotiating to buy. Tweed doesn't care much for such charades, because he's always expected to portray Henry VIII or Falstaff or even Captain Kidd. Once he went as Robin Hood, with us as his Sherwood boys. Connolly was Friar Tuck, and I was little John. It was good fun and sport."

He laughed in retrospect, and Devon smiled, her eyes and teeth brilliant in the sunlight. Suddenly he sobered, and his face was intensely serious in the shadow of his tall silk hat, as much a mark of the Americus Club as the tiger pin. "Some sage once wrote that God proves Himself most effectively in the creation of a beautiful woman," he said. "If that's true. He surpassed Himself in you, Miss Marshall. Do you know your eyes have gold flecks in them? You're sort of a golden girl, hair and all, and you should have a bright future."

"You make it sound so easy, Mr. Sweeny."

"It is, my dear, with the right connections. In any case, what have you got to lose?"

"Well, I'm not exactly adrift, if that's what you mean."

"Not at all. I'm simply saying, nothing ventured, nothing gained. That's one of the oldest axioms in the world, but also one of the soundest, and more futures have been built on it than any other."

The *Water Witch* was preparing to dock, her paddles churning slowly toward Greenwich landing. Sweeny removed a card from his wallet and scribbled an address on the reverse side. "If you decide to come, and I hope you do, this will serve as your invitation. Good day, Miss Marshall." He tipped his hat and went back inside, presumably to rejoin his friends.

Devon pondered his laconic advice and philosophy. "You get what you want by going after it." The creed of an unscrupulous politician, or pearls of wisdom cast upon the Hudson?

Chapter 32

To go, or not to go. That was the question, and Devon debated it with herself fervently. Surely it couldn't hurt her, and it might help her in the elusive career she still craved. How else was she ever to succeed, if she did not heed Sweeny's advice, hunt down opportunity, seize it by the scruff of the neck, and shake it for all it was worth? *Seek and ye shall find.* Even the Bible advocated that, as well as helping oneself.

Keith, of course, imagined that her ambition had been permanently squelched in motherhood, that she had no choice now but to spend the rest of her life in the country, as a helpless leech on him.

She fixed tea to go with the croissants she had bought from a baker's cart. Then she opened the *Herald*, which had lured her with sensational headlines of a society scandal. But the principles involved in the lurid triangle were only names to her, and she turned to other news. An article on the third page, to which Catholic editor James Gordon Bennett had devoted six long columns, caught her interest. NEW MIRACLE AT LOURDES? Her heart froze as she began to read:

Mrs. Keith H. Curtis, wife of the prominent New York capitalist, today rose from her wheelchair at the sacred shrine, apparently cured of a spinal affliction that had incapacitated her a number of years. The alleged miracle was witnessed by an estimated three hundred pilgrims to Lourdes, who fell to their knees and kissed the consecrated ground, where, according to Roman Catholic belief, the Virgin Mary appeared to the young peasant girl, Bernadette Soubirous, in 1858. Since that time numerous miraculous cures have been reported by the faithful, and crutches and other votive offerings have been left at the Grotto of Our Lady of Lourdes by grateful supplicants relieved of their maladies and infirmities. Mrs. Curtis' expensive wheelchair has joined these tributes.

Mr. Curtis, with his wife at the time, was too astonished to comment for the press. But it was known that the couple had gone abroad to consult a prominent Vienna nerve specialist about the patient's persistent paralysis, resulting from a previous accident. Dr. Frederick Tabor could not be reached for comment, but, according to Mrs. Curtis, he had not given them much hope for improvement in her condition, much less a permanent cure. Thus, in last-resort desperation, they made the pilgrimage to Lourdes, an ancient hamlet in the foot of the Pyrenees, whose origins are lost in antiquity.

According to witnesses, Mrs. Curtis appeared radiant, as though bathed in mystic light, as she rose from her chair unaided and walked toward the grotto, to her husband's and her attendant's amazement. Priests and nuns at the scene would not confirm this purported illumination, however. (Ed. note: Mrs. Curtis is of Protestant persuasion, a member of Grace Episcopal Church of New York City.) But Mrs. Curtis was presented with a blessed rosary and vial of holy water, and will be received at the chancellery of the local diocese by the bishop of Tarbes, who is a member of the Papal Commission of Inquiry. This is a courtesy extended only to pilgrims who have "presumably received the Holy Ghost," and only when efforts are to be made to verify a miraculous recovery.

Asked to describe her reaction to the apparent revelation, Mrs. Curtis replied: "I felt suddenly strengthened and energized and motivated, as though a powerful spirit had entered my mortal being, and I was further conscious of an inner urging to rise and walk. But so often had I tried it before and failed, I was naturally afraid and reluctant. Yet the voice persisted, assuring me that this time I would succeed, and I did. Truly, I feel that I received divine assistance and blessing."

Then, smiling lovingly at her handsome and

wealthy husband, who has stood faithfully by her side through all her trials and tribulations, Mrs. Curtis remarked softly, her beautiful violet eyes glowing like stained glass windows: "Only his great love and devotion could have sustained me in my agonies, dilemmas, and nightmares. Now we shall have a second honeymoon in Europe, as we had our first. We shall dance together again for the first time in six long years. And Oh! how we will dance!"

From Lourdes the couple will journey to Rome for an audience with Pope Pius IX. Thence to Paris, where they will be the guests of the Baron de Rothschild and attend a bal masque at the Tuileries. In London they will be received by Queen Victoria at Buckingham Palace, and then visit Heathstone Manor in Sussex, seat of the earls of Heathstone for three centuries, and birthplace of Mr. Curtis' late mother, Lady Anne, daughter of William, Lord Heathstone, a grand old gentleman of ninety.

There was more, but Devon's eyes blurred and she couldn't continue. The paper slid from her hands to the floor. She was numb. But she did not for a moment credit a miraculous cure. There had been no need for miracles, because the creature had never been paralyzed. It had all been an act, an incredible drama played for an incredibly long run in Gramercy Park! Pretense to bind her husband as nothing else could, and she had simply tricked and deceived him again. She had never intended to divorce him, no matter if he bought her a dozen castles in Europe. And how could he leave her now, with the aura of Lourdes upon her, practically a beatified saint proclaiming his eternal love and devotion to the world! The "miracle" would be recounted in all the New England journals, with embellishments in New York and Boston, and Esther would trade on it for years to come.

And so the witch had won, after all. Why hadn't Keith at least prepared her for the shock? There'd been time enough, according to the dateline on the story. He could've sent a cablegram! How could he *not* inform her?

A sinister presence seemed to have invaded the apartment, taking possession, and Devon couldn't exorcise it with tears or frustration or fury or despair. She had to escape for awhile. Go somewhere, do something. Walk. Shop. Yes, that was it. Shop for a costume. And a mask.

The home which James Fisk provided for Josephine Mansfield was the envy and aspiration of every mercenary mistress in Manhattan. Including decoration and furniture, the imposing four-story-and-basement brownstone mansion on Twenty-third Street represented an investment of one hundred thousand dollars.

The foyer was Breche rose marble, the walls paneled in fine woods and brocades, the ceilings delicately frescoed. Some of the furniture was inlaid with ivory and mother-of-pearl and bronze, some carved and glazed and gilded. There was much silver and crystal and cut glass in evidence, and sculptures, paintings, *objets d'art*. New ornaments were continually added, for Josie was a compulsive buyer, acquisitive as a squirrel, and it pleased her infatuated lover to indulge her fancies.

Her household staff included a cook, two chambermaids, a butler, a coachman, a footman, and a black waiterboy. She could summon any of the dozen conveyances from Fisk's nearby stables, and preferred the opulent blue clarence upholstered in cloth-of-gold, and the big bright red barouche sleigh with leopard skin cushions during winter snows—all this while the naive and unsuspecting Mrs. Fisk lived in comfort and ignorance in Boston.

At twenty-nine Josephine Mansfield was still a spectacular beauty, with pearly pink skin, large deep dark eyes, and luxuriant black hair worn tonight in massive coils. She was Cleopatra in silver lamé and genuine diamonds and emeralds. Her corpulent Mark Antony affected a green satin toga bordered in gold. Fisk was thirty-four, the partner of Jay Gould and Daniel Drew in numerous financial adventures, most of them shady.

Bought at a theatrical shop in a tragic mood, Devon's costume was the traditional Juliet-Camille-Isolde white drapery, easily converted with accessories to portray an unfortunate heroine of stage or legend or history. With it she wore a becoming gold mesh headcap, gold waist cord, and gold vizard. And though identities were to remain secret until midnight, Peter Sweeny recognized her when she presented his card at the door; he had evidently been watching for her. He approached and took her arm reassuringly, a broad grin on his swarthy face, his villainous eyes masked in black, but otherwise uncostumed.

"So you came," he whispered.

"You're not supposed to recognize me," she chided, spreading a golden fan before her face, and he laughed.

"Look around you, my dear. You'll never be surrounded by more powerful people in your life. See that trio over there, hoisting champagne? Tweed, Oakey Hall, and Dick Connolly. Mayor Hoffman will probably show up later—he's attending the August Belmonts' reception tonight. Belmont will be chairman of the Democratic Convention. The pasty-faced fellow with the bristling black beard is Jay Gould, in conversation with some Erie Railroad men. Of course Jim Fisk is Mark Antony—isn't he a sight? God, what a paunch! But he loves costumes and uniforms; he's a colonel in the national guard, and a self-commissioned admiral on his steamboats. Why not, he says, if Vanderbilt is a commodore? Jim has the best sense of humor of any man on Wall Street."

"He does look jolly," Devon agreed.

"Particularly so tonight. He and Gould are celebrating the victory of the long battle of Erie, against no less an adversary than Commodore Vanderbilt. They had an ally in Tammany, however. But I assume, being a journalist, you read the papers. Tweed and I will become members of the Erie directorate at the next board meeting." He smiled down at her, for her dimunitive figure made even his medium height seem impressive. "By the way, I took the liberty of speaking to a friend about you yesterday. He owns the New York *Record*, and you are to call at your convenience for an interview."

His prompt action astonished her. "Not really?"

"Yes, really. And he'll employ you, I can practically guarantee it. Tammany advertises heavily in the *Record*, and I'm city chamberlain."

"I don't know what to say, Mr. Sweeny, how to thank you."

"You can begin by calling me Pete," he said. "Oh, Christ! The Bowery Fox has just come in. Maybe he won't recognize you masked. There's the music. Shall we dance?"

Devon nodded, her head spinning without benefit of wine. He was an excellent dancer, as light and graceful as

Keith, who was probably dancing at some palace or castle tonight. A pain stabbed her heart, and she tensed in Sweeny's arms.

"You're not afraid of Donahue, are you?" he asked. "If so, I assure you I can handle him."

"No, it's just a little warm in here."

"New York in July. Most people get out at this time, if possible, and so would I except for the convention."

"Who do you expect to get the presidential nomination?"

"Horatio Seymour, if some dark horse doesn't upset his political cart," he said. "Chief Justice Salmon Chase is one of the hopefuls. But Grant is going to be hard to beat." His smile neither humored nor patronized her. "Don't tell me a pretty little thing like you is interested in politics?"

"I grew up in Richmond," Devon said, "which was the Southern political arena before and during the war. I read transcripts of the Lincoln-Douglas debates when I was fourteen. My father published a newspaper, you see, and I worked on it with him for several years. He's dead now . . . he took his own life the day Richmond surrendered."

"I wish I'd had this information when I spoke with Samuel Fitch yesterday," Sweeny said. "I'm sure he had doubts about your qualifications and experience, and thought I was just applying pressure, which I was."

"Are there any ladies on his staff?"

"A couple, I think, for the feminine news."

"Token concessions, naturally. And how do you feel about women in politics, Mr. Sweeny?"

"I don't approve, although I know they exert plenty of power and persuasion behind the scenes. Many a politician has been compromised through a petticoat, his reputation made or lost through one, and his honor bought or sold the same way. Kings never underestimate the influence of women in their courts, because thrones have been preserved or destroyed by them. Some day they may be a force in this government too, but not in the foreseeable future, despite the efforts of Susan Anthony, Victoria Woodhull, et al. Have you seen the new Wigwam yet, Miss Marshall?"

"Only the exterior. Females are taboo there, aren't they?"

"In the inner sanctums, yes. But I could give you a tour. Be my guest."

"I'm tempted, of course . . . as a journalist," she added. "But since I can't vote in the election—"

"You wouldn't be old enough, would you?"

Devon smiled noncommittally, and he said, "You have the loveliest mouth in the world. Fisk thinks Josie has, but he's wrong; yours could conquer and enslave any man. I suppose I'll have to let the others have a dance with you, but only one. And I'll give odds that Donahue will be the first to claim his. No, by God, it's Slippery Dick coming over now."

"Who?"

"Connolly. That's what the anti-Tammany press calls him. You might as well learn the soubriquets, my dear. They call me Squire Sweeny; also Brains, Bismarck, and Buccaneer. And all of the sachems are known as tigers, due to this." He indicated the symbolic emblem in his black satin lapel. "All right, Dick. I recognize you. Once around, no more. I'll break in if you don't release her. Got it?"

"Got it," Connolly nodded, whirling away with her. "Who are you?" he asked without preamble. "I can't place you?"

A coy smile. "Isn't that the purpose of a masquerade?"

"Oh, yes. Jim and Josie like such games. Sweeny seems to consider you his personal property, however, although he didn't bring you. Why should he think you belong to him?"

"I can't imagine, sir."

"Are you an actress? You can tell me that much."

"I'm not an actress."

"I didn't think so. You're quality if I ever saw it." Behind her back he signaled the orchestra to prolong the music, but the maestro was myopic, and it faded away. "The Boss is next on your program," Connolly said. "He's a fine dancer, despite his bulk. So's Fisk, if he can tear himself away from Josie long enough to ask anyone else. Thank you for the pleasure, Miss." He bowed agilely and surrendered her to the Grand Sachem.

Tweed was especially skillful in the waltz. So was Mark Antony when he spun by with Cleopatra. And the elegant Oakey, wearing formal clothes and a pince-nez clipped on his black velvet mask, might have been a duke or baron incognito. But other than Sweeny, only Tweed seemed to suspect her identity. Shrewd blue eyes peering through the slits in his mask, he said, "I think we've met before, young lady."

"Perhaps."

"Shall I be more specific?"

"Oh, no! Don't take the fun out of it. We're supposed to pretend and guess until midnight."

"You're not guessing," he said. "You know damn well who I am. Everybody here knows me."

"Well, anyone so distinguished could scarcely remain anonymous, even masked, Senator."

"God forbid I should ever need a disguise, then," he said jovially, pleased with the compliment. "But I think Sweeny has committed an act of piracy on Donahue, and I'm surprised the Bowery Fox hasn't realized it yet. I thought he was sharper than that, and had a keener eye."

Devon feigned innocence. "I'm sure I don't know what you mean, sir."

"I'm sure you do, Miss, and I hope those two feisty Irishmen don't tangle over it. You're probably much too good for either of the rascals, anyway. I gather you don't belong in that acting company from Pike's Opera House, so where do you belong? Are you a refugee who came North during the war and forgot to return?"

"In a way," she murmured.

"Which state?"

"Virginia."

"One of the three which haven't yet rejoined the Union, and so can't help to vote our man into the White House in November."

"Oh, but they'll be rooting for him, sir! Can you imagine any loyal Southerner, particularly a Virginian, favoring Grant?"

"Cheer up," he consoled. "Maybe the old boozer'll die of corn or lead poisoning before then, or be lynched on a magnolia tree. If not, my braves hope to scalp him at the polls." He ended "The Blue Danube" on a graceful flourish. "Well, here comes your self-appointed mastiff again, looking fierce as a Cerebus," he said, as Sweeny reclaimed her.

"What were you telling Donahue just now?" Devon asked him.

"To keep his distance."

"Will he?"

"I don't know. He's hard to insult. But he still hopes to make the Americus Club, and I'm president this year. His membership will depend on his Ward record, however ... how many ballots he delivers to the precinct boxes."

"Is Mr. Fitch here?"

"No, he's not much of a social lion. Practically a hermit, in fact. Just don't let him bluff or scare you. He's beholden to Tammany, therefore vulnerable. One word to the wise is sufficient. One word from the right source."

One word, and yet Keith would never speak it for her. But no matter now. That was over, it had to be, there was nothing for them together any more, not even hope. She had to forget him, get free of her emotional entanglements, and make a new life for herself and her child. There was no alternative.

Thinking of it made her sigh and falter, and assuming it was the heat again Sweeny ushered her out to the terrace and into the walled garden. There was a glimmer of moon and stars and Japanese lanterns, the scent of roses and carnations and potted gardenias. Sweeny removed his mask and then hers and stood looking at her, his savage eyes glowing like coals in the faint light. Wordlessly, he drew her to him and kissed her, gently at first, then with lingering intensity, until she gasped for breath and swayed involuntarily against him. "I've wanted to do that since we met on the boat," he said. "Don't be angry with me, Devon. I think I'm in love with you. I *know* I want you."

Devon shrank from another such involvement. "I'm sorry, Mr. Sweeny."

"Pete," he reminded.

"I'm sorry, Pete."

"Think about it, darling. That's all I ask."

"Does my job depend on it?"

"Of course not. I'm not that kind of bastard, regardless of what my enemies think."

She smiled, straightening his cravat. "You're not such a pirate, after all, are you?"

"Oh, I'm ruthless, make no mistake. But not with

women. I can't, however, be responsible for what others might think of our association. You understand that?"

"Yes—but I'm a good reporter, Pete. I can prove myself to Mr. Finch. And I don't care where he starts me. In obituaries or classified, the files or the library, or just running errands."

"My dear, you underestimate your assets, and my interest. You'll be in the ruffles and flourishes department. Society, fashions, entertainment."

"Wonderful!" she cried. "That's how Kate Field and Jenny June and Minnie Squier started."

His arms and mouth captured her again, and she could feel his male hardness against her uncrinolined body. "God, you are an adorable little doll, and I'd like nothing better than to spoil you! What do you want, Devon? Tell me, and I'll give it to you. Anything, gratis."

"Just be my friend, Pete."

Chagrin edged his voice, making it unintentionally gruff. "I lay my heart at your feet, and you ask my hand in friendship! All right, I'll settle for that, now. Just remember, if ever you need me, I'm at City Hall. Now I think we'd better remask and return to the party before we're missed."

Donahue was waiting for them. He crossed the ballroom floor as soon as he could escape a clinging creature in a gaudy gypsy costume, jingling with beads and bangles. "Don't be a hog," he said with the kind of fraternal clap on the shoulder that Sweeny despised. "Give another Irishman a chance."

"It's up to the lady," Sweeny deferred, and Devon only shrugged helplessly. She would have danced with Lucifer himself to avoid offending him or creating a scene. Too late she realized her mistake, for Donahue recognized her.

"Richmond," he said quietly, peering into her mask.

"Beg pardon?"

" 'Tis no use pretending Miss Marshall. I've heard your voice before and seen you masked before. Shall I be refreshing your memory, me beautiful little bird of paradise?" He scowled ruefully. "Oh, St. Paddy! Did the wolf ever outsmart the fox!"

Devon was properly indignant. "I don't know what you're talking about, sir! I'm a reporter."

"So the Tammany Tiger tells me. Is he knowing about the Wall Street Wolf?"

"I have no knowledge of any such person," Devon denied doggedly, "so please don't badger me about it, sir. I don't think Mr. Sweeny would like it."

"Don't worry, honey. Your secret's safe with me. Sure I'm not fool enough to twist *that* tiger's tail. Is this little shindig appearing in the *Record*?"

"If Mr. Fitch says so."

"If Mr. Tweed says so, you mean."

"Well," Devon shrugged, her eyes beckoning Sweeny, who promptly rescued her from her recalcitrant partner. The two men exchanged fierce glares, and Devon thought Donahue might protest, but he only bowed mockingly and sauntered back to the gypsy.

"Trouble?" Sweeny asked in repossession.

"He recognized me."

"Your voice, naturally. It's as memorable as your mouth. And his gambler's vision probably penetrated your disguise. It's almost midnight, anyway. Forget him, Devon. Some of the men plan to play poker later on, and Josie would like you to keep her company. I'll see you home afterwards."

After the unmasking and buffet, the theatrical troupe left to make early rehearsals the next day, and while the men gambled for high stakes, Devon and Josie got acquainted in the upstairs parlor. The adjoining bedroom was an unabashed chamber of love. Roses and cupids, carved and gilded, decorated the massive bed, and the mirrored ceiling seemed the ultimate in voluptuous abandon, the significance of which made Devon blush. Toile de Jouy covered the walls, the mantel was Florentine porcelain painted with nymphs and satyrs, the carpet soft and lush as flower petals, and French perfume and Oriental incense hung in the air.

Miss Mansfield was neither secretive about her liaison with the Prince of Erie, nor inquisitive about Devon's connection with Squire Sweeny. Devon appreciated that, and was surprised to learn that they had something in common, for both were daughters of newspaper publishers.

"My father was killed in a duel with another editor," Josie confided. "In Stockton, California. We had moved there only a few years earlier, from Massachusetts."

"Mine killed himself," Devon said, and filled in a little of her background, including her education.

"Rosewood Female Academy, in Charlottesville? Sounds elegant. I went to convent school in Lowell, and Mama put me with the nuns again in California. I was a precocious child, and she thought I needed discipline, which I'm sure I did. Not that it helped much. I ran away, at fifteen, to marry an actor, who was living in the boardinghouse Mama opened after Papa's death. It didn't work out, however, and I left him in San Francisco and came to New York, where I managed to get an annulment. I married again—another failure that ended in divorce. I was trying to act for Tony Pastor when I met Jim, and he understood and encouraged me. He's going to buy Pike's Opera House and redecorate it as the finest theater in New York. We plan to introduce opera bouffe to America. Jim's really a clown at heart, you know. They call Tweed Falstaff, but the soubriquet fits Jim better."

They talked for hours, but Devon could not confide any intimate secrets in Josie. Nor had she been able to do so with either Janette Joie or Mally O'Neill. Her housekeeper was the only woman who knew the truth, which had spilled out in an impulsive confession after her baby's birth. And Anna, in virtually the same situation some years earlier, did not judge or criticize her. Perhaps Josephine Mansfield would have been equally understanding and discreet, but Devon offered no confidences or revelations that night. Somehow, inadvertently or otherwise, they might pass on to Sweeny, and for some inexplicable reason she did not want to disillusion him. It was mortifying enough that Donahue had discovered the truth, or at least guessed at it.

Chapter 33

The New York *Record* was a three-story red brick build-ing on Printing House Square, adjacent to City Hall Park, and the publisher was a tall spare man in his late thirties, with a thin jaundiced face and disillusioned smile. Devon sensed what he was thinking: that she was Peter Barr Sweeny's woman and, talent or not, he was obliged to ac-commodate her. It was a matter of economics: publish, or perish.

There were some eighty metropolitan journals—dailies, weeklies, periodicals—in cutthroat competition, and the majority were in perennial financial difficulty, struggling for mere existence. Some were indebted to the city treasury for support. Municipal news, including the mayor's and other official messages, was printed at one dollar per line. Organs which did not deliberately affront or antagonize Tammany Hall were additionally subsidized with handsome monthly fees, depending on the amount and nature of their cooperation. Minus this subsidy, the *Record* would have long since faded into obscurity and oblivion. Nevertheless, Samuel Fitch resented this continu-ance, which subordinated his judgment and restricted his freedom, bribed his conscience and literally bartered his soul. It was prostitution of the press, that which there was no worse sin or disgraceful service, and he felt like a whore beholden to political pimps. He drowned his shame and professional pride in alcohol, and vented his repug-nance and frustration on his helpless employees. He had hired Tammany proteges before, but this was the first time one of the Tigers had sent him a female cub—pert, pretty, and obviously pampered. It displeased him mightily.

"Tell me about yourself," he began, inviting Devon to be seated in his office. "Your experience, I mean."

She told him, while he toyed with a quill, as if bored

and certainly unimpressed by her verbal résumé. "So your father published the Richmond *Sentinel*? Small potatoes, Miss Marshall, compared to the *Enquirer* and *Examiner*, but I was aware of it, because Hodge Marshall was a damned good editor. One got the feeling, however, reading his paper, that there were some emotional restraints on his personal comments; that he was not always in complete accord with what he printed and had to juggle some hot and potentially explosive political potatoes to provide food and shelter for his family."

"Perhaps he did," Devon allowed.

"Ah well, we can't all be Benjamin Franklins or Horace Greeleys, can we? Exactly what did you do on the *Sentinel*?"

While she explained, he slashed some words in an editorial he was writing, as if cutting his own veins, bloodletting his conscience, purging his soul to admit alien and contaminated material to which he was allergic. "I may as well tell you frankly that I don't believe women have much place in this profession, Miss Marshall, or at best, a minor one. But since we do have a woman's page, we can fit you in somewhere there. If you reported social trivia in Richmond, you can serve similar tripe here. Females everywhere, it seems, even in the hinterlands, are afflicted with an incurable mania for fashion and frivolity, and some will read little, if anything, else." Surveying her chic costume, from the Milan straw hat to the French kid slippers peeping from under her apple-green mousseline skirts, he abruptly inquired, "How well do you know Squire Sweeny?"

"He's a friend," she answered, and his presumptuous smile incensed her.

"Well, tell your 'friend' that you now wear the *Record*'s badge. But it's not a sinecure, Miss Marshall. You'll be expected to earn your keep here, and your salary will be commensurate with your ability. Nor can I guarantee how long you'll last. Journalistic careers, as you undoubtedly know, are often notoriously short. Editors especially have a high mortality rate, and Park Row is littered with the bones of bankrupt publishers. The first editor I replaced was a victim of poor circulation, and rafts of first-rate reporters have been sunk in seas of red ink. How any of us survive to longevity is a mystery to me. But perhaps your lifeboat will prove more secure, and I wish you success in the perilous waters of publishing." He rose wearily from his desk. "Report at eight o'clock tomorrow morning. The woman's editor, Mrs. Carrie Hempstead, will brief you and give you your assignments. That's all."

"Thank you, Mr. Fitch. I'll try hard to do a good job."

"We'll see," he said simply. "Good day, Miss Marshall."

His attitude did not discourage Devon, for she sensed that he was not as cold and insensitive as he pretended. Cynical, disenchanted, perhaps, but then many journalists were; cynicism and disenchantment were occupational hazards. At that moment, however, nothing could dismay or disillusion her. She had a job on a newspaper, a genuine journal!

Carrie Hempstead was a pleasant, plump widow of fifty, with dun-colored hair and a bosom like a shelf. Samuel Fitch had once worked on her husband's paper in Providence and courted her elder daughter, who was killed in a sleighing accident. She had another child, a son crippled by some mysterious disease, whom she had to support after her husband's death. Out of pity and charity, Fitch created a place for her on the *Record*. Most papers maintained a "petticoat page" to satisfy distaff readers, as they included a "parson's pulpit" to please the pious.

As Carrie Hempstead edited it, the feminine section was a potpourri of home, hearth, garden, childcare, health, fashion, beauty, etiquette, and cooking—all seasoned with pungent feminism whenever and wherever it could be judiciously inserted. She had one assistant, Tish Lambeth, underweight and overworked, with a face like a fallen pudding. Both welcomed a helping hand, for in addition to their editorial duties, they did the janitorial work in their office, and when Tish went on assignments, Carrie was inundated by miscellaneous chores. Now she could send Miss Marshall, who would certainly make a better impression than poor homely Tish, who could not affect style no matter how hard she tried. This lovely creature would be an asset to the *Record*, on the order of Kate Field and Jenny June.

"Good morning," she greeted her. "Welcome to the *Record*, Miss Marshall. I'm Carrie Hempstead, and this is Tish Lambeth. We know a little about your background and experience, my dear, and I'm sure we'll get along famously together."

"Oh, yes! It's a pleasure having you, Miss Marshall." The assistant, relieved to share the burdens, smiled sincerely and offered her hand, as Devon stripped her gloves to shake it. "How about a cup of tea? I just made it, fresh."

"Fine." Devon removed her bonnet. "Is there a locker?"

"Just the stationery closet," Carrie replied, "and it's communal. I fixed a peg and hook for you."

Her desk was next to Tish's, in the center of the bare oiled floor. Mrs. Hempstead's office occupied a corner of the room, neither private nor partitioned. She gave Devon some notes she had scribbled at a soiree and told her to condense them into a single paragraph. Space was limited, and the hostess wasn't prominent enough to receive or demand much attention. Tish was busy on an Astor affair, which naturally took precedence, particularly since the family was known to be friendly to Tammany Hall. Despite her space handicap, Devon produced a social vignette that anyone would be proud to paste in a scrapbook. Carrie was pleased and complimentary. "It's like distilling perfume, my dear, and you've managed to capture the essence." And she handed Devon a sheaf of similar projects.

Devon worked six days a week, Sundays off. Society worshiped on the Sabbath, Blue Laws suspended business, and there were few entertainments other than church activities. Sunday, then, would be her day in the country. And when she arrived, on an early train, Anna had a letter for her bearing a Rome postmark. A mere note, actually, of cablegram brevity, scrawled in haste and apparent anxiety: "Please disregard anything you might read in the press. Sailing for America in a few weeks. Happy Birthday! Best wishes. KHC." That was all, and only initialed, like an office memo. Devon took it up to the master chamber, flung herself across the bed clutching the message in her hand, and bawled until she woke her son in the nursery, who promptly joined her.

Bringing his bottle Anna did not ask what was wrong; she had read the *Herald* article herself. She suspected it was the reason for the job, of which she disapproved, but made no comment on that, either. "I've baked you a premature birthday cake." she said cheerfully. "It's next Tuesday, isn't it?"

Devon nodded, sobbing. "I hope it's a tipsy cake, Anna, with plenty of rum."

"It's a Lady Baltimore, with fruit filling, and if you don't dry your tears they'll drown the candles."

Except for leaving the baby, Devon was eager to get back to the city. Work was a nepenthe, if not a panacea. Arriving at the office Monday morning she found Tish Lambeth, who was thirty-two, in the throes of periodic pain, sipping a hot herb brew, and unable to go on her scheduled assignment: a project about which every red-blooded newsman in town was joking and laughing, including Jenny June's husband, David Croly, managing editor of the prestigious New York *World*.

The lady journalists, excluded from the New York Press Club, had organized one of their own. Croly's own wife had conceived the idea in February, when her sex had been barred from the press banquet honoring Charles Dickens, who had just arrived for his second American visit and lecture tour. The literary event of the year, and yet some of the most intellectual women of the century had been denied admission! It was an indignity not to be meekly borne, and thus the Sorosis Club was born. The ambitious charter was ridiculed by their male counterparts as the Crinoline Bill of Rights and the Mauve Magna Carta. "We have tipped the teapot," declared Alice Cary in the inaugural address at Delmonico's, where Dickens had been feted, and male ego was scalded.

Fated by Tish's troublesome menses, Devon Marshall sailed into the meeting as an envoy of the *Record*, and was hailed as a long lost comrade-in-arms by those who knew her. "Wherever have you been, dear?" asked Phoebe Cary, kissing both her cheeks as if presenting the Croix de Guerre.

"Crusading in the field," Devon lied facilely. "I returned only last month and miraculously landed a job on the *Record*."

"It seems to be the season of miracles," Kate Field mused, referring to the recently reported one at Lourdes. "Isn't that something about Mrs. Keith Curtis? Naturally, I'm happy for them, even if the *Herald* did scoop us all on the story. No doubt the Curtises are making up for lost time abroad, and Gramercy Park'll be a busy place when they return. No rest for the weary society reporters!" And confidentially to Devon, "Does his bank still hold your mortgage?"

"Well, I've paid the interest regularly and expect to redeem it soon."

"Good, and you must let Woodhull and Claflin invest your extra cash for you. Lord, they've even got Jay Gould, Jim Fisk, and Daniel Drew as their financial aides-de-camp now! In addition to the Commodore."

Jenny June rapped for silence, and the meeting came to order. Devon noted the agenda, the speakers and proposals, the clothes and coiffures, the luncheon menu of crab croquettes, watercress salad, asparagus tips, and cherry tarts. What she brought back pleased Mrs. Hempstead immensely in its freshness, style, insight. But the compositor and make-up man conspired to squeeze the article between two patent medicine advertisements, one for female complaint and the other for pruritis. Devon was furious, but Carrie assured her it was nothing personal, just the men's idea of a practical joke.

Devon frowned. "Some sense of humor."

"Gentlemen of the press," Tish hissed. "Hah! Chauvinist beasts. I'd like to slay them all with the jawbone of an ass."

"What we need is a blast from Woodhull and Claflin," said Carrie. "But they're so busy coining gold in Wall Street, they haven't taken notice of Sorosis yet. Heaven help the male monsters when they do." She grinned and handed Devon a cartoon in another paper. "Have you seen this?" It was the Bewitching Brokers driving a cart and cracking whips over the hitched teams of bulls and bears, some of whose identities were recognizable.

"Hooray!" cheered Tish.

"Hooray," Devon murmured.

Now it was September and presumably Keith was somewhere on the high seas, en route home. Should he arrive in the country during Devon's absence, Anna was to say that she was shopping in the city. She wanted to tell him about the job herself, and the servants, acquainted with the master's temper in his confrontation with the Virginian, were only too happy to let her do so. "The privilege is all yours, Ma'am," said Anna.

Scotty was six months old now, sitting up and crawling. Devon brought him numerous toys and lavished love and affection on him during her visits. Was she trying to compensate for six days of maternal neglect in one? Nonsense! He was healthy, happy, thriving on substitute milk and domestic care. A beautiful child, conceived in Keith's image, so that it was impossible to look at the son without seeing the father. Devon liked to bathe him, feed him in his highchair, rock him to sleep with lullabies. Scotty loved to go outside and view the domestic menagerie, which included the cow and her calf, the nanny goat and her mischievous kid, the big gentle brown-and-white collie, and several lazy tabby cats, but he seemed to prefer the horses over all.

Sometimes, with Enid at the reins of the pony trap, they would drive along the lanes of Washington Heights, through Inwood Valley to Spuyten Duyvil Creek, crossing King's Bridge to Marble Hill. The landscape glowed under autumn's first faint blush. Sunset colors tinged the woods, holly berries were tipped with scarlet, and dry leaves rustled under the hooves and wheels. They splashed through shallow brooks, clopped over rustic wood and stone bridges, passed picturesque Dutch and Colonial cottages behind gardens of chrysanthemums, asters, fall roses.

Why wasn't it enough? Devon wondered, cuddling her sleeping babe to her breast. The peace, the beauty, the solitude. She should be happy in the country, content in the lovely old house on the Hudson. Yet she regarded it as a holiday retreat, a temporary refuge from the clamor and chaos of the city, and the pressures of Printing House Square. Anxious for Sunday, equally anxious for Monday. But, then, why shouldn't motherhood and a career be compatible? Why should one be sacrificed for or jeopardized by the other? As for marriage, why worry about *that*? She would never be a wife—not to Keith, anyway. There wasn't a hope or prayer of that any more. And she wouldn't ask for a settlement, either. He could provide for them or not, as he wished. She wouldn't demand anything, except an end to the relationship.

Chapter 34

Ignoring Mrs. Hempstead's suggestion that a woman be sent to meet the luxury liner carrying the Curtises home, the city editor gave the Lourdes assignment to the male reporter on the Battery beat, and for once Devon was glad of the sexual discrimination in the profession. She had been sick with fear that Carrie would assign her instead of Tish Lambeth, and she would have resigned or died rather than accept.

The resulting interview was essentially a cribbed rehash of the now stale *Herald* story, but Devon read it avidly, noting that once again Mrs. Curtis did most of the talking. Comments attributed to Mr. Curtis were terse, cynical, and extracted as reluctantly as teeth.

"Naturally, we're pleased at her complete recovery, however it occurred."

"Miracle? That's a moot question. The Church hasn't established one in this case; that requires intensive investigation, you know, similar to that conducted by the devil's advocate on candidates for sainthood."

"Yes, we did visit His Holiness, and he was most gracious. The Vatican is a splendid place."

"No, I don't believe much in miracles—at least, I never did before. Yes, it's good to be home again. That's all for now, gentlemen. Thank you."

A fashion trailer was appended for the benefit of the distaff readership: "Mrs. Curtis was wearing a Worth travel suit of gold French faille trimmed with black passementerie, matching bonnet and gloves. Mr. Curtis, debonair as usual in British tweeds, stands tall among the Wall Street giants."

"Stupid idiot!" Carrie criticized in exasperation. "A woman would've described her costume in detail. Was the suit bustled? Was she wearing crinolines, or has Paris finally

386

abolished them? And surely there were some jet beads and soutache in the passementerie—that's a Worth trademark! Was her hat veiled? Was she wearing slippers, shoes, or the new ankle boots? I suppose we'll have to read Kate Field and Jenny June to find out! Any of us could've done a better job than this and I doubt if Mr. Curtis would've been so curt and uncooperative with a lady. Jack must've irked him somehow, for ordinarily he's a paragon of courtesy."

Had she not been in the office, Devon would have burst into tears or tantrums, or both. But she must learn to control her emotions and impulses, and to treat even personal news impersonally. She folded the paper neatly and laid it with her reticule to take home and clip and file with the others on the subject.

There was a felicitous message from Sweeny in her mailbox: "Saw Fitch at City Hall this morning. He says you're doing a good job. Congratulations! Keep it up. From little cubs, big reporters grow. Best wishes. Pete." And a postscript: "Anytime you want that guided tour of the Tigers' lair, this one is at your humble service."

Smiling, Devon tucked it away in a bureau drawer. For what? she wondered. Posterity?

The next day she covered the fall showings at Demorest's Emporium, and bought a new hat in the hope of improving her morale. It didn't help much, however, and she still was not sure that she liked it. Well, she could always return or exchange it. Madame Demorest understood the inherently vacillant female mind and moods and catered to its prerogative.

Entering the apartment, Devon thought she smelled tobacco smoke and chided her imagination. It was late afternoon, dim and shadowy, and an elm branch scratched against the window in a sudden autumn breeze. Lighting the gas sconces flanking the hall pier table, she tried on the new cloche again. It was pearl-gray velvet, very chic and feminine, with one large pale pink silk rose on the brim, and a wisp of illusion that wreathed her face in an opal mist. She preened herself, angling for best profile, still dubious about the effect.

"Charming," said a familiar masculine voice from the parlor shadows. "Enchanting."

His reflection appeared in the mirror, and Devon had a

glimpse of glowing eyes and flashing teeth before swirling darkness enveloped her. She woke on the sofa, the bonnet off, a satin cushion under her head and solicitous hands chafing her wrists.

"Keith?" she murmured.

"Yes, darling, yes."

"What happened?"

"You swooned on me, and I had no smelling salts handy."

"You startled me! I—I thought I was hallucinating."

"I'm sorry, Devon. It was stupid and clumsy of me, surprising you that way. But I thought you might be expecting me. I've just come, not an hour since, from the country. Anna said you were in town, shopping."

Recovered, Devon sat up cautiously, avoiding his eyes. "How do you like your son?"

"What a question! He's wonderful, Devon, just the little boy I've always wanted. And how he's grown! We had a great time getting reacquainted. I finally wore him out playing with him. He fell asleep just before I left." He hesitated. "You've seen the papers?"

She nodded. "Why didn't you warn me, Keith? Write or cable? You could've spared me that shock!"

"Didn't you receive my letter to disregard it?"

"Letter? Those few words! They told me nothing."

"I wanted to tell you personally, Devon."

"But that was months ago, Keith! And I'd already read about the miracle at Lourdes in the *Herald*."

"Miracle, hell! It was just the greatest drama of Esther's whole goddamn dramatic life, and she went abroad with a well-rehearsed script in mind. What a performance! The pilgrim audience was convinced that she was aglow with celestial light, some kind of apparition or revelation herself. A travesty, of course, but I'd have seemed like Satan mocking it."

"And was the second honeymoon a mockery too?"

"Good Lord! You didn't *believe* that?"

"She said—"

He interrupted impatiently. "I know what she said, Devon. I was there, remember. So were some international correspondents. Could I call her a liar before the world? What kind of fool or imbecile would publicly deny intimacy with his wife? I trusted you to *know* better."

She bounded to her feet, eyes blazing. "Then what were you doing with her all this time?"

"Trying to persuade Esther to keep her end of the bargain," he said. "Tempting her with mansions in Paris, chateaux on the Loire, Roman villas and Spanish castles—and the witch let me think I was succeeding."

"Nevertheless, you were royally entertained together!"

"My dear, it's lèse majesté to decline such invitations, and not every American abroad receives them. You simply don't send your regrets to the Emperor of France, or the Queen of England."

"Oh, sure, the royal summons! I suppose you were bored dining and dancing at the palaces, romping at the resorts, riding and hunting and yachting all over the Continent and the British Isles? Mere courtesy and protocol. And patronizing the restaurants, theaters, ballet, opera, and shops was just reciprocal trade, Mr. Goodwill Ambassador? And of course the mean old witch forced you to take her to Heathstone Manor!"

"More bribery," he insisted, frowning, "and persuasion that failed. She couldn't find a home in Europe to please her and decided that she wanted to live in England, after all. She thought a town house in London might be nice, and I almost bought one in Mayfair. Then she wanted to look at country estates and sea cottages. At Brighton, she finally told me that all she really wanted from me was a child and would release me when she became pregnant. I knew then I'd been played for a fool. As Barnum says, there's a sucker born every minute, and I was the champion of sucker husbands." Pausing, shuddering at the memory, gritting his teeth, he said, "I was angry enough to kill her that night."

"What did you do?"

"Well, I didn't oblige her in bed and try to make a baby, if that's what you think! I went to a pub, got royally drunk, and riddled a dart board. The next morning I booked return passage and hoped some catastrophe at sea would sink the ship. I doubt I'd have tried to save her. But with my luck she would probably have survived, if she'd had to swim a thousand miles and eat the sharks along the way."

"Poor darling—and this is the homecoming I gave you." Her fingers caressed his face, tracing the planes and angles; a leaner face than she remembered, more sardonic and embittered, and the intense gray eyes were smokier too. "You look tired, Keith, and you've lost weight."

"I've been through hell, Devon, and no wonder I frightened you. I must look like the devil."

"Oh no, darling! A little thinner and much tanner, as if you'd lived on deck, but handsome as ever."

"You're just prejudiced. Wait till you see me in bright sunlight. I have some new lines in my face and even some gray in my hair. I'm getting old, darling."

Her smile teased him. "Are you?"

"Well, not *that* old."

Their mouths fused in swift urgent hunger, trying to compensate for months of starvation in a few ravenous moments, before he swung her off her feet and headed for the bedroom. Devon knew well enough that she shouldn't let the thing happen between them again, that it would only make it harder to end the affair. Oh, God, could she ever really end it? She wanted the reunion as much as he, was as eager and desperate and lustful, unable to think of anything else until the first violent demanding passion was appeased. Then she lay languidly in his arms, lamenting her abandon and wishing she had been born cold-natured. Sensuality was a curse in a woman. And yet, according to Victoria Woodhull, the female sexual instinct was as strong and aggressive as the male, as natural and normal and vital, and were it granted the same freedom of expression, most of womankind's vague ailments, vapors and frustrations would subside and ultimately vanish in health and happiness, serenity and vitality.

Decanters of liquor and wine stood on the bedside table, and Devon suggested lighting the candle and having a drink.

"I don't need it now," Keith said. "The tension's gone."

"Have some brandy, anyway, darling. I'll take a little claret." While she fluffed the pillows against the headboard, he struck a match to the wax taper and then poured the drinks. They touched glasses in a silent toast, smiling intimately. Experience had taught her that disagreeable subjects were best broached under expedient conditions, such as the warmth and indulgence of sexual afterglow. "I have something to tell you, Keith."

"Unhuh?"

Fortifying herself with wine, she recited in a single breath, "I'm working now on a newspaper, the woman's page."

He gulped his brandy. "Which paper?"

"The New York *Record*."

"The *Record*? That's a Tammany tool."

Devon shrugged. "I don't care about its politics. Besides, the *World* and *Herald* and plenty of others support the Democrats. Just because you're a Republican—"

"That has nothing to do with it! I'd object if you were on the *Sun* or *Times* or *Tribune*, and you know it. Why did you do this behind my back, Devon? Wasn't I taking adequate care of you? And what about the baby?"

"Does he look mistreated? Anna and Enid are excellent nursemaids. I see him on weekends. When he's older, and the proper arrangements can be made, I'll bring him to town. But for now, he's better off in the country."

"While you pursue your silly ambition?"

"It's not silly."

"It is silly, Devon. Social reporter! What drivel. I want you to resign immediately."

She shook her head vehemently. "No, Keith! I want to work, I need to work. I can't just languish in the woods, like a parasitic growth on you!" The sheet fell away from her body; she clutched at it frantically, as if he'd never seen her naked before. "And this has to stop too, Keith. You know as well as I that we're never going to be married. What's the use beguiling ourselves? It can't be, that's all."

"It can and will be," he said doggedly. "It'll just take time, Devon."

"Time," she mocked. "How often you've said that, Keith. Meanwhile, our child is six months old and still nameless."

"I'll begin adoption proceedings immediately."

"Oh, no you won't! We've discussed that before, and I haven't changed my mind."

"I could take him, Devon."

"You'd better not try."

"Oh, darling, for God's sake! Do you honestly think I would? I'm just trying to reason with you. How did you get this damn job, anyway?"

"I applied, and Mr. Fitch hired me."

"Just like that?" he asked skeptically.

"Yes, just like that!" She snapped her fingers.

"What's your salary?"

"Twelve dollars a week."

"That much? My!" He whistled in apparent amazement at this stupendous sum, and then laughed. "And you expect to be independent on fifty dollars a month?"

"It's a start," she bristled, for it was actually high wages for a woman and more than many men earned. "I have to begin somewhere, and get some experience somehow."

"Why?" he demanded angrily. "I don't understand, Devon. If you must scribble, I should think the peace and quiet of the country would be the ideal atmosphere and inspiration. Write a novel, some poetry, any kind of book. I'll get it published if I have to buy a printing press."

"And what would that prove?"

"Why must you prove something, Devon? What is this mania, this panic to succeed? You're a mother. That should be career and success enough for any woman."

"I'm an unwed mother, Keith, supported by a married lover. A kept woman with a bastard child! No, it's not enough." Her hand trembled as she finished her claret. "And this liaison can't continue, because I'll get pregnant again—and you'll scream bloody murder at the idea of abortion. You can't expect me to bear an illegitimate family for you, Keith."

The linen slipped from her body again, but this time she ignored it. He stared at her bare breasts heaving in agitation, the pink nipples proudly puckered. "You've weaned my son," he said, "and now you want to castrate me."

"That's not true, Keith. I'm just afraid of another illicit pregnancy."

"We'll be more careful, Devon. Take extra precautions. I'll use condoms, and Dr. Blake can insert a pessary in you. It's a simple contraceptive device known for centuries in the Old World, ever since a clever Egyptian camel driver discovered that an intra-uterine apricot seed would prevent conception in female camels and prevent delays in the desert caravans."

"Oh, fine! So all I need is a fruit pit in my womb, and we can diddle without fear. That'll solve all our problems, won't it?" She laughed, a little hysterically. "May I have a choice between apricot, peach, plum, or cherry?"

"Hush," he muttered. "It's nothing so crude as that, but

an ingenious invention, similar to a gold collar-button or shirt stud, and no larger. Once every six months or so, the doctor checks its placement. Meanwhile, it's comfortable and effective and can be ignored."

"By whom?"

"Both of us."

"I'll think about it," she agreed to placate him.

"And you'll quit the paper and go back to the country?"

"No, Keith. I'm sorry."

"Goddammit, Devon! You torment me as much as she does, and buck me even more."

"Poor man. You do have your petticoat problems, don't you?"

"I'll get you fired," he threatened. "I know Sam Fitch. He's for sale—to Tammany and Wall Street and anyone else with the money to buy and influence to bribe him."

Her chin quivered. "If you do that to me, Keith, I'll never see or speak to you again. I mean it! And I won't starve or go ragged, either."

"Just what in hell does *that* mean?" His eyes glittered dangerously. "What've you been up to in my absence, Devon? Have you met a benefactor?"

Devon bit her tongue. Oh, Lord, if he'd found Sweeny's note! She must be more careful.

"Stop this inquisition, Keith. You don't own me, body and soul. I'm not accountable to you or anyone else for my every breath and thought and movement. Please try to understand, darling. I love you, but until we have a life together, I must have one of my own. And it's not just a matter of money or morality, either. Marriage and homemaking can absorb and content a woman, but I don't have these satisfactions—and I'll die emotionally without substitutes. I'll wither into a dead clinging vine! Is that what you want?"

"No, of course not," he said grimly. "But neither do I want to be considered a poisonous weed in your garden, interfering with the cultivation of your character. I get that impression sometimes, Devon. That you feel I've debauched as well as deflowered you, and precipitated you on that primrose path. You're not ruined, you know."

She forced a tremulous smile. "Society would disagree with you, lover. I'm a 'scarlet woman' deserving the big red A in the eyes of the pulpit."

"Rubbish."

"Did you think it was 'rubbish' when your wife was an adulteress?"

"That's different. She was married."

"Woodhull and Claflin call that marital rationale the single standard of the double-bed, tying the female partner to the post, while the male is free to explore other territory."

"They're whores," he said. "There's no comparison."

"Thank you, I think. And I can keep my job?"

"If I can keep you," he compromised, reluctantly. "You can't possibly manage on your meager wages, Devon."

She was as aware of her feminine handicaps as she was of his masculine need to support her and their child; denying him the privilege of fiscal responsibility would be tantamount to mutilation, and she had no wish to destroy his manhood.

"I know," she conceded, laying her head on his strong hard shoulder. "I need you in many ways, Keith. This is just one of them. I couldn't function as a woman without you."

"Hey now, don't cry, darling! I almost forgot something." Reaching under the bed, he produced a velvet jeweler's box. "A little belated birthday gift, my love."

It was an exquisite diamond and topaz parure: necklace, bracelet, earrings, brooch. "Little?" she cried. "It's fabulous, Keith! They look like crown jewels."

"And so they were, in the collection of Louis XV's Queen Maria. I bought them at auction in Paris." He fastened the necklace about her throat, while she donned the ear and arm pieces. "There now, you're not naked any more. Too bad I can't pin the brooch on your breast."

"Oh, you rogue! Are you sure these belonged to Queen Maria, and not Madame Du Barry or de Pompadour?" she asked, and he grinned at the allusion. "Did you meet Napoleon's mistress at the Tuileries, Keith?"

"Which one?"

"The Comtesse de Castiologne."

"I danced with her."

"Is she as beautiful as they say?"

"Yes, and Napoleon is wild about her and insanely jealous of her. To flirt with La Castiologne is to risk the Bastille and guillotine. I narrowly missed execution." She pushed him away petulantly, and he laughed and caught her to him. "Is that the thanks I get for the present?"

"You want appreciation, Mr. Curtis? Well now, how much did the jewels cost you?"

"Thousands, and you're worth every penny."

Suddenly, in the midst of laughing, teasing, playing, Devon sobered and sighed. "How wicked we are, Keith, behaving this way, making love with this fortune on me! We'll be punished. Wait, I'll take them off—oh, darling, darling. . . ."

Chapter 35

One mild autumn evening they drove out to an old inn Keith knew in Yorkville, where his family had once owned a country estate and where he had ridden and hunted in his youth. Built of stone and hoary timbers, the tavern predated the Revolution, and was still a stage station for villages on the Boston Post Road. The host, a descendant of the original British proprietor, served the best kidney pie, roast beef, and Yorkshire pudding in New England, as well as Keith's favorite Beef Wellington. The taproom, decorated with ancient armor and shields, featured imported ale. Devon had enjoyed the long ride under the harvest moon, round and bright as a ripe pumpkin, and the excellent food, although Keith seemed seriously preoccupied.

After supper, driving leisurely back to town, he suddenly pulled the chaise off the Post Road onto a wooded winding lane to the East River, familiar to him in boyhood. At that section of the island, a sheer rock precipice overhung the river. From its precarious heights to the northeast, Hell Gate was visible, a narrow treacherous channel of dangerous rocks and tidal currents, the despair of navigators and the doom of countless vessels. Directly across was Long Island and between, casting dark shadows on the silver water, lay the grim institutional buildings of Blackwell's Island: the county penitentiary, the charity homes and hospitals, and pesthouses. Far below, the myriad lights of Manhattan gleamed and twinkled.

Thinking that he merely wanted to show her the spectacular view, which she had never seen from this vantage at night, Devon said, "It's beautiful, Keith. The town looks like a gigantic Christmas tree aglow with candles."

He did not answer. Throughout the evening his mood had been somber and contemplative; now it was grave, desperate, omnious. Abruptly he said, "I've decided to resort to fraud to get a divorce, Devon."

"Fraud?"

He nodded, his face saturnine, his eyes glowing like the Hell Gate danger beacon. "It's a fairly common practice in situations like mine. I'll spare you the ugly details."

"No, you won't spare me, Keith. I want to know."

"Well, there are people who specialize in obtaining the kind of evidence necessary in this state. I intend to hire some and let them set it up."

"Set *what* up, Keith? Tell me!"

Her journalistic curiosity and persistence annoyed him. He scowled. "False adultery evidence, Devon!"

"And just how do you propose to arrange it?"

"That should be easy enough, considering her vanity and eagerness for reconciliation. I'll invite her to accompany me on a business trip. We'll register at a hotel, and while I'm out the plant across the hall will enter with a duplicate key, pretending to be intoxicated and in the wrong room. I'll return on cue and find him there. She'll realize she was tricked, but there'll be a witness—and she won't dare fight it in court. The alternative will be to divorce me. You get the idea?"

"I do, and it's reprehensible, Keith! I will not conspire in such sordid intrigue."

"You won't be involved, Devon."

"How can you say that? I *am* involved, Keith, directly and indirectly. And if trickery fails, then what? Murder?"

"No, of course not! Do you think I'd implicate you in a crime ... leave such a legacy to my son? That I want to hang or rot in prison? Her parents still hold that sealed incriminatory statement. She denies its existence now, but I'm sure she's lying, and any fatal accident or violence to her person could convict me, regardless of who was guilty—" His hands toyed with the whip, twisting the rawhide into a noose, flicking it restively against the dashboard, finally snapping the handle violently over his knee. "I don't know what in hell to do, Devon! Maybe I should remove myself from the picture—jump off this cliff and let the river solve the problem—"

His anguish was genuine and intense. She knew she had to help him somehow, soothe him some way, and she could think of only one effective, if temporary, alleviation. "Why don't you make love to me instead?"

"Here, now?"

"Isn't it possible in a carriage?"

"Possible, but not practical. I may disappoint you."

"I'll make allowances."

"We could get a room at the inn for tonight."

"I'd love to, darling. But I have an early assignment tomorrow."

"Damn that job! Sometimes I think it's more important to you than me or the baby or anything else in the world."

"That's absurd, Keith, and you know it."

"But you'll admit it interferes with our relationship and causes unnecessary friction. It's difficult to plan our lives to suit the *Record*! I'd buy it and fire you, but you'd probably just go to another paper, and I can't buy them all."

"Such tyranny." She smiled, caressing his face. "Let's not quarrel, darling. That's exactly what she'd want."

"I know, and I'm sorry. It's just that it all seems so hopeless and futile, Devon."

"Love will find a way," she said.

"Ways like this?"

"Lovers can't be choosers."

"That's beggars."

"Well?"

He clung to her, his face in her hair, mouth and hands seeking, finding, possessing. "I need you, Devon."

"I'm here, Keith. I'm here. . . ."

The next evening, on the way to his tobacconist to pick up the special mixture of Latakia he smoked in his pipe, Keith sensed that he was being followed. The man, inconspicuously dressed and transported, stayed at a discreet distance, and appeared to be merely taking the air. He drove nonchalantly past the shop where Keith stopped, and was out of sight when he emerged. But a few minutes later, he was again lagging behind. Keith returned to Gramercy Park. The dark rig turned off a block shy of the house, and disappeared.

Coincidence, perhaps, but he had to be sure. A deliberate test the following night convinced him, for soon the stranger was trailing him—a dark-garbed horseman this time with a slouch hat shielding his face, his black mount clopping leisurely behind Keith's cabriolet. There was no mystery. Contrary to his warnings and her promises, Esther had hired a detective. Having long ago put the cuckold's horns on him, the cunning bitch had now added a tail.

He drove to the nearest telegraph station and sent a message to Rhinelander Gardens, asking Devon to come to the bank at her earliest convenience. She came the next day, and his secretary, a small bald man with a busy air, showed her into his office. It was a suite of large impressive chambers, paneled in teakwood, richly furnished but not at the expense of dignity or comfort. Above the black marble fireplace hung a portrait of Keith's great grandfather, Cameron Curtis, founder of the Curtis Countinghouse. She met his distinguished father and grandfather, Angus Curtis, on other walls, and visualized his own image and that of his son in the vacant spaces.

"I got your message," she said.

"I had to send it, Devon." His voice was low and guarded, although the thick walls blocked sound, and his secretary, who had also served his father, was perfectly trustworthy. "There's a new development. I'm being followed."

"Are you sure?"

"Positive."

"Then the other night—" She paused, mortified to think some stranger had been in the shadows, listening and watching, witnessing their intimate act.

But he reassured her. "No, he wasn't there, Devon. He's not a very smooth operator. Not Pinkerton quality, anyway, because they don't take such domestic cases."

"But don't you suppose he's watching the bank now?"

"I haven't noticed him on the premises and don't think he'd dare. This is private property and under constant surveillance by my own security agents, who are a hell of a lot sharper than this character. I suspect he's in the vicinity, however, to record my activities off Wall Street. But since neither of them know you, Devon, he must still *cherchez la femme*."

Devon sighed wearily, discouraged, defeated. "Why is she doing this, Keith? What does she want? Not evidence for divorce, so what?"

"To know your identity, of course. To threaten and intimidate you with exposure and scandal, and frighten you out of my life. To break us up, what else! Now do you think collusion on my part would be such a terrible solution?"

"Wrong never makes right, Keith."

"And what can't be cured must be endured? If you have more than axioms to offer, my dear, I'd like to hear it."

She shook her head, wordlessly.

"I'm sure I could buy him off, Devon, but she might hire someone more efficient."

"Perhaps we should stop seeing each other for awhile, Keith."

"That's what she wants, Devon."

"Well, what's the alternative?"

"This," he said, "as a temporary expedient."

"And lock ourselves in the vault?"

"Hardly. Money is not a very buoyant bed." Gesturing toward the large soft leather couch, "I think that would be more comfortable, darling. As you said, love will find a way."

She stared at him in astonishment, unable to believe he was serious. "During business hours, with your secretary in the anteroom!"

"Don't worry about that," he said. "Mr. Stacy is a permanent fixture, slightly deaf, partially blind, and completely loyal. In thirty years with Father, he never once betrayed a confidence. But why should he even suspect? This is a bank, open to the public. You have every right to come here, Devon."

"Whenever you send for me? I have a job, Keith! I can't obey your sexual summons like some strumpet on assignation! I'm supposed to be covering a tea on Fifth Avenue right now—"

"The bloody *Record* again! Always your goddamn career to consider first! And naturally a Fifth Avenue tea is of paramount importance. Well, don't let me detain you, Miss Marshall."

"If you talk that way, I'll cry—and what will your secretary think then, Mr. Curtis?"

"That I foreclosed your mortgage," he muttered, opening the cellaret, extracting a decanter of Scotch and a hobnail glass. "Some Madeira or Montrachet for you?"

"I'd better not."

"No, it wouldn't do to go to tea with wine on your breath, would it? Mrs. Prude and Mrs. Puritan might object and blackball you from future events. Run along, Devon. Mustn't keep the social martinets of Manhattan waiting."

"Will you come to the country this weekend?"

"If I can escape my shadow."

"You're angry," she accused.

"No, just disappointed."

"If it's any consolation, darling, so am I." And with a significant glance at the couch and a blown kiss, she left.

They were not long inconvenienced, however, for Keith soon devised devious strategies. The simplest was to go to one of his clubs, stay an hour or so, then slip out the back and hail a cab to Greenwich Village. When Sleuth suspected this trick and took up vigilance at the rear of the buildings, Subject escaped via a side or front entrance, alternating clubs and exits, until Sleuth was too confused to know where to post himself. Other members, becoming suspicious of their wives, resorted to similar stratagems, aiding and abetting one another, so that occasionally Curtis' hound took off after the wrong man, providing additional sport and amusement for all, plus an extra fillip to their love affairs; they joked and laughed about it over their liquor and cards and conspired in jovial camaraderie.

Keith practiced his ploys at restaurants, theaters, concerts, lectures, casinos, and even arranged with Josephine Woods to enter and depart her establishment in similar fashion, pleased to imagine Esther's reaction when she read these particular episodes in the dossier. And the fellow who spent his weekends in the country was never tailed at all, for he traveled incognito, mustached or bearded, or both, sometimes wearing spectacles or pince-nez or a monocle, sometimes with an arm in a sling or limping on a cane. The disguises amused him, none more than the villain image with black waxed handlebar mustache and long black cape, and he was constantly devising new ones. Baffling his pursuer delighted him as much as if he were a youngster eluding a truant officer.

"I'm leading the poor bastard a merry chase! He's confused as a rat in a maze, and his client must be equally frustrated by his reports. Next week I'll rent a scull and sail up here if the weather serves. So expect a seedy seaman in peajacket, striped jersey, and black eye-patch."

Devon smiled over her notebook. "Are you having fun playing games, darling?"

He had brought the baby a jumping jack and was operating it for him, while Scotty chuckled and reached out for it, squealing with delight each time the bright object popped up from the box. "You've been scribbling for an hour, Devon. Deadlines?"

"No, I've begun a series on the Five Points missions. I hope to convince Mr. Fitch that I have some versatility, and can also do general reporting and features."

"You've been going to Five Points?"

"Just to the various missions," she said, "including the House of Industry."

"Jesus Christ, Devon! Do you want to get yourself killed? Robbed and raped, at the least?"

"I haven't been bothered, Keith. I wear the *Record*'s badge, and the people there respect the press, especially when they think it's trying to help them better their lives. And when word reached precinct headquarters, I was given a police escort. Also, the ward master sent a welcoming committee."

"Don't you mean ward heeler? That's Tammany territory!"

She shrugged. "The whole town is Tammany territory, Keith. Aren't their men in City Hall, and the Capitol at Albany? But the Republicans are in the White House and shouldn't begrudge the Democrats their city and state victories. I despise Grant and predict he'll be a sorry president. He's not intelligent enough for such a position. General Lee was his mental superior in every way, far more brilliant and a greater soldier too; he was overwhelmed by material strength, not military prowess. Grant was elected on his war record, but battle heroes are not necessarily civil giants or geniuses. Leading an army and leading a country are two different things."

A mocking grin twisted his mouth. "Thank you, Miss Marshall, for that enlightened observation. I, of course, wasn't aware of any of that. Nor will your clever digression deter discussion of the issue at hand. Who arranged this Five Points tour for you? I know the *Record* supports Tammany, but a ward heeler's welcome suggests orders from one of the sachems. It could also explain your safe conduct in the most notorious milieu in Manhattan. Nobody would dare harm or molest anyone under the protection of the ruby-eyed tiger! Is that the case? Did Fitch ask Tweed's henchmen to provide security for you?"

What could she say? That she was under the aegis of Peter Barr Sweeny? "I don't know. Perhaps. But this isn't an assignment, Keith. I'm doing it on my own, and it has nothing to do with politics. It's human interest."

His eyes rested on her long and intently. "Everything in Five Points has to do with politics, Devon. And don't you think the poor and oppressed of this town have been written about before?"

"Does the Chamber of Commerce admit that poverty and oppression do exist in this fair city, and that human misery is commercialized, exploited as a profitable commodity?"

"Answer my question."

"Which one? Yes, I know the district has been described before, many times, and by some famous writers, including Washington Irving and Charles Dickens. But not from the feminine viewpoint, and I've met some women willing to talk frankly about subjects they wouldn't readily discuss with a male reporter."

"Prostitutes?"

"A few. They came forth voluntarily when they learned a female journalist was in the area. But mostly my sources are wives and mothers of large families living under some of the most deplorable conditions imaginable, worse than Hogarth's London, and factory girls working harder than any slave ever did on a Southern plantation! Have you ever actually been there, Keith?"

"Not in the gutters and sewers of Murderers' Alley or Cow Bay, or the dens and dives of the underground! Nor has any other respectable and rational citizen. And so now, in addition to advocating female suffrage and social reform, you're going to crusade against crime and sin and vice?" He smiled indulgently. "That's all very noble and courageous, darling, but also naive and foolhardy. And you're probably working for nothing. I doubt that Fitch will oblige or humor you in print."

He was right, but Devon did not realize it until after she had expended considerable time and energy on the project. She turned out a five-part series that would have done credit to any journal interested in humanity, and Mrs. Hempstead lauded it, saying she had not suspected such perception and depth in her. "How do you think it'll affect Mr. Fitch?"

"Like a cold enema," replied the candid Carrie.

"You don't think he'll approve it?"

"I'm afraid not, Devon."

"But *why*, Carrie?"

"Several reasons. Your sex, for one, and the fact that no male reporter on the staff could have done better. But primarily because you tread on some Tammany toes when you hint, however vaguely, that the law is lax in the slums and crime and vice are either tolerated or ignored, and even assisted. That smacks of political corruption. They control the sheriff and police departments, you know, including the officers of the ward precincts. You'd have stood a better chance at print had you stuck with your original theme, and concentrated on the missions and missionaries—the good rather than bad aspects of the community."

Devon sighed. "They're related, Carrie, interrelated, and almost inseparable. One is the natural enemy or victim of the other, and victims predominate. The strong always prey on the weak where jungle law prevails. Barefoot children eating out of garbage cans make willing thugs and thieves. Girls forced into prostitution at puberty accept it as a way of life and survival. Not one child in twenty goes to school, and half of them can't even speak English. There are sweatshops paying fifty cents a day for fourteen hours of labor, part of which must be kicked back to the supervisor, and some girls sacrifice more than money to hold their jobs. Streetwalkers have to pick their customers' pockets in order to pay their panderers and brothelkeepers, and the police, or they're threatened with arrest and violence. And what goes on in the subterranean hives! Dear God! One source told me that hundreds of men, women, and children lived together in semi-darkness, without fresh air or sanitation, sleeping on bags of rotten rags and straw, or the bare floor, worse than animals in cages. Mothers and daughters prostitute themselves to the same men, little children are sexually molested and abused, and some fathers use their daughters incestuously—"

"I know, dear. It's all in your articles, which would create a sensation even under a male byline. But you also found some good things, Devon."

"Not enough to outweigh the bad, Carrie, or even approach a balance. The missionary work is marvelous, of course. And the philanthropists contribute generously, many anonymously. At least there's an orphanage and a hospital, and the House of Industry provides manual training and incentive for a few lucky people to find better jobs and eventually leave Five Points. It's something, a little help, but it barely scratches the surface of that civic cancer, and certainly doesn't cure it, or alleviate its suffering. Because the trouble, the fault, is in the basic structure of a society that can breed and foster such a malignancy in the first place, with so little effect on community conscience. Contrast those wretched tenements with the mansions of Fifth Avenue, Washington and Madison Squares, Murray Hill and Gramercy Park! Small wonder that most of the epidemics germinate in that cesspool. It's a plague on the whole town."

Gathering up her story, Devon took it to the city editor. It lay on his desk for days, unread because it was unauthorized. He did not, however, reject it summarily, but passed it on, sans comment, to his boss. Samuel Fitch finally read it and summoned her to his office.

"Has your friend in City Hall seen this?" he asked.

"Mr. Sweeny? Why no, sir, why should he?"

"I don't think he'd like it, Miss Marshall."

She realized she was gaping in bewilderment. "I don't even mention Tammany Hall, Mr. Fitch!"

"Only by inference." he drawled. "Mrs. Hempstead gave me to understand you were interested in the sunshine, not the shadows, of that slimy sump."

"What sunshine? It's all shadows and slime."

He whacked the sheets of foolscap. "Nevertheless, this won't do, Miss Marshall! It's out of your realm, your category. Stick to women's stuff, to frou-frou, bon mots and bagatelles. Don't try to push any part of this through, because it'll be promptly killed. What kind of heading is that, anyway? MISSIONS IN HELL? Holy God, I never knew you had it in you!" A wave of his hand dismissed her. "You might catch Victoria Woodhull's lecture at Cooper Union tomorrow, and see if you can put enough antidote in that serpent's poison to make it harmless. She has a forked tongue, and needs her fangs milked and pulled."

"Yes, sir."

Devon was abashed, devastated. All that work! And it was good, Carrie said so, and she knew it herself. She hadn't studied under her father without learning anything; he would have approved that series, and printed it, possibly editing out some of the harsh realism, separating the wheat from the chaff, but the hard kernel of truth would have remained.

She filed the articles in a drawer of her desk and sat gazing morosely out the window at City Hall Park and the massive marble building, its finial a figure of Justice. Despite his proximity to the *Record*, Sweeney had never intruded on her there. Sometimes she glimpsed him, and Dick Connolly and the elegant Oakey, on the way to and from their offices. And once she had met Sweeny while strolling across the park, and they had stood chatting by the fountain, while he tossed popcorn to the pigeons. His black eyes had peered at her hungrily, fastening on her mouth, and Devon blushed, remembering his ardent embrace in Josie Mansfield's garden. When he again invited her to tour Tammany with him, she dimpled and dissembled. "Just as soon as I can vote, Pete." He had laughed, squeezed her hand, said seeing her had brightened his day, and that he still meant what he had told her at the ball. She was tempted now to test his friendship and influence with her Five Points story—his approval would sway Mr. Fitch—but resisted in fear of Keith.

Carrie tried to console and cheer her. "There's an interesting assignment coming up in January, dear, and an even more important one in March. Would you like to cover the inaugural social affairs in Albany and Washington?"

Her spirits revived. "Oh, yes, Carrie! Do you think the ogre'd let me?"

"I'll insist on the woman's angle in the entertainment and fashions, and I'm sure you could do justice to both."

"What about Tish? Doesn't she want to go?"

"Not particularly. She's getting married."

"Oh? I didn't know she was serious about that fellow she's been going with."

"She isn't, really. But Tish's thirty-three now, and afraid she might never have another opportunity. That's not much of a reason to marry a man one doesn't love, but it's amazing how many women do so, even emancipated ones like Tish. As if there were some stigma or disgrace attached to celibacy."

"Well," said Devon, "I hope she'll be happy."

"Don't we all? Unfortunately, the Holy Grail so many of us seek in matrimony often evolves as a chamberpot."

Chapter 36

Excited over her prospective assignments in the state and national capitals, Devon was preparing herself with historic facts and interesting anecdotes, precedents, and protocol. And all was joy and enthusiasm until she learned that the Curtises were on the guest list of the President and First Lady. She should have realized this herself, before confirmation by the Associated Press, when the Washington correspondents began speculating on the cabinet appointments, and the name of Keith Curtis loomed as one of the three potentials for secretary of the treasury, the others being Manhattan merchant A. T. Stewart and Philadelphia banker Jay Cooke. The trio, all of whom represented tremendous wealth and monetary experience, had been generous contributors to General Grant's election campaign. Cooke and Curtis had also acted as financial advisers to President Lincoln, floating huge loans to help support the war effort. Devon had discovered this data in the *Record*'s files and library, along with information that Keith had declined several ambassadorships during Lincoln's administration because of his wife's health. But when she asked him point-blank about the current rumors and speculations, he denied having been approached by the President-elect or any of his representatives in that capacity and assured her he would not consider or accept any such offers.

"But why not, Keith? It would be a great honor."

He shrugged, glancing away. "I'd have to divest myself of my banking, oil, and other commercial interests—ostensibly, at least—and I don't propose to do so. Cabinet posts are generally thankless and temporary, anyway, and I'm not interested. Nor in any other kind of government service, either."

Sensing rationalization, her journalistic mind probed.

"That's not quite true, is it? I think you are interested, Keith, and would like to accept."

"Well, if you're interviewing me, Miss Marshall, you should be aware of the Senate investigation necessary to confirm a cabinet appointment. And while I believe my honesty and capability are sufficient and unimpeachable—" He hesitated, and her face flamed at the allusion.

"You mean your honor and integrity wouldn't pass muster, because of us?"

Now he was striding the floor, hands jammed deep into his trouser pockets. "As a newswoman, I assume you know the answer to that! There are ferrets in your profession who specialize in exhuming and dissecting skeletons for the benefit of gossip mongers. Such scandal is potent ammunition for character assassins, and there wouldn't be anything either of us could do about it. You'd be crucified on the cross of convention."

"The wages of sin," she lamented. "There's a moral accounting, after all, isn't there? And a penalty. You're paying it now, Keith, and it's a high one. The opportunity for a distinguished place in history, perhaps even immortality, lost to you forever, sacrificed on the altar of adultery."

Her dramatic moralization elicited a rueful smile. "Strange you should use that word, Devon, rather than love, and even equate it with lust. What happened to your romantic illusions? Have you buried them in the ruthless realism of your career?"

How cynical and disillusioned he sounded! "No, I just feel I've deprived you of some greatness, Keith. Diminished you in some respects, as a man and a person. That our illicit love has lessened and betrayed us both."

"I don't feel either diminished or betrayed that way, Devon. Deprived, yes—but not of greatness or glory, to which I've never seriously aspired. Deprived only of you and my son. And peace and happiness. Contentment."

"Mutual deprivations," she assured him. "Naturally you'll go to the inauguration."

"Naturally. You should know, Devon, that in this country a presidential invitation is tantamount to a command."

Her next inquiry was reluctantly forced, "Will she accompany you?"

"Wild horses couldn't stop her," he muttered. "She's already assembling her wardrobe."

Devon chewed her lip. "How does she feel about a possible cabinet position?"

"I haven't discussed it with her in detail," he said. "But she'd like it fine, as well as an ambassadorship to England or France. Anyplace where she could shine as hostess."

"I suppose you'll stay at your suite in the Clairmont."

"I suppose," he nodded. "And you?"

"Wherever the press is housed," she replied. "The *Record* will make the reservations and pay my expenses." But her pretense at nonchalance failed, and feminine petulance emerged. "I shall ignore her presence in my social reports."

"That's your prerogative, my dear, although I doubt your colleagues will ignore her."

"Oh, Keith! I know I sound like a jealous wretch, but I'm not sure I can bear seeing you together in public. Dancing at the Inaugural Ball and—"

"Do you think I'm happy about it, Devon? Or that I want you there as a reporter? And worse yet, in Albany in January, where I won't be at all?"

"It's my job, Keith."

"Let them send someone else!"

"There's no one else to send," she said. "Tish Lambeth got married recently, and is probably already pregnant. Mrs. Hempstead can't go herself, because she's the woman's page editor and has a crippled boy who needs her care at night. There are only three of us on the staff. I simply can't let them down."

"But you can let me down?"

"That's not fair!"

"Then we'll just have to endure the ordeal, won't we?"

"You could go to Albany," she suggested tentatively, "even if you didn't attend the political functions."

"And do what instead? Wait in a hotel room for you to come off the Democratic circuit? No, thanks. That'll be a Wigwam powwow, anyway. Let the braves hail their new state chief." He picked up his hat and gloves.

"You're not leaving!"

"I think I'd better, Devon, before this gets out of hand, and we say things we'll regret later."

"But you just got here!" she protested. "And I wanted to fix dinner for you."

"I'll dine at my club."

Her eyes moistened. "No goodbye kiss even?"

He smiled wryly. "It won't work every time, Devon."

"What won't?"

"Tears, kisses, sex. Isn't that how we usually resolve our differences and grievances?"

"When will I see you again?"

"I'll be in the country Sunday. Perhaps then, if you're not too busy and involved." His gesture took in her research, the papers, and notebooks.

Devon started toward him, but his hand was on the doorknob. "Sunday," she agreed. "We'll put up a tree for the baby. Will you spend the Christmas holidays with us, or her?"

"Does it matter?"

She stared at him, abashed, eyes glistening, then turned and walked away. He waited several long hesitant moments, remorseful and indecisive, before following her.

"Go away," she sobbed. "To your damn club, or whatever!"

"Don't cry, darling. Please. I'm sorry." He heaved a heavy sigh, shaking his head, feeling himself weaken. "Oh, God! I guess it does work every time, after all."

The newswomen—a mere handful—kept to themselves in the parlor car on the Albany-bound train, chatting and sipping hot tea. Frost sparkled like granulated sugar on the pine woods through which they passed and glazed the roofs and fretwork of the gingerbread houses. The bleak slate sky was almost the color of Hudson bluestone, and it was chilly in the coach even with the coal stove glowing cherry-red. Devon was warmed by Keith's Christmas gift, a sable-lined cloak and muff and toque, which made her the fashion equal of Kate Field in chinchilla and Frank Leslie's Minnie Squier in mink. All Manhattan journalism was aware of the romantic rumors concerning the attractive Minnie and her employer, both married, but respected the tacit gentlemen's agreement regarding its own members.

Aboard the same news caravan, one of many converging on the state capital to witness the inauguration of Tammany's triumphant governor, John T. Hoffman, were numerous male journalists including the *Record*'s Jack Hiller, boisterously entertaining themselves in the smoker with liquor, cigars, cards, and jokes. Hiller, assigned to the political aspects, resented Miss Marshall's access to the social functions that precluded him, particularly the scheduled private party of State Senator Willaim Marcy Tweed. Her inclusion could only have been sanctioned by one of the Wigwam sachems, possibly the top totem himself, although office scuttlebutt hinted that it was Squire Sweeny.

Detecting her champion at the governor's ball was difficult, however, for Devon concentrated on her business, and did not even join in the cotillion, as did some of the ladies of the press. Nor was the fact that she was quartered at the same hotel conclusive, since the fashionable Delevan House was headquarers for all the discriminating distaff correspondents.

Here, in a sumptuous suite fit for a potentate, the Boss lived and held court during legislative sessions. Here he received his constituents and petitioners and dispensed or denied his favors, entertained his colleagues and cronies, consulted his confidants and cohorts, and devised and executed his political plots and schemes. His sybaritic bedchamber, hung with crimson and gold and featuring an enormous canopied bed, was strictly private, but the other six rooms were handsomely equipped for business and entertainment. The massive mahogany sideboards were burdened with silver, crystal, and cut-glass decanters of exotic liquors, including Holland gin and Jamaica rum, French brandy and Scotch and Irish whisky; and a fabulous feast was spread on the banquet tables. There were steel engravings on the walls, and vases of fresh flowers, potted plants, and canaries in decorative cages. The porcelain cuspidors, painted with roses and gilt, were strategically placed to protect the luxurious carpets. No one who was not expected could get past the vigilant guards at the doors. Miss Marshall's open sesame, presented on her earlier arrival at the Delevan House, was initialed by the squire, and declining it would have offended the man responsible for her being there in the first place. But she intended merely to make a courtesty appearance, and not to linger or engage in any friendly familiarity.

"How nice to see you again," Sweeny welcomed her. His stature seemed to expand visibly at sight of her, his inherently sullen countenance to automatically brighten, and his natural reticence to disappear.

Devon smiled, letting him hold her hand briefly. "But I'm not sure why I'm here, Pete, if not to report this for the *Record*. Can't I even mention it in my dispatches? It seems like a lovely party."

"But private, my dear. Just enjoy yourself, and forget work for this evening. It's pleasure time. Can I get you something? Punch, champagne, caviar, oysters?"

"Just punch, please."

As at all of Tweed's receptions, politicians predominated. Women were a novelty, usually mistresses, entertainers, and ladies of pleasure. Wives, except on state occasions and in rare cases of individual obstinacy, were left at home to tend the hearth and family. Mrs. Hoffman, however, attended with the governor, along with the Horatio Seymours who had lost their bid for the White House, and Congressman Johnny Morrissey and his lovely wife Susie, up from Washington to pay their respects and insure the continued smooth operation of his Saratoga casino.

But the only familiar female face Devon saw was that of Josephine Mansfield with the flamboyant James Fisk. Josie affected demureness this evening, in dark flowing silk with masses of Valenciennes lace, her only jewelry a simple gold cross. Men feasted on her voluptuous femininity like bees on nectar, fascinated by her deep dark mysterious eyes and amorous smile. She was party to many masculine secrets, intrigues, alliances, and numerous business and political deals had been consummated in her Manhattan menage. But not even her quixotic lover suspected the true depth of her sensuality and passion for life, nor that she actually lived in fear of ultimately betraying him. Like Victoria Woodhull, Josephine Mansfield possessed a visible aura of celebrity and notoriety, and Devon could visualize her creating sensational and perhaps scandalous headlines.

Once, while the politicians were temporarily diverted in a spontaneous caucus, Miss Mansfield came to chat with her, to ask where she'd been and why she hadn't accompanied Sweeny to her last dinner party. Devon blushed and almost stammered, "Oh, it's not serious with us, Josie. We're just friends. Mr. Sweeny was kind enough to help me get on with the *Record*, and that's why I'm in Albany now. On assignment."

"But surely you realize how he feels about you? Your

presence literally transforms him—he's a different person around you. And you could do worse than the squire romantically, believe me. He has wealth, power, influence, and an absolutely brilliant mind. Tammany picks his legal brains, and Tweed won't make a legislative move without consulting him. He's here now to scan some new bills about to be introduced in both houses, one affecting the Erie Railroad and some other Fisk-Gould interests, which accounts for Jay's presence here this evening, for he's really a Republican, you know, as Jim is basically. But Tweed and Sweeny are on Erie's directorate, which is known as expedient back-scratching. I think that's what the impromptu cloakroom smoker is about now. Did you cover Mrs. Hoffman's tea for the press ladies?"

"Yes, it was delightful. She showed us through the executive mansion, and gave me an exclusive interview."

"Naturally," said Josie with a wink of her long lustrous lashes. "Look who introduced you! I'm anxious to read it, and hope you'll cover the opening of the Grand Opera House next month. We'll have Toastee and her company for the premiere, and then Irma—and other great and glamorous stars that will make the Academy of Music green with envy." She chuckled pleasedly, anticipating herself in the glittering galaxy. "You can interview all of them, darling, starting with me. I presume you're also the *Record*'s drama critic?"

"Well, the woman's page is a mixed bag, including a little of everything. Press potpourri."

"Or ragout?" Josie punned, and they both laughed. "Don't forget now, Devon. You'll have a reserved seat opening night. Oh, Lord, there's that obnoxious Bowery Boy who warted you at my masquerade . . . excuse me, won't you?"

Donahue, who had been huddling with his old Saratoga gambling partner Morrissey, moved in during Sweeny's absence. "Sure now, it's the Southern bird of paradise, all decked out in velvet and sable! I take it the Tammany Tiger has bested the Wall Street Wolf?"

Devon sipped her punch, uncommunicative, noticing that his lapel still lacked the coveted Americus Club emblem, indicating his failure to deliver his quota of votes in the past election, and his continued trial. "Shall I quote you, Mr. Donahue?"

"Quote? Isn't this affair off the record?" Suddenly comprehending, he grinned gingerly. "Oh, I see. Sweeny's the *Record*, right, and its unofficial censor?"

"You might ask him that question, sir. Here he comes now." But Donahue only bowed sheepishly, and backed off.

"Enjoying yourself, my dear?"

"So much I wish I could stay longer," Devon said, "But I must get some sleep. I'm taking an early train home tomorrow."

His disappointment was obvious. "Must you, Devon? I can fix it with Fitch. Stay a few days, and let me entertain you."

"I have other assignments waiting, Pete."

The crease between his dark craggy brows deepened. "And I'll be tied up here another week or so, on business." He insisted on escorting her to her room, however, which was on the same floor as his own suite, although Devon preferred to believe this was coincidence rather than contrivance with the hotel management. "I'm just down the corridor," he said at her door. "May I come in a few minutes?"

"Oh, Pete, I don't think—"

"Just to say good night, Devon. Please?" He had taken her key and was inserting it into the lock. The chambermaid had thoughtfully left a lamp burning, and he turned the jet down to a glimmer and drew her into his arms. Devon did not resist but responded to his kiss, parting her lips, surprised at her cooperation, astonished at the desire his eager probing mouth and caressing hands aroused in her, and embarrassed by it. Sweeny held her gently away from him, his own face darkly flushed, his black eyes glittering carnally. "I don't suppose—"

She shook her head negatively.

"That's not what your lips say."

"My lips need discipline. My body needs discipline. I'm ashamed of myself, Pete."

"I think you love me, Devon. A little, anyway."

"No, Pete. I just have this terrible weakness, this awful need and drive—"

"There's nothing terrible or awful about it," he said. "On the contrary, it's rather rare and wonderful. I love you, Devon. You know that. I've thought about you so often these past months, hoping you would get in touch with me. We are so near, just across City Hall Park, and yet so far apart. Oh, God, I want you so much now, I'm half crazy!"

"There's someone else, Pete."

"Who? That Bowery bastard? I'll kill him!"

"It's not Donahue."

"Fitch?"

"Nor him, either."

"You love this man, Devon?"

She nodded miserably. "But he's married."

"It's always that way," he muttered. "You find someone you really want, and there're obstacles and barriers. Marriage, family, religion. I'm Catholic."

Devon was trembling. "You'd better go, Pete."

"Darling— Oh, goddamn it all! Do you know the real irony of this, Devon? I don't have anything I really want in life, except money."

"Well, I don't even have that, Pete."

"You could, Devon. There's nothing I wouldn't give you."

"You'd better leave, Pete."

"May I see you in New York?"

"It wouldn't help either of us," she said, "and I don't want to hurt you."

"I'm hurting now, and it's the devil's torment."

"I'm sorry, Pete. Forgive my impetuous affection. I'm afraid it misled you. Good night."

He nodded and kissed her quickly before opening the door. "Pleasant dreams, darling. I expect hellish nightmares."

When he had gone Devon stood with her back braced against the door, still shaking. Dear God, what was wrong with her? Loving one man with her whole being, she had yet responded sexually to another. Out of frustration, despair, hopelessness, what? Not pyhsical attraction, surely, for Pete did not strongly appeal to her. Did she imagine, somewhere in her desperate conscience, that infidelity to Keith would automatically sever her moorings to him, scuttle the precarious vessel they were sailing together, and launch her on a separate course, detached, independent, uninvolved? And would it, in effect? Was it perhaps the essential release, the ultimate escape, the true finality? She was tempted to experiment, tempted, tempted. . . .

She returned to New York feeling as guilty as if she had actually yielded to the tempation, succumbed in flesh as well as spirit. Mrs. Hempstead praised her reports, and even Mr. Fitch paid her some gratifying compliments.

"You seem to have a knack for this sort of thing," he said. "Think you'll do as well in Washington?"

"I hope so, sir."

"Would you believe we had some requests from other papers to reprint your interview with Mrs. Hoffman? Perhaps Mrs. Grant will be gracious enough to extend the same courtesy, although I imagine you'd much prefer to see Mrs. Jefferson Davis or Mrs. Robert E. Lee in the White House."

"I interviewed both of these ladies for the *Sentinel*," Devon recalled, "and covered their social affairs. I'm very happy for Varina Davis, that the treason charges against her husband have been dropped. Mrs. Lee, poor soul, is partially crippled with rheumatism, and in constant pain. I've never met Mrs. Grant, although she lived with the general in Virginia during his campaign there, and many journalists and editors did meet her. I have no idea what manner of First Lady she'll make, but almost anyone would be an improvement over Mrs. Lincoln. Even the Northern press criticized her, you know. They called her a shrew and termagant, and said she was violently jealous of the President, suspected every woman who came into his presence of coveting him, and made ugly public scenes. Some considered her mentally unbalanced by the death of her son, and finally driven mad by her husband's assassination. No wonder she has gone abroad to live. She's to be pitied, I suppose."

"Well," Fitch shrugged awkwardly, "I don't delve much into the intricate personality of peculiar females, Miss Marshall, which is one reason Mrs. Hempstead insists— and possibly with some justification—that every paper needs a woman's section. I just want to say, I'm glad you're with ours, Miss Marshall."

"Thank you, Mr. Fitch. That's the nicest thing I've heard today. Now I think I'd better go home and get ready for the opening of the Grand Opera House."

He grinned. "Kind of expensive way for Fisk to put his

inamorata on the boards, wouldn't you say? But I guess the Prince of Erie can afford it, and that million dollar marble palace should go down in history as one of the greatest erections to woman since the Taj Mahal. Run along now, Miss Marshall. Our distaff readers will be panting to hear about Miss Mansfield's debut in opera bouffe."

Chapter 37

The chaos, clamor, and confusion of Albany in January were mild compared to Washington in March. Hotels and inns, rooming and boarding houses, had been solidly booked months in advance. Transients were putting up in carriagehouses and stables and squatting in parks. A disreputable colony mushroomed on the Mall. Some crossed Long Bridge to Arlington, others rode the ferries to Alexandria. Many New York correspondents, including the *Record*'s Devon Marshall, were registered at the famous Willard Hotel, political and social hub of the capital during inaugurations and sessions of Congress.

Ironically, Washington had always been more Southern than Northern in aspect and character, holding slaves until the Emancipation Proclamation, and planters and their ladies had ruled its government and society when the Virginia dynasties occupied the White House. The antebellum atmosphere still prevailed in many Georgetown mansions staffed with black servants, where grace and leisure reigned, and balls and riding were the principal diversions. But Devon still thought, as she had on her first visit there with Keith, that Richmond would have been a better capital for the nation.

The memory of that brief summer interlude at the Clairmont made her wistful and reminiscent. Had she not known that his suite contained two bedrooms and the trip to and from Washington would be made in daylight hours, she would have been miserable with jealousy and despair. When would they arrive, and how would she react at her first sight of them together? Suppose, somehow, in a look or word or irresistible touch, they both betrayed themselves? Would he dare try to see her alone, despite their firm agreement to the contrary? Love did not always behave rationally, nor desire discreetly. She pondered these dilemmas her first long lonely night at the Willard, remembering the epicurean supper at Dijon's while dining conservatively on her expense account, and the rapture in his arms while tossing restlessly in her chaste single bed.

From her windows she could see lights burning in the White House, while Andrew Johnson was preparing to vacate to his hated successor, whom he would refuse to accompany to the inauguration. She could also see the fifty-foot lantern glowing in the Capitol dome, signifying that Congress was in urgent night session, possibly hoping to enact some last-minute legislation before the expiration of the Johnson Administration.

Fascinated by her assignment, Devon was also frightened by a sense of inadequacy. She was, after all, a rank novice among the veteran females of the Washington press corps, some of whose past accomplishments and exploits amazed and even awed her. The powerful middleaged Jane Swisshelm, for instance, first woman to crash the Capitol news galleries back in 1850, whence she had become the conscience of Congress and persistent gadfly of Daniel Webster. Intellectual spinster Gail Hamilton, whose work appeared in the New York *World* and distinguished literary magazines. Pert and vivacious Nellie Hutchinson, who sent her witty newsletters to Horace Greeley. Sophisticated Mary Clemmer Ames, correspondent of the prestigious New York *Independent*. Charming and brilliant Grace Greenwood, whom even Abraham Lincoln had admired. And devastating Olivia, dean of the gossip columnists, who could destroy a reputation with a few deft strokes of her adroit pen.

But the people who came and went at the Willard were rank strangers to Devon. She saw not one familiar Virginian, not one famous Southern statesman or politician who had frequented the Confederate capital wearing broad-brimmed planters' hats and drinking mint juleps at the Spotswood Hotel, Richmond's counterpart of the Willard. Reconstruction kept Dixie Democrats away, and all but the scalawags boycotted the inaugural of the general responsible for their defeat and humiliation.

Devon did have a piece of luck, however, by being in the lobby when Washington's most famous hostess, Kate Chase Sprague, entered with her husband, William

Sprague, former governor of and now senator from Rhode Island. The daughter of Chief Justice Salmon P. Chase, Mrs. Sprague had made herself well known in New York during the last Democratic Convention, where she had worked diligently but fruitlessly behind the scenes to get the presidential nomination for her father, who would now administer the oath of office to Grant. A titian-haired beauty still under thirty, with wide gray eyes and flawless white skin, she was also vain, haughty, and inordinately ambitious. Women feared her, and Mrs. Lincoln had despised her. But men—with the possible exception of her husband, who was being driven to drink and other vices by her ruthless ambitions for her father and herself—admired her political knowledge, her subtle machinations and persuasions, and her almost sibylline predictions.

"Senator and Mrs. Sprague?" Devon approached and presented her presscard. "Would you care to say a few words for the *Record*?"

Publicity was food and drink to Kate Chase Sprague. "Delighted, Miss Marshall. Shall we get acquainted over tea?"

The less enthusiastic and compliant senator excused himself and headed for the bar, while the ladies went into the tearoom. Devon noted her lime-green velvet suit and smart Watteau hat pinned with artificial spring flowers. She talked animatedly and freely over tea and croissants, saying nothing libelous, but getting in a few judicious criticisms of people and things that annoyed or displeased her, and Devon had her first interview with a Washington female celebrity, plus an invitation to the forthcoming Sprague reception, which would take precedence over any but a White House affair. It was a heady experience, exhilarating as a glass of champagne.

"Thank you so much, Mrs. Sprague. You've been a great help to me. This is my first assignment here, you see."

"Well, let's hope it won't be your last, dear. I was happy to oblige, and expect I'll be seeing you around town often for the next week or so. But you must excuse me now—I have another engagement." And summoning the captain as if he were a congressional page, she bade him fetch the senator from the saloon.

*

Inaugural Day dawned bleak and overcast, with cold gray mists blowing off the Potomac, threatening rain or snow. Spectators along Pennsylvania Avenue were bundled to their ears. Some sat and stood on balconies and hung out of windows. Others perched in trees and clung to fences and monuments. Armed security guards and military marksmen were posted atop the buildings lining the processional route from the Grant residence on I Street to the East Portico of the Capitol, for the town was reputed to be virtually swarming with rabid Southern patriots and sympathizers—former Rebel soldiers, Ku Klux, and Knights of the White Camellia, all gunning for Grant.

Devon viewed the military parade passively, her mind a hundred miles away in Richmond. The new blue uniforms of the crack infantry, the scarlet plumed artillery and finely mounted cavalry, the gold braid and polished brass, varnished boots and rattling sabers only recalled the battered beaten beleaguered brigades of Confederate gray. For the Dixie journalists on the press platform, watching General Grant assume the Presidency of the United States was like witnessing their own execution from a scaffold draped with Union flags.

Devon knew the Curtises were in the privileged group on the presidential dias, but she disciplined her eyes not to focus on them, concentrating instead on Kate Chase Sprague, whose face registered bitter disappointment as her father swore in President Grant. The inaugural address, brief and undistinguished, was scarcely audible over the wind and noise. And when the tumult and shouting died down, and the captains and the kings departed, Devon returned to the Willard to compose her impressions for the *Record*. Then she tried to relax and rest for the evening activities.

By nightfall the Capitol dome was obscured in skeins of pale woolly sleet, and even in her fur-lined cloak and muff Devon shivered on her way to the inaugural ball. Ironically, it was held in the newly completed north wing of the Treasury, which Keith would occupy should he yet accept the cabinet plum still in his grasp. The architecture was classic Greek: fluted columns and templelike halls, tessellated marble floors and an impressive gallery of marble and bronze statuary. Garlands of spring greenery decorated the second floor balcony of Sienese marble, where the President and First Lady would receive the diplomatic corps and other dignitaries. The Marine band, resplendent in scarlet uniforms, played in the temporary ballroom hung with flags and evergreen festoons, and busy caterers hovered over the vast supper tables—all somewhat marred by the paralyzing cold and the choking dust in the air from the still unfinished building.

With the exception of dowdy Jane Swisshelm, who scorned feminine vanity and frippery as inappropriate to the profession, the press ladies were as voguish as the pages of *Godey's* and *Demorest's Mirror of Fashions*. Devon wore amber velvet and creamy *point aiguille* lace with topaz jewelry. Queen bee Olivia, in black-and-gold striped taffeta, buzzed around the room, jotting down bits of information and gossip, costumes and coiffures, and Devon followed her example. There were senators and congressmen and their ladies flaunting their finest raiment, and gold-laced generals and admirals, some of whom had menaced and ravaged Virginia. But she must remember her purpose there, not her politics. There was no room for partisanship in journalism. And yet, could she ever be truly impartial, completely unbiased and objective in reporting the Washington scene, or would her war memories always affect her vision, occasionally blur and even distort it?

At ten-thirty President Grant, Vice President Schuyler Colfax and their wives arrived, and the foreign ministers in full ambassadorial regalia were presented. Also in the presidential party were members of their respective families and hometown friends, Chief Justice Chase and his daughter and her husband, some important members of Congress, and prominent New Yorkers, including the A. T. Stewarts, Hamilton Fishes, and Keith Curtises.

Esther was regal in silver brocade, the skirt draped with glittering gossamer. Diamond dust shimmered in her raven tresses, and she wore elbow-length gloves of silver lamé. How tall she was, how slender and graceful and imperious! Beside her, even the radiant Worth-gowned Kate Chase Sprague dimmed slightly, and the chubby crosseyed First Lady in her heavy white French satin and rosepoint lace, her diamonds and pearls, was virtually eclipsed. Although not the same jewelry Devon had worn on their Hudson holiday, Esther's diamonds and sapphires had also belonged to his mother, and for some reason this hurt and depressed her. Naturally his wife had to look her best and reflect her station in life, but this knowledge did not mitigate Devon's jealousy and resentment. In a sense she felt betrayed, for she had considered Lady Heathstone's jewels her private property. Was it a subtle punishment for defying him in her job? Was he actually capable of such petty reprisals?

Devon stared up at the Olympian balcony. Keith stood near the marble balustrade, his eyes reconnoitering the crowded hall, and she imagined he spotted her, for he moved toward the stairway and began to descend. Her heart beat a deafening staccato in her ears, swelling fit to burst in her breast, and suddenly she felt weak and queasy. Bent on escape, she rushed into the press corridor and leaned against a laurel-entwined pillar, quivering, afraid she would do something feminine and foolish like bawling or fainting, or both. Oh, Lord! She was behaving like the doomed heroine of a Greek tragedy!

"Anything wrong, Ma'am?" A shadow fell across her, and a tall young man stood beside her, a Westerner by his voice and clothes. "Reed Carter," he introduced himself, sticking out a friendly hand. "The Dallas *Post*."

Devon composed herself as best she could before accepting the hand he offered like a staff of support. He had long lean fingers, and the firm but gentle grip of an experienced rider. He was cigar-slim and trim, his smooth-shaven skin only a shade lighter than his sun-bronzed hair. His tight narrow breeches and high-heeled boots made him appear even taller than he was, so that he towered over her by a foot or more, and she had to look up into his clear sky-blue eyes. In the eastern haberdashery of the clothes-conscious capital, amid the formal black suits and white ties, he was a sartorial anachronism.

"Devon Marshall," she murmured. "New York *Record*."

"What's the matter, honey? You get stomped on in there?"

She knew he wasn't being fresh; in his part of the country that colloquial endearment was probably as natural as his drawl. "Sort of, Mr. Carter. I'm a Virginian, you see, displaced by the war."

"Aren't we all?" he reflected grimly. "And this isn't our celebration, is it—or, as we say in Texas, not our night to howl. My father was a rancher on the Trinity, fought the Indians and the Mexicans for his land. He was at Jan Jacinto with Sam Houston, and later in Congress with him. Now he's scratching out a living on a few acres, and I'm operating a printing press. You plan to do any dancing this evening, Miss Marshall?"

"Only if they play the Virginia reel, Mr. Carter."

Irony touched his slow rueful smile. "No, I think it's the Washington quadrille tonight. The band hasn't once struck up *Dixie*. The whole thing's a fiasco, if you ask me. Too many heads and not enough leg room. They're trampling one another like corraled cattle, and there's a regular stampede to the food troughs. Look at their military bulls out there! Sherman, Sheridan, Meade still taking bows for Gettysburg, Fighting Joe Hooker who terrorized your James peninsula, and that bloody Beast of New Orleans, Benjamin Butler, now in Congress. Farragut, Dupont, Porter, and all the others responsible for our wreck and ruin. General Sheridan was military governor of Texas for awhile and did his damndest to make Reconstruction as much hell as he made war."

"Did you meet him on the battlefield?" Devon asked.

"Not personally. I rode with a volunteer troup of Texas Rangers. We saw cavalry action in Tennessee, against the Rock of Chickamauga, George Thomas. Sort of returning a favor to Crockett, Bowie, and Travis for the Alamo. You expect to be in this Yankee territory long, Ma'am?"

"Washington? I'm not sure, Mr. Carter. A few days, possibly more. At least until Mrs. Grant holds her first press levee."

"Where're you camping?"

"Camping? Oh. The Willard."

"I hear they got a right good chuck wagon there," he said, "albeit a little rich for my wallet. I pitched tent by Rock Creek—only place I could find and afford. Figured it'd be somewhat crowded and expensive here, so I came prepared with haversack and bedroll."

"But it's freezing, and there's ice on the ground!"

"Oh, sleeping outdoors in bad weather doesn't bother me," he shrugged. "I used to drive our cattle to market. Carter campfires marked the Chisholm Trail to Abilene, and the Shawnee to Kansas City. Had a bonfire glowing on Rock Creek last night, and it was real cozy. I could hear singing water and varmints in the brush, almost like home."

Was he really that naive and rustic? What a boy he would seem on Broadway, what a rube on Wall Street. A lamb to be fleeced. And yet she sensed that he was none of these things—no simple trusting soul easily beguiled or taken, and any man who so rashly misjudged him would regret it. It was probably just the characteristic pose Westerners assumed in the East while "sizing up the situation."

"Is the Dallas *Post* a daily, Mr. Carter?"

"Lord no, Ma'am! Publication depends on our shipments of newsprint and ink, which come by wagon train from Louisiana. Sometimes it's a weekly or biweeky or monthly. Doesn't matter much—folks are glad to read it whenever they can. Pa writes and edits some of the editorials and political stuff. He was a damned good senator—maybe even a statesman in his homespun, common horse sense fashion. He still parleys and caucuses around the creek and crackerbarrel."

Someday, perhaps, she would tell him about her father, and herself. But there seemed no point now; she might never see him again. Texas was a long way from New York, and right now she had an article to write.

She smiled. "I've enjoyed meeting you, Mr. Carter. But now I'd better get back to work. Hadn't you?"

"Shoot, I'll dash this shindig off in two shakes of a lame Coyote's tail!"

Later, as Devon was struggling to find a hackney or omnibus with room for one more passenger, pummeled and about to be crushed by the milling horde before the Treasury, the Texan emerged and silently took her arm, ushering her to a private carriage and ordering the liveried coachman to drive to the Willard.

"You's in the wrong carriage, sir," the Negro informed him. "This here's Sentah Bryce Horton's 'quipage.'"

"I know that, Hercules. I'm the senator's nephew. You're to take me where I wish, and then return for your master."

"Yessir."

Devon relaxed in the luxurious interior of the clarence with a grateful sigh. "Gee, I thought I'd have to walk to the hotel in this wretched weather! How fortunate that the senator from Ohio has such a gallant nephew."

Grinning, he leaned close to whisper, "Can you keep a secret? I don't know the pompous old goat, never even met him. But I saw him arrive earlier—and what the hell! The North borrowed enough of our transportation without leave, didn't they? Stealing horses, and confiscating anything with wheels. They made Quantrill's Raiders look like choirboys on angelic behavior! This'll be good for a few horse laughs back home, anyway. Too bad it's not Sherman's or Sheridan's equipage—or better still, Grant's!"

"Too bad," Devon agreed and laughed with him. She decided that she liked this brash young man, his unorthodox clothes and daring manner, and especially his delicious sense of humor.

"They've got some stables out in Georgetown," he said, "and it'd pleasure me mightily if you could find time to ride with me, Miss Marshall."

The wind was gusting against the carriage, ice pricking the windows, yet Devon felt warm and cozy and completely at ease. "How did you know I like to ride?"

"That's easy, honey. You're a Virginian—and next to my state, yours is the horsiest one in the Union."

"Ah, but Virginia's not in the Union now, Mr. Carter, and neither is Texas."

"Which is just one more thing we have in common, isn't it?" They had reached the Willard, and he leaped out to assist her, escorting her into the lobby and to the desk for her key. "I'll be moseying around the Capitol tomorrow, but I might ramble over here for noon chow, and if you're in the vicinity—"

"Well," Devon hesitated, "I can't promise anything, sir. I have a busy schedule, and another assignment might crop up at any moment. You understand?"

"Sure, I'm in the same business, you know. And in case you didn't know, we have some lady reporters and editors and even publishers out West. What's more, females in the Montana Territory have the franchise, which puts them far ahead of their eastern sisters in suffrage, I believe. The pioneers are not as backward as some folks like to think."

"That's good news," Devon said, "Good news indeed!"

Chapter 38

So many statesmen, diplomats, and millionaries thronged the Chase-Sprague mansion at Sixth and E Streets, the correspondents had difficulty listing them. Devon had already filled several notebooks and fairly exhausted her fashion vocabulary on the splendid attire of the ladies of the embassies.

Madame Catacaxy, the tall striking blonde wife of the Russian minister, whose past was somewhat unsavory—she had abandoned her spouse in Russia and lived with her lover while both were being divorced for adultery—was most impressive in purple velvet and sables and jewels fit for a czarina. Madame de Noailles, whose debonair husband represented the Second Empire, epitomized French elegance in bronze-green moiré antique and mink. The imperious Lady Thornton, arriving on the arm of the distinguished British ambassador, Sir Edward Thornton, wore Queen Victoria's favorite Honiton lace and ermine, as she might to the Court of St. James. And Madame Garcia, an exotic Latin beauty with dark sultry eyes and glossy black hair, would have created a sensation in her fluttering white ostrich plumes even without His Excellency, the minister of Peru.

Nearly every cabinent potential and hopeful was present, except the one Devon prayed not to see. But as postmaster general was the only slot filled so far, no one knew whom to congratulate or console, envy or pity, cultivate or ignore. Expedient Kate had assembled them all in her magnificent home as if for a family portrait, determined to include herself if only in the background. Devon was scribbling rapid desultory notes about Mrs. Cooke's turquoise satin gown and peacock aigrette, and Mrs. Stewart's watered silk and Oriental pearls, when she heard the butler make the dreaded announcement:

"Mr. and Mrs. Keith Heathstone Curtis!"

Murmurs, mostly feminine and feline, coursed through the salon as the couple entered, for surely Mr. Curtis would be the handsomest man in any cabinet, and Mrs. Curtis a formidable rival for any woman in beauty, charm, and elegance. She was *en train* in the latest Worth dictum, her shimmering gold Empire gown designed with panels of gold and silver embroidery. Diamonds and rubies blazed at her throat, ears and wrists, and flashed in the coronet of tiny gold acanthus leaves on her dark proud head.

The diplomatic corps immediately gravitated toward this obviously independent wealth and prestige, and covert glances caught the hostess' anxious expression, for Mrs. Sprague plainly did not relish the possibility of such competition in her social realm. And to have this ravishing creature appear at such an unpropitious time, with Kate beginning her second pregnancy and rumors of marital discord in her union running through the drawing rooms and Capitol corridors, was enough to bring on an attack of vapors. Hoping to divert the columnists' attention from Mrs. Curtis, she failed with all but the *Record*'s Miss Marshall, to whom she would be eternally grateful.

As the Curtises approached, Devon bent her head diligently over her pad. Her opal jewelry and costume of creamy peau de soie appliqued with Alençon lace and seed pearls was exquisitely conservative, yet she felt as conspicuous as if she were wearing a scarlet letter, and she feared her emotions were transparent as gauze. She knew that Keith was also uncomfortable, with Esther clinging possessively to his arm, perhaps even suffering a little, and she pitied him. But still she refused, as she had on that other wretched occasion in Gramercy Park, when she was half naked in a boudoir ensemble, to meet his eyes and commiserate. How could she, without betraying them both?

Esther was soon charming the French minister and chargé d'affaires with her clever wit and repartee, speaking their tongue fluently, and the Italian and Spanish ambassadors were also intrigued admirers. Despite Keith's affected nonchalant dialogue with Sir Edward Thornton and Hamilton Fish, rumored to be the choice for Secretary of State, Devon could sense his guarded glances, and only the supper announcement saved her from possible catastrophic response. Mrs. Sprague informed her that Gautier, famous for his carved ices of capital edifices and monuments, was the caterer; that the gold-embossed dishes had come from France, and the unusual bowls of garnet-dust from the palace of the shah of Persia. Surely, she hinted, the Curtises boasted no finer home or possessions!

Between notes Devon managed to consume a delicious oyster patty and cup of Roman punch, before she was interrupted by Mrs. Curtis, still at her husband's side. "It's Miss Marshall, isn't it? I've seen your byline in the *Record* and wondered if you were the same person—and so you are!"

"So I am," Devon acknowledged. Was she supposed to apologize for the coincidence?

"My compliments on your versatile talents, Miss Marshall. As I recall, you also have a penchant for modeling, and your former employer, who seems unable to keep any mannequin for long, has lamented your loss at length to me. Although I could go to her boutique now, she still gives me private showings at my home. My doctors curtail my activities, you see, fearing a relapse, which is why we haven't been entertaining much and certainly not lavishly. We hope to begin soon again, however, and you must cover our affairs."

"With pleasure, Mrs. Curtis, if my editor assigns me."

"Well, if you'd like a description of this gown, it's cloth-of-gold from Damascus, and the train is embroidered with crystals and semiprecious stones. Of course you saw my costume at the inaugural ball?"

"Yes, I was present." Devon said.

Esther nudged her silent glowering husband. "You remember Miss Marshall, don't you, dear?"

"Vaguely," he nodded.

"Only vaguely?" Her skeptical smile mocked him. "I thought you were well aware of her that day, darling, and certainly there was plenty to notice—"

At that moment, to Devon's intense relief, the orchestra struck up "Hail to the Chief"! The President and First Lady had arrived. The crowd hushed expectantly, and Devon seized the opportunity to occupy herself professionally.

They were not a luminous pair, somewhat dull and countrified among these glamorous sophisticates, gauche

and almost pathetic in this coterie of cosmopolites. Neither
of the Grants had ever been abroad. They lacked the luster and confidence of personal affluence, the patina of aristocracy, and the savoir faire which were the birthright and
heritage of most of the assemblage. An impressive figure
uniformed and mounted, the general was less so in his ill-
fitting black formals, his off-center white tie, his white-
gloved hands nervous for reins, a glass, a cigar—anything to
occupy them. And his wife was short and plump, so full-
breasted her garnet velvet bodice appeared stuffed with
cotton, a partridge among peacocks and birds of paradise.
Surmounting this matronly figure was a plain middle-aged
face with irregular features and small gray eyes habitually
narrowed to minimize their congenital affliction. Even
without malice or prejudice for what the Grants represented to Richmond, Devon taxed her journalistic integrity to
describe them honestly. But prudence ultimately triumphed
over pettiness, especially when she realized that Julia Dent
Grant was not only painfully aware of her unattractiveness
but humbled and possibly even humiliated by it; and out
of compassion emerged a flattering portrait which the First
Lady would proudly paste in her personal album and note
in her diary.

Absorbed in her task, Devon had almost forgotten the
Curtises until Keith, temporarily eluding his wife, murmured sotto voce, "What happened to you at the Inaugural Ball? One minute you were there, the next vanished.
Where did you go in such haste, and why? I wanted to
dance with you."

"We agreed—"

He interrupted, "To hell with that agreement! Do you
honestly think we can be in the same town and not see
each other?"

"I have assignments," she reminded. "Do you want to
make her suspicious? Move on, or turn your back. Ignore
me."

He did neither, persisting, "I'll come to you tonight, after I take her to the Clairmont."

"No! You'll ruin everything. Oh, God! Here she comes!
Go away, Keith, please?"

"All right, but I hope you have a restless night, Miss
Marshall. I *know* I will."

*

While waiting for Mrs. Grant to announce her first press levee, Devon was occupied with other public and private functions, sightseeing, and sitting in the Capitol press galleries, where Jane Swisshelm and Grace Greenwood spent most of their time when Congress was in session. She noticed Kate Chase Sprague in the ladies' balcony of the Senate, observing her husband and his colleagues on the floor, primarily Senator Roscoe Conkling of New York, a flashing auburn-haired and bearded man unanimously acclaimed the Apollo of the Senate. A brilliant speaker and close friend of the President, Conkling was expected to rise to prominent political heights on the Hill. Women adored him, and he encouraged their adulation by conveniently leaving his wife in Utica. Gossip in the capital hinted at a romantic attachment between the handsome Conkling and the beauteous Mrs. Sprague, but the columnists could not confirm the rumors and would not have dared create and circulate false ones about two such powerful personalities. Lack of confirmation did not, however, prevent off-the-record speculation.

"How do you like Washington, Miss Marshall?" someone asked.

"It's interesting," Devon replied, and the veterans smiled indulgently at this naivete.

"It's a mad marathon with the White House as the trophy," Jane Swisshelm said, "It's havoc and turmoil, dilemma and dynamite and often disaster."

Grace Greenwood assented, adding, "It'll mature and age you faster than marriage and childbirth, my dear. Are you leery of the First Lady's press premiere?"

"Terrified," Devon confessed, hoping they would volunteer to coach her.

"No more than she is of us," Olivia drawled.

"Well, I've read the protocol manual and—"

"Just be kind to the poor soul, and tolerant of her shortcomings," Olivia advised. "I'm afraid she was more at home in their crude log cabin, Hardscrabble, outside St. Louis, and their humble abode in Galena, Illinois, where her husband sold lumber for a living, and perhaps even in his quarters on the battlefronts than she is in the White House. Kate Chase Sprague would be the first to agree on that."

"Undoubtedly," said Gail Hamilton, who was kin to the

wife of the Speaker of the House, and a staunch friend of the First Family. "God knows she has coveted that position herself since her teens, and gave Mrs. Lincoln a difficult time during her tenure there."

"Actually, Gail, it was the other way around. Mary Lincoln was insanely jealous of Kate—her youth and beauty and position. Didn't she refuse to attend her wedding?"

"She was still in mourning for their son Willie."

"Nevertheless, Lincoln went alone—and kissed the bride! One wonders if his wife ever forgave him that gallantry."

"Expediency, Olivia. What else could the President do, when the bride was the daughter of the chief justice and the groom the governor of Rhode Island? And such airs her father gives himself, you'd think he was on the high tribunal of Heaven!"

Mary Clemmer Ames intervened. "Oh, dear! Senator Sprague is about to make another of his dreary speeches. Brace yourselves for boredom, ladies."

Browsing around the building during the noon recess, Devon met Reed Carter in the Rotunda, where Constantino Brumidi, the so-called "Michelangelo of the Capitol" was painting the epic frieze, sixty feet above the crypt. Although his scaffolds had been permanent fixtures in the dome for seventeen years, his historical work was still only partially completed. This didn't surprise the Texan, who had previously inspected the incomplete Washington Monument, whose cornerstone was laid July 4, 1848. He shook his head wonderingly. "Reckon he'll ever get done up there, and Old George's corncob shaft out yonder will ever be more than a nubbin? Jesus, can't they ever finish anything around here!"

"Apparently not," Devon said, "If so, they tear it down and start over."

Her acerbity amused him. "Pressures getting to you, honey?"

"Frankly, Mr. Carter, I feel as if I'd been crushed, pressed, and pureed through a sieve."

"For me, it's like being tied spread-eagle with wet rawhide in a red ant nest, and the thongs are shrinking in the hot sun," he said, "Say, I don't think there's gonna be any real action in the Senate arena this afternoon—no more'n the usual strutting and pawing of the herd bulls flexing their muscles. What say we cut out for the rest of the day, grab some grub, and then hit the trail to Rock Creek? I find the saddle more relaxing than a hammock in the shade. You'll have to doff those fancy duds, though, for sturdier gear."

Suddenly it seemed imperative that she escape, at least temporarily, the Washington bedlam, the giddy whirling carousel of activity, lest she fall victim to its perpetual madness. A leisurely ride offered the ideal rest and recuperation for both spirit and perspective. "Capital idea, cowboy," she agreed. "And you can have a drink at Willard's saloon while I change."

On rented mounts they cantered along the bridal paths of a peaceful wilderness only partially developed, although it was to Washington what Hyde Park was to London and the Bois de Boulogne to Paris. There were tangled woods and thickets, deep gorges and ravines, and towering boulders—a sanctuary for wildlife including deer, racoons, opossums, rabbits, muskrats, squirrels, and numerous foxes, red and gray.

"I reckon you used to hunt those critters with hounds," Reed said, as a bushy tail streaked past into the underbrush.

"A few times."

"Plenty of skunks and possums around here too, I've noticed. All sorts of varmints, including the two-legged species of wolf and coyote, which are probably as indigenous to this bank of the Potomac as the bulls and bears are to Wall Street. I saw a whole herd of Manhattan mavericks lobbying on Capitol Hill this morning, and some fancy blooded and branded Boston Brahmins too. They say Grant admires millionaires, and this is apt to be a money-changers' administration ruled from the treasure temples of the East. The poor fella will be left to shift for himself."

"Hasn't he always been, Mr. Carter? Hasn't the average man either survived or perished in his own sweat and blood? Money is a mania in New York, and people count dollars, rather than friends or blessings."

"You don't like living in Midas country?"

"I must earn a living," she shrugged.

"There're other ways, and other places. But I suppose you'd find 'em mighty dull now."

"Oh, I don't know, Mr. Carter. I've always considered people more interesting and important than places. Don't most journalists? After all, people, not places, make news. What would Washington be without the President and the politicians? London without the queen and parliament? Paris without the emperor and his court? New York without capitalists and celebrities? Just cities, that's all. And though you don't have any great towns in Texas, I'm sure you have many interesting folks."

"Oh Lord, yes! It'd be hard to find more unusual characters anywhere on earth than some of our Texans."

His laughter suggested some native joke, and Devon joined him in reminiscence. "We had some quaint ones in Virgina too, and New York fairly bristles with them."

After an hour of riding they dismounted and walked to Rock Creek, a tributary of the Potomac, where ferns were beginning to sprout in tiny fronds like curled green plumes, at the water's edge and among the mossy rocks, and arbutus bloomed often under snow, and violets clustered in patches of moist shade. March sunlight filtered through the bare trees, and the sky was clear, but spring was far from imminent. Her broadcloth habit felt good, albeit incongruous beside his western trappings. And it amused him to compare her elegant veiled British postilion to his battered, sweat-ringed Stetson.

"That outfit wouldn't last long on the prairie," he said. "It'd turn gray with dust, and if the wind didn't rip off that pretty gauze frippery, the chaparral would."

"Chaparral?"

"Brush. You'd have to dress more practically."

"In homespun and sunbonnets?" she mused.

"If that was the best your man could afford. You'd have to learn to ride astride too, in britches and chaps and sombrero, lest you get thrown off into cactus and barbecued by the sun. Damned if I see how you hang onto that blamed sidesaddle, anyway. I keep expecting you to slip off under the hooves, and it gives me the jitters. You make a fetching picture, though, and you'd be quite a novelty in Texas, so angel-fair. Not many milk-and-honey blondes there. The women are mostly brunettes. Some Mexican mixtures, half-breeds, and savages too."

"I've read that it's still largely a wilderness, and San Antonio is the only civilized city in the state."

"If you can call what happened at the Alamo civilized," he said. "Laredo, Brownsville, El Paso are wild border towns. Houston down on Buffalo Bayou is far from New Orleans. Waco is a raw tough pueblo, but Austin, on the Colorado, is a right nice little place, quiet and peaceful except when the state legislature is in session. Most of the settlements are on the rivers and the gulf coast, the big plantations are in the eastern section, the great ranches in the west and farms everywhere. Indians still roam the high plains and mountains, and Mexican bandits hang out on the Rio Grande. Not much law west of the Pecos."

"Then it is still wild?"

"Well, it's a frontier, and parts of it will always defy and reject civilization. The hide-hunters haven't slaughtered all the buffalo yet, and there're vast herds of longhorns and mustangs that belong to whoever can capture and domesticate them. The ranges are thick with deer and antelope, and sometimes the sky is dark with pigeons and geese and ducks. It's a sorry shot that can't keep food on his table. On the Sabine and Red River, where the rainfall is plentiful, you find great forests of pine and cypress and liveoak tangled with moss, and water lilies and purple hyacinths choke the swamps and bayous, and the rich moist soil encourages jungle growth. By contrast there are barren mountains in the west and deserts so hot and arid nothing but rattlesnakes and gila monsters can survive. And just when you get to thinking it's the most God-forsaken country on earth, and the devil's own territory, a blooming prairie or gorgeous sunset or moonlit night will convince you otherwise."

His remote wistful eyes and soft, almost caressing voice, betrayed his long and passionate love affair with his native land, and Devon said quietly, as if intruding on a romantic reverie, "You make it sound fascinating."

"Challenging," he mused. "The whole West is a challenge, a duel with nature, and as in any such contest half the challengers are inevitably defeated. Lured by dreams and promises, men come expecting to embrace mother earth like eager lovers, only to find she can be formidable and impregnable—a temperamental bitch screaming in the wind and spitting sand, flooding in tears, drying up in drought, freezingly frigid in winter. A vixen and a hellcat, and it takes a mighty determined hombre—or loco one—to even try to tame her. But for those with enough guts and perseverance to try, the rewards can be great and satisfying. It's a good place to begin a new life, or reconstruct an old one, especially since the war—one reason so many wagon trains are rolling from the South now. For me Texas is the most alluring coquette west of the Mississippi, offering more hope of surrender and fulfillment than the Territories. Nothing for her to do but grow and prosper, and I aim to do it with her. She has a big bountiful bosom, tremendous energy and resources, an unconquerable heart and spirit, and a man could do worse than entrust his future to her. Dallas is only a prairie cowtown on the east fork of the Trinity now, but someday it'll be a big city. Maybe I won't live to see it, but my kids will."

Devon was leaning against the trunk of a great oak, toying with her crop. "How many children do you have?"

"None yet. I'm not married. That's all in the future too." He paused, his blue eyes surveying and calculating from under the tall gray hat. "When I find the right woman, which won't be easy, because she has to be something special."

"Don't worry, you'll find her, eventually. Is that your camp over there?"

"Yeah, but not for long. I'm pulling stakes tomorrow. Bending he scooped up a handful of pebbles and tossed them singly into the stream, pondering the widening circles. "Any chance your paper will ever send you to Texas?"

She smiled at such an unlikely prospect. "I can't foresee any circumstances."

"Nor I," he lamented. "But Easterners do visit the West, you know, and many like Texas well enough to stay. We have a number of transplanted Virginians, and even some New Yorkers. I reckon you've read Washington Irving's *Sketchbook?* What I'm trying to say, Ma'am, is you'd be mighty welcome in Dallas."

"Thank you, Mr. Carter. And should I ever travel that way, I promise to look you up."

"In Texas we call strangers Mister," he said. "Friends don't stand much on ceremony."

"Are we friends, Reed?"

"I hope so, Devon. I sure do hope so."

"Shall we finish our ride, then?"

Back in the saddle, she challenged him boldly, "I'll race you to the stables."

"Not in this thicket, honey. You might get hurt. That's a sport for the wide open spaces, and rescuing maidens from runaway horses is a favorite pastime on the prairie. Matter of fact, I'm tempted to spook your cayuse now, just for the privilege."

"You think I need a hero?"

"Not as much as I need an excuse to get familiar," he said. "You see, I want to say adios with more than a handshake."

Devon said nothing, listening to the creaking leather and crunching leaves, and he thought he understood her silence. But he was mistaken, for she didn't understand it herself. A part of her was sad and reticent at the thought of his leaving, while another part wanted to encourage his familiarity, to feel his touch, his arms and mouth in farewell. To give him something to remember, or to keep him from forgetting?

She didn't know, and it didn't really matter, for when she thought of Keith, the Texan's image suddenly dimmed, blurred, and faded, receding into the emotional mists that so often fogged her mind and memory and even her soul.

Chapter 39

Until the swearing in of Massachusetts' George S. Boutwell as secretary of the treasury, Esther had not actually believed that Keith would decline the honor of serving in the cabinet, and her disappointment was keen and frustrating. She had anticipated a new and exciting life in Washington, supplanting Kate Chase Sprague as its most influential hostess and conducting an even more brilliant political salon, such as the Mesdames de Stael, Récamier, and Roland had once conducted in Paris. Her horoscope indicated great and marvelous changes for her this year, which a perverse spouse seemed determined to foil. Furious with him, Esther began to nag the moment their train pulled out of the Baltimore & Ohio station for New York.

"I suppose you're also going to turn down a foreign ministry?" she demanded petulantly, and his nod dashed even that glimmer of hope. "Oh, my God! What's wrong with you, Keith? Where's your patriotism? It's your civic duty to serve your country in whatever capacity your President desires!"

"I don't need you to quote my patriotic duty to me," he responded quietly. "I'm just not interested, Esther."

"And I know the reason for your disinterest, Keith! You're afraid your private life might become public, aren't you? That your mistress and child would be flushed out of the bushes, or wherever you're hiding them, with attendant consequences. Isn't that it? Well, perish the thought, darling. I wouldn't think of exposing family secrets or rattling ancestral skeletons under such circumstances."

Unlocking his portfolio, Keith sorted among its contents. Esther visualized an attache case containing vital government papers, documents, state secrets. His Excellency, the ambassador to Great Britain ... France ... Italy ... Russia ... Austria ... Spain.... Traveling, entertaining, being entertained in all the great European capitals. London, Paris, Rome, St. Petersburg, Vienna, Madrid. It was an illusion of grandeur not easily vanquished, a dream of glory reluctantly relinquished.

"Keith, listen to me! I had a detective on you last fall. I was determined to learn the truth about your affair, despite your warnings to me. But I removed him when rumors began to circulate that you were on President Grant's list of cabinet potentials. I didn't want factual evidence then, nor anyone else to have it, for fear the agent might be unscrupulous enough to blackmail you. See how solicitous I am of your reputation and future? How much I still love you in spite of everything, and want only the best for you?"

Cynicism twisted his smile into mockery. "For me? Your solicitude and ambitions are for yourself. Esther. Well, perhaps if you employed your charms and seductive arts on the President, you might persuade him to give you a ministerial appointment."

"Don't be vulgar—especially when you know very well that's impossible for a woman in this benighted day and age! If not, Kate Chase Sprague would be an ambassadress. Why can't the almighty male realize that the female is equipped with a brain as well as a body, and capable of serving him in other areas than the boudoir and other positions than horizontal. Oh, you're not even listening!"

"I've heard it all before, Esther. Ad infinitum. And the abuse and oppression of your sex is a familiar cud too, chewed incessantly in public. As for the sleuth, I spotted that clumsy, incompetent hound immediately and led him a merry chase. How did you like his reports—particularly the evenings I spent at Josephine Woods'?"

Her skin flushed hotly. "I couldn't believe it. A whorehouse, Keith! I told him he must be mistaken, following the wrong man, and dismissed him. Not that it displeased me to discover that you were also cheating on her; on the contrary, I was quite heartened. Such perfidy is inherent in the male animal, who never has been nor ever will be monogamous. Few of your American contemporaries could censure you with impunity, and your European brothers would salute and esteem you. The bordello is a way of life there, and the mistress a mark of success."

"Esther, I'm too busy to be amused by your babble. I'd appreciate it if you'd just hush and let me work in peace."

"You're a fool," she fumed. "Passing up a golden opportunity! Success in the cabinet or other high government service could catapult you into political prominence, Keith. The prospects are unlimited, the horizon infinite. The governorship, Congress, even the White House! Surely the Presidency appeals to you?"

Suddenly he bolted out of his chair, scattering portfolio and papers. "Goddammit, Esther! If you don't shut up, I swear I'll throttle you!" His breath was labored, eyes fierce and nostrils distended—an angry bull goaded beyond endurance.

"My word," she mocked, "but you're touchy! Is this the effect of a week's separation from your whore? If so, you should have relieved your tensions in a capital brothel, darling. They must have some comparable to Josephine Woods', for 'gentlemen only,' where the risks of blackmail and venereal disease are minimized. No doubt you've patronized them before, on your numerous junkets to Washington."

After his initial outburst Keith had regained his composure and returned to his work, ignoring her as if she were invisible. Esther chattered awhile longer, determined to penetrate his indifference, if only through aggravation, then gave up and summoned Rufus to serve luncheon— anything to interrupt him and compel attention and congeniality before the servant. Then she would rest on the bed, which they had never yet occupied together, and attempt once more to seduce him. She had almost succeeded, she believed, one evening at the Clairmont, when she had emerged from her bath stark naked and proceeded to tantalize him in his bedroom. He had just finished shaving and was stripped to the waist, applying facial tonic before the dresser mirror. He had stopped and stared at her in disbelief, then turned quickly away, muttering, "You're in the wrong room, Madam."

"On the contrary, Mister. Where does a wife belong, if not in her husband's bedroom?"

"Put some clothes on, Esther!"

"Keith, look at me, please. How long since you've seen me nude? Am I not still desirable, still slender and supple? And my breasts are larger now that I've gained some weight. Oh, darling, you don't have to love me to want me! Do you love the women at Josephine Woods' house? If you can take a whore, why not your wife? And if you can betray your mistress with a harlot . . . besides, she may not be faithful to you, either! She may be with another lover right now. When the tom's away, the pussy will sometimes play the alley cat, so why deprive yourself? You want me now, Keith, I *know* you do!"

"Wishful thinking," he scowled, reaching for the whisky decanter beside his bed. "Get dressed, Esther. We'll be late to the Sprague reception."

"Will you lace my stays?"

"That's what maids are for," he said. "Call yours."

"Very well, darling. Perhaps next time?"

But he had wanted her, then. She'd had enough experience with male passion and lust to recognize the symptoms —the obvious physical response and disturbed emotions seeking alleviation in alcohol. Deny it to eternity, he'd been erotically aroused by her nudity, and diverting his mind had been as difficult as averting his eyes. Moreover, he'd been restless and edgy at the reception, focusing his frustrated desire on that pretty young reporter, Devon Marshall, whom he'd once shamelessly coveted in their home in Gramercy Park.

What had he whispered to her? Esther wondered now. Pleading with her, perhaps, for an assignation? She was lovely, of course—any potent man would desire her. But evidently she'd refused him, for Keith had returned to the Clairmont with his wife, and she had heard him pacing his room and later tossing in bed.

Still, Esther was confident that complete capitulation was only a matter of time and effort. If only she could persuade or provoke him to touch her even in anger or violence, to take her even in rape—preferably rape resulting in pregnancy, remorse, guilt, amends. He was only a man, after all, the most sexually susceptible and lustful of all God's creatures. Tease and torment him enough, and he would vault the wall between them, or batter it down. Then she would employ the artful tricks Mallard had taught her in bed, make him realize what he'd been missing and foolishly denying himself, and hopefully forget his little bitch and her bastard, whoever and wherever they were. . . .

That same afternoon, in the Capitol press gallery, Olivia remarked to her female colleagues, "Well, our darling Kate can relax—the Curtises have finally left town. I went to the depot, curious to see that majestic coach I'd heard about—and it's true, they do travel like royalty!"

"Nevertheless," Mary Clemmer Ames deprecated, "I doubt if anyone could ever successfully depose Queen Kate; she's reigned too long. Mrs. Lincoln couldn't, nor Andrew Johnson's White House ladies, and neither will Julia Dent Grant. What are you going to wear to her press premiere tomorrow?"

"I haven't decided yet. Anyway, it's supposed to be a very public affair, open to just about anybody on the street. Shopkeepers, government clerks, housewives, farmers, and former slaves will all be welcome. Grant has a feeling for the common man, acquired no doubt in conquering Southern aristocracy, and he plans to initiate a democratic regime at least in matters of entertainment. Naturally, the military will have his blessing too. I think just about every man who fought under his command attended the inauguration." She nudged the *Record*'s correspondent, who was listening attentively to a scalawag senator speak on Reconstruction. "Is he saying something significant?"

"No, just another Judas Iscariot selling his state for thirty pieces of Yankee silver," Devon replied.

"Oh, such betrayals are common in Congress, my dear. Loyalty and integrity are negotiable commodities on the chamber floors. You should have witnessed the debates on secession! Tempers clashed and exploded, culminating in brawls and challenges to duel. Nearly everyone carried a weapon, and some still do. And any illusion that the country has been peacefully reunited and unified can be dispelled by observing one joint session of the legislature and beholding the houses divided against themselves. Right, Jane?"

Mrs. Swisshelm nodded. "I predict the Congressional conflict of Reconstruction will continue for years, particularly when those three fiery Rebel states are again represented, and I'll wager Virginia will be the last to rejoin the Union."

"I'll bet on Mississippi," Gail Hamilton drawled.

Nellie Hutchinson cried, "I'll take Texas! Did any of you girls happen to meet that divine young fellow from the Dallas *Post*, whose father once served in these hallowed halls?"

"Yes, he's very nice," Devon murmured.

"Nice? My, you're conservative! I found him fabulous. So tall and lean and bronzed and virile-looking! Mexicans would call him macho and muy hombre."

Grace Greenwood smiled. "I didn't know you habla español, Nellie."

"Oh, you pick up a few words here and there at the Spanish-speaking embassies. I know a beauty like Devon Marshall would be described as bella and bonita, and a handsome male is considered hermoso and potente."

"Most Western men qualify in those categories," said Jane, who had traveled in the Territories. "I've never seen a short pale fat one. They're all thin, tanned, and tough—especially the ranchers and cowboys. Heavy drinkers and hard fighters, some of them; gentle with women and horses but suspicious of strangers—on the whole, dangerous devils to anger or antagonize. And the clothes they fancy! My God, Carter covered the Inaugural ball in buckskin jacket, canvas breeches, and range boots. A latter-day Sam Houston, or Daniel Boone."

"Or Davy Crockett," Nellie mused.

"Whoever," Olivia shrugged, "he was the only hombre there who dared to be different—and it took mucho viscera to wear that outfit."

"Maybe it's all he had," Devon reasoned.

"Maybe," Jane agreed, "but I think he'd have worn it regardless, in defiance of tradition and custom. Texans have never been noted for formality or conventional behavior. As I remember, his father, Jason Carter, was one of the most colorful characters ever to sit in Congress. Very powerful and effective legislatively. His colleagues nicknamed him the Texas Argonaut, and when he rose to speak, they'd say, 'There's Jason again, after the Golden Fleece for his state!' Why so quiet, Devon? You're not still worried about the White House assignment?"

"A little," she admitted.

"Don't be," Grace encouraged. "You'll do just fine. I've read some of your articles, and you seem to have both the flair and finesse to handle the capital social scene. A born writer, and you should have a bright future in the profession."

"Undoubtedly," Olivia declared, "although, at her age, she might prefer more adventure. If I were young and single, I'd be tempted to follow Horace Greeley's advice and go West. Cover a migration by prairie schooner . . . cross the Great Divide . . . watch a railroad tunnel blasted through a mountain . . . interview a Pony Express rider and Wells Fargo detective, a frontier general and Indian chief . . . witness a Longhorn roundup, buffalo stampede, even accompany a cattle drive on one of those rugged trails to Kansas or Missouri, or wherever. The Territories are full of fascinating stories begging to be written, an endless source of material and inspiration, a rich gold lode still to be mined. But except for Jane, most of us have never ventured west of the Mississippi. And it's such a glorious challenge to femininity—how can any spirited young and liberal woman in this game refuse it? Go West, dear girl, to Texas!"

"Texas is southwest," Devon said.

"Wherever, the maidens among us should go in that general direction, and let the cow-chips fall where they may."

"Ignore her," Jane advised. "Olivia's only trying to scatter her competition, always encouraging the rest of us to embark on adventurous safaris into the wilderness, while she remains in the safe comfortable fort. *She* wouldn't have accompanied the Lewis and Clark Expedition, or Ives' exploration of the Grand Canyon of the Colorado, and is terrified even of reservation Indians, much less the savages." The suppressed dissension between these two ladies occasionally flared into open hostility. "Of course her incessant prattle would be hazardous in a land where silence is often vital to security, and loose lips can bring disaster. I swear she could patent her mouth as a perpetual motion machine!"

Olivia's rebuttal was interrupted by a sudden commotion in the ladies' gallery, and then Mrs. Sprague entered in a cashmere cloak with a pierced gold heart pinned over her left breast, and a miniature jeweled Saracen blade stuck in her matching turban—the jewelry symbolizing, perhaps,

defiance of her husband and surrender to Cupid. Senator
Conkling immediately requested the floor from Sprague,
who was haranguing on some innocuous issue, to perform
for her.

"Sprague's furious," Olivia observed, while the others
scribbled notes. "He must suspect something! He's looking
daggers at Roscoe. 'Et tu, Brute?' There may be more than
verbiage in the American Forum today. Some fisticuffs,
possibly, or even bloodshed. Remember the '59 duel in
Lafayette Square, Mary, when Congressman Daniel Sickles
challenged his wife's lover, Philip Baron Key, son of Fran-
cis Scott Key?"

"It was murder," Mary reflected, "and Sickles not only
got away with it but became a decorated Union general
and has just been appointed minister to Spain."

"But why didn't he just get a divorce?" asked Devon.

"Divorce in the District requires an act of Congress,"
Grace explained. "Murder by duel is simpler, quicker, and
rarely penalized if the provocation is sufficient. No man
will ever convict another for killing his cuckold in an affaire d'honneur. Talk about barbarism in the wild West, it
still exists, even flourishes, in the tame and civilized East
too."

"Oh, shoot," Olivia muttered in disgust. "The spineless
Sprague is yielding to his potent adversary. Listen to this
man speak, Devon. He's not only the Apollo of the Senate, but its Cicero too. A tremendous orator, positively
mesmeric."

"He does have a magnificent voice and powerful delivery," Devon agreed.

"Yes, indeed! The senator from New York can make
trivia sound important, build molehills into mountains,
give a cloakroom water closet titantic proportions and
prime priority. And it's all to impress Kate. He plays the
whole scene to her, as though she were the only lady in
that balcony. And that's what the others have come for, to
observe and share vicariously and perhaps envy the budding romance of this mature Romeo and Juliet. Sometimes, when Senator Sprague is not present, Roscoe sends
Kate notes by the pages. She acknowledges them with a
nod or smile or wink. Once she returned a message and
was later seen in the corridor near his office, giving

credence to the rumor that it's their rendezvous. Oh, there's going to be an amorous scandal on the Potomac before long! You'll probably witness it, Devon, if you're not on the Mississippi or the Rio Grande by then."

Chapter 40

For Devon the White House represented the ultimate journalistic challenge and experience. Entering it, she could not help feeling proud of herself, and thinking that her ancestors would be proud of her too. Suddenly she remembered her father's last visit to Washington, as a delegate to the peace conference that had failed its purpose, and what he had said about President Lincoln, how courteous he had been to the Southerners, and how sad and worried he had seemed during the long tense discussions.

Journalists had always enjoyed access to the executive mansion, wherever its location—New York, Philadelphia, the District of Columbia. President Washington had paid them the tribute of saying that the War of Independence couldn't have been won without the loyal support of the Whig publishers and editors, and Devon had always been proud that a Marshall had been present to report the British surrender at Yorktown. No Marshall had witnessed Appomattox, however! How long ago it all seemed now, and yet how near. Eons in the past, and only yesterday. . . .

Mrs. Grant received the ladies of the press in the beautiful Blue Parlor—a celestial chamber, at least in aspect. Walls, furniture, carpet, all were blending shades of cool azure, clear or misty or muted, reflected in the multiple crystals of the illumined aurora borealis chandelier. There were masses of flowers from the conservatories, their fragrance heightened by the warmth of the pure white marble fireplace. And the First Lady was gracious beyond hospitality, with no suggestion of noblesse oblige. She was eager to please and to placate her critics, and above all to reflect credit on her position and her husband, who wandered in from his office to extend a personal welcome. As he shook hands, smiling his slow shy smile, it was hard for

Devon to realize the fear and hatred his name had once struck in the civilian Confederacy, and the horror and violence it had symbolized on the battlefields. She had expected his touch to be cold and hard, but it was warm and gentle.

The levee evolved as a friendly, almost intimate, brunch with tea and refreshments, during which their hostess recalled her early life, sharing wistful memories about her courtship and marriage, the birth of her children, her often difficult times at Hardscrabble and in Galena, while tactfully avoiding any mention of the late war, except to quote the President's laconic comment upon his nomination: "Let us have peace." And even those who had come with malice or mischief in mind were subdued, dissuaded, totally disarmed. Julia had conquered with kindness and humility.

She accompanied the reporters through the White House like a proud mistress showing her new home, revealing its beauty and lesser attractions, its pleasures and problems, comforts and discomforts, its housekeeping handicaps, and the imperative renovations which were already in progress. "Some of the ornaments I previously selected at Brown and Spaulding Decorators in New York have arrived," she announced. "Those in the East Room represent Night and Morning and the Union."

Viewing the East Room, Devon wrote in the shorthand she had devised: "Magnif. 4 white marble mantels, 8 Ven. mirrors, 3 elab cut glass chandes. Frescoed walls, ceiling. 8 life-size oil portraits of former Prez including Gil Stuart of Washington saved by D. Madison in fire of 1814, and I'm vis-a-vis with Old Abe! Sofas, chairs, crimson brocatelle. Drapes same, gilt cornices bearing U. S. coat-of-arms. Immense, exquis carpet gift from sultan of Turkey. State receptions, grand balls, soirees held in this chamber. Music by Marine band."

In the striking Red Parlor she noted: "Prez receives Foreign Min., other dignitaries here. Large, impressive. Oval shape. Bow window looks out on park and Potomac, to blue hills of Virginia. Light dim and rosy, reflecting vivid walls, furniture, carpet, hangings . . . all crimson in fireglow."

On another page: "State Dining Room adjoins, 40×30 ft. Banquet table seats 36, Julia will enlarge. Massive mahogany sideboard with carved eagle supports. Two consoles with same. Walls, carpet neutral colors; green satin damask drapes. Passages lead to large aquarium, grapery, 3 greenhouses in mansion gardens, wine cellar. 11 rooms in basement for kitchens, pantries, butler, servants, etc. Washington's dishes—fine old Cantonese platters, plates, cups—on display. Also Prez Madison's French china, deep buff, border of white-leaf wheels on black background. Lincoln's lovely Haviland. Monroe's gorgeous gold service. USG will add to china, silver, crystal."

The elegant simplicity of the Green Parlor appealed to Devon. She found it, "Cozy, almost homelike. Lace curtains, rosewood fur. covered in green-and-gold brocatelle. Silver wall-sconces, delicate, lovely. Mrs. G says mantel clock made of ebony and malachite, and ornate punch-bowl on cen. table gift from Emperor of Japan. Many tasteful ornaments."

There were thirty-one rooms in all, including the President's office, secretarial antechamber, audience room, cabinet room, public reception rooms, library, and billiards room. The spacious, handsomely columned corridor, which opened off the vestibule, extended the entire length of the house; along its walls were ferns and other greenery, mirrored French consoles, and ornate gilded and glazed benches with velvet cushions. Designed to impress visitors upon entrance, it succeeded overwhelmingly.

Although the presidential apartments were private, Mrs. Grant broke precedent by allowing the reporters to view them. The state bedchamber was grandly hung in purple and gold; damask curtains from a large gilded hoop draped the high massively carved bedstead, and the foot cushions were crimson velvet. The furniture, including two great wardrobes, was rosewood. The chandelier, depending from a frescoed and medallioned ceiling, formed a glittering cascade of crystal. And as in every room in the house on this chilly March day, a cheery fire crackled on the hearth.

The ladies' parlor was charmingly feminine, with delicate ebony furniture covered in blue satin. The daughter of the house had a dainty blue boudoir lined with mirrors, white organdy curtains, and a pale blue carpet strewn with pink rosebuds. Nellie Grant was a pert and pretty adolescent, with the promise of great beauty, and said to be her father's pet. Her proud mother showed a Brady portrait of her eldest son, Fredrick, a West Point cadet. Ulysses Junior was preparing to enter Harvard, and Jesse, the youngest boy, was still in knee breeches.

A stroll through the burgeoning spring gardens, under magnolias and catapultas, completed the tour. The First Lady bade them a cordial goodbye until her next levee, which was to become a regular ritual during her tenure there. The journalists could make what they would of her character and personality, and what they made was generally complimentary, forgetting the squinting eyes, the elongated nose and imperfect teeth and almost peasant buxomness, concentrating instead on the corona of dark lustrous hair, the sincerity of voice and smile and manner, the stylish gray moire gown trimmed in rose velvet, the genuine pearl jewelry. Combining her observations and information with sketches of the White House and its history, Devon produced an admirable article for the *Record*, and somewhat regretfully concluded her Washington assignment, arriving back in New York just in time to celebrate her son's first birthday.

Her reunion with Keith was both happy and sad, however, for Mrs. Hempstead had hinted that a permanent correspondency in Washington was in the offing. Tish Lambeth, who had refused to take her husband's name professionally, was recovering from a miscarriage and would soon be able to assume the metropolitan social beat again, releasing Devon Marshall for traveling assignments. But she did not know how to prepare Keith or herself for such an eventuality. He had arrived on the *Sprite*, with a cargo of expensive toys, most of which were beyond the baby's ability to appreciate, and Devon accused him of buying them for himself. He grinned, setting up the train. "Of course! That's half the fun of fatherhood."

"You bought enough for an orphanage, Keith. And all that candy! He'll be toothless before he's ten. You mustn't spoil him so, darling. It only makes it more difficult for Anna and Enid when we're away."

Keith was laying tracks, assembling tunnels and bridges, winding keys to make locomotives and cars run. Scotty sat in the middle of the floor, clapping his hands with infan-

tile delight, as if aware that he was the center of attention.
"I can't help it, Devon. I have to make the most of my
time with him. Perhaps we should hire a nanny to help
out."

"I wouldn't dream of offending Anna and Enid that
way! They are perfectly capable nursemaids. Next you'll
be talking about tutors and college and the grand tour!"

"Tempus fugit," he said. "Actually, it's not too soon to
consider a governess. A child is never too young to learn,
and early training is the best foundation for the future.
With good enough tutelage, he could qualify for Harvard
at fourteen, and possibly even younger."

"And under what surname will he register?"

"He'll have one long before then, Devon. He'd have it
now if you—" But her look stopped him. "Isn't the Shet-
land pony a beauty? As soon as he can sit saddle, I'll
teach him to ride. *That* should please his Virginian
mother."

"Oh, Keith! He can hardly manage his wooden hobby-
horse. Even the rocking duck is a challenge. He's still a
baby, one year old today, and the party's over, so take off
that silly Yankee Doodle Dandy hat!"

"What? Oh, I forgot it." But when he removed the
cocked crepe-paper triangle with its patriotic stars and
stripes and red feather, Scotty picked it up and stuck it
back on his father's head. "He wants me to wear it,
honey."

Devon laughed. "I give up. You're two of a kind."

"And you love us both?"

"And I love you both," she agreed, biting her lips.

"You seem anxious, darling. Problems?"

Hesitating, "Not exactly."

"Tell me."

"It's nothing," she insisted. "Play with your train."

Immediately he stood, flung off the party hat, and summoned Enid to take the child. "All right now. What's
wrong?" Lowering his voice, "Are you pregnant?"

Devon sighed, shaking her head, dreading a revelation
she knew would displease him far more than another pregnancy, which he would probably have welcomed as a
timely anchor. "No, nothing like that, Keith. It's just
that—well, I may have to leave New York again."

"So soon? Where to this time, and for how long?"

"Washington, and perhaps permanently."

His facial muscles tensed and flickered. "Well, you just won't go, that's all! You know how I feel about your career, Devon, and I've been humoring you. But not to that extent!"

"It would be a great opportunity for me, Keith, and possibly the best thing for all of us."

"How can you say that! What about Scotty?"

"That worries me," she admitted. "I mean, explaining his birth to a censorious world. I suppose I could say he's a war oprhan—the South is full of them now."

"Not soldiers' orphans of his age," he argued, "even if his father were supposedly killed on the last day! That was four years ago, Devon."

"You needn't remind me, Keith. I'm not likely to forget the date it ended! But perhaps it'd be more logical and credible to say he's the product of a Union rapist during the military occupation. The Yankees are still in Richmond, you know."

"That barb was a double-edged Rebel sword," he said, "and I resent it."

"Well, don't try to corner me, Keith, when I have no weapon to defend myself."

He stared at her, anger mounting. "You've been planning this, haven't you? Actually figuring how to pass off our child as someone else's! Perhaps a nonexistent sister's or cousin's? Goddammit, Devon! What do you think I'm made of—putty and straw? You're not going anywhere else to live, and certainly not taking my son with you."

"He's my son too, Keith."

"You didn't want him, I did."

Her eyes misted, then blazed. "You dare throw that up to me, knowing the reasons?"

"All right, I'm sorry. Just the same, I won't let you take him away from me now or ever, Devon."

"But it's not a foreign correspondency, Keith. We can still be together, when you come to Washington on business."

"No! That's final, Devon. This issue is not negotiable under any circumstances."

"Not even in bed?"

"Especially not in bed. I won't be led that way."

"What way?"

"By the penis. If you want to make love now, fine. If you expect to bargain with your assets, forget it."

"I thought I was the one being compromised," she said.

"Not entirely, my dear. I just declined a cabinet post and ambassadorship, remember?"

"And I wanted you to accept, remember?"

"You know damned well I couldn't! So far I've had no regrets, Devon. Don't give me any now, please."

"Oh, darling, I don't want to quarrel!" She put her arms around him, laying her head on his heart. "This is our baby's birthday . . . shouldn't we celebrate somehow?"

"What was the cake, ice cream and presents?"

"*His* celebration," she said, rising on tiptoe to kiss his sullen mouth. "Now let's have ours—"

"If you think I don't know I'm being beguiled and manipulated right now, my cunning little minx—"

"Oh, I know you're not made of putty and straw, Keith, and I'm glad, because I wouldn't want to change the master mold even if I could. No woman wants a dummy to dominate, any more than she wants to be a dominated dummy. Such a life would be intolerably dull for both sexes, don't you think? An occasional fight adds fillip to the relation—it's such fun making up! Spank me, Keith, but don't scorn me." She kissed him again, more ardently. "I love you so, darling. I was wild for you in Washington. The Sprague reception was sheer torture for me. I hoped you'd come to the Willard afterwards."

"You forbade it!"

"I know, and suffered for it that night. I wrote my piece for the *Record*, and then lay awake hopefully, and finally cried myself to sleep. I was even jealous and fearful that you might go to bed with her, or she might try to seduce you—"

His arm was guiding her toward the stairway. "I suppose Anna and Enid will be shocked. Lovers in broad daylight!"

"You once told me that love was too beautiful to be made only in darkness."

"You remember that?"

"I remember everything, Keith. Everything." Sometimes

there was more pain than pleasure in her reveries, and more grief and sorrow than joy, but she did not tell him that; nor did she mention her ominous premonition that their love was doomed.

Chapter 41

The staff of the *Record* were gathered around the office telegraph. Three thousand miles away, in the Utah Territory, a gold spike was about to be driven into a laurel tie to link the East and West by rail. The blows of the silver hammer, transmitted via the telegraphic key, would announce the feat to the country. The men were drinking coffee from mugs with their names stenciled in printer's ink, and smoking cigars and cigarettes. The three ladies occupied a corner of the room, out of range of the spittoons and ribaldry, sipping tea and nibbling cakes. All were tense and expectant, awaiting the momentous signal. The front page of the *Record* was ready for the special edition, lacking only a headline for the masthead dated May 10, 1869.

Travel space on the Union Pacific bound for its rendezvous with the Central Pacific at Promontory Point, north of Great Salt Lake, had been limited and allotted to the railroad tycoons and their guests, and only the most experienced journalists from the most prestigious papers. Nevertheless, Devon knew, had she requested it of Peter Barr Sweeny, he would have pulled enough strings through Jay Gould or Jim Fisk to get her aboard, even though Tammany had no interest or stakes in Territorial politics. The reason she didn't was because Keith Curtis, a large stockholder in the Union Pacific, was among the chosen few to witness the historic occasion. He would have been suspicious of her presence, if only because there were no women among the reporters, and she couldn't have borne crossing the continent with him under circumstances of suspicion and forced formality.

Suddenly Samuel Fitch leaped up and shouted, "There's the alert, boys! Quiet, everybody! Here it comes! Listen now, and count the blows!"

They listened to the sound of progress, counted its pounding pulse. After the gold spike was set, the two engines representing East and West were moved together and christened with champagne. A wiseacre cracked, "The twains have met!" and the nation received the message in Morse code: "Done!" The men then jumped up, each rushing to his particular job in publishing the *Record*.

When Devon returned to the calmer ladies' department, Mrs. Hempstead informed, "We have a note from Mrs. Keith Curtis in the mail. They are planning a ball to celebrate the first anniversary of her miraculous cure at Lourdes. She mentions that she has read and admired some of your features and would like you to cover the event."

Devon blanched. What could she say, do, how avoid it? A special request from someone of such social status was essentially a command. "She's certainly giving advance notice, isn't she? If memory serves, that 'anniversary' falls in June."

"The twenty-fifth, to be exact. I suppose she expects prepublicity, and we must oblige. Her husband may still end up in the cabinet or a foreign ministry. He's one of the dignitaries at Promontory Point now, you know."

Devon nodded. The papers had lists of the personages aboard both trains. She reasoned that Esther's premature public announcement was deliberately made during Keith's absence, precluding protest or cancellation. But such self-administered soothing syrup provided little comfort for Devon's anxiety and distress. She glanced out the windows, at the white marble bulk of City Hall, wondering if Sweeny were in the chamberlain's office. Then, unbidden, her mind drifted westward again, to Utah. Had Reed Carter covered the story for the Dallas *Post,* or was his paper too small and unimportant to acquire a seat in the coveted news caravan? It surprised her to think of the Texan now, for she never expected to see or hear from him again. It only showed how lonely she was for her beloved, and how disturbed by the ridiculous celebration in the offing.

By the time Keith returned, the papers had all been notified and Esther's invitations had been sent to Boston, Philadelphia, and Washington, even one to the White

House. Furious, he demanded, "What do you mean, planning this thing without my knowledge and consent?"

Esther smiled, polishing her long pointed nails with orris root and a buffer of Chinese jade. "Don't you think the occasion of your wife's cure is worthy of commemoration, darling? Besides, our friends are curious about our lack of entertainment; I've used the 'doctors' orders' excuse long enough. It's high time we started repaying some of our social obligations, and this will be a brilliant beginning. I've invited the President and Mrs. Grant, the cabinet, some ambassadors and senators and congressmen, my parents . . . oh, many important people!"

"Everybody except God, apparently."

"Well, I wasn't certain of His address," Esther quipped.

"Do you expect to crowd them all into this house?"

"No, dear. I've reserved the grand ballroom of the Fifth Avenue Hotel. It's really a dual celebration, since our wedding anniversary falls on the same date . . . or had you forgotten?"

"I should live so long," he muttered, rage receding in resignation, frustration dissolving in despair, "and be so lucky."

But acquiescence wasn't enough. Esther wanted a firm commitment, assurance that he could not possibly renege at the crucial moment. She said, "If the Grants accept, they may be our house guests. I enclosed a personal note to Julia."

"They'll accept," Keith said. "The Treasury is under pressure to redeem the war bonds in gold, and if the banks demand the same specie on their certificates—well, Grant is going to need some friends on Wall Street. Just be prepared to put up his retinue and bodyguards."

"Imagine actually having the President in residence! Isn't it exciting?"

"If you enjoy the prospect of a privacy invasion and possible assassination, my dear."

"Oh, I should think a general would know how to avoid such hazards and contingencies, strategically."

Esther began methodic preparations, determined to make an immaculate and perfect household more so. She screamed at the servants, finding fault with their work, donning white gloves to inspect furniture and mantels for dust, fanatically straightening pictures and shades and blinds, books and bibelots, criticizing perfection until, emotionally exhausted, she collapsed in tears on the parlor sofa. There were still menus to plan, fittings on her gown, discussions with the hotel management on decoration of the ballroom, the music and collation—the enthusiasm and excitement waned into worry and apprehension.

What was wrong with her? Why was she so tired, so nervous and irritable and distraught? It wasn't as if she were actually recuperating from a long and debilitating illness, for she had never been ill. Furthermore, she'd had six years of bed rest! And she was only thirty-two years old! But of course that wasn't young any more for a woman, who was considered middle-aged at thirty-five, and old at forty. Wrinkles, gray hair, and flabby flesh often appeared long before the crucial climacteric, at which time, like the Chinese mandarins and African tribal chiefs, many other men also relegated their wives to the archives of their lives, as if taboo, and acquired young concubines. Esther dreaded menopause and its attendant miseries more than smallpox and even death. But there were ways to preserve the illusion of youth long past its bloom, through clothes and cosmetics, tonics and diet. She would make a cult of beauty and dedicate herself to it. Ripen she might. Mellow, perhaps. Deteriorate, eventually. Decay, never!

Observing Keith she thought resentfully how much kinder age was to men. At thirty-four, he had not even reached his prime. His skin was still firm and tanned, and he had his full quota of teeth and hair. The few crinkles at the corners of his eyes and the few threads of silver at his temples only added maturity to his other attractions. His physique was still magnificent, wide straight shoulders, arched chest, flat belly, narrow hips. Still the athlete and sportsman, agile and alert, fencing at his club, riding, hunting, sailing, racing in Harlem Lane again or at least driving his rigs in that direction, and invariably the best dancer in any ballroom. By comparison men in their twenties seemed immature, callow, and insipid as schoolboys. Unfortunately, he was also still adamantly resisting her overtures, impervious to her charms and even her sorcery.

Ten dollars that old Spanish gypsy had charged her for the tiny vial of tincture of Old World herbs, guaranteeing the efficacy of the basic ingredient, mandrake root. Esther

had managed to slip it into his coffee one evening, and
waited expectantly for the effect. But it had succeeded only
in making him ill and frightening her. Suppose he accused
her of trying to poison him? She had paced the hall outside his suite, wondering if she should summon a physician. When finally he had ceased vomiting, she had
prepared a milk caudle and sent it to him by Hadley. He
was all right the next morning, but glowered at her suspiciously throughout breakfast and he drank only black
coffee, serving himself directly from the pot. At last he
spoke in low angry tones, "Did you underestimate the
product or its potency, Madam? If ever you try it again,
make sure it's a fatal dose!"

She feigned innocence. "I don't know what you mean,
Keith. You probably had a touch of ptomaine. Perhaps
the shellfish was tainted. I felt queasy myself, although I
didn't eat as much as you, and had to take bismuth and
paregoric for relief."

"You're lying, bitch! I know it was in my demi-tasse.
Will you tell me what it was, or must I choke it out of
you?"

"All right, but it wasn't poison, Keith. Just a harmless
herbal concoction, mostly mandrake root."

"An aphrodisiac?" He stared at her incredulously. "Did
you get it from a witch or witch doctor?"

"A Romany woman in Chelsea."

"She must have cooked it in Hell's Kitchen, using the
devil's own recipe!" Suddenly the effect struck him as a
comical fiasco, a scheme that had boomeranged, and he
smiled ironically. "Good Lord, you are desperate, aren't
you? Was it supposed to turn me into a rutting bull, panting and pawing at your bedroom door? You stake too
much on my animal appetites, Esther. I'll never be that
hungry for you again."

"Liar," she chided. "You were starving that evening in
Washington, and you know it. But you wouldn't accept my
food, for fear of developing a taste and craving for it
again."

He laughed, shaking his head. "Sorry to disappoint you,
Mrs. Curtis. If that 'magic potion' was guaranteed, demand your money back. You'd have had better luck with
your derringer!"

*

In addition to the government operatives, Keith hired a complement of Pinkerton detectives to protect the President and his own property. For when news broke that the Grants were in Gramercy Park, hordes of curiosity seekers drifted into the area, spectator madness set in, and near-riot. And Grant made matters worse by insisting on mingling with the masses and shaking hands with "my friends and fellow countrymen."

"Mr. President," his host warned, "they'll strip you for souvenirs and leave you in your union suit."

The anxious agents agreed and looked at Curtis gratefully. Theirs was a job of continual strain and responsibility, uncertainty and fear. But the general, accustomed to personal risk and danger on battlefields, only smiled and continued pumping hands, waving, greeting, until the metropolitan police forced back the mob, blocked off the street, and surrounded the house into which the genial President was finally and safely ushered.

"Precautions are necessary, I suppose," he told Keith over brandy and cigars in the library. "But my theory about assassination is the same as Lincoln's. We discussed it together once, when the South had a price on both our heads, and agreed that we must live with it as normally as possible. He even walked the streets of Richmond after it surrendered, and spent a night there. Of course Admiral Porter and a guard of ten sailors accompanied him, but any marksman with a rifle could have shot him down. And I was always uneasy when he reviewed the troops or came to the front, for fear some disgruntled draftee or deserter would seek revenge. Because if they really want to get you, they can. Nothing can stop 'em!"

"That may well be, sir. But if you don't mind, I'd prefer that they didn't get you here," Keith said, and Grant grinned in his peppery beard, hoisting his glass in a salute.

"It's a damn nuisance, isn't it, having the President for a guest? Bet it was your missus' idea, eh? No sane man would want such a bother and burden. The A. T. Stewarts entertained us one night and called it the Ten Thousand Dollar Honor. Ten Thousand Dollar Headache might have been more accurate. And I'm sure the amount of wear and tear on the nervous system are incalculable. But the ladies, God bless 'em, including my Julia, don't seem to realize that the President's presence anywhere is more apt to be an imposition than a privilege," he said, and promptly headed off any protest from his host by praising his hospitality. "Great brandy, my friend. Napoleon quality. And Bismarck should smoke such cigars."

"Permit me to send you a case of each, Mr. President."

Grant nodded appreciatively. All sorts of gifts were pouring into the executive mansion and being accepted, with no thought of propriety or ethics or bribery. If the country could receive presents from foreigners, why not from its own citizens? He was, in fact, hurt when his personal friends forgot him, disappointed when they offered no more than felicitations, which awareness had prompted Keith's gesture.

Now his hostess appeared on the threshold, wreathed in smiles. "Forgive me for intruding, gentlemen. Keith, I think we must get ready for the ball. Mrs. Grant prefers to rest awhile and come later, if that's all right with you, Mr. President?"

"Quite," Grant agreed, always deferring to his wife in such matters. "Go ahead, Keith. I'll relax here awhile longer, if I may."

"Please do, sir. A carriage will be at your disposal whenever you are ready. If you need anything meanwhile, just tell the butler. His name is Hadley."

"And a fine major domo he is—I'd like to appropriate him for the White House. But I'll help myself, thank you."

The presidential entourage included a personal maid and valet. Every room in the house was occupied, with guests and agents and servants, and the overflow, including Esther's parents, were dependent upon the hospitality of friends and neighbors. Hadley was in charge of the entire ménage and managing excellently. Thank God for English butlers trained in noble service! Serene, steady, meticulous, cognizant, Esther knew she would have failed or blundered without him. And surely the President was only joking about confiscating Hadley for his household!

Lurline and Monsieur Dubonnet hovered over Esther, attending to her toilette. The Frenchman was ecstatic at the prospect of assisting with Madame Grant's coiffure, possibly persuading her to allow him to employ some of his subtle arts and artifices. The dear lady needed some improvement on nature, something more than the elegant Venetian velvet gown he had glimpsed her maid steaming

over a boiling kettle—if only the wrinkles could be so easily erased from her simple face! No competition for the
Worth creation of Madame Curtis—iridescent moire antique and Florentine lace—but then there was no comparison of face or figure, either. And certainly not éclat.

Esther was alone in her boudoir when Keith knocked
and entered looking puzzled. "I can't find my diamond
studs and links," he said, and Esther chuckled. "What's so
funny?"

"You, darling. A houseful of detectives, and you can't
find your jewelry. Try looking in my case."

"What the devil would they be doing in *your* case?"

"I put them there earlier, so we could have some privacy and conversation. I'm afraid your rooms must be
given to the Pinkerton men tonight, Keith. And don't
blame me, *you* hired them! You will just have to sleep in
here."

"Such subtlety! Set the trundle up in the parlor."

"Suit yourself," she shrugged. "Do you like my gown?"

"It'll do, I guess."

"Monsieur Dubonnet raved, said it's *exquis* and *enchan-
teresse*."

"Monsieur would say that, yes."

"Oh, I know he's somewhat eccentric, Keith, but a marvel in other respects. And he has offered his services to
Mrs. Grant."

Visualizing Grant's reaction to the fluttering fop, Keith
could only smile. Esther picked up a black velvet jeweler's
box, opened it on a diamond riviere, bracelet, and pende-
loque earrings. "Your anniversary gift, I presume, Mrs.
Curtis?"

"I remembered, Mr. Curtis, even if you forget."

"They go back to Tiffany's tomorrow," he ordered.

"Very well, but I intend to wear them tonight. Keith,
and to say you gave them to me." Her purple eyes cast a
warning glance. "Don't make a liar or fool of me!"

"You've already made both of yourself, Madam. And
now, if you have no further edicts, we had better get on
with the masquerade. That's what it is, you know. A bal
masque sans costume. It was pretense at Lourdes, and this
wedding anniversary celebration is pretense too. Don't you
ever tire of pretense, Esther?"

"Don't you? Aren't you acting now, jolly good fellow,

genial host to the President? Weren't you acting in Washington, at the inaugural ball and all the receptions? Aren't we both living a lie, a farce, a fantasy? What makes you think yours is any better, more honest, holier than mine?"

"You're right," he said grimly. "We're a pair of goddamn hypocrites! Worse, cowards. But at least I think I have a valid reason for my masquerade: protecting an innocent child. Yours is sheer selfish vanity and vindictiveness."

"Your 'reason' is a year old now, isn't he? How much longer do you think you can protect him and his mother, Keith? Five years, ten, forever? You should be grateful for my understanding and cooperation. Not many wives would be so considerate under the circumstances."

"Nor many husbands so patient," he muttered, setting his studs and links. "And if we don't get out of here, we'll be late to our own deception."

"Reception."

"No, my dear. Deception."

Madison Square before the Fifth Avenue Hotel was packed with people, standing on boxes and barrels, hanging like monkeys out of trees and off lampposts, hoping for a glimpse of the luminaries arriving in the carriage procession. The police had put up ropes and barricades and formed a cordon with the military. Security agents were stationed in the lobby and ballroom, where admittance was by invitation only. Small fortunes had been offered for cards, some had been counterfeited, and a few sold at auction.

Reporters were required to present credentials. It was the most coveted social assignment in town, and the press sent its best representatives. Devon saw Kate Field, Jenny June, Fanny Fern, Minnie Squier for Frank Leslie's numerous publications. Olivia, Mary Clemmer Ames, Gail Hamilton, and Ben Perley Poore had come from Washington, and there were journalists from Boston, Philadelphia, Hartford, Baltimore, and other cities.

Reluctant as Devon was to attend, she could neither shirk duty nor let personal feelings interfere with her career. If she could bear seeing them together socially in Washington, she could bear it in New York, or wherever assigned. And this time she wouldn't try to avoid facing him, talking, even dancing if he dared. He mustn't know how adversely these public meetings affected her, lest he intensify them to induce her resignation. She had bought a new gown from Madame Demorest for the occasion, white satin and Chantilly lace, the skirt a mass of frothy flounces falling from a tightly molded basque whose decolletage enhanced her smooth fair shoulders and high full breasts. A delicate white lace mantilla, a new vogue popularized by the Empress Eugenie from her native Spain, lay like mist on her golden curls, and she wore Keith's pearls and favorite jasmine scent.

Esther stared at her from the receiving line, greeting guests perfunctorily, wishing the Grants would arrive so the ball could begin. "Miss Marshall doesn't dress much like a reporter," she remarked to Keith during a respite. "She looks now as if she were modeling a bridal ensemble ... and don't tell me you haven't noticed, Casanova."

"I've noticed, Madame Bovary. Beautiful, isn't she? And so young."

Esther gave a wistful sigh. "Yes, so young. But I doubt as pure and innocent as her virginal gown—she has the rosy glow of a woman in love. Strange, she's still single. But perhaps the man in her life isn't, or she's wed to her career. She's really quite talented and versatile, though, and undoubtedly dancing is one of her accomplishments. Ask her later on, if you wish. Just remember, your wife is able to dance again now."

"This replica of Lourdes' grotto spouting champagne is in execrable taste, Esther. The French minister will be affronted. Nor will the Virgin's statue of carved mozzarella please the Italian minister."

"I don't see why. France exports more wine than holy water, and the empire is publicizing the shrine now; even Napoleon and Eugenie have visited it. Italy has graven images in every church, including St. Peter's, and consumes tons of cheese. I understand the Pope's favorite is mozzarella, prepared from the Vatican's own recipe. But surely you can't criticize our anniversary cake. The chef did himself proud, don't you think?"

"A sweet monument to many years of bitterness," he replied of the towering, elaborately frosted edifice. "Is the punch safe to drink, or contaminated with your witch's brew?"

"Damn you," she muttered.

Some guests approached. They smiled, shook hands, accepted congratulations and well wishes. Keith was amused, annoyed, bored by the mockery, the whole ironic travesty.

"I wonder what's keeping the Grants," Esther whispered. "As if they had to make an entrance! Well, *finally*," she breathed in relief, as the orchestra hailed the chief. "Oh, poor Julia! How drab and dreary. Well, not even Monsieur Dubonnet can perform miracles. Perhaps *she* should go to Lourdes."

Chapter 42

The ball, opening with the traditional promenade followed by a quadrille d'honneur, was soon in full swing. Devon recognized many of the same faces and figures, domestic and foreign, that she had seen in the capital. The same formal black tails and white ties, the gold braid and fringed epaulettes of the military, the bright ribbons and medals of the diplomats. With the President, vice president, and most of the cabinet, the Speakers of both Houses, and ranking generals and admirals in New York, she wondered who was minding the country's business in Washington. But such journalistic impertinence would have been expediently stricken from her report. Society, not government, was her primary concern, although sometimes the two seemed harder to separate than church and state.

The voices, the chatter and laughter, the coquetry and flirtations, the music and refreshments all seemed familiar. Strauss and Lanner waltzes, Joseph Gungl's wistful *Dreams of the Ocean* collection. Devon saw Keith dancing with the First Lady, while the President favored Mrs. Curtis. Then Grant and Mrs. Hamilton Fish, and Esther in the arms of the secretary of state. Esther and the French ambassador, and Keith and Madame de Noialles. The combinations were endless. She glimpsed Senator Conkling's flaming head in the crowd, but pregnancy had forced Kate Chase Sprague to decline. During intermission dozens of waiters passed trays of champagne, punch, and hors d'oeuvres. Then came an intricate German cotillion at which the Prussian ambassador excelled, a gay Polish polka and merry mazurka, a sprightly schottische—everything but the Highland fling and Irish jig.

A room had been prearranged for the press, and the presence there of James Gordon Bennett Junior, heir apparent to the New York *Herald* empire, created considerable excitement and wonder, for no one could predict or even imagine what this fantastic young man might do on whim or impulse.

Devon had never met him before, although he was already a legend on Park Row. She had seen him around town, a tall strapping ginger-haired rake in his late twenties, with an aquiline nose and walrus mustache over a frankly sensual mouth. Educated abroad, where he had spent most of his childhood and youth, he was intelligent, sophisticated, arrogant, and utterly dissolute. On Printing House Square they said his odyssey in the Paris fleshpots began in puberty, that he was a voluptuary in his teens and a drunkard before twenty; that he was spoiled, selfish, and completely uninhibited, given to orgies and violence and verging on insanity. But he was also a flamboyant sportsman, possessed of the kind of extravagance and derring-do so admired by male Manhattan, who winked at his revelry and praised his reckless racing in the yacht regattas, his wild coaching copied from the duke of Beaufort, on which he whipped his horses into foaming frenzy and occasionally to death. He was notorious for night-coaching in the nude, tearing along the shadowy roads of the upper island like some moon-mad phantom pursued by the Furies. Nevertheless, he had been admitted to three of the most coveted and exclusive gentlemen's clubs in the city—the Yacht, the Jockey, and the Union—which still ostracized his father, who was generally considered to be the most contemptible and repulsive man in New York. And though Junior had not been on the Curtis guest list, he had simply used his press-card as his invitation.

Now, observing the ladies with an expert eye, he remarked to Devon, "What a fine display of female flesh! I haven't seen so many half-naked bosoms since I left Paris."

"Most of their gowns were designed there, Mr. Bennett."

"Yours too, Miss Marshall? It's gorgeous. You're gorgeous, the cream of this bumper crop." His gaze stripped her. "I'd heard the *Record* had a great beauty on its staff, your purse now, and let's see if you dance as well as you write—" and for once rumor understated truth. Tuck that pad in

"Oh, I can't, sir! I'm here on business, not pleasure."

"Can't you combine them, like Minnie Squier and Olivia, et al? I know Fitch is a slave driver, but he wouldn't fire a pretty little thing like you, for fear some other publisher would snap her up. Me, for instance. I suppose you know what makes poor Sam so testy? He's a kept man, supported by Tammany, and it piques his masculine pride and ego. But he's in rather precarious straits—similar to a proud prostitute forced to solicit for survival, and his rag would go down the red ink drain into oblivion without Tweed largesse."

"I try not to mix in politics," Devon said demurely.

Bennett's ribald laughter turned some heads. "Honeychile, that's what the free press is all about, and we couldn't exist without our Constitutional rights. But those statesmen were also politicians, you know, and one suspects they wrote the First Amendment to give them the liberty of verbally and otherwise redressing their enemies and opposition. Whigs, every last one of 'em, looking to their own political advantage in addition to the country's welfare. The Revolution was a war between political factions as much as the Crown and Colonies, and for independence of mind and spirit as well as body and pocketbook. Politics brought the pot to boil at the Boston Tea Party—and don't tell me you thought it was only taxes. But enough of this ancient history and shop talk. Come now, dance with me. If you refuse, I'll make a nasty scene and embarrass you."

Aware of his reputation, Devon acceded. He had been drinking champagne, which he consumed like water, and his eyes were somewhat glassy in his flushed face. But drunk or sober he danced expertly, if indecorously, his arm too tight about her waist, his hand hot and moist on hers. His passions were spontaneous, as combustible as his temper, and he was accustomed to satisfying his appetites and desires; nor was he ever abashed by his natural male responses to a pretty young female. Devon tried to remain reticent and aloof, but his ardor was aggressive.

"Are you a virgin?" he asked unexpectedly. "Oh, don't blush! That's a beautiful word, used every day in the Catholic Church. Virgin Mary, Blessed Virgin, Immaculate Virgin, Holy Virgin; litanies, rosaries, prayers, hymns extoll her virginity. My mother's Catholic, and I'm sort of—baptized, but not practicing. I'm more atheist than anything, like my father, who has only contempt for organized religion and blasts them all in his editorials. I'm just curious about your chastity, since you're not married. Consider my curiosity a compliment, my dear. Believe me, I wouldn't bother if I weren't interested."

How respond to such dubious chivalry? "Well, thank you, I guess."

"But you won't satisfy my curiosity?" Grinning, "Well, I can't blame you. Obviously my reputation has preceded me, and you've heard of my escapades and exploits. All true, Miss Marshall, and I offer no apologies. It is my good fortune to possess an insatiable libido, and my Eros dream is to find a female of similar sexual temperament. A nymphomaniac, to be specific. Now you really are blushing! And such a lovely pearly pink—boxed, it'd be worth a mint." Bending closer, so that his droopy mustache brushed her cheek, he whispered, "Why don't you slap my arrogant face? It'd attract attention. A shame for Grant to hog it all. I never did cotton to him much, and my father not at all. Ah, this waltz is over—aren't you relieved? I want to ask Kate Field now, I'm trying to woo her away from old Greeley to the Bennetts. But I shall stalk you again, pretty pussy . . ."

As Devon stared after him in mute indignation, Keith approached with smoking eyes. "I didn't know you danced on duty, Miss Marshall."

"Sometimes, Mr. Curtis."

"May I have the pleasure, then?" On the polished floor, which had received a coating of shaved wax during an intermission, they glided as gracefully as swans on water. "Did you find young Bennett so charming you forgot your work rule?"

"There are exceptions to every rule."

"Oh . . . and you made one for him?"

"He threatened to make a scene if I refused."

"He would too, the bastard. Always hunting a new thrill or new woman. I assume he propositioned you?"

"Oh, really, Keith!"

"He did, didn't he? The sonfabitch! I ought to kill him."

"Keith, he asked me for a dance, not an assignation."

"That was next. I know him, Devon. He's conceited and overbearing, and thinks himself irresistible to women. A decent one is not safe in his company. He'd still be a social pariah, like his old man, if his schooner *Henrietta* hadn't won the transatlantic run from New York to Needles, England, in December of '66. The purse was ninety thousand dollars, and the winter seas were raging, so he became something of a conquering hero. That's how he got into the best clubs. But he's no good, Devon. Stay away from him. He brags about his conquests and debaucheries, and has a yen for virgins."

"Well, I'm not a virgin."

"But he doesn't know that, does he? Every single girl is a challenge to his sexual prowess, and every seduction another notch on his monstrous ego. Don't give him any encouragement, that's all."

"Encouragement? Oh, my God, Keith!"

"Smile, Devon. People are watching."

"Including your wife," she snapped. "She must realize we're quarreling, Keith, and strangers don't argue in public."

"Would you like to meet the President?"

"Don't you remember, or read my stuff? I met him in Washington, at the Sprague reception. And I shook hands with him at Mrs. Grant's first press levee."

"Well, would you like to dance with him?"

"Not especially."

He smiled faintly. "No doubt you'd prefer Jefferson Davis or Robert E. Lee. Incidentally, I hear Davis is in seclusion at the Bennett estate in Washington Heights. Seems there was some truth to the Copperhead rumors about Bennett Senior during the war, and he was a treasonous turncoat in his libelous attacks on Lincoln."

Tears glistened in Devon's eyes, and her voice quavered, "How cruel you are sometimes, Keith."

"No, Devon, you mustn't think that. I'm just jealous and resentful of other men's attentions to you. I don't want anyone else touching you—and especially not that odious character!" He drew her closer, almost intimately so, forgetting or ignoring discretion. "You're lovely, as always, but particularly so this evening. Esther mentioned earlier that you look like a bride, and you do. Radiant, and that reprobate saw the glow. I want to kiss you now, make love to you. I wouldn't go home tonight if we didn't have company."

"Poor darling. Sometimes I think the rich and famous

are more to be pitied than envied. If you were an ordinary man, none of this would be happening now. And we wouldn't have our personal problems, either, because we would never even have met, would we? You wouldn't have come to Richmond hunting bargain property, and I wouldn't have tried to sell you mine."

Only vaguely aware that the music had ended, Keith still held her in the waltz position, gripping her hand and gazing raptly into her face, which was pale and lovely as a moonflower. And next to them stood Esther and Mayor Hall—the elegant Oakey in baronic attire and monocle, the only invited Tammany sachem. Recognizing Devon, he smiled and bowed. "It's nice to see you again, Miss Marshall. How are you?"

"Quite well, thank you, Your Honor." She held her breath, lest he betray secrets, but he was too shrewd and suave to commit such a faux pas. Dimpling in gratitude, Devon explained at random, "I met Mayor Hall in Albany, at the Governor's Ball. Would you care to say a few words for the *Record* about this one, sir?"

"Only that it's brilliant, and I'm enjoying it exceedingly, although," he smiled humorously, "I've never been at such a political disavantage, numerically. I feel somewhat like a Democrat at a Republican convention."

"May I quote Your Honor?"

"Why not? My constituents would surely agree."

Esther touched her husband's arm. "I'm sure the mayor and Miss Marshall will excuse us, dear. The caterer would like to serve the buffet now, I think. It's rather warm, and he's afraid the ice molds might melt prematurely. Wait till you see the masterpieces of ice sculpture!"

Idle chatter. Forced gaiety. The evening had suddenly lost its luster for Esther and began to pall. The dancing, the crush tired and even bored her. The superficial smiles and laughter and inane conversation were actually debilitating. A torturing headache came on: demons of pain plucked at her brain, relentless and vicious, darting in and out of her skull, stabbing with hot pokers at her temples, behind her eyeballs and ears, in her neck and spine. Her armpits and palms were moist and clammy, and her perfume had evaporated. She felt hot, sticky, unfastidious, flesh-and-bone weary. Perhaps a respite in the ladies' lounge would revive her.

Fortunately, it was empty. Esther locked the door and virtually collapsed on the bench before the vanity table. Monsieur Dubonnet's artistry was not as subtle as she had imagined. The powder had begun to cake, and against its unnatural whiteness the black beauty patches stood out like disfiguring moles. Too much mascara and eyeshadow and lip rouge! The glue he had used on her hair had weakened and a few tendrils fallen down, straggling on her neck. She resembled a painted bisque doll whose glaze had cracked to reveal the common clay.

That French fop! That Parisian pimp! Fifty dollars she had paid him to make her look like a fifty-cent whore! Oh, Lord. If only she didn't have to go back out there and face all those people, be calm and poised and charming and perfect when she was about to shatter into fragments. Did their friends suspect? Had they seen, noticed, guessed? Were the female hypocrites gossiping now behind sly hands and handkerchiefs and fans?

She repaired the facial damage as best she could, applied more cosmetic camouflage and essence, almost panicking at the knock on the door. My God, but her nerves were frazzled to fiddle strings, and about to pop! "One moment, please!" She leaned closer to the cruel mirror. Were those circles under her eyes, or shadows? A parenthesis enclosing her mouth? No, just the garish lighting. She must order the gaslights dimmed in the ballroom, and more candles. At last Esther opened the door and there she stood, the young and beautiful bitch! "Oh, Miss Marshall! I hope I didn't inconvenience you. I trust you're accumulating enough news for your column?"

"More than space will permit print," Devon replied.

"Well, if you'd like a private audience with Mrs. Grant, come to tea in my home tomorrow afternoon, at four."

"That's very kind of you, Mrs. Curtis."

"Not at all," Esther protested. "Pardon me, please. My guests are waiting."

Should Devon mention the invitation to Keith? No, he'd probably forbid her to accept—and it was an opportunity she couldn't afford to miss. Somehow, some way, she'd navigate the emotional reefs of Gramercy Park, and get the exclusive interview!

Devon left before the finale of the ball, while the lights were being dimmed in the romantic tradition for the last waltz, and the husband-host was inextricably caught in the wifely web.

They were alone in the brougham. The Grants and two operatives occupied the clarence behind them, and more agents followed in other Curtis vehicles. The Pinkertons had suggested the sandwiched arrangement—Curtis vanguard and detective flank—and Esther resented the jeopardy in which Keith had so willingly placed them. Prime targets for any crackpot with an urge to kill, and if he didn't value his own safety, he might at least have considered hers! Preoccupied or obsessed, he had not spoken since the armed caravan had left the hotel for Gramercy Park.

"Miss Marshall is coming to tea tomorrow," she announced as casually as possible.

His face was in shadow, concealing any reaction other than the same somber sardonic profile. "Why?" he asked quietly.

"I invited her to interview Mrs. Grant."

"At tea? Esther, you know damn well they're leaving for Long Branch in the morning!"

"So I hoodwinked her! That should give you a clue that your mystery woman is no longer a mystery to your wife. It's Devon Marshall, isn't it? I should have guessed long ago, the day she came to the house with Madame Josie. Your emotions were as nakedly revealed then as her body! Thinking it was just lust, I teased and taunted you with her. But I caught that same expression at the Spragues' reception in Washington—that same admiration and desire whenever you looked at her, and then tonight—what were you quarreling about? Your jealousy of Jimmy Bennett? Say something, Keith!"

"What should I say?"

"That's it's true or false. Admit or deny it, or something. All right, then. Keep your silence. I'll have my answer tomorrow, one way or another."

"She may not come, Esther."

"Oh yes, she will, Keith—unless you warn her, which would constitute confession! She's too ambitious to pass up such a golden opportunity to further her career. Too bad there will be a 'sudden change' in the presidential plans. How disappointed she'll be!" she gloated.

"No sane woman would want such a meeting, Esther."

"On the contrary, darling. A wife without curiosity about her husband's mistress is abnormal. This affair concerns me too, you know. My life, my marriage, my future. I want to know what she expects of you. And me."

Keith ground his teeth. "You really are a bitch, aren't you? A genuine bona fide bitch!"

"And so is she, or she wouldn't be involved in this sordid mess, would she?" The brougham halted before the brownstone mansion bastioned with police. "Well, here we are, at our happy little home! Naturally, you'll offer the President a nightcap. I doubt he could sleep without it. Evidently those stories about his intemperance in the military were not exaggerated. He certainly does seem to enjoy his liquor, and have a prodigious capacity for it. Perhaps Julia will share some sherry with me."

Chapter 43

After weeks of agonizing over the menus, Esther was disgusted to discover that the President had a plebeian palate and would have been just as pleased with common fare as the royal dishes set before him. Moreover, he had installed an army quartermaster as White House chef, who served such hearty mess as boiled mackerel, beefsteak, bacon and fried apples, hominy grits, buckwheat cakes, and potent coffee for breakfast. The First Lady's tastes were more refined, although she confided a fondness for Southern cooking, particularly that of Virginia and Carolina. To the Boston-bred New Englander, these revelations were heresy.

The whole thing was something of an ordeal, and Esther was rather relieved when it was over, and the Grants and their entourage departed for their cottage at Long Branch. But still she could not relax and longed for one of Hilde's soothing massages. The brilliant success of the state visit and ball was overshadowed by her personal discovery, so diminished and tarnished by it that in retrospect it seemed like a failure. And her dilemma was now monumental. Devon Marshall was no ordinary rival, no temporary convenience to be dismissed with scorn and contempt. Not only was she young and beautiful and obviously genteel, but Keith was deeply and desperately in love with her, totally involved and committed. His fierce jealousy and possessiveness had betrayed him despite his secrecy and precautions to protect her. Now he was brooding in the library, his conviviality having vanished with their guests.

Had he warned the wench? This seemed unlikely with the President's presence requiring his own as host. How awkward it must have been for him last night, with the house under guard inside and out. Sneaking off even in disguise would have been difficult and embarrassing if detected. No, Esther was satisfied that Keith had not been in personal contact or communication with his inamorata since she had invited Devon to tea. But he was devious enough to have dispatched a footman on an errand this morning, or alerted her some other way.

Neither of them slept well. Having waited for Keith to come up after his nightcap with the President, Esther had again disrobed before him and flaunted her nudity as flagrantly as she had in Washington. But this time he ignored her completely, impervious, immune in self-isolation, and she knew his restless trundle-tossing was not due to smoldering passion and desire. Her suspicions and accusations had only further estranged and annihilated him, destroying all hope of reconciliation. A gross mistake, perhaps, but too late now to rectify. And since she could neither retract nor retreat, she must proceed, advance.

The sun was beaming on Gramercy Park, flowers blooming, birds singing, children playing behind the iron pickets and locked gates. A perfect day for Devon's new mint-green linen dress, one of Madame Demorest's career designs, feminized with white lace collar and cuffs and flowery bonnet. She arrived precisely at the appointed hour, remembering the cold misty November day she had first seen the great brownstone house guarded by recumbent granite lions holding ornate bronze gaslamps between their forepaws. But where were the crowds and police? Presumably the President had gone somewhere, and hopefully Keith had accompanied him.

Memory impressions of the luxury and splendor in which he lived included the liveried butler, who opened the door, and the magnificent foyer with its tessellated black-and-white marble floor and richly paneled walls arrayed with ancestral portraits in elaborate frames. "Miss Marshall, of the *Record*," she said, presenting her card. "I'm expected."

"Yes, Miss. This way, please."

But as he led her toward the parlor, Keith stepped out of the library, surprise in his expression. "A message was sent to your office, Miss Marshall. You didn't receive it?"

"Why no, I didn't, Mr. Curtis. I was out on assignment."

Hadley said, "Mrs. Curtis is in the parlor."

"The spider waiting for the fly," Keith muttered, and Devon glanced at him curiously.

"Miss Marshall," Esther cried, coming forward with a cunning smile. "I presume Mr. Curtis has explained the sudden change in the President's plans. Unfortunately, they left earlier than anticipated. But do stay to tea, anyway, won't you?"

Comprehension appalled Devon; she felt like a trapped fool, momentarily abashed. "Thank you, but I really don't think I have the time, Mrs. Curtis—"

"Nonsense! You cleared your schedule for this appointment, didn't you? And it needn't be a journalistic loss. Why not interview me? After all, I was hostess to the First Family, and I'm sure your readers would like to know how one prepares for such a momentous occasion. Sit down, please. How do you like your tea? Cream, sugar, lemon?"

"Lemon, please."

"Mr. Curtis takes both his tea and coffee black—or is that superfluous information, Miss Marshall? I assume you're acquainted with his tastes and habits and preferences?"

"Stop it, Esther," Keith said. "You're not going to play this out like some English drawing room satire! Tell her why you invited her here this afternoon—that you knew at the time of your invitation that Mrs. Grant would not be present."

Esther ceased pouring, put down the Wedgewood cup with a tiny clatter. "I doubt that explanations are necessary, Keith. I suspect Miss Marshall is aware of my reasons."

"Vaguely," Devon acknowledged, "but puzzled, Mrs. Curtis. What do you hope to achieve with this meeting?"

"What do *you* hope to achieve, Miss Marshall, by your liaison with my husband!" Esther countered.

"That's enough, Esther!"

"Enough? I haven't started yet, Keith!" She stared malevolently at Devon. "I asked you a question, Miss Marshall, and would appreciate an honest answer, if you're capable of truth and honesty. What do you expect of my husband?"

"Nothing," Devon replied, sick with humiliation.

"Nothing?" Mockery gurgled in Esther's throat. "He's

keeping you, isn't he? You have a child by him, don't you? He wants to marry you, doesn't he? You call that nothing!"

"I'm cognizant of the circumstances, Mrs. Curtis, which is why I don't expect anything of him ... or you. But I am curious about what you expect of me."

"What any wife would expect and demand of her husband's mistress, Miss Marshall. An end to the affair!" There was no equivocation in her voice or manner; it was an edict, and she awaited the sledgehammer effect, pleased at the staggering blow to the other woman's equanimity.

Her response was barely audible, eyes downcast. "It's more than just an affair, Mrs. Curtis, and it may surprise you to learn that I have tried to end it." She avoided visual contact with Keith, sensing that he was displeased with her humility, resentful of her acquiescence.

"Not hard enough, evidently," Esther quipped. "But I'm sure it's only the child that binds him, Miss Marshall. Naturally, he is concerned for his son's welfare and future. If you would consent to surrender him—"

Keith interrupted angrily, "Just who do you think you are, Esther? A judge in domestic court awarding custody? Don't say any more, Devon—you've said too much already. She wasn't actually sure of any of this, only speculating, until your admission. You walked blindly and obligingly into her web, and she'll do her damndest now to devour you!"

"I'm sorry for my vulnerability, Keith. I'm just not very good at intrigue."

"Well, she happens to be a past-mistress at it!" He rose, gigantic in his fury. "But you needn't endure this inquisition and indignity any longer, Devon. Come, I'll take you home."

Esther sprang off the sofa and wedged herself rocklike between them. "It's not that simple, Keith! This thing has to be settled, one way or another."

"I settled it years ago, Madam!" Brushing her aside, he took Devon's arm. The gesture infuriated Esther. She grabbed at Devon's sleeve, ripping the lace trim. "You brazen bitch! Do you think you can just walk out of my home with my busband? I'm warning you, Devon Marshall! Leave him alone! Get out of his life, or I'll destroy you and your child!"

Keith urged Devon toward the door, but Esther pursued. Something demonic had taken possession of her, releasing all caution and restraint. Suddenly she lunged at Devon like an enraged cat at evasive prey. Startled, Devon gave a short cry and raised her arms protectively. Keith stepped swiftly between them, and Esther's sharp nails raked his face instead. He caught her wrists and shook her furiously. She struggled with him madly, twisting, moaning, shrieking at Devon, reiterating her threats of violence and destruction. Her purple irises had dilated and darkened murkily, nostrils flaring viciously, lips receding from her teeth. Devon shrank from the sight of her, stripped now of all beauty and rationality—ugly, evil, maniacal.

"Esther!" Keith shouted, trying to penetrate her blind-deaf frenzy and utterly senseless rampage. "Esther, for God's sake! Hush! Stop!" Blood smeared his face and shirt; he was pouring sweat and trembling violently. He slapped her to bring her to her senses, but her emotions were beyond control. She retaliated wildly, frantic for revenge, hitting, kicking, scratching, biting, profanity and vile epithets spewing from her salivating mouth. Keith raised a fist to knock her out, and Devon cried, "No, Keith, no! Don't hurt her!"

She watched the hideous spectacle, bewildered, mortified with shame and disgust. Dear God, to think that she was the unwitting cause of it! Esther tried to gouge his eyes. Failing this, she grabbed a vase to smash his skull. Keith ducked and it crashed against the marble mantel, narrowly missing Devon. Keith's face was darkly flushed, his eyes glittering savagely, the veins of his temples and neck protruding like heavy blue cords. He seized Esther's shoulders, she clasped his waist, and they whirled about in some macabre dance, bumping into furniture, knocking down ornaments. His face was raw and bleeding, her hair streaming grotesquely. They paced and menaced each other for awhile, and then he shifted positions, spun her about swiftly and cracked her neck in a whiplash. She promptly spat in his face. His hands encircled her throat strongly, lethally. Esther gasped, eyes popping, tongue extended. Her hands clawed helplessly at his.

Devon stared in petrified horror. My God, he was choking her to death! She had to stop him somehow—and with a piercing scream, Devon rushed to Esther's rescue. "Keith! Let her go! Keith, you're killing her!" She clutched his arm. "*Keith!*"

Esther was limp, legs buckling, skin livid. She appeared dead already, although she was still breathing. Suddenly released, she crumpled to the floor and lay there prostrate, panting like a rabbit, saliva drooling from her gaping mouth. Keith gazed at her coldly, as if the inert creature sprawled at his feet were an unrecognizable stranger. Bitter, ruthless, remorseless, chilling Devon's blood. "Help her," she implored his mercy. "Can't you see she's ill?"

"Mad," he muttered, wiping blood and spittle from his face, contemplating the teethmarks on his hands. "She bit me, and I'll probably die of rabies."

Esther was whimpering now and still slobbering, helpless and pathetic as a wounded animal.

"She needs a doctor, Keith.

"She needs a straitjacket and a padded cell. She's insane Devon. If ever I doubted it before, I'm convinced now. I'll send for Ramsey Blake. He's familiar with the situation. You can testify."

"Testify to what, Keith? The horror that happened here? I almost witnessed a murder! She was nearly a victim, not a patient. I won't testify at a sanity trial."

"Devon, be reasonable. She has to be committed, for her own safety and protection, if no other reason."

"I've seen the asylums, Keith. They're dreadful: dungeons and torture chambers."

"This will be a private institution, and expensive. She'll be comfortable and have good care."

"No, Keith. I don't want that on my conscience. I have enough mental and emotional burdens now—please don't ask me to assume another one of such gargantuan proportions. We can't buy your freedom with her confinement."

"You're distraught, darling. Perhaps you should leave, go home and rest. I'll order a carriage for you."

"I'd rather walk, Keith. I need to walk. And think. "

"All right. I'll come to you when I can." He would have kissed her, with Esther's dazed eyes focused on them, but Devon repulsed him.

"Help her!" she cried and left, wondering where the servants had been during the debacle. Naturally they would not dare intrude, but why hadn't either master or mistress summoned assistance rather than try to cope or kill each other?

Trunks were open on the floor, valises and bandboxes on the bed. Devon was flitting between armoire, bureau, chests, gathering clothes, bonnets, lingerie, shoes, so preoccupied she did not hear Keith's chaise arrive, or his key in the lock, and she was somewhat startled when he entered the bedroom. His eyes took in the signs of flight but registered no surprise.

"I expected to find something like this," he said quietly. "Running again, Devon?"

"Yes, I am, Keith."

"Because of this afternoon?"

"That was only the climax—the catalyst that finally forced a decision. Esther was right about one thing, you know. I never tried very hard before to end the affair."

"And you think I'll let you do it now? Let you walk out of my life and take my son with you?"

"Oh, don't act so stricken, Keith, as if I'd betrayed you with another man! It's because of your son—our son!—that I must leave. What future has he here?"

"I've told you before, Devon, leave his future to me. I'll take care of him."

She was folding wisps of gossamer to tuck into the portmanteau. "You have a wife to take care of, Keith. Go home and look after her."

"She's under sedation with a nurse and her mother's in attendance," he said.

"Where were her parents during the storm?"

"Across the park, guests of some neighbors," Keith replied. "Dr. Blake thinks Esther's mind and nerves are shot. She was twitching and muttering incoherently when he arrived, oblivious of her surroundings, unable even to give her name or answer the simplest questions. Shock, possibly, or hysteria." He did not mention the other medical possibility—that the pressure of her windpipe and jugular had deprived her blood too long of oxygen, damaging the brain irreparably. "Hopefully, she'll recover her physical health and strength under treatment. But her sanity remains in doubt. At this point the prognoisis is guarded.

She attacked me and threatened to destroy you, which also makes her psychotic."

"And you almost destroyed her," Devon reflected, shuddering. "It would have been homicide, Keith."

"Second degree, perhaps, manslaughter lacking premeditation." Still no visible compassion or regret, which astonished Devon. "And no more than she deserved."

"Unpremeditated, Keith? Truthfully now, haven't you considered it before, many times? Don't her parents have a statement accusing you of wanting to harm her? You'd be in the Tombs right now, if I hadn't interfered."

"Oh, I doubt that, with my battery of attorneys."

"You mean your money, power, prestige? Gold is invincible in New York, isn't it? Above the law, or able to buy it. No doubt the scale that weighs justice here is made of gold."

Keith smiled sardonically. "Would you prefer to see me hang, darling? Write the story for the *Record*?"

"Don't be cynical about this tragedy, Keith."

"Well, surely you'll admit I had some provocation? I didn't intend to touch her, Devon. I only wanted to get you out of there before she could hurt you. You're no match for her; you lack her malice. You think she wouldn't have brained me with that vase, or used a dagger or derringer on you?"

She nodded mutely but continued her packing. "I may as well tell you, Keith. The Washington assignment is definite for this fall. Meanwhile, I'll be traveling a good deal with the First Family. I am scheduled to go to Long Branch tomorrow."

"And if I forbid it?"

"I'll disobey."

"So Esther was right about something else, then—your ambition and dedication to your career. She said you were wedded to your profession. Is it a satisfactory spouse, Devon, and the only one you want?"

"Whether it is or not, it's the only one I have, Keith, or likely to have as long as I'm involved with you."

"You may be right, unfortunately. And I see a compromise is in order. We'll keep our present arrangement, Devon, which means the child stays in New York when you go to Washington."

"And not see him for months at a time!"

"It's not that far away," he said. "Eight or nine hours by train, and you'll have time off. I'll be practically commuting to the capital and can occasionally bring him with me. You know that makes more sense than setting up a household there, trying to create an identity for Scotty and explaining his existence. You only see him once a week now, anyway, and sometimes less. Besides, eventual separation is inevitable when he goes to boarding school—that's a fact of life. It's also years away, and a lot can happen before then."

"That's rationalization, Keith. Meanwhile, you'd be in charge and possession, his guardian, and if you decided to adopt him I wouldn't have a prayer in court, because you could make a case of legal abandonment against me."

"Good Lord, Devon! If you don't realize by now that I want his mother as much as him, then you don't know or understand me at all, and I don't know or understand you, either. We're strangers who happen also to be mutual parents and lovers. And how you can lie in my arms and say you love me and want me to be happy—"

"But I do, Keith! And I believe you love me and want my happiness too. I'm just so mixed up now and unnerved—"

"I know, darling. That was a hell of a thing for you to witness. I must have seemed like a monster, frightening you more than Esther." Emotion crept into his voice, but he suppressed it. "Nevertheless, she belongs in a sanitarium, and I intend to put her away, Devon. Dr. Blake will consult with some colleagues and, if necessary, we'll obtain a court order for commitment. Her parents can't do anything about it, because they're citizens of Massachusetts and have no authority in New York. And even if introduced into the proceedings, that statement of Esther's would only help to confirm paranoia—abnormal fears of persecution—and, in effect, commit herself."

It was another milestone in their rocky relationship, another compromise in a corporation of compromises. Both a beginning and an end, a realization and a resignation: committing his wife would not solve the problem, only complicate it. Devon was ready to concede defeat and accept destiny, but Keith seemed determined to hang on to illusions with bulldog tenacity.

*

Mrs. Stanfield stayed on to help attend her daughter and supervise the household. The story Hortense gave the public and press was that Mrs. Curtis was suffering from exhaustion and would require a long quiet recuperation. But she informed her son-in-law in no uncertain terms that she would vigorously oppose any attempts at institutional confinement, and that he had best also perish any thoughts of divorce.

"I am aware of your mistress and illegitimate child," she said. "You may adopt the boy if his mother agrees. You may even continue your adultery with her, but you will never marry her. Not while my daughter lives! And I tell you quite frankly that I shall never again leave her alone in your presence. When she is sufficiently recovered, I shall take her home to Boston for awhile, then back to Lourdes, and on a long Mediterranean cruise. But you must never touch her again! She has told me, you see, that you tried to strangle her."

"She was babbling."

"I think not. There were marks on her throat, I saw them! Furthermore, I know that she has been in fear of her life for several years now. I am also aware of your insidious threats and tormentations, your sinister insinuations of poison and asphyxiation. Your wife was so terrified of you, she had the gas jets in her rooms sealed and turned her maid into a food taster. Well, let me warn you, Keith Curtis. Her father and I have a statement—"

He interrupted, "I know all about it, Madam."

Her eyes widened. "And still you—oh, what a fiend! And what a monstrous temper! But you'll never have another opportunity to murder her! And if you attempt to commit my poor little girl over my wishes, it'll be the greatest cause celebre this country's courts have ever seen!"

"You would only hurt your daughter, Mrs. Stanfield."

"She is beyond that kind of pain," Hortense said sadly. "It is your mistress and son who would suffer the worst wounds in a legal battle, Keith. Think about that before you proceed to confine her in a cell, condemn her to a living death!"

PART VII

The question that has never been answered, and which I have not yet been able to answer despite my thirty years of research into the feminine soul, is: What does woman want?

Sigmund Freud (1856–1939)

What is now called the nature of women is an eminently artificial thing—the result of forced repression in some directions, unnatural stimulation in others.

John Stuart Mill (1806–1873)
The Subjection of Women

Men and women were created equal; they are both moral and accountable beings, and whatever is right for man to do, is *right* for women.

How monstrous, how anti-Christian, is the doctrine that woman is dependent on man! Where, in all the sacred Scriptures, is this taught?

Sarah M. Grimke

Whatever the theories may be of woman's dependence on man, in the supreme moments of her life he can not bear her burdens. We may have many friends, love, kindness, sympathy and charity to smooth our pathway in everyday life, but in the tragedies and triumphs of human experience each mortal stands alone.

Elizabeth Cady Stanton (1815–1902)
Solitude of Self

Chapter 44

Devon and Keith saw little of each other that summer, most of which Devon spent in Long Branch, New Jersey, in one of the hotels on Ocean Avenue occupied by the contingent of correspondents who followed the First Family.

The presidential cottage at Elberon, called the Summer White House, was two and a half stories high, with dormers and double gingerbread verandas on all four sides. The curious quadrangular architecture was humorously described as a cross between an English villa and a Swiss chalet. Members of both the Grant and Dent families were frequent guests, and there were many friends and important visitors as well, including members of the cabinet and Congress. For distinguished company, formal dinners and luncheons were the rule and protocol was observed. But Julia Grant preferred informal entertainments and picnics with her children, and even more the rare peaceful seclusion on the gallery, reading or writing letters, planning menus and visualizing the White House renovation, or merely rocking in her rattan chair enjoying the view and cool ocean breezes. When the President was in residence, as indicated by the hoisted flags, American vessels veered toward shore and saluted. Occasionally a navy ship anchored, and the captain came to pay his respects; and once the President was piped aboard for a conference with the secretary of war, when French troops began to move in Mexico, toward the Texas border.

When summoned to the capital on urgent business, Grant went alone, for the summers there were abominations of heat and insects and fevers to which he did not care to subject his family. Then Mrs. Grant would receive female delegations calling on various missions to enlist her aid and support. She was amenable to all charities, sympa-

thetic with woman suffrage, condemnatory of sweatshops
and child labor, genuinely interested in the plight of the
poor and disabled and insane and otherwise unfortunate
and afflicted. The cottage was staffed with Negro servants
in white coats and aprons, and a small repast was always
served to the callers and press: tea or lemonade, finger
sandwiches, biscuits, cakes made from her favorite recipes.
For the *Record*'s fashion column, Devon reported the First
Lady's smart summery wardrobe of sheer voiles and crisp
linens and tissue silks, her flower-trimmed sunbonnets and
nankeen croquet dresses and lawn shoes. Although having
no objection to females frolicking in the sea, Julia did not
engage in this sport herself, and someone asked her opin-
ion of the segregation of the sexes on the beach.

"Why, I've never given it much consideration," she answered, her natural squint increased in contemplation. "I
suppose it's a case of deference to feminine modesty, a
mark of respect. But it does seem rather absurd, doesn't it,
that even husbands and wives can't mingle or bathe together on public beaches, and fathers must attend sons and
mothers daughters, thereby separating families. It's a moot
question, and I shall ask the President what *he* thinks
about it."

Ridiculous, indeed. For certainly there was nothing im-
modest or immoral about a bathing costume that enveloped the body from bonneted head to canvas-slippered
feet, too voluminous to reveal the most voluptuous figure
even soaking wet, and hardly a source of embarrassment
or threat to feminine virtue. Devon and some of her colleagues enjoyed the surf, holding hands and jumping
waves, splashing one another, tossing rubber balls, and intermittently writing and lounging under the umbrellas. Nor
were the men too solicitous of the ladies' delicacy to dis-
port themselves in knee-length torso trunks and tight jer-
seys, strutting vainly in their bailiwick and flexing their
muscles like wrestlers and pugilists on exhibition, trying to
attract attention. The boors might wink or whistle or flirt,
but never dared molest, for there were always a few self-
appointed lifeguards in attendance.

An early riser, Grant could be seen driving his buggy at
dawn along the shore, the hooves of his swift trotter flying
as if in a race against the sands of time; but he drove so
recklessly that Julia refused to accompany him, and once

actually forced him to stop and let her out to walk. Arriving at the cottage in a huff, she complained to her father, Colonel Dent: "Ulysses is going to wreck his rig! He drives as if he were leading a charge! Will you speak to him, Papa?"

"Reprimand the President?" The old colonel, still a distinguished man with gray hair and military bearing, smiled in his beard. "I'll defer to his own father. Jesse's fishing off the wharf, if he's not hunting quail or rabbits in the woods again. Strangest fellow I ever saw, can't sit still a minute. Reckon that's where Ulysses gets his restlessness."

"Where are the children, Papa?"

"Romping on the beach, with the agents nearby. The excursion boats just delivered more gaping, gawking vacationers, and the parlor's full of press people. Lord, Julia, it's like living in a glass house and being a specimen on a microscopic slide, constantly under observation."

"Well, if it upsets you, Papa, go back home." Although Julia loved him and all her family dearly, she knew her father had never approved of the shy young lieutenant who had first requested her hand in marriage and had been cool to him for years afterwards, even when he became a general, relenting only upon his election to the presidency. Furthermore, imposing relatives on both sides were causing charges of nepotism in the administration.

Colonel Dent chose to placate rather than vacate. "Soothe your ruffled feathers, daughter. I'll ask Mr. Grant to remonstrate with his son on safe driving. . . ."

Spectators on holiday trespassed on the property hoping for a glimpse of the First Family; Long Branch citizens encroached, and occasionally a plague of petitioners descended. Commercial greed intruded on peace and privacy, bringing a midway atmosphere in summer: cheap hotels and boarding houses, saloons and gambling halls and racetracks, hucksters and harlots, garish concession stands and gregarious vendors hawking soft drinks, gingerbread, hot corn, popcorn, peanuts, salt water taffy, souvenirs. Bullets exploded in shooting galleries, calliopes ground away, people yelled and pushed and fought. Umbrellas, blankets, tents, and makeshift dressing houses lined the shore. The Grants accepted it all philosophically.

There were brief interludes at Newport and Saratoga Springs, during which Devon learned how to travel lightly and live out of a trunk; how to manage her own baggage, bribe porters and bellboys for information, and how to decipher tenuous rumors and pursue elusive leads, until she fancied herself as adept as Olivia at such journalistic intrigue. In Saratoga the Grants stayed at the Grand Union Hotel (Oh, the memory embers that stirred!), and held receptions in the great glittering ballroom. And Devon was actually awed by the splendor of some of the summer palaces of the Newport colony which feted the President. By comparison the Long Branch cottage was as humble as the log cabin, Hardscrabble, and the Grants seemed relieved to return there in late August. Devon resettled in her hotel room, which had been reserved for the season, and tried not to dwell on her autumn move to Washington.

Senator Roscoe Conkling's visit to the cottage created a wave of excitement among the female reporters, for he came alone, even though his wife Bessie was a close friend of the First Lady. Was Mrs. Conkling sulking in Utica? Had the rumors concerning her spouse and Mrs. Sprague, who was summering at the family castle, Canonchet, on Narragansett Bay, penetrated her lonely seclusion? Julia, adverse to malicious gossip but not impervious, having been both target and victim herself, was in sympathy with Bessie Conkling, especially when wild suspicions about the paternity of the expectant Kate's offspring suggested the virile senator, who was said to have left a trail of broken hearts and bastards from the Mohawk to the Potomac. And Senator Sprague was behaving like a suspicious husband fearing cuckoldry, no longer concealing either his drinking or his extramarital amours and having acquired not one but two mistresses.

"Well," declared Olivia, spooning tartar sauce over her broiled flounder in the hotel dining room, relishing the prospect of a good juicy scandal as much as she did gourmet fare, "the fall season promises to be one of the most interesting in ages! I wouldn't miss it for anything!"

One mid-September day pregnant with autumn, another of the President's friends arrived, in a yacht. Devon was standing at a window in her room when she noticed the familiar white-and-green vessel steaming into harbor, and immediately grabbed her opera glasses and focused them on the bow. It was the *Sprite,* all right, and the President was waiting on shore to welcome Keith! Had he been summoned for financial consultation? There was some talk, most of it out of her realm, about Wall Street being bullish on gold, and Jim Fisk and Jay Gould being in some kind of conspiracy to corner the market on bullion.

Back in June, as the press knew, the Grants had gone to the Boston Peace Jubilee on one of Fisk's elaborate Fall River steamboats. Also aboard and lavishly entertained were the President's sister Virginia and her husband, Abel Corbin, Jay Gould, Cyrus W. Field of Atlantic cable fame and fortune, and other prominent citizens. Upon returning to New York, the presidential party had been further feted by the Prince of Erie, at Delmonico's and the opera, hearing Les Curaz and the famous Irma sing *La Perichole* from his ornate box at the Fifth Avenue Theater. Devon's only interest in that occasion, however, was to report the gowns of the First Lady, daughter Nellie, and Mrs. Corbin. She remembered seeing Josephine Mansfield in the audience intermittently raising her jeweled lorgnette and smiling intimately at her lover, who winked back and fondled his blond mustache waxed in points like the Emperor Napoleon's, for Julia was occupying Josie's seat—and the spectators were far more interested in the characters and performance in the private box than on the public stage.

Although it was unlikely that his wife would ever travel with Keith anywhere again, Devon could not breathe easily until she saw that he was alone, walking down the gangplank to shake hands with the President. They stood a few minutes in apparent serious conversation, nodding gravely, and then boarded a carriage. That same afternoon, Jay Cooke arrived by rail from Philadelphia and treasury secretary Buell from Washington, and lights in Grant's study burned late into the night. But there were no ladies present and no formal entertainment, nor could the male reparters cooling their backsides on the gallery rails, get much significant news.

The social correspondents were at leisure to shop, surf, take in the carnival, or go on short excursions. One of them, a Nantucket native who knew how to sail, took a few friends sculling in a borrowed craft. Another group, including Devon Marshall, cantered along the shore on rented mounts. Parts of it were bleak and barren desert, shimmering in the sun, grass and scrub cedar bristling among the desolate dunes. No woman who valued her complexion dared venture out in the wind and heat without proper protection, and veils and scarves floated and fluttered like colorful banners behind the small sidesaddled troop.

"Wonder what's transpiring in the cottage?" Nellie Hutchinson mused. "An emergency or something? A crisis in gold, maybe?"

Olivia sighed. "Lord, I hope not! The country's just beginning to recuperate from the war; it couldn't cope with a Wall Street panic. And poor Grant, only a few months in office and so inexperienced in government and economics! I think I know more about both than he about either."

Jane Swisshelm smirked at that and coughed, as if she'd just inhaled some blowing grit. "Perhaps you should offer him your counsel, dear."

"Now, dear," Grace Greenwood temporized, "let's not quarrel among ourselves, or deal in personalities. Heaven knows there're enough public figures to engage our tongues and talents. You and Olivia really should call a truce in your feud before it becomes a vendetta. Mercy, this wretched sand and heat and the flies! I think the others were wise to choose sailing; that boat can't possibly be as hot and uncomfortable as this saddle. I'm so tightly stuck I couldn't fall off in a gallop."

Nellie wished aloud that she knew a banker, preferably one on the gold board, who could personally explain the intricate mechanics of finance to her. "Doesn't anyone here know Mr. Cooke or Mr. Curtis?" she asked.

"We all know them," Devon said.

"I mean really know them, darling. Frankly, I'd adore the Curtis assignment! Did you see his sumptuous yacht? And that gorgeous tan! Maybe he'll spend some time on the beach, and we can somehow surround him—"

Devon chuckled. "And do what, fickle creature, who only last March was raving over a tanned Texan? Sunworship with the New Yorker? How is that going to increase our knowledge of economics? Anyway, that's not our beat. I know of no place on earth more adverse to petticoats in our profession than Wall Street, and the Stock Exchange and gold room are taboo to us."

"Then how did your astute lady brokers manage to set

up shop in the heart of the verboten district and not only survive but flourish like green bay trees in that infernal region?" demanded Jane, who specialized in crashing male strongholds and admired the Claflin sisters' strategy.

"Through Cornelius Vanderbilt," replied Kate Field, who had thought this was common knowledge even in Washington. "But he may not be coaching them much longer. Now he's courting a certain Miss Crawford, who's not only as lovely as Tennie Claflin but even younger, at least fifty years his junior. I saw them together at Saratoga, chaperoned by her widowed mother, who had hoped to land the Commodore herself. But apparently he prefers her twenty-year-old daughter, and the betting odds are ten to one the old boy'll propose before the season's over. I guess Tennie really did imbue him with eternal youth!"

"Right now, I'm more interested in the fiscal stability of the Street than its fickle romances," declared Jane. "I'm worried about my savings, the value of the dollar—"

"Just have faith in the motto of our currency," Kate advised. "In God we trust—and believe me, you could get closer to heaven than the gold room!"

They rode awhile longer and then returned to the hotel to check their boxes for mail and messages, and with their network of personal "spies" for information. Thus they learned that Jim Fisk, who kept a seasonal suite at the nearby Continental Hotel, was expected there shortly—and Josephine Mansfield's presence or absence would be a fairly accurate barometer indicating pleasure or business.

The Colonial House, situated on the Ocean Avenue bluff, afforded a fine view of the harbor lights, which Devon was watching later that evening from the third floor piazza outside her room. She sat in a wicker rocker, opera glasses in hand. There was some activity aboard the *Sprite*, which seemed to be preparing to sail. Perhaps Keith was taking the President for a cruise tomorrow, or out for some deep sea fishing. If so, and the First Lady went along, the presswomen would probably be invited too, and how could she cope with that?

The moon streaked the sea with phosphorescence, and she could see the lighted silhouette of a ship on the dark horizon moving like a pantomime figure across a monolithic stage. Below the piazza fireflies darted mercurially, and frantic moths fluttered about the gas streetlamps. Soon after dusk Keith came aboard wearing white tropicals and a low-crowned Panama with a black band. He disappeared, presumably into the master cabin, reappeared minus hat and jacket, and sat down with binoculars in a canvas chair.

Rufus brought him a drink, which he did not quite finish before rising to tread the deck, as if disturbed or agitated. Suddenly he paused, setting his glass on the bulwark and reconnoitering with his binoculars. Naturally he knew where Devon was staying, and he was searching the Colonial House now, as though he could penetrate its walls and invade her room. Devon ducked her head, haloed in a porch lantern, lest his lens discover her own reconnaissance, and slipped promptly inside. She still had an article to write, much of which would have to be improvised and embellished for lack of real news.

Devon was ready to retire when a bellboy knocked and delivered a sealed message. "A sailor from that yacht out of New York, the *Sprite,* brought it, Ma'am. Might be a story in it for you."

"Which makes it exclusive and confidential," she said, tipping him generously. "Thank you, Todd. There's no answer."

Closing the door, she ripped the envelope and read the note scrawled in his bold hand. "Important that I see you. Please come aboard. An escort is waiting outside for you. If you don't come to me. I'll come to you. K."

From her windows Devon could distinguish a dark figure in the shadows, seacap pulled over his eyes, one of the crew. She draped a concealing scarf over her head and slipped out the exterior stairway used by bathers when wet and sandy. Couples were strolling the moonlit beach, hand in hand. Several driftwood bonfires were glowing, with picnickers and choral groups harmonizing around them. The silent pair heading toward the waterfront attracted no special attention. Nevertheless, Devon felt conspicuous as a harlot going on assignation, and entered Keith's quarters on a wave of indignation. "How dare you issue such an ultimatum at this hour of the night!"

"It's only ten o'clock," he said.

"I was preparing to retire!"

"I saw you on the gallery earlier with your lorgnette, watching me as I was you." He grinned at her blush.

"Now run down your storm signals, and hear this. I'm sailing at dawn. Jay Gould and Jim Fisk are coming in, and I want to be away before they arrive. A monetary crisis is developing on Wall Street. If it isn't stopped, many banks will be ruined."

"I don't understand, Keith."

He tried to explain in simple terms. "There's a great speculation in gold, Devon. It's being bought in the market in tremendous quantities, on time contracts. All the business of the country is done in gold, you know—the transactions of importers and exporters are liquidated through the Gold Exchange. This averages from five to ten million dollars daily, including government purchases and bonds sold abroad, and the fluctuating price between gold and legal tender makes an attractive speculative market for the precious metal, which is bought and sold for future delivery like cotton and wheat and corn. Presently, the Treasury has about one hundred millions in bullion, which is released to banks and business concerns at the rate of two million or so per month to cover their foreign and domestic commitments. Gould and Fisk have a plan to corner the gold market, but it's unfeasible unless they can persuade Grant to prohibit the sale of government gold. Is any of this getting through to you, Devon?"

"Vaguely."

"Well, suffice it to say there'll be some explosions in the Exchange before long. Gold is selling at one thirty-two now; it might jump to one seventy-five or even two hundred in a bullish movement, and the men buying on paper will be left holding the bag. The entire nation, farmers and stockmen, merchants and industrialists and everyone else will be affected in some measure. You know what happens when an overinflated balloon bursts? Kaput!"

"Can't the President do something?"

"That was my purpose in coming here," Keith said. "To warn him about the scheme and also that his brother-in-law, Abel Corbin, is their willing tool and supposed to have White House connections. Unfortunately, Grant is no financial genius. I don't think he comprehends the gravity of the situation, the manipulations and chicanery of which those two unscrupulous scoundrels are capable, nor the trouble and scandal that could devolve on him and his administration. But all this is off the record, Devon. Don't carry it back to your colleagues."

"And just how would I do that, Mr. Curtis, without revealing my source?" she demanded petulantly, affronted. "Anyway, I'm not a market analyst, like the Bewitching Brokers."

"Those cunning Amazons will lose some of their expertise if the Commodore takes a bride," he said. "According to Street scuttlebutt, he's romancing more than gambling at the Saratoga tables and track, and plans to elope to Canada shortly. Can you imagine eloping at his age? Vicky's Colonel Blood is beginning to sweat real blood, although Tennie doesn't seem much concerned one way or the other. She already has several other old fossils begging to be sparked by her magnetism."

"What about Esther, Keith? Is she any better?"

Despair darkened his face, haunted his eyes. "She's barely functional, Devon. Sometimes she acts like two different persons and personalities imprisoned in the same body and alternately emerging—gay or morose, talkative or reticent, triumphant or defeated, on top of the mountain or down in the valley; no in-between, no happy medium or even keel. Occasionally her mind seems to wander and even hallucinate; then again she appears rational and lucid. The physicians are more puzzled and curious than ever, and convinced now that she actually did imagine that she was paralyzed all those years and experienced a miraculous cure at Lourdes. It's weird, as if she's under some kind of spell. Her mother's still with her. She hopes to take Esther back to Lourdes and, if she's able, on a long Mediterranean cruise." He paused, frowning. "Let's forget it now and concentrate on something else. Did anyone notice you leave the hotel?"

"I don't think so, but the crew saw me come aboard."

"Darling, we've been through this crew sequence before." He smiled, shaking his head. "You still expect seamen to be shocked at a romantic rendezvous in port?"

"That sounds cheap, Keith."

"Well, you know better, Devon." He drew her close against his groin, without shame or apology for his physical urgency. "Feel me? I'm ready as a sailor after a long voyage at sea. Spend the night with me?"

"Oh, Keith, I don't know—"

"Please, darling. The Grants are leaving soon for the Cooke estate in Pennsylvania—I don't know when we'll see each other again." His kiss was long, deep, desperate, his tongue tasting, probing, demanding reciprocation. "God, I've missed you! Do you realize how much, and how long?"

"Thirty-three days, nine hours and twenty minutes," she replied. There had been a week in New York, while Mrs. Grant and her daughter shopped for their personal wardrobes, the President and the White House.

"You count too?"

Devon nodded, although her calculation was done on a different calendar, and for a different reason. It was time for Dr. Blake to check the pessary again, which hardly seemed necessary at all any more, considering her limited love life and the law of averages. "I'm counting now, Keith."

"And we're wasting precious time," he said, proceeding to undress her.

As always it seemed to Devon that she lived for these vital precious unions, that she could not survive without these periodic infusions and replenishments of love, and would simply dry up and wither away. When continence made Keith avid and greedy, she responded in kindred ardor and lust; and when his repressed passion was excessive, her deprived sensuality complemented it .A rare sexual relationship from its inception, it had progressed to a marvelous, cohesive, completely compatible one in which their bodies were in perfect harmony and communication.

When he was on her, and inside her, concentrating with his peculiar intensity on the act, silent except for occasional endearments and erotic expressions whispered against her lips and into her ears, his hands and mouth caressing her breasts and belly and every intimate and private part of her, evoking almost unbearably exquisite sensations, she cried out in climax, and he gloated over her pleasure and then his own, and it was over.

Drowsing later in his arms, warm and languid, loath to move so much as a muscle, he mentioned as casually as an afterthought that he had started adoption proceedings. Surprised, Devon recoiled as if she'd been unexpectedly and indefensibly struck, or dashed with cold water. "How can you, without my consent?"

"I have a paper for you to sign."

"Well, I won't sign it, Keith."

"It's just a formality, Devon. Not absolutely essential, but I would like your signature."

"Take me first, and then my child. Is that it?" Her sweet reverie was shattered; abruptly she severed his embrace. "Why didn't you tell me this before, Keith?"

"Before what? I've been telling you for over a year. Devon. I told you before Scotty was born. So don't imply now that I tricked you aboard this evening to seduce and intimidate you, in that order."

"I still won't sign your damn paper!" she cried defiantly. "Lock me in the brig, throw me to the sharks—oh, what did you do with my chemise?"

"Hung it on the mast."

"I wouldn't doubt it. You're a pirate, Keith Curtis, and your ship should be flying the jolly roger!"

He laughed. "Well, unless you'd rather walk the plank, come back to this bunk immediately! Try to understand, Devon. This is best for the child. But I won't take him to Gramercy Park, if that's what you fear. He'll stay right where he is for the present. Nothing will change, except that he'll have a name."

Qualms of guilt assailed her, and she felt wrong, selfish, even vindictive in her attitude. Moreover, she knew, ultimately and inevitably, she must make a decision. She could not conceal Scotty's existence forever; nor could she be brazen enough to advertise it to the world, as had the Bohemian mistress of pianist Louis Moreau Gottschalk, via a defiant card on her Greenwich Village door: Miss Ada Clare & Son.

Miss Devon Marshall & Son? Oh, no!

And it wasn't as if she would be surrendering him to his wife, or another woman. Why then should she feel this desolation and despair, this tragic sense of loss and deprivation and betrayal, because her child's father wanted to secure his future and place in society? She was still searching for her elusive lingerie, a pale golden naked nymph in the moonlight. "If I don't sign, will you take me to court?"

"Jesus Christ! Of course not! This isn't a subpoena."

"Then why do you want everything so legal?"

"For his sake, Devon. In case something happens to me.

I want to make him my incontestable heir. Ample provisions will also be made for you and my other obligations."

"I don't want your money," she murmured, finding the thing at last and struggling now with tangled ribbons and lace.

"Stop that!" he commanded, and she dropped the garment. "Be a little realistic, Devon. There's no such thing as complete idealism in this mundane world. And nothing—nothing!—ever turns out exactly the way we hope and plan. You should realize this yourself, after your experiences. Is bastardy the kind of heritage and legacy you want to leave our son?"

She sighed hopelessly. "No . . . I'll sign the document."

"You sound as if you were on a torture rack. Is that how you feel?"

"How should I feel?"

"Happy, glad, relieved."

"As if I'd had a painful tooth extracted by a solicitous dentist?" Unexpectedly, she said, "The circumstances of his birth wouldn't matter so much away from censorious society, on the liberal frontier—"

"The frontier! What put that in your head?"

She shrugged bare shoulders, unsure herself. But it was a fertile thought, and perhaps a fruitful solution.

"I don't know," she said truthfully.

"Well, the West has its share of bastards, all right, natural and otherwise. And just how do you think a nameless man defends himself out there when called a sonofabitch? He'd have to learn to be a coward or a gunslinger, Devon, because his life would depend on a fast draw."

He was right, of course. He was always right—practically, logically, maddeningly right!

"Give me the paper, Keith. Get it over with."

"Later," he said, grasping her outthrust hand. "First we make this quarrel up properly. Sometimes you drive me to distraction, Devon, and I despair of ever convincing you of my love and devotion and total commitment—or of winning yours completely."

Chapter 45

The gold crisis culminated in Black Friday, September 24. The Stock Exchange was verging on riot when finally Secretary Boutwell wired the sub-treasury in New York to release two millions in gold, suddenly flooding the market, and the frantic buying ceased in frenzied selling. Half of the Street was already ruined. The legitimate commerce of the country was paralyzed. The mood was panic and despair, as men went from kings to paupers, and riches to rags. Some dropped dead; several blew their brains out; one leaped from the balcony into the cockpit, striking his head fatally on the bronze cupid holding a dolphin in the fountain, where others were bathing their hot flushed faces; many went berserk. Angry voices muttered threats of reprisal and even of lynching the conspirators, who had promptly fled to the Erie Railroad offices in the Grand Opera House and barricaded themselves under heavy guard. Jim Fisk, who had dropped millions, took his losses philosophically. But Gould, with his mysterious alchemy for profiting from the misfortune of others, added millions to his already bulging coffers, for he had secretly double-crossed his partners and liquidated most of his contracts before the market bottomed. Both men accused the President, members of his family, and high-ranking government officials of complicity in the cabal. Black Friday was the first major scandal of the Grant administration, and it left an ugly and indelible mark.

For weeks Wall Street languished in a funereal atmosphere, as business was suspended and doors of banks and brokerages and other firms closed, some somberly draped in black crepe. Fortunately Keith had risked little of his own wealth in speculation, but many of his large customers and depositors, some with vast loans and mortgages outstanding, and against his counsel and better judgment, had gambled and lost heavily. He tried to help his bankrupt friends recover, but there were expedient limits even to the compassion and generosity of friendship.

"I feel sorry for the victims," he told Devon. "But I can only do so much, and I should ignore those who resented and even ridiculed my advice. How many booms-and-busts and financial panics do some market men have to experience before they learn! What infuriates me most is that the culprits haven't been punished at all, and still retain their seats on the Exchange. Gould didn't even suffer financially, and Fisk will recoup his losses in watered and bogus stock issues in his railroad and steamboats. They ought to be hanged higher than Haman!"

Devon was watching the autumn leaves drift past the windows like bright feathers on the wind. How quickly the seasons passed! Her trunks were packed. She had given Anna and Enid superfluous instructions on the care of the child and household. She had ceased trying to persuade Keith to let her take Scotty with her, reluctantly convinced that he was right in refusing. Explaining him with lies and dissimulation would be awkward, and the truth more so. There was no sympathy for women who committed such sins, regardless of circumstances, only suspicion and contempt. Her career would be jeopardized, if not ended, for an unwed mother could be dismissed even from a menial job and blackballed in the few honorable professions open to her sex. There were two alternatives, either of which would please Keith: decline the capital assignment, or resign from the *Record*. And though she contemplated both, one would be as much punishment to her as the other. Working was essential to her morale, vital to her sense of dignity and individuality—and she must continue until they were a bona fide corporation of man and wife and family.

But even temporary partings were agonizing experiences, for there was some emotional destruction in every physical severance, something final in every separation, something lost and irretrievable in every spent day and hour. The mournful farewells of the familiar Hudson steamers on that last weekend in the country brought her close to tears and capitulation. She clung to Keith in bed, and he tasted salt on her lips.

"You don't want to go," he said hoarsely. "You know you don't, Devon."

And she sobbed, "Of course I don't!"

"Then why—?"

"Make love to me, Keith."

"Darling, I just did and wish I could again, immediately. But I'm not a Jack-in-the-box to spring up on command. Besides, we still have two more days together.

"When will you come to Washington?"

"Next month. I'll let you know. Where will you be?"

"In a hotel, until I can find a suitable boarding house. That's where most correspondents live, you know. Other transients too, including many senators and congressmen."

"Why not live in my suite at the Clairmont?"

"And just how would I explain *that* on my salary?"

"Set yourself up as an heiress."

"From Richmond? A Southern heiress now would have to be on the carpetbagger side of Reconstruction. Anyway, I'd rather save the Clairmont for special occasions ... you know?"

He knew, and the mere thought of it stimulated him again. His mouth closed over hers, his hands pushing her swiftly back on the pillows, and she delighted in his sudden fierce demanding urgency. "Jack changed his mind?"

"He has a head of his own," he grinned, taking her vigorously, forcing several orgasms in her, leaving her both depleted and rejuvenated, and once again she felt the human need and necessity of these physical contacts and exchanges. Love, not bread, was the staff of life, and mutual sex its sustaining juices. Deprived long enough, would they be driven by nature to seek other partners and compensations? Washington was three hundred miles away!

The staff gave her a bon voyage party, as if she were sailing on foreign assignment, which indeed appeared to be her next promotion. Most of the men attended, and all had contributed to buy her a "going-away" present: a fine monogrammed leather notebook and silver pen. Sweeny wandered over from City Hall to congratulate her, wishing aloud that she were going to Albany. Overhearing, Fitch said, "If you think she would serve the *Record* better there, Mr. Sweeny, it can be arranged."

"No, her talents are broad enough for Washington. I'm

just afraid some national politician might steal her away from us, Fitch." A friendly clap on the publisher's shoulder propelled him forward and away. "See how unselfish I am where you're concerned, my dear? I was tempted, however, to press your transfer up the Hudson, at least until Tammany gets more power on the Potomac. It seems I'm spending half my time in Albany now—the Boss has endless need of legal counsel. And now an anti-Tweed faction, the Young Democracy, is giving us trouble at home. Sheriff O'Brian has betrayed us, and state senator Genet is aiding him. Congressman John Morrissey is their aide-de-camp in Washington. Can you beat that? All three of those ingrates owe allegiance to Tammany—not one could have been elected to office without our help! Politics not only makes strange bedfellows but often treacherous ones too."

"Is any of this for publication?" asked Devon.

"I gave the facts to Fitch earlier," he nodded. "They'll be in the next edition, but it's nothing for you to bother about. Would you like to extend this celebration to supper at the Astor House or Delmonico's?"

Devon hesitated. "I'd love to, Pete, but my train leaves at dawn, and I'm still not quite ready."

"Let me help you."

She smiled, wagging an admonitory finger. "I'm afraid that would only delay me."

"Well, you wriggled out of that nicely, but I expect a bon voyage kiss, darling. That's not too much to ask, is it?"

Devon thought of all he'd done for her, how none of this would have happened without him, yet Pete had never demanded anything in return. There were no debts of gratitude or any other kind to settle with him; she was free, unfettered. A kiss was a ridiculously small request, and platonically granted in the presence of the staff, what harm could it do? But he was an obsessively private person, and his black eyes scanned the City Room for a private place, spying Fitch's vacant office. Ignoring the covert glances, Sweeny took her hand and led her there and closed the door and kissed her as he had in Albany. Silently, seriously, intensely, yet with the same astonishing deference and restraint that belied his reputation as a ruthless rogue—and now, as then, Devon felt an innate response she dared not vent or pursue.

There was a light frost on the White House roof the day she arrived in Washington, and the occupants were under a social chill until the Congressional investigation of the gold scandal exonerated them, establishing Gould and Fisk as the crafty lions, Corbin their jackal, and the country the victim.

The New Year reception, a state affair with the East Room appropriately decorated, formally launched the fall-winter season. Julia Grant wore a sophisticated gown of black Lyon velvet trimmed with black lace, and her beloved diamonds and pearls. Mrs. Hamilton Fish, in dark satin and jet ornaments, her steel-colored hair tortured into corkscrew curls, stood in the receiving line; this grand old dame, whose memory encompassed the whole of the Social Register, was Mrs. Grant's social mentor and arbiter and bulwark, as her Knickerbocker husband was Grant's most important statesman and ally. When Mrs. Fish suggested that a mess sergeant was not a suitable White House chef, he was replaced by an excellent Italian steward named Melah, and the cuisine became famous for quality and extravagance.

Devon covered the event which Keith Curtis attended alone, confident that no one present could have guessed that they were lovers. She had found a room on Virginia Avenue, the address appealing to her more than the accommodation. Keith, contemptuous of all such establishments as microcosms of prying communities, still could not persuade her to accept a key to the Clairmont and use it in his absence, if only as a retreat. "The lady is supposed to give the gentleman a key to *her* place, not vice versa," she protested. "I'm not quite *that* liberated, darling."

Offhandedly, he inquired if she knew that the President had received and respectfully declined an invitation to witness the opening of the Suez Canal. "Why no," Devon said, surprised. "Apparently your sources are better than mine."

"Why not, my pet—I'm closer to them."

Mrs. Grant's weekly levees brought the female press coterie together regularly, as well as the important public and private functions, and the gatherings in the Capitol press galleries. Devon was friendly with them all, though not intimately so, lest they invade her privacy. One of the penalties of an illicit romance was its imperative secrecy, the fear of discovery that precluded sharing it with even a trusted friend. Fortunately, capital activities kept her too busy and involved to think or brood much about matters in New York. And Anna's regular letters, with cute postscripts from Enid, minimized her wonder and worry although not her lonesomeness for the baby.

Public receptions at the White House were almost as democratic as in President Jackson's time, with citizens of all classes mingling in the parlors: gentlemen in fine suits and beaver hats, and shopkeepers and workmen in plain clothes and sturdy boots; ladies in silks and furs, and government clerks, shopgirls, and domestics in faded cloaks, frayed shawls, worn bonnets. The wives of the cabinet assisted the First Lady in making them all as welcome in the executive mansion as embassy dignitaries.

The first royal guest of the season arrived in late January. The question of the Crown's violation of neutrality in the British-built *Alabama-Florida-Shenandoah* depredations on United States' shipping during the War Between the States was about to be submitted to arbitration in Geneva; and Queen Victoria, anxious to alleviate the lingering tensions and bitterness, sent her third and favorite son, Prince Arthur, as a sort of good will gesture. But while charming and tactful, the young prince, barely twenty, was hardly a statesman or diplomat, and his arrival during Virginia's readmission to the Union was sheer coincidence. Nevertheless, the White House was decorated with British and American flags, the visitor was accorded all the pomp and circumstance due royalty, and feted at a twenty-nine-course dinner. Hostesses, especially those with eligible daughters, fought to entertain him. Kate Chase Sprague gave an elegant *dansant à la chandelle* in his honor, and Ambassador Thornton hosted a grand ball for the sovereign son. Devon was in the news caravan that followed the prince and his retinue everywhere they went.

In February a number of anxious bankers thronged the capital to protest the Supreme Court's decision on the Legal Tender Act of 1862. They convened at the Willard Hotel, raising voices and glasses and the roof of the White

House. Devon saw Keith only once during the three-day conclave, and he complained bitterly about dimwits and bumblebrains in high places.

"Chief Justice Chase wrote the decision on that act himself in '62, to ease the critical monetary situation. Now he declares it unconstitutional, and once again Wall Street is the loser. Eight years of promissory notes, mortgages, and other obligations incurred prior to the act have already been paid off in paper currency; if that decision stands, receipts will be invalid, payments in arrears, and they'll have to be liquidated again in gold. Can you imagine the chaos and consternation that would cause in the banking system? I'm convinced that this country is in the hands of incompetents and imbeciles out to wreck the economy and financial institutions!"

Devon, in the forest on such issues, was immeasurably relieved that she did not have to report on the political aspects and complications of the administration. "But that's the Supreme Court, Keith! What can the President do about it?"

"Number one, he could appoint two justices not in their dotage to bring the Court to its full bench of nine."

"You mean pack it?"

"No, staff it with men who might have some savvy of the import and implications of their decisions! The financiers are here to persuade the President that it's his duty to fill the vacancies promptly and capably and responsibly, and get that damnable decision reversed before it results in another financial avalanche—and brings another mountain down on the White House! We absolutely cannot go back on the gold standard now . . . it would mean recession and ruination. We must stick with currency. The greenback financed the war, and it can finance Reconstruction. If only Grant would listen to fiscal advisors who actually know and practice their business!"

It became increasingly clear to Devon that when he turned down the cabinet post it was not only a loss but a disservice to his country, and she could not dismiss or negate her role in it. Their combined debt to posterity was no small obligation, and it mounted with interest every day they continued their liaison. Gazing out of the Clairmont windows at the Capitol, and the Treasury next to the White

House, she lamented, "You should be secretary of the treasury, Keith. You should have accepted."

"We'll, I'm not, and I didn't, so no postmortems, please." Opening the cellaret, he brought out a decanter of Scotch. "I've ordered dinner sent up, but we're meeting again later this evening at the Willard, to burn the midnight oil on this new monetary enigma. We have only a few hours together, Devon, so let's make the most of them. . ."

The President saw the light, and appointed two intelligent associate justices, Strong and Bradley, whose votes on yet another legal tender matter reversed the previous ruling. The greenback was safe for the present, although Grant obviously preferred the gold standard, and soon Congress would be toying with the kindred Specie Resumption Act to reestablish gold and render currency transactions redeemable in coin. The frustrated bankers would be frequenting Washington for years, lobbying and besieging Congress, the White House, and the halls of justice.

During the current furor, Mississippi's reentry into the Union in late February was scarcely noticed. Then, on the thirtieth of March, Texas had the dubious distinction of being the last of the strays to rejoin the fold, and Reed Carter returned to Washington to witness the historic seating of the Texas delegation, appointed puppets of the carpetbagger-scalawag regime in Austin, in a hostile Reconstruction Congress. His only smile came when his eyes encountered Devon Marshall's in the ladies' press gallery, and he immediately sent her an invitation to lunch with him. She read the note, smiled, nodded. At noon they went to a small cafe on Capitol Hill, with a view of the still rising Washington Monument. The menu displeased him both in price and content. "Bean soup our specialty," he read, frowning. "Who the devil eats bean soup?"

"The senators—it's their favorite dish."

"We eat beans in Texas, but not in soup. Sure wish I could find some good hot chili con carne."

"Chili?"

He nodded. "Next to beefsteak it's practically our state dish. It's slow-simmered meat seasoned with peppers, cumin seed, and other spices. Cooking it is a culinary art only a native can master, and he never reveals his secret recipe. I'll make it for you sometime, if I can find the right ingredients here." Abruptly, he said, "Hardly a day passed in Dallas that I didn't think of you, and I hoped every mile of this trip to see you again. How've you been, honey?"

"Fine."

"You look great. More beautiful than I remembered, if that's possible. It's true, what they say about Virginia girls; all the Southern soldiers agreed they were the prettiest."

"All the Virginians, anyway," Devon laughed.

"Well, I reckon we're citizens again, aren't we? Americans. But I bet my best boots it'll be a long time before we're called anything but Johnny Rebs and Susie Belles and Dixiecrats. Have you met any of your state's new legislators?"

"No, and I don't care to, because they don't really represent Virginia. They're bought and controlled and manipulated by the radical forces in Richmond."

He nodded gravely. "Same with Texas. We've got the damndest regime out there! A Unionist governor and illiterate Negroes in the state House and Senate. Mass corruption, dishonesty, lawlessness, injustice, violence, vigilantes. If things don't change soon, if they don't stop rubbing our noses in the manure of defeat, all hell's gonna bust loose!"

"Can't the press do anything?"

"Only at the risk of life, limb, and property. The State Printing Bill wiped out our Constitutional freedoms and privileges, providing for a state journal and official printer and requiring all regional newspapers to print quote 'official' unquote news. The Enabling Act gives Governor Davis power to appoint whomever he pleases in mayorships, district attorney, sheriff, and even aldermen, putting him in the position of a despotic king handing out sinecures to his sycophants. And the State Police Bill provides the legal enforcement of all these vicious laws."

Devon picked at her food. "It's probably just as bad in Virginia and our fellow states, Reed. I wouldn't want to be in Richmond now. How long will you be here?"

"Till the *sine die* of Congress," he said. "Pa's minding the press now, and stringing along with the tyrants in Austin to keep from getting the place busted up and himself maimed or killed. I'm here to see just what, if anything, the stooge senators and representatives are going to do for Texas at the Federal level. We intend to play the game with Austin—Pa's a shrewd politician, he knows you have to scratch some crooked backs and shake some thieving hands. But we plan to toe the mark until we have free elections again, and I can run for Congress. Folks in our district know where the Carters really stand, and I don't think I'd have too much trouble winning an honest election, even without Pa's past reputation for political integrity. Other men are also biding time, and playing ball, with the same intentions. Eventually we'll be able to help Texas, and save her from plunder and ruin, if there's anything left by then to salvage. The land grabs and giveaways and swindles and tax confiscations are outrageous. Hardly a plantation, ranch, or farm remains in the hands of the original proprietors."

"I think Congress is reassembling," Devon said, and he reached for his familiar nutria hat, which had grown a bit more battered since she had last seen it, as had his boots and cowhide coat. But he was wearing a clean white corduroy shirt and natty black string tie, and he seemed taller and handsomer than before, his eyes a deeper blue and his skin more bronzed.

"Well, well," Devon's colleagues teased her on her return to the gallery. "Is Virginia ceding to Texas, being annexed, or vice versa? What a delightful pair you two make—the Cowboy and the Belle! Cactus and Magnolia."

Devon proudly announced, as though she had some stake in his future, "He plans to run for Congress!"

"Bravo!" cried Jane Swisshelm. "Congress needs an honest man like Diogenes needed a lantern. May the handsome hombre realize both of his dreams and ambitions. I can see him now, carving warm sentiments on little wood hearts, as did Sam Houston, and sending them to the ladies' press gallery."

All Devon could visualize was a compatible riding partner in Rock Creek, where dogwood and laurel and redbuds bloomed along the trails, and ferns and violets clustered in damp shady places. It became a Sunday morning ritual with them, and when once Devon remarked that she felt guilty riding instead of attending church, he alleviated her conscience. "Look at that sky, blue with lavender and pink and saffron streaks! You ever see prettier stained glass windows? A higher vault than heaven? Finer spires than those tall pines, mightier pillars than those great oaks? Ever hear a more beautiful choir than the birds? Nature is God's outdoor cathedral, and the only one they had in Eden."

"Which is probably why they went wrong," Devon surmised, "and the snake had nothing to do with it."

He laughed, a hearty echo in the woods. "You think maybe He should have built a temple before creating man and woman?"

"Sometimes I think He should have stopped with the world. As a wise philosopher once said, man was His first mistake and woman His second."

"I can't agree with that sage, honey. Nope, looking at you, I just can't agree. You're a masterpiece of humanity if there ever was one. And at this moment I'm mighty damned glad He made us both and even happier He brought us together. You got the prettiest profile I ever saw, and the most fascinating eyes. I can't decide their color—a mixture of jade and topaz, emerald and amber—but they're compelling and intriguing as a mirage."

Slanting the gold-flecked green orbs at him from under her postilion, and dimpling slightly, Devon brought her crop down on her mount's flanks, startling the frisky little beige mare into a gallop. He watched her a few moments, giving her a good lead, before spurring his stallion and swiftly overtaking her. And Devon remembered that she couldn't beat Keith, either, when they raced in the country. It chagrined her, for she wanted to ride, if not better than a man, at least as well.

When they dismounted, Reed broke off several sprays of frothy dogwood and placed them in her arms. Her habit was pearl-gray faille with a velvet collar and misty gray veil trailing down her back. White kid gloves encased her small delicate hands, which held the white boughs as gracefully as a bride's bouquet. The effect devastated and demoralized him. "Let's get out of this brush, pronto," he said brusquely. "There's bound to be some snakes in here!"

"Oh, I shouldn't think so, Reed—and it's such a lovely day. Can't we walk awhile?"

He glanced away, squinting his clear blue eyes at the sun. "Believe me, honey, it's better to ride."

Chapter 46

Summer again, and the annual exodus from the hot steaming capital, where several cases of malaria and other swamp fevers had already been reported. Long Branch for the President and First Lady, with junkets to Newport, the mountains of Vermont and Pennsylvania, Saratoga Springs, and the baronial Hamilton Fish estate, Glenclyffe, on the Hudson River.

The journalists lived out of trunks like troupers, always partially packed and ready to travel on a moment's notice. And though it still seemed to Devon exciting and interesting, and she was ever more enthusiastic about her career advancements, it was also often tedious and exhausting and occasionally frustrating. Sometimes she felt like a whirling dervish, simultaneously stimulated and obsessed, too tired to eat and too tense to sleep, and she had to consult a physician about a tonic and sedative. The brief respites in the country with Keith and the baby, during interims when the First Family were cruising on some private yacht or navy vessel which prohibited reporters, were eagerly anticipated. Never had she appreciated solitude and serenity so much, nor enjoyed leisure and relaxation more, which only proved that even glamour and excitement could jade and pall.

Although they seldom discussed his wife, it was difficult to forget her. Esther continued to invade their most remote rendezvous, to interrupt many of their most private unions, to haunt them like an uncanny emissary from another world. And indeed she seemed to be slowly progressing in that direction, in a continual physical and mental decline. She was thin and hollow-eyed now, gaunt, and haggard, in a deep lethargy and depression from which she only rarely and briefly emerged. She clung to her rooms and stared blankly at the walls, lacking interest or initiative of any kind. She no longer read, worked jigsaws, corresponded or kept a diary, and botched any needlework she attempted. Her beauty had vanished with her figure, leaving an emaciated rack of skin and bones, and she cared nothing for clothes or appearance any more. There was no desire for Hilde's sensuous massages, nor need for Madame Joie's seductive lingerie. Attendants kept her clean and neat, and she submitted to their ministrations like a meek, docile, retarded child.

Keith could easily have committed her to an asylum, since even her obstinate parents finally acknowledged that she was beyond help or hope. That he did not put her away esteemed him considerably in their eyes, although Keith took no credit for conscience or compassion. He simply could not bear to confine anyone so forlorn and pathetic and helpless with strangers who might only frighten and further depress her. He paid her brief perfunctory visits but could not in any sense converse with her, for she seemed scarcely aware of him or her straits, and he invariably left her chambers filled with despair and hopelessness himself. One day, he expected and fervently hoped, she would simply disappear as a shadow lacking substance.

It was easier to concentrate on his son and contemplate his future, now that the adoption was final. His fatherhood occasioned little comment, curiosity, or suspicion among his friends and associates who were aware of it; a child, however obtained, seemed a logical and just compensation, if not substitute, for a hopelessly ill wife.

If Devon sometimes felt that his gain was her loss, and his solace her sorrow, she tried to conceal her sentiments. He had, after all, only done what was right and best for the child, and she knew it. So why then did she continue to feel resentful and deprived and coerced, as if he had somehow tricked her and taken her baby under duress? And why was she often jealous because he could spend more time with Scotty? Wasn't one parent preferable to none, and paternal love equal to maternal? He adored his son, and Scotty was obviously delighted with his doting father, whom he now knew better than his mother. Perhaps this was what hurt most and started the vicious little imps gnawing at her sore and aching sensibilities.

*

There was a whirlwind of news that summer. The Yellowstone expedition in the Wyoming Territory. Troublesome Indians on the frontiers. French troops on the Mexican borders. Increasing migrations from the East and South to the West. A spectacular steamboat race between the *Robert E. Lee* and *Natchez*, from New Orleans to St. Louis, a distance of 1,210 miles on the Mississippi River, which the general's namesake won handily by six hours and thirty-three minutes. Baseball, fast becoming the national sport, attracted large crowds of fans to the games at Elysian Fields, New Jersey, and on Long Island, although no one expected it to surpass horse racing in popularity, and ladies still preferred croquet. In New York, two great construction projects—Brooklyn Bridge and Grand Central Station—so engaged press attention that the systematic looting of the city treasury by the Tweed Ring was scarcely noticed.

In July, Napoleon III unexpectedly declared war on Prussia, and fashion columnists were primarily concerned with its effect on haute couture. *Godey's, Leslie's,* and *Demorest's* advised their readers to rely more on American modistes for their wardrobes. And women's liberation that season concerned the Claflin sisters: their weekly newspaper, their continued success on Wall Street (under the Commodore's helm they had not only weathered the Black Friday storm but profited handsomely out of the wreckage of other fortunes), their invasions of fine restaurants unescorted after dark and demanding service, their free-thinking lectures at Cooper Union and Steinway and Apollo halls, and above all Victoria's incredible announcement of her candidacy for the presidency in '72. Even the most liberal members of the Movement reeled under the impact of this unprecedented female ambition. Mrs. Woodhull, however, saw nothing unreasonable, presumptuous, vain, or inordinately ambitious about it. If queens could rule kingdoms and empresses succeed to empires, why should not an ordinary woman govern a republic if she could be elected to the office? What was the objection: prejudice and discrimination against her sex, or her common blood? And which, then, was the superior system of government—monarchy or democracy?

While her opposition pondered these pertinent and provocative questions posed from platforms and the columns of *Woodhull & Claflin's Weekly*, Victoria prepared to present a memorial to Congress, under the sponsorship of no less a chauvinist than Congressman Benjamin Butler, the same Beast Butler and Bluebeard of New Orleans, who had declared Southern women fair game for his Northern legions. What sorcery Beauty had conjured on the Beast could only be imagined, but he had succumbed to her charms and fascination to the extent of arranging her future presentation to the House of Representatives, and suffragettes everywhere hailed this vigorous new blood and bold spirit in their midst.

Devon's return to Washington in October was marred by the tragic death of General Lee, in Virginia. Nostalgia overwhelmed her, and for days she languished in the doldrums of reminiscence.

The capital social calendar began and ended with the first and last official entertainment at the White House, always red-letter days. In between were the embassy balls, society soirees, and charades on Capitol Hill. Posturing in the Senate, gesticulating in the House, lobbying everywhere. Regional conflicts flared in Congress, as the odious Reconstruction laws continued to oppress and exploit the South; violations of the Amnesty Act were widespread; and white Southerners were maliciously deprived of their civil rights in the elections controlled by scalawags and former slaves bent on revenge and political pogrom. President Grant was still smarting over the Senate's refusal to ratify his treaty to annex Santo Domingo, one of his pet projects, which he had negotiated without consulting his cabinet, infuriating the secretary of state almost to the point of resignation, and incurring the eternal wrath of the omnipotent chairman of the Foreign Relations Committee, Senator Charles Sumner.

It was an era of conspicious consumption and epidemic villainy, of greed and graft in business compounded by nepotism and incompentency in government, and the country was mired in a morass of corruption and immorality, foundering without strong leadership or guidance. Unfortunately, the evils were fostered by Grant's almost slavish worship of gold and his admiration of success without regard to principle or propriety. Legislation aided and abetted profiteers, as the Protective Tariff Act and expanding civil service brought numerous superfluous and nepotistic appointments. Congressional debates raged fiercely, the opponents verbally at one another's throats, sometimes physically, and it made Devon sick to watch them tearing at her native land as if it were a piece of raw bloody meat in a tiger pit.

In the men's press galleries she saw Dixie correspondents wince grimly and shake grave heads over the reports they must send home. She searched for Reed Carter, their eyes met and mutually commiserated. Gradually she realized that he was important to her morale, that his mere persence could give her comfort and courage; that she actually anticipated their cheap meals together, their long Sunday rides, and the entertainments to which their presscards provided free admission. He seldom bothered with social affairs, which could have little importance to faraway Texans, nor the theater, except to escort her to Ford's and Grove's when she reviewed a new play, or covered the Grants' attendance at a premiere.

On these occasions she was conscious of Reed beside her in the dark theater, his long sinewy legs cramped in the narrow space between the seats, his male warmth and scent—his utter and unabashed masculinity. And she sensed his attention frequently straying from the characters on the stage to her person, his quickened breath inhaling her fragrance, his eyes covertly admiring and coveting, his restless hands clenched in restraint. He had never kissed her even platonically, nor touched her except to assist her in and out of the hackneys, and on and off horses. Yet he aroused shameful sensations in her, and she admonished herself in disgust. How could she respond to other men, as she had to Pete Sweeny and now Reed Carter? Was she cut from the same carnal cloth as the Claflin sisters, imbued with the same abominable sexuality unbefitting a decent woman? Whatever her erotic curse, she longed for Keith, and when next he came to town was frantic in her embrace, demanding and consuming like a wild fire, and he was pleased and gratified, confiding, "I thought of this for three hundred miles and wish it could last forever."

"We'd kill ourselves, lover."

"Well, what better end to life than the act that creates it," he mused. "In the ruins of Pompeii a couple are preserved in sexual embrace, caught in copulation when Vesuvius erupted. At least their last moments on earth were happy, and perhaps the death agony only seemed like the final coital ecstasy. Human beings die a little with each orgasm, you know."

"I wonder if I shall ever go abroad."

"Of course, darling. On our honeymoon."

She smiled wistfully, at a promise often made but never kept. "I hope we won't be too old to enjoy it, Keith."

"People are never too old for love, Devon. Age should mellow that emotion, not diminish or destroy it."

"Yes, dear." But intuition told her that these ersatz honeymoons were all that a disapproving heaven was going to allow, or a contrary fate bestow. He had said that once himself, in the Catskills—had he forgotten? How long ago and far away it seemed here and now, phantom lovers on holiday, embracing on an evanescent cloud in an impossible dream.

Reality was her inability to get to New York for Christmas, and his to come to Washington.

Another horror had happened at Gramercy Park, in the brownstone mansion that had become a house of horrors. In an unguarded moment the mad mistress had attempted suicide by slashing her wrists with the master's Sheffield razor, and lay comatose from loss of blood, physicians and nurses laboring over her. The tragedy was kept out of the papers, but Keith wrote a long letter to Devon during his vigil, medically assured that she would sleep peacefully into eternity. He found himself praying as fervently for his wife's death as her mother for her life, contemplating euthanasia if divine mercy failed, wondering if he could induce his friend Ramsey Blake to practice it, or do so himself. In the end he couldn't do either, and the patient recovered, miraculously, it seemed. She lived and he remained her prisoner, as tightly shackled to her in sickness as ever he had been in health. And his staunchly Protestant mother-in-law, who in desperation had beseeched the Lady of Lourdes for another miracle, erected a small Catholic shrine in her daughter's chamber with a plaster image, votive lights, and tiny font of holy water.

Meanwhile, in Washington, the White House cancelled its New Year reception out of respect to secretary of war Belknap, whose lovely young wife, a former Kentucky belle, had died on the twenty-sixth of December. Her funeral was stately and impressive, with the President and Mrs. Grant, the cabinet, and other dignitaries in attendance. But the perceptive female reporters couldn't miss noticing the bereaved husband's furtive glances at his pretty single sister-in-law (so kittenishly cute and cunning she was nicknamed Puss) across the velvet casket during the eulogy. How contemptible, Devon thought, and yet how typical of some widowers she had known in Richmond. And like them Mr. Secretary Belknap would probably remarry before the grass had effaced his "dearly beloved" wife's grave, much less her memory.

The arrival of Victoria Woodhull early in January provided considerable diversion and excitement in the petticoat press, as the male journalists humorously referred to the woman reporters. A genius at timing, Vicky had planned her memorial to coincide with the annual capital convention of the National Woman's Suffrage Association, from which her scandalous morals and philosophies had previously precluded her. A personal appearance before a congressional committee was an honor never before accorded to a woman—a tribute and triumph for which Victoria gave Demosthenes and destiny full credit.

The gallery was packed with the stalwarts and standard bearers of the Movement, plus every sympathetic sister who could make it to Washington. Devon also recognized some wives of congressmen and cabinet members, for Mrs. Grant was tacitly allied with the cause, although not with Mrs. Woodhull's aspirations to replace her husband in the presidency. And since Victoria had already proposed to wear a suit of purple velvet with mannish trousers, white frilled shirt and black necktie to her inauguration, there was much speculation about her apparel for her congressional debut, and some disappointment at the conservative dark street costumes of both sisters, not to mention their perfect decorum. Vicky's glossy brown bobbed hair curled gently from under a modish Alpine hat, and she wore her favorite ornament, a white tearose, at her waist. Under the gaslights, her flawless skin gleamed opalescently, and she was somewhat nervous, possibly in awe of the august assembly she was scheduled to address even with the great Greek orator's inspiration and guidance.

She needn't have worried. Her brief but impressive speech (believed to be Butler's composition), her eloquent voice and delivery captured her male audience, and her beauty and femininity detracted from even Kate Chase Sprague's presence in the gallery. Her thesis, clear and concise and dramatic, at once intrigued, challenged and appealed—but not enough, unfortunately, to carry her petition, even as Demosthenes' famous Philippics denouncing the tyranny of King Philip had failed to conquer the Macedonians, and the Woodhull memorial was voted down with only two dissents, including the sponsor's.

Nevertheless, Mrs. Woodhull was the sensation of the hour in Washington, a name now and a celebrity with influential friends in Congress, and that was primarily what she had come for: publicity and recognition. Ladies who had previously scorned or ostracized her for her improper behavior now followed in her perfumed wake, vicariously sharing her glory and victory. She and Tennie were feted at a luncheon at the Willard, and then escorted to the opening of the Suffrage Convention at Lincoln Hall. On the bunting-draped platform, they sat with Susan Anthony, Elizabeth Cady Stanton, Lucretia Mott, Isabella Hooker, sister of Reverend Beecher and Harriet Beecher Stowe, several senators and congressmen, and the prominent Negro leader, Frederick Douglass. But everyone agreed that the beautiful, bewitching Victoria Woodhull was the star and heroine of that particular drama.

"Ye gods!" cried Olivia in the Lincoln Hall pressbox. "I'd heard about those two and read their astonishing newspaper, but they surpass imagination and defy belief. I wouldn't have missed this show for the world, although I don't believe that superstitious nonsense about Demosthenes and her clairvoyance."

"I do," said Kate Field, winking at Devon. "How about you, Miss Marshall?"

Remembering the seance off Fire Island, Devon only smiled. She would never be sure herself exactly what had or had not happened on that fantastic occasion.

Chapter 47

In late May Devon was summoned to New York to cover the wedding of William Marcy Tweed's daughter, Mary Amelia, to Ambrose Maginnis, son of a famous New Orleans family. Nothing at the White House, Samuel Fitch reasoned, could be more important to his own welfare in publishing than the proper reportage of this affair. Tweed had been striving for years to enter Manhattan society and hoped to succeed with this combination of sentiment and extravagance. Who could resist a candlelight ceremony in the revered Trinity Chapel, attended by the city fathers, esteemed judges and legislators, the Astors and Belmonts, and other wealthy and influential citizens?

The fabulous gifts of silver and jewels, appraised at one million dollars, were compared to those received at the marriages of the daughter of the khedive of Egypt, and British princess Louise to the duke of Argyll. Peter Barr Sweeny gave diamond bracelets valued at forty thousand. Jim Fisk sent an enormous frosted silver dish shaped like a iceberg for serving frozen desserts, apropos perhaps of his current mood, for his beloved mistress had just put him on ice for his younger, more handsome friend, Edward Stokes. His romantic troubles were about to be aired in court, and the calloused press had little sympathy for the disillusioned lover. But Devon felt genuinely sorry for him, not only betrayed but blackmailed by the woman he loved, for the pair were in collusion to extort a vast sum of money from the Prince of Erie to prevent public exposure of his love letters. Jim's refusal to be so coerced was admirable—but, Lord, what an ugly mess it was going to create! Josie's behavior horrified Devon, for it seemed at variance with her character, and she thought Stokes must have an evil influence on her. Her previous premonitions about Miss Mansfield's making lurid headlines were

imminent, and she sincerely hoped she would not have to
report them for the *Record*.

Devon was recording the high noon ceremony in Trinity
Church, trying not to think of the Curtis Bank virtually in
its shadow, and Sweeny's furtive glances at her across the
aisle. In her pale green organza gown and misty malines
chapeau, her fair beauty eclipsed that of the dark-
haired, somewhat sallow bride in white corded silk,
décolleté and court-trained, her Brussles lace veil and
crown of fresh orange blossoms and diamonds. Sweeny,
immaculate in formal attire, could not resist a sly wink
and smile under his Bismarck mustache. Devon responded
faintly, then bowed her head while the minister read the
nuptials in the glow of hundreds of candles. The sun pouring through the vivid sapphire and ruby stained glass window above and behind the reredos, bathing the chapel in
an illusion of mystic radiance, seemed like a special
blessing from heaven, and a good omen for the Tammany
chiefs and warriors alike.

But later, at the reception in Tweed's opulent Fifth Avenue mansion, when the squire managed a few discreet
words with her, Devon thought something in his manner
and expression, and in the mein of all the sachems, indicated worry, wariness, tension, and anxiety. Perhaps they
were watching what one perceptive editor called "the hand-
writing on the Wigwam wall." Were their days of power
and glory numbered, their doom and destruction at hand?

"What a beautiful bride you're going to make for some
lucky man," he said. "Ah, you still blush at compliments,
after all this time out in the competitive dog-eat-dog
business world! Such refreshing modesty does my heart
good, Devon."

"May I mention your lovely wedding gift in my report,
Pete?"

"Of course, my dear. Just don't forget that the Boss's
five hundred thousand in jewels topped us all."

Devon had a brief blissful interlude in the country before taking off on the presidential summer circuit of sea
and mountains and spas. Her three-year-old son was talking now, riding his pony and sailing with his father, crying
when his parents left him and begging his mother to stay.
His cries and pleas wrenched Devon's heart, and she ac-

cused Keith of prompting him in his tearful little drama. But he insisted that it was spontaneous and unrehearsed . . . proof that Scotty needed a governess.

"Do you want to interview her, or shall I?" he asked.

"Shouldn't we do it together?"

"Ideally, yes. But I wasn't sure you—"

"Would care to under the circumstances? Well, I'm not exactly eager, so perhaps you'd best handle it alone, although I don't see the necessity yet."

"Well, if you're worried that I'll engage a governess on beauty rather than brains—"

"Why should I worry about that? I expect her to be chosen strictly on fitness and qualifications!"

He grinned blandly. "If I thought it'd bring you back here permanently, I'd resurrect Cleopatra."

"You do, Caesar, and I'll find myself a Marc Antony in the capital!" she threatened.

Cynicism promptly vanquished humor. "I'm only surprised that one of the Capitol Forum hasn't discovered *you* already, or is that a moot question?"

"Open to debate but not filibuster, which is your procedure in such issues," she said petulantly.

"On the contrary, my love, I prefer cloture. Just don't have any secret caucuses, because I'd only have to eliminate my opposition, one way or another, and it could get messy." His allusion sent shivers up her spine. "You ever see or hear anything of your Tidewater planter? Now Virginia's under the flag again, perhaps he'll be appearing with the tobacco lobbyists. I rather expected to receive another cartel from him, but apparently he has forgiven his grievances and forgotten our postponed meeting on his own ground. Such Southern hospitality!" Keith's voice was silky smooth, his features impassive, his hands working on an intricate scale model of the embryonic Brooklyn Bridge now appearing in building sets, joining the Lincoln cabin "split rails," Union Pacific locomotives, and Hudson River steamboats as little boys' favorite toys, and giving fathers fun and frustration testing their engineering skills and ingenuity in assemblage.

But all too soon the Hudson hiatus was over, and Devon was in Long Branch in another hotel room reserved for the season. The *Sprite* put into port twice at the President's behest, and she and Keith managed a few

hours alone together but no more. The summer holiday
ended in late September, and she was en route to the autumn–winter social circus on the Potomac. Current news
concerned the Great Fire in Chicago, the Tweed Ring in-
vestigations in New York, the Franco–Prussian War in
Europe, while capital society was aflutter over the prospective visit of the Grand Duke Alexis, third son of Czar
Alexander II, expected in November.

He arrived at the White House in far greater splendor
than his royal predecessor, Prince Arthur, wearing an im-
perial uniform of rich dark blue cloth with gold epaulettes,
a light blue silk sash over his shoulder, and a priceless
jewel-encrusted sword. His retinue was also in court attire,
with much garniture of gold braid and decorations, as was
Russian minister Catacazy, who presented the duke to the
President in the Blue Parlor. Grant, always in awe of royalty, shook hands cordially and exchanged pleasantries in
a barely audible voice, after which the party was escorted
to the Red Parlor to join the ladies.

Devon noted the palpitating bosoms and fluttering eyelashes as they curtsied to the grand duke. A strikingly
handsome man, tall and regally erect, with dark wavy hair
and aristocratic features, smooth-shaven except for long
fanciful sideburns, he was the most eligible bachelor in the
Russian empire. Mrs. Grant was radiant in ruby velvet
and diamonds, Mrs. Fish frumpish in purple satin with a
black lace shawl and rosette headdress. Miss Nellie Grant,
dazzled by His Royal Highness, was in demi-toilette of
point lace and rainbow ribbons, a dainty pearl choker
about her fair young throat. But hoops were finally and
definitely passe, relegated to the archives of haute couture,
and bustles and trains were now the ultimate in fashion
elegance.

A grand ball at the Russian embassy climaxed the
duke's visit to Washington, and Devon was on the train—
decorated with American and Russian flags—that carried
him back to New York, where he was immediately
mobbed by hysterical admirers. His ship left port as it had
been welcomed, with music and flowers and flags.

From the pier Devon went to the *Record* to file her report, and met gloomy faces in the city room. Tammany
was in trouble, and the staff were apprehensive of the future of the paper. Tweed and Connolly had already been

arrested and bails set at over a million dollars each, met for the Boss by Jay Gould, but Slippery Dick was still trying to raise his from his cell. Sweeny had resigned his office and reportedly fled to Canada ahead of the sheriff's warrant for his arrest. The charges were fraud and graft, and long beguiled and delayed county justice was now moving with swift and devastating vengeance.

Devon could scarcely believe and comprehend these new apocalyptic developments, although the telegraph wires had relayed them to Washington while she was involved in her assignments. How would it affect her job? Mr. Fitch told her not to worry, circulation and advertisements had increased considerably in the last few years, there was a surplus in the bank account—and, besides, the squire had "provided" for her.

"Provided?" she repeated, coloring. "For me? I'm afraid I don't understand, sir?"

Fitch explained: "He left some money in trust for you, Miss Marshall. A tidy sum, in fact. Fifty thousand dollars. I suspect he'd prefer that you spend some of it to join him in Canada, and eventually sail with him to Europe, although I rather imagine he's going to be disappointed. In lieu of that, I'm to use the money for the paper, of which he's the benefactor, you know, provided I keep you on in your present status as long as you wish to remain. So you see, there's nothing for you to worry about, my dear. Your future is fairly secure, no matter your choice. Besides, you have enough experience and recognition in the profession now to obtain another, and possibly better, position with one of my competitors."

Nevertheless, Devon worried and wondered. She could visualize Keith gloating, waiting complacently for the ax to fall on Tammany's neck, and consequently the *Record*'s. Was he going to win, after all, by default?

He had hired a Miss Heather Vale as governess. She was a spinster of thirty-seven, with drab brown hair parted in the middle and bunned in back, a Roman nose and thick-lensed spectacles, and she wore dark simple gowns with neat white collars and cuffs, sedate pokebonnets, and sensible shoes—precisely the type Devon had always associated with female pedants. And although her education and personal references were impressive and flawless. Devon considered her contract a token concession to her own jealousy, for surely there had been more comely applicants equally qualified. Keith was polite and formal with her, apparently interested only in his son's scholastic progress. And certainly the woman knew her proper place in the menage and did not trespass or presume on the housekeeper's domain. Devon need have no fear that Miss Vale would supplant her either in the master's or the servants' affections, but what about her son's?

She was pensive and moody on her return to Washington, staring glumly out the windows at the misty countryside, scarcely touching her luncheon in the dining car. At the next table some men were laughing and joking over a clever cartoon depicting the Tweed Ring either in jail or flight. Were the Thomas Nast caricatures in *Harper's Weekly* accurate, and the astonishing accusations in *The New York Times* true? Were the sachems all crooks and thieves, and Pete Sweeny a coward who had escaped capture and prosecution by running away? Was she as mistaken in judging his innate character as she had been in Madame Joie's and Ephraim Joseph's and Josephine Mansfield's? Either her human insight was woefully impaired, or her faith in humanity dreadfully misplaced.

It began to rain in Baltimore, and continued all the way to Washington.

The yule season kept her busy, traipsing from one luminous event to another. The embassies celebrated according to their national origin and custom. The First Family enjoyed the traditional tree and turkey. Senator Sumner hosted a holiday costume ball at his Georgetown mansion in which the guests were obliged to portray Christmas characters, literary or legendary. Kate Chase Sprague held open house at Edgewood, her father's estate on the Potomac, its beautiful landscape enhanced by falling snow. Kate no longer tried to conceal her romantic interest in Senator Roscoe Conkling, who now seemed more like the host at her entertainments than her frequently inebriated or absent husband. It was the most sensational affaire d'amour since Dolley Madison and Aaron Burr. Her enemies marveled at the cool confidence, the almost reckless defiance with which Kate jeopardized her reputation, marriage, and social position, while her friends feared that she was about to sacrifice herself to an impetuous, hopeless, forbidden love. Devon was sympathetic, aware of the intense torment and anguish she must be suffering.

On January sixth, she received another terrible shock via the telegraph system from New York, when the Fisk-Mansfield affair climaxed in violence and tragedy. STOKES SHOOTS FISK ON STAIRS OF GRAND CENTRAL HOTEL. TWEED, RELEASED FROM JAIL, PAYS VISIT TO DYING PRINCE OF ERIE. BODY TO LIE IN STATE IN GRAND OPERA HOUSE. NINTH REGIMENT PLANS MILITARY FUNERAL FOR COLONEL FISK. STOKES IN JAIL CHARGED WITH MURDER. JOSIE IN SECLUSION. The story came in piecemeal, at intervals over the next few days, big news in Washington, where it recalled Black Friday. Flamboyant in life, Fisk was equally so in death. Notorious in love, he had died in notoriety. And apparently all New York loved a rascal and a lover, for his funeral was long and spectacular, six black-plumed horses pulling the hearse, a riderless mount with boots turned backwards in the stirrups, dirges and banging drums and hundreds of marching troops, and thousands of weeping mourners.

Poor Jim, Devon thought. Poor Josie. Poor fools and victims of love and passion everywhere. . . .

A new social hierarchy surrounded the White House, creating an aura it had not possessed since the illustrious Dolley Madison's reign. But the insidious worm of bureaucracy continued to gnaw at government, inciting new censures, complaints, and criticisms of extravagance and nepotism, as the President's son, Lieutenant Grant, a recent graduate of West Point, sailed to the Mediterranean as an aide to General Sherman, and daughter Nellie also went abroad under the chaperonage of friends. Washington followed the Grant heirs, who were welcomed like crown prince and princess in the European capitals, via the foreign correspondents. They were received at the courts of Lisbon and Madrid and Berlin, and by King Victor Emmanuel in Rome. Nellie was presented to Queen Victoria at Buckingham Palace, and feted by English nobility at balls and garden parties. But there was no royal reception at the Tuileries, no emperor and empress to fawn over her in Paris. Napoleon had surrendered to Prussia in January, and France was once again a republic. Devon wondered if

Sweeny had been in Paris when it had fallen to the ruthless Bismarck, one of his idols, to whom he himself had been compared.

It seemed that she wrote and mailed reams of copy to the *Record,* telegraphing only the most momentous news, and she was also keeping a voluminous personal journal. Someday, perhaps, she would put her journalistic experiences in a book similar to Grace Greenwood's popular *Washington Leaves.*

Mark Twain, a friend of the President, was a frequent guest at the White House, where Devon also met Louisa May Alcott, Anna Dickinson, and other literary figures. But although Walt Whitman was still a resident and often glimpsed on the street, he was seldom if ever invited out socially, burdened still by poverty and debt, his genius unrecognized even after his brilliant memorials to Abraham Lincoln. His bachelorhood and apparent preference for male companionship combined to make him suspect in the eyes of moralists, and he was considered "strange" and "peculiar." And indeed he did have odd eyes, hooded, fathomless, the eyes of a mystic. He could be seen with naturalist John Burroughs in the Potomac woods, and on the Pennsylvania Avenue horsecar collecting fares for his young conductor friend and former Confederate soldier, Peter Doyle. And though literary critics predicted obscurity and ultimate oblivion for his poetry, Devon still enjoyed it and cherished the two autographed volumes he had sent her at Joseph's bookstore. Once she mentioned a conversation with him on a capital horsecar, but her editors deleted it from her column as inconsequential chatter.

Another major scandal erupted in the administration, threatening Grant's renomination, for it was a presidential election year, and his record hardly inspired confidence or enthusiasm. Vice President Colfax was among many high government officials profiting from the malfeasance in the credit mobilier and the fantastically high stock dividends of the Union Pacific Railroad on its transcontinental venture, and had to be dropped from the ticket in favor of Henry Wilson. Horace Greeley was the Democratic candidate, and Victoria Woodhull the choice of the People's Party supposedly composed mostly of wild radicals and crazy women.

Grant did little campaigning that summer, but when he

did Julia accompanied him like Penelope following her Ulysses, and the female reporters naturally tagged along. The First Lady, grown accustomed to her press retinue, remarked that she would miss it when she was no longer a news figure. But Devon thought it would have been infinitely more exciting to follow Mrs. Woodhull's fiery campaign trail, her gaily decorated bandwagons, and battalions of suffragettes. Occasionally her mind wandered to Texas, where Reed Carter was running for Congress in the first free elections there since the war. Then again there were times when she longed for nothing except the peace and quiet of the house on the Hudson, her child, and his father. Oh, if only a merciful Providence would take Esther, who had degenerated into hopeless lunacy and vegetation in Gramercy Park!

Greeley lost the election, beaten worse than any man who had previously aspired to the office, apparently defeated by his zealous idealism and lofty unrealistic proposals for turning America into utopia. Two weeks later, broken in health and spirit, he died in a sanitarium, and President Grant went to his funeral in New York, which was almost as impressive as Jim Fisk's.

His fellow newsman in Texas had also lost his political race, but had run a close second. And Reed had a theory for his defeat, which he rationalized to Devon when he arrived early in '73 to report on the victor.

"The only advantage my opponent had was a family. Somehow folks just don't cotton much to bachelors in politics. Fact is, I think I'm better qualified in some respects for that office than he is, and I aim to challenge him again next year. But first I've got to get me a wife. That's the greatest asset a politician can have, it seems: a fine pretty spouse at his side and maybe a sprout or two in his image. And I give you fair warning, Miss Devon Marshall, I intend to puruse you with all I've got, which unfortunately isn't much. You see, I was counting on that big seventy-five-hundred-dollar congressman's salary to dazzle you into marrying me for my money."

Reed grinned and Devon laughed, pretending that he was teasing, knowing otherwise, wondering how she could reject his courtship and still retain his friendship. She had missed him a great deal, more than she had realized, or imagined possible, and was glad he was back. Despite the glamorous assignments and the numerous people she met, she sometimes felt alone and lonely, and it took a while to discover that this feeling of loneliness and isolation in the midst of a crowd was characteristic of the capital.

Chapter 48

The press platform shook precariously in the wintry gale. Flags and decorations were torn to shreds, or ripped from their moorings. The temperature hovered near zero, the capital was crystallized in ice, with floes on the Potomac. Even in thick wool mittens Devon's frozen fingers could scarcely move pencil on pad. Reed Carter sat beside her on the scaffolding, and for some curious reason she was more aware of the fluttering fringe on his rawhide jacket and the wind-bent brim of his tall Western hat, than the President's honor guard marching stiffly past in dark blue uniforms trimmed with bright yellow and black-plumed caps.

Reed was covering Grant's second inauguration for a number of Texas journals, including his own Dallas *Post*. In need of funds to maintain himself in Washington, he had arranged to act as correspondent for papers in Fort Worth, Waco, Austin, San Antonio, Houston, and Galveston. At ten dollars per subscriber, this was considerably cheaper than they could buy national news from the Associated Press. Thus, he had established his own syndicated service and enabled himself not only to live comfortably in the capital but save some money to finance his next congressional campaign. He was intent now on the President's speech, copies of which the news corps already possessed. Ice crystals glistened in Grant's graying beard—he had aged ten years in the past four—and he could barely speak or be heard above the wind, for neither his voice nor words were sufficiently strong or significant. But somehow he mumbled and stumbled through his second inaugural address from the Capitol portico, noteworthy only for his pettish carping complaints about the slander and abuse to which he had been subjected by both the people and the press.

Devon thought the gaunt and haggard chief justice, administering the oath of office, looked like a patriarchal ghost risen from a deathbed, and indeed he had been seriously ill. His fur-wrapped daughter was on the dais sans husband, but Senator Conkling, rumored to be in line for a cabinet portfolio, was only a few feet away. The gossip columnists noted this public proximity, but more so the frequency with which they danced together at the inaugural ball in the Muslin Palace, a makeshift building decorated with myriad yards of pink cambric, and inadequately heated.

The blizzard had delayed or marooned trains from the North, and many invited guests were not present. Devon imagined Keith stranded somewhere on the railroad tracks, if indeed he had left the city at all. Like many financiers now, he was disillusioned with Grant's domestic policies, particularly those of the economy. He had once remarked to Devon that Hamilton Fish was the only real asset to the cabinet, and that the secretary of state's brilliance and competency in handling foreign affairs was all that saved the administration from total disaster.

Reed balked at the ball coverage, muttering, "Hell, I'm no good at writing this frivolous stuff!"

"Use my notes," Devon offered.

"Crib, you mean? I got a better idea. Let my subscribers pay for them. Just write up a brief column, highlighting the glamor ladies like to read, and I'll sell it for you at five bucks per shot. How's that?"

She agreed, enthusiastically. "Gee, we've got an enterprise going, Reed! Maybe we could set up a sort of 'syndicated feature' service and give AP some competition?"

"Oh, I doubt that. AP's a fairly well established organization, you know. But we can sure make ourselves a little extra dough. Shall we discuss the partnership over a dance?"

"Later," Devon demurred, as the Marine band hailed the arrival of the chief. "I've got work to do now, podner."

The First Lady was shivering in her mink-banded cloak, which she reluctantly removed to reveal an elegant gown of white and silver brocade designed from material presented to her by the emperor of China. The skirt was fashionably bustled and trained, the shaped bodice lavishly trimmed in Chantilly lace. Daughter Nellie, home from her European travels, sweet sixteen and in love with a handsome young junior diplomat of the British legation, Algernon Sartoris, whom she had met on shipboard, wore bouffant white silk and tulle, with fresh white camellias in her long, dark, loose hair. Mrs. Fish was swathed in satin and ermine, and Mrs. Henry Wilson, wife of the new vice president, wore sapphire velvet and sables. Mrs. Sprague gleamed in a yellow satin Worth with turquoise ornaments in her titian hair, which was almost the same color as her romantic idol's.

Most of the guests danced in their wraps, and the floor swirled with dark mannish capes and bright feminine cloaks. The President, never a Beau Brummel or master of the dance, shuffled awkwardly through his paces under Julia's patient encouragement. But Sheridan's "Gallop" and Sherman's "Lancers" were something to behold; only the dashing General George Custer was said to outshine them in a ballroom. But Devon remembered the Confederate balls in the executive mansion in Richmond, the graceful waltzing of President Davis, the gallantry of General Lee, Jeb Stuart, Joseph Johnston, and Stonewall Jackson before his death in the long terrible bloody Seven Days Battles.

She wrote with chattering teeth and numb hands, while Reed tried to warm her with hot chocolate and himself with coffee. The frosted champagne and punch bowls were largely ignored, along with the icy food. Over a hundred caged canaries had been brought in for the occasion, but were too cold to sing. The diplomatic corps, rigid as frozen marionettes, departed as early as protocol would permit. There was endless coughing, sneezing, wheezing, and several attacks of asthma and bronchitis on the floor, one fatal. When finally Devon had accumulated enough copy, she danced with Reed to circulate her blood and was pleasantly surprised at the lightness of his booted feet, the easy grace and skill of his maneuvers. Reading her mind, he smiled.

"Surprised, my dear? You didn't think Texans could dance? I assure you we can and do, every chance we get. Anywhere, anytime, on any pretext. Barn-raisings, barbecues, roundups, political powwows, spring plantings and autumn harvests, weddings, christenings, everything but wakes. We favor reels and squares, and we invented the

Western Stomp. But we love to waltz too, and are sentimental about Stephen Foster melodies." His face and
voice sobered, and his hand tightened on hers. "There's
something else I do fairly well, Miss Marshall."

"Oh? And what is that, Mr. Carter?" she asked archly,
flirting, teasing him with formality.

Bending, he whispered in her ear, "I'd rather show you,
honey, and hope someday to have the privilege."

"Oh, Reed—this has been a long day! Thank you for
helping me get through it, being there when I needed
you."

"Devon—darling, it's the other way around! This evening would have been sheer hell for me without you."

Spring again, and the beckoning blue hills of Virginia,
and nostalgia. As a child drawn to its mother's bosom, Devon felt an instinctive urge to cross the Potomac and stand
on her native soil again, if only briefly. When she confided
this longing to Reed, he confessed a similar homing instinct for his birthplace.

"It's inherent, Devon. We never forget where we were
born and grew up, no matter how cosmopolitan we might
eventually become. Right now, this country boy is yearning for the greening hills and prairies of Texas, and would
like very much to show you the purple sage in bloom, the
bluebonnets and Indian paintbrush and wild verbena, and
even the cactus. It's all so damn beautiful in spring, even
Washington Irving had difficulty describing it, and so vast
not even the gifted Spanish artists can capture it completely on canvas. You have to see Texas to believe it." He
mentioned trees and plants of the plains and deserts as
rare and exotic to Devon as if they grew in foreign lands:
retama, huisache, mesquite, yucca, peyote, tumbleweed,
woolly loco which literally drove cattle and sheep that ate
it crazy. In some respects Texas sounded like another continent, indeed another world.

"But it's a far piece to ride," she said. "Would you settle
for a nice long drive in Virginia?"

"You bet! I've been wanting to see General Lee's plantation at Arlington, anyway. I know it's a national cemetery now, but I've seen the manor house from Capitol Hill
many times and thought of paying a visit."

Early the next morning they set out in a rented buggy,

rumbling across the boards of Long Bridge, beneath which the blue Potomac flowed toward Alexandria and Mount Vernon, on to Chesapeake Bay and Hampton Roads and the Atlantic Ocean. "I understand the general traveled this way twice a day when he was in the war department," Reed said, interrupting her reverie.

"Yes. My father visited him at Arlington before the war. I went with Pa once to see Stratford Hall, where Lee was born. His ancestral plantation, also on the Potomac and very English in character, rather like a noble estate, was much larger than Arlington, brick with wings and clusters of chimneys. Of course when Stratford was built in 1729, it had to serve as a fort as well as a country seat, defendable against Indians and pirates and other outlaws. But Lee lived there only three or four years before his family suffered financial reverses due to severe drought and depletion of the tobacco land in overplanting. His father, Light-Horse Harry Lee, loaned his friends money which was never repaid, and was arrested and imprisoned for debt, where he wrote his memoirs. Then the family moved to Alexandria, where Robert Edward spent his boyhood."

"You know a lot about him, don't you?"

"It's a sorry Virginian that doesn't," she said. "I reckon, next to Washington and Jefferson, he's the most famous and best loved man in the state. His death is still being mourned there, and all the South, and monuments to him are rising everywhere below the Mason-Dixon Line."

"Revered like the heroes of the Alamo in Texas," Reed mused. "Every little hamlet has its memorial to Crockett-Bowie-Travis, or Sam Houston, if only a painted adobe statue or clay fountain no bigger than a birdbath. People everywhere practice hero and ancestor worship, and we all have our sacred cows too." He paused, smiling in reminiscence. "Pa had an old red longhorn bull named King Roho that he just couldn't bear to sell or kill for meat. When the ornery critter finally died of old age, he dragged his carcass out to the prairie to bleach in the sun, and then buried his bones on the ranch with his own horns, which had an enormous span, as his monument. But he'd have rawhided anyone who accused him of doing it out of sentiment."

"I'd like to meet your father, Reed, if ever he comes to

Washington again. And when I get some free time I'm going to read up on him in the Library of Congress."

"He'd be flattered, Devon, because he's quite proud of his congressional record. Did I forget to tell you how pretty you look in that yellow dress?"

"It's the color of the jonquils that bloom in the Shenandoah meadows," she said.

"Reminds me of 'The Yellow Rose of Texas.' You ever hear that song? We marched and rode and fought to it. It was the Texas battle hymn as much as 'Dixie.' "

"Dixie." How long since she'd heard it played, sung, danced to it, or watched a parade march to its lively tempo? One more memory consigned to the sepulcher of memories.

She quieted as the buggy rolled off the bridge onto the Virginia shore and wound up the rutted road toward the great white Greek pillars of the mansion, now in disrepair, one wing providing living quarters for the caretaker. Crossing the Chesapeake & Ohio Canal on which the Custis-Lee tobacco had been shipped to market, they rode past the vacant slave cabins and tumbling barns and outhouses, the fallow fields and blighted orchards, where Union troops had camped and trained after confiscation of the property. Accustomed to such pilgrims, the caretaker paid no attention and let them wander at will. Most of the plantation buildings had been destroyed, and rows of graves stood in their places. They paused at the common Confederate monument marking the remains of soldiers collected from the battlefields. The dense woods, which Lee had so loved, were full of shadows but serene and somehow peaceful. Cardinals chirped in the trees, and robins sang, but mostly Devon heard the mockingbird's mockery. It was a pilgrimage of sadness and irony.

"He should have been buried at Arlington," she said, "rather than Washington College. He was a general, not a professor!"

Reed slipped a comforting arm about her shoulders. "He was both, Devon. And more, much more. He was a _man_."

"Oh, Reed! Why did any of it have to happen? The war, the killing, the horrors, the aftermath!" She was thinking of her father now, and Reconstruction. "Why couldn't slavery just have outlived the times and passed peacefully into history?"

"I've asked myself that same question many times, although we didn't use slaves on the ranch, and our household servants were Mexican. Still, every time I ride out to the Carter spread, once the largest and finest on the Trinity, and see that goddamn fat-ass Yankee spilling out of the saddle like over-risen sourdough and his poor pony sagging under the load, I want to fight the war all over again. If only Pa had buried gold instead of Confederate bonds to pay the taxes! Can you imagine how much worthless treasure is cached all over the South? I don't know why any of it happened, Devon. It just did, that's all. A century from now, historians will still be studying and analyzing the causes and effects of that civil conflict. And all we have to show for it now are ruin, grief, and monuments."

"Take me away from here, Reed. Drive in any direction, as long as it's south."

"Sure, darling, sure."

But to travel south was to travel toward Manassas, Chancellorsville, Fredericksburg, Spotsylvania, Richmond—and Appomattox. A grim journey for any Southerner, and particularly a Virginian. After some miles the horse began to plod, and Reed squinted at the noonday sun. I could do with some vittles? How about you?"

"I'm not hungry," Devon said.

"You have to eat, though. I'll try to find a tavern. Holler if you see chimney smoke. This isn't a well traveled road, in case you haven't noticed."

"It's a wilderness."

"Good hunting, I bet."

"Do you have a gun?"

"A pistol in my haversack."

"Derringer?"

"Honey, that's a toy for ladies. I use a Colt forty-five."

"Have you ever fought a duel?"

He hesitated before nodding. "Had to, was called out."

"Obviously, you won."

"Well, he was a good shot, but I was faster on the draw. Luckier too, I reckon."

"They say challenges are common out West, and that's how most men settle their differences."

"Not most, no. Surprisingly few, in fact. We're not as bloodthirsty and barbaric as we're pictured. But now and then you run into an hombre who just won't be satisfied any other way, and then you have to fight him, even if you know he might kill you. Coward is the worst brand a man can wear in the Territories and can never be lived down, because even if he could forget, nobody would let him. He'd have to leave the country."

They traveled another hour without sighting an inn, and now the sun had disappeared behind scudding clouds. "Just like Texas weather," Reed remarked. "Changes without warning, temperamental as a filly in season."

Devon smiled for the first time since they had left Arlington. "It wouldn't be April on the Potomac without sudden showers. Springtime and thunderstorms are synonymous in Virginia."

"In Texas, it's tornadoes. We'd better get off this dirt road before rain turns it into a wallow and gets us stuck. Doesn't seem to be any civilization at all in this region."

"I should have packed a picnic basket."

"Don't worry, we won't starve. Luckily I threw in some emergency rations: hardtack, beef jerky, and a canteen of water. Force of habit. An experienced traveler wouldn't venture anywhere in the West without such provisions, because he would probably regret it if he did."

The sky darkened and the density of the woods increased, so that they seemed to be tunneling through the arched and embracing branches. But here and there Devon glimpsed a vivid splash of blooming redbud, the rosy glow of rhododendron and the white froth of dogwood, all familiar, and caught the sweet scent of violets and honeysuckle and wild roses. Suddenly they came upon a small abandoned cabin in an overgrown clearing, and Reed suggested that they take shelter there until the ruckus blew over.

"I won't melt if I get wet, Reed. I'm not made of sugar."

"That's a matter of opinion," he said. "Anyway, I wouldn't want to spoil that pretty yellow dress."

Drawing rein, he got her into the refuge quickly, and then went back outside to tether the horse and gather some firewood. There were a few sticks of furniture, splintered chairs, a hacked-up table, a homemade bed with pine needle mattress, and dead ashes on the hearth.

Devon watched him from a paneless window and held the door open when he carried in a load of wood and twigs. Soon he had a cozy fire roaring. "Welcome to the Willard of the Woods, Ma'am! Dinner will be served as soon as your host can shoot and roast it. I saw a nice plump partridge out there, and if the storm doesn't scare him off ... or would you prefer a tender young rabbit or juicy squirrel?"

She puzzled, playing the game, forefinger tapping chin. "I think I'd like to try the jerked beef first, sir. It sounds rather exotic."

He laughed. "Tastes exotic too, but hardly gourmet, and I don't recommend it. Ever chew on salty dried-out leather? You'd think you were gnawing an old seaboot."

"Just the same, I want to try it," she insisted. "Another experience to enter in my personal log."

His eyes sought and held hers, admiringly. "You're a venturesome lass, aren't you? I like that. Where I come from spirit and adventure are important in a woman, along with a sense of humor. Without them, she'd be as dull to live with as a spiritless pony to ride."

"Are you comparing the two? I've heard that Texans put their womenfolk third, behind their horses and cows."

"Not this Texan," he said.

Devon shivered slightly, hugged her shoulders. "This is a lonely place, and sort of spooky. I wonder who owns it."

"Some hunter, probably, or hermit flushed out by the war. And it's haunted by the Yankee ghosts, who left these mementos." He emptied some rifle shells from his pockets. "Union caliber and markings. And those are saber-cuts and bayonet scars on the furniture. The blue devils were here, all right."

"They were everywhere in Virginia," Devon reflected grimly. "There's no place you could go in this state without seeing such evidence. Dear God, some of the grisly souvenirs the scavengers used to find on the peninsula!"

"Don't think about it now, Devon." With his jackknife he whittled off a ration of jerky. "Here. Chaw on this awhile, if you can. Had it in my saddlebags so long, reckon tanned buffalo hide would be tastier and easier to digest. But it's nourishing, and without it the West would never have been opened. Lewis and Clark ate it, and their successors on the Montana and Arizona expeditions, and every explorer and pioneer in the Territories since."

"Is it true that convoys of covered wagons cross the country every day, and the billowing canvas of the prairie schooners look like ships in full sail on seas of waving grass?"

"Well, that's a mite poetic and romantic. Some of those armadas don't make it past the midwest plains, and further west whole flotillas have been scuttled in the mountains and deserts, by winter snow, summer sun, or Indians and outlaws. Their flotsam and jetsam are scattered everywhere: stoves, bedsteads, bureaus, and other jettisoned household cargo mark the trails, and the milestones are crosses and mounds of rocks over graves, sometimes tiny graves. But for those who do succeed, it's worth it. It must be, because they keep coming in spite of everything—heat, cold, suffering, dying."

Devon had managed to sever a piece of the stringy beef and was trying to chew and swallow it. Ironically, she remembered Keith's favorite filet mignon at Delmonico's, and chateaubriand at Dijon's, and wondered if she were quite mad to be in an isolated shack with a cowboy riding out a rainstorm and chomping on something that tasted exactly as she imagined sweaty rawhide would. More incredible, enjoying it, and envisioning herself traveling in the West and writing about it, a pioneering journalist. Articles, features, perhaps a book for posterity. For she knew now that she could never write about Virginia and the war objectively: pain, heartbreak, sentiment, and sorrow would always intrude, interrupt, stay her pen.

Her wistful expression, as if she were viewing distant horizons, encouraged Reed and her beauty enchanted him. She was every girl he'd ever dreamed of, desired, longed to possess as his own. He'd had visions of such loveliness and femininity while riding the plains, lying in his bedroll under the stars, hunting and fishing, and leading a cavalry charge. Sometimes that fair image was all that kept him going when things got tough and struggle seemed futile. Yet there was more, so much more, to her than just a lovely face and fine figure. There was wit and brains, courage and determination, and another quality he could only define as humanness. Not a mere doll, a pretty plaything to amuse a man, but a genuine *person* who happened also to be female and beautiful.

He admired her grit in eating the jerky, which she obviously did not relish. "Seems to expand, doesn't it? The harder and longer you chew, the bigger and tougher the cud gets." He extended the canteen. "Better wash it down with water, honey. The hardtack's a bit stale, but you know our soldiers lived off it on the battlefields. It was in every mess kit, and toward the end about all we had to eat. You can imagine how it affected bellies already sore and griping with dysentery. But remember, it's not our staple diet in Texas, not even on the trail. And I'm still going to cook you a pot of mouthwatering chili con carne one of these days."

The wind-driven rain deluged the shanty, leaking through the bullet-riddled roof, splashing in the unprotected windows. Devon ignored it, as she did the mouse that peeked curiously from under the floorboards, saw he had unwelcome company, squeaked in alarm or protest, and disappeared again. When she passed the canteen back, Reed put it immediately to his mouth, tasting her lips. "Almost as good as a kiss," he said.

"Is it?" she asked directly, with none of the silly mincing and simpering he found irritating in immature females.

"Almost, but not quite."

Devon knew, intuitively, that he was going to make love to her, and she was going to let him—and not feel guilt or shame or remorse, because it was normal and inevitable, and the only viable solution to her dilemma with Keith. It came to her, almost as gospel revelation, that her salvation lay in the hope of loving another man. When he drew her into his arms it seemed natural and right to respond, to feel and express the same emotions he was feeling and expressing. But when he mentioned marriage, she hesitated. "Let's not think of that now, Reed."

"What better time to think of it, Devon?"

"You don't know me well enough."

"I know all I need to know," he said. "I'm in love with you, and have been from the beginning. I don't have much to offer you now, but someday I will. I promise you that, Devon. I'll do anything for you—and with you at my side, there's nothing I couldn't do. Nothing!"

"Oh, Reed. I'm not the girl you think I am! I'm a

mature woman, I've been out in the world alone for some years, and I've done some things—"

He interrupted brusquely, "I don't want to hear about it, Devon! I don't care what you've done, even if it's murder. You went through a war the same as I. No doubt you were cold and hungry and desperate, like the rest of us. People do what they must to survive, and sometimes that means compromising honor and virtue, and bending custom and convention. I gather there was a man who helped you—maybe a rich man, maybe even a Yankee. I'd just rather not hear about it, Devon."

"Not even if I loved him?" Why had she used that tense? She loved him still, didn't she?

"Especially not if you loved him! That's the past, Devon. I'm interested in the future. Our future, together. Someday, when I'm old and gray and too feeble to sit saddle any more, you can tell me the rest of the story. But let's put a heap of living and loving behind us first. Let's get married and take a honeymoon cruise down the Potomac, then hit the trail to Texas, and not travel this way again until I go to Congress—"

"Couldn't you do more for Texas in the state legislature, Reed? Why don't you try for that first? It'd be good experience and make your name well enough known possibly to insure election to federal office, perhaps even the Senate. Why not aim your sights high?"

"Well now, you might have a point there! See what a helpmeet you'd be to me? Sure, I think I could capture a state seat and make my voice heard in Austin—enough to get some recognition and accomplish something worthwhile for Texas in the process. But I won't try it without you, Devon. Hell, one of the main reasons I wanted to return to Washington was to woo you, anyway. I want you with me, wherever I am, whatever I do. Otherwise, none of it would be very important to me, or make much sense. A man needs more than a cause and goal to fight for, you know. And if you wouldn't mind waiting a few years to come back East—"

"I wouldn't mind, Reed." Maybe by then she could bear it, if she had another child. Maybe by then she could endure living in Washington, knowing *they* were only three hundred miles away. . . .

"I love you," he said intensely, with a desperate embrace. "My God, I love you! I'd like to find a backwoods preacher or judge right now and make it legal—"

"Oh, it can't be that fast, Reed! I have things to do and settle first, with my paper and—"

He nodded understandingly. "Sure, honey, I know. Don't let me stampede you. I can wait, if it's not too long."

"You needn't wait unless you want to," she said.

"Lord knows I don't want to, darling, but I think I'd better. Because I want you to be sure, Devon, in your own heart and mind. I don't want anything as important as that to happen on sudden impulse. Maybe I'm a strange critter, but I'd like it to be something special for you too. Hell, what am I saying! It *will* be something special. So I'll wait, dammit, if it kills me!"

Chapter 49

Wisely or not, for better or worse, she had made a decision and intended to adhere to it, even more firmly convinced now that it was the only possible way to end her involvement with Keith, and the salvation not only of her soul but her sanity. She simply could not endure the anxieties and frustrations of the past five years indefinitely, for the remainder of his or her or Esther's natural life. Already they had taken their physical and emotional toll. She had lost pounds she could neither spare nor regain, and suffered digestive upsets that would have made her suspect pregnancy had she the accompanying symptoms which, thankfully, she did not. But insomnia plagued her increasingly, adding stronger sedatives to her medicine chest. She tried valiantly to conceal these ailments from Keith, but her weight loss and the occasional dark smudges under her eyes were apparent. He remarked that she must be driving herself too hard and needed more rest and nutritious food. "I like you slender, darling, but don't overdo it. Severe dieting will affect your health, and ultimately your beauty." And he stuffed her at Dijon's, ordering the richest cuisine, the most tempting desserts, on the menu.

He was in Washington for another conference with the treasury secretary. The department was in such a muddle Grant was contemplating staff replacements. Congress had gone money-mad, doubling the salaries of the President, cabinet, and Supreme Court, increasing their own handsomely, and making it all retroactive. The press and taxpayers were grumbling, the spectators in the Capitol galleries shouting threats and obscenities at the gladiators in the congressional arena. The national debt was mounting alarmingly, inflation and interest rates rampant, farmers in a quandary, labor striking, industry and merchants confused, and Wall Street up in arms as it had not been since Black Friday.

"The country's already in a recession," Keith said. "We're heading for another crash and panic. I predict it'll hit this fall, no later than winter. There won't be much for people to be grateful for on Thanksgiving, and even less cheer in some homes at Christmas."

"Would the West be affected?" Devon asked.

"Not immediately, since the Territories are less dependent on commerce and industry. But eventually, yes, and progress would be slowed, stalled, possibly halted completely, even reversed and set back a generation. Depressions have an insidious way of spreading. In '37 and '57, the repercussions were felt all over the civilized world." He paused, studying her with knitted brows. "What's your interest in the West?"

Devon shrugged, affecting nonchalance. "It's part of the country, isn't it? A journalist should be concerned with the whole nation. The entire universe, in fact."

He smiled, amused. "Darling, you're a social correspondent concerned with society trivia. The capital has a surfeit of such chroniclers, and while they're necessary to record contemporary life-style for cultural history, the White House has its own historians and would hardly sink into ignorance and oblivion without your erstwhile efforts and contributions."

"Nor would the treasury perish without your estimable advice!" she retorted defensively, furious that he still did not take her work seriously, still regarded it as petty and superfluous.

"Will you ever understand economics, Devon? Ever realize how the monetary systems functions? How the Confederacy went bankrupt, and why the South is lagging now in Reconstruction? You still don't comprehend the causes of fiscal crises and their effects on national security, how tariffs work and affect business and agriculture, manufacture and labor and gross product, why foreign trade agreements and payments must be kept in balance—it's all Greek to you, isn't it? Which is precisely as it should be, for the female brain was never designed or intended to cope with such intricate problems."

"Oh, I don't know, Master! Some of us understand the

almightily dollar system well enough, and there just might even be a female treasurer someday."

"When the cow jumps over the moon," he said.

"Why not? The most stupid woman could hardly do a much worse job of running the country than some brilliant men!"

"Ah, Devon, sometimes I think you must have been the inspiration for Stephen Foster's 'Beautiful Dreamer.' Just don't delude yourself that reporting who wore what at the latest White House soiree is the most important news in Washington today."

"I've never thought that!" she bristled. "But perhaps you're right, and I should seek assignments of more substance and consequence."

Some fine newspapers were emerging in the West, and some courageous frontier editors were making names for themselves. Reed had told her of progressive journals in Chicago, Kansas City, Denver, and San Francisco. Even the Dakotas, the Arizona and Utah and Nevada territories had oracles of some renown. And he wanted to put the Dallas *Post* on the journalistic map too. Well, maybe she could help. A small country clarion printed on a hand press and shoestring budget, an organization in which every member was familiar with every phase of operation, including type setting and inking—that's how the Marshalls had started in publishing, wasn't it? That's how, during the war, the *Sentinel* was printed, on the back of wallpaper when no newsprint was available. Her father would have encouraged her. Her grandfather, and all her journalist ancestors would applaud her!

"What the devil does that mean, Devon?"

"I have an opportunity to work in Texas, Keith, on a Dallas newspaper."

He shook his head in confoundment. "*Where* do you get these hare-brained ideas, Devon? You'll do no such damned thing!"

"It's not hare-brained," she protested, "and I'm serious, Keith. I want to do it." Any previous doubts were suddenly resolved, dispelled. But she hesitated about further enlightenment. Somehow it seemed indecent to tell one man, while lying in his bed, that she was going to marry another. The words formed on her lips, but she couldn't speak them. She coughed, choked, and tears surfaced in her eyes.

Keith caught her to him, all but crushing her in his fiercely possessive grip. "For God's sake, don't anger and excite me that way, Devon! You want to give me apoplexy? If you must work, stick with your frou-frou job here. You're far too delicate to survive the rigors of the frontier. You'd die out there in a year or less!"

"I doubt that, Keith. Richmond wasn't exactly a bed of roses during and after the war, and I didn't die there."

"You were anxious enough to escape, though," he reminded her brutally. "Desperate, in fact. Also younger then."

"And greener," she added ruefully. "But I'm hardly a feeble old woman now!"

"My dear, of course not, and I wasn't implying any such thing. My God, you're touchy tonight! And tart. Was it the cherries flambé you had for dinner?" His grin teased, his finger flipped a vivacious curl. "And do you imagine you would feast on such gourmet fare in Texas? That gown you wore to Dijon's, how much did it cost? Five, six hundred? It was on your last bill from Lord & Taylor, but I forgot. You want to exchange it for calico and gingham hubbards, and your Paris chapeaux for prairie sunbonnets? I've pampered and spoiled you, Devon, and you know it. You're not the naive little girl you were in Richmond, and you couldn't be content to live in poverty and privation again. You've acquired affluent tastes and at least a patina of sophistication."

"That's just it, Keith. I'm mostly veneer, patina. Like a pretty polished but hollow shell. Maybe it's time I acquired some core or, in Western lingo, guts."

"Lingo, guts? I didn't know those words were in your vocabulary. Where did you pick them up? More important, from whom?"

Suddenly it was spilling out, a torrent of words rushing, gushing, as if through a broken levee. He listened, deadly calm, a nerve flickering faintly in his rigid jaw, refusing to help or lead her when she faltered and stumbled and seemed lost in dismay and confusion. Then his arms released her so unexpectedly she fell back on the pillows with an abrupt jolt, bumping her head slightly against the velvet-padded headboard.

"How far has it gone?" he demanded hoarsely.

"Not that far, Keith. He's a gentleman."

"Oh, spare me that, Devon! Some mangy cowhand with manure on his boots and sagebrush in his hair is too chivalrous to take a woman in the woods?"

"Incredible as it may seem to an urbane Wall Street wolf, yes! And you forget, I'm going to be his wife."

"Like hell you are! I'll see the sonofabitch dead and in hell first!"

"You don't mean that, Keith."

He reached for the decanter on the bedside table, sloshed Scotch into a glass, bolted it in a gulp. His mouth twisted ironically. "Here I've been fearing that planter would resurface in your life and carry you back to Ole Virginny, while a goddamn Texas wrangler was cutting me out! Surely you realize the Virginian would be a more suitable mate for you, Devon? Haverston's your kind, at least."

"How can you say that, without having met the Texan? He's really a very fine person, Keith, kind and considerate. Intelligent, too—he was educated in New Orleans. His family was once wealthy; his father was a rancher, also a representative and a senator. And like Jason Carter, his son is going to be in Congress some day."

"More dreams, Devon! Meanwhile, you'll live in a hovel and eat pinto beans, waiting for them to come true. Didn't you have enough hardship and misery and suffering in Richmond? Do you honestly imagine you could be happy in those circumstances, even if you loved him, which you don't!"

"I will, eventually—when I forget you!" But her voice quavered, broke into sobs.

"You'll never forget me, Devon, any more than I'll ever forget you. Even so, can you forget our child? Because that's what you'll have to do, my dear. There's no way you can take him to Texas and give him a stepfather!"

"I know," she wept, "and if anything kills me, that will. But I don't really have him now, Keith. He belongs to you, legally. And he's beginning to think the governess is his mother!"

"And whose fault is that?"

"Mine. It's all my fault, everything. And I deserve to be punished, and suffer."

"Darling," he relented, "it's not that bad. Nothing's happened that can't be undone. I think this is just another of your conscience convulsions and will pass like the others. Despite your liberal notions, some puritanical ideals still linger in your flesh and blood, and force these periodic purifications. They're somewhat annoying and inconvenient to romance, but not fatal. Shall we kiss and make up? We haven't been together like this in weeks. I need you, Devon. I'll always need you.

"You'll find someone else, Keith. I've accepted that. A man your age must have a woman."

"I thought I did," he said wryly. "You know I love you, Devon, and all this is gutting me. But why Texas, of all places? Is that as far away from me as you can get? If you feel you must put some distance between us, go to California or Alaska. It won't matter, you know." His finger touched her left breast. "I'll still be with you, in there. You can't lose me that easily, Devon. You can't lose me at all."

From the windows she could see the lights of the Capitol, the White House, the city, blurred through the mist in her eyes—and, in the dark sky to the west, a shimmer of stars. "I'm going to try," she murmured doggedly. "Oh, God, I'm going to try!"

"Come here," he said, opening his arms.

She shook her head reluctantly, sighing.

"Come on," he coaxed. "This is how it began, Devon. See if you can end it the same way."

"You think I can't?"

"I'm hoping you can't," he said.

"Don't bet on it, Keith."

"You don't want me now."

"I didn't say that."

"And would be lying if you did."

While she hesitated, her hands clenching and twisting the sheet helplessly, his moved stealthily under it and over her body, evoking familiar sensations, fires, desires. Oh, she was carnal, wanton, and Reed would know it the moment he touched her intimately! He should have realized it when she offered herself to him in that shanty in the sticks. . . .

She began to writhe, moan, clutch at Keith. He lay on his side and continued to touch, stroke, probe, tease with lips, tongue, fingers—the delicious love ritual that was at once sacred and profane. She felt his tongue in her mouth, her ears, on her breasts and nipples, her navel, the inside of her thighs. She shivered in a sexual spasm. When she thought she couldn't bear any more, he mounted, penetrated, plunged, rotated, until she, clinging in wild passionate delirious abandon and undulating unison, climaxed just before him.

"You think he'll ever make you that happy, Devon? Give you that much sexual pleasure? You think you could lie in his arms and not remember me? Sleep on gunnysacks and make love on hay and shucks, and not long for silk and satin and eiderdown?"

"Why do you torture me, Keith?"

"Was that torture? I thought it was ecstasy."

"You know what I mean."

"Yes, and any torture is your own, Devon. You seem determined to punish yourself for your 'sins' with me. It's foolish, this self-martyrdom, and running away to Texas would be tantamount to immolation. How much more proof do you need that we belong together?"

"God's blessing," she murmured.

"A formal ceremony and wedding ring? That's going to make it right to marry a man you don't love and have his children? I shouldn't have used a shield—another pregnancy might bring you to your senses."

"The pessary's still intact, dear."

"And just how will you explain *that* to the cowboy?"

"I don't think I'll have to," she replied.

"Oh, he's so goddamned understanding, is he? And in addition to his gallantry, he's content to wait for the nuptials, even though he knows his predecessor didn't?"

"You brute!" she cried, turning her face into the pillow. "Go away, damn you! Leave me alone!"

"Jesus, darling, I'm sorry. I'm being a bastard."

"Yes, you are! Do you think this is easy for me, Keith? I'd rather die than give up you and the baby! But this has been going on over five years, and it can't continue forever. Your wife's still in her thirties and could outlive either or both of us! But I can't live this way any longer, Keith—it's killing me! I'm giving up my child. Isn't that enough? You want my blood, my life? Don't crucify me any more."

"What about me, Devon? You don't think I'm suffering too? You expect me to congratulate him? Make the beau geste and give the bride away?"

"Now you're being cynical."

He heaved a long heavy sigh. "I'm tired of sparring, Devon. Your mind is made up, and I can't change it. So go to Texas and pioneer with your hero! Fight Indians with him, herd wild horses and brand longhorns. Live in a sod shanty or adobe hut with coyotes howling at the door, and bear his kids on buffalo hides. Cook his beans and sourdough biscuits, wear rags and brogans, and follow him on the trails. Watch your fair skin grow dark and wrinkled, your eyes and hair fade, your beauty vanish. Oh, Christ, I don't want to discuss it any more! Just don't let me know when or where it happens. If you need or want anything before or after, it's yours. And if it doesn't work out—"

"It will," she sobbed.

"If not, I'd be the last to know?"

"It'll work out," she insisted.

"Yes, somehow I think it will, if he's half as desperate and determined as you. Will you come back to New York to say goodbye to Scotty before—?"

"No," she shook her head vehemently. "I couldn't leave if I did. Oh, God, why did you ever come to Richmond!"

He held her tenderly, kissing the soft golden crown of her head. "For the same reason your Texan came to Washington, I guess. It was meant to be, Devon."

"I was supposed to give you a son?"

"My sweet little Puritan is surely aware of that pertinent passage in Ecclesiastes? 'To every thing there is a season, and a time to every purpose under the heaven. A time to be born, and a time to die. A time to plant, and a time to pluck up that which is planted. A time to kill, and a time to heal. A time to break down, and a time to build up. A time to weep, and a time to laugh. A time to mourn, and a time to dance. A time to cast away stones, and a time to gather them together. A time to get and a time to lose. A time to weep, and a time to cast away. A time to rend, and a time to sew. A time to keep silence, and a time to speak. A time to love, and a time to hate. A time of war, and a time of peace.' "

His fine voice fell gently on her ears, and the Scripture was somehow soothing and inspirational. "I—I didn't know you could quote the Bible, Keith. I didn't even know you read it."

His faint smile eluded her. "I'm not a heathen, darling, even though I may have some pagan philosophies. But I think that verse suits our situation now very well, don't you?"

Devon swallowed the painful lump that had risen in her throat. "Except for that one line: a time to love, and a time to hate. I could never hate you, Keith. You know that."

He nodded, pressing her tearful face into his shoulder to conceal his own. "I know, Devon. And somewhere inside me, I think I always knew it would end this way. That passage doesn't mention a time to marry and a time to divorce, because that would contradict and void the Commandments. And because I've been unable to put my wife asunder or away, I must lose you. That's my punishment, my penalty. As you said when I declined the cabinet post and ambassadorships, none of us gets off scot free. There's a moral accounting, and we have to pay a price for our transgressions. But I never expected to pay such a godamned high one!"

"Nor I," she whispered.

"So what do we do now, my love? Tally our respective tabs? Recant and repent? Take the holy vows? Have one last orgy? What, Devon? Tell me. *What!*"

"I don't know, Keith. I don't know."

"You want a drink?"

"Please. Oh, yes, darling, please—"

Chapter 50

Samuel Fitch persuaded Devon to remain through the summer, and she agreed out of a sense of loyalty and gratitude. After all, he had given her a chance, albeit under pressure from Sweeny, and she owed whatever journalistic reputation she now possessed to the *Record*, along with some allegiance. The First Family's vacation travels were about to begin, and her faithful distaff fans followed the itinerary via her byline. Carrie Hempstead and Tish Lambeth lamented losing her, and even the city editor and some of the other men agreed that she had done a good job "for a woman" and added "class" to the paper. Moreover, when news of her resignation circulated Printing House Square and Park Row, she received several attractive offers, including one from young Bennett to join the *Herald*, and another especially tempting bait to take a European assignment for Leslie's Magazine Corporation— Minnie's way, according to the grapevine, of removing beautiful young talent and competition from her husband's roving eyes, now that she and Frank Leslie had married after succeeding in divorcing their respective spouses for adultery. And with his keen understanding of the profession, Reed Carter agreed that obliging her publisher was the proper thing to do, regardless of the delay and inconvenience to their own plans. It was all very flattering and gratifying, except when she thought of the motivation.

On the summer circuit the ladies talked of the many exciting prospects on the capital autumn–winter calendar. The annual presidential reception for the diplomantic corps was always a brilliant affair, if only because of the spectacular uniforms and decorations of the foreign ministers and splendid attire of their ladies. Equally colorful and elaborate were the seasonal entertainments of the embassies, which were steadily moving up Connecticut Avenue toward Admiral Dupont Circle, as society spread its tentacles beyond Lafayette Square. The whole social structure of the city was changing, along with the architectural quality and design of its residences, in a way that would not have pleased the aristocratic Washington and Jefferson, Madison and Monroe. The dynasties of the Federal period had died out, and with them their life-style of order, beauty, leisure, simplicity. The new rulers were aggressive, often ruthless, some rude and crude and avaricious, others ostentatious and flamboyant: fame-and-fortune grubbers who bent and twisted government to their own advantage. Ornate, ponderous, pretentious dwellings replaced the gracious mellow red brick Georgian and Colonial houses and gardens. Times were changing along with morals and mores.

Nellie Grant's engagement to Algernon Sartoris had been announced, and though no wedding date had yet been set by her reluctant parents, it would certainly be an event of the first magnitude in the social firmament of the capital. The President's frank objection had already created some sensation, for in addition to considering his precious daughter too young and immature for marriage, he disapproved of her choice of a groom and had publicly stated that he preferred an American son-in-law. This wounded the proud British lion and affected diplomatic relations almost as much as the Alabama Claims Treaty, finally resolved at Geneva and resulting in the Crown's paying over fifteen millions in shipping damages to the United States.

Devon had covered Nellie's glittering debut and the numerous bethrothal parties, and rather hoped she would still be around to witness the wedding—also the forthcoming royal visits to Washington already announced, among them the king of Hawaii. There was much sympathy for Kate Chase Sprague, who was mourning her beloved father, whom she had lost in May, and much wonder about Senator Conkling, who had declined the chief justiceship purportedly out of sentiment for her.

"Isn't that the most romantic thing you ever heard?" cried Olivia. "Imagine refusing an appointment to the Supreme Court, because he thought it might hurt Kate's feelings!"

"Oh, I doubt that was the primary reason," said Jane

Swisshelm, in one of her argumentative moods. "I suspect more ambition than romance was involved. The senator's '76 presidential aspirations are not exactly secret, and he'd much rather be in the White House than on the bench, which he'd have to resign."

"He's a fool, then," declared Nellie Hutchinson. "The Court is a permanent office and honor. The presidency, at best, is temporary and not always honorable."

"Justices can be impeached too," reminded Jane. "What did you girls think about our not being invited along on the President's trip to the Colorado Territory?"

"I suppose," said Devon, "since Mrs. Grant didn't accompany him, we'd have been considered excess baggage. I'd like to have seen Central City, though, and those sidewalks actually paved with silver bricks!"

Mrs. Swisshelm, who had left her overbearing and penurious husband and was seeking a divorce, admonished, "It serves us right, being left behind. Not one of us had the nerve to *demand* our professional rights to be in the press caravan with our male colleagues! Of course I'm getting a trifle old for such gallivanting, and ready to pass the torch to youth—but that's no excuse for Nellie and Devon. Would that one of us had the late Anne Royall's spirit and audacity when she determined to get that interview with President John Quincy Adams. Lord, that must have been something! The President caught in his early morning swim in the Potomac, naked and shivering in the icy waters, while obstinate Anne sat complacently on his clothes, demanding that he give her his views on the Bank of the United States controversy then raging. I've always admired Mrs. Royall, even though she was considered a termagant and her *Paul Pry* a slander-sheet, and think we all owe much to her endeavors for our positions today."

They were lounging under umbrellas on the Long Branch beach near the gingerbread cottage, nibbling dainty sandwiches and sipping cold lemonade, watching the restless gulls wheeling, diving, begging for crumbs. Devon's mind wandered frequently up the Atlantic coast to the Isle of Manhattan and the house on the Hudson. To think Keith and Scotty were only thirty miles away, and she had not seen her son since his fifth birthday in March. Her eyes moistened; she pretended it was the salt spray and sun glare on the water, and rearranged her protective

veil more concealingly about her face. She lived in wary
fear of the appearance of the *Sprite,* wondering how effectively she could resort to incognito.

And then one morning, from the hotel piazza, she
sighted a familiar silhouette on the sea. Was Keith just
cruising, or had the President summoned him? Perhaps the
financial panic the Wizard of Wall Street had predicted
was imminent. There were rumors in the press that the
Philadelphia house of Cooke, considered a veritable Gibraltar in banking, was quaking and the vibrations were
emanating to its Manhattan branch. Keith would have
this information, as well as any other precarious rumblings
on the Street, and the President would be anxiously awaiting it. Grant was such a dunce about finance, and so dependent on his economic advisers, for he still had not
found a competent secretary of the treasury. Conceivably,
he might again offer this cabinet portfolio to Keith Curtis—and possibly this time he might accept.

They had not seen each other since their poignant parting in Washington—that bittersweet farewell after which
Devon had been actually ill for several days, too distraught to give full attention to her assignments. Reviewing
Laura Keene's new play at Ford's Theater was almost a
chore. She could barely concentrate on the eloquent
readings of Fanny Kemble, who was related to Miss
Grant's fiancé, at the Grove, or Anna Dickinson's powerful lectures on women's rights at Lincoln Hall, which even
Mrs. Grant attended. In her preoccupation Devon ignored
the chatter in the Capitol galleries concerning new scandals in the administration: something about a Whisky Ring
defrauding the government of revenue from distilleries,
and something else about Indian Territories' post-trader-
ships involving Secretary of War Belknap, whose pretty
young wife and former sister-in-law, Puss, was challenging
Mrs. Sprague's social supremacy. Devon had even missed
the colorful ceremonials at the White House for the Indian
delegation from the Dakotas consisting of the great chiefs,
Sitting Bull the Minor, Swift Bear, Spotted Tail, and Red
Cloud, and had to crib from Reed's notes.

Although involved with his newsletters to the various
papers he represented in Texas, Reed had nevertheless noticed Devon's malaise and insisted that she consult a doctor, which she did to please him. As usual when baffled by

a woman's health or behavior, the medical diagnosis was anemia and female complaint, the treatment iron pills and elixirs of various herbs and roots; she gagged on the thick bitter syrup of aloes. They both hoped that the seashore would prove beneficial to her, improve her strength and color and mood, which it did. After a few weeks at Long Branch, she felt much better, almost herself again . . . until she saw the puffing stacks of the *Sprite* steaming into harbor.

She watched it approach through her binoculars, the national and state flags flying from its tall masts—it was also equipped for sailing—along with that of the New York Yacht Club, and his own dignified standard. Oh, God— there was no one else in the world like him, and never would be! Was it true, as he had warned her, that she never would or could forget him? Was she making a grave and tragic mistake in marrying Reed Carter? Would any other man, even one as rugged and masculine and adventurous as the Texan, eventually seem a mild and even pallid imitation by comparison? And what would she do if he tried to see her, put her resolution and mettle to the acid test!

She recognized Keith in the pilot-house, standing beside Captain Bowers, who was at the helm. Soon the ship was docking. Several other well-dressed men, presumably also bankers, appeared on deck. Perhaps the situation was more serious and alarming than believed in Washington. But, thank heaven, he wasn't alone! It would make it more difficult for him to invite her aboard, and easier for her to resist and decline.

And then she saw the woman and child! The governess, Heather Vale, in a prim gray gown and fluted bonnet tied under her chin like a Quakeress, holding the hand of a little boy in a blue sailor suit and jaunty white seacap, a replica of his father. Devon stared avidly, longing to run down the stairs and along the beach to the pier, up the gangplank to the deck, to scoop Scotty up in her arms and hug and kiss him. The desire made her weak and faint. She hurried into her room, grasped the bedpost for support and leaned her head against it, her heart throbbing in her breast and echoing like a bass drum in her ears. How could he do this to her! Deliberately torment her this way!

Vaguely, gradually, reason penetrated her mental fog of

fury and despair, and she realized that she was being unfair to him, for he couldn't necessarily know that she
would be in Long Branch. She might have been hundreds
of miles away, in Texas. Hadn't he asked only that she not
let him know when or where she married the cowboy, as
he had persisted in calling him? And now that adoption
had removed all obstacles from his fatherhood, and all
secrecy and shadow from his son, he was free to show him
off in public. Did he intend to bring him ashore and
present him to the First Family? Why not? He had a surname now, a very old and very fine one. He was Master
Scott Heathstone Curtis, and there was noble blood in his
ancestry. The great grandson of Lord and Lady Heathstone! She should be proud of his lineage, happy about his
heritage, and pleased at his father's pride in him. And she
should despise herself for her maudlin tears and brooding
and self-pity, ashamed of this contemptible compulsion to
throw herself into the sea and let the tides decide her destiny. . . .

The men sat vis-à-vis in the official landau conveying
them to the summer White House. Formal entertainment
had been suspended due to the death of the President's father in late June, and Grant himself was recovering from
a respiratory ailment contacted in the rain at the funeral.
He had been further saddened to learn that General
George Meade, the victor of Gettysburg, was suffering
with a terminal disease, and that Vice-President Wilson
was also reputed to have some form of serious and often
fatal debility, possibly consumption. As always the press
pursued such morbid rumors cautiously, lest it be accused
of indulging in prognostication and even witchcraft. Nevertheless, thoroughly researched obituaries were ready in
the files. And one by one, the Civil war giants and heroes,
Union and Confederate, were falling in the greater and
unconquerable battle of life and age.

Soon the steward and two servants, shopping baskets
over arms, were bustling to market in the provision cart
kept at the kitchen door. As every other hostess, the First
Lady was not always prepared for extra or unexpected
guests, whom her busy husband had forgotten or neglected
to mention to her.

Following a lengthy conference in the President's study,

the group assembled on the lower veranda to catch the ocean breezes. A white-coated Negro passed cigars and tall cool drinks among them. Nearby a platoon of male reporters waited, kept at bay by security guards unless the President signaled otherwise. Grant was still enough of a military strategist to prevent or circumvent surprise attacks and sieges by newsmen, and was no longer as accessible, amenable, or amiable as he had been during his honeymoon with the people and press. The female coterie never dared invade Mrs. Grant's privacy without invitation, and Devon prayed that they would not be summoned now. If so, she would invent some excuse, if she must take to her bed.

Sleep without a soporific was next to impossible that night. She could think of nothing but her baby so near and yet so far away, in the care of another woman. After hours of forlorn and fretful tossing she swallowed a bitter potion, which induced hideous nightmares, vivid and disconnected as the bits and pieces of a kaleidoscope.

First she was alone and wandering in a wilderness of strange trees and plants; then the unfamiliar landscape changed to a hot dry windy desert crawling with poisonous snakes and monstrous lizards, and she was dying of thirst and pursuing water mirages that never materialized; then climbing and falling off mountains into tangled ravines, trapped in a boxed canyon, stampeded by longhorns and mustangs and buffaloes, chased and scalped by wild Indians, and finally running blindly in a dense fog toward a dark roaring sea, at which point she woke soaking wet and shivering in the damp night air blowing through the windows, clutching her pillow and crying Keith's name. And if some night the same dreams plagued her in Reed's bed, haunted her in his arms, what then? Maybe it was madness, sheer lunacy to imagine she could escape, relocate, forget. And even worse insanity to try.

In the morning, ordering her breakfast sent up, she sat at the desk and composed a brief article to send to her editor. It required extreme effort to affect sparkling wit and gaiety in her desolate mood, but somehow she managed in the tradition of the trade to keep her personal emotions out of her stories. This, her father had taught her, was the mark of the true journalist: the ability to write one's own obituary without weeping. But what about a mother surrendering, relinquishing her child!

When Nellie Hutchinson knocked and asked if she would be riding with them this morning, Devon pleaded menstrual cramps. Nellie made a sympathetic grimace. "I just finished Eve's curse myself. Will you be coming down to the beach this afternoon?"

"Probably not—it's real revenge this month! I think I'll stay in bed with my hot water bottle. I trust there's nothing urgent on the First Lady's agenda?"

"Not to my knowledge. It's all masculine business at the Cottage now. That Wall Street delegation is meeting with the President again. I didn't know the Curtises had a child, but one of the yacht crewmen told me that's his little son aboard. And a governess. He also said that Mrs. Curtis is seriously ill in some mysterious way."

"Mysterious?"

"Well, confined to their home in Gramercy Park. He said she never goes anywhere, or has any visitors, and there's a kind of pall over the house. Peculiar."

"How does a crewman know these things?"

"Backstairs gossip. Seems he courts the scullery maid, who told him that the mistress is considered hopelessly insane. I wonder if it's true."

Devon shrugged. "Could be, Nellie. People do lose their minds, you know. The asylums are full of lunatics."

"That's just it. The maid says all the servants fear her and think she belongs in a cell, yet he keeps her at home under constant attendance. I guess he must love her too much to put her away somewhere in a cage, which is what most of those places are. Isn't it awful, though, a man like that burdened with such a heavy anchor. Plenty of husbands would jettison such a cargo, one way or another. And according to the household scuttlebutt, in her fits of raving, Mrs. Curtis accuses him of trying to poison her, and sometimes refuses to eat or drink anything for days. She forces her maid to taste her food, and won't allow any potted plants in her rooms for fear of noxious vapors. She even had the gas jets there sealed long ago, before she entered that pitiful state, and kept a derringer handy."

"Fantasies, Nellie. The vagaries of a mad imagination."

"What a living hell it must be for both of them! Hopefully, the child won't inherit the tainted seed."

"He's adopted," Devon said, unexpectedly.

"Oh? Where did you hear that?"

"In New York, when I lived there."

"Well, I'm happy for Mr. Curtis. He deserves something out of life, and he's obviously wild about the cute little tyke. He's a lucky boy to get such a father instead of an orphanage. Boone—that's the crewman's name—said Mr. Curtis maintains two residences, the town house in Gramercy Park and a country estate on the Hudson, where he keeps the child and spends most of his free time."

"That sailor is a regular encyclopedia, isn't he? And you must have had quite a tête-à-tête with him, Nellie."

"Not intentionally. I mean, I wasn't trying to pump him, and he might only have been spouting bilge, anyway, siphoned from a disgruntled domestic. I really wanted to talk with the governess, Miss Vale, but she's a tight-lipped creature, flat-chested and plain as porridge, who tends strictly to her business of minding the child. The gregarious seaman volunteered the information while swabbing the deck, but insisted he wasn't betraying any confidences or secrets, because the servants had already spread it around town. He also said his wife's condition had kept Mr. Curtis from accepting any high offices with the government. Gee, honey, you look quite pale. Better hop into bed with your hot water bottle before you swoon. And don't worry, if anything newsworthy happens at the Cottage, we'll get word to you—"

"Thank you, Nellie. Enjoy your ride."

"Oh, you're the best horsewoman among us," declared Nellie unequivocally. "The Virginian expert. And I bet you miss riding with your handsome Texan at Rock Creek. You make such a darling couple—you in your fancy British habits, and him in his rugged western duds. Anyone can see he's in love with you, Devon. Do you like him?"

Devon nodded, wishing she'd leave. She liked Nellie, but wanted no company this morning. And though she considered confiding her future plans, if only for reassurance that she would adhere to them, she kept her silence and secret. "Do you mind, dear? I'm really in pain and misery."

"Oh, of course. Get some rest, girl."

Rest. She sighed slightly, closing the door. Was what that blabber-mouthed Boone said true, and the Curtis situation common knowledge and gossip in Manhattan society? Was there something strange, peculiar, mysterious about Esther's illness and even some foundation for her maniacal accusations? Of course not! She was delirious and having delusions! And he, poor darling, must be experiencing perennial nightmares more horrible than hers, and perpetual torment greater than any she could possibly imagine or endure.

A few inquiries could determine her presence at the Continental Hotel, and she wondered if he would bother to make them, or had resigned himself to the finality of their parting at the Clairmont. She waited, half in hope, half in dread, not at all certain how she would react to a message from him. Perhaps he was aware, and simply did not want to disturb healing wounds. He was a proud man, who had pleaded eloquently and lost his case, and he refused to reduce himself to begging and groveling. You fool! she chided herself. You got what you wanted, now take it if it kills you! And maybe, if you're fortunate, it will.

Not once did she catch him on deck with binoculars, as she had on previous occasions, scanning the hostelries along Ocean Avenue, or the pedestrians on the beach and boardwalk. But later that day Keith and the other men sat in conversation under the deck awning, while Rufus served them food and drinks. Then his guests went ashore toward town, and while Devon watched behind the curtains of her room, the governess came out with her charge. Heather Vale was in a dark poplin gown softened with a creamy lace fichu, and Scotty was adorable in a white linen suit and white straw hat with a rolled brim and streamer. Keith spoke to Miss Vale, and then bent to say something to his son, who clapped his little hands. Apparently the three of them were going to visit the President, for the landau was waiting at the wharf. Oh, if only she could witness that! But he couldn't have forgotten her yet—and what would she do if he ran to her and cried, "Mommy!" Die on the spot, that's what.

She timed the visit, thinking he would be brought back shortly for his nap. Or had he outgrown naps? Perhaps his regular routine had been suspended for the holiday. Miss

Vale was stern stuff, but Keith had always spoiled and indulged him.

Devon kept her lonely vigil and surveillance until the carriage delivered them to the *Sprite* again. But not for a nap. The trio changed clothes, Miss Vale into some sort of striped seersucker beach costume, and Keith and Scotty into jersey bathing suits and terrycloth robes. They were going into the surf. Be careful, my darlings, be careful!

The finest of the resort hotels, the Continental also boasted the largest and best beach, which Keith naturally chose, and for over an hour Devon watched them frolic, through glasses when she longed for a close-up of their faces. Miss Vale did not go in the water; she occupied a canvas chair shaded by a huge orange umbrella, an open book in her hands, while Keith romped and played with his son as if they were the same age. In and out of the surf, jumping waves together, his hand always securely on the exuberant child's, who was laughing and screaming with delight. Then he fastened a pair of tiny water wings on Scotty and let him paddle in the calm troughs, hoisting him to his broad shoulders when a breaker rolled in, and frequently bear-hugging him. Next they trotted along shore a piece, pausing to pick up shells, which Scotty brought to his governess to put in one of his daddy's cigar boxes. Finally they sat down almost directly beneath Devon's windows to build a sandcastle, and she quickly released the drawn curtain lest Keith notice her surveillance.

Still peering through the mesh, longing to go down and join them, she suddenly realized that he had known all along she was up there and had been trying, not to torment her, but do her a great favor. Aware that she could not publicly acknowledge the child, he had given her this wonderful opportunity to observe him, to see and know that he was well and happy and content—a fine robust youngster. Oh, darling, thank you, thank you!

Tears spilling down her cheeks, she watched a sandcastle rise, complete with towers and moat and bridges, wondering if it were a replica of Heathstone Manor in Sussex, which she had always hoped to visit and now probably never would. She could hear their musical voices like a choral duet, Scotty's lilting tenor asking numerous questions—"Daddy what, Daddy why, Daddy how, Daddy when, Daddy where—" And Keith's deep baritone patiently responding, satisfying his childish curiosity. Fatherhood came naturally to him; he should have a dozen children!

The building project completed, the architects lay down on the sand and proceeded to cover each other. A symbolic gesture? Was he saying bury us in memory, forget us if you can? Had he reassessed the whole situation, in all its emotional aspects and ramifications and entanglements, and concluded that her decision was, after all, the best for all concerned? Practical, sensible. Wise, judicious. The answer would lie in whether or not he sent her a message, tried in any manner whatever to communicate and make physical contact. . . .

Exhausted, Scotty fell asleep, and Keith carried him back to the yacht. Miss Vale followed a few paces behind, befitting her station, carrying her books and Scotty's treasure chest of shells. Of one thing Devon could be certain—no personal relationship whatever existed between master and governess.

Later, presumably after Scotty's nap, they set out again toward the midway and the carnival. Devon could visualize them riding the carousel and hobby horses, and Keith indulging Scotty's appetite for candy and soda pop despite Miss Vale's protests, and then worrying wildly if he developed a bellyache. Within two hours they were back and aboard the *Sprite* for supper with Keith's guests.

Devon ate hers alone off a tray by the window, binoculars handy. Sunset tinted the sea crimson, and twilight brought that peculiar mauve cast over the New England coast. The crew lighted the ship's lanterns before the obliterating shadows of dusk, and Devon took up nightwatch. The moon rose in a silver halo, signifying rain or other change in weather. She waited apprehensively for some sign of Keith, some signal from him, since he certainly knew how to operate the lamp signaler. There was no visible activity whatever on deck, not even a game of shuffleboard or ring-tossing or rope tricks, for the crew was at liberty on the town. And evidently Keith and his guests were in the salon, possibly playing cards. Nevertheless, they could have met somewhere later, on the beach or at the carnival. There were ways if he were determined enough—God knows he'd found them often enough before! And she, as she had so often before, would probably weaken and respond, run to him with open arms and aching heart.

Her agonizing was in vain, for she was spared the crucial decision. No summons, no supplications came. She retired at midnight, surrendering herself to the horrors of another violent dream that racked her senses and emotions.

The *Sprite* sailed the next morning, and Devon watched the steamer until it was out of sight from the piazza. Keith's presence on deck, and the child in his arms waving toward shore, could not have been coincidence. They were bidding her farewell.

THE IMMORTAL LOVE EPIC

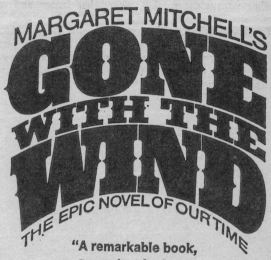

MARGARET MITCHELL'S
GONE WITH THE WIND
THE EPIC NOVEL OF OUR TIME

"A remarkable book,
a spectacular book,
a book that will not be forgotten."

Chicago Tribune

#30445/$4.95

Margaret Mitchell's unsurpassed romantic story—that has thrilled a quarter-billion readers and moviegoers worldwide—is now available in a permanent deluxe Avon/Equinox paperback edition.

Wherever paperbacks are sold, or order directly from the publisher. Include 25¢ per copy for handling; allow 3 weeks for delivery. AVON BOOKS, Mail Order Department, 250 West 55th Street, New York, New York 10019.

GONE 9-76